PRAISE FOR
POSEIDON'S WAKE

"Reynolds's scientific education is on full display, as the novel permeates a sense of realism throughout, from the scientific ideas—even the most far-flung ones—to the nature of the characters and their relationships, which eschew the normal 'dark,' Hollywood-like trend of action heroes in literature, with a sense of optimism and discovery . . . It's grand, involving and full of light and wonder. *Poseidon's Wake* is one of the best sci-fi novels of the year."
—*SciFiNow* (UK)

"Concluding in a tense rescue mission reminiscent of writers like Arthur C. Clarke, *Poseidon's Wake* is a novel unafraid to ask big questions about human nature and, for that matter, about the 'truth of life's fate in the cosmos.'"
—*Irish Examiner*

ON THE STEEL BREEZE

"For SF fans, the possibilities and imagination that has gone into the book will remind them of the heady days of Asimov and Clarke, of an age where imagination and people were more important in telling the story of humanity and guessing about its future."
—The British Fantasy Society

"This is imaginative, ambitious and visual science fiction . . . An intelligent novel, with strong dialogue and stunning visuals."
—Fantasy Book Review

BLUE REMEMBERED EARTH

"Engrossing . . . Demonstrates Reynolds's genre mastery."
—*Los Angeles Review of Books*

"Reynolds's near-future is so brilliantly extrapolated, with original ideas fizzing off every page, that the reader is left awestruck at what further wonders await in the following volumes. Excellent."
—*The Guardian* (UK)

Ace Books by Alastair Reynolds

REVELATION SPACE
CHASM CITY
REDEMPTION ARK
ABSOLUTION GAP
DIAMOND DOGS, TURQUOISE DAYS
CENTURY RAIN
PUSHING ICE
GALACTIC NORTH
THE PREFECT
HOUSE OF SUNS
TERMINAL WORLD
BLUE REMEMBERED EARTH
ON THE STEEL BREEZE
POSEIDON'S WAKE

POSEIDON'S WAKE

Alastair Reynolds

ACE
New York

ACE

Published by Berkley

An imprint of Penguin Random House LLC

375 Hudson Street, New York, New York 10014

Copyright © 2015 by Alastair Reynolds

ISBN: 9780425256343

Gollancz hardcover edition / April 2015
Ace hardcover edition / February 2016
Ace mass-market edition / September 2016

Printed in the United States of America
1   3   5   7   9   10   8   6   4   2

Cover illustration by Dominic Harman
Cover design by Sarah Oberrender

For my wife, who once fell in love with an elephant.

I have come to the borders of sleep,
The unfathomable deep
Forest where all must lose
Their way, however straight.
—Edward Thomas

CHAPTER I

Early one evening, Mposi Akinya went to visit his sister. He took a car from the parliamentary building in the heart of Guochang, out through the government quarter and across the residential districts, until at last he reached the secured compound surrounding her house. He walked to the gate and presented his identification, even though the guards were ready to usher him past without a second glance at his credentials.

He made his way to the entrance, knocked on the door and waited until Ndege opened it. For a moment she blocked his entry, standing with her arms folded across her chest, her head cocked to one side, her expression betokening neither warmth nor welcome. She was still taller than him, even in their mutual old age. Mposi had spent a lifetime being looked down on.

"I brought greenbread." He offered her the paper-wrapped loaves. "Still fresh."

She took the package, opened the paper, sniffed doubtfully at the contents. "I wasn't expecting you until later in the week."

"I know it's a little unexpected, but I promise this won't take long."

"Good. I have reading to be doing."

"When do you ever not have reading to be doing, sister?"

After a moment, Ndege relented and admitted him into her house, then led him to her kitchen. She must have been sitting at the table, for she had her black notebooks laid out on it, open to reveal their dense scribbled columns of strange symbols and the sketchy relationships between them. Except for the notebooks and a small box of medicines to counter oxygen toxicity, the table was bare. Mposi took a chair opposite the one Ndege had been using.

"I should have told you I was on my way, but I couldn't keep this to myself a moment longer."

"A promotion? Another expansion of your powers?"

"For once, it's not about me."

She looked at him for a moment, still not sitting down. "I suppose you're expecting me to boil some chai?"

"No, not today, thank you. And save that greenbread for yourself." He patted the plump padding of his belly. "I ate at the office."

Before easing her tall, thin frame into the chair, Ndege gathered the notebooks off the table and set them carefully on her bookcase. Then she faced him and made an impatient beckoning gesture with her hands. "Out with it, whatever it is. Bad news?"

"I'm honestly not sure."

"Something to do with Goma?"

"Only indirectly." Mposi settled his hands on the table, unsure where to start. "What I'm about to disclose is a matter of the highest secrecy. It's known to only a few people on Crucible, and I would be very glad if it remained that way."

"I'll be sure not to mention it to my many hundreds of visitors."

"You do receive the occasional visitor. We went to a lot of trouble to allow you that luxury."

"Yes, and you never let me forget it."

Her tone had been sharp, and perhaps she realised as much. She swallowed, creased her lips in immediate regret. In the silence that ensued, Mposi found his gaze wandering around the kitchen, taking in its blank, bare surfaces. It struck him that his sister had begun to turn her life into an exhibit of itself—a static tableau reduced to the uncluttered essentials. His own government had made her a prisoner, but Ndege herself was complicit in the exercise, happily discarding her remaining luxuries and concessions.

Somewhere in the house a clock ticked.

"I'm sorry," she said, finally. "I know you worked hard to help me. But being here on my own, knowing what the world thinks of me—"

"We've picked up a signal."

The oddness of this statement drew a frown from Ndege. "A what?"

"A radio transmission—very faint, but clearly artificial— from a solar system tens of light-years away that no one from any of the settled systems is supposed to have reached or explored yet. Interestingly, the transmission's strength definitely tailed off the further you moved from the system's centre—meaning it was aimed at us, not broadcast in all directions. More than that: it appears to concern you."

For the first time since his arrival he had at least a measure of her interest, guarded and provisional as it was.

"Me?"

"Quite unambiguous. It mentions your forename."

"There are lots of people called Ndege."

"Not lately there aren't. It asked us to send you. *Send Ndege*, in Swahili. That's the extent of the message. It began, continued repeating for a matter of hours, then shut off. We're keeping an eye on that part of space, of course, but we've heard nothing since."

"Where?"

"A system called Gliese 163, about seventy light-years from us. Someone or something there went to the trouble of lining up a radio transmitter and sending us this message."

Ndege absorbed the information with the quiet concentration that was so thoroughly her own. Over a lifetime together, Mposi had learned to recognise their differences as well as their similarities. He was a speaker, a reactor, a man who needed to be constantly on the move, constantly engaged in this business or that. Ndege was the reflective one, the thinker, taking little for granted.

She opened the medical box, plucked out one of the hypodermic sprays and touched the device to the skin of her forearm.

"The oxygen gets to me these days."

"I'm the same," he said. "It was hard in the early years of settlement, then for a long while I thought I had adapted—that I could live without medical assistance. But the blood carries a memory."

She put the hypodermic back into the box, snapped the lid down and pushed the container aside.

"So who sent this signal?"

"We don't know."

The clock kept ticking. He studied Ndege, measuring her visible age against his own, wondering how much of her frailty was the direct result of time passing, of the physiological stress of adapting to a new planet, and how much the consequence of her imprisonment and public shaming. She was thinner in the face than Mposi, and there was still an asymmetry there from the minor stroke she had suffered three decades ago. Her hair was short, thin and white—she cut it herself, as far as he knew. Her skin was a map of old lesions and discolorations. She looked tremendously old to him, but there were also days when he caught a glimpse of his own reflection and stared back in startled affront, barely recognising his own face.

Then again, the light could shift, her expression could change, and she was his sister again, just as she had been during their brave young years aboard the holoship.

"You think it might be our mother."

Mposi gave the slightest of nods. "It's a possibility, nothing more. We don't know what became of the Trinity—Chiku, Eunice, Dakota."

"And you reckon they want me to go out there and meet them?"

"So it would appear."

"Then it's a shame no one told them I'm a decaying old crone under permanent house arrest."

Mposi smiled sweetly, refusing to rise to the provocation. "I've always held that every problem is also an opportunity. You know of the two starships we're building?"

"They do let me look at the sky sometimes."

"Officially, their intended function—when they're completed—is to expand our influence and trade connections to other systems. Unofficially, nothing is set in stone. Feelers have gone out concerning a possible expedition, using one of the two ships. Given the specific nature of the signal, there would be a certain logic to having you aboard."

"Are you serious?"

"Perfectly."

"Then you understand less about politics than I thought.

I'm a pariah, Mposi—hated by millions. They'll have my head on a stick before they let me leave Guochang, let alone the system."

"For now, it's all hypothetical. The expedition won't be ready for four or five years even if we accelerate the preparations. But if you agree to join, and I work to make it look as if you're offering yourself up for . . . I don't know, the selfless betterment of Crucible, there could be an immediate improvement in the terms of your detention."

"Working on people's opinions—you're good at that."

"I have my uses. My point, though, is that even by agreeing in spirit, you would not be automatically obliged to go on the expedition itself. Any number of things might happen between now and then. We may run into problems with the ship, or lose the argument to reassign it. We may discover that the signal is a fluke. You may fail the medical criteria for skipover. You may even—"

"Die."

"I was not going to put it in such blunt terms."

"I've had my share of adventures, brother. So have you. This is where mine brought me—locked up and hated."

"You made a single miscalculation."

"Which killed four hundred and seventeen thousand people. You reckon one act will atone for that?"

"No, but I do believe you have already paid back more than your share. Think it over, Ndege. There's no immediate rush."

"And am I allowed to discuss this with Goma?"

"For now, I'd rather you didn't. If and when the expedition becomes likely, certain aspects of it may be made public. But until then, let this remain between you and me. Brother and sister, sharing a great responsibility—the way it has always been."

Her look was sympathetic but also slightly pitying. "You miss the old days."

"I try not to. It's an old man's habit, and I don't very much enjoy being an old man."

"Would you go, if the opportunity came?"

"They'd never allow it on medical grounds. I'm about ready to be pickled and stuffed into a jar."

"And I'm not?"

"You forget, Ndege: they asked for you by name. That rather changes things."

She gave a lopsided squint, her expression of puzzlement. "What do I have that you don't? We grew up together. We've experienced the same things."

Mposi scraped back his chair and stood with a click of knees and a little involuntary groan of effort. "The only way to find out, I suppose, would be to respond to the signal." He nodded at the package he had arrived with. "Eat that green-bread, while it's still fresh."

"Thank you, brother."

She rose from her chair and walked him to the door; they embraced and kissed each other lightly on the cheek, and then she was back inside and he was alone, outside the house.

He looked beyond the perimeter wall of her compound, out towards the greening domes and ellipsoids of this early district of Guochang, with the later structures rising rectangular and pale beyond. The sky had darkened with the onset of evening and now the rings were starting to become visible. Present during the day, too, but almost never seen except at night, they rose from one horizon, vaulted over the zenith and descended to the opposite horizon—a twinkling procession of countless tiny bright fragments, each following an independent orbit, but nonetheless organised into a complex banded flow. A spectacle that could be beautiful, even enchanting, if one were not aware of its true meaning.

The rings had not been present when people first reached Crucible. They were a scar—the lingering evidence of a single calamitous mistake. The error had been made with the noblest of intentions, but that did not render it any more forgivable. In those hot and heady days, when the laws of this new world were still being formulated, many were prepared to see Ndege executed.

Mposi had done well to keep his sister from the gallows. But he could do nothing about the sky.

The airstrip was within the compound but screened off from the elephants. After she landed and secured the old white aeroplane, Goma grabbed her things, climbed down and made her way to a heavy gate set into the four-metre-tall electrified fence. She opened the lock and pushed through into the separate enclosed area which held their study buildings and vehicles. Over the years the camp had expanded, but the core remained a group of closely set domes, linked together like a cloverleaf. She walked the short distance to the first of the domes, then ascended the metal stairs leading to the entrance. Her lace-up boots rattled on the openwork treads.

Inside, where the heat and humidity were kept at bay, Tomas lay on his preferred bunk bed. He was eating greenbread out of a paper bag and leafing through expensively printed research notes. He peered at her over the top of the pages, smiled cautiously.

"Home is the hunter. How'd it go?"

"As well as expected." Goma took off her sunglasses, stuffed them into a hip pocket. "They said my request was very well presented, case well made, expect our decision in the fullness of time."

Tomas nodded sagely. "In other words, the same old brushoff."

"All we can do is keep trying. How are the numbers on Alpha herd?"

He pinched at the bridge of his nose and squinted at a column of figures, scribbled over in ink. "Down two on last season. Measurable impairment across a battery of variables, all significant at three sigma. I'll run the results again, just to be sure, but I think we know how the curves are trending."

"Yes." She was about to tell him not to bother rerunning the analysis—the outcome would be the same, she was sure—but a tiny part of her hoped there might be a glimmer of good news buried somewhere in the numbers. "I came to speak to Ru."

"She's with the elephants. Beta herd, I think—study area two. You look exhausted—want me to drive you out there?"

"No, I'll be fine—it's Ru I worry about. Look, run those numbers again, will you? Isolate the Agrippa subgroup, too—if there's a signal to be found, I don't want it smothered by the noise."

"Will do. Oh, and well done—however well it went."

"Thanks," Goma said doubtfully.

Outside the dome, she took the second electric buggy,

dumped her gear in the rear hopper, buckled herself into the driving seat and headed through the automatic gate in the secondary fence, into the main part of the sanctuary. She picked up speed, bouncing in her seat as the buggy followed a rough, undulating path. The sanctuary's terrain ranged from level ground to gentle uplands, with areas of grassland and heavier tree cover. On Earth, an elephant population of the same size would have stripped the vegetation back to its roots, but Crucible's plant life grew with astonishing vigour all year round. Without the elephants to hold it in check, this whole zone would have returned to thick forestation within a few years.

Goma passed the occasional small building or equipment store along the way. Here and there she spotted elephants, sometimes partly screened by intervening trees and bushes. Glossy from a recent rain shower, they sometimes looked like boulders or rocky outcroppings—the exposed geology of an ancient world. Mostly they kept their distance, wary if not actually afraid. She spied a lone bull or two, isolated from the larger herds. She gave them a wide berth. Drenched in testosterone, bulls could be unpredictable and dangerous. Over generations, and with the dwindling influence of the Tantors, the old herd dynamics were reasserting themselves.

Soon enough she was at the study area, and there was the Beta herd—lured in with enticements of fruit and greenbread, then persuaded to take part in cognitive games. Goma and Ru had designed the research programme, but it was mostly down to Ru to shape the individual challenges. Of necessity, these had grown increasingly simple as the elephants' average intelligence baseline slowly declined. The complex tests—those that demanded a high degree of abstract reasoning—were now obsolete. Only Agrippa could pass them with any regularity, and Agrippa was too old and canny to be a reliable test subject.

Ru was standing up in her own buggy, back ramrod straight, a cap jammed down over her eyes. With a notebook wedged into the angle of her right arm and a stylus in the other hand, she was recording observations.

Goma slowed so as not to disturb the experiment. She stopped the buggy, grabbed her things and walked the rest of the way.

The herd comprised thirty members, give or take, led by

the matriarch Bellatrix. There were older females under the matriarch, but the only males were infants and juveniles.

In a clearing, Ru had set up the day's sequence of cognitive puzzles, and one by one the elephants were encouraged to try their luck. There were mirrors, to test recognition-of-self. There were pots with food under them that could be moved around, or blinds that served a similar purpose. There were sturdy upright boards set with movable symbols—simple problems of logic and association and memory, with clear rewards for a correct answer. There were piles of objects and tools that could be combined to solve a problem, such as extracting fruit from a container. With her usual diligence, Ru had been working through combinations of these tests all day. The elephants were generally obliging, but only up to a point. Goma knew how frustrating it became when the rewards stopped being sufficiently attractive.

"I could use some good news," Goma said when she was within earshot.

"How about you go first. Did you batter those idiots into a pulp?"

"Metaphorically."

"So we get our brand-new fence?"

"It's pending, but I think I made a good case."

"I wouldn't expect anything less of you. Still, arseholes, the lot of them."

"I wouldn't go *quite* that far."

"Oh, I would." Ru hopped down from the buggy. "They're just playing with us. They could give us ten times the amount we've asked for and it wouldn't make a dent in their funding budget. We're just down in the noise."

They walked towards each other.

"Speaking of noise," Goma said, "Tomas tells me the numbers aren't looking great."

"Dismal, more like. But why are we surprised? Three years ago I could draw a chequer-board in the dirt and play a passable game of Go with Bellatrix. Now she just scuffs her trunk through the squares—it's as if she almost remembers, but not enough to understand the point. That's not an intergenerational decline—that's a single elephant losing intelligence almost as we speak."

"We should expect some age-related cognitive deterioration. It affects people, so why not pachyderms?"

"We never used to see such a sharp tail-off."

"I know—just trying to find a slightly less depressing way of looking at it. Have you been out here all day?"

"Got caught up. You know how it goes."

They met, embraced, kissed. They held each other for a few seconds, Goma straightening Ru's cap. Then Goma stepped back and appraised the other woman, noticing the stiffness in her posture and the slight tremble in her hand, the one still holding her notebook. Ru was bigger and taller than Goma, but for all that she was also frailer.

"You're done for the day. Let's pack up and drive home."

"I need to finish this batch of tests."

"No, you're done." Goma spoke with all the firm authority she could muster, knowing full well that her wife would not take well to being pressured.

"It's just been a long one. I'll be fine after a night's rest."

They packed the study items into the rear hoppers of their two buggies. Goma slaved her buggy to follow Ru's, then joined her in the forward vehicle. Goma opened the storage compartment by the passenger seat, unsurprised to see that it was empty.

"Did you even bring your medicines?"

"I meant to go back for them."

"You never miss a detail with elephants—why is it so hard to extend the same care to yourself?"

"I'm fine," Ru said. But after a moment, she added, "Can we detour to swing by Alpha herd? I'd like to take a look at Agrippa."

"Agrippa can wait—you need your medicine."

But it was pointless arguing, especially as Ru was driving. She steered the buggy onto a narrower track, the rear vehicle following, and soon they were cresting a low hill to overlook the favoured gathering spot of Alpha herd. It was near the greened-over corpse of a Provider robot, frozen where it had been when the information wave hit Crucible.

They stopped. Goma hopped out first, then went around to help Ru step down.

"There she is. Binoculars in the back, if you need them."

"No, I'll manage." Goma levelled a hand over her eyes, screening out the platinum glare of the clouds. It only took her a few moments to pick out Agrippa, the matriarch of the Alpha herd, but her usual pleasure at recognition was offset with disquiet.

Something was not right with Agrippa.

"She's very slow."

"I noticed that a couple of days ago," Ru said. "Some lameness for a while, but this is different. I know she's old, but she's always had that underlying strength to get her through."

"We should take some blood."

"I agree. Bring her in, if necessary. Maybe it's just an infection, or a bad reaction to something she ate."

"Possibly."

But neither cared to admit the obvious truth: that Agrippa was showing the signs of extreme age rather than of any underlying malady that could be treated with drugs or transfusions. She was simply an old elephant—the oldest of the herd members.

But also the smartest, according to the cognition measures. The only one who could still pass most of the tests, proving that she had an inner monologue, a sense of her own identity, an understanding of cause and effect, of time's arrow, of the distinction between life and death. Agrippa could not generate speech sounds, but she could understand spoken statements and formulate symbolic responses. She was the last of the Tantors—the last elephant to carry the fire of true intelligence.

But Agrippa had grown old, and although her immediate offspring were cleverer than the common herd, they were not as bright as their mother. Her children had produced grandchildren, diluting her genes even further, and these elephants were barely distinguishable from the others. So weak was the signal, it took careful statistical analysis to prove they had any cognitive enhancements.

"We can't lose her," Ru said eventually.

"We will."

"Then it ends. We'll have failed."

"There's more work to be done. Always will be. We'll still have all these elephants to look after."

"They don't even care. That's the part that really gets me.

We do. It tears us apart to see them losing what they had, year by year. But to them it's nothing. They don't miss being Tantors—give them wide-open spaces, food to eat, some mud to roll in—why should they?"

"Being Tantors was not a normal part of elephant development," Goma said. "We can't blame them for not caring. Do dogs care that they're not as clever as bonobos? Do ants care that they're not as smart as dogs?"

"*I* care."

Goma squeezed her shoulder, then hugged her silently for a few moments. She shared Ru's creeping despair—the sense of something bright and precious and mercurial slipping through their fingers. The more they tried to measure it, to preserve it, the more quickly it was fading. But she needed Ru to be strong, and in turn Goma needed to be strong for Ru. They were like two trees leaning against each other.

"Let's go home," Goma said. "I have to call my mother—I told her I'd visit tomorrow but Agrippa's bloodwork is more important."

"I can take care of that," Ru said. "You know how much Ndege needs her routines."

"Can you blame her?"

"Not me. I'm the last one who'd blame her for anything."

A few days later, when early evening business brought Mposi back to the parliamentary building in Guochang, he found a visitor waiting for him in the annexe to his office.

"Goma," he said, beaming. "What a pleasant surprise."

But his words drew no corresponding sentiment from her, nor even a smile.

"Can we speak? In private?"

"Of course."

He let her into the office, still maintaining a façade of polite conviviality even though nothing in her manner suggested this was a social call. That would have been out of character, at least lately. When she had been less busy in both professional and private spheres, Goma had often visited him for a stroll around the parliamentary gardens, both of them trading stories and titbits of innocent rumour. He realised, with a swell of sadness, that he had almost forgotten how much pleasure those simple encounters had brought him, unencumbered by professional obligations on either side.

"Chai?" he offered, drawing the office blinds against a lowering sun as fat and red as a ripe tomato.

"No. This won't take long. She can't go."

He smiled. They were both still standing. "She?"

"My mother. Ndege." Her hands were planted on her hips. Goma was small, slight of build, easily underestimated. "This stupid expedition of yours—the one you think I don't know about."

Mposi glanced at the door, making sure he had closed it on his way in.

"You'd better sit down."

"I said this won't take long."

"Nonetheless." He raised a hand in the direction of the chair he reserved for visitors, then eased his plump frame into the one on his side of the desk. "She was under express instructions not to mention it to anyone."

"I'm her daughter. Did you think she'd be able to keep something like that from me for long?"

"You were to be informed when matters were on a more stable footing."

"You mean when everyone else learned about it."

"I'm not a fool, Goma, and I do understand your feelings. But secrecy is secrecy. What else did she mention?"

"There's more?"

"Please, no games."

After a silence, Goma said, "A signal, from somewhere out in deep space."

Mposi rubbed his forehead. He could already feel a knot of tension building behind his eyes. "My god."

"Some possible connection with the Trinity—with Chiku, Eunice and Dakota. I can understand why that would be of interest to her. She lost her mother—watched as she was spirited away by an alien robot. But it's Dakota I'm interested in."

"The elephant?"

"The Tantor. If you received a signal from Eunice, then maybe Dakota's out there as well. Do I have to explain why that's of interest to me?"

"No, I think I can guess." Mposi had always found Goma's

scientific reports too technical to be easily digested by a non-specialist like himself, but he could skim the abstracts, get the thrust of her argument. "It was just a signal. It never repeated, and we've been listening for it again for six months."

"But you believe it was a real message, and that it was meant for us. You think it might have some connection with the Trinity."

"This is what I told your mother. In confidence."

"If you start blaming her for the leak of your little secret, you'll have a much bigger problem on your hands."

"Goodness, Goma. That almost sounds like a threat."

"You need to understand my seriousness."

"I do. Fully."

"Then I'll cut to the point. Whatever that message says, Ndege's not going."

"I rather think that choice should be your mother's."

"It isn't, not now. I'm going in her place. I'm a quarter of her age and much stronger."

"Be that as it may, Ndege is still alive. She has also consented to join the expedition."

"Only because you gave her no choice."

"I merely pointed out that volunteering for such an expedition could be turned to her immediate advantage."

"You dangled the idea of a pardon in front of her. I thought better of you."

"It was meant with all sincerity." Mposi picked up the paperweight he kept on his desk—the skull of a sea otter, polished to a pebble-like glossiness. It had been sent across space, a gift from his half-brother. "You have a nerve, Goma, lecturing me on my treatment of Ndege. If you doubt that, ask your mother."

His outburst—delivered calmly enough—had an immediate and chastening effect on his visitor. She looked contrite, sad, momentarily ashamed at herself.

"I just don't want her expectations raised."

"Nor do I," Mposi answered softly. He put down the skull; it made a pleasingly solid thunk. "I would never put a false hope before your mother, not after all she's been through. Are you serious, though—would you consider going in her place?

You love this world, you love your work. You have a fine companion in Ru. Why give all of that up?"

"Because I'd rather it was me than Ndege. And I've seen those ships of yours, swinging overhead like a pair of new moons. They're huge. You can't tell me there isn't room for thousands of people on them."

"In their original design," Mposi answered. "But if one of the ships were to be refitted for a long-range expedition—and that's still not a given—a great deal would need to be re-organised."

"I bet you could still find room for Ru."

Mposi could hardly believe his ears. "You've spoken to her as well?"

"Out of respect for your secret, no. In fact, I haven't spoken about it to anyone except Ndege. Does that make you happier?"

"Marginally."

"But I will put it to Ru. She'll feel the same way about Dakota. We lost the Tantors, Mposi. We lost the most beautiful, surprising thing ever to happen to us as a species. New friends—new companions. And we let them die. That's all Ru and I have ever done—chart the decline, the tailing-off of their intelligence. But now we have a chance to recontact one of the original Tantors, or at least her offspring. Even if all we recovered was fresh genetic material, that would give us something new. Ru knows that, too. She'll want to come with me."

"Does Ndege know of your intentions?"

"I told her I'd speak to you about it."

"And did she approve? No—you don't need to answer that. Ndege would try to protect you just as you're trying to protect her. She wouldn't want you to leave."

"Ultimately, though, the choice would be yours, uncle. Commit your sister to something she won't survive, or take a chance on your niece?"

"When you put it like that, it sounds so simple."

"That's because it is. Agree to my being on that ship, uncle."

He felt himself on the brink of consenting. But he would not—could not—allow the decision to be made in haste. Too much was at stake. It was vastly more complicated than Goma understood.

"I wished to do something good for your mother."

"You still can. That ship won't be ready for a while, will it?"

He sighed, seeing where this was heading. "Another five years, so I'm told."

"Then that's five years in which you can make things easier for Ndege. Are you ever going public with this?"

"Some sort of limited disclosure will be required once it's clear we've altered our plans for one of the ships. A year or two from now, perhaps."

"Then you can tell the world that Ndege has volunteered for the mission. Let her have that moment. Only the three of us need know that she won't be going."

"It would be more than three of us. Your medical suitability for skipover would need to be assessed. There are no guarantees."

"I'm still more likely to cope with it than my mother."

"You place me in an unfortunate position."

"Then I'm glad you understand how it feels. Put me on the expedition and reserve a space for Ru. I won't ask again, uncle. And my words earlier?"

"Yes?"

"They weren't a threat. But if you want to think of it as a robust bargaining position, be my guest."

He smiled fondly, simultaneously proud and a little terrified. "You were wasted on science, Goma. We could have made a fine politician of you."

CHAPTER 2

In the early spring of the northern hemisphere of Occupied Mars, in the year 2640, on the evening of the day before he died, Kanu Akinya stood at a tall fretted window with his back to Swift. He had his hands behind him but not quite clasped, a slim-stemmed goblet dangling loosely from his fine-webbed fingers. It had been years since he was a true merman, but his anatomy retained traces of that phase of his life. Muscles corded his mountainous neck; his shoulders had a swimmer's top-heavy broadness. Kanu's mouth was small, his nose flat, his eyes large and expressive, optimised for light-gathering in conditions of low visibility. Grey now, he still wore his hair long, gathered into a pleated tail that hung halfway down his back.

"Your move," Swift reminded him.

Kanu had been watching the sunset. The sky at his eye level was an extremely deep blue, virtually black at the zenith, shading to purple and then salmon pink as his gaze tracked down to the horizon. This ancient volcanic summit had been the obvious location for the embassy: the closest point to space, and the furthest from the confusion and danger of the forbidden surface.

"My apologies," he said, turning from the window.

Kanu resumed his position at the table facing Swift and set his goblet next to the board. They were playing chess, that most ancient of African games.

"Troubled?" Swift asked.

"Thinking about my brother, actually. Wondering if it wouldn't hurt the universe for us to swap places, just for a year or two."

"Your brother is twenty-nine light-years away. Also, technically speaking, he is not your brother."

"Half-brother, then."

"Not even that. Your mother died on Earth. Mposi's mother may or may not be dead, although the balance of probability points in that direction. I'm sorry to belabour these unfortunate facts, Kanu, but I have difficulty enough understanding human affairs without you complicating things."

"I'm sorry it's not simple enough for machine comprehension. I'll make a note of that for future reference."

"Pray do so, your memory being as fallible as it is."

Swift had adopted scrupulously human anatomy and dress for the purposes of diplomatic relations, his face, outfit and bearing approximating those of a young man of learning of the late eighteenth century. He favoured a frock coat, a white scarf around his neck and pince-nez glasses through which he was inclined to peer with his chin cocked at a high, imperious angle. A head of thick, boyish curls was combed and oiled into some sort of submission.

After a moment, while Kanu continued staring at the board, Swift added, "Seriously, though—you would swap places with Mposi, if that were an option?"

"Why wouldn't I? A backwater colony, a modest but growing economy, easy relations between humans and machines . . . no Consolidation breathing down my neck, no great concerns about the Watchkeepers. I bet Mposi even has a room with a view."

"I feel obligated to point out that it's easy to maintain cordial relations between humans and machines when there are hardly any machines. Are you planning to make that move, incidentally, or would you like a few more months to think about it?"

Kanu had evaluated his narrowing options and was about to move his piece. But as he raised his hand towards the board, a chime sounded from across the room.

"I'd better take that."

"If it helps delay the inevitable, be my guest."

Kanu rose from his chair, walked to the console and angled its screen to address his standing form. The face of Garudi

Dalal, one of his three human colleagues on Olympus Mons, appeared before him.

"Garudi. I'm late for dinner, I know. I'll be on my way up shortly."

"It's not about dinner, Kanu. I take it you haven't heard the news?"

"That Swift is terrible at chess?"

But the normally amiable Dalal—his best friend among the other humans—did not respond in kind. Her face was grave. "There's been a development in the last few minutes."

"That sounds ominous."

"It may well be. Something's come in. Slipped right through interdiction."

Kanu glanced at Swift again. Technically, this information was confidential, a communication between ambassadors. But if something had happened close to Mars or on it, Swift would not be ignorant of it for long.

"Normally we worry about things *leaving* Mars."

"Not this time. It's a supply shuttle, inbound from Jupiter. Semi-autonomous. Sometimes they put a crew inside, but not for this run. It wouldn't have got close to us except it was scheduled to dock with one of the fortresses. Approach clearances all checked out. Then at the last minute it veered off and slipped into the atmosphere."

"In which case there won't be much left of it. Do we have an impact point yet?"

"I'm afraid," Swift said, rising from his chair to stand behind him, "that you have rather more than an impact point."

Kanu turned to his friend. "What do you know?"

"The news has just reached me—by somewhat different channels, of course—the ship made it down." Swift directed his own face to the screen. "Good evening, by the way, Ambassador Dalal."

Dalal acknowledged Swift with a nod but did not reciprocate the verbal greeting.

"Swift's right. Most of it's still in one piece. The guns hit part of it, and then the atmospheric friction did some more damage, but that's when things got strange."

"Strange? In what way?" Kanu said.

"It slowed down. Used thrust after it was in the atmosphere. By the time it hit the surface it was hardly moving at all."

"Sounds like a deliberate attempt to land."

"That's the theory," she said. "Reclamationist sabotage, maybe. If they intercepted and boarded it somewhere between here and Jupiter . . ."

"Do you think Reclamationists were inside it?"

Dalal gave a weary shrug. "Who knows. What I *do* know is that someone's going to have to find out, even if all they end up doing is recovering corpses. I'm convening the others to discuss how we handle this."

Kanu nodded—he shared exactly her misgivings over the whole business. "Let Korsakov and Lucien know I'm on my way. So where did it come down? Please say it was the other side of Mars, that this doesn't have to be our problem."

"I'm afraid it's just within range of a flier."

Kanu closed the console and returned to the chessboard. He moved his piece, setting it down with a decisive *clack*.

"More fool me."

Swift looked puzzled. "For what?"

"Hoping for some drama in my life. This is what you get."

It was always cold on the landing deck. The dome at the top of the embassy was sealed, the air pressurised to a breathable norm, but it never got warm enough to be comfortable. This was the literal summit of the human presence on Mars—the embassy rising like a small pinnacle of its own from the monstrous upwelling of Olympus Mons.

In the cold it was easy to believe that space was a hop and a skip away.

"Garudi tells me you allowed Swift to eavesdrop on her conversation yesterday," said Korsakov, standing next to Kanu, the two of them with their helmets tucked under their arms.

"Swift knew about it before we did."

"Nonetheless, Kanu. It's hardly protocol, is it?" Korsakov spoke slowly, as if each word needed consideration and that the patience of his listeners could be expected. "What is it about that one, exactly? What do you see in *that* machine, compared to the others?"

"I enjoy Swift's company. Anyway, why do I have to explain myself? Isn't that what we're here for—to communicate with them?"

"Communication is fine," Korsakov said, his fine grey eyes surveying Kanu from beneath an imperious brow, surmounted by a sweep of long grey hair which he wore combed back. "But it can't be more than that. These machines stole Mars from us. It was *our* world, *our* inheritance, and they tore it from our control."

The flier, powered up and ready, was turning on a platform after being serviced.

"I'm broadly aware of recent history, Yevgeny."

The tall, stooping Korsakov began: "I can't speak for the United Aquatic Nations—"

"Then don't."

"But *your people* have an expectation, Kanu. A tacit understanding that your sympathies, when put to the test, will always fall on the human side of the equation."

"Is anyone saying they don't?"

"The robot is using you, Kanu. Machines don't understand friendship. This is leverage, pure and simple."

Kanu was glad when the other two ambassadors arrived at the landing deck. They were also wearing surface suits, although their outfits hinted at their differing allegiances within the solar system. Kanu wore a blue-green suit patterned with starfish, their arms linked together in a kind of synaptic net. Korsakov, who stood for the United Orbital Nations, wore regolith grey, embossed with a representation of craters. Dalal, the representative for the United Surface Nations, carried the motif of a single tree, its branches hung with birds and fruit.

Lucien, the recently appointed ambassador for the Consolidation—everything out to the Oort Cloud that was not Earth, the Moon or Mars—wore a suit threaded with a ripple-like design of complex interlocking orbits.

"Swift will be joining us?" Dalal asked of Kanu.

"Yes. He should be here in a moment."

"I don't care for this arrangement," Lucien confessed. "We should be free to conduct our inspection without having a robot along for the ride."

"It's what's been agreed," Kanu answered, just as Swift

appeared from a door leading onto the deck. "Transparency. Cooperation. It's bound to help."

"Them, or us?" Korsakov muttered, stooping to avoid scraping his head on the underside of the vehicle.

Once the flier was sealed, the air was pumped out of the deck and the dome opened to the sky. The passengers took lounge seats and tucked their helmets between their feet. By consent Garudi Dalal took the controls. She vectored them east, maintaining altitude at the agreed value. In the cabin, a soft automatic voice reeled off indices of airspeed, temperature and pressure. Kanu turned around in his lounge seat to view the receding spire of the embassy, the dome clam-shelling tight once they were gone.

The embassy was a dark fluted spire with broad, rootlike foundations. It corkscrewed a kilometre and a half from the summit of Olympus Mons, a unicorn's horn jammed into Mars. With the four ambassadors now aboard the flier, the place was completely devoid of human inhabitation. In fact, since the ambassadors were in the sky, there was now no human presence on the surface of Mars at all.

They had been under way for an hour when Dalal raised her voice, though without any particular urgency. "Something coming up. Three envoys, standard approach formation."

Korsakov moved to look over her shoulder, studying the console displays. "Weapons readiness?"

"Nominal," Dalal answered.

The flier itself carried no armaments—that would have been an express violation of the terms of the embassy settlement—but they were under constant surveillance and cover from the orbital fortresses. Kanu had been expecting the escorts, though. They were a normal feature of their occasional inspection flights.

"They won't harm us," he said. "Not with Swift as a hostage."

Swift looked affronted. "I trust that is meant as a joke."

"You'd make a very poor hostage given what you've always told me about your massively distributed nature."

Swift touched a hand to his frock-coated chest. "I am still very attached to this body. It would be a nuisance to have to make a new one."

Korsakov scowled in annoyance.

The three flying things were smaller than the ambassadorial vehicle, each a bronze ellipsoid with blue and red lights glowing through from within. How they flew was open to conjecture. Once, humans would have harvested their technological cleverness for profit, but those days were long behind them. The three machines enclosed the flier in a triangular formation.

"You are free to descend," Swift said.

Dalal took them down to an altitude of only two kilometres above the mean surface level, close enough that the robots' workings were in plain view. At periodic intervals, the machines had built towering diamond-faceted citadels on the face of Mars. They studded the surface like anthills, beehives or ice-cream cornets. They were huge, candy-coloured, aglow with secret purpose. Tentacular tubes linked them, hundreds, maybe thousands of kilometres long. Glowing corpuscular things shot along these tubes, or occasionally moved through the air between the citadels.

Undoubtedly there was much more going on beneath the crust, beyond the easy scrutiny of orbital sensors.

"Coming up on the impact site," Dalal announced. "Twenty kilometres dead ahead. Visual on it now. Dropping speed to minimum. Swift—please remind your friends of our agreed intentions?"

"All is in hand," Swift said.

Still accompanied by their machine escort, the ambassadors made a slow approach to the object of their interest. It was bigger than Kanu had expected—skyscraper-sized. An ugly squared-off thing never designed to move through air, it resembled a grey metal filing cabinet and was jammed into a sand dune like a surrealist art installation. He thought of his grandmother's sculptures, and wondered whether Sunday would have appreciated the comparison.

"An hour is an insult," Korsakov said, tapping life-support instructions into his suit cuff.

"We'll make the best of it," Kanu answered.

"Always the optimist, merman."

"I try, Yevgeny. There are worse habits."

They could not land on or dock with the tilted, damaged wreck, but orbital surveillance had identified a possible entrance just above the point where the ship met the ground. It was a tiny airlock, but it would have to suffice. They circled once, verifying that the lock was as it had appeared from space, and then settled down about fifty metres from the wreck.

All in hand, as Swift had said.

When the flier was down, Dalal pumped the air out of the cockpit and lowered the boarding ramp. Korsakov and Lucien were the first to exit, followed by Kanu, then Swift—Swift, of course, had no need of a spacesuit—and finally Dalal, once she had secured the flier. The ramp folded up behind her, but the little vehicle was ready and waiting for their return.

"Sixty minutes and counting," Lucien said.

"Fifty-six minutes," Swift said, almost apologetically. "I am sorry to insist on a point of diplomacy, but the agreed time began the moment your skids touched our soil."

They made a beeline for the side of the wreck—a shadowed slab, dense with machinery. The side where the entrance point had been identified curved back over their heads. Kanu had the dizzy sensation that it was in a constant slow topple, about to bury the ambassadorial party.

"That lock is tiny!" Dalal said.

"Emergency egress only," Lucien said. "The cargo locks are buried, or much too high up for us to reach in the time we have."

Even the emergency lock was some distance above their heads, and they had to scramble up to it one at a time using pipes and handholds projecting from the wrecked hull. There was a narrow ledge beneath the lock and extending to one side of it. Korsakov was the first to reach the ledge, its width just taking his feet. He traversed sideways, one hand reaching to his left, the other hanging on to a rail over his head.

Dalal and Lucien went next, and then Kanu. Swift monkeyed up alongside them with dismaying agility, pausing only to scuff dust from the collar of his coat.

"Lock power is still active," Korsakov announced. "I am going to try and open it." Continuing to brace himself with his right hand, he folded aside an armoured panel to access a bank of controls.

"Well?" Lucien asked.

"Cycling," Korsakov said. "But this is, as Dalal said, a very small lock. I doubt it will hold more than one of us at a time."

"We'll see you on the other side," Kanu said. "It shouldn't take more than a few minutes."

"Under the terms of our arrangement," Swift said, "I must not be the last to enter."

"We weren't about to forget you," Lucien muttered.

Korsakov was soon inside the lock with the outer door sealed and the chamber pressurising. His voice sounded as clear as before. "The lock is reaching normal pressure. I will not, of course, be so foolish as to remove my helmet, and I advise the rest of you to follow my example."

"Tell us when the inner door opens," Dalal said.

"It is doing just that, Garudi. I am stepping through into the ship. There is heat and power and emergency lighting, but no immediate sign of life."

"Garudi is next, then Lucien," Kanu said. "I'll allow Swift to enter before me. Is that arrangement acceptable to all parties?"

There was no dissent, and so Dalal cycled through the lock next. She joined Korsakov on the other side, confirming his initial observations. "Much less structural damage than I was expecting. Everything looks straight and there's still power, as Yevgeny says. The lower levels must have absorbed a lot of the impact."

"Bad news for anyone down there," Lucien said.

Kanu waited for the Consolidation ambassador to pass through the lock. Save for himself, the breathing members of the party were now all inside the wreck. It was just Kanu and the robot, alone under the sky of Mars.

"Now your turn," he told Swift.

"Thank you, Kanu. It's rather irksome that I must use the lock in the first place, but there's no avoiding it."

"When robots build ships, you can show us how it's done."

"We shan't build ships, Kanu. We shall become them."

He waited on the ledge until Swift had gone through, and then counted the long seconds until the lock was ready to admit him. He cursed himself for forgetting to zero his suit clock the moment they landed on Mars.

"How long have we been here?" he asked Dalal when he finally joined the others.

"Thirteen minutes just to get this far. And we'll need to allow the same amount of time to get out."

Kanu nodded within his helmet. Panels and signs were still aglow, and dim yellow service lighting offered glimpses into adjoining passageways and compartments.

"We'll never sweep the whole thing," he said, "so we won't try. For a start, I think we can rule out survivors in the lower levels. But we should be able to reach the control core easily enough."

"It would be unwise to raise your hopes," Lucien said.

"I'm not."

"Regardless, Kanu is correct," Dalal said. "For the sake of making our governments look good, we must go through the motions."

"Steady with talk like that," Kanu said. "They'll hang you for honesty."

Dalal grinned back at him through her faceplate. "Being hanged is the least of my present worries."

The slope of the floor made progress tricky, but they found their way to the central trunk elevator without too much trouble.

Korsakov found the control panel and punched the big manual button to summon their ride. It came rattling and groaning along its shaft, squealing and protesting. Kanu supposed that they were lucky the elevator was working at all, after the impact the craft had sustained. But he would have welcomed any excuse to abandon the search and return to the flier.

The ambassadors entered the elevator, followed by Swift, and the car began to ascend, bucking and jerking as it hit some obstruction.

"It is not easy to see what these Reclamationists were hoping to achieve," Swift said, as if he felt an obligation to make conversation.

"It might be a symbolic gesture," Kanu said. "Reclaiming a piece of Mars, if only for a few days."

"With their corpses?" Swift asked.

"Maybe they hoped to survive long enough to issue some kind of statement, a declaration of sovereignty or suchlike."

"I still fail to see the logic. What use is this dry, airless world to you?"

"No practical use at all," Kanu said as the elevator halted and the doors opened. "But we can't bear the thought of someone else having it."

The control deck was a semicircular room with passages branching off it and a wide armoured window occupying one arc of the curved wall. Some of the console displays were still active, and Korsakov was confident enough to start flipping the heavy manual control switches. With a clunk and whine, the window's armoured shuttering began to retract.

They were higher on Mars now than when they landed, a good twenty levels up, and from this elevation—surveying the oddly tilted landscape—Kanu could easily make out the luminous, pastel-shaded anthills of three distant robot cities. Even closer, one of their connecting tentacles formed a distinct glowing ridge-line, like the spine of a half-buried sea-monster. He watched, partly mesmerised, as lights raced along the spine with the speed of shooting stars.

"Do those cities have names, Swift?"

"I am not sure you would perceive them as 'cities,' Kanu. 'Nodes' or 'hubs' would be more accurate. Functional modules, like your own brain compartmentalisation. But yes, they do have distinct signifiers. Although again, 'name' may be stretching things a little—"

"When you're done chatting," Korsakov said, "we could begin searching the ship with these internal sensors." He was bending over a console, tapping keys. Displays were coming online, showing blueprints and cross sections, and he drew their attention to a couple of them. "These areas appear to contain air, and these are where the ship seems to have lost pressure."

"Given the lack of time available to us," Dalal said, "it'll be a token search. But at least we can go home saying we did the best we could."

"Should my compatriots find organic material," Swift said, "we would treat it with the utmost respect."

"Thank you, Swift," Kanu said, "but I'm not sure being shredded and incorporated into your neural-logic networks is the fate we'd want for our loved ones. Even if you did it respectfully."

"I can, nonetheless, assist with your search."

The ambassadors looked at each other. Korsakov started to say something, but Kanu raised a hand.

"No, it makes sense. One of him can do the work of four of us in about a thousandth of the time."

"I would not go quite that far," Swift said, "but I can certainly make a difference, given the time you have remaining."

"Yevgeny," said Dalal, "can you call up the sensor search on different consoles?"

"It's done. Five consoles—four for us and one for the machine. I'm already running a visual and infrared search on decks twelve to eighteen—don't bother duplicating my efforts."

"We won't," Kanu said.

The consoles were simple to use, and it did not take long to run at least a cursory search on each deck. They were looking for the obvious: survivors or bodies, in plain view. If people were hidden away in lockers, out of the reach of the sensors, there was nothing the ambassadors could do about it.

"In ten minutes we'll need to be on our way back down," Dalal announced. "And that's assuming we cut our margins to the bone."

"Our margin is still good," Kanu said. He had searched half of his allotted area of the ship, seeing only empty corridors and service shafts, plus the occasional vault-like cargo bay. Since some of the bays retained pressure, there might be survivors hidden among the ranks of cargo pallets. But unless they made themselves known, they were going to remain there.

"Wait," Lucien said, stepping back from ver console, ver gloved fingers spread wide. "I've just been locked out."

After a moment, Dalal said, "And me."

"The fault has spread to my console as well," Swift said, his hands becoming a blur on the controls.

Kanu was also unable to continue his search, and he noticed Korsakov suffering the same problem. The schematics had vanished. All the displays were showing the same thing: a block of Swahili, appearing and disappearing over and over.

IN THE NAME OF HUMANITY WE RECLAIM THIS WORLD FOR PEOPLE! LET THIS BE THE FIRST LIGHT OF A NEW MARTIAN DAWN! LET FIRE CLEANSE THE FACE OF MARS IN READINESS FOR THE RECLAMATION!

"The message was almost certainly meant to be read by robots, rather than humans," Swift said. "They would have been counting on us reaching the wreck in advance of any diplomatic party. Had you not arrived first, we would have triggered exactly this response."

"We're leaving," Dalal said. "This instant."

"For once," Kanu said, "I think you'll find the four of us in unanimous agreement."

The elevator returned them to the level where they had boarded. They still had to pass through the airlock, but for the first time Kanu allowed himself to hope they might yet make it out alive.

"Lucien is the newest ambassador," Dalal said. "Ve should go first. It's only fair."

"Agreed," Kanu said. "It's settled. Lucien first. Then you, Garudi. Yevgeny next, then me. Strict order of hierarchy, and save the arguing for later."

Korsakov said, "You mean to be last, Kanu?"

"Makes sense—I've been on Mars the longest."

"I won't leave this ship with a robot still inside it, free to do what it likes with a human asset."

Kanu had to stop himself seizing the other man by the shoulders. "Get some perspective, Yev. We were about to hand it over to the machines anyway."

The lock was ready to receive Lucien. As the door closed, Dalal said, "Don't wait for us outside. Get back to the flier and prepare to leave."

Lucien gave a nod through ver visor as the door closed. Kanu watched the airlock indicators crawl through their automatic cycle.

"I'm clear," Lucien said, after what felt like an eternity. "Jumping off." There was a thump, an intake of breath. "Down and moving. Flier is intact."

"Lock's cycling for Garudi," Kanu said.

"I could attempt to force the mechanism to open both doors at the same time," Swift said.

"And risk jamming it completely?" Korsakov said. "No. We'll leave the way we came in."

Finally the lock was ready to accept Dalal. She stepped inside, turned away from the door and initiated the cycle. The door sealed and the interminable process recommenced. Air out, door open, air in again. Kanu cursed the intransigent stupidity of the airlock for not understanding their deeper predicament.

"I'm out," Dalal said. "Crossing ground. Lucien is at the flier. Are you all right?"

"Yes, we're fine. Yevgeny's next."

It could only have taken as long for Korsakov to cycle through the lock as the other two, but to Kanu it felt like at least twice as much time. Now there was so little to lose, he wondered if perhaps Swift ought to force the lock after all.

But the air was pumping back in now. Korsakov was outside.

"Are you clear, Yev?"

"I see the flier. Lucien and Garudi are aboard. She should have moved it by now—why is she delaying?"

"Out of some misplaced concern for your well-being, perhaps?"

"You should be next," Swift said.

"No," Kanu answered. "You're a witness to this and I want you to survive. If and when you make it back to your friends, they need to know that this was a terrorist act."

"My friends already know, Kanu."

"Maybe they do. But for my peace of mind, you're still going first."

Swift gave a perfunctory nod. "If you insist."

"I do."

The lock was ready to accept Swift. He was on the verge of entering it when there came a sudden sharp blur of motion and Swift was on the other side of Kanu, the airlock vacant, and

Kanu was being pushed—shoved was closer to the truth—into the waiting aperture.

"Swift, no!"

"It is within my capability to help you, Kanu. Therefore I have no option."

Before he could act, Swift had pushed enough of himself into the lock to be able to activate the automatic sequence. It was a snakelike striking motion, almost too fast for the eye to follow. Kanu barely had time to register what had happened, let alone abort the lock sequence. Swift withdrew, the door sealed and the exchangers began to drag air out of the chamber.

"The terms of our inspection visit are still in force, Swift! We have our one hour! It has not expired!"

"Which is precisely why I will be joining you on the other side the moment the lock allows it."

When the door opened, Kanu had to stop himself toppling out. He had climbed up on the way in but now he chanced a jump, hingeing his legs to absorb the impact and trusting that the reduced gravity of Mars would spare him any injury. He hit the dirt and sprawled, nearly burying his visor in the soil. He grunted, gathered air into his lungs and pushed himself to his feet. He was still alive, and Korsakov was just vanishing into the belly of the flier. "I'm clear!" he called. "But Swift is still coming through."

Korsakov and the others would have heard something of the exchange between Kanu and the robot, even if its meaning were unclear. "Why did you allow—"

"I didn't!"

Kanu set about crossing the ground to the flier. It really was not very far, but after a dozen paces he felt compelled to turn back, anxious to see Swift appear in the open lock. He wanted Swift to be true to his word, to be the sincere and honest friend he had always believed in.

The ship blew up.

It was not a nuclear blast or metallic-hydrogen phase change; it was not the flare-up of a runaway Chibesa motor. It was not the swallowing whiteness of an unbound post-Chibesa process, the kind of catastrophic event that had destroyed entire holoships.

It was still an explosion.

The detonation tore through the ship about a third of the way up the exposed part of the vessel. Above the blast zone, the already leaning edifice started buckling over. Kanu had thought it on the verge of toppling before; now it was fulfilling that promise. Debris, flung in all directions by the detonation, began to rain down around Kanu.

"Kanu!" someone shouted.

"Take the flier!" someone shouted in return, and it was only when the words were out that he recognised his own voice.

Kanu started running, or what passed for running in the soft, slipping dust under his feet. In the distance, the flier was taking off. The boarding ramp was still lowered, dragging across the ground, and the flier was turning to meet him.

"No, Garudi," Kanu called. "It's too dangerous."

Kanu glanced back again. A lengthening shadow loomed over him now. The wreck was coming down, bowing to meet him. He could see no sign of Swift, and with an exquisite clarity he knew he stood no chance of reaching the flier.

CHAPTER 3

The seas were heavy, the boat's rise and fall testing Mposi's delicate constitution to its limits. For an Akinya, he had always been a poor traveller. Chai and greenbread and paperwork, four square walls and a horizon that stayed still—that was all he really wanted from life.

Even without the tracking device, it was not usually too hard to find Arethusa. They knew her haunts, her favoured latitudes and familiar places. The only large living thing anywhere in Crucible's waters, she could be tracked using the ancient and venerable methods of submarine warfare. She gave off a mass signature and distorted the waters above her as she swam. Her songlike ruminations, when she talked to herself or recounted Chinese lullabies, sent an acoustic signature across thousands of kilometres. Networks of floating hydrophones triangulated her position to within what was normally a small volume. During times of heavy weather or seismic activity, though, she had stealth on her side.

Nonetheless, the merfolk had narrowed down her location, and swimming out from the hydrofoil they had finally sighted their quarry. But that was as close as the merfolk could get. They owed their very existence to Arethusa—she had been involved since the start of the Panspermian Initiative. Some obscure bad blood lay in their mutual past, however, and she would not deign to talk to them any more.

So Mposi had to swim alone. The merfolk fitted him into a powered swimsuit equipped with a breathing system and launched him into the darkening swell. He gave chase, and of course Arethusa indulged in her usual games, allowing him to come very near before swimming away faster than he could follow. She could keep this up until the cells in his suit ran out of energy.

But Mposi knew that curiosity would eventually prompt her to relent.

"It's me," he sent into the water ahead of himself, using the suit's loudspeaker. "We need to talk. It's nothing to do with the tracking device—I'll never ask such a thing of you again. This is something else, and I need your advice."

But it always paid to flatter Arethusa.

"More than your advice," Mposi added. "Your wisdom. Your perspective on events. No one has your outlook, Arethusa, your breadth of experience or insight."

It was hard to talk. The suit was powered, but it still required some effort to drive and coordinate his movements. His lungs burned, even when he turned up the oxygen flow in his mask. She would hear his weakness, he felt sure. She would hear it and mock him for it.

"Something's happened," Mposi carried on after he had swum a dozen more strokes. "A signal's come in from a long way off. We don't understand why it's been sent to us, or what we should make of it. There's a chance it has something to do with—"

"That dolphin-torn, that gong-tormented sea."

She had answered, in her fashion, and his suit had picked up the emanations and converted them into natural Swahili. Arethusa did in fact speak Swahili, or at least she had been able to in the past. Lin Wei, the girl she had once been, had attended school in East Equatorial Africa.

Dolphin-torn, gong-tormented.

He was doing the one thing he had meant not to do—getting on her nerves.

But she slowed, allowing him to narrow the distance between them, and he was soon approaching her great fluked tail. His mask showed her body, two hundred metres away, as a whiskered oval. She had been two hundred metres long when she hurt him; now she had grown by a third as much again. Arethusa was the oldest sentient organism, as far as Mposi knew. But the cost of that sentience was an endless need to grow. To grow, and to move further and further from the epicentre of human affairs. The murmurings the hydrophone network picked up were increasingly strange, increasingly suggestive of a mind that had slipped its moorings.

And yet he would still risk all for an audience.

"The signal," Mposi persisted, "was aimed at us, unidirectional. Low power, even allowing for the transmission distance—and while it repeated long enough for us to recover the content, it was only active for a short while. Doesn't that interest you, Arethusa? I'll tell you something else. The message mentioned Ndege. That's a name you recognise. My sister, of course. Another Akinya. And while you might not be blood, our business is always your business."

Arethusa had stopped in the water, so Mposi slowed his rate of approach, painfully conscious of what those flippers could do to him. Like a great spacecraft making a course adjustment, the whale turned gradually until Mposi was hovering just before her left eye. Scarcely any light now reached them, so Mposi was reliant on his goggles' sonar overlay. He shivered, as he had shivered before, at the magnitude of her—and the very human scrutiny of her eye, looking at him from a cliff of grooved flesh.

"I thought I killed you once, Mposi."

"You gave it a good try. The fault was mine, though. I understand there was nothing personal in it."

"Do you?"

As large as she was, she could move with surprising speed. He had allowed himself to enter her sphere of risk.

"Gliese 163," he said. "That's the name of the star in the other solar system. We know a little bit about it: Ocular data, a few later observations."

"No one has mentioned Ocular in a very long time."

That was true, but Mposi had not made the reference thoughtlessly. The vast telescope had been Lin Wei's brainchild, and she had seen it hobbled by Akinya interference. There was danger in bringing that up, he realised. But he was also seeking a direct connection to her past.

"Eunice was your friend, before it all turned bad over Ocular. That's true, isn't it?"

"You never knew her. What right have you to speak of her?"

"None, except that I'm her great-great-great-grandson. And I think she may have some connection with the message."

Arethusa's flukes stirred, moving tonnes of water with each stroke. "You *think*?"

"There hasn't been time for any human ship to get that far out, and send a return transmission. But the Watchkeepers? We don't know how they move or how fast they can travel. What we do know is that they took three of us with them—the Holy Trinity. Chiku Green, of course. Dakota. And the Eunice construct."

"The map is not the territory."

"I understand that the construct isn't the same thing as your flesh-and-blood friend. But she was getting closer, becoming . . . what's the word? When a curve meets a line? Asymptotic?"

"Your point, Mposi?"

"Someone has to go out there. We can't just pretend this message never arrived. Someone went to the trouble to send it. The least we can do is respond."

"Just like that."

"We're getting a ship ready. It'll make the crossing, with some modifications. Wheels are turning. The expedition will happen—it's just a question of who goes on it."

"You have your answer. Send Ndege."

"That's the problem. My sister is very old."

"So are you."

"But I haven't been wasting away under house arrest for more than a century. Aside from the political complications, there's another headache. Ndege has one child, a daughter named Goma. She wishes to take her mother's place."

"Either this Goma is very old herself, or Ndege was allowed conjugal visits."

"Neither. The child was conceived long before Ndege's incarceration, but Ndege and her husband chose not to have their daughter until later in the colony's settlement. They kept the fertilised egg in the facility in Guochang—it wasn't an unusual arrangement in those days. But her husband died, and Ndege pushed herself into her work, and the Mandala event changed everything. For a long while afterwards she could not bring herself to consider the unborn child, but eventually she relented."

"Did you play some part in that, Mposi?"

"I was concerned for my sister. The arrest was taking its toll on her and I felt that raising a daughter would be good for her soul."

"Soul. Listen to you."

"Soul, spirit, state of mind—whichever term you prefer. The point was, Goma gave Ndege something else to think about. The government allowed her to have the child and to raise her while remaining in detention. It was an odd upbringing for Goma, I'll admit—very cloistered. But it did her no harm, and Ndege is still with us."

"And now this Goma becomes a thorn in your side."

"She wasn't supposed to find out about any of this. But on the face of it, Goma is the better candidate—young and strong enough that there is no question she can endure the skipover interval. It means I won't be sending Ndege to her almost certain death."

"Then your conscience can be clear. I do not see the difficulty."

"Goma's safety is hardly guaranteed. She might survive the skipover, a hundred and forty years of it, but then what?

What will she find around Gliese 163? For all we know it's a trap of some sort—maybe a fatal one."

"It sounds like a very long-winded way of killing someone."

"That's my hope."

"Then you must send Goma. She consents, and she is an Akinya. Why do you ask me?"

"I want to know that I am doing the right thing. Regardless of whether I back Ndege or Goma, I'll still be separating a mother from her daughter."

"You are an inveterate meddler, Mposi. Always have been, always will be. You Akinyas can never leave well enough alone, none of you. You meddled in Ocular, you meddled in human technological development, you meddled in the fates of elephants, you meddled in first contact, you meddled with Mandala. Is your sister's happiness really any of your business? You didn't cause her incarceration—she did, by being rash. And yet you made her bring a daughter into the world because you thought it was what she needed. And now you meddle again—mother, daughter, who shall you send? Whose life shall you cast to the winds?"

"I'm just trying to do the right thing," Mposi protested.

"You can't. It's not in you. The only thing you Akinyas can be relied on to do is make new mistakes, over and over. The more you try to do right, the worse your choices. You're a corrupting influence. It's what the universe made you to be."

"Is that really what you think of us?"

"Give me a reason to form a different opinion. Give me a reason to think there's a single one of you who doesn't have their eye on the main chance. Even you, Mposi."

"I didn't ask to be placed in this position. If Goma insists on taking her mother's place and has a better chance of surviving the trip, who am I to stand in her way?" But then a sudden, shivering insight overcame him. If Arethusa wished to doubt his good intentions, his hopelessness in the face of an impossible choice, he would give her pause for thought. "I'll go," he said, simply and quietly, as if it were the smallest thing.

"In her place?"

"No. I'm not much stronger than Ndege, and besides—I'm not her daughter. But I can be there for her."

"Brave intentions, Mposi. I know what this world has come to mean to you. But you won't stand by these words. The moment you're out of the water, out of my presence, you'll pretend they were never spoken."

"I won't. I'll talk to the doctors. They'll find me fit enough. I'm swimming with a sea-monster, aren't I?"

"Be careful with your words."

"And you be careful who you doubt, Arethusa. I came to you for your wisdom, not your scorn. You're wrong about us, especially Goma, and especially me, and I mean every word I just said."

"Go on, then, Mposi Akinya." She uttered his name with sneering condescension. "Prove me wrong about you and your kind. I'll be here, waiting to hear what becomes of you."

"If you're still sane by the time we get back, I'll be glad to tell you. But frankly I have low expectations."

He turned from her without another word, thinking of the boat and the dry and distant sanctuary of Guochang.

Ndege had prepared chai for the two of them. She took a sip, pursed her lips in a habit of familiar distaste. Ndege, who had been born on *Zanzibar*, maintained that boiled water always tasted wrong on Crucible. Goma had learned to humour her, but the fact was that sooner or later water tasted like water. How long had her mother been on Crucible, that she could not learn to like the taste of it?

"He's a fool."

"But a fool with the medical authorisation to do whatever he wants. Anyway, you shouldn't speak ill of your brother."

"He's still a fool."

"He's only doing this out of some misguided sense of obligation." Goma worked at her own tea. "Since I'm going in your place and he can't do anything about it, he feels he has to be there to take care of me. I can't blame him for that. He's wrong, of course—I don't need him looking over my shoulder—but I can't begrudge him the adventure."

"No good will come of it."

"Then you try arguing him out of it."

"Not much chance of that, Mposi's like an asteroid—once he's set on a course, there's not much to be done. If only we could swap Ru for Mposi, both our problems would be solved. How are things with Ru, by the way?"

Goma studied her mother's face, searching for clues as to the intent behind the question. There were lots of new lines lately, complicating the map.

"Nothing's changed. I'd have told you if something had."

"But you still speak to each other?"

"We're colleagues. We work on the same project. It would be difficult not to speak."

"I mean as wife and wife."

"What do you want me to say—that it's all fine between us?"

"It looked like it was, to begin with. You said Ru was accepting of your decision."

"Maybe she was, at first."

"So what changed?"

Goma worked at her chai. She thought, for a second, of finishing it in a gulp and storming out. Her mother had requested—no, demanded—this meeting. It had come at an awkward time and Goma had struggled to alter her plans to accommodate it. She assumed Ndege had something more important on her mind than rubbing salt into recent wounds.

"Ru was just deluding herself, that's all. Can we talk about something else?"

"I'd rather we talked about Ru."

Recognising that she was now too deep into the conversation to back out gracefully, Goma said, "When there was a chance of the expedition losing approval, Ru thought she could talk me out of it gradually, or trusted I'd eventually lose my nerve. But it's going ahead, and I haven't changed my mind."

"It's my fault—I should have been more steadfast, refused to let you and Mposi talk me out of the expedition."

"None of it's your fault. It was always a bad idea, you going. I'm your daughter—why shouldn't I stand up in your place? I've even had the medical examination—I'm as fit as any skipover subject. You'd never have passed the first test. When you failed—as you would have—we'd be exactly where we are now, with me going in your place."

"I just wish something would persuade her."

"It doesn't matter what Ru decides now. You know how

sick she's made herself. Her nervous system's a wreck—she neglected the medicines for too long, and now it's a case of patching up the damage. She hasn't been formally tested, but my guess is she wouldn't obtain skipover consent. It'll be hard enough for Mposi."

"Chiku and Noah put us through skipover many times aboard *Zanzibar*," Ndege said. "It was hard. I won't lie. Like dying back into life every single time. You never get used to it. But it would still be good if you and Ru came to some understanding, so that you could at least be friends again. I can't bear the thought of you parting with this distance between you."

"I don't think there's anything to be done about Ru, any more than you can turn Mposi around."

"I hope things aren't that desperate for either of us."

"I can't speak for you and Mposi, but Ru and I are past any point of reconciliation. We've said everything, had every argument. There's nothing left for either of us. Sooner or later—certainly before I leave—we're going to have to talk about formalising our separation."

Ndege looked stunned, as if she had never foreseen this development.

"Divorce?"

"Kinder on both of us," Goma answered, with an easygoing shrug that still left her ripped inside. "Ru can get on with her life back on Crucible. One day she might even be able to forgive me."

"There's nothing to forgive."

"You would say that."

"You're my daughter, and I'm allowed to think the best of you. You'll always be in my thoughts, Goma, even when the ship's left—even when you're too far away for communication."

"I don't want to think about that day."

"That's not going to keep it from happening." Ndege let out a sigh. "With that in mind, there's something else I want to talk to you about."

"Something besides Ru?"

"Yes, and I wish you weren't so glad of the fact." Without warning, Ndege scraped back her chair, rose from the table and moved to one of the bookcases. "It's a delicate thing and it could get both of us in trouble, so you'd best keep it from my brother for now. Did I ever speak to you about Travertine?"

Goma nodded vaguely. "Some old friend of yours."

"Much more than that. A staunch ally to my mother, on the holoship. Then a loyal friend to me, after your father died and the world decided I needed burning. Other than Mposi, Travertine was one of the few people who'd still give me the time of day. I could never pay ver back for the love and loyalty ve showed me."

Goma had seen public images of Travertine in the government halls of Namboze and Guochang. Peevish and stern, severe of countenance, it was hard to square the face she remembered from those pictures with warmth and companionship.

"What has Travertine got to do with any of this?"

"Ve shared my interest in Mandala—it was a scientific puzzle, after all. Catnip to Travertine. Ve helped me design the communications protocol—the shades and illuminators we used to project light and darkness onto the walls. We cobbled them together with solar panels, mirrors, dome material, sheets of agricultural membrane—anything we could get our hands on and rig into place quickly. All very crude, but it worked."

Goma managed a smile at her mother's customary understatement.

"After the event," Ndege went on, "I did my best to obscure Travertine's involvement. Ve already had a stain on ver character from the *Zanzibar* days—this would have been too much. I took more than my share of the responsibility, but since I was going down anyway it was a small price to pay. Regardless, Travertine remained my friend and never allowed me to forget ver gratitude. That is why ve gave me the list."

"What list?"

Ndege's fingers hovered over a row of books, finally settling on a slim, dusty-looking volume. She brought it to the table, holding it upright between both hands, like a shield.

"*Gulliver's Travels*," Ndege said. "Have you read it?"

"No."

"Good—I wouldn't recommend it." Ndege sat down again, then opened the book and paged through it until a slip of paper fell out onto the table. Goma saw a list of handwritten names running down one column, and numbers in the other.

"What are those?"

Ndege coughed to clear her throat, touching a hand to her windpipe. "After the Mandala event—after my crime—a great deal of attention was paid to the destruction of *Zanzibar*."

"There would be."

"Well, yes. It was clear that I had triggered some sort of response from Mandala. The public focus was on the obvious— the destruction of *Zanzibar*. But Travertine dared to look beyond the obvious—dared to ask verself a different question. What was Mandala pointed at when the event happened?"

"The sky."

Ndege smiled patiently, well used to Goma's sarcasm by now. "Beyond that. Crucible itself rotates, and revolves around its star. Mandala's gaze sweeps the heavens like a lighthouse beam. At the precise time of the event, Mandala was directed towards a specific patch of the sky. That region happened to include Gliese 163."

This was news to Goma—she had heard no mention of this association from anyone else—but she was careful not to accept the information without question.

"You haven't said how big the patch of space was, or how many other stars were in it."

"You're right to be suspicious of coincidences. Then again, you're a scientist too, so I shouldn't be surprised." Ndege's fingers tapped the paper. "But so was Travertine, and ver methods were rigorous. That's the point of this list. Travertine identified a few hundred candidate stars in the direction of Mandala's gaze. They were all at different distances, of course—some of them hundreds, thousands of light-years away. Travertine ignored all of those. Ver only interest was in the nearest stars—those from which we might expect to receive a return signal."

"A return signal?"

"What if *Zanzibar* got in the way of something? An energy pulse, yes—but not something meant to be destructive. Something meant to cross interstellar space from one solar system to another? Travertine's next question was: when might we expect a response? These are the numbers—the dates."

Ndege's finger moved down the list to the entry for Gliese 163, her too-long fingernail scratching against the paper. "Do you see the significance? My crime happened in 2460, so the earliest response from that system couldn't arrive until one hundred and forty years later. That's 2600."

"Twelve years ago."

"Long before Mposi came to me about his signal—agreed. But close enough to Travertine's prediction to raise goosebumps. And you see how ve underlined this star in particular? Out of all the candidates, Gliese 163 was the nearest, the most likely to have habitable worlds. Travertine always suspected it was the target of the Mandala signal."

Goma was silent. There was a possibility, she supposed, that the list of stars and dates was a hoax, recently engineered by her mother. But Ndege had no history of that sort of fabrication. More than that, a hoax would serve no obvious purpose, benefiting neither of them.

"I don't know what to make of this."

"Someone sent us a signal, Goma. It was a human message. Personal. It said, 'Send Ndege.' Someone knew my name. How could that have happened if there were no people in the Gliese 163 system? And how could people have got there, if not aboard *Zanzibar*?"

"*Zanzibar* was destroyed!"

"Some of it, maybe, but not necessarily all of it. How much rubble is in the ring system, anyway? Travertine didn't think the mass added up. Ve believed there was a significant discrepancy—that a huge chunk of *Zanzibar* was never accounted for. Of course, no one else gave a damn."

"Because it's madness."

"Someone still needs to go there and find out. I would, if I were younger. But instead my brave daughter will take my place. Don't think I'm not proud of you, Goma, but you'll allow me a little jealousy."

"I'm jealous of *you*. You had the chance to live and walk among the Tantors. You knew them."

"I did, and it was wonderful. While we're on the subject, though? When the event happened, most of the Tantors were still on *Zanzibar*. We've assumed all this time that they were killed, lost to history. A wonderful promise squandered. Believe me,

I've felt my share of that loss. But if something survived the translation, then there's a chance the Tantors did, too." Ndege looked down at her fingers, lost in herself for a few seconds. "It occurred to me that perhaps Ru would find this of interest."

Goma had gone so long without allowing herself hope that it was rather odd to feel that all the doors were not yet locked. But Ndege knew both of them well enough. Tantors were the answer to any argument.

"She might not believe me."

"She doesn't need to. The mere possibility that there might be Tantors will be enough. Admit it, Goma—you're the same."

"You said this could get both of us into trouble."

"I did, and I meant it. But if it made a difference to Ru's decision, then I think the risk would be worth it, for both of us."

"I . . ." Goma began.

"You don't know what to say. That's understandable. You don't know whether you've been given a bomb or a gift. My suggestion? Use it wisely. You'll only have one chance with Ru."

"Thank you," Goma answered.

Ndege returned the slip of paper to *Gulliver's Travels*, tapped the book against her table and then rose to replace it in the bookcase. She flashed a quick smile and then it was gone. "I await developments, daughter."

CHAPTER 4

Kanu and the robot trod water next to each other. They were in a wide, calm sea, nothing but ocean and sky to the limit of vision. Swimming was natural enough for Kanu—he was always happier in water than on land—but the thought of the robot having to share the same unforgiving element struck him as both comical and ludicrous, a profound violation of all that was right and proper.

"Aren't you made of metal?" he kept asking. "Aren't you too heavy for this sort of thing?"

"So are you," Swift answered every time. His frock coat looked heavy and sodden.

"But I only have to swim a little bit to support my weight."

"That's your problem," Swift said. "You're not moving at all!"

It had been Kanu's move for quite some time, but whenever he felt himself on the threshold of committing, some doubt stayed his hand. The longer he delayed his move, the worse the indecision became.

"Well, then," Swift said, obligingly enough, "I shall simply make another move while you think about it."

"Is that in the rules?"

"Different rules for different times. We have to think innovatively now. It's no good being held back by old patterns."

Swift picked up one of his own pieces, a knight, preparing to place it on the floating board. The chessboard rose and fell on the gentlest of swells, hingeing in the middle in a manner that made Kanu think of the languid wingbeat of a giant manta ray.

It was odd, now that he paid proper attention to it, that all the pieces were the same colour. Kanu did not appear to have any of his own on the board.

Then Swift lost his grip on the knight. It slipped from his fingers, bounced off the side of the board and vanished under the water.

"I'll fetch it," Kanu said.

"Would you be so kind?"

Kanu submerged. The sun's dazzle was kinder under the waves and its trembling light fell on the sinking chess piece. As the knight descended, a string of bubbles left the horse's mouth. Kanu snatched for it, but his fingers closed on water. The knight was still falling.

Kanu followed it into darker, cooler waters. Never mind, he was made for this. He could stay submerged for as long as a sperm whale and dive just as deep. Already he could feel the old engine of his heart beginning to slow, the blood leaving his extremities.

But even with his webbed hands and feet, it was becoming

harder to match the speed of the knight's descent. The water was almost totally black now, the chess piece's progress marked only by the silvery thread of its bubbles.

There was something below him.

It was a huge form, a concentration of deeper blackness, ink upon ink. He thought for a moment that it was a pinnacle, a summit pushing up from the ocean's bed. But the black thing was rising to meet him. It was a wonder he could see it at all; even more of a wonder that the trail of bubbles was still silver-bright. He redoubled his efforts, grasping for it even as he pulled himself deeper. The knight was headed straight for the rising blackness. Within the blackness, a mouth began to open and kept opening, angling ever wider, a tunnel of blackness within blackness. The knight descended into it and the mouth clamped suddenly shut, scissoring the chain of bubbles.

"You ought to turn around, Kanu."

He knew her voice, and he knew her name.

Arethusa.

"I have your knight. I've swallowed it. I've Jonahed it into the belly of the whale. Would you like it back?"

"It's Swift's knight, not mine."

"You can have it if you swim into me. Look, I'm opening my mouth again. Just swim inside and collect what's yours. Or give up and turn back to the light."

"I don't know what to do."

"You could die. That would solve a lot of problems. You want to die, don't you? You were hurt so very badly, Kanu— no one would blame you."

"I wasn't hurt."

"You died on Mars. Or don't you remember?"

He pulled himself away from the whale. The knight was unimportant. He rose and rose. His heart quickened, his blood resuming its normal circulation. He caught up with the knight's bubble trail and clung to it like a rope, so that it hauled him all the way to the bright trembling of the surface waters.

And then he broke free into air and daylight, except that Swift was gone and so was the chessboard.

There was a boat nearby. He swam to it, and a beautiful

woman with a broad face and kind eyes leaned over the side and made to help him out of the water.

"I'm strong enough to do it myself."

"No, you're not," she said. "You're on Mars, and you're dead."

"Kanu," the voice was saying. "Can you answer me? The neural traces suggest the presence of deep-level comprehension, but I would be very happy to have it confirmed. Try to speak. Try to say a word or two."

After an age, he felt he had the strength and focus to oblige. "Swift."

"Yes!"

"What happened?"

"*That's* your question—what happened? Not where am I? What kind of condition am I in?"

"I'm alive."

"You are alive, yes. But only by the narrowest of margins."

After a while, Kanu repeated: "What happened?"

"Do you remember the terrorist incident? There was an explosion, quite a big one."

Kanu did his best to remember. "Dalal . . . Korsakov. Lucien."

"It was very bad."

Something important occurred to him. "I can't see."

"You will, shortly. Some wiring still needs to be reconnected."

"What about the others?"

"Regrettably," Swift said, "there were fatalities."

A room, this time. He thought for a moment that he was in the embassy, but the view through the window was wrong. Beyond the glass was a kind of cityscape, except it was no city he had ever known. There were illuminated buildings, conforming less to human architecture than the flanged, angular proportions of ancient radio components. Between the buildings, and linking them, were thick, glowing arms. In place of a sky was a rising vault of excavated rock.

Swift was sitting opposite him. A low table had been set between their chairs, but it was mercifully free of a chessboard.

"I had the strangest dream."

"I feel obliged to point out that not all of your dreams were dreams." Swift gestured at a pitcher of water and a glass on the table. "If you're thirsty."

Kanu continued looking around. "Am I really in this room, or are you feeding information into my skull?"

"This is real. That thing you are wearing is your actual body. It needed rather a lot of repair, so I trust you still find it to your liking."

Kanu looked at his forearm, the loose fit of the green-embroidered sleeve. He spread his fingers. The webs between them were still present.

"I'll ask again: what happened?"

"You were seriously injured in the Reclamationist incident. It killed you, in fact. But we brought you back to life, stabilised you and set about rectifying the damage."

He felt he needed a drink now. He tilted some water into the glass and brought it to his lips.

"The others?"

"Garudi and Lucien were killed outright—the flier was too close when the wreck came down."

Kanu absorbed this news, but for the moment it was just there, unprocessed.

"And Korsakov?"

"Injured, but not too severely. He made it out of the wreck of the flier and his suit retained its life-support capabilities until he was rescued."

"But you saved me."

"It took a tremendous concentration of machine resources. We might have attempted to save one of the others, but the likelihood of failure would have been greater." After a silence, Swift added, "I am sorry to lose both Garudi and Lucien. But I am very glad we were able to save you."

"Does the world know I'm here?"

"Not yet. We issued a statement through the usual diplomatic channels shortly after the incident. That was almost three weeks ago. We said we had recovered human remains and that they would be returned to the rightful authority in due course. Now we can proceed with the significantly better news that we have brought you back to life."

"Why didn't you say so sooner?"

"We didn't wish to raise false hopes. Your survival was far from guaranteed."

"I'll need to speak to my people."

"Of course. Your great powers are still knocking heads over the whole incident, deciding who is and isn't to blame for wiping out three-quarters of an intergovernmental diplomatic party."

"Half," Kanu corrected. "I didn't die."

"For long," Swift replied.

When the machines deemed him well enough to leave their care—which was only two days after his first intimation of consciousness—Kanu was provided with transport back to the embassy. He was glad when the flier brought him to the summit and the embassy's landing deck opened to welcome him home.

Swift accompanied him from the flier.

"We've issued the formal announcement concerning your survival," the robot said as they made their way down to the level of the main staterooms. "News is spreading, and of course there is criticism of our actions. I trust we can count on you to argue our side of things?"

"I'll give them the truth, Swift—no more, no less. You have nothing to apologise for."

"I hope it will not create difficulties for you in the wider sphere of human discourse."

Kanu pushed open one of the heavy oak doors and stepped through into a room that felt larger and colder than he remembered. "Why should I care what they think of me beyond Mars? Everything that matters to me is here. This is my life. Pretty soon they'll assign new ambassadors and we'll carry on as we were before."

"But you must be mindful of the opinions of others. We have not often spoken of private matters—surely you have friends and loved ones elsewhere in the system?"

"Not as many as you'd think."

"But you have lived a great many years."

"Thanks for reminding me. The truth is, though, that you burn through friends and lovers when you live as long as I have. I am what I am, Swift—an old merman. Too ancient and strange for most people to feel comfortable around." He paused to survey the stateroom, finding everything exactly as it had been before the expedition to the wreck, but at the same time every note of the room jarringly off-key.

Dalal had left a book open on one of the tables. Kanu walked to it and stroked a finger across the pages. The text was in Urdu, one of her four or five languages. He stared at the script, trying to remember how it felt to have the words resolve before his eyes, mysteries disclosed. How it had been before the Age of Babel.

"I'll miss Garudi."

"So shall we. But out of this calamity, perhaps some greater good can come?"

Irritated by the triteness of this sentiment, Kanu snapped shut the book. This in turn made him feel irritated with himself, as if he had lost Dalal's place in the text. Where on the Earth did her family live? he wondered—Madras? Perhaps he should make a point of returning the book to them. It would be a small kindness, and his bones could do with a dose of Earth gravity now and then.

"And they say I'm the optimist."

Swift was at the high-fretted window. "There has always been disunity regarding how best to deal with extremists. Now, perhaps, it will not be so hard to make a persuasive case for clamping down on the Reclamationists."

"Be careful someone doesn't make an equally persuasive case for clamping down on you."

"I thought that had already occurred."

A console chimed with the small, annoying tone that indicated a stored message was waiting. Kanu guessed it had been making that chime for some time.

"This might be a private diplomatic matter, Swift. Do you mind stepping out of the room?"

"I would be overjoyed to accommodate your request."

"And don't try to listen in, either."

"Very well." Swift made an impatient gesture with his hand as he headed for the door. "Pray take your precious call."

When he was alone, Kanu stood before the console and used his diplomatic authority to accept the message.

A face appeared above the console. It took Kanu a second or two to recognise it as belonging to his old colleague Yevgeny Korsakov. The ambassador for the United Orbital Nations had changed quite markedly in the three weeks since the terrorist attack. His hair had been shaved to the skull, perhaps in connection with emergency surgery. His face, craggy and gaunt at the best of times, now looked ghoulishly drawn.

The recording began to play.

"May I offer my warmest congratulations on your return to life, Kanu. Given the circumstances, it is remarkable."

"Thank you, Yevgeny." The playback paused as soon as it detected Kanu's intention to speak. It would embed his response into the flow of Korsakov's words exactly as if the two men were speaking normally, without the hindrance of light-minutes of separation and time lag.

"But I am afraid I must temper my congratulations with news that you may find less than agreeable," Korsakov allowed. "You know full well that your relationship with Swift had become problematic. It was possible to turn a blind eye to that error of judgement, at least until now. The machines should have handed you over to human medics, but instead they opted to heal you themselves. Worse, they neglected to keep us properly informed of your condition."

"I'm sure you were most concerned."

"I can only speak for my delegation, Kanu. You are compromised. I have even heard it said that you have been tainted—that your basic loyalty to humanity can no longer be relied upon. I do not believe that myself—of course not—but it is the wider perceptions that count. And because of those perceptions I am sorry to inform you that you must reconsider your position as ambassador. We are seeking a unanimous cross-governmental vote to have you replaced, for the sake of confidence in the embassy. I do not think we will have too much trouble. Even your own government has come to view you as a soft-liner."

Kanu was not surprised; he had been expecting as much from the moment Korsakov began speaking.

"I will resign if I am required to do so by the United Aquatic Nations or the intergovernmental panel," Kanu stated. "Until then, I will continue to fulfil my duties as ambassador."

While his reply was on its way to Korsakov, Kanu called Swift back into the room.

"I'm sorry for shutting you out of that."

"Forgiven and forgotten. Judging from your demeanour, though, the news wasn't good?"

"Not exactly. That was Korsakov calling to tell me there's a vote to have me removed as ambassador. There's no reason for it not to go through. When it does, they'll ship me back to Earth."

"This is official?"

"As good as. Korsakov wouldn't have called unless he was certain of the outcome."

"But your own government will defend you!"

"Until it becomes politically expedient to switch me out for someone with a harder attitude to your kind."

Between them was the table and Dalal's book. Kanu felt a swell of sadness rise up in him like a tide. They had disagreed on many things, but he felt sure that Dalal would have spoken up for him.

"We placed you in this unfortunate position, Kanu."

"It's not your fault. And this isn't about you—it's about ignorance and fear."

"Will returning to Earth be so bad? There must be a great many people there who would value your diplomatic experience."

"I think I might return Garudi's book to her family. Beyond that, it depends on how 'tainted' I'm perceived to be."

Swift looked down. "Oh dear."

"You needn't worry. I'm adaptable. I'll find something to occupy myself with."

The robot nodded solemnly. "Of that I have no doubt whatsoever."

CHAPTER 5

Goma was suffering another medical examination by the expedition's physician, Dr. Saturnin Nhamedjo, when the call came in from Ru. She was to leave Guochang and return with all haste to the sanctuary. Goma made her apologies to the gentle, accommodating Nhamedjo and was soon on her way back to the elephants. A year ago she would have taken the aeroplane, but her role in the expedition brought a number of new perks, chief among which was the ability to hire a government flier at short notice. She took the little beetle-shaped machine from Guochang, vectoring around Mandala to avoid a bad weather system. When Goma arrived at the facility, Tomas explained that Ru was already out with the Alpha herd.

"That bad?" she asked.

"Worse, I think. You'd better not hang around. Take the buggy—it's already loaded up for the day."

Goma raced back out into the heat and humidity. She gunned the electric vehicle hard, nearly tipping it over on the bends, dust pluming up from its wheels as she sped away from the compound. It only took her twenty minutes to reach Alpha herd. She slowed and then stopped, taking in the scene from a slight elevation. From the disposition of the elephants, it was obvious that something was wrong. They were turned inwards, an audience facing some central spectacle. Goma left her buggy and walked the remaining distance, passing Ru's vehicle on the way. They were so deeply preoccupied that she was nearly with them before any of the elephants deigned to acknowledge her presence.

Goma paused to allow the young mothers and calves to accept her arrival. A calf brushed against her with boisterous disregard, but the older elephants shared none of its exuberance.

They were making low, agitated rumbles, with much mutual trunk-touching taking place, as if the herd members sought constant reassurance.

Goma scanned the familiar forms, noting body size, tusk disfigurement, ear shape.

She moved carefully between the adults, conscious of their size and heightened mood. She had rarely been the target of elephant aggression. In their present state, though, it would not take much provocation to draw a bad-tempered response. She was small and they were large, and nothing in the universe would change that basic asymmetry in their relationship. They could crush her between breaths.

At the focus of the gathering lay a dying elephant. Goma recognised her immediately: the elderly Agrippa, the herd leader. Even as she moved through the standing elephants, Goma had been aware of Agrippa's absence among their ranks, so unlike this dutiful matriarch.

"You're in time," Ru said.

Agrippa lay on her side, her breathing laboured. Ru knelt at her head, one hand on Agrippa's forehead, the other dabbing a wet sponge around the elephant's eye. Agrippa's trunk lay limp as a hose on the ground, only the end twitching up as Goma approached.

She knelt next to Ru. Ru had brought a pail of water and there was another sponge in the pail. Goma wrung most of the water from the sponge and then touched it gently to the end of Agrippa's trunk.

"When did this happen?" she asked, keeping her voice low, as if there was a risk of the elephants understanding.

"She was on her feet at dusk yesterday. Overnight, this."

Agrippa had been ailing for many seasons, slowly losing her strength. But she had retained her authority as matriarch, and Goma had allowed herself to think that the elephant would go on until at least after her departure, that her death was a problem she need not face.

"Thank you for calling me."

"I knew you'd want to be here." Ru recharged her sponge, the water in the pail already turning dusty. "As soon as I saw how bad things were, I called you."

"There's nothing we can do, is there?"

It was a rhetorical question. She knew the answer as well as Ru.

"Make things as easy as possible. Keep her eyes from drying, keep the sun off her. I should have told Tomas to send some blankets out with you."

"I think he did. The buggy was pretty well loaded."

"She's been so strong," Ru said, pausing at a catch in her voice. "I thought she'd endure longer than this. Even when I knew she was ill, I didn't think it would be so sudden."

"She was putting up a show of strength," Goma said. "For the sake of the herd."

"As always."

After a moment, it occurred to Goma to ask, "How long have you been here, Ru?"

"You're cross I didn't call you sooner?"

"No, I'm worried that you've been here hours and hours without thinking of yourself. You brought water for Agrippa, but I don't see anything for you."

"There's water in my buggy."

Goma had passed the other vehicle long before she reached the herd. She doubted Ru had been back to it since reaching the fallen matriarch. "Wait here," she said, risking placing a hand on Ru's shoulder by way of comfort.

She was as quick as she could be, but not so hasty that her movements would further disconcert the herd. In Ru's buggy she found water flasks and a wide-brimmed hat. A little further back, where she had parked her own vehicle, she found a pair of survival blankets and a box of emergency rations. She bundled everything into the blankets and headed back to Ru.

Ru took her flask distractedly at first, as if being reminded to drink were a nuisance. But after she had swallowed a mouthful, she gulped the rest in sudden thirst.

"Thank you," she said, with a certain wariness, as if the words might put her in some unspecified debt to Goma.

"It's all right. I've got these blankets, too. They should keep her a little cooler."

The blankets only covered part of the elephant, but they did the best they could to make her comfortable. Goma opened the ration kit and showed Ru the contents, then tore the foil from an energy bar and bit into it.

"I wonder if there's more we should do," Ru said, wiping her mouth. "Then I wonder if we're already doing too much. Prolonging something that shouldn't be prolonged."

"You couldn't just leave her," Goma said. "I know you. And this is a kindness, so don't start doubting yourself. All you're doing is easing things for her, not making it worse. Seriously, how long has it been?"

"Seven hours. Maybe eight. I arrived just after sunrise."

"Then in a little while I want you to go back to the buildings. I bet you didn't bring your medicines, did you?"

"She's what matters now."

"No, you matter, too—to me, anyway. You drive back and I'll stay here. We can take turns holding vigil."

"I won't leave her."

"She could be like this for days."

"I think it will be faster. Her breathing's weaker than it was a few hours ago."

"All the same, you still have to think of yourself." Goma allowed her hand to rest on Ru's shoulder again. It was what one colleague would do for another, she told herself, a gesture of emotional support that had nothing to do with their shared history.

"I'm all right. But I was getting a little dehydrated. I didn't realise it until now."

Two of the senior females had come closer while this exchange took place, testing their trunks against the rise and fall of Agrippa's ribcage. It was as if they needed validation that their matriarch had not yet taken her final breath, drawing the air of this alien world into her lungs one last time.

"They know," Goma said.

"Of course."

Of all the animals, only elephants had a sophisticated understanding of death. They knew the difference between breath and bones. They had their own customs of grief and remembrance. More than once, Goma had found herself wondering if it was precisely this apprehension of mortality that had primed the elephants for taking the next step on cognition's ladder, a rung up to language and sentience. To know death was to know time, to know the past and the future. Most creatures were bound entirely to the present moment, blissful prisoners of an ever-moving now. They knew hunger or anger, contentment or lust, but they did not know doubt or longing or regret.

Elephants knew that their tomorrows were not numberless, that each day was a gift. In that awareness lay both their majesty and their tragedy.

Ru would not be persuaded to leave her vigil for more than the few minutes necessary to wander to the bushes to relieve her bladder. On the way back, she stopped at her buggy, washed her hands and face and hair and scraped dust from her eyes. She refilled the portable water flasks and found extra rations, tucked into a forgotten compartment. As the sun moved, they adjusted the blankets.

Ru was right, Goma decided. After two hours, even she had noticed that Agrippa's breathing had deteriorated.

The knowledge had communicated itself to the other elephants, too. The next-oldest Alpha-herd females, Arpana and Agueda, appeared to be assuming the role of matrons at a deathbed, ushering the other elephants to their matriarch's side and ensuring that none lingered at the expense of another. Even the younger males looked more sombre in mood than when Goma had arrived. Armistead, the male calf who had nearly knocked her down, was emulating the trunk-touching of the older animals. He might not have understood the significance of the affair any more than a human child grasped the deeper implications of a human funeral, but Goma could not help but be moved by the sense of shared observance. Ru was right. They knew.

What were we thinking? Goma wondered to herself. *Why did we ever think that elephants needed to be more like us and less like themselves?*

Soon the hour was upon Agrippa. They had moved the blankets again and again, but during the course of the afternoon her breathing had grown progressively less detectable, her eye responses weaker, her trunk almost still. They continued their ministrations, sponging her skin and eyes, offering what solace they could with the gentle laying on of their hands. Until the moment when Ru said: "She's gone."

Goma had felt it, too, but not had the courage to say so for fear that voicing her suspicion might be enough to make it real.

"Yes, she is."

Ru could not stop moving the sponge across Agrippa's face. Feeling the same impulse, Goma shifted the blankets again. There had been no convulsive final breath, no obvious marker of life's passing. It had simply happened, as steadily and irrevocably as the movement of the sun.

But she noticed a shift in the other elephants' behaviour. The laying on of trunks had become more desperate. They were touching and prodding her with trunks and feet now, evidencing a forcefulness that to a human's sensibilities appeared almost indecent. It was as if they were angry at what she had done and wished to scold her back to life. *They know*, she thought again. *They know but they do not fully understand. That will take time.*

"Thank you," Ru said, and for a moment Goma thought her words were addressed to the matriarch. Then Ru added, "I wanted you to be here. I hoped you'd come, but I wasn't sure you would."

"I'm glad I made it in time. I'm so sorry, Ru. We knew this day was coming, but that doesn't make it any easier."

"She was a good elephant. Whoever accepts her place will have a lot to live up to. I've changed my mind, by the way— I'm coming with you."

Ru barely drew breath between sentences. Goma heard the words, but her natural reaction was to doubt them, or search for a different meaning.

"With me where?"

"To Gliese. I made my mind up a couple of days ago, and I would have told you sooner or later." Ru was at last able to rise from the ground, scuffing dirt from her knees. "I suppose I wanted to live with my decision for a while, to see if I still liked it."

"I'm . . . sorry." Goma barely knew how to respond. "Of course I want you to come, but I don't think it's possible now. They've filled all the slots."

"I've already spoken to your uncle. He was the first person I discussed this with." Ru gave an easy shrug. There were dark patches under her armpits, inverted triangles like two little maps of Africa. "I know I was meant to be removed from consideration, but I think leaving me on the list was Mposi's way of giving us a chance of reconciliation."

"I don't—" Goma started.

"They had offered my slot to another candidate, but it turned out there was a question over his commitment—when push came to shove, he didn't want to go, so they've been scrambling around to find someone else. When I asked Mposi if I could be allowed back onto the expedition, he said it would solve a number of difficulties."

Goma shook her head, caught between joy and irritation. "I talk to Mposi almost every day—he never said a thing!"

"I told him not to until I'd thought things over. He was just doing as I asked. You can be cross, if you like, but don't blame him." She squinted at Goma with her tired, dirt-kohled eyes. "You *are* pleased, aren't you?"

"I'm . . . shocked. And pleased, yes. More than pleased. I'm delighted. This is . . . the best news I could have hoped for. Please tell me you're certain about this. I couldn't bear the disappointment if you change your mind."

"When I make my mind up about something," Ru said, "it tends to stay made up."

"But medically—"

"Mposi arranged for Doctor Nhamedjo to visit me. There's not much he doesn't know about Accumulated Oxygen Toxicity Syndrome—the man practically wrote the textbook on AOTS. Saw exactly how screwed-up my nervous system is, too. But he says with the right medicines, the right care, I could make it through skipover like the rest of you."

"It was the Tantors, wasn't it? What I told you about Travertine's theory?"

"I don't know whether to believe in that possibility or dismiss it out of hand. All I know is that if there's even the faintest chance of it being true, I want to be part of that."

Goma looked at Agrippa's body, wondering if the matriarch's death had been the decisive factor in Ru's change of heart. Perhaps she had not truly made up her mind until now.

"You'll miss the herd, watching how they move on," Goma said.

"Not really. We haven't left yet and, in any case, it will be years before we totally lose contact with Crucible. I intend to stay awake for as long as they'll let me."

Goma hardly dared ask the next question, the one uppermost in her thoughts. If Ru had committed to the expedition, did that mean she had also renewed her commitment to their relationship? To ask now, even in the most indirect of ways, would be unforgivable. There was opportunity enough for that, in their last months on Crucible.

Goma felt herself beginning to cry, an expression of both joy at Ru's news and inexpressible sorrow at the loss of the elephant. But the joy and sadness mingled, each colouring the other, and she knew all would be well, given time.

"I could never have faced this without you."

"Yes you could," Ru said. "Because you're strong and stubborn and you don't need me as much as I need you. But that's all right. You get me as well. And if it's okay with you, I'd still like to be your wife."

Soon the last months were upon them, and then the last weeks. Goma expected Ru to express misgivings as the day of departure approached, but in fact she was resolute, refusing to admit to the slightest of doubts. Perhaps it was a bluff, but if so it was an exceedingly persuasive one.

Goma wished she shared the same resolve. As the days counted down, the prospect of departure began to take a steepening toll on her emotions. She found herself dwelling on aspects of her world that she had until then taken for granted, appreciating them anew now that she knew they would be taken from her: the specific seasonal tang of the sea breezes at this time of year, heavy with their cargo of microorganisms; the swollen sun at dusk, ripening as it met the horizon; the horsetail patterns of clouds; the glint and glimmer of the rings, which—their origin aside—were unquestionably beautiful. Even the constellations, disfigured and displaced from their classical forms—they would suffer a further estrangement from the vantage of Gliese 163. Soon there would be a final morning, a final afternoon, a final sunset. She measured her life by these thoughts and then reprimanded herself for not simply enjoying such pleasures while she still could. The thought of leaving Crucible left her numb with self-recrimination, stung by a sense that she was committing an act of grave betrayal to the world itself.

She usually felt better after speaking to Ndege.

"You adjust," she told her daughter. She had said the same thing, time after time. "That's what happens. My mother left Earth and never saw it again. But she lived a life, and she never looked back over her shoulder. You'll do the same."

"It's going to tear me apart, the day I go."

"It will. But you'll heal. We all heal."

They had been allowed to walk in the park, under discreet surveillance, but for some reason Ndege had insisted on Goma coming back to the house. Now they were alone at her table, Goma quietly aware of the hour and the fact that she wished to be at the elephant sanctuary before evening.

"I have to be in Namboze tomorrow," she said, "but I'll be back in Guochang in a few days."

"I'm sure you will. But before you go, there are a few things I'd like to give you."

"You don't have to. I won't be able to take very much with me on the ship."

"Won't be able to, or won't want to?"

Goma did not have an answer for that.

Set on the table was a dark wooden box which Goma did not recognise. Ndege opened its lid, disclosing a nest of tissue paper. She pulled the paper away carefully, setting the wads down next to the box, and then produced six individually wrapped forms. She peeled each from its tissue cocoon and set them down on the table in order of size. They were a family of six wooden elephants, each mounted on a rough black plinth.

"Have you seen these before?"

"I'm not sure."

"They're very old and very well travelled. They belonged to Eunice, and then Geoffrey, and then my mother, and then me. They've never been split up before, this family. But I think the time is right." Ndege grouped the elephants into three pairs, each of which consisted of a larger and smaller elephant. She stared at the permutation for a few seconds before making a substitution between two of the pairs.

"Two will remain with me. Two will go with you, and two will go with Mposi. Good luck charms. I hope the universe bends itself to bring the elephants back together one day. I'm not inclined to mystical thinking, but I'll allow myself this one lapse."

"Thank you," Goma said, quietly relieved that the gift was nothing likely to embarrass her. The elephants were small and charmingly carved, and she appreciated the gesture.

"There's something else."

Goma settled back into her chair, chiding herself for thinking it was ever going to be that simple. "Is there, now?"

Ndege creaked up from her own chair, went to the bookcase—the same one where she kept the note from Travertine—and came back with three of her black-bound notebooks. She set them down on the table next to the box and the family of elephants.

She offered one for Goma's inspection. "You'll have seen me with these, but I doubt you've ever looked at them closely."

Goma opened the pages. They were unlined and filled with her mother's hand. Very little of it was orthodox writing. There were pages and pages of winding angular glyphs, like the patterns made by dominoes. Sometimes there was a line down the middle of a page and symbols on either side of it, cross-linked by a tangle of arrows.

"This is the Mandala grammar," Goma said, stroking a finger down the right-hand column on one of the pages. "The language of the M-builders. Right?"

"You recognise it."

"Yes, but that's not the same as understanding it, the way you can."

"You needn't blame yourself. They've made it difficult. Books locked away in libraries, direct access to the Mandala tightly controlled . . ." Ndege shook her head in disgust.

"What are these other symbols?" Goma asked, indicating the left-hand column, which appeared to be made up of stick figures in various poses, headless skeletal men with squiggles and zigzags for limbs. "They're not part of the Mandala grammar, are they?"

"No—these are elements in the Chibesa syntax."

"Which is . . . ?"

"The set of formal relationships underpinning both classical and post-Chibesa physics."

"I don't understand." Goma was staring at the cross-linking lines, the arrows and forks implying a logical connection between the two sets of symbols, the Chibesa syntax and the Mandala grammar. "One of these is the alien writing we found on Crucible. The other is . . . there *can't* be a connection, Mother. It's a human invention. Chibesa invented the syntax to work out her calculations."

Ndege shot her a look of stern reproval. "I know it was a long time ago, but you could at least do Memphis Chibesa the dignity of remembering that he was a man."

Goma was not sure she had ever heard Chibesa's first name. It was rather odd to think of this mythical figure being born, like any other human being.

"Did you know him?"

"Goodness, no. Memphis died . . . Well, it was a ridiculously long time before I was born. Eunice knew him, though. Look, there's no need to rake over old ground here. Just accept that Chibesa was lent a helping hand in formulating his theory—that it had its origin in some scratches Eunice found on a piece of rock on Phobos, one of Mars's moons."

"Scratches?"

"The keys to the new physics. Cosmic graffiti, if you like—a kind of irresponsible mischief-making left by someone or something who neither knew nor cared what the consequences would be, thousands or millions of years later."

Goma considered, at least provisionally, that her mother might be delusional. Not a word of this had been mentioned in any previous conversation between them, at any point in Goma's life. But nothing in Ndege's manner suggested confusion.

"How . . . Phobos?" Goma shook her head, trying to clear a thickening mental fog. "What does *Phobos* have to do with Mandala? The Mandala is the product of a hypothetical alien civilisation—the M-builders. For all we know, the Watch-keepers are something else entirely. Now you're asking me to accept that Eunice discovered the remnants of another alien culture, centuries before any of this?"

"We do like our family secrets."

"Or our tall stories."

"If it was a tall story, it wouldn't have told me how to talk to Mandala." Ndege tapped the notebooks again. "It took me years to make that connection, to see the links between the two linguistic structures. Once I did, though, it was like being given a key. I was able to unlock huge tracts of the Mandala's inscriptions. I understood that the inscriptions were a kind of control interface, an invitation to start making the Mandala work for us."

"And that turned out well, didn't it?" Goma said, knowing her mother would not take her sarcasm to heart.

"Accept that I had my insights," Ndege said, with a tolerant smile. "I realised that the rock carvings were an ancestral form of the Mandala inscriptions—that whoever or whatever left the scratchings on Phobos was there a long, long time before Mandala came into existence." Ndege pushed all the notebooks over to her daughter's side of the table. "You'll take these with you, too."

Goma looked at the books. Even with the elephants, they only added up to a negligible fraction of her mass allowance. It would cost her nothing to take them on the ship, nothing except pride.

"I am a biologist," she said slowly, as if her mother might somehow have forgotten this salient detail. "I know elephants, nervous systems, cognitive tests. I don't know a single thing about physics or alien language systems."

"We're cut from the same cloth, Goma. If I could make sense of these connections, then I expect no less from my daughter."

"You do have copies, don't you?"

"I destroyed them shortly before I was detained. I thought it would be safer that way."

"Then I can't take them!"

"They're of no conceivable use to me, not now, so I would rather they were in your care. Even if they do end up halfway across the galaxy."

Goma sensed an easing in her mother, the relief of a burden discharged. She began to wonder how long it had been playing on Ndege's mind, this business with the books.

"I can't go with you and Mposi—that's settled—but it would have been nice to get some answers. You'll just have to be my eyes and ears. Rise to the occasion. Roar like a lion. Be an Akinya, like Senge Dongma herself."

At the door, with the notebooks and two of the elephants in her possession, Goma said, "One day they'll see they were wrong. You never deserved this."

"Few of us get the things we deserve," Ndege said, "but we make the best of what we're given."

CHAPTER 6

Kanu was in no hurry to reach Madras; equally he knew that he would not be able to settle into the rhythms of his new life until he had discharged his obligation to the family of Garudi Dalal.

His port of entry was Sri Lanka, the nearest land mass to the Indian Ocean vacuum tower. From Colombo he took the high-speed train up the western side of Sri Lanka, passing under the Gulf of Mannar and heading up the eastern coast of India. On its way to Madras, the train surfaced into the hard silver glare of an overcast sky, speeding through a string of moderately affluent coastal communities: Cuddalore, Puducherry, Chengalpattu, each a blur of white buildings, pagodas, domes and towers hemmed by a blue-green rush of sea and jungle.

In Madras, the sun was hot and unforgiving and indecently large in the sky.

"You'll have read the official reports," Kanu said, when they were sitting around a metal table in the back garden of the Dalals' home, surrounded by trees and birds. "I was there, in a sense. I can tell you that Garudi acted courageously and that her death would have been virtually instantaneous. It was an honour to have known her."

"These terrorists," Dalal's father said, pouring fresh chai into their cups.

Kanu felt their grief as an invisible, silent presence at the garden table, acknowledged but uninvited. He supposed that the worst sting of it had passed by now, in the six weeks since the incident, but there were still months and years of quiet pain ahead of them.

"You represented different interests," Dalal's mother said, offering Kanu a dish of dried and sweetened fruit.

"We did, but we always respected each other. Besides, we were both from Earth. We had far more in common than we had to divide us."

"I am sorry to hear that you have lost your ambassadorship," said Mr. Dalal.

"It was right to bring in new blood. Marius is a very safe pair of hands."

"Garudi wrote to us when she was able," said Mrs. Dalal. "She thought highly of you, Mister Akinya."

"Kanu, please."

"She would not have thought it fair, that you should be considered . . . What is the word they use?" asked Mr. Dalal.

"He doesn't need to hear that," said Mrs. Dalal.

Kanu laughed aside the awkwardness. "Tainted. It's all right—I've heard it already."

"I do not suppose this is a time for idealists," said Mrs. Dalal.

"No," Kanu said ruefully. "I don't think it is."

They asked Kanu what had happened to him since the terrorist incident. He told them how the machines had healed him, keeping him in their care for twenty-two days before releasing him to the embassy. "Then I was told that my services were no longer required. Soon after, a shuttle arrived to take me away."

"And you came straight to Earth?" asked Mr. Dalal.

"No, there were some administrative formalities first. I was subjected to the most intensive medical examination you can imagine, just in case the robots had planted something in me while I was under." Kanu nibbled at one of the dried fruit slices. Overhead, the blades of plants scissored in an afternoon breeze. He was glad to be in the shade. Here the sunlight struck the surfaces of things with a hard, interrogatory brightness. "I had to disappoint them, though. Other than some scars, the robots hadn't left any trace of themselves."

"Then you should be allowed to continue with your work," Mrs. Dalal said, her tone indignant.

"In a perfect world."

"Do you have plans?" asked Mr. Dalal.

"Nothing terribly detailed. I thought I might visit some old friends now I'm back on Earth. After that, I have enough funds that I don't need to make any immediate decisions. Also, I've been meaning to look into the history of a relative of mine—my grandmother, Sunday Akinya?"

"She has the same name as the artist," said Mrs. Dalal.

Kanu smiled at this. "She *is* the artist. Or rather was. Sunday died a very long time ago, and we never had the chance to meet."

Mrs. Dalal nodded, clearly impressed.

"When Garudi mentioned your name, I did not make the connection," Mr. Dalal said. "But I suppose Akinya is not all that common a surname. I should have realised."

"The odd thing," Kanu said, "is that Sunday never made much of a name for herself when she was alive—not through her art, anyway. Her grandmother was the famous one."

"Eustace?" asked Mrs. Dalal.

"Eunice," Kanu corrected. It was a perfectly forgivable error, this long into her afterlife.

After a silence, Mr. Dalal said: "More chai, Kanu?"

He raised his hand, webbing his fingers apart. "No—it's very kind of you, Mr. Dalal, but I need to be on my way."

"Thank you again for bringing Garudi's things," Mrs. Dalal said.

They needed groceries so decided to walk him back to the railway station. Beyond the shade of their garden the afternoon was still warm and now virtually breezeless. Kanu thought of the ocean and wished he could be in it.

"I was hoping you might set our minds at ease," Mr. Dalal said.

"About what?" Kanu asked.

"During the day you don't usually see it, but at night, it's hard to ignore. When it passes over Madras, over India, it's hard to sleep. Just the thought of that thing up there, wondering what it's thinking, planning. I imagine it's the same for everyone."

"I suggest we take encouragement from the fact that the Watchkeepers have not acted against us," Kanu said delicately, drawing on one of a thousand diplomatic responses he kept in mind for questions such as this. "It's clear they have the capability to do so, but they haven't used it. I think if they meant to, we would already know."

"Then what do they want?" asked Mrs. Dalal, her tone demanding. "Why have they come back if they don't want something from us?"

"I don't know," Kanu said.

Noticing his unease, she shook her head and said, "I am sorry, we should not have pressed you. It's just—"

"It would be good to know we can sleep well in our beds," Mr. Dalal said.

From Madras he travelled west to Bangalore; from Bangalore he took a night connection to Mumbai; from Mumbai at dawn a dragon-red passenger dirigible, ornamented with vanes and sails and a hundred bannering kitetails. The dirigible droned at low altitude across the Arabian Sea, a thousand passengers promenading through its huge windowed gondola. In the evening they docked at Mirbaţ, where Kanu found lodgings for the night and a good place to eat. Over his meal, alone at an outdoor table, he watched the boats in the harbour, recalling the feeling of rigging between his fingers, remembering how it felt to trim a sail, to read the horizon's weather.

In the morning he drew upon his funds for the expense of an airpod, an ancient but well-maintained example of its kind, and vectored southwest at a whisker under the speed of sound, across the Gulf of Aden and down the coast towards Mogadishu. He veered around fleets of colourful fishing boats, lubber and merfolk crews gathering their hauls. Their boats had eyes painted on their hulls. It was good to fly, good to see living seas and living land beneath him, people with jobs and lives and things to think about besides robots on Mars and alien machines in the sky.

Presently a seastead loomed over the horizon. Kanu slowed and announced his approach intentions.

"Kanu Akinya, requesting permission—"

But the reply was immediate, cutting him off before he had

even finished his sentence. "You of all people, Kanu, do not need to seek permission. Approach at leisure and be prepared for a boisterous welcoming party."

He recognised the voice. "I'm that transparent, Vouga?"

"You're almost a celebrity now. We've been following developments since we heard the good news about your survival. I'm dreadfully sorry about the Martian business."

"I got off lightly."

"Not from what I heard."

The seastead came up quickly. It was a raft of interlocking platelets upon which rose a dense forest of buildings packed so tightly together that from a distance they resembled a single volcanic plug, carved into crenellated regularity by some fussy, obscure geological process. Several of the structures were inhabited, but the majority were sky farms, solar collectors and aerial docking towers. By far the largest concentration of living space was under the seastead, projecting into the layered cool of the deep ocean.

The airpod was not submersible so Kanu docked at one of the towers, nudging past a gaggle of plump cargo dirigibles. The reception was, mercifully, not quite as boisterous as Vouga had warned, but warm and good-spirited for all that. These were his people, the merfolk he had joined and served and later commanded. Some were like Kanu—still essentially humanoid but for some modest aquatic adaptations. For the sake of practicality, Kanu had even allowed some of his own adaptations to be reversed prior to his Martian assignment. There were some among the welcoming party who bore no merfolk characteristics at all: recent arrivals, perhaps, or people who shared the ideology but not the desire to return to the sea.

Others were unquestionably stranger, even to Kanu's eye. He had been away for long enough to view matters with the detachment of the émigré. Genuine human merpeople, their legs reshaped into fish tails, were the least remarkable. A few resembled otters or seals, furred or otherwise, and several had taken on different aspects of cetacean anatomy. Some had lungs and others had become true gilled water-breathers, never needing to surface. Some greeted him from the water-filled channels around the docking port. Others made use of mobility devices, enabling them to walk or roll on dry land.

"Thank you," Kanu said, unable to stop himself bowing to the assembled well-wishers. "It's good to be home, good to be among friends."

"Will you be staying with us?" one of the merwomen called from the water.

"Only for a little while, Gwanda." They had worked in many of the same administrative areas before his ambassadorship. "There's a lot to keep me busy away from the aqualogies."

Now that he had returned, he felt a profound sense of belonging, a connection to the sea and its cargo of living things—everything in the great briny chain of being, from merfolk to plankton.

But he knew he could not afford to stay long, if he did not wish to be pulled back into his old life. Not that the prospect was unattractive—far from it. But even though he could not quite articulate the reasons, Kanu felt a deep sense that he must be moving on, attending to business that was as yet unfinished. What that business was, what it entailed, he could not quite say. But nothing would be gained by submitting to the lure of the merfolk.

"Would you like to swim with us?" Gwanda asked. "We can take you to Vouga. Ve will be done soon, I think."

"I think I remember how to swim," Kanu said. And then smiled, because he realised it had sounded like sarcasm. "No, genuinely. I *think* I remember. But it has been a long time— please be gentle with me."

He left his clothes in the airpod and joined the other swimming things in the water. For a moment he sensed their eyes on him. They had no particular interest in his nakedness—few of them were wearing anything to begin with beyond a few sigils of rank and authority, equipment harnesses and swimming aids—but they had surely heard about his injuries on Mars, if not the specifics.

"The machines did a good job on me," he said, disarming their curiosity. "I suspect they could have avoided scarring altogether, but they left me a few as a reminder of what I'd survived—not as a cruel thing, but to help with my psychological adjustment. Given that they've had remarkably little experience with human bodies, I don't think they did too badly, did they?"

"We heard that you died," said Tiznit, all whiskers and oily white fur.

"A spaceship fell on me. That'd take the shine off anyone's day."

Vouga was done with ver work by the time Kanu arrived. They met in a private swimming chamber, a bubble-shaped turret high in the topside seastead.

"Judging from the evidence, they put you back together very well. No one on Earth has that sort of surgical capability any more, you realise? Not even us. If you'd suffered a similar injury here, we'd have fed you to the fish by now."

"I suppose that puts me in their debt."

"Is that how you feel—indebted?"

"Mostly, I'm just grateful to be alive. In my more cynical moments I tell myself that the robots did rather well out of it, too. They got to handle a human subject—took me apart like a jigsaw, put me back together again. We were trying to stop them getting their hands on corpses, and I gave them one for free!"

Vouga appraised him carefully. "The problem, Kanu, is that you're not a natural cynic. You don't wear bitterness or distrust particularly well."

"Perhaps I'm changing."

"No one could blame you after what you experienced. For myself, I'm happy the robots did one good deed, regardless of their deeper motives. Have you kept up with the news since you left the embassy? Things have been stirring up on Mars—your former friends are behaving provocatively. The Consolidation's hard-liners want a decisive response, and frankly I don't blame them. It's no good just shooting the machines down when they try to reach space."

Kanu smiled, although he felt a sourness in his belly. "So we endorse Consolidation policy now, do we? More's changed here than I realised."

"Our anti-robot stance is as old as the movement, Kanu—I shouldn't need to remind you of that."

After the warmth of his welcome, the last thing he wanted to do was argue with Vouga. "Lin Wei would have found them marvellous. She'd have wanted to embrace them, to share the future with them."

"It's a little late for pipe dreams. We had our chance, we blew it. These are post-Mechanism times, Kanu—we make the best of what we have and wander sadly through the ruins of what might once have been." But after a moment, Vouga added, "I know—we should all try to be positive. There's always a place here for you. Those modifications you had reversed—it's a trivial matter to have them reinstated. You should rejoin us, embrace the ocean fully. Put all that Martian business behind you like a bad dream."

"I wish that's all it had been," Kanu said.

"Is there anything we can do for you in the meantime?"

"I thought I might drop in on Leviathan, if it isn't too much trouble."

"Trouble? No, not at all." But Vouga sounded hesitant.

"What is it?"

"Nothing. I'll make the arrangements. He'll be very pleased to see you again."

The great kraken's haunt lay in the deep waters of the Indian Ocean, about a thousand kilometres south of the seastead. They went out in a sickle-shaped Pan flier, a machine nearly as old as the airpod that had brought Kanu from Mirbaţ, but larger and faster.

Vouga and a dozen other high-echelon Pans came along for the ride and a grand old time was had by all. They spent so much of their lives in the ocean that it was a novelty to see it from above, from outside, and they rushed from window to window, goggling at some extremely subtle demarcation of colour and current. Once they passed a tight-wound whorl of fish, spiralling about some invisible gravitational focus like stars at the centre of the galaxy. It was hard not to see the shoal as a single living unit, purposeful and organised, cheating the local entropy gradients. Kanu felt a shiver of alien perception, as if he was also momentarily seeing organic life from outside itself, in all its miraculous strangeness.

Life was a very odd thing indeed, he reflected, when you really thought about it.

But then they were on the move again, over reefs and smaller seasteads, over clippers and schooners and schools of dolphin, and then there was a darkness just beneath the surface, an inky nebula against turquoise.

"Leviathan," Vouga said.

They slowed and hovered above the kraken. It was as large as a submarine. In the years since Kanu had last spent time with Leviathan, the kraken had easily doubled in size.

"Who works with him now?"

"You were the last, Kanu," Vouga said, as if this was something he ought to have remembered. "The need for construction krakens has declined significantly compared to the old days. Most of them were put out to pasture, until they died of old age. Some live longer than others. We try to keep Leviathan suitably occupied."

Kanu had discovered an aptitude with the construction krakens not long after he joined the merfolk. There were some who found the genetically and cybernetically augmented creatures daunting, but Kanu had quickly overcome his misgivings. In fact, the huge and powerful animals were gentle, obliging and fond of human companionship—elephants of the deep, in many regards.

The most adept partners worked with their krakens so closely that an almost empathic bond was established, the kraken responding to the tiniest gestural commands and the partner in turn utterly sympathetic to the kraken's own postural and visual-display communication channels. Kanu and Leviathan had established one of the most productive and long-lasting bonds between any such pairing.

But the years had rolled by, and the escalator of power had taken him to the top of the Panspermian Initiative and then to Mars, and he had never quite found the time to ask after Leviathan. Not even the minute or two it would have taken to formulate the enquiry and transmit it back to Vouga.

It was much too late to put that right now. But he still had to make the best amends he could.

"I'd like to swim."

"Of course. Do you need a swimming suit, accompaniment?"

"I don't think so."

"Then we'll hover until you need us. Good luck, Kanu."

He dropped the short distance from the flier's belly into the water. He hit the surface hard and was under before he had taken the shallowest of breaths. He fought back to the surface, coughing, the salt stinging his eyes.

When the coughing fit passed and he had gathered enough air into his lungs, he chanced another submersion. He fought for the depths. Leviathan was further below the surface than he had appeared from the air. Kanu wondered what had drawn the kraken to this particular spot in the ocean. Given the chance, krakens were free-roaming and fond of the cool and lightless depths.

Kanu's augmented eyes dragged information from the ebbing light. Leviathan was a pale presence below—much paler than he had looked from the air. The iridophores in his body shifted colour and brightness according to mood and concentration. Kanu watched a wave of amber slide along the main body, from eye to tail—a guarded acknowledgement of his presence. But Leviathan's eye was looking obliquely past him, as if he did not care to meet Kanu's gaze directly.

Kanu bottled up his qualms. The kraken was huge and he was small, but Vouga would never have allowed him to swim if there was the least chance of injury.

He noticed now that something was occupying Leviathan. The kraken had not chosen this spot randomly. There was a structure here, pushing up from the depths. Massive and ancient, its outlines were blurred by coral and corrosion. Kanu made out four supporting pillars, thick as skyscrapers, and a complicated metal platform like a tabletop. He could not tell how far down the legs went, but the entire thing was slightly lopsided.

It had become a kind of toy for Leviathan. The kraken used his arms to move things around on the upper deck of the platform like a child playing with building blocks. The kraken had a shipping container pincered between two arms, some maritime logo still faintly readable through layers of rust and living accretion. Another pair of arms moved a jagged and buckled crane through the water, then jammed it down on the platform. He placed the container next to it. Even through metres of water, Kanu felt a seismic thud as the objects hit the hard surface.

He swam into clear view of the nearest eye, wider than his body was tall, unblinking as a clock face. Still using the air he had drawn into his lungs, Kanu allowed himself to float passively. He wanted some show of recognition from Leviathan, but the eye appeared to look right through him. The kraken was still moving things around, picking the same things up, putting the same things down.

"You know me," Kanu mouthed, as if that was going to make any difference.

The kraken hesitated in his labours. For a moment he was as still as Kanu, poised in the water, arms moving only with the gentlest persuasion of the ocean currents. Kanu would need to surface again shortly, but he forced himself to remain with Leviathan, certain that a connection—however fragile— had been re-established.

I was away too long, he wanted to say. *I'm sorry.*

He just hoped that the mere fact of his being there was enough to convey the same sentiment.

But Leviathan could not tear himself from the puzzle of the drilling platform. He picked up the container again, moved it like a chess piece to some new configuration. With a shudder of insight, Kanu grasped that the activity was as unending as it was purposeless. It satisfied the kraken's need to be moving things, to find permutations of space and form.

At last his lungs reached their limit. He surfaced, conscious even as he ascended that he had slipped beyond the horizon of Leviathan's attention. The kraken might have been dimly cognisant of his presence for a few moments, but no more than that.

He broke into daylight. The flier was over him, ready to take him back to the seastead. Vouga did not ask if he wished to dive again, and he was glad of that.

The following morning, Kanu was on his way north.

CHAPTER 7

Goma had long held a notional understanding of the starship's size, but it was quite another thing to be coming up in the shuttle, gaining her first true understanding of the scale of her new home. It was four kilometres long, about five hundred metres across, and resembled a thick-barred dumb-bell with equal-sized spheres at either end. The forward sphere was patterned with windows and access hatches—cargo bays, shuttle docks, sensor ports—while the rearward globe was contrastingly featureless. That was the drive sphere, containing the post-Chibesa engine. Its exhaust, hidden around the sphere's curve, would eventually boost *Travertine* to half the speed of light.

Constructing a starship, or indeed a pair of such craft, was still beyond the economic reach of all but a few governments, in all but a handful of solar systems. Two hundred years after Travertine's work on *Zanzibar*, the mechanics of a PCP engine still presented fiendish challenges. The new generation of engines were faster and more efficient than the old, but they were no less dangerous to work with, no less unforgiving of error.

But Crucible had committed itself to building two of these ships, banking its future on their construction. It had hoped to tap into the still-young extrasolar trade networks and do business with its stellar neighbours. These ships gave it legitimacy, proving that it had the financial and technical maturity to join the league of spacefaring worlds.

All that had made tremendous sense until the Watchkeepers returned.

The shuttle approached *Travertine*'s forward sphere where they docked and transferred inside. There was artificial gravity, provided by the rotation of the ring-shaped interior sections. Ru wanted to see the cabin, but before any of them were allowed to their rooms—or given access to the personal effects shuttled aboard days ago—there was the necessary formality of a meeting with the captain and her technical staff.

All of the crew and passengers—fifty-four souls—convened in the largest lounge, its windows shuttered against the glare of day.

"Welcome aboard," said Gandhari Vasin, spreading her arms wide as if to embrace all of them, technical crew and passengers both. "This is a great day for all of us—a monumental day—and a privilege for those of us fortunate enough to be riding the ship. I would like to wish us all a safe voyage and a productive, bountiful expedition. I also extend our collective gratitude to the people of Crucible, for their kindness and generosity in making this expedition possible. It is nothing that we take lightly, any of us. Let us hope for good fortune, for ourselves and for our sister ship, and those who will travel aboard her."

Goma had already met Gandhari Vasin. She was a good choice, extremely satisfactory to all parties. It helped, perhaps, that she had not been born on Crucible. Vasin had arrived on the planet via the same quarterlight vehicle that had brought Arethusa. A senior propulsion specialist, she had decided that she wished to remain behind on Crucible when the QV departed. She was regarded as non-partisan, and Goma believed that Mposi had favoured her candidature for exactly that reason, aside from her obvious competence.

She was also a cheerful-looking woman with a broad smile and a habit of wearing colourful wraps and headscarves, disdaining titles and the regalia of hierarchy at all times. "I am your captain," she said, as if it were a kind of confession. "This is the role they have given me, and I will do my utmost to be worthy of it. But I am also Gandhari, and I would much rather you call me that than Captain Vasin. We are all going to be aboard this ship for a very long time. Formalities will begin to fade sooner or later, so we might as well dispense with them immediately."

All well and good, Goma thought, but Gandhari was also in charge of a starship, a massive and lethal piece of technology, and before long they would be on their own, independent of external support. She could be their friend up to a point, but Gandhari would also need nerves of steel and an iron will to go with it.

Gandhari said a few more words, then set about introducing the key members of the expedition, trusting that everyone else would get to know each other over the coming days.

"I must first mention Goma Akinya, who did not have to join us, but chose to out of selfless consideration for her mother." Gandhari pointed both hands at Goma, palms nearly together, the gesture almost worshipful. "It is true that we have all made sacrifices, but many of us were long committed to the idea of an interstellar voyage—it is the ambition to which we have bent our professional lives. Not so with Goma. She had no desire to leave Crucible, no desire to abandon her friends and work. Yet here she is. I do not think we can speak highly enough of her loyalty to Crucible."

Then Gandhari pivoted slightly, shifting the focus of her attention to Ru.

"While we are speaking of sacrifices, let us also remember our friend Ru Munyaneza, Goma's wife, who has left behind her beloved elephants to come with us. Ru's loss is our gain, however."

Gandhari turned to introduce Dr. Saturnin Nhamedjo. It was a formality: the physician was already known to most of the party since he had been involved in assessing their suitability for skipover.

"Saturnin brings with him a small but highly capable medical team, all multispecialists and all—like the rest of us—volunteers. They are to be our doctors, our first line of defence against illness and injury, but above all else they are to be our friends, full members of the expedition."

Next, Gandhari introduced Nasim Caspari, head of the eighteen-strong technical section and, like Gandhari herself, an expert in post-Chibesa theory. Caspari was a slight, unassuming man who clearly did not relish being in the limelight, visibly relieved when Gandhari moved on to her next introduction, who was sitting close to Caspari. Aiyana Loring was a multispecialist, heading the astrophysics and exoplanet group, which also included biologists and ecosystem experts. Loring would have little data to work with until they reached their destination, but Goma doubted that ve would have difficulty keeping verself occupied, especially given ver willingness to cross between disciplines.

"Ve's good," Ru whispered, as if there had been any doubt. "Came up with some of the algorithms we use for our own studies. Turns out that what works for galaxy clusters also works for elephant neurones."

"Thank you, Captain Vasin," said the willowy, graceful Loring, who moved like a cat and was by all accounts a fine dancer. "I mean Gandhari. My apologies. And please, everyone—I am Aiyana. My door is always open. I hope to get to know you all very well."

Technically, Goma and Ru were both subsumed into Loring's team of specialists—they were now the resident experts on large fauna and interspecies communication. But in practice (as Mposi had assured Goma) neither would be required to answer to anyone but Gandhari. That said, Goma took an immediate liking to the elegant Loring and looked forward to contributing to the team.

Next was Maslin Karayan, head of the twelve-member Second Chance delegation. Maslin Karayan was a bullish, barrel-chested man, bearded and patriarchal, perhaps the oldest person on the ship after Mposi. He had been close to *Zanzibar* when it was destroyed, narrowly avoiding death, and by all accounts took the whole incident personally.

"I don't know why she's bothering introducing them," Goma said to Ru. "It's not like we'll ever need to talk to each other."

Ru smiled. "Everyone's useful—even believers."

"Thank you, Gandhari, for your kind sentiments," Karayan said, sweeping the room with wide, challenging eyes set under a prominent brow. So much of his face was covered by his beard that it was hard to read his expression, which was perhaps the intention. "I speak for my family and friends when I say that we are very glad indeed to have assumed our place in the expedition. The hand of history lies heavy upon us, and its retribution will be merciless should we fail in any respect. We must have courage, yes"—he was still looking around the room, his gaze settling for a moment on Goma, or so it felt to her—"but courage is not in itself sufficient. We must also exercise prudence and caution—those higher faculties of judgement—to the very limit of our abilities."

Officially they were a coalition of conservative political interests with a common desire not to repeat the errors of the past, from the Mechanism to the Mandala event. They had been instrumental in keeping Ndege under lock and key when more enlightened voices called for a relaxation in the terms of her incarceration. Unofficially, they tolerated—even encouraged—a strain of superstitious thinking which Goma considered profoundly objectionable. She had nothing against untestable belief systems per se. She just did not care to share a ship with people who subscribed to them.

"God-botherers," she whispered.

If Karayan heard her, no sign of it perturbed his leonine mask of a face. "Great challenges lie ahead of us. Scientific puzzles. Mysteries and wonders, no doubt. Temptations."

Goma rolled her eyes.

"But with the right frame of mind, the right spirit, we may overcome our worst appetites for mere knowledge. The moderating influence of my friends may never be called upon, yet—"

"You've won your victory by being on the ship," Goma said, finally unable to contain herself. "Now will you let someone else have their say?"

"I think we can all agree," Mposi said, rising from his seat, "that these last few days have been extraordinarily taxing. Against our better nature, we may say things that we regret an instant later. Isn't that right, Goma?" He was looking at her with fierce intensity, as if branding his thoughts directly into her brain. "*Isn't that right*, Goma?"

"Yes," she said, at a prod from Ru. "Yes."

"I accept your apology," Maslin Karayan said, making a tiny bow in her direction.

"I would add," Mposi went on, "that I entirely echo Maslin's sentiments. We must all do our best to act with intelligence and caution. We will be tested, I know, but I do not doubt that we have it in us to succeed."

"Mposi speaks wisely," Gandhari said, her voice slow and oratorical. "There will be challenges, certainly. But if we can avoid tearing each other limb from limb, at least for a few weeks, I think that would make for an excellent start." Then, with a deliberate shift in tone, she added, "We will remain in orbit, completing final system tests, for another five or six days. You have until then to decide your place in this expedition. From the moment I light the Chibesa drive, no force in the universe will make me turn this ship around."

In that promise, Goma saw, was a glint of the steel she had guessed must be there. Gandhari be damned—this was Captain Vasin in all her pomp and authority, and she was all the more magnificent for it.

"I do not think," Mposi said, "that any of us will take you up on that chance to leave, Gandhari, but it is good to know it is there."

Their captain made a few more introductions before wishing the best for everyone, thanking the people of Crucible again and finally dismissing the assembly. "Go! You have a ship to explore. But don't explore too much of it in one day— we all need to leave a few surprises for later!"

Like all the married couples on the expedition, Goma and Ru had been given a cabin to themselves. It was a decent size, with an en suite bathroom and toilet, even a small kitchen area where they could prepare food when they did not feel like eating in the communal spaces. The walls were capable of displaying any colour or pattern, and pictures and murals summoned from the central library. Goma had already taken out the two wooden elephants Ndege had given her and set them within a low alcove.

The room was large enough, but there was also a ship to explore. There were many levels, many sections, and not all of them would be routinely accessible. Instead of keys, Goma and Ru had bangles around their wrists which opened the doors they were allowed to use. Every crew-member's bangle was set to allow different levels of access. Only Nasim Caspari's technical crew were permitted anywhere near the rear sphere, and there were few good reasons for an ordinary passenger to enter the connecting spine. But this still left hundreds of rooms and bays to explore, some of them as large as any enclosed space Goma had known on Crucible.

The Knowledge Room quickly became one of her favourite

haunts. She quickly began to feel a claim on its territory, especially as it was not often visited by Ru or the other crew-members. Perhaps that would change when they were under way, but for now it was hers. The room itself was a circular chamber, the centre of which was occupied by a well-shaped projection device. The device was about four metres across, walled around by an opaque material and virtually filled to the brim with a level transparent substance.

Beneath the surface of the well—embedded in the transparent matrix—floated a representation of their current total knowledge of the Gliese 163 system. In its neutral state, the display had the form of an orrery, with the star at the middle and its family of worlds ticking around on their orbital paths. Much was known about the star, but then stars were simple things, their physical natures dependent on only a handful of parameters—mass, metallicity, age. The essential nature of Gliese 163 had been common knowledge for over half a millennium.

Worlds were a different matter, however, their histories contingent on a billion random factors. They did not fit into neat categories; they did not readily disclose their secrets, especially across many light-years. All of the larger worlds in the Gliese 163 system had been studied from Earth's solar system using the swarm of telescopes called Ocular. Ocular data had proven the existence of Mandala and sent the first wave of holoships on their way.

But that data had been deliberately tainted, and when people eventually learned the truth, they tore Ocular apart in their fury and fear. Nothing like it had been constructed since, in any solar system. That said, the data was still archived and available for analysis. Goma was given to understand that it had been cleansed of any bias, intentional or otherwise.

Gliese 163 was nearly twice as far from Earth as Crucible so the images were never going to be as sharp. Crucible had also been observed more intently over a longer period of time, allowing for data to be synthesised across many planetary rotations and season cycles. No such effort had been expended on the more distant system since there had been no reason to expect any benefits from such extended study. The planetary globes looked sharp enough, delicately jewelled marbles, but when Goma pushed her hand into the image—feeling the cold suck of the membrane as it slid over her fingers and up her wrist—she could conjure any of the planets or moons to a much larger size and pluck them out of the well like apples, at which point the fuzzy nature of the data became very obvious.

Near the star, for instance, was something the annotation labelled a "superterran waterworld" called Poseidon. It was the second world out from Gliese 163, and the first that was habitable by any stretch of the definition.

They knew the size of this planet and could infer its surface conditions and predict the make-up of its atmosphere even from a distance, but none of its features was sharp. "Habitable" was also a relative term. Poseidon was hot—its coolest areas were equivalent to the warmest parts of Crucible—and its surface gravity was half as strong again. On its ocean-covered surface, conditions would be near the upper limit for the long-term viability of multicellular creatures, although that did not preclude the existence of extremophile organisms. There was oxygen in the atmosphere, so presumably some form of photosynthesis was occurring in or on the ocean, and since the planet had apparently escaped a runaway greenhouse effect, there must be thermal-regulatory mechanisms in play, keeping the atmosphere from turning into an incinerating furnace. While humans could endure such an environment for a short period, it was no place to consider making a home.

There were gas giants and smaller, rockier worlds in orbits circular and eccentric, some close to Gliese 163, some much further out. Since no hard data was available on the gas giants' moons, it was difficult to say whether they might have any connection with the signal. Goma thought it more likely that the answer might lie with one of the terrestrial planets—worlds with names like Paladin and Orison. They moved in small, circular orbits—this was a very compact solar system. But there was little or no data on them or such moons as they might possess, or on the many smaller bodies orbiting Gliese 163.

The well, Goma knew, was actually a soup of nanomachines. When her fingers closed around a marble, the well sensed her intention and organised its resources—the Knowledge itself— to produce a "solid" image, a ball composed from nanomachines at a much higher density than those in the transparent matrix. When she hauled her glowing prize from the well, the machines making up the sphere were reflecting the horizon of human knowledge at that moment in time. She could tear away a rind of crust, expose the best-guess for the planetary interior—cherry-red core or stone-dead, nonmagnetic heart.

But the nanomachines guarded themselves jealously and the prize was as ephemeral as a fairy-tale gift. Even as she held it in her hand, the machines began to seep through her grip, back into the pool. If she tried to take her prize beyond the limit of the device's rim, the globe would collapse into liquid and drain away in a gush of colour. There was no harm in trying to beat it, and she tried again and again, hoping to hold a tatter of a world in her palm. But it was to no avail, for the machines were swifter than thought.

It pleased Goma that no one else appeared to be interested in the Knowledge Room—at least not yet. She enjoyed tossing the worlds back into the well, watching them shrink and return to their proper orbits. Which of these planets or moons, she wondered, had sent the signal to her mother? No one knew.

Exiting the room after one visit, she saw two men come bustling along the corridor on which it was situated. Both were Second Chancers, obvious from their dark red clothing. It was not quite a uniform—the styles varied from Chancer to Chancer—but close enough to convey a sense of kinship and shared purpose. One of the men was the burly, bearded Karayan, the other a younger and slighter man.

Goma desired no contact with these people, so her first instinct was to duck back into the Knowledge Room. But that would have been far too obvious and cowardly a gambit. She decided to brazen it out—they were going to keep bumping into each other, after all.

"Ah," said the bearded man. "The redoubtable Goma. Could you not have stayed your tongue, at least for the duration of Gandhari's introduction?"

"I said what was on my mind."

"Yes, we noticed." Maslin Karayan's eyes narrowed at her from beneath his formidable brow. "Crucible is a democracy, in case you didn't realise. And we are aboard this ship by mutual consent—as entitled to our places as you or any of the other scientists."

"I didn't say you weren't."

"You also made no secret of your ill-feelings," Karayan said.

"I'm entitled to them," Goma said, feeling a certain shameful thrill in her own studied belligerence.

The younger man had been silent until now. He had a pale complexion and a mop of blond hair which sat on his scalp in tight curls, save for a cowlick covering half his forehead.

"Do you really hate us that much, Goma? Just because we have a slightly different set of values from your own?"

"I must go on ahead and meet my wife," Karayan told the other man. "I will see you at the evening gathering, Peter."

"Thank you, Maslin."

Karayan touched a big hand to the younger man's shoulder and proceeded down the corridor, leaving Goma alone with the man named Peter.

"I'm not stopping you from leaving," Goma said.

The man smiled, although there was more sadness than amusement in his expression. "I am Peter Grave, for what it's worth. Yes, I'm a Second Chancer and I respect Maslin, but I'm also hoping you and I might become friends, at least while we're stuck inside this ship."

"Why would you want that?"

"Because I admire you. Because I know what you did, to spare your mother from this."

"The last thing I want to hear is a Second Chancer talking about my mother."

"Ours is a broad alliance. Not everyone holds Ndege to the same accountability."

"So what do you think?"

"I think there are always grounds for forgiveness."

"Then you're wrong. My mother didn't need forgiveness. Forgiveness is only required when you commit a crime."

"And your mother's deeds don't count as a crime?"

"She was trying to do something good."

"I don't dispute that, but good deeds alone can't excuse mistakes that kill hundreds of thousands of people." Grave offered her the palms of his hands. "Look, the last thing I want is to get into all that. I just feel that if we can at least agree to rub along together, it's going to make life a lot easier for all of us. Maslin's not such an ogre, you know—none of us is."

"Do you believe in a god, Peter Grave?"

"My beliefs or otherwise don't lend themselves to simple answers."

"That's a yes, then."

"You are doing me a disservice, Goma." He averted his eyes, looking regretful. "Honestly, I was hoping for better from you. Open-mindedness, a willingness to accept differing viewpoints—"

"There's only one viewpoint."

"The infallible wisdom of science?"

"Call it what you like."

"It might surprise you to know that I'm a great admirer of science. I've even read some of your work."

"I suppose it helps to know your enemy."

"Oh, please." At last he raised a surrendering hand. "Never mind. Point made. Point very excellently made. I'm sorry I detained you—sorry one of us wasn't ready to begin building a bridge. You're wrong, though—wrong about me, wrong about all of us. I just hope it doesn't take the rest of the voyage for you to see your way past your prejudice."

Goma blinked in surprise. "*I'm* the prejudiced one?"

But Peter Grave was already easing past her. "Goodbye, Goma Akinya."

CHAPTER 8

Kanu had been travelling on Earth for a week by the time he reached Lisbon. That time seemed improbably full of incident: the visit to the grieving Dalals, the airship flight across the Arabian Sea, the warm reception in the aqualogy, his dismay at the plight of his old friend Leviathan. With his obligation to the Dalals discharged, and having paid a courtesy visit to the merfolk, he at last felt that he could afford to slow down and spend some time in one place. Finding lodgings had taken the better part of a day; now, rested—and no longer finding Earth's light and gravity quite so burdensome as when he had first arrived—Kanu had no grand plans for his day beyond a trip to the quayside and a visit to an art show. He set out in a water taxi, a buzzing electric thing that conveyed him and a handful of fellow travellers the short distance to the concrete jetty, built around the feet of a Provider robot.

The towering, crane-sized robot had been there since the Mechanism fell, still poised halfway out into the Tagus River, where it was working at the time. Much too vast to move or economically dismantle, it now formed a permanent if unintentional sculptural installation. Accepting the inevitable, the city had put a landing deck on top of the Provider and jetties around its feet, then run elevators and staircases up the inside of its tripedal legs. Within its body and the bulges of its limbs' articulation points, thousands of tonnes of useless machinery had been torn out to make way for multipurpose event spaces. It was here, inside the Provider, that one of the most significant Sunday Akinya retrospectives in recent years was taking place.

Kanu had bought a ticket and joined the line on the jetty waiting for the elevators. Despite his diplomatic status on Mars and the link between his name and artist's, he was no kind of celebrity on Earth. He moved through Lisbon in blissful obscurity, barely attracting a second glance. If he was noticed at all, it was only because merfolk always drew a certain amount of attention wherever they went. He had dressed in simple clothes, slung a shabby second-hand satchel over his shoulder and bolstered his anonymity with a pair of antique sunglasses. He was not even the only African-Aquatic in the line.

He entered the cool of the lift, which carried him up the leg to the exhibition level. He lingered in the windowed entrance lobby for a few moments, enjoying the view of Lisbon from this elevated vantage point. There was nothing to rival it anywhere in the city itself, and as he traced the maze of streets and squares around his pension, he felt the slow uncoiling of old spatial memories. Many years had passed since his last visit, but Lisbon was like the sea. It could change, and change again, yet in its eternal changefulness, the city would never be entirely unfamiliar to him.

Kanu crossed the lobby and entered the event space. Although the exhibition was sold out, the organisers had kept the numbers at a manageable level. The retrospective was divided into three main sections: paintings, sculpture, and decorative pieces and public works. Within each section, the pieces had been organised in approximate order of completion.

Kanu dithered over where to start. He had no real sense of how these works slotted into the larger narrative of Sunday's life—whether she had been a sculptor before a painter, a decorator before a sculptor. With some trepidation, he dug the brochure out of his satchel. Unfortunately it offered little help on the matter—it appeared to be written with a tacit assumption of knowledge he had not yet acquired. Even the floor plan appeared to have been drawn in a deliberately counter-intuitive way, so that he had to hold it upside down to orientate himself with respect to the point of entry. Kanu observed the other patrons, who were strolling around with an air of cultured self-confidence, casually pointing out this and that to each other as if the landmarks and milestones of Sunday's career were too obvious to mention.

Never mind. He had to start somewhere.

Near the entrance, preserved on a plinth, was a section of wall that had been cut and removed from the Descrutinized Zone on the Moon. It contained a piece of psycho-reactive graffiti done by Sunday in or around 2163. Kanu wandered over and tried to make sense of the piece. He stared at the smear of clashing colours, daring it to show some acknowledgement of his presence. According to the accompanying text, the "paint" was in fact a kind of licensed nanotechnology infiltrated with invisible attention-tracking devices. Those parts that were "looked at" the most intensely would resist being overpainted by other hands. Areas of the art which suffered attentional neglect were liable to be changed. Kanu was free to drag his finger across the piece's surface, altering colour and texture—but the installation always reset itself on the hour, reverting to the form it had taken when it was last on the Moon.

He moved to a selection of fired earthenware stained with glazes incorporating the greys and fawns of the Lunar surface. In Kanu's eyes there was nothing to link these pieces to the graffiti, but he supposed better scholars than him had done their homework.

The earthenware could not hold his attention—ultimately it was just so many pots and vases. He moved to an upright glass cylinder which held a realistic-looking mannequin of a human figure, sitting in a grandly appointed armchair. The family likeness was inescapable. This was not Sunday, though, but rather her grandmother, the redoubtable Eunice Akinya. According to the annotation, Sunday had invested a lot of time programming a construct "tribute" to the real space explorer.

Kanu could not tell if this was the actual construct or just a good copy.

A sudden sense of purposelessness overcame him. What was he doing here, going through the motions of art appreciation? Art had never spoken to him before, not in any meaningful way, so what was he hoping to get out of this experience? It was absurd to feel that he owed his dead ancestor anything. Sunday was gone—she could not have cared less whether or not he had an appreciation of her work. *A merman in an art gallery*, he thought to himself, *a fish out of water in all but the specifics*.

"The real problem for us," someone was saying in clear, high Portuguese, "is to imagine ourselves inhabiting Sunday's world of four hundred and fifty years ago—she's as remote from us as Vermeer was from her. But if we're going to understand the impulses behind her art, we have to bridge that mental gap—to see her as a fully formed human being, a woman with friends and family, confronted by the same mundane problems of love and life and work that we all face. How to pay the bills. Where to eat, where to live, who to approach for her next commission. She's not a remote historical figure, floating in a cloud of pure inspiration. She was a real woman, with the same cares and fears as the rest of us. She even visited Lisbon—how many of you knew that?"

The speaker was an older woman, lecturing a group of well-dressed young people gathered around her in a loose circle, notepads, pens and crayons at the ready. She wore a dark green jacket over black trousers, with a scarf of a lighter shade of green tossed over one shoulder. She almost had her back to him, and from his present angle he could only see the side of her face. Over the shoulder of one of her audience, Kanu observed a creditable sketch of the graffiti wall rendered in bold diagonal strokes. It was a copy, but it had a vigour about it that captured something of the original.

"In her day," the woman continued, "Sunday wasn't famous at all. It's true that she was born into a rich and powerful family, by the standards of the time. But she didn't want any of that. She went to the Moon, set up shop in the Descrutinized Zone—that's what they called the commune in which she lived—and more or less wrote herself out of ever being rich. She surrounded herself with like-minded souls who couldn't have cared less where she came from. Artists, tinkerers, gypsies, renegade geneticists—every piece that didn't *quite* fit into the ordered jigsaw of the Surveilled World."

Kanu was intrigued now. He had no difficulty understanding the woman. Her diction was very good, but regardless he had spent enough time in Lisbon during the earlier phase of his life to have gained a decent grasp of Portuguese and its commoner dialects. But there was something more to this. It was not just the words the woman was speaking, but rather the precise cadences of her speech. It was as if he had heard her speak on many occasions, to the point where his brain was already ahead of her words, anticipating their flow.

He moved slightly and the angle of her face altered. She was an attractive woman with broad features and very appealing eyes. She was older than the people she was addressing, certainly—perhaps as old as himself. There was a fineness in her features, the definition of her cheekbones, temple and jaw. Her hair was nearly white but still thick and long, and she had allowed it to grow out naturally.

Kanu could not believe his eyes. He knew her.

"Nissa," he said quietly, as if he needed to say it aloud before he could be sure of it.

Nissa.

Nissa Mbaye.

She had been a high-ranking technocrat in the United Surface Nations, not quite his opposite number, but close enough in their respective hierarchies that their paths had crossed many times. During the difficult years after the Fall, when the world had to learn to live without the Mechanism, without the aug, without instantaneous translation and instantaneous virtual telepresence, without absolute security and oversight, without the promise of limitless life extension, Kanu and Nissa had worked together on many of the intergovernmental emergency-response measures. They had their differences, but each recognised that the other was striving for the same thing—to help heal a wounded, traumatised world as best they could. Later, when the Watchkeepers came, Kanu and Nissa had cooperated on the formulation of a pan-governmental response, urging caution and non-aggressive interaction with the alien machines.

They had been opposites, rivals, colleagues, obstinate opponents. They had also come to be friends. Later, more than friends.

For thirty-five years, Nissa Mbaye had been his wife.

"This is weird," she said, when they both had drinks and pastries.

"Weird doesn't begin to cover it," Kanu replied, smiling as he recalled Nissa's old habit of masterful understatement. "If I didn't know better, I'd say I was hallucinating, or stuck in a dream."

"If it's a dream, then I'm stuck in it with you." They were alone, sitting opposite each other at a corner table in the upstairs café. Nissa had sent her students off with an impromptu drawing assignment that she was confident would keep them busy for a half-hour or so. "Shall we switch to Swahili, or would that be bad manners?"

"It would be very bad manners."

They switched to Swahili.

"Let's get one thing out of the way," Kanu continued, faltering over the consonants until his tongue got the message that they were no longer doing Portuguese. "It's odd enough us bumping into each other, but at least I'm here as a member of the public. What are you doing teaching art history?"

"There's no law against it."

"You were a career politician, like me!"

"Please," she said with a smile, "we're in polite company."

Kanu smiled in return. It was banter, but of an old and familiar form that would not have been possible had she not been comfortable around him. But he still felt that there had to be a catch to their meeting.

"Civil servant, technocrat, functionary—whatever you want to call it. Unless my memory's failing me, you had nothing to do with teaching art—and still less to do with my grandmother."

"All right, I'll come clean—I'm not really a teacher. But they're stretched here and I've agreed to help out the exhibitors by leading guided tours, mostly school and student parties."

"That doesn't make it any clearer."

"I'm a scholar now. Don't look so surprised—we're allowed to do more than one thing with our lives. You of all people ought to know that."

"I do—and I agree. But I'm still reeling. You say 'scholar'—"

"Sunday is one of my principal interests. By helping out with the retrospective for a few hours a day, I get almost unlimited access to the archives—the rest of the collection and its documentation. I also assist with some of the cataloguing and annotation along the way."

Kanu was still having trouble with the concept. "So you really are an art historian now?"

"It's not a complete stretch. Even when we worked together, I had other interests—antiquities, deluge architecture, pre-Mechanism cultural semiotics—"

"All of that's still a long way from being an expert on my grandmother."

"There's the small detail that we were married. Is it such a surprise that I know a few things about your grandmother?"

"I hadn't forgotten that we were married." But in truth, it had been months, perhaps even years, since he had last called her to mind. Not because they had parted in bitterness, or that he wished to erase her from recollection, but simply because his life had changed in so many ways that the years with Nissa belonged in their own compartment, one that he seldom had cause to open.

"Sunday was always looming there in your ancestral background. You didn't have to take an interest in her, but that didn't preclude me from doing so."

"I don't remember any such thing."

"It was mostly after we split up. She was a bit of a niche interest then, so her stock hadn't really begun to rise. Look, don't tell me you've completely forgotten. What about the divorce settlement? You agreed to let me have some of her pieces."

"I'm afraid they can't have meant much to me."

"More fool you, merman. You gave away a small fortune. Actually, sizeable fortune would be more like it, with the prices she's fetching now. You could buy a spaceship with those pieces. In fact, that's exactly what I did. But who knew, back then?"

Kanu feigned a glum look. "Not me."

"And you wouldn't have cared even if you'd had an idea what those paintings might be worth. It was just family clutter to you. Money was never your motivator." She appraised him from across the table, doubtless taking in his unostentatious choice of clothing. "I'm guessing it still isn't."

"At least one of us did well out of Sunday."

"Oh, I've done more than well. I see you have a brochure. You didn't read it very closely, did you?"

Kanu blew away table crumbs and spread the brochure out before them. He could see it now, right at the end: a paragraph of acknowledgements in which Nissa's name figured prominently. Not just Nissa but *The Nissa Mbaye Research Foundation*.

"I'm amazed."

"And you're seriously telling me you were wandering around here without a clue I was involved?"

Kanu hesitated. It was quite possible he might have turned away at the jetty if he had seen Nissa's name and realised there was a good chance of bumping into her.

"I didn't know. Genuinely."

"Then your own interest in Sunday . . . that's real?"

Kanu took a deep breath. "I'm at a bit of a loose end these days so I thought, why not take an interest in Sunday? You're right—she never mattered much to me before. But that was wrong. It's odd—she's just my ancestor, but I started to feel as if I owed it to her to learn a little more about her life and legacy. I thought this might be a good place to start."

"We always liked the city. Was that a factor, too?"

Kanu lowered his voice, although there was no chance of

them being overheard in the noisy café. "I'm lucky they didn't lynch me the minute I set foot in the place. They have long memories here. Lisbon is where it all started—or all *ended*, more accurately."

"You didn't personally bring down the Mechanism, Kanu. Also, it was merfolk tecto-engineering that kept Lisbon safe from another tsunami. Anyway, I'm not sure memories are as long as you think. Not these days. It's an old world now. Too much to remember, too many lives. I mean, take us, for example."

"You don't look any older."

"That's very kind, but you were never much of a liar. Really, though—what happened? I'll admit, I saw your name in the news. Some bad business on Mars."

"I was in an accident—injured, quite badly. But I'm all right now. They fixed me."

"They?"

"The machines of the Evolvarium. I was hurt on the surface and taken into their care." After a moment, he said, "I still bleed. They didn't turn me into a robot. I wouldn't have got far from Mars if they had."

"My god. I had no idea it was that serious."

"Two of the other ambassadors were killed, so I got off lightly. But the robots' intervention made it hard for me to carry on in that line of work—there's a perception that I got too close to the robots. Which is why I'm at a loose end."

"So you came back to Lisbon?"

"Madras first—one of my colleagues had family in India. But how could I resist the pull of this old place?"

"This *is* too strange, you and I sitting together. I feel as if the universe has pulled a nasty trick on us both."

"Nasty?"

"All right—unfair. We weren't expecting this, were we?"

"I certainly wasn't." Kanu started to fold the brochure and slip it back into his satchel. After the oddness of this encounter, he had lost what little enthusiasm he had for the rest of the exhibition.

"What are your plans in Lisbon?"

"I didn't have any, beyond visiting the exhibition." Kanu patted the satchel. "Early days, you see. I thought this would be a good way to get my bearings before digging deeper into her legacy. I suppose you'll be in town as long as the exhibition's here?"

"There are only a few weeks left. You did well to make it back to Earth in time."

"There'd have been another one sooner or later, I suppose."

"And doubtless our paths would have crossed eventually. I know this wasn't something either of us planned, but it is nice to see you again, Kanu."

"I feel the same way."

There was a silence. He felt certain that Nissa could sense the inevitable question, floating in a state of unrealised potential between them. She had almost voiced it herself when she asked about his plans in the city. Perhaps she had meant him to go further in his answer.

"We should meet up again," Nissa said.

"Yes," he agreed. "We should definitely do that."

CHAPTER 9

Goma had been aboard *Travertine* for more than two weeks. Each morning she woke to find that the light-speed delay between the ship and Crucible had increased by many seconds compared to the previous day. She preferred not to be reminded of that during the waking hours, for if she dwelt too much on the widening separation between herself and her home, it would have been more than she could easily endure. But it was happening whether she cared for it or not. With the ship under constant thrust, they had locked down the centrifuge wheels for the remainder of the acceleration phase. The fact that she could still walk around, eat and drink, wash and shower, was testament to the force of the Chibesa drive dragging her deeper into the void.

No one was immune to it, including Ru. They'd both had

bad moments—a breakdown, a sobbing fit, a spasm of misdirected anger. Fortunately one had always been there for the other. Goma worried what would happen if they both lapsed at the same time. It did not take much to set it off—a news report from home, a smell or a taste that triggered some sequence of memories that in turn related to something they would not experience again, at least until their distant, largely hypothetical return. Goma only had to pick up on some sadness in Ndege's communications, real or imagined, and she herself was a wreck.

"Sometimes I wake up back on Crucible," she told Captain Vasin, "and I'm overwhelmed with joy to discover that the whole thing on the spaceship was just a bad dream. And then I wake up again, for real this time, and I'm here."

Vasin tilted her head in fond sympathy. "If I told you that just about everyone on the ship will have experienced something similar, including myself, would that make it a little easier to bear?"

They were in Vasin's cabin, drinking chai. The room was slightly smaller than Goma and Ru's own accommodation, but then again Vasin had no one to share it with, and she had obviously chosen the space and furnishings to reflect her own modest needs. A small annexe with a bed and washing facilities was visible through an open doorway, and the main cabin contained a low coffee table, a console, some chairs and soft cushions. The main feature, spread across most of one wall, was a painting of the sun rising over a lake framed between grey and purple crags. At least, Vasin had told her that the name of the painting was *The Sun*. To Goma's eyes, it might as well have been a depiction of some destructive stellar event, or even the violent birth of the universe itself—a primordial explosion of light and matter.

Their captain made a point of arranging these little social occasions. As far as Goma could tell, she was not being singled out for any special favours.

"Even you, Captain?"

"Gandhari, please."

"All right, Gandhari. But I can't believe you have weak moments."

"More than my share. Not necessarily to do with Crucible,

although I was happy enough during my time there, but I have fears enough of my own. I would not be a very effective captain if I did not. Our fears keep us on our toes."

"Are you worried about the ship?"

"Oh, I trust the ship with my life. I'd better! Of course, a lot could go wrong. But then again, we have the best technical crew Crucible could muster. No, my fears are external—directed at the factors I can't control."

"Like the Watchkeepers?"

"They have certainly been uppermost in my concerns. It was always a gamble, taking a ship out on an interstellar heading. We couldn't guess how they'd respond. So far, though . . ."

Behind Vasin, on the wall next to the one displaying the painting, was a schematic of the solar system. It was a real-time image, updated according to new data as it became available to *Travertine*. The arc of their trajectory formed a bold, straightening stroke, arrowing out from the middle. The orbits of Crucible and the other major planets were squeezed into increasingly tight ellipses, crowding around 61 Virginis. But there were also cone-shaped symbols dotted around the schematic, each of which indicated the known location of a Watchkeeper.

"They've not moved?" Goma asked.

"No response that appears directly connected with our departure. In a way, it's almost too good to be true."

"Don't say that."

"I expected to draw some interest, at the very least, but I won't complain if they leave us well alone. Perhaps we've been too cautious, all these years?"

"One in the eye for the Second Chancers, in that case. They've been the main fear-mongers, haven't they? Going around telling everyone that the instant we leave Crucible, we'll feel the wrath of alien judgement."

"In fairness," Vasin said, "that viewpoint isn't just shared by Maslin and his disciples."

"It's a point of view. It's also idiotic."

Humans had first encountered the Watchkeepers around Crucible as the holoships slowed down from crossing interstellar space. After the agreement brokered by Chiku Green, the Watchkeepers had departed Crucible space—to all intents

and purposes vanishing from human affairs and leaving the
colonists free to explore the Mandala. So it had remained for
a century. But they were back now in significantly larger numbers. Not just in Crucible space, but also in Earth's solar system and around every extrasolar world where humanity had
staked a significant presence.

No one knew what to make of them. In the early days of
their return some ships had been destroyed. But whether that
was because those ships ventured too close to the alien
machines or because they were imposing a general injunction
against interstellar travel, no one was quite sure.

Interstellar travel had continued but at a much reduced
level. Once or twice, the Watchkeepers had acted to destroy or
incapacitate in- or outbound ships, but there was no obvious
pattern to their interventions. The result was nervousness and
a growing political conservatism. Each system had its own
specific manifestation of this trend, whether it was the Consolidation of Earth space, the Bright Retreat of Gliese 581's
colonies or the Second Chance movement of Crucible. Interstellar travel was deemed a risky provocation, with the more
extreme voices calling for its complete abandonment, at least
for a few centuries. None of those voices was louder, or more
strident, than the Second Chancers'.

"You really don't have a lot of time for Maslin's people,"
Vasin said.

"And you do?"

"I'm a pragmatist. So's your uncle. Getting Crucible to
agree to hand over this ship to an expedition took a lot of
doing, Goma. The Second Chancers were dead against it."

"So why the hell are they here, stinking up the place?"

Vasin wrinkled her nose as if the bad smell were right
before her. "That was Mposi's masterstroke—and the only
reason he secured agreement for the mission. They'd have
organised a block vote against us, and that would have been
the end of it. But offering them a place on the expedition as
observers?" She shook her head in admiration. "Even I
couldn't have come up with that, so hats off to Mposi."

"Compromise. What about sticking to your principles?"

"If it's a choice between the expedition happening or not,
I'll take compromise over principle any day. Incidentally, I've

heard about your run-ins with Karayan and Grave. I'm trying to maintain a happy ship—are you going to keep making more work for me?"

"I can't stop being a rationalist just because it upsets some people."

"Nor would I expect you to. But you appear far more upset by them than they are by you."

Goma looked down at her chai. All of a sudden the temperature in the room felt cooler than when she had arrived. She set the cup on the coffee table. The liquid surface threw back her reflection, but the mirror was imperfect, blurred by the tiny but constant vibrations that worked their way along the ship from the relentless, roiling furnace of the Chibesa engine.

Another reminder that home was falling further away with each breath.

"I didn't realise I'd been called here for a dressing-down."

"You haven't. You're the most critical member of this expedition and I respect your opinions. I trust everyone else to do the same. But I also need cohesion. Believe it or not, the other scientists are looking to you to take the lead on this. No one's asking for the world here—I don't expect you to start embracing Maslin's beliefs. But if you could at least make a gesture towards mutual cooperation, accepting that they have as much right to be here as we do?"

"You know what they did to my mother."

"And I know what it must mean to you to have left her behind. But the Second Chancers weren't the only reason your mother was locked away, Goma. You have to allow that she had her critics from all corners of Crucible, people of all stripes, all persuasions—even hard-nosed scientists like yourself."

"You weren't there."

"I didn't have to be—I know my history." Vasin offered a conciliatory smile. "Difficult, I know, all this. But just do your best. Who knows? There may be friends among the Second Chancers you've yet to meet."

"I doubt it."

"But time will tell. Set an example, Goma. Reach out. What's the worst that could happen?"

* * *

The days continued passing—Crucible becoming first a star-like dot and then a mote of light so insignificant that Goma could not readily separate it from its star. Distance and then more distance—time opening up like a wide swallowing mouth. The ship functioned with an almost merciless reliability. Some part of Goma almost willed it to malfunction—hoping for some serious but not fatal glitch, sufficient to make them turn around.

But the ship did not oblige.

Goma, meanwhile, did her best not to disappoint Vasin. Reaching out was a step too far, but she avoided the Chancers when she was able and bit down on her worst impulses when she was forced to talk to them. Most of the time, it was not too difficult. She had learned a lot of self-control around elephants as well as people.

She continued to enjoy the solitude of the Knowledge Room, delighting in the endless, childlike pleasure of dipping a hand into the well and scooping out worlds. But soon even that simple pleasure was tested. Aiyana Loring and the other scientists began to show up with increasing frequency, using the well to explore speculative ideas about the Gliese 163 solar system. Goma and Ru were also expected to join in, offering their insights and opinions. Goma was rankled to begin with, feeling that she was no longer at liberty to organise her day as she wished. But it was hard to stay annoyed with the elegant, obliging Loring for very long. Goma was fascinated by the way ve moved, the sense that the slightest, most trivial gesture had been considered and choreographed. There was also something captivating about Loring's androgynous beauty, even the deep, calm register of ver voice.

"This is the central mystery, as far as I'm concerned," Loring was saying, kneeling at the well, reaching into it with one hand to scoop out the blue ball of Poseidon. "Our superterran waterworld. Maybe the origin of the signal? Not necessarily from the surface, but somewhere in orbit? If there aren't moons around it, we'll have an equally fine time explaining their absence."

"Why not the surface?" Ru asked.

"There won't be one?" Loring had a way of phrasing ver

statements as questions, even when they were not. "Just a continuous layer of water, much deeper than any terrestrial ocean? A true waterworld?"

"Sounds boring," Goma said.

"Would be, if we didn't already know that something's going on there. No detailed imagery of the world itself yet—this sphere is conjecture, nothing more—but we know enough to be puzzled. There's oxygen, to begin with—spectral lines in the atmosphere, green tints and chlorophyll signatures. So, life? Not necessarily multicellular, but enough to sustain an oxygen cycle?"

"In the oceans?" Ru asked.

"Or maybe on top of them? Blooms, mats, entire floating land masses and ecologies?"

Goma delicately extracted the sphere from Loring's hand. It still felt odd to know that there was nanotech between her fingers—feared, fabled nanotech. And yet it felt as innocent and harmless as clay.

"Why not dry land?" she asked.

"Because there won't be any. Poseidon's too massive, with too much surface gravity. Continents, mountain ranges? They get flattened out, smothered by water. Push one up and it'll be gone again before you can blink."

"By which you mean over tens of millions of years," Ru said.

Loring smiled. "Think like an exobiologist. A million years? That's nothing. There and gone. Anyway, I don't expect dry land. But it'll be exciting to see what *is* there. Not the real mystery, though."

"No?" Goma asked.

"Question is why it hasn't cooked itself to death. Runaway greenhouse effect—water vapour boiling off that sea, trapping heat in the atmosphere? Feedback cycle—more heat, more vaporisation?"

"That obviously hasn't happened," Ru said.

"No. Hot but not too hot. Bearable for us, with tech. Maybe even limited exposure without. So: some thermoregulation process. Life by itself maybe not be sufficient to achieve that. Also, Poseidon ought to be tidally locked by now—keeping one face to Gliese 163. Hot one side, cold the other. Why isn't it? What's keeping it spinning? Need to get in closer, find out."

"Maybe it's not even the world we're interested in," Goma said, thinking only of the signal and its point of origin.

"I am," Loring answered.

"It's just a planet," Goma said, "a rock and some gas and liquid, and—if we're very lucky—maybe some scummy green organisms."

"Scummy green *living* organisms!"

"The clue's in the name," Goma said, taking a malicious pleasure in pedantry.

"But life—doesn't that fascinate you in and of itself?"

"I'd have to say it doesn't," Goma answered. "Life's commonplace. We understand the basic processes—the originating principles of self-replication, the chemistry, the metabolic pathways. The same story plays out over and over again."

"Doesn't make it any less marvellous."

"No, but it makes it less novel. Plant cells on Crucible aren't exactly like plant cells on Earth, but neither are they unrecognisably different—there are only so many molecular transport mechanisms, only so many energy cycles, only so many ways of organising cells into larger structures. Biologists didn't take long to solve the major mysteries of Crucible—much less time than it took to figure out how everything worked on Earth. They already had the tools, the ideas, and they knew the right questions to ask. Where's the intellectual thrill in solving a puzzle twice?"

"Elephants, though? Just another manifestation of those same principles?"

Goma glanced at Ru before answering. "There's a difference. Elephants are intelligent. They have consciousness, self-awareness, a notion of self."

"It's true," Ru agreed. "We've seen that they can acquire language, with some minor genetic enhancements. They can even speak, given the right prosthetic tools."

"But those elephants are gone now," Loring said. "They've lost the ability to speak, haven't they? What did you call it— the cognitive decline?"

"They're gone on Crucible," Goma said, "but that doesn't mean they've gone for good."

"I have read your work," Loring said. "The circumstances that produced the genetic breakthrough—the emergence of the Tantors? They're not at all clear, are they? It happened in secret, across many generations? Hard to replicate, even if you had the tools?"

"Maybe we don't need to replicate it," Goma answered. "The gene stocks on Crucible were too small to sustain a viable population of Tantors. Genetic dilution—the averaging out of the Tantor traits across successive generations. But if we could locate a larger group of Tantors . . ."

"Elsewhere in human space?" Loring said.

Goma shrugged, equivocal, as if she had given the matter no great thought. "Perhaps."

"But no one has spoken of such a thing. If there were an independent Tantor population back in Earth space, would we not know, after all this time?"

"Maybe they're somewhere else."

"You'll forgive me," Loring said, "but that does not sound like science to me."

"So what does it sound like?" Ru asked.

"Faith," Loring answered.

A day later, Goma was called to Vasin's quarters again. She went there expecting another kindly lecture about the need for harmonious relations between the crew, but when she arrived it was immediately apparent that the purpose of this summons was very different. In addition to Gandhari Vasin, Mposi was also present, as was Aiyana Loring, Dr. Nhamedjo, and Maslin Karayan. None of them looked at ease.

"Come and join us," Vasin said, indicating a space at her coffee table, which was set with a formation of playing cards, evidence of an interrupted game. "This will be made public within the hour, but given your centrality to the expedition, I thought you should know about it immediately."

Goma settled into the seat between Mposi and Maslin Karayan, the only vacant position.

"It's a Watchkeeper, isn't it?"

Vasin nodded at the schematic of the solar system still on her wall, clotted with symbols and numbers. "I suppose that's a bit of a giveaway. Apparently we finally have their interest. Taken long enough. As I said to you the last time we spoke, I almost dared to hope we'd managed to slip under their radar."

"Not very likely," Goma said.

"With hindsight, not remotely. Aiyana—do you want to summarise the findings, for the benefit of Goma and Maslin?"

"This Watchkeeper broke its position eight hours ago," ve said, touching a stud on ver bangle that made the schematic spool back in time, then begin moving forward again, covering hours of movement in seconds of real-time. "Nothing unusual in that? They move around. Acceleration small to begin with, but increasing? Hard to extrapolate trajectory to begin with, but numbers firming up. Course intercepts our own—no chance of that being coincidence."

"When?" asked Karayan, scratching idly at his beard.

"Best guess, Maslin, fifty hours?"

"I'd sooner it were five. At least let the judgement be done with."

Goma made to speak, intending to quibble with that choice of term, but a glance from Mposi convinced her to think better of it.

"Crucible will send us better figures," Vasin said. "That may shift the projection by a few hours. But for now we work on the assumption that it will be on our position in just over two days."

Goma looked at Mposi. Her uncle was impassive, his emotions bottled. She wondered how long ago he had been informed of this news, hoping it was minutes rather than hours. She did not like the idea of him keeping it from her, even if that had been Vasin's express instruction.

"Can we change course, outrun it?"

"It would be a gesture, nothing more," Vasin said. "We know from the records that they can easily outpace and out-manoeuvre us, probably without breaking a sweat. The only thing we can do is maintain our intended course."

Goma's eyes settled onto the landscape painting again, with its shards of light emanating from a bright central focus. It was like a hammer-blow against brittle glass, a spidery fracturing along radial lines.

If the artist had meant to celebrate the sun's return after night, they had instead produced an image of brutal cosmic obliteration. It struck Goma as less a depiction of renewal than a fierce cleansing annihilation—space itself breaking down, or returning to a more primal, basic condition.

"And what happens when they get here?" she asked.

"As your captain, I wish I had something concrete to offer you. If pushed, I'd say there are two distinct possibilities. The first is that we are scrutinised and then ignored, in the same way that the Watchkeepers appear happy to ignore almost all of our day-to-day activities." Vasin moved two of the playing cards which were still set out on her coffee table.

"And the second?" Goma pressed.

"It destroys us. From what we know of previous encounters, it will at least be quick, and probably painless. Chances are we won't even have any warning."

"We'll take our mercies where we find them," Mposi said.

"What are you hoping to get from Crucible?" Goma asked the captain.

"Chai and sympathy, not much more than that. Really I am waiting for them to tell me not to attempt evasive action, because we all know how much good it would do." She moved another card. It was a coping strategy, Goma decided, not a reflection of her lack of concern. "Of course we will transmit our intentions to the Watchkeeper, in every language they have ever been exposed to—for all the good that will do: 'Please ignore us, we mean no harm.'"

"What about the other Watchkeepers?" Karayan asked. "Are they doing anything?"

"Just this one," said Aiyana Loring.

"Maslin is right," Vasin said. "Better five hours than fifty. But better fifty hours than have this hanging over us for the rest of our expedition. None of us wants this fear inside us all the way to Gliese 163."

"I think we'd all agree with that sentiment," Nhamedjo said. "I have fifty-four largely sane individuals to look after—including myself. Confined surroundings, the routine dangers of space travel, the knowledge that whatever world we return to, it will no longer be *our* home—those are bad enough stressors for the human psyche. I would much rather not add years of anxiety to the melting pot. Whatever that Watchkeeper means to do with us, let it be done, and let it be quick."

CHAPTER 10

By the time the exhibition wrapped up Kanu was not sad to be moving on from Lisbon. He had always been fond of the city—it had provided sanctuary to his mother for many years, and much of her own affection for the place and its people had rubbed off on him—but after his time in the embassy he had no desire to be rooted to one place for very long. As it transpired, Nissa had a gap in her commitments, so they agreed to be tourists for another three weeks. Nissa, for her part, had identified a number of small museums and galleries they could visit during their travels, each of which contained works by his famous ancestor Sunday Akinya.

"Not the real treasures," she cautioned. "They've all been sucked up by the Lisbon show, and it'll take a few months for those pieces to get back to their home collections. But there should still be enough to broaden your education."

"I have a lot of catching up to do," Kanu said. But his frame of mind was agreeable and receptive.

From Lisbon they travelled to Seville and Gibraltar, riding the great suspension bridge to Morocco. In Tangiers they visited a small private collection housed in the lower rooms of a salmon-coloured town house constructed around the cool geometry of a lovely shaded courtyard. Kanu had been doubtful about intruding on someone's privacy, but the family owners were flattered to have the attention of the renowned scholar Nissa Mbaye and threw open their doors accordingly. Kanu and Nissa were treated splendidly, finally conceding to remain as guests of the household so they might enjoy a little more of Tangiers.

Their hosts, the Al Asnam family, were born on the Moon but had returned to Earth fifty years ago. After selling a tract of valuable Fra Mauro real estate, they moved into art, a shared fascination.

"I'm as pleased as anyone to see Sunday receive the recognition she was due in her lifetime," said Mr. Hassan Al Asnam as they dined on couscous in an upstairs room, its walls hung with carpets. "But as a relative, Mr. Akinya, you must wonder how it would have changed her, to have received this acclaim when she was alive."

Kanu chose his thoughts and words carefully. They were speaking French, since their hosts were fluent and Kanu's French was not as dreadful as his Arabic.

"I barely knew my grandmother," he said. "She visited Earth precisely once in my lifetime, and that was only very near the end of her life. But I can tell you this." He took a moment to pour more honeyed mint tea for Nissa and their hosts. "She did not feel for a second that her genius had been overlooked. She spent part of her life being an artist and she made a modest living from it, but when the time came she was perfectly willing to turn away from it."

"It has to be said that Sunday's position was exceptional," Nissa put in. "It was her choice to leave the family business, but that money was always there if she chose to return." She glanced at Kanu, as if seeking his approval.

Kanu nodded. "Yes. She was a struggling artist, but she always had that safety net. And when the time came, she felt she had no choice but to take on her share of the family responsibility. But it was not a surrender. From what I understand—and Nissa is the historian here, not me—Sunday could have carried on creating art indefinitely."

"She was prolific enough as it was," said Mrs. Karimah Al Asnam. "Imagine how hard it would be to get to grips with her work if she'd continued for another century!"

"Picasso produced around fifty-two thousand works of art," Nissa said, "and Vermeer fewer than fifty, yet they are of equal interest to us. It's true, though: Sunday's legacy is already more than enough for most of us. And that's before we start worrying about all the lost pieces, scattered around Earth and the solar system."

"I am just sorry she could not share in this," said Mr. Al Asnam. "It would have been a blessing on her life. What is the point of having all this fame and prestige if you are not alive to share it?"

"You think about death too much," chided Mrs. Al Asnam, placing a hand on her husband's wrist. "It's not a healthy preoccupation."

"I think about death to stare it in the eye," Mr. Al Asnam replied, with a sudden fierce enthusiasm.

There was a formulaic quality to this exchange which led Kanu to suspect it had been aired before, perhaps many times. The Al Asnams appeared cosily settled in their routines, as comfortable with each other as a pair of gloves.

"You must tell us again how you came to meet," said Mrs. Al Asnam. "Nissa explained quickly, but I do not think I quite understood. You were married once, and now you have met again because of your mutual interest in Sunday?"

"We met in Lisbon," Nissa said. "Accidentally. But had it not been for Sunday's work, it wouldn't have happened."

"And you were aware of Mrs. Mbaye's scholarship beforehand?" Mr. Al Asnam asked.

"How could he not have been?" asked Mrs. Al Asnam, as if this was the silliest thing he had ever said.

"Actually, I wasn't," Kanu said, smiling. "It's a terrible confession, I know, but I've really only developed an interest in Sunday since I got home. And it was a coincidence, our meeting again."

"The world still has the capacity to surprise us," said Mr. Al Asnam, visibly pleased with himself at the expression of this sentiment. "This gives me hope."

"Sooner or later," Nissa said, "our paths would have crossed. In some ways, perhaps it's not such a coincidence. I developed an interest in Sunday's work because of our marriage, and it must always have been at the back of Kanu's mind, something he meant to look into."

"I'm glad it happened, though," Kanu said. "I didn't realise how much I'd missed a friend until I was back on Earth."

With a certain inevitability they had become lovers again a week after their reunion in Lisbon. It was tentative at first, both of them recognising that their new-found friendship could just as easily be broken as reinforced. Equally, neither had much to lose. If they became lovers and then decided it was not working, no great hurt would have been done to either party. They could still part on good terms, better for the experience. In the meantime, as in all things, Kanu opted to trust the compass of his instincts and hope for the best.

Both had changed in the century since their marriage ended. Kanu was much older than Nissa—very old indeed even by the modern measure. He had benefited from his merfolk genetic transformation, which protected him against the worst effects of the Mechanism's fall. Nissa was less advantaged, but as she approached the turn of her third century, it was clear she had made the wisest use of her wealth and contacts, seeking out the best prolongation therapies available in this harsher, simpler world. They both carried their allotment of scars, inside and out.

"I have work to do," she said as they were lying next to each other in one of the guest bedrooms. "Too much work and not enough time. I'm not ready to give in just yet."

"I was thinking back to what Mr. Al Asnam said. He had a point, didn't he? What's the sense in all this glory if Sunday's not around to be a part of it?" Kanu kept his voice low, not wanting to disturb the other sleepers in the household. It was late and the night silent. He felt himself at the epicentre of an almost perfect stillness, as if Tangiers was the unmoving pivot around which the rest of the universe revolved.

Perhaps it was the wine.

"Half of all the great art and literature in existence went unrecognised during the lifetimes of its creators," Nissa answered in the same low murmur. "I know, it's a terribly unfair state of affairs, but that's just life. At least your grandmother wasn't unhappy, or starving, or persecuted. That's more than some of them managed."

"I'm not ungrateful. We'd both be poorer without her work."

Nissa rolled over into his belly, straddling him. She began to draw lazy spiralling designs on his chest, circles within circles, wheels within wheels. "Reputation's everything to you Akinyas, isn't it? You've always got to push at the boundaries, looking to the horizon."

"Not all of us."

She stroked his neck. "What happened to the gills?"

"I didn't need them on Mars and they're a bother in a spacesuit." Kanu began to stroke the side of her face, testing the line of her jaw against his memory. "Perhaps I should grow them back. I think my space-travelling days are over."

"That's a shame. I thought you might like to see my ship."

"You really have a ship?"

"A terrible waste of money, most of the time—just sits up in orbit, depreciating."

"Then sell it."

"I would, except it's not exactly a seller's market right now. Hello, would you like to buy a spaceship? Nearly new, one careful owner? The only drawback is you'll need to spend a month filing flight applications even if you only want to go to Venus and back. Oh, and there are huge alien things floating out there which might be about to kill us. Most people can't be bothered." She was working her way down his abdomen, slowly and with care, as if mapping an alien territory. "Besides, I'm going to need it again. All I'm waiting on is the permission."

She had been vague about her plans for the future. Kanu began to understand why.

"You mean to go somewhere?"

"Not far—just an exploratory expedition, following up a line of enquiry."

"To do with Sunday?"

"From the right angle, everything is to do with Sunday. I'm serious, though—I thought you might like to see the ship."

"I'll think about it."

"Well, don't overdo the enthusiasm."

"No, really—it would be nice. Where exactly are you going, anyway?"

"You don't get to learn all my secrets at once, Kanu Akinya."

He smiled at her coyness. "Nor would I wish to."

They fell into wordless, near-silent lovemaking, after which they lay back in their bed and tried to sleep.

But Kanu found it impossible. After a few restless hours he rose, dressed, left the room as quietly as possible and began to stroll the moonlit corridors, stairs and courtyard of the house. When the shutters were thrown wide, the windows turned out to be wooden carvings cut with tremendous skill into mesmerising Islamic patterns. By day, they cast interlocking designs across the courtyard's tiles, developing across the hours like a slowly revealing mathematical argument. At night the same theorem repeated itself in the paler hues of moonlight.

But the absence of glass left Kanu oddly unsettled, as if it had been omitted purely to throw him off-kilter. On Mars, a thumb's width of glass had stood between him and death. He had come to depend on the sanctity of glass, to sleep well in its care.

He tried not to disturb Nissa when he returned to their bed.

"You can't sleep?"

"Still on Mars time," Kanu said.

"You've been back on Earth for weeks."

"It takes a while. Perhaps it's the Moon. It's very high and full tonight and I've never slept well when it's bright. I'm a marine organism—we live by the tides."

"You mean you're a creature of water."

"Something like that."

"Then you should come with me when I take the ship. I'm going somewhere wet."

He smiled. "There aren't many wet places in the solar system."

"Do you like surprises or not?"

"Sometimes." But after a silence, he added, "Surely not Europa? Don't tell me you're going there?"

"You're no fun. You guess too easily."

"It was just a guess."

A cat shrieked across the night. Kanu knew that his chances of sleeping were now hopelessly lost. It would be best to resign himself to that. Before very long, from the telephone masts and solar towers of old Tangiers, the faithful would be called to prayer.

The Al Asnams had been marvellous hosts, but Kanu and Nissa had a world to see and limited time in which to do so. From Tangiers they took the coastal express to Dakar; from Dakar they crossed the Gulf of Guinea to Accra, riding a sleek old clipper ship that had once navigated autonomously but whose sails were now trimmed by a boisterous crew of sea-hardened merfolk. In the evening, as the ship cut through wine-dark waters, Nissa and Kanu sat on deck. They listened to happy shanties about foolhardy mariners and troublesome sirens and fell asleep under equatorial stars. Kanu slept better on the ship than he had in the household, even when they ran into heavy seas off Freetown.

In Accra there was a museum to visit, a modest public affair but nonetheless bright and well maintained. They had six Sunday pieces on permanent display—three paintings, two Maasai-inspired sculptures and a ceramic jug she had bought in a Lunar flea market and glazed with her own designs. Nissa patiently explained the various provenances of these pieces and their relatively minor significance within Sunday's wider output.

"Really," she said, when they were out of earshot of the museum's hosts, "it's just an excuse to visit Accra. It's lovely at this time of year."

It was, but since Tangiers a disquiet had settled over Kanu's mood. It was with him at all hours of the day. If it began to slip away, the mere observation of its departure was enough to bring it scuttling back.

They had been married, but that was an earlier part of his life and for years Nissa had barely troubled his thoughts. He would never have wished harm upon her, but equally he had taken no interest in her day-to-day affairs. If she wished to place herself in peril for the sake of intellectual curiosity or academic reward, that was her right; he would have resented Nissa telling him he was taking an absurd risk by living on the surface of Mars. Now they were lovers and companions again, and it was natural that he should take a greater interest in her well-being. But he did not think this breezy affair would last for the rest of their lives. It would come to its natural conclusion, as their marriage had, and they would go their separate ways again. And in time there would be a day during which he did not think of Nissa, and eventually a week, and sooner or later what she did with herself would cease to concern him.

And yet here they were, wandering Accra's public gardens, and the thought of her travelling to Europa alone drove a knife into him.

Kanu was staring at the jangle of light through a fountain when his anxiety shifted into focus.

It was not precisely Europa that worried him, he realised. Nor was it the notion of Nissa going there in her little ship.

It was a fear of not being there as well.

They caught up with *Fall of Night* over the Horn of Africa. It was parked in the orbit where Nissa had left it, quietly minding its own business. Like all spacecraft, it had a level of autonomy that would have been unusual or forbidden on the Earth's surface.

"I warned you it was small," Nissa said as their transfer shuttle completed its final approach.

"I wasn't expecting a holoship." Kanu was floating at a porthole, restraining himself by his fingertips. "Actually, it's bigger than you led me to expect. Quite an old ship, isn't it?"

"Old is good, they say. It's served me well enough over the years. I've splashed out on a few modifications since the last time I used it."

Fall of Night was a charcoal-coloured arrowhead, sharp at one end and swelling out to a fistful of engines at the other. They docked and boarded, transferring their luggage at the same time. Nissa completed some basic checks and then signalled that the shuttle could be on its way. Kanu quickly orientated himself, exploring the living quarters, the two separate cabins, the command deck. For an old ship, *Fall of Night* was bright and modern inside. There were a couple of skipover caskets, but they would not be needing those on the hundred-hour cruise out to Jupiter space.

"I can tell this is your ship," he said.

"I should hope so. There'll be hell to pay if we've docked with someone else's."

"The smells and colours remind me of our old house. I'd forgotten them until now. You chose everything in here, just as you did back then."

"You never had much of an opinion, Kanu. It was up to me to make the decisions."

There were more system check-outs to complete. Kanu could operate a ship but it was clear that Nissa had a great deal more experience than he did, especially with *Fall of Night*'s particular idiosyncrasies. He watched over her shoulder, weightless, as she sat buckled into the pilot's position and reviewed status updates. Screens had petalled around her, bright with diagrams and scrolling tables of numbers as the ship roused itself to full life. Pumps whirred, fuel lines ticked, engines ran through start-up cycles.

"Why don't you go and do something useful?" Nissa asked, twisting away from the screens to look at him. "Make us some chai. You'll be on tea duty until we reach Europa."

Kanu obliged.

Nissa cut in the engines for departure. They broke orbit at half a gee, then ramped up to one and a half until they were clear of UON jurisdiction.

"Can you tolerate two gees?" Nissa asked.

"If I start make choking noises, you'll know the answer."

The engine reached maximum sustainable output. They would be on two gees all the way to Jupiter, flipping for a thrust reversal a little more than halfway to their destination. Nissa had programmed in an aerobrake passage to shave off the rest of their speed. "That'll be bumpy," she cautioned, "but no worse than those seas off Freetown."

At night he had the dream again. They were on the converted cyber-clipper, weathering the swell off Freetown. By the dream's disfigured logic the stars were blazingly bright and clear overhead, even as the sea moved to the thrust and parry of storm winds. The merfolk were singing sea shanties. Nissa and Kanu lounged in deckchairs, a small table set between them. Although the ship rolled and pitched, they were still soldiering on with a game of chess.

The game had reached a decisive moment. Kanu was about to move his knight. He reached to pick up the piece, victory in his sights. But the ship tilted and the knight began to slide across the board, square to square, even though the other pieces were curiously unaffected. Kanu tried to stop it, but his hand moved sluggishly. The knight sped to the board's edge and toppled off. Still Kanu attempted to catch it. But the knight fell to the deck and continued its slide, out to the drainage slot cut into the ship's gunwales. Kanu rose from the table and went to the side of the ship. He saw the knight drop into the waves. In an instant he was overboard, in the water, chasing the chess piece. It was sinking again, down into still, stormless black. Kanu could not swim fast enough to catch it. The water was thickening, resisting his passage, turning to iron.

He watched the knight's descent into darkness. And woke with a single phrase on his lips.

Fall of knight.

CHAPTER 11

Goma was worried, but at least she no longer had to keep her emotions to herself. News of the Watchkeeper was now public, and Goma's apprehension was now something shared by the entire crew. The Watchkeeper had drawn a horizon across their fears, making it pointless to think beyond the next couple of days. Every other consideration—the performance of the drive, their chances of surviving skipover, the mystery around Gliese 163—was now secondary.

Captain Vasin called a special assembly. It was early morning by the ship's clock and not everyone was fully awake. The night-shift technicians, on the other hand, were red-eyed with weariness and keen to return to their cabins. Goma could not help noticing that Vasin looked more tired than she had been at the start of the voyage, a dark puffiness under her eyes, a weariness in the set of her mouth.

"An hour ago, I was approached by Maslin Karayan." She nodded at the Second Chancer, seated close to her podium. "Maslin wished to share his concerns about the Watchkeeper. That was his right, and I agreed to listen. Maslin—would you like to state your request now, so that there need be no ambiguity?"

Karayan rose and stood next to the captain. "In the light of the Watchkeeper's approach, I asked Captain Vasin—I mean

Gandhari—to disengage the drive and make preparations for our return to Crucible." Despite his powerful build, he was not quite as tall as Vasin and had to cock his head when addressing her. This gave him a questioning, pugnacious look. "I believed it would be a prudent action, given our circumstances."

"Exactly what were your fears, Maslin?"

"I wouldn't characterise them as fears, Gandhari. Reasonable concerns, perhaps. This expedition has been years in the making and the construction of this ship has taken decades. There is no haste to make it to the other system." He was looking around at his audience, nodding in agreement with himself, encouraging everyone else to nod along with him. "A year here, a year there, it will make no difference. Until we have a better understanding of the Watchkeeper's intentions, we should take no unnecessary chances. We have barely left our home! There would be no shame in returning now."

"No shame, and also no point," Vasin said. "If we return to Crucible, the Watchkeeper may leave us alone. But we'll have gained nothing, and sooner or later we'll have to try again. And then what? We'll be back out here, having exactly this conversation."

"Always knew there was a chance this would happen—" said Loring.

Vasin raised a gently silencing hand. "I think it fair that I explain my decision to Maslin—and the rest of you. We will not be slowing, or turning around. Not while I remain in command. I have sent another transmission back to Crucible and stated my position. If our government dislikes my choice, I will turn the ship around. I will even resign, if it comes to that. But until then, we hold our course and hold our nerve."

"We should debate this," Karayan said. "Put it to the vote."

"I am not silencing debate, but this is a starship, not a democracy. We have barely begun to be tested, and already this is too much?" Vasin shook her head in dismay and frustration, and an edge entered her voice. "No. We hold the line. Let the Watchkeeper do with us as it will, but we will not be cowed or intimidated. We have as much right to move through space as they do—and while my hand is on the wheel, we will exercise that right."

Mposi coughed gently and rose from his seat. "Thank you,

Gandhari. And thank you, Maslin, for raising your concerns in the manner you did. We respect your right to do so and sympathise with your position. This is a difficult moment for all of us, regardless of ideology or belief. And I do not mind admitting that I am fearful of the Watchkeeper." He turned his hands palm up, emphasising the sincerity of this confession. "We would all be mad if we were not fearful. But Gandhari is right: to turn back will gain us nothing. Not a shred of new data. But if we succeed in leaving the system, we will acquire useful knowledge. And if we fail, if we are destroyed, that will also be useful knowledge to our friends back on Crucible. They have another starship. It will help them decide how best to use it."

"This was never meant to be a suicide mission," said Peter Grave, the young Second Chancer Goma had already spoken to.

"No, but it was never without risk," Mposi countered. "We've all accepted that. When Nasim switched on the Chibesa drive, there was a chance of it blowing up in our faces. What were the odds, Nasim?"

"One in a thousand," said Caspari. "Maybe a little worse."

"Those are not great odds! I wouldn't bet my life on the roll of a thousand-sided dice! But we all did exactly that when we boarded this ship. And skipover—some of us won't make it out on the other side, after one hundred and forty years. That's a statistical certainty! Isn't that the case, Saturnin?"

Dr. Nhamedjo smiled at Mposi's question, but he looked uncomfortable about being drawn into the argument. "There are risks," he said. "On the other hand, my team will be doing their utmost to minimise them—and I do not believe you could find yourselves in safer hands."

"Fine," Mposi went on. "But what if we were to run into a piece of debris at half the speed of light? Our shielding will absorb the most likely range of collisions, but it won't protect us against a freak event. The Watchkeeper is the same—just another calculated risk."

"Sooner or later, though," Grave said, "there will be a risk that we should turn back from."

"I don't disagree," answered Vasin. She waited a breath, gathering the silence she wanted. "I have a mission to execute, but I also have a ship and a crew to protect. Always those considerations must be balanced. That is what I do. That is what a captain is for, and why none of you really wants my job."

True to her word, Gandhari allowed everyone a chance to have their say. Goma sat back and held her silence, unsurprised by anything she heard. The Second Chancers were all of the opinion that turning around was the thing to do, but then again none of them thought the expedition was a good idea to begin with. Of course there were nuances within that uniformity of opinion, but nothing that altered her basic view of them. On the other hand, all the other technicians and passengers were in broad agreement with Vasin. Again there were nuances. Nasim Caspari was willing to attempt a course change, if it were deemed wise. Mposi was adamant that they should not deviate a hair's width from their intended trajectory. Dr. Nhamedjo appeared anxious to project an image of scrupulous neutrality and merely reiterated his earlier statement that the medical provisions were as good as they could possibly be.

Ru looked bored—she just wanted the whole thing done with.

The hours stretched, with sleep offering little respite. Everywhere Goma went, the Watchkeeper was the only subject of conversation. The common areas, the lounges and galleys, were busier than they had been since departure, full of people trading rumour and opinion. Meanwhile, intelligence and analysis arrived from Crucible, but it brought little solace. The government had backed Captain Vasin, and that vote of confidence ought to have silenced Maslin Karayan. But the Second Chancers were still not placated. Goma saw them gathered in twos and threes muttering and whispering. She hated them for being so brazen about it, when they could easily have kept their plotting behind closed doors.

Against all that, it was good to hear from Ndege.

"I can't be with you, daughter, and I wish it were otherwise. But you will be all right. I am sure of this."

How could she be sure of anything? Goma wondered.

"When we were first on Crucible, the Watchkeeper took my mother into itself. When it was over, she said she felt as if she had been probed, dissected and deduced. That was the point when they would have destroyed us if they hadn't liked what they found in Chiku Green. They knew us then, and they know us now. I have no idea whether they have our best interests in mind, or if they really care. But I do not think they fear us, not yet. I think we may be useful to them, on some level we don't yet understand—or may never understand. But while that usefulness lasts, they won't harm us."

Snakes are useful to people, Goma thought. *We milk them for venom. But usefulness has its limits.*

She thanked her mother for her kind words, told her not to worry, that the mood on the ship was actually quite positive, that most people were more excited than frightened, that it was in fact something of an honour and a privilege to be offered this close-up view of one of the aliens . . .

Ndege would know she was lying, of course. But it was the thought that counted.

Machine eyes, spread throughout the system, tracked and imaged the Watchkeeper. Nothing on *Travertine* could compare with the capability of the system-wide sensor network, with its huge baselines, but even their own instruments were able to acquire a steadily sharpening picture of the approaching machine. They showed it on the walls in the commons, accompanied by a dismayingly tiny barbell-shaped silhouette which was the true size of their own ship in relation to the alien robot. Goma stared at it with listless fascination. Fear was almost beside the point now. Whatever the Watchkeeper meant to do with them was surely already ordained.

She spent time in the gym, finding that exertion was good for blanking out bad thoughts. Usually she had the place to herself, even Ru preferring a different schedule.

One hour she arrived at the door to find Peter Grave sitting on an exercise cycle. He was finishing a programme, mopping at his brow with a towel.

"Goma," he said, smiling. "At last, fate brings our orbits back together."

"I wouldn't call it fate, Peter. I'd say there aren't enough gyms on this ship."

"Cutting."

"I'm not one for sugaring my pills. I'll give you the time of day, but that's as far as it goes."

Grave's smile was pained. "If this is you giving me the time of day, I'd hate to see your idea of a cold shoulder. Are you irritated because Maslin said what we're all feeling, and I had the temerity to agree with him?"

"I expected nothing else from you."

"Whatever you think, we're going to have to start getting along. I've been talking to Aiyana Loring, you know. While I'm aboard, I'd like to at least sit in on some of the scientific meetings. Aiyana says that request is reasonable."

A kind of dread opened up in Goma. She had come to think of the scientific gatherings as the one area of shipboard life where she would not have to put on a diplomatic face in the presence of Second Chancers.

"What interest do you have in science?"

"The same interest any of us has! When we reach Gliese 163, I want to feel capable of sharing in the same spirit of discovery as the rest of you. Why is that so hard for you to grasp?"

"You're with Maslin."

"Yes."

"Then what else do I need to know? That makes you a believer, doesn't it?"

Grave climbed off the exercise cycle and threw his towel into a disposal slot. He filled a glass of water from the wall spigot and sipped quietly before answering. "Belief is a complex thing, Goma. We both agree that the universe is comprehensible. Where we differ is in the point of that comprehensibility. Forgive me if I sound like I'm putting words into your mouth, but you'd agree, wouldn't you, that in your view there is no ultimate purpose to that comprehensibility—that it's just a happy accident, a chance alignment between the laws of physics and the limits of our own sensory capabilities? Our minds come up with mathematics, and the mathematics turns out to be the right tool—the only tool, in fact—for making sense of anything? That we happen to be smart enough to figure all this out, but there's no reward at the end of it for all that smartness? No higher truth, waiting to be illuminated? No deeper reason, no deeper purpose, no greater wisdom, no hint of a better way of being human?"

Against her wiser judgement, she allowed herself to be drawn in. "And your take is?"

"I cannot accept a purposeless universe. Science is a wonderful edifice of knowledge, beautiful in its self-consistency. But it cannot simply be the means to its own end. Nor is it an accident that mathematics is supremely efficient at describing the play of matter, energy and force in our universe. They fit together like hand in glove—and that cannot be coincidence. Our minds have been given science for a reason, Goma—to guide us as we progress towards an understanding of the true purpose of our own existence."

"There is no purpose, Peter."

He studied her with a certain shrewd detachment. "You say that, but do you really mean it?"

"I'll decide what I mean, thanks."

"You accept the uncanny connection between mathematics and phenomenology without question—and yet you can't begin to admit that there might be a purpose to that interdependence?"

"I don't need a spiritual crutch to deal with reality."

"Nor do I. But you say that you accept a purposeless universe. Deep down, though, are you sure you understand the implications of that statement?"

"I think I do."

"Then why would you even bother with science, if there is no purpose to anything?"

"To understand it."

"But there would be no point to that understanding. It would be an empty, futile act—like miming in a cave."

"Maybe the point is to understand. For matter to start making sense of itself."

He brightened. "A teleological position, then. Implicit purpose in the act of the universe turning an eye on itself?"

"I didn't say that."

"Perhaps," Grave conceded. "But something drives you to this task. The satisfaction of adding a small piece to the larger puzzle, maybe. Placing another stone in the fabric of the cathedral even though you'll never live to see the thing finished. But would that matter if your name was enshrined, passed down through the ages?"

"I don't care about posterity."

"Then you'd be content for your work to be published

anonymously? Perhaps it already is?" He looked suddenly thoughtful. "No, it can't be, or else I wouldn't have heard of it, wouldn't have been able to read it."

"You think you know my work?"

"Well enough to be impressed by your intellectual integrity."

If that was meant as a compliment, it had a backhanded quality that left her bristling. "I have no idea what you're talking about."

"Your honesty in facing up to the worst. You of all people must have wanted nothing more than to find evidence that the elephants' cognitive decline wasn't permanent, that it could be arrested or even reversed. Who would blame you for that? Yet you've done the good and noble thing—you've presented the data and allowed it to speak for itself. None of your strategies has made any difference to the elephants—and yet you haven't tried to gloss over that, or to present the data in a way that suggests a more favourable outlook. That's admirable."

"Fuck off."

This outburst drew a blink from Grave, but he looked more puzzled than offended. "I'm sorry—did we get off on the wrong foot again? I was praising your work, not criticising it."

"You know exactly what you were doing."

Grave's smile was all innocence. "Do I?"

"Rubbing my nose in the truth, at least as you see it. You're so happy about that, aren't you? Look at you. You can barely contain your joy that the Tantors won't be coming back. They were an affront to your view of things because they dared to displace humanity from the centre of the universe. Well, fuck that as well. They were something marvellous and beautiful, a new possibility—but you can't handle that."

"I see we're going to get on tremendously." At last the smile faded, replaced by an expression of quiet sadness and resignation. "I know you disagree with Maslin's position and I don't blame you for that. But most of us are just trying to see both sides." He combed his fingers through his hair, pushing it back from his glistening forehead. "How well do you know everyone else?"

"What sort of question is that?"

"Not an unreasonable one." His eyes were pink with sweat.

"It's only human nature to divide everyone into groups and cohorts, but it's not always like that. The Second Chance delegation was thrown together at the last minute, with a lot of disagreement and compromise. You see twelve of us and think we're all exactly alike, but I feel I know you almost as well as I do some of my colleagues.

"On the other hand, we sometimes feel beleaguered and believe the rest of you are thinking in lockstep. I'd wager that isn't true, either. We're just people, all of us. Thank goodness for your uncle, I say. Mposi is a very good man—we all like him."

"I'm thrilled for you."

"So much for that, then. I'm trying to offer an olive branch—I thought you'd respond well to a little intellectual discourse. Shall I let you in on a secret? There's no chance of Vasin changing her mind and Maslin knows it. He's stated his case, and now he'll go along with whatever she decides."

"All right," Goma said, slowly, as if she had to consider each word. "You and I are never going to be friends. Your people screwed up my mother's life and you've gone to a lot of trouble to screw up mine. Collectively, I mean, with your stupid, repressive, backward-looking, antiscientific ideology. But I do have to share this ship with you."

"If we both took the time, Goma, I'm sure we'd find a lot more in common than divides us. But I'll say one thing for that Watchkeeper. It unifies us in one very important sense."

"Which is?"

"We're all equally terrified."

They could see it with their own eyes now. It was forty-five hours since Goma learned the news; five more hours until the projections said the Watchkeepers would be on them.

They crowded the windows, lights turned low. It was approaching on a nearly parallel course although not moving in the manner they might have expected—with its blunt or sharp end aligned with the direction of travel—but rather sideways, showing the utmost alien disdain for sensible human notions of physics and propulsion. And indeed, as the distance narrowed to tens of thousands of kilometres—the mere span of a world—so the Watchkeeper compassed around with a terrible grindstone slowness. Blue light spilled from the gaps in its pine-cone coating and from the "signalling" aperture at its thick end. The light abated just as the beam was about to sweep over *Travertine* and then resumed on the other side of the ship.

By then no one was sleeping and all but the most essential housekeeping duties were being postponed. It was hard to eat, hard to talk about anything other than the unignorable presence outside.

Goma was on her way to Mposi's cabin when she heard raised voices coming from behind the door. They were the voices of two older men and she recognised both. Not quite a blazing argument, but as close to one as she had yet heard aboard *Travertine*. She considered turning around, but a fierce compulsion made her continue, knocking hard on the door until Mposi answered.

"Ah. Goma. Maslin and I were just . . ." But her uncle trailed off, surely knowing she would not be assuaged by any explanation he could offer.

"What were you discussing?" Goma asked, still standing on the threshold.

"It's not too late," Karayan said, dressed in his usual formal attire. "We have a few more hours. A gesture from us, a small change of course, that would be sufficient."

"As far as I can tell," Goma said, "Captain Vasin has made up her mind."

"Of which you doubtless approve."

"I approve of doing what we came here to do, which is carry on into space. Were you hoping to bend Mposi to your view, Maslin?"

"That would be for your uncle to decide."

"I think my uncle knows what's best. Why do you even talk to these people, Mposi? They've got their concession—they're on the ship. There's no need to give them any more ground."

"I am sorry for troubling you," Karayan said, directing his statement at Mposi. "Sorry also that your niece would prefer disharmony and factionalism to cooperation and mutual advancement. But she is young. It would be wrong to expect too much from someone with so little experience of life." Something moved under his beard: a smile, perhaps. "You'll convey my sentiments to Gandhari, Mposi?"

"Of course."

"That's very good of you."

When the Second Chancer had gone, Mposi held an uncomfortable silence before speaking. "He was within his rights to speak to me, Goma. You didn't have to take such an automatically hostile tone. He has strong feelings. Why shouldn't he?"

"You were arguing."

"We were being frank with one another. At our age, I think we've earned it." A sudden weariness appeared to overcome him. "Oh dear. The last thing I want is to exchange harsh words with you, of all people." He gestured for her to enter his cabin. "Shall I make us some chai? I fear it may have come to that."

"I was angry, and I'm sorry. I just . . . don't like them."

Mposi closed the door on the rest of the ship. "None of them?"

"I make no exceptions. They've chosen their ideology; I'm free to choose mine in response."

"They can't be our enemies for the entire trip, Goma. Sooner or later we'll have to do the unthinkable and start liking each other. They're as nervous of us as we are of them! And Maslin doesn't have the automatic authority you imagine. His selection was controversial, even within Second Chance circles. He barely knows some of his own people, several of whom were actively critical of his appointment. All that rhetoric of his? He has to do that to bolster his strength within the delegation. But in person he's perfectly reasonable and open to persuasion."

Goma sat down on the chair Mposi kept for visitors. "It didn't sound that way."

"I would not have admitted him into my cabin if I did not trust the man, Goma. Anyway, there's a lot we needed to talk about. Might I ask you something?" Despite her lack of encouragement, Mposi was fussing in his kitchen, boiling water for chai.

"It depends."

"It's about Peter Grave. You know him?"

"Yes, we've spoken once or twice." She was looking around the room, comparing Mposi's efforts at personalisation with her own. The room was slightly smaller, but Mposi had it all to himself. She spotted the two elephants, the other pair Ndege had insisted travel on the ship. Goma had the matriarch and a calf; Mposi the bull and another juvenile.

"What do you make of him?"

"He's a Second Chancer. What more do you need to know?"

"They're not all cut from the same cloth, Goma. There are pragmatists and hotheads and zealots, just as in any other calling. How well do you know Maslin?"

"How well am I meant to know him?"

"He was ill, once, and I did him a small favour. He's never forgotten that. Deep down, beneath all the bluster, he is a decent man. And his doubts and fears are ours. The odd thing is: Maslin was asking *me* what *I* know of Peter Grave. Now why would Maslin quiz me about one of his own people?"

"As you said, they don't all know each other particularly well."

The chai was ready. He set a cup before Goma and took his own seat.

"I have a slightly unusual position on this ship. The captain isn't a politician, and because she's an outsider she doesn't have strong ties to the Crucible political structure. Whereas I do, which makes me the natural point of contact, I suppose you would call it, for those friends and colleagues concerned with our mutual welfare." Mposi spooned honey into their cups, drawing from his precious personal ration. "When intelligence comes to light . . . intelligence relating to us, to our expedition, I am the trusted party. And there *has* been intelligence, Goma. This Watchkeeper isn't my immediate concern. Or, to put it another way, I am obliged to look beyond it. There is a deeper threat to our success."

"What kind of threat?"

"Call it a sabotage plan, although it's likely a lot more complicated than that."

Goma was momentarily lost for words. She had spent enough time around her uncle to know when he was making idle play with her and when he was serious. There was nothing frivolous in his manner now.

"You're serious?" she asked. "Actual sabotage—a physical threat to the ship?"

"My sources on Crucible believe we are carrying something we should not be. A weapon, perhaps—smuggled aboard with the rest of the cargo. Thousands of tonnes of equipment and supplies, much of it for inscrutable purposes—it wouldn't have been that difficult to slip something through. And by implication, there must be someone—maybe several someones—with the wherewithal to use that weapon. Or maybe the weapon is *us*, and we just don't know it. This crisis places us under a lot of stress. But that's the perfect time to observe our individual reactions. I may have said too much. Have I said too much?"

"I've no idea." Goma was still unsettled. "Why would anyone put a weapon aboard? What's the point?"

"The expedition has never sat well with everyone."

"You mean Maslin and his nutcases?"

"Perhaps." But Mposi's answer was not the automatic affirmation she might have hoped for.

"What do you know?"

"Enough to keep me awake at night. As you can imagine, I need to tread very, very carefully. The wrong word, a note of misdirected suspicion—it could sour everything."

"Have you spoken to Gandhari about this?"

"Not yet. To the best of my knowledge, she isn't aware of the issue, and our captain has enough to worry about for now. When I have definite answers, I'll go to her."

"So who *does* know?"

"You, for a start. You're my extra pair of eyes and ears, Goma, but I don't want you to do anything out of the ordinary or change your routine in any way. Just carry on as normal."

"With that thing out there?"

"You know what I mean. But be alert, watch other people— and not just the obvious candidates. If you see or hear anything that you think might be of interest to me . . . well, my chai may not be the best, but my door is always open."

"And Ru?" Goma asked. "Can I tell her?"

"It might be expecting too much of an Akinya, asking one to keep a secret," Mposi said. "Certainly your mother found it beyond her. But you would be doing me a great favour if we could keep this between ourselves, just for now."

* * *

At last the alien machine had turned to face the same direction of travel as the ship, matching their course and acceleration precisely. Goma wanted to do something, and she knew she was not alone in that compulsion. The instinct was to talk, to negotiate, to offer explanation. To beg for clemency, or pray for salvation. But what was the point of even attempting communication after all the years of failure and silence? Negotiating with the Watchkeepers was like negotiating with geology, or some vast, indifferent weather system.

She had been at a window, watching for long, silent minutes, thinking herself alone, when Peter Grave announced his presence at her side.

"Does it frighten you?"

As irritated as she was at being jolted from her contemplation, she had vowed to be civil with the Second Chancer.

"It would be strange if it didn't. They're an alien machine civilisation, they've probably been in space longer than we've had tools and language. They could dismantle our entire culture in an afternoon if we did something they didn't like. We barely know what they want, or what they really think of us. And they're back, hanging around as if this is judgement hour. Which part shouldn't I be frightened by?"

"I agree, totally. And maybe, as you say, this is the hour, the moment. No one has operated a ship like this in this system for decades, and certainly not a ship as fast as *Travertine*. Perhaps this is the point where we cross a line with them? Some algorithm trips inside them, a decision path, and that's it? Extinction for the monkeys?"

"Would you like that to happen?"

"Do you think I would?"

"At least you could say you were right all along."

"I don't think that would be much of a consolation. How about you? With your family connection, your grandmother and the Watchkeepers—do you feel you've earned some kind of special treatment from them? Your mother must have, when she went poking into Mandala's secrets."

"First," Goma said, trying to keep her voice as level as possible, "she wasn't 'poking.' She was conducting a structured scientific investigation based on a profound theoretical breakthrough in the understanding of the Mandala grammar. Second, I didn't ask for a deep, meaningful conversation about my ancestors."

"Ah, and there was me thinking we'd turned a page."

"Don't hold your breath."

"Regardless of what you think of me, I honestly admire what your grandmother did for us. All of us do—every human being on Crucible. Chiku's martyrdom—"

"Don't put martyrdom on her—she deserves better than that."

"You speak as if she might still be alive."

"No one's proved that she isn't."

"Someone sent this message to us. No one would blame you for presuming a family connection. But it *has* been a very long time, Goma."

"Meaning what?"

"I know many of us were alive at the time of the first landing, but your grandmother was already old by then." For a few seconds, Grave studied the alien machine, some of its holy blue radiance anointing his face. If it had not been so dark in the room she would never have tolerated him being so close to her. "I hope you find answers, anyway. I meant everything I said to you, when we first met. I do have great respect for your work."

"So you say."

"Believe me, Goma—nothing's as black and white as you think. Our feelings towards the elephants are much more complex than you imagine. We regret what they were, we regret the mistake of them, but we also mourn for what became of them."

"Hate the sin but not the sinner?"

"If you wish to put it in those terms. It was a terrible day, in any case—a stain on our collective history. Yet Mandala's retribution could have been much more severe."

"You think this was about retribution? That Mandala was somehow acting *against* the Tantors?"

"The facts are all we have," Grave replied. "Mandala was provoked, Mandala acted, and the uplifted elephants ceased to exist. I make no inferences. It is up to each and every one of us to draw such conclusions as we see fit."

"I've changed my mind," Goma said, after a silence. "I was starting to think I might be able to stand being in the same room as you, let alone the same ship. I was wrong."

"And I am very sorry that we cannot find common ground."

"There isn't any. There never will be."

She was speaking when the blue radiance increased its intensity by many factors. There was barely time to react, barely time for anyone in the room to do more than draw breath. Goma had an impression, no more than that, of the gaps in the Watchkeeper's layered, armour-like plating opening up, the way a pine cone changed with the weather, permitting more of its internal blue glow to gush out into space. And then it was gone—not just the blue glow, but the entire alien machine.

It had simply disappeared.

CHAPTER 12

Kanu was unsettled. While Nissa slept, her ship operating itself, he made his way from window to window, pausing at each to survey his reflection—the cabin lights were dim but not totally off—and attempt to convince himself that he had not begun to slip into madness. What he saw in the reflection was the face of a profoundly troubled man with a desperate, searching stare in his eyes—as if the face in the glass expected answers of him, the man least capable of giving them.

He thought about what happened to him on Mars and everything he had been through since—the deaths of his colleagues, his own recuperation, the end of his political career. It would have been odd if he did not look troubled, like a man cast adrift from every certainty. But there was more to it than that, and as much as he tried to rationalise, he could not find a way to explain what he had dreamed. He had not known the name of her ship until she told him. So how was it possible that it had been prefigured during his dreams on Mars, when he never had the slightest intention of recontacting Nissa Mbaye?

Coincidence, he tried telling himself. His dreams had contained a set of random symbols, the senseless output of his subconscious mind, and by chance they gained an uncanny significance now that he knew the name of her ship. Had the name been different, he would never have returned to the content of those dreams—of him and Swift playing chess in heaving seas.

But that explanation was not sufficient. He felt that the symbolic connection was significant—a true portent of what was to come. Since he did not believe in precognition, that left an even less-palatable possibility: he must have known about Nissa's ship somehow before he even left Mars.

And yet he had no recollection of thinking about her—and certainly no foreknowledge of her ship's name. Could he have been thinking of Nissa, and her ship, and somehow misplaced the memory?

He thought back to Lisbon, to that moment of surprise when he recognised first her voice, and then her face. That memory was much closer to the present than his confused and episodic recollections of Mars. He could still see the sunlight in the gallery, the faces of the students gathered around Nissa, the strokes of their sketches. He could bring to mind the exact texture of the pastries they had shared in the upstairs café, when they had got over the shock of meeting. The shock had been genuine—he had faked none of it.

But something did not tally.

There was still the odd coincidence of their meeting in the first place. Life threw up its share of chance encounters, that was true. But to suddenly take an interest in his grandmother's art and almost immediately stumble upon his ex-wife at the first exhibition he visited? He had been ready to put it down to caprice until now, but was it possible that their meeting had been intentional all along?

Kanu tore himself away from the reflection. None of this was helping. It was just sending his thoughts down ever-tightening spirals of paranoia and self-doubt. He had to trust himself. There had been no ulterior motive on his part.

He was sure of that.

His movements stirred Nissa. He was trying to be as quiet as he could, but it was her ship and her sleeping senses must have been acutely attuned to the presence of another human being.

"What is it?" she asked, laying a soft hand on his cheek. "You're sweating like you're running a fever. Shall I turn down the cabin temperature?"

"I don't think it's that."

"Something's bothering you. Bad dreams? No one's going to blame you for having flashbacks, Kanu—not after what happened."

"I'm all right."

They went up front. Nissa made warm chocolate for them both and insisted Kanu clear his head before returning to bed. She put on some music—an early recording by Toumani Diabaté, which she knew happened to be one of Kanu's favourites. With the cabin lights back up to full strength, the readouts and navigational displays a riot of bright colours and symbols, and the reassuring chime-like cadences of the music, he started to feel the phantasms releasing their hold. He was just rattled, that was all. If anyone had a right to be, he did.

"We should go back to Lisbon," Nissa said.

"Now?"

"I mean when we're done with all this."

"I thought you were fed up with the place, after the exhibition."

"I'll admit to being fed up with the routine of teaching those students, but it'd take more than that to put me off Lisbon."

"I like it there, too. It's almost a second home to Akinyas."

They made small talk, Nissa very deliberately steering the conversation away from anything directly connected to Mars or Kanu's recent experiences. They spoke of favoured cafés, restaurants, the property prices in various quarters, the wisdom or otherwise of renting, all the while speeding through the solar system aboard a clever little dart of a spaceship, inside a bubble of six-hundred-year-old music.

Kanu felt some sort of ease. He wondered if she had slipped a mild barbiturate into the chocolate. Perhaps.

But when his dreams came again, they were no better.

* * *

He was in a white room, flat on his back on an operating table. He knew this because he was looking at his own body from the outside, seeing his own mangled form spread out on the sterile surface of the ellipse-shaped table. Surrounding the table, almost encasing it, was an array of surgical devices. They were also white, clearly medical, but their individual functions were unclear to him. Some of them were hinged or bent over, holding curved parts to his ruined body or pushing other parts of themselves through his flesh, or into the open horrors of still-raw wounds. The machines moved with deliberation. There was urgency, but not haste. They sucked at the wounds and he heard the occasional crack or flash of some cauterising process. Around the room, on the walls, diagrams of human anatomy flickered past at almost dizzying speed. They were black and white, drawn in ink, annotated with handwritten Latin.

Beyond this encirclement were more machines, all different shapes and sizes. There were pipes and tubes, white on white. Still another rank of machines stood behind the second, androform but otherwise featureless. They resembled snowmen, except thinner in proportion. Kanu sensed that his point of view must originate with one of these standing figures. He was among them, looking back at his own body.

He had never enquired too deeply of Swift as to the exact severity of his injuries, and when the human medics finally got their chance to look him over, it was hard for them to be sure how badly he had been hurt. In places, the traces of the robots' surgery were easily discernible. In others, there was only the faintest hint that he had been worked on at all.

But Kanu could see himself now, and the human remains on that operating table made him want to scream. It had been worse, far worse, than even his gravest imaginings.

A voice said: "Threshold of consciousness."

Another: "Inhibit commissural traffic."

A third: "Inhibiting."

The second: "He must not wake until completion."

The second, he realised, was himself. And it was not language he was speaking, at least not in human terms, but rather a rapid exchange of symbols which served the same communicational function.

Threshold of consciousness. Not long now, and then he would be well again—or at least well enough to be spoken to in the human manner.

He glanced down at his white forearm. The blank material of his anatomy gained texture, form and colour. It became fabric and flesh—a hand and a sleeve, the garb of a man of learning of the late eighteenth century.

"There's something wrong with me," Kanu told Nissa when they were sharing breakfast, spooning grapefruit out of a bowl, the engines throttled back to a gee while they ate.

"A few bad dreams? I think you're allowed."

"It's more than just bad dreams. Ever since I returned from Mars, nothing's been quite right. I thought I was fine to begin with, but I was deluding myself. I feel on edge, not quite in tune with things. Have you ever had déjà vu?"

"Once, but I had the oddest feeling it had happened to me before. Sorry—I can see you're bothered by something."

"I don't know what it is. It's been worse since Tangiers. A sort of continuous feeling of . . . dread, dislocation, premonition."

"Premonition? Are you serious?"

"Perfectly. And then there are these dreams. I'm not one to attach significance to such things, Nissa, but when a dream of mine appeared to prefigure the name of this ship? That was bad enough, and I can't easily rationalise it away. But now I've started getting flashbacks to when I was injured."

"You were more than injured, Kanu. How can you have flashbacks to being dead?"

"I don't know. Except they're vivid, detailed, and I'm not watching from my body's point of view. I'm seeing myself being repaired—with machines standing around debating my state of consciousness. I've had nightmares but never like that. I've never seen myself from outside, a barely conscious thing on a slab."

"All right—I can understand why you're bothered. Who wouldn't be, by something like that? But it's still just dreams."

"I'm worried they're symptomatic. That sense of not being in my own body—maybe it's telling me there's something wrong in my brain's wiring? That some core sense of my own identity isn't quite working the way it should?"

"The odd thing would be if you didn't feel a little strange, given everything you went through. You lost friends and colleagues on Mars; you lost your vocation and the trust of people who matter to you. It's no wonder if something's snapped, Kanu— you wouldn't be human otherwise. When I met you in Lisbon—"

"I'm glad you mentioned Lisbon. We bumped into each other by coincidence. How is that not supposed to make me feel a little strange?"

"Coincidences happen all the time. You took a late interest in your grandmother's art and I'm one of her highest-profile scholars—our paths were on a collision course."

"When we were married, did I ever show much interest in Sunday's work?"

"People change. Especially after something bad happens to them."

Kanu was silent. He wanted to accept this version of events, the smooth plausibility of this offered narrative.

"I hope that's the answer."

"The more you dwell on it, the stranger you're going to feel. You think too much, merman."

"Fine words coming from you."

"I'm not the one twisting myself in knots with introspection and self-doubt. Look, an adventure will do you good. We're going to Europa! We have Consolidation authorisation to land on the ice and attempt contact with the Regals! How can that not stir the soul? Surrender to it, Kanu. Let some fun into your life."

He smiled meekly, though she had done nothing to assuage his doubts. "I'll try."

Nissa tidied the breakfast bowl away. "I was going to notch up the engines but we can leave them for a little while. You need something to take your mind off yourself."

The transmission came in on a routine civilian frequency and encryption protocol—nothing about it to suggest the slightest diplomatic connotation. It was aimed at *Fall of Night*, but beyond that contained no clue as to its origin or purpose.

Nissa accepted it, expecting it to be from a friend or colleague, perhaps concerning some aspect of her ongoing curatorial work. Instead, she was confronted by a man she did not know but who carried the automatic assumption of authority that only came from high office. He was as grey and grave as a statue, and looked worn away, somehow, as if he had been left out in the weather.

"I am Yevgeny Korsakov," the man explained, belabouring the syllables of his name, when Nissa established a two-way send. "I was a friend . . . a colleague . . . of Kanu Akinya. We were both on Mars—both of us hurt in the terrorist incident. I wanted to see how he was doing."

Nissa explained the request to Kanu while her response—that Kanu was indeed with her—was crawling its way back to the sender.

"Did I do the right thing? He said he knew you on Mars."

"He did," Kanu said, struck by an apprehension he could not quite pin down. "He was also largely responsible for the end of my career."

"I think your accident had a lot to do with that."

"Maybe, but Korsakov was the first to argue that I'd been tainted by my experiences. Of all of them, why did *he* have to survive?" But the uncharitable nature of this sentiment left a sour taste in his mouth. Dalal, Lucien . . . they deserved better from him. "I'm sorry—you were right to answer the call, and you can be sure Korsakov knew I was here whether you confirmed it or not."

"Do you hate him?" Nissa asked.

"He's not a bad man, it's just that we were on opposite sides of the fence. Never really saw eye to eye."

"He sounded concerned."

"That's what concerns me."

But when Korsakov spoke to Kanu directly, he appeared genuine enough. "I hope I did not violate your privacy by tracing you to Nissa Mbaye's ship," the man said. "It was easily done, all public information—Nissa had to name you as a passenger in her flight plan, of course."

"Of course," Kanu whispered in return, although the words would form no part of his actual reply.

"I am very glad to see you getting on with your life, Kanu. After Mars, we feared the worst. It was one thing to know you had survived, been repaired by the robots . . . but to regain your spirit, your sense of life? That was by no means guaranteed. I heard about your kindness to the Dalal family. In truth, I expected you to spend more time on Earth. I would have thought you'd had enough of space travel."

Kanu smiled tightly as he formulated his response. "Thank you, Yevgeny. It's good to see your face again, and to know you are well. I'm touched by your concern. As for the Dalals, it was the least I could do. I see from your time lag that you're on the Moon. I must come and visit sometime. It would be good to catch up."

He hoped that might be the end of it, but Korsakov was not quite done with him.

"Of course you would be welcome on the Moon—indeed, anywhere in UON sovereign space. Your flight plan tells me that you have business in Europa—quite unusual, if you do not mind my saying. Very difficult to arrange those permissions. Might I ask the nature of your business there?"

"Art," Kanu replied, as succinctly as he dared. Then he smiled again. "Well, Yevgeny—it's very kind of you to track me down. And I'll be sure to get in touch when I return."

"I have my eye on you now," Korsakov said, in tones that sounded friendly enough. "No escaping your old friend, Kanu."

When it was over, Nissa floated opposite him, cross-legged. "What was all that about?"

"I wish I knew."

"Why would he care what you're up to now? If he's the one who had you kicked out of the diplomatic service, hasn't he already got what he wanted?"

"I don't think Yevgeny is completely satisfied with my behaviour."

"What business is it of his?"

"I've no idea. It's very odd."

"Well, here's something else that's odd. Did you say he was transmitting from the Moon?"

Kanu nodded. "He never said as much, but the time lag fitted. Why—did you get a better fix?"

"*Fall of Night*'s cleverer than he assumed. That time lag was a spoof. He was bouncing the signal through a dozen mirrors, but I could still backtrack to its real point of origin. It's a ship, a Consolidation enforcement vehicle, and it's much closer than the Moon."

"That makes no sense at all. Yevgeny was the ambassador for the United Orbital Nations, not the Consolidation."

"In which case, apparently you're not the only one starting a new chapter."

Beyond the orbit of Mars they passed within visual range of a Watchkeeper. Kanu wondered if Nissa had bent their course to make it possible, seeking the thrill of a close encounter, something to take their minds off the puzzle of the Consolidation ship—even his own mind off his troubled dreams.

"The moratorium is stupid," she was saying. "Look at the size of that thing, the power it must contain. If the Watchkeepers didn't want us to be flying around in spaceships, does anyone think we'd still be able to?"

"They make people nervous," Kanu said as *Fall of Night*'s cameras relayed an increasingly sharp image of the alien machine. "Perhaps it's sensible not to do anything too provocative until we have a better idea of their intentions."

"Maybe they don't have any intentions—maybe they're just going to sit in our solar system like rocks until we bore ourselves to death waiting for them to do something."

The Watchkeeper was a thousand-kilometre-long pine cone, interlaced and overlapping black facets wrapped around a core of glowing blue mystery. There were eleven Watchkeepers in the solar system now; some of them in orbit around planets, others floating in free space. Occasionally they moved, changing orientation or position. They swung like weathercocks and slid from orbit to orbit in mute defiance of parochial human physics. Occasionally a beam of blue light would pass from one Watchkeeper to another, or stab out of the solar system entirely.

They had communicated not the slightest thing to any of the human powers. What they wanted, what they would permit, what was forbidden, remained within the realm of increasingly fraught speculation. It was clear only that they were here for something—observation, perhaps, or a reckoning, which lay at some point in the future.

Kanu was glad when their course began to take them further from the Watchkeeper.

"It never hurts to give them a wide margin," he said, feeling he needed to defend his qualms.

"Did your friends on Mars feel the same way?"

"My friends on Mars were three human beings, two of whom are dead now—and you've met the other one." But that was a harsher answer than her innocent question merited. "I had good relations with the machines through Swift. It was exactly that good relationship that Yevgeny Korsakov disapproved of— he felt it was tantamount to treason against my own species."

"Extreme. But given that we know so little about the Martian robots—who can say what they're really up to? How can we be sure they're not in secret cahoots with the Watchkeepers, plotting our downfall?"

"Believe me, it's not like that at all. I spent enough time with Swift and the other machines to know how they feel about the Watchkeepers, and the truth is they're as in the dark as the rest of us. They don't feel some distant kinship with the Watchkeepers. They're as alien and frightening to the Evolvarium as they are to us."

"You think."

"You have a great many genes in common with an oak tree. Do you feel an intense kinship with oak trees?"

"They're both robots, Kanu. Try seeing things from our perspective for a while, not theirs."

That was as close to arguing as they got. It was only four days from Earth to Jupiter space, hardly enough time to start getting on each other's nerves. *Fall of Night* was certainly not large, but the provision of two cabins meant there was more than enough privacy available to keep irritation at bay.

After their breakfast discussion, Kanu had been careful not to raise the matter of his disquiet again. It was better that way. He allowed her to believe she had settled his misgivings, putting them down to the unpleasantness of his recent experience on Mars. And, indeed, Kanu was ready to concede that a component of his feelings could be explained away as a kind of post-traumatic episode. But he knew there was more to it than that.

On the third day, twenty-four hours from Jupiter, he was alone in his cabin when he became unaccountably certain he was being watched; that he was sharing the room with a silent observer. Out of reflex he twitched around, and for an instant he was convinced he had seen something, a figure or the shadow of a figure, out of the corner of his eye.

In any other situation he would have gladly put the matter behind him. But it was just Kanu and Nissa and her little spaceship, and there was nothing between them and another human being except millions of kilometres of vacuum. Nissa aside, he was more alone here than he had been on the surface of Mars. Nor had he ever been one to jump at shadows.

And yet there had been someone—some*thing*—there.

Perhaps it was just a glimpse of his own reflection in the mirror above his private washbasin.

Yes. Just the mirror.

That was it.

But now a question pushed itself to the forefront of his mind. He voiced it aloud, but in a quiet enough whisper that it was easily drowned out by the noise of *Fall of Night*'s systems.

"What did you do to me?"

Because his thoughts were following the groove of a different, darker orbit now. Not that the machines on Mars had somehow erred in putting him back together, botching part of his brain wiring, but that this might be deliberate.

That all of this might suit some purpose of which he was not aware.

A day later they reached Jupiter. Nissa put extra power into *Fall of Night*'s electromagnetic deflectors, cocooning them from the worst effects of the Jovian magnetosphere. They were still moving quickly, about five hundred kilometres per second of excess speed, but Nissa had allowed for that with the aerobrake passage, knifing her ship through Jupiter's extreme upper atmosphere at an oblique angle. It was as bumpy as she had predicted, but—she assured Kanu—the buffeting and heating were well within tolerable margins, and the dodge had shaved many hours off their flight. In fact he found the experience more bracing than unpleasant. By the time they reached clear space again, their speed was down to a manageable hundred kilometres per second, more than sufficient for operations within Jupiter's system of moons.

Nissa was on the flight deck, confirming that their approach authorisation was in order. The certification was complicated and in a state of continuous adjustment and review, with a chance that it might be rescinded at any moment.

"Something giving you cause for concern?" Kanu asked, rubbing his face with a moistened towel. "I thought you had all the details covered."

"So did I, but there's a heavier Consolidation presence than I was expecting. After that business with Yevgeny . . . what's his surname?"

"Korsakov."

"Him, yes. I'm starting to feel rattled. Sure, I've bent a rule or two, but I haven't done anything to deserve this kind of attention."

"Nor have I."

"Well, of course *you* haven't." She gave him a quizzical look. "Unless there's something you haven't told me."

Kanu thought about it for a few moments. "I don't believe those enforcement craft are anything to do with us. They're here for some other reason entirely."

"And Korsakov's interest in you? The Consolidation ship from which he's transmitting is here, too."

"Really?"

"Yes. I tracked its heading, and here it is. Doesn't that concern you?"

"He must be on diplomatic business, intergovernmental work. Europa's a constant background problem for all the governments. That's why those permissions are so difficult to arrange."

"I've fought long and hard for this, Kanu. No one's taking it away from me now."

On their fall to Europa they were interdicted by two of the Consolidation enforcement craft, pincering *Fall of Night* from either side. Kanu had a good view of the official vehicles— dark, shark-shaped ships with the interlocking ripples of the Consolidation's emblem glowing along their sides.

"If it came to it," he said, "do you think you could outrun them?"

"Down to the ice, maybe. But I'd be in a world of trouble when I came back out."

It was a formality, more or less. Her authorisation was queried, then re-queried. Even though she had filed all the necessary requests, the Consolidation ships still insisted on signalling for confirmation. Kanu and Nissa endured long hours of waiting while photons bounced around the system, pinballing from one encrypted router to the next. Meanwhile Nissa tried to get a signal through to her contact in Europa, informing them of the delay, but the omens were not propitious.

"Something's not right down there," she said when the response was late returning. "The last I heard, the Margrave was having trouble with border control. I hope the situation hasn't worsened."

As abruptly as they had arrived, though, the Consolidation ships broke off. Kanu watched them fall away with a vague feeling of resentment. No apology for detaining them, or for wasting hours of their time. Not even a *bon voyage*.

"Rude."

"Planetary geopolitics looks a bit different when you're one of the little people, doesn't it?" Nissa said.

"I'm getting used to it."

Europa had no atmosphere, so they were able to come in hard and fast until the last moment. The moon was an almost perfectly smooth sphere, an off-white eyeball crazed and veined by healing stress fractures, but with no mountains, valleys or craters. Abandoned cities littered the Europan plains, spires buckled and domes cracked, sagging down into the ice on their stilts and buttresses like drowning cathedrals. It was much too expensive to return these cold, airless, radiation-sleeted ruins to viable habitats. Besides, their economies had always depended on the cities and markets under the ice, in the blood-warm ocean. The abandoned cities were merely the ports of entry to the hidden kingdom, and now the kingdom was lawless.

"Looters have stripped out almost anything useful," Nissa said as they vectored low over one of the tilted ruins. The clustered vanes and docking towers of the abandoned settlement brought to Kanu's mind the image of a sailing ship, hemmed in by pack ice, its masts and rigging angled closer to the horizon than the zenith. And the thought shaped itself: only the ice traps that ship. She could still sail again, if only she could break free of its hold.

"Kanu?"

"I'm sorry."

"I was saying that looters have stripped out almost anything we might be able to use in those cities. Power, computer systems, elevator links through to the ocean. The ice has shifted, anyway. Unless those elevator shafts are constantly maintained, the ice soon severs them."

"Are you expecting the Regals to come up and meet you on the surface?"

"No—they almost never show their faces."

"Then you have a problem."

"Only if I hadn't done my homework first."

Nissa had preselected a landing spot near the equator and where the ice was thinner. Jupiter's swollen one-eyed countenance lorded it over the sky, as if it had them pinned beneath its singular gaze. A case could be made for the beauty of Saturn, Kanu supposed, but never Jupiter. It was as ugly as an ogre, and it guarded its moons with an ogre's mad-eyed jealousy.

Fall of Night settled onto the ice without landing legs, letting its hull take its weight. Europa's gravity was barely a seventh that of Earth, less even than Mars, and after the two gees of their flight out to Jupiter, Kanu felt nearly weightless. It did not escape his attention that Nissa had put them down nowhere near any of the empty cities.

"This is where I start testing the letter of the law," she said. "We're not about to violate the terms of my authorisation—but we *are* going to make use of them in a way the Consolidation didn't expect."

"Continue," Kanu said.

"I was given forty-eight hours of surface time. That would be just enough to get in and out of the ocean if the elevators were working, but they're not, and the Consolidation knows that. So they don't believe I'll be able to reach the sea."

"You, on the other hand, have your own plans."

Nissa patted the couch adjoining her own. "Strap in next to me. I think you're going to like this part."

Kanu did as he was told, apprehension and curiosity vying for control of his emotions. Nissa was selecting navigation options he had not seen before, and beyond the enclosure of the command deck he sensed the ship going about some urgent new business. The hull was doing something. He felt the thud and whirr of activating mechanisms.

"Heating elements in the outer skin," Nissa said, directing his attention to one display. "They'll turn the ice to slush right

under us and we'll start sinking through. That won't be fast
enough, though." She tapped another diagram. "Active traction
mechanisms. They'll drag the slush from one end of the ship to
the other, pulling us deeper—just like a mole burrowing into
soil. Pitch-and-yaw stability, angle of attack, all under my
direction. We'll make about a metre a second at full crank."

Kanu was dumbfounded. "You've turned your ship into a
tunnelling machine."

Nissa settled her hands on two lever-shaped controls which
had emerged from the sides of her couch. "So let's tunnel."

She pushed the controls forward and Kanu felt *Fall of
Night* begin to burrow into Europa.

CHAPTER 13

The moment of the Watchkeeper's vanishing was too sudden
and inexplicable to bring any sense of relief. It felt, instead,
like the prelude to something else, one step in a conjuring trick
which had yet to reach its conclusion.

It was only after hours of analysis and communication with
Crucible that the disappearance began to be believed and understood. First and foremost, the Watchkeeper had not disappeared
at all—it had simply moved away at unbelievable acceleration,
somewhere in the region of twenty million gees according to
the best estimates. This was in stark contrast to the normal
movement of the alien machines as they travelled around Crucible's system, but it did accord with the documented manner of
their return, decades earlier: an almost instantaneous apparition. It was also the way in which Chiku Green's Watchkeeper
had "vanished" after its departure from Crucible.

"We always thought they had this other mode of propulsion," Mposi said, a day after the vanishing, "but it's one thing
to hypothesise about it and quite another to see it up close. The

good news is that the radiation burst, all that blue light, doesn't appear to have done us any harm. The ship is intact. In fact it's slightly better than intact, if the technicians are to be believed."

Ru frowned. He was addressing both of them, the trio sitting at one of the galley tables. Goma's appetite had been slow to return, delayed by a sense that they were not quite beyond the Watchkeeper's sphere of interest.

"I don't see how it can be better," Ru said.

"It's our acceleration: we are not using as much fuel as we expected. Which, of course, is impossible. But the technicians have double-checked their numbers."

Goma picked up a pepper pot, allowed it to fall the short distance from her fingers to the tabletop. "Aren't we at half a gee?"

"Slightly less," Mposi said, "but we're not losing any speed. Something is helping us along, so the engines have been dialled back a little. It will make life easier when we reach Gliese 163 if we don't have to scramble around immediately to refill our initialising tanks. Even a Chibesa engine needs some fuel occasionally."

"This makes no sense," Goma said.

Mposi delighted in having the upper hand. "There's something ahead of us. We've imaged it, but the quality is very poor—it's at the absolute limit of our resolution. They haven't had much more luck on Crucible, using synthetic data from the system's monitoring devices. But we don't really need better data, do we? It's obvious what the thing must be."

"The Watchkeeper, I suppose," Ru answered.

"The scientists have projected its course based on the acceleration burst. If it stays on that trajectory, it may end up on the same flight path we're taking. It isn't outpacing us, though—it's matching our acceleration precisely, keeping about one hundred and fifty million kilometres of separation between us."

Goma almost had to laugh. These numbers—accelerations of twenty million gees, distances wider than Crucible's orbit around its star—were almost too absurdly large to bother trying to comprehend. Physics, with its exponents and Planck lengths and Hubble distances, left her feeling diminished, as if it would not be satisfied until she felt vanishingly irrelevant, annihilated between the tiny and the enormous.

You knew where you were with elephants.

"What is it doing?" Ru asked.

"There are several possibilities. Clearing space ahead of us like a cosmic snowplough, perhaps. Space isn't a perfect vacuum. If it holds this trajectory, we'll have a much better chance of reaching Crucible without running into interstellar debris. Then there's the acceleration boost. It's as if we're benefiting from whatever the Watchkeeper does to make itself move—we're caught in its slipstream. The technicians want to make some measurements on the local vacuum, see if there's anything different about it."

"It's helping us?" Goma said.

"That's one interpretation," Mposi answered, as if it was his duty not to alleviate her qualms. "Another is that these are accidental benefits, and that it neither knows nor cares what becomes of us."

"But it is moving in the same direction," Ru said. "That has to mean something."

Goma felt her earlier apprehension reassert itself. "We'll know when we arrive, I suppose. If it lets us."

Within a few hours it was common knowledge that the Watchkeeper lay ahead of *Travertine*. From what Goma could judge, the other passengers shared her equivocal feelings. There was relief at not being immediately destroyed. Given the opacity of the Watchkeepers' deeper motivations, though, it was hard to know whether to be comforted or unnerved by the continued presence of the alien robot.

There was some debate about how best to exploit the advantage provided by the slipstream effect. Ru felt that the technicians were being too cautious in their response. If they ran the drive at the planned level, they could exceed fifty per cent of the speed of light and reach their destination a number of years ahead of schedule. On the other hand, they would then be banking a lot on the Watchkeeper's continued assistance. The holoships, travelling to Crucible, had made a similar gamble and been caught out.

Goma took Mposi's view, which considered it better to keep to the existing schedule, saving fuel and engine life in the process. *Travertine* was not built to travel faster than half the speed of light, and to exceed that margin would be to place an additional burden on its hull insulation and navigation systems.

The point was argued, and Crucible weighed in. Messages

crawled back and forth, stretched out by ever-increasing time lag. Eventually the verdict was in and Mposi's cautious view won out. They would use the Watchkeeper to their advantage, but they would not make the error of trusting it.

It was a fault of the human condition—or perhaps a blessing—that there was no situation which did not eventually become the normal state of affairs. All the people on *Travertine* knew it would be centuries before they made it back to Crucible, if indeed there was a world left to recognise upon their return. By turns, though, their psychological adjustment was slowly completed. The ship was their world now, and they had better learn to like it. Most found a way.

So life on *Travertine* fell into a comfortable rhythm of sorts. Mposi had said nothing more about the sabotage rumour and Goma was content to assume that the theory had been quietly discredited. All the same, she chose to keep out of the way of the Second Chancers, especially Peter Grave, and with Ru's collusion it was not so hard to structure her routines around that principle of avoidance. Their differences, the years of tension and separation on Crucible, were now fully behind them. They spent long hours together in their cabin, sharing warmth and silence and intimacy. Goma began to feel that at last there had come a healing, a point beyond which no more apologies or excuses were necessary. History and circumstance had done what they would to them, and they had been stronger. It was good to be loved, good to love another human being—even in the belly of a starship arrowing for unmapped space.

Ru and Goma both maintained an interest in news updates from the elephant reserve, and they shared a genuine eagerness to see how the Alpha herd had reshuffled itself in the wake of Agrippa's passing. But over time, Goma found that she had to work harder and harder to sustain her intellectual engagement. She sensed the same thing in Ru as well. It was not that they had ceased to care about the elephants, but the direction of their concern now had a different, outward focus. What happened to Crucible's elephants was increasingly not their business—Tomas and the others were managing their affairs with predictable efficiency. But Goma and Ru had a chance to offer some constructive help to the Tantors, and so the weathervane of their sympathies had swung to a new bearing.

Three months into the trip, with 61 Virginis now no more than a bright star in their wake—and the world they had known squeezed into that same dwindling glint—life on the ship began to change. With the drive running steadily and the Watchkeeper holding its position, some of the technical staff had already gone into skipover. So had a number of passengers, and more followed by the week. This was true also of the Second Chancers, who had no option but to submit to the skipover caskets even though (Goma did not doubt) they regarded them as a pernicious form of life-extension technology.

Goma and Ru were free to enter skipover whenever they chose, but neither was yet ready. Goma's communications with Ndege had grown steadily less frequent as the distance increased, but at least there were communications. That would cease when she entered skipover, and cease for ever. Since the time was to be of her choosing, she could not bring herself to make the decision. She could spend years awake if necessary—there would always be someone else around for company, and no shortage of rations—but to die before reaching Gliese 163 would entirely defeat the purpose of her being on the expedition in the first place. For now, she had agreed with Ru that they would remain awake at least until *Travertine* stopped its acceleration boost and resumed spin-generated gravity. Very little could go wrong during the cruise, and when the drive was restarted to slow the ship down again, the technicians would have the benefit of all the knowledge they had gained during the acceleration phase, making a catastrophe that much less likely. It was a good plan, Goma thought. They were not yet bored with the ship, not yet bored with each other, and not yet ready to surrender to sleep. And if either of them changed their minds, skipover was waiting.

But Goma need not have worried about boredom.

"Do you remember that business we spoke about a little while ago?" Mposi asked.

Goma was alone with him. Once or twice a week he dropped by their cabin for a brief social visit, often contriving to make it look like he was simply stopping in while on his way elsewhere. Goma went to his room more often than he came to theirs, but she was inclined to draw no negative conclusions from that. It was simply Mposi being his usual shrewd self.

Living in such a confined environment, it was virtually guaranteed that nerves would begin to fray over the span of the expedition. Being asleep for much of it would make very little difference; there would still be months or years of wakefulness when they reached their destination. Given that even the best of friends could grate on each other if pressed into the same space for too long, it made no sense to hasten that process.

Still, when Mposi came to see her that evening, it was immediately obvious that his mood was unsettled.

"Hard to forget," she said. "Although I was hoping it had dropped off the agenda."

"So was I," Mposi answered, gravely enough. "Indeed, it was starting to look as if that might have been the case. Updates from Crucible—a suspicion that the original intelligence was no more than malicious rumour-mongering."

"And now?"

He sucked breath through his teeth. "It turns out there might be some truth in it after all. A while ago I asked you to be my eyes and ears. Have you picked up on anything?"

"Not really. Then again, I haven't been going out of my way to mix with the Second Chancers."

"I wouldn't dream of blaming you for that. Here's the thing, though. Let us suppose someone on this expedition has a very real desire to see it fail, one way or another. Very possibly someone prepared to die to serve that end. When the Watchkeeper took an interest in us, there was a chance that the saboteur wouldn't need to do anything at all."

Goma reflected on the prospect of imminent destruction they had all felt, followed by the uneasy sense of a stay of execution once the Watchkeeper vanished.

"You mean the saboteur was hoping the Watchkeeper would destroy us?"

"Not *hoping*—but allowing for the possibility, certainly, waiting to see what transpired. Why risk acting and being detected in the process if the aliens are going to achieve the same ends? It needn't have been total destruction. For all we knew—for all the saboteur knew—the Watchkeeper might have just forced us off course, or damaged us enough to make us abandon the expedition and return home. There was every good reason to lie low and see what happened."

"And now?"

"Things have stabilised. The Watchkeeper didn't destroy us, and it appears to be content to hang ahead of us, clearing our path. Meanwhile, the ship seems to be working properly—well enough that people have already begun to go into skipover. Crucible's intelligence is that the saboteur may have been instructed to resume working towards the original plan—whatever that might be."

"And you still don't know?"

The door began to open. Goma had closed it as Ru's return was unexpected.

Goma groped for the thread of a plausible conversation—anything to give the impression that they had just been passing the time of day rather than discussing a secret conspiracy against the expedition. She felt paralysed and looked to Mposi in the hope he had come up with something.

"Am I interrupting?" Ru asked.

"Not at all," Mposi said, rising to leave. "We were just . . ."

"What?"

"Just catching up on gossip," Goma said, with what she hoped was the right note of breezy innocence.

Ru kept looking at them. She had opened the door but come no further into the room. "Fine."

"Ru . . ." Goma began. "It's not what—"

But Ru had shut the door, already on her way somewhere else. "I'm sorry—" Mposi started.

"We should have told her. *I* should have told her. If there's anyone on this ship I trust . . ." But before she could complete her own sentence, Goma was on her way out of the room. The door closed behind her, leaving Mposi alone. Ru was nearly at the end of the corridor, about to reach one of the stairwells. "Ru!" Goma called out. "Stop, please! You've got to let me explain!"

Ru halted, but when she looked back her expression was icy. "Explain what? Why you feel the need to talk behind my back?"

"It wasn't about you!"

Ru started up the staircase. For a moment, Goma was torn between possibilities—return to Mposi to hear the rest of what he had to say, or repair things with Ru?

Her decision was as impulsive as it was heartfelt. Mposi would return, but she could not count on Ru forgiving her unless she made immediate amends. Ru's footsteps rattled away up the staircase and Goma followed as quickly as she was able.

Ru could not have escaped her for long, and within a minute or so she stopped, squaring off against Goma on the next level up from their own.

"Whatever it is, I'm not interested. I gave up everything to be on this fucking ship." Ru had raised her voice, but it was such a subtle modulation that only Goma would have noticed it. "My work, my world, my life. And this is my reward? We've barely begun and already there are secrets?"

"Please be quiet," Goma said, speaking the words with soft authority.

"Don't tell me—"

"No," she said. "I will tell you. This is not my doing. I promised Mposi that I wouldn't tell you because he asked me to and I respect him. It was not about keeping anything from you, but from everyone else—the rest of the ship." She glanced around even as she spoke these words to make sure they were as alone as they appeared to be. "So I kept my mouth shut, and guess what, Ru? Mposi wasn't kidding around. There is something serious happening—something I don't want any part of, but now I know about it and I wish I didn't, because I was just getting used to being here. And by the way, everyone gave up their old lives for this—including me and Mposi." But now Goma glanced down, her indignation burning itself out. "He was wrong, though. I should have spoken to you, and I'm sorry I didn't. Actually, given what he just told me, I'd have insisted on sharing it with you now."

"So what did he tell you?" Ru asked.

"We can't talk here. It's best if you hear it from Mposi—I'll make him tell you."

Some of Ru's fire had died away now, too. Perhaps she sensed Goma's sincerity and her obvious anguish at being forced to conceal something from her.

"What is it?"

"Someone wants to hurt us."

"Who?"

"That's all I know. As I said, we'd be better off talking in our room. Mposi knows more—that's why he came to see me."

After a lengthy silence, Ru said, "Whatever it is, you should have told me."

"I know."

"Never again. No more secrets. Understood?"

"Believe me, I've learned my lesson."

"Good." But Ru laid a hand on her shoulder. "I can understand how you'd feel, with Mposi putting you on the spot like that. Fucking politician—I'm sorry, but that's still what he is—they think they own the rest of us. Mostly because they do."

"If he wasn't my uncle, maybe I wouldn't have listened."

"That only makes it worse. Relying on family loyalty—playing the same old Akinya tune. When will you lot get over yourselves?"

"I already have," Goma said.

"I'll need a lot more convincing of that. How long has this been playing out?"

"Since before the Watchkeeper."

"Fuck."

"It's not as bad as it sounds. Mposi mentioned it once, then it appeared to die away. I almost stopped thinking about it. That's the honest truth."

"Until now?"

"He's received some news—that's why we were speaking."

They made their way back to their room, the tension between them lessened but still there, Goma feeling she was only one mistake away from never being forgiven again. And perhaps that was justified, because Ru had surely earned better than this.

At their door, Goma realised she had left the room in such a hurry that—against her usual habit—she had not snapped her bangle on. Ru had hers, though, and the door opened for them.

But Mposi was gone.

"He said he had something to tell me," Goma said.

"And maybe he decided we'd need some time alone after that little incident. It's late, anyway, and I'm tired."

"I think I'll go and see him."

"Whatever it is, it can wait until morning."

Ru was right, of course, and Goma was in no mood to find something else to argue about. She conceded the point with a weary nod, glad that at least they were back in their room and speaking. She would talk to Mposi tomorrow, and all would be well.

CHAPTER 14

The ice was twenty kilometres thick; twenty thousand seconds of travel once Nissa's ship had reached a vertical-descent angle. From the first moment of immersion, the melted ice screening windows and cameras, there was nothing to see except the graphs and numbers of cockpit displays tracking their progress. For the most part they were heading straight down, but now and then Nissa steered them around some rocky or metallic thing entombed in the ice, preferring caution to bravado. "There are whole ships down here," she said, with a sort of reverent awe in her voice. "They crash-landed, began to melt into the ice whether they wanted to or not. They'll still be here when the sun swallows Mars!"

After a while, Nissa felt she could rely on the automatic pilot. She had not slept since their arrival at Jupiter and wanted to be as alert as possible once they were through the ice.

"We'll pop out in another two hours unless the radar picks up something we need to steer around. You should grab some rest, too. We'll be busy little beavers once we break through, and our forty-eight hours will be over before you know it."

It was sleep she meant rather than two hours of lovemaking. Agreeing with the eminent good sense of this proposal, Kanu retreated to his cabin. He doubted he would be able to sleep for the entire two hours but decided to make the best of what was on offer. Everything was flipped now, up and down reversed compared to deep space, and the noise of the heating and traction devices was louder and less regular than the inflight systems. But he would adapt to one set of circumstances as readily as another.

* * *

"It's time."

The voice was clear, quiet and quite unmistakably his own.

Kanu froze—every doubt, every bad thought confirmed in that one impossible utterance. He was alone in his chamber, Nissa doubtless already asleep in hers. There was no immediate sense of another presence in the room. But he knew how the voice of his own thought processes sounded, and this was different. An acoustic and spatial shift, the auditory information reaching his brain along the usual sensory and neural channels, as if it had been whispered into his ear.

"I said, it's time."

He whispered back, "I heard you."

"You don't have to speak aloud. That would get awkward very quickly. Simply think your responses clearly." The voice paused—almost as if giving him a moment to adjust to its presence. "How much do you understand or remember?"

"I remember Mars. I remember nearly dying on Mars. This is about that, isn't it?"

"Of course."

"You've done something to me. I've been feeling as much for days. You put something in me, changed me in some way. My meeting Nissa—that never was a coincidence, was it?"

"If you are a puppet, Kanu, then you should know your puppeteer. Will you do me a small favour?"

"Do *you* a favour?"

"All right, for both of us, then. Move to your private washbasin and run the hot water until the mirror steams up. Can you do that for me?"

Of course he could. If it meant getting an answer, or even just the beginning of an answer, he would oblige. He allowed the mirror to begin to mist, greying out his reflection.

"Now—neatly and precisely—draw an equilateral triangle in the steam, flat side down. Position yourself exactly in front of the triangle and look at nothing else."

"Why?"

"It's a visual mnemonic trigger. Your memories will unlock in their own good time, but this will accelerate the process. Do it, Kanu. What do you have to lose?"

* * *

He recognised the room instantly. It was where Swift had first allowed him sight, and where he had first learned of the deaths of Dalal and Lucien. He recalled sitting in a chair, and a view of the robot city beyond the window.

Now he was in the chair again. This time there was a difference, though: he was looking at himself, seeing his body from the outside.

Seeing himself, he realised again, from Swift's point of view—as he had during the dream of the operating theatre.

"This is complicated." The version of him seated in the chair was addressing the version haunting his own memory.

"Very complicated, and very delicate, but we need to get the essential facts straight before we go any further. Something bad happened to you on Mars. Call it a terrorist incident, call it a stupid accident. Either way, the machines did not engineer it. But there are never truly any accidents, just unforeseen opportunities."

"Who am I?"

The seated counterpart of himself raised a silencing hand. "I'm you. I am you before some of your memories are—or were—deliberately blocked from conscious recall. That's so you can leave Mars and pass our colleagues' scrutiny before returning safely to Earth. It's your choice. My choice. *Our* choice."

Kanu had a hundred questions, but he allowed the speaker to continue.

"After your accident but before your return to the embassy, Swift confided something in you. Swift revealed to you knowledge obtained by the Evolvarium, knowledge of a potentially destabilising nature. Shall I remind you of what Swift told you, Kanu? Briefly, then. The machines have intercepted a signal from deep interstellar space. No one here knows about it—yet—because it was never aimed at our solar system. The signal was directed at Crucible, around Sixty-One Virginis. Its point of origin, as near as can be determined, is *another* solar system about seventy light-years from Crucible. That system is Gliese 163. It has never been of interest to you, the machines or anyone else. No human expedition has gone anywhere near it. And yet someone there has sent a message, and the message was aimed at Crucible, and the message appears to be urgent."

The speaker allowed itself a silence before proceeding.

"You may wonder how this information reached the Evolvarium. Isn't the Evolvarium supposed to be quarantined on Mars, denied access to the rest of the universe? All of that is correct, but it underestimates the ingenuity of the likes of Swift. The machines have never established a physical presence beyond Mars. But their capability for obtaining information? It is vastly superior to even the best estimates of the Consolidation. When they put you back together, Kanu, the machines made some *deliberate* mistakes simply so that their work would not look too perfect!"

The figure laughed, stiffening his back in the seat.

"I mean no disrespect. I couldn't very well disrespect myself, could I? The point, anyway, is that the machines are able to tap into a very extended informational network with peripheral branches extending all the way to Crucible. And they picked up on the existence of this transmission before it reached the intelligence networks of any of the major powers in this solar system, including our beloved merfolk, Kanu—there are limits even to their omniscience."

Kanu could not begin to see where this was headed.

"The mere existence of this message would be surprising enough," his shadow-self continued, "especially as the message is framed in human terms, for human comprehension, because there should not be anyone out there to send a message in the first place! But there's a deeper mystery here, and a direct reason why the message is of specific interest to our friends on Mars. They think another machine may have sent it. And the likely identity of this artificial intelligence should be of specific interest to *you* as well since there's a strong family connection. Do I need to spell it out?"

"Eunice," Kanu breathed.

He remembered the exhibition in Lisbon, the construct simulation of his great-great-great-grandmother, enthroned in glass. Except what he had seen was a copy of a copy, not the construct itself. According to the annotation, nobody was certain what had become of the real thing.

"If you believe the rumours," the speaker went on, "the

actual construct—the illegal, unlicensed artilect emulation of Eunice Akinya—hid aboard one of the holoships and travelled to Crucible. Then, shortly after the settlement, it disappeared again. The rumours—as before, make of them what you will—say that it was abducted by the Watchkeepers, spirited away into interstellar space, or taken as part of some agreement in exchange for the settlement and exploration of Crucible. Either way, there is a direct connection to the aliens. And now *something* pops up around Gliese 163, but instead of announcing itself to the universe, it chooses to communicate only with Crucible."

The figure shifted in the chair. "I don't know about you, but I put some stock in those rumours. Our *other* mother—one of our other mothers, anyway—was also involved in that supposed business with the Watchkeepers. They took Chiku Green with them, too. Surely that holds some significance for you? Anyway, the Evolvarium has declared an interest. The collective consciousness of the machines must now confront the possibility that there may be another artificial intelligence out there, an artilect old enough to predate the fall of the Mechanism. Furthermore, it's woven around the personality of the woman who might have single-handedly initiated the Evolvarium. Machines don't believe in gods, Kanu—but if they did, she'd be a good candidate. Naturally, they'd like to know what's happening around Gliese 163. That's where we come in."

"We?"

"Your injuries were definitely the unfortunate result of terrorist activities, but the incident also provided an opportunity. You are still who you were, but you now serve two masters. When the machines remade your nervous system, they encoded a tiny part of themselves into you. Not via implants—that would have been much too crude and easy to detect—but via the actual topological map of your idiosyncratic connectome. There has always been great redundancy in the human brain, Kanu. Now some of that redundancy has been co-opted, given over to the Evolvarium. You are carrying part of it inside you, influencing your actions and intentions. Influencing, not determining—you still have free will, but the epicentre of your sympathies has shifted. You have not turned traitor to the human species, but from now on the interests of the machines will be of equal importance to you. You stand between two worlds, Kanu."

Kanu felt an immediate and visceral revulsion, but also a kind of relief that he now had an explanation for his sense of dislocation. He was neither mad nor traumatised—or no more than might be expected given his ordeal.

But what had been done to him was still profoundly wrong.

"Here's the important thing," the speaker said. "This state of affairs was not forced upon you. It was arrived at by mutual agreement. During the early stages of your recuperation— long before you remember coming back to consciousness— Swift explained to you the nature of the crisis, how the message relates to the machines, and the Watchkeepers, and our ancestor. How they are anxious to know more—anxious to respond—but cannot share this information with the conservative, machine-phobic governments of the solar system. Swift suggested a solution: use *you* as the means for the machines to extend their influence beyond Mars. You become their vehicle and their agency, Kanu. Both of you understood that it would be the end of your diplomatic career. But that was actually a blessing, as it would hasten your return to Earth— and make it possible for you to set in motion the second part of the plan. Europa is the key. Europa has always been the key. You only had to find a way to get here, a way to get under the ice. But you had already solved that particular problem on Mars. You just needed to reconnect with Nissa Mbaye, to whom you'd once been married . . ."

They broke through the crust on schedule. He was sitting with Nissa on the command deck, waiting as the radar began to detect the imminent transition from ice to water.

"Suitably refreshed?" Nissa asked.

For an instant, Kanu hesitated on the verge of confession.

It would feel good, to unburden himself—to submit to her understanding and forgiveness. But if his newly uncovered memories were correct, he had come here for a reason. If his confession forced Nissa to turn back, he would have learned nothing about himself, nothing about the grander objectives of the machines. He had to keep the truth hidden for a little longer.

"As a matter of fact," he answered, despising himself, "I've never felt better."

"Good, because the clock's been ticking since we landed. I'm testing the law but I don't want to break it, especially with that heavy Consolidation presence in orbit. To be back on the surface within the agreed window we'll need to allow enough time to chew through the ice again." She was working the controls, preparing for the shift from tunnelling machine to submarine. "We'll be going fast and deep, and we need to cover a few hundred kilometres to reach our objective." She looked at him with sudden eagerness. "What's the deepest you've ever gone on Earth? Ten kilometres, maybe?"

"Only as a passenger. A lot less under my own power."

"We're going down much further than that—more than a hundred kilometres of vertical descent. I know that sounds impossible, but this is Europa, not Earth, and the pressure builds much more slowly. We'll top out at about two hundred megapascals—easily within the hull's crush tolerance."

"I sincerely hope so," Kanu said, not for one moment doubting her words.

She flashed back a quick smile. "Well, if I'm wrong—it'll be quick."

Not a stray photon of starlight made it down through the twenty kilometres of icy crust. *Fall of Night* was swimming now, its motion smoother than when it had been tunnelling. Their angle of descent was shallower and the only sound beyond the ordinary life-support systems was the whirr of water-thrusters. They could have been in the most perfect starless vacuum, adrift between the galaxies.

"Nissa," he said. "There's something I need—"

"Can't you turn off your anxieties, merman, just for a few hours?"

"I don't think so, no."

And there was the first flash of real irritation.

"What's troubling you now?"

"More than we have time to cover at the moment. This objective of yours—can you tell me a little more about it? I understand you wanting to keep things as close to your chest as possible until we got here, but we're on Europa now. Shouldn't I know the full picture?"

Nissa gave a small sigh and called up a map of the Europan surface, peeled open like an orange. "We're here," she said, jabbing with a finger. "All these dots, these are abandoned cities. Abandoned doesn't mean empty, of course." Her finger skated to a knot of ruins, settling on one bloated dot. "This is Underthrace. It was one of the biggest subsurface settlements before the Fall—a bubble economy, skirting the brink of what was legal or ethical elsewhere in the system. You can see why it would have appealed to your grandmother."

"You have proof that Sunday was here?"

"Concrete. I've seen the paper trails. When your family's finances were on the slide, it looks like they tried to move a lot of their more questionable holdings into Underthrace's independent credit system. My guess is Sunday was shrewd enough to want to safeguard her art as well."

Kanu nodded slowly. "I'm sure you're right. It wouldn't surprise me in the slightest if she banked some of her artworks here. If nothing else, she wouldn't have wanted the market flooded with her work after her death."

"I'm glad you approve of my theory. It would be a little disappointing to be wrong."

"I don't think you are. But I suspect there might be something else in Underthrace."

Nissa twisted to face him again. "Something to do with Sunday?"

"I doubt she would have had direct knowledge of it. It's more likely to have been initiated by the next generation—my mother, her contemporaries. They'd have had the time and the knowledge."

"The time and the knowledge for what?"

"Nissa, it's time I spoke frankly. This isn't what you think it is—there's something much bigger going on. You've come to Europa on some pretext, but so have I—our meeting wasn't coincidence after all."

"What do you mean?"

"I always knew you'd be in Lisbon, and that there was a good chance we'd run into each other."

"No," she said flatly. "I was there. I saw your reaction. You were as surprised as I was."

"At the time I believed it was a genuine coincidence."

They had descended twenty kilometres since breaking through the ice—deeper than any part of Earth's seas—and mindless black fathoms lay beneath them still. From the hull there came not a murmur of complaint as it bore the smoothly rising stresses.

"Only yesterday," Nissa said, "you told me you didn't feel quite right. I reassured you it was to be expected and dismissed your concerns, but it's obvious now that I was wrong, for which I apologise. I should have listened to you. But we're on Europa because I chose to come here, looking for art. Not because of some grand conspiracy you dragged me into. Can you hold on to that simple truth for a few hours?"

Kanu closed his eyes, opened them again, hoping that the world would have done the decent thing and changed into a less problematic version of itself.

"I want to."

"So do me a favour and try. There are some floating structures coming up soon which we'll cut through to save time. We may stir up a few Regals as we pass and I don't want to be distracted if that happens." Then added, under her breath: "The four days home are going to be interesting."

There was no point in stealth. *Fall of Night*'s searchlights pushed out at all angles into the surrounding water, turning the little ship into a neon-spined pufferfish. Nissa did not care who knew of her arrival, only that she did not startle the unwary.

They nosed through looming dark structures still secured to the ocean floor, ovals or spheres for the most part, strung along the tethers like baubles. Each of the ruins was large enough to be considered a city in its own right, and indeed—according to the maps and records—many of them had been autonomous enclaves, bubbles within the bubble, exploring their own fringes of the edge economy.

Nissa was justifiably nervous. There were hot spots and pressure gradients, evidence of recent or ongoing inhabitation. Kanu felt the tension boiling off her.

"They talk about the Regals as if they're one thing," she said, keeping up a commentary as if it was the only thing holding them both on the right side of sanity. "In truth, there are about a hundred different factions down here, and most of them hate each other more than they hate us."

"Who is your contact? What are you hoping to exchange for the artworks?"

"My contact is the Margrave. As for leverage—money's useless down here. There are no economic ties to the rest of the system, no way of moving credit in or out." But then she noticed something. "Oh, what's this?"

"Show me."

"Movement. Warm objects." She tapped her finger against a smudge of thermal signatures emerging from a fissure in one of the tethered structures.

The thermal signatures were Regals, but moving too swiftly to be swimming under their own power. There were a dozen of them, organised into an arrowhead squadron. *Fall of Night*'s sensors picked out the powered drones they were using for propulsion, each Regal drawn along by one of the machines. They could swim, of course—all of the Regals had tails and flippers rather than legs—but machines would always be faster. They were armed and armoured, but it all looked makeshift, cobbled together from technological junk and detritus—the scavenged titbits of what had once been a thriving submarine economy.

"The Margrave's people?"

"Probably. We're in his sphere of jurisdiction, more or less."

"You don't sound certain."

"I was told I wouldn't be contacted until we reached Underthrace itself."

"Could we outrun them?"

"Oh, easily. Wouldn't gain us much, though. If you don't do business with the Regals, you don't do business with anyone."

The Regals carried their own lights. They had glow-sticks and luminous paint, some of which flickered and changed in a way that reminded Kanu of Sunday's psycho-reactive graffiti. Their submarine armour was horned and bladed. They also carried long, spearlike weapons with triggers and gas canisters.

Nissa allowed them to approach. She did not increase *Fall of Night*'s speed or take evasive action. Equally, she did not deviate from their original course.

The Regals split their formation and surrounded Nissa's ship. They had no difficulty matching pace. Kanu heard clangs and thumps as they knocked carelessly against the hull, followed by the long fingernail scrape of a spear or harpoon being drawn down the length of the ship.

"It's intimidation," Nissa said. "That's all."

A Regal suddenly stationed itself in front of the command-deck window, grappling on with plate-sized suction clamps. Kanu had a much better view of its armour and equipment now. It was a very muscular creature, with a powerful tail and torso, strong-looking arms, wide, webbed hands and barely any neck. It was hard to see its face behind the partial mask covering its nose and mouth, which he guessed was either a breathing apparatus or part of some water-intake and oxygenation system. Its eyes were hidden by strap-on goggles, pushed into the dough of its face like two black eggs. Its visible skin, where the armour did not cover it, was an off-white or pale green.

The Regal unclipped something from its utility belt that looked like a smaller version of the suction clamps, which it pushed against the glass before fiddling two tubes into holes on either side of its skull. Then it took another item from the belt, a metal cone, and jammed the open end of it hard against the glass. Kanu flinched as the Regal bent its face to the narrow end of the cone.

Indistinct, watery sounds came through the glass. It was language, possibly even one of the common tongues, but mangled beyond recognition by cultural isolation and the forbidding physics of this environment. Kanu thought he could make out a word or two, in what might have been Swahili—*identify*, *ocean*, *exclusion*, *anger*—but it was very difficult to be sure. He began to open his mouth, but Nissa raised a cautioning hand.

"They can hear us now, through that stethoscope," she said in a low voice. Then, projecting her voice with theatrical clarity: "I am Nissa Mbaye. I have come to Europa on peaceful business under a Consolidation permit. The Margrave of Underthrace is expecting me. May I have safe passage?"

An answer came back. To Kanu's ears, it was no more comprehensible than the first. But Nissa must have prepared herself for dialogue with the Regals.

Speaking for Kanu's ears only, she said, "They say the Margrave won't speak to me, so I'm wasting my time."

"That's a good start."

"They also say they're happy for me to waste my time provided I pay a tribute or a toll for passing through this part of the ocean."

"Were you expecting to pay a toll?"

"I anticipated the demand." Nissa shifted her voice into her louder register. "I am honoured to offer tribute. I am opening my dorsal cargo hatch. Please take what you will, with my respect and gratitude."

She made the hatch spring open. Kanu watched her silently, impressed by her preparedness. The Regal detached its stethoscope and unsuckered itself, then swam around the ship to join its fellows by the cargo hatch. The knocking and scraping had intensified around that area.

"What did you bring?" Kanu asked.

"Medicines. Vitamins and food supplements." But in her voice he heard trepidation. It was all very well speculating on what the Regals would consider an acceptable tribute; it was quite a different matter to put that idea to the test.

Angry thumps and knocks sounded along the hull.

"Could they damage us?"

"Jam the thrusters and steering gear, maybe. Block the water-cooling intake. Not much else."

"That already sounds bad enough."

Nissa's expression tightened. The main Regal had returned to the window holding a fistful of small white pills, which were already beginning to dissolve into the water. The Regal mashed the soggy pills and hammered the pulped remains against the glass. It barked some oath into the water, the sound strong enough to reach Kanu even without the speaking cone. Then it gave a jerk of its tail and flicked away into the water.

The hammering and scraping abated. One or two strikes more, a dismissive final clang, and then they were free of the Regals.

"Did we pass or fail?"

"If we'd failed, we'd know it," Nissa said. "That was just their way of letting me know they were being generous, that my offering was at the lower threshold of what they consider acceptable."

She touched a control and the window glass cleaned itself. The Regals had departed. They were alone again, still moving ever deeper into the ocean. Kanu did not allow himself to relax—there was too much on his mind for that—but they had cleared one hurdle and Nissa's ingenuity led him to hope they would be capable of clearing more if they arose. If all else failed, he supposed, they always had the option of drilling their way back out of Europa. The Regals would not be so foolish as to try to hold them hostage . . . would they?

But they could only have travelled another few kilometres closer to Underthrace when their lights picked out a familiar masked and goggled face rising in the waters before them, as if to block their passage.

"No," Nissa said, with anger this time. "We did a deal. We had an arrangement!"

But her concerns were misplaced. It was the same Regal, certainly, but there was no actual body accompanying its face. The Regal's head had been cut off and skewered on a pike.

Holding the pike, hovering before them, was another humanoid aquatic creature. It carried no lights and its mostly black armour was both more functional and less ostentatious than that of the earlier Regals. It looked, to Kanu's eyes, no less dangerous or forbidding.

But the creature waved its arm, indicating that they should follow it. With one flick of its tail it was under way, the Regal's skewered head still in its grasp.

"Finally," Nissa said. "Someone with manners."

CHAPTER 15

Goma rose early, by routine, with Ru still deeply asleep on her side of the bed. She had slept only fitfully, knowing that her mind would not be fully at ease until she had picked up the thread of last night's aborted conversation. Not wishing to disturb Ru, she washed and dressed quietly before leaving the room. She went to one of the galleys and poured herself coffee. The galley was empty and she had passed hardly anyone else on her way there. *Travertine*'s lights were still dimmed to their nocturnal level, encouraging its human crew to continue following a diurnal sleep pattern. The ship was all shades of brown and amber now, and as quiet as a spacecraft could ever be. Non-essential life-support systems had been turned low or switched off completely and the noise of the drive—conducted through the fabric of the ship—amounted only to a distant, waterfall-like roar, as lullingly soporific as a white-noise generator.

Mposi would be awake, though. He was a creature of extreme habit and was always up and working before anyone else. Granted, he no longer had the duties of his political life on Crucible, the pressures and obligations of high office. But he would find enough to keep himself busy no matter where he was, and Goma knew he currently had the matter of the saboteur to occupy his thoughts. No, Mposi would be awake by now and probably anxious to resume their conversation.

When the coffee had restored some clarity to her thoughts, Goma moved through the ship until she reached Mposi's cabin. She knocked quietly on the door, not wishing to disturb anyone in the adjoining cabins, presuming they were occupied.

She waited a decent interval, then knocked again.

Two possibilities presented themselves: Mposi was profoundly asleep or had already left his room. She risked a harder set of knocks but there was still no sign of life.

Fine: he was already up and about.

Goma searched the obvious alternatives—the galleys, lounges and public spaces—and still there was no sign of her uncle. She went to the gym and found it empty. She checked the medical bay, just in case, but there was no one inside the glass-doored area.

By the time she got back to her own cabin, Ru was drowsily awake.

"About last night—"

"I can't find Mposi."

Ru scrunched her still-sleepy eyes. "Where have you looked?"

"Just about everywhere. No sign of him in his cabin, no sign of him anywhere else."

"That still leaves a lot of the ship—places you and I can't get into."

"I know. But Mposi shouldn't be able to get into them either, not without special authorisation."

Some alertness was returning to Ru. She dug dust from the corners of her eyes, inspected it with a sleepy fascination. "For which he'd need to go to Gandhari. You want to talk to her? For all we know, she and Mposi might be sharing a cabin by now."

"I'd have heard," Goma said, not particularly in the mood for humour. "Let's leave her out of it for the moment. I'm concerned for him, but I don't want to cause an unnecessary panic."

"You look panicked already."

It was true, but Goma closed her eyes and forced a kind of calm upon herself. "He can't have gone anywhere. It's a ship, and there are only so many places he could be. I probably missed him. We'll search thoroughly ourselves before we go to the captain."

"That'll take a while. We'd better divide up the sections, meet back at our room every hour."

"Make it every thirty minutes," Goma said.

"Fine, thirty minutes. And we *will* find him—probably at some porthole, gazing back at Crucible and wondering why the hell he ever signed up for this."

Try as she might, Goma could not be cheered by this. "I'm worried for him."

"So am I, but he'll be fine."

Ru washed and dressed while Goma made chai. They drank it quickly, nothing much to say to each other, too much still unspoken from the night before. But when they were nearly ready to leave, Ru reached out and touched Goma's wrist.

"He'll be all right. And I still love you."

"Thank you," Goma said.

They separated and searched the ship. The lights were beginning to warm up for the day cycle now, but the transition was gradual and there were still relatively few people moving around. This made it easier to look for Mposi, but also made Goma feel more conspicuous. She was going into parts of the ship she would not normally visit at these hours with no ready explanation for her presence there. She did not want to have to tell anyone that she was searching for her lost uncle. But as she searched the corridors, stairwells and passageways, no one minded her, or even engaged her in anything more than passing conversation.

Goma searched all the permitted areas in the lower half of the forward sphere, and then as much of the spine as she had access to. Since *Travertine* was still accelerating, entering the spine felt like descending into the supporting tower of some huge sphere-capped building, with another sphere at its foundation. Beyond a certain point, though, the lower levels were open only to technicians. Mposi might have had a way of getting through those locked bulkheads but she certainly did not.

Some doors offered access—via airlocks, disposal vents or cargo bays—to open space. But Goma was certain that Mposi could not have opened any of those doors without Gandhari Vasin being informed immediately. There would have been alarms, emergency procedures, staff dashing to the affected area. No; Mposi could not have left the ship—or been pushed off it, for that matter.

The thought was there, then. The possibility of murder. Was that melodramatic of her, given so little evidence of misfortune?

But Mposi had been aware of a possible sabotage plot, and he had spoken to Maslin Karayan only recently.

So yes, murder: why dismiss the obvious?

But she found neither Mposi nor his body. When she and Ru checked in with each other, at half-hourly intervals as agreed, Ru was having no more success.

"I've accessed every room I can get into," she said. "That excludes all the private quarters, unoccupied rooms and various areas closed to anyone who isn't on the technical staff. To get into those, we'll need to see Gandhari."

"Maybe now we have cause," Goma said.

"Have you double-checked his room, just in case he was sound asleep after all?"

"Twice. And I'd have woken the dead the second time." She regretted the choice of words immediately. "I don't think he's in there. But again, we'd need the captain to open that door."

"Then we go to Gandhari. I had my doubts to begin with, Goma, but you're right—we should have found him by now."

"One more sweep," Goma said. "If we were unlucky, he could have been taking one set of stairs while we were using another. Did you check the Knowledge Room?"

"No, it was locked. Who ever uses that place, anyway, other than you?"

"A few," Goma said. "And I've never known it to be locked."

Still, Ru was right: Goma very rarely met anyone else in the Knowledge Room. Even after other people had started spending more time there, she had managed to hang on to the idea of it as her personal kingdom, an enclave of privacy and solitude where not even Ru was likely to wander.

"I've changed my mind," she said. "We go straight to the captain now."

"I agree."

Gandhari Vasin was readying herself for the day when they disturbed her, although still in her nightclothes. If Goma had expected resentment at their early arrival, none was evident.

"You were right to tell me," she said, after taking a few moments to dress for the rest of the ship. "You ought to have found him by now, and I doubt he had the means to get through any of the sealed doors. Rest assured, though—he's still on the ship, and we will find him."

Goma mentioned the Knowledge Room. They had checked it again on the way to Vasin and found it still secured.

"I've given no orders for it to be locked and I can't see why it would be. Was it somewhere Mposi went very often?"

"I don't think so," Goma said.

And it was true. As the data in the Knowledge Room had hardly altered since departure, few people saw any reason to go in there at all. It would be different when they neared Gliese 163, but for most of them that was decades of sleep away.

"Mposi's not a scientist anyway," Ru said.

"I know. And thank goodness for that," Vasin said. "He's the one person on this ship the scientists and Second Chancers can both talk to."

"There's you," Goma felt obliged to point out.

"Next to Mposi, I'm a rank amateur. Your uncle's liked and trusted by all parties, and that makes him as invaluable to me as any part of this ship. I shudder to think how we would ever have managed without him."

Vasin opened a drawer and snapped a bangle around her wrist. "We had some lengthy discussions about the functionality of these devices. They allow access to the rooms, but they're clearly capable of much more than that. Have you ever wondered why we didn't make provision for communication, for localisation?"

"I am now," Goma said.

"The truth is, the bangles can do all of that and more if they need to, but our psychologists were against the idea. The dynamics of a ship aren't the same as those of a city or even a planet. They considered it unwise to implement the full functionality. Sometimes it's good to have the choice not to be found, not to be spoken to—especially on a starship. There's enough to drive us mad without engineering the last traces of privacy out of our lives." But she offered a semi-smile. "Still, rank has its privileges. My bangle can locate any one of you if the need arises."

"You didn't need to tell us that," Ru said, Goma sending a nod of agreement—both of them aware that Vasin had shown her trust in them with this confidence.

"You'd have figured it out sooner or later." Vasin touched a stud on the bangle's rim and raised her wrist to her lips. "Find Mposi Akinya, please. Throw his location onto my wall and open a vocal channel to his bangle."

A diagram of the ship appeared on a blank portion of Vasin's wall, outlined in glowing red lines. Lilac cross hairs appeared over part of the forward sphere, and then the whole thing zoomed in on that section.

"That's his room," Goma said, "but he isn't answering his door."

"Mposi? This is Gandhari. Are you there? Speak, please. We are concerned about you."

There was no answer.

Vasin lowered her wrist. "We'll visit his room first, then look at the other possibilities."

There was no need for a search party—Vasin had all the tools and authority she needed. They went quickly to Mposi's quarters, where a touch of another stud on her bangle unlocked his door. Goma braced herself for the worst as they entered his rooms, but it was clear after a moment or two that he was not present. The bed was only slightly rumpled, a cup of honeyed chai standing cold on a table.

Vasin found his bangle tucked under a cushion.

"He may have left it here by mistake," she said. "None of us was used to these things on Crucible."

That was true, but after so long on the ship, Goma now felt naked without her bangle. She could not imagine Mposi feeling differently. Still—absent-minded old Mposi. She supposed it was possible.

"I'd like to look in the Knowledge Room," Goma said.

"Of course."

They were there in minutes. Vasin opened the door, bidding Goma and Ru wait at the threshold while she went inside. Not only had the door been locked, but the room was totally dark. A second or two passed before the lights came on.

Goma caught Vasin's intake of breath, a single sharp sound in the silence.

"Gandhari?"

She came out again, visibly shocked, and in the gentlest of ways prevented Goma from entering or looking into the Knowledge Room. She closed the door and elevated the bangle to her lips. "Gandhari," she breathed, as if the shock had taken all the air from her lungs. "We have a technical emergency. Doctor Nhamedjo . . . Nasim, Aiyana . . . anyone who's listening—come to the Knowledge Room immediately."

"What's going on?" Goma said.

"I am sorry, Goma. I saw Mposi in there. In the display . . . in the Knowledge itself. He's dead, Goma."

"Open the door."

"You do not need to see this. I want my technicians here, people who understand—"

"Gandhari. Open the door. I want to see him."

It was Goma speaking but the words almost felt like someone else's, stuffed into her mouth. No, she did not want to see him at all. The last thing she wanted was evidence of her uncle's death, plain and undeniable. She wanted to run away, to bash her head against a wall until she woke up from this awful dream. But the brave thing, the noble thing, was to pretend otherwise. To let everyone think she was courageous enough even for this.

Ru took her hands. "Let us in, Gandhari. It's better that we see."

Gandhari gave a regretful nod and opened the door. "You should not touch anything," she said, "no matter how much you want to. Something bad has happened to him. It may not be safe." And then, as if the words demanded a second utterance: "Something bad has happened."

Mposi was in the Knowledge. Goma knew instantly it was him even though he had his back to the door. He was leaning against the side of the display tank, head lolling, left arm hanging over the side so that his fingers brushed the floor on which Goma now stood. There was a gash on his forehead, traces of dried blood around the wound, but no sign of any more grievous injury. He looked supremely relaxed—like a man who had dozed off in a jacuzzi.

"Mposi," Goma said.

Her instinct was to rush to him, but she knew better than that. Something was very wrong with the well. As she circled around to his side, she saw that no part of Mposi was visible beneath the well's surface. Instead of being transparent, the matrix of nanomachines had turned opaque and muddy. The colour quivered before her eyes, and the surface—normally flawless—rippled and surged. Mposi, what she could see of him, was unclothed. She moved around the tank for a better view of his lolling head. His eyes were closed, his expression slack, as if he had indeed drifted into sleep. But he was much too still for that, and their presence would surely have roused him by now.

She looked down his angled torso to the point where it met the well's troubled, turbulent surface. His right forearm was submerged below the elbow. Goma could not resist. She would not touch any part of the well, but she had to touch her uncle. Her fingers stroked his upper arm.

"Uncle."

Not because she expected an answer, but because to say nothing was worse.

"Goma," Vasin said quietly. "You should step back now, until the technicians come."

It was the gentlest of touches, scarcely any contact at all, but the press of her fingers had upset some equilibrium. Mposi began to slump away from her, leaning further into the well. As he tilted, so the steepening angle drew his right arm from the surface. Beneath the elbow, the arm was nearly gone. Goma stared in wordless horror. It had not been severed or burned, just dissolved away, leaving milky strands, the liquidising remnants of bone and muscle, nerve and flesh. And as Mposi slumped further, so it became clear that a similar process had affected the rest of him.

Ru slapped a hand over Goma's eyes, snapped her head around.

"Don't look," she whispered.

CHAPTER 16

The Margrave of Underthrace was, naturally, apologetic for the inconvenience they had suffered on their way through Europa's waters. "There was a time when Regals stood for something," he lamented. "We had our differences, yes, our disagreements over territory and negotiating rights with the Outside, but we had far more in common than we had to divide us. We knew where we stood with each other. These hooligans barely know they're born. How dare they charge you to pass through *my* waters!"

"I don't suppose they'll do it again," Kanu said.

"They've had their gentle warnings," the Margrave said. "Unfortunately, we're long past the point of reasoning with these ruffians. Force is the only language they understand—and if it isn't brute force, you're wasting your time. You've done me a favour—I would have had to nip those incursions in the bud sooner or later, so it might as well be today. I'm just sorry you had to get caught up in all that unpleasantness."

"I almost thought we wouldn't make it," Nissa said. "Those Consolidation ships in close orbit—is that all connected with the trouble down here?"

"If they touch this moon, they will learn a valuable lesson."

"I hope for your sake," Kanu said, "that the lesson isn't too painful for either party."

"Spoken like a true ambassador. No water so troubled that it can't be oiled."

They were breathing the dry air of Underthrace, in a room furnished for the needs of Outside visitors. The Margrave's Regals had escorted *Fall of Night* all the way in, easing through a thickening forest of submarine structures until they came to a kind of enclosed glade, a bubble of ocean in the fortified heart of Underthrace. The Regals had docked Nissa's ship and connected an underwater airlock so that Nissa and Kanu could disembark.

The Margrave remained fully immersed, under deep-ocean conditions. In the middle of the room, rising from floor to ceiling, was a glass tube armoured to withstand a differential pressure of hundreds of megapascals. The glass was tinted, the Margrave no more than a shadowy form. Kanu made out a suggestion of some kind of headdress or helmet, a hard, ridged shape, but he could not decide if it was an adornment or some kind of bony extrusion of the Margrave's altered anatomy. Of the face, he saw only the glint of goggles above a kind of mandrill-like snout or mask.

"I never meant to cause you any trouble," Kanu said. "There's been enough of that already where my family's concerned."

"The trouble was coming whether we liked it or not, so please do not feel bad on my account, Kanu."

"Wait," Nissa said, raising a hand. "Let's clear this up right now, shall we? Kanu is my guest. He only came along for the ride, so can we please stop talking as if this visit is for his benefit, not mine?"

Kanu shifted in his black and purple chair. It was scarcely any bother to stand in Europa's gravity, but the chairs had been provided as a courtesy. The guests had even been served chai, brought to them by air-breathing aquatics.

"The art is here," Kanu confirmed. "It's been here since Sunday first brought it to Europa. That's the reason for Nissa's visit."

"Good," she said. "At least we agree on that."

"You'd have come here with or without me," Kanu went on. "But because I knew of your interest in Sunday, and Sunday's connection with Europa, I knew you would eventually make this trip. It was imperative that I travel with you. You had the ship and the legal clearance to land on Europa. I had none of those things, and if I had begun to seek them . . . well, there were already enough questions surrounding my integrity. We could not stand that sort of scrutiny."

"We?" Nissa and the Margrave asked simultaneously, the moment of unity surprising them both equally.

"The machines and I. The robots of Mars. Margrave? Nissa

still doubts me. I don't blame her in the slightest, so would you mind telling her about the ship?"

The form in the water did not answer directly. Nissa looked at Kanu, and for an instant he was on the cusp of doubting himself as well. Perhaps this was the moment when his delusions reached the point of fracture, their grand absurdity becoming apparent even to Kanu.

But the Margrave said, "You'll forgive me for thinking no one would ever come. It has been such a long time."

"It has," Kanu agreed. "But now we need it. Is the ship intact?"

"Yes."

"Wait," Nissa said. "What *ship*? What are you talking about?"

Kanu tried to answer as reasonably and openly as he could. "It's around a hundred years old. It was built here, out of sight, and left to repair and upgrade itself as necessary. It was fast for its day and is even faster now."

"You lying . . ." But then she shook her head, words inadequate to express her disgust at him, at the degree to which she had been used. Kanu knew he deserved worse. He had done a vile, hateful thing.

"There was no other way. And I haven't turned traitor against humanity. This concerns us all—flesh, blood, steel."

"What do you know?" the Margrave asked.

"The robots are still confined to Mars, but their information-gathering capability is much more extensive than any of us ever suspected. And they've found something, Margrave—a signal, from another solar system. It wasn't even aimed at this system. It was picked up by human listening systems around Crucible, but in the process it also came to the attention of the robots' intelligence-gathering apparatus. News of the message was kept secret by Crucible's government, but it's already reached the robots on Mars."

The Margrave stirred in his tube. "And this is of interest to the machines because . . . ?"

"The most probable source of that signal, at least according to their analysis, is another artificial intelligence. Years ago, a simulation of Eunice Akinya travelled to Crucible along with the first colonists. The Watchkeepers permitted human settlement on Crucible on the condition that three subjects went with them into deeper interstellar space. The Eunice construct was one; the other two were my half-mother Chiku Green and an elephant named Dakota. A machine, a woman, an elephant. The Trinity, they were called. The organic members of the Trinity may or may not still be alive—who knows? But the construct was effectively immortal. For the robots on Mars, this realisation presents opportunities on two fronts. They can re-establish ties with the closest thing they have to a creator—communion, if you will. It's also a chance to come to a better understanding of the Watchkeepers. They're bound to have communicated with Eunice on some level, and she's bound to have learned something about them. The possibility of gaining insight into what the Watchkeepers want of us is as significant to humans as it is to robots."

"So your intention is to respond to that signal," the Margrave said, "for which you need your ship. But only Nissa could get you to Europa. I can understand how she might feel . . . aggrieved."

Kanu turned to face his companion. "Nissa—no apology can begin to atone for what I've done to you. You've every right to feel mistreated, to loathe the moment I came back into your life. But you *must* understand the stakes. We stand at a threshold, all of us—people, merfolk, machines. You and I." He looked down at his knotted fingers, shaking his head. "I don't expect forgiveness, but if you can at least bring yourself to understand that what I've done—"

"There's nothing to understand. If you trusted me, if you felt anything for me as a human being, you'd have told the truth from the moment we met."

"I didn't even know the truth myself at that point," Kanu said, persisting despite a rising sense of hopelessness. "I wasn't allowed access to my own memories. I thought we'd met by chance. I was overjoyed . . . I loved you, Nissa. I still do."

"No, you find me useful. Or did, until I'd served my purpose."

"A moment, please," the Margrave said, not impolitely. "We have much to discuss, I know, but I must attend to a matter of immediate and pressing importance. Will you excuse me momentarily?"

Kanu watched the Margrave descend back down the tinted shaft and disappear beneath the level of the floor. Oddly, now that the glass contained nothing but water, he was more acutely aware of the pressure it held back. He imagined it shattering, Europa reclaiming this room quicker than either of them could blink.

"I died," he said eventually, when Nissa said nothing. "On Mars. The accident was genuine and I had no right to survive it. It was only by the grace of the machines that I was put back together. I had a friend among them, a robot called Swift. When they'd restored enough of my mind that I could understand my predicament, Swift offered me a choice. It was very simple."

"To live or die?" Nissa asked finally.

"No. To live, or to live. Swift said that the machines would do what they could for me and send me back to the world of people, and that would be an end to it. I'd still be tainted, of course—I'd still lose my career, my sense of purpose—and my colleagues who died on Mars would still be gone. Shall I tell you about Garudi Dalal? She loved poetry. I took her belongings back to her mother and father, in Madras." But Kanu sighed, beyond explaining himself. "I believed Swift—trusted him. I thought I could help the machines. That's why I agreed to the second option—to allow a part of them to escape Mars inside me—doing what they could not do alone. Allowing them to use me, the way I used you. Life, again—but life serving a deeper purpose."

"You agreed to it," she said flatly.

He nodded, accepting the distinction. "I chose to put my trust in Swift, and this is where it has brought me."

"Conscience clear, then."

Kanu gave a final, defeated shrug. "I know there's nothing I can say to fix this. But I am sorry it happened and with all my heart, I wish you well. These last few weeks—"

"You regret that they happened?"

"No! I regret that it took me so long to find you again. I regret that it took Mars, my death and Swift's bargain to make it happen. I regret losing you in the first place, and I regret that *this* will always stand between us, worse than anything that ever happened before. I am truly sorry, Nissa, but there is nothing more I can offer beyond my apologies." After a moment, he added, "You needn't worry about your return. The

Margrave will take good care of you and make sure you reach the Outside in one piece."

"That's it, then? My usefulness is over, but you've very thoughtfully considered my future welfare?"

"It's not like that."

"I'll tell you what it's like." Nissa stiffened her jaw. Her voice was calm initially, but anger was building behind it. "You saw me as a means to an end—a convenience. Had there been anyone else with the ability to get you to Europa, you'd have lied and schemed your way around them as well."

"That isn't how I feel—"

"I don't give a shit how you feel." Now her voice turned into a snarl. "You've treated me like a piece of disposable equipment, a tool. Something you use once and throw away. And no matter what crocodile tears you manage to dredge up now, no matter what ersatz contrition, you went into this with cold-blooded calculation. You knew exactly what had to be done and exactly who had to be manipulated. You thought it through—planned it like a campaign. The happy accident of us meeting? Two old lovers reconnecting? Sleeping with me? You probably have it all worked out on a diagram."

"All of that was sincere—"

"You're a snake, Kanu. An emotionless reptile. It sickens me that I ever thought you possessed a human conscience. And do you know what? You haven't just lied to me; you haven't just betrayed me and wasted my time. You've fucked up my work. You've fucked up everything I planned to do on Europa—years of planning, years of devotion to the memory of your stupid dead grandmother and her fucking art."

"I'm sorry."

"I'm sorry, I'm sorry, I'm sorry." She parroted him with a sneer. "That's all you've got, isn't it? But what more should I expect? You're a diplomat. You're used to words making everything right. Not now, though. You don't get out of this with a few spoken charms. But why am I even bothering? Why am I deluding myself that this conversation means a damn thing to you? As soon as you're on your ship, you'll be off and away—and you won't have to give me a second's consideration after that."

"I will. You're wrong about me—wrong about how I feel. If there's a way I can make this right—"

"There isn't. Not now, not ever."

A rising, piston-like movement caught his eye. It was the Margrave returning to the room. Kanu's vision had adapted to the gloom since his arrival and he spied more of the Margrave's dark anatomy and regalia, gaining a clearer sense of bony integuments and hard, hornlike growths.

"I had hoped they would see more sense," their host said. "Our rash friends, the ones who hampered your arrival?"

"The ones you skewered?" Kanu asked.

"We only skewered one," the Margrave countered, as if this was acceptable. "The ringleader. To send a message to the others not to trouble my jurisdictional waters again."

Nissa asked, "And did it work?"

"Not *quite* as I had intended. I am afraid that they have been gathering in greater numbers around the limits of Underthrace ever since your arrival. Of course, this happens from time to time and they are always rebuffed. But the present concentration . . . I regret that I may have precipitated something closer to civil war."

"Are we in danger?" Kanu asked.

"No! Not in the slightest. Underthrace will hold. The lines will not be crossed."

The king's grip was faltering, Kanu sensed. It might have been faltering for months or years but their arrival must have quickened some underlying process of collapse.

"Can you guarantee it, Margrave?"

"As my life is my word. The Consolidation forces are of no concern to you, either."

Kanu looked at Nissa, then back at the Margrave. "What about them?"

"They've landed. Six of their enforcement ships are now on our ice. I believe they intend to exploit the internal difficulties we are currently facing. Foolish beyond words—and displaying their utter contempt for the mutual respect of treaties and rights!"

"This isn't a coincidence, is it?" Nissa said. "The Consolidation hasn't just randomly chosen this exact moment to retake Europa. We've brought it about, just by coming here."

"You may have provided the distraction they were hoping for," the Margrave said.

"Nissa's safety is paramount," Kanu said. "Whatever it takes, she mustn't come to harm."

"Nissa can take care of herself," Nissa said. "In fact, I'm leaving now, before this whole fucking moon blows up."

"What about the art?" the Margrave asked.

"You think I give a damn about that now? Get me back to *Fall of Night*. If I have to fight my way to the ice, I will."

"The art belongs to Nissa now," Kanu said, rising effortlessly from his chair. "Look after it, Margrave—it's hers when she returns. And I know she will, one day. Nissa spent years putting this trip together—she deserves better than to have it end like this."

"Will she be in trouble?" the Margrave asked. "Your departure will not go unnoticed, Kanu, especially not now."

"When I'm on my way and safely out of reach, I'll issue a statement clarifying that Nissa was an innocent party in all this."

If he had expected some token of gratitude for this promised gesture, none was forthcoming. Her anger was still there, contained like the water in the glass—megapascals of it.

"Don't waste your precious breath, Kanu."

The Margrave escorted Kanu deeper into the bowels of Underthrace, until at last they reached the flooded vault in which the Akinya ship lay waiting, entombed these past hundred years. They viewed it from a gallery, floodlights scratching out across the water to compensate for the feebleness of Kanu's eyes. The Margrave, floating next to him in an extension of his water-filled pipe, had placed another pair of goggles over those he already wore. This must be a sun-bright blaze to him, Kanu thought, like the inside of a furnace.

"Thank you for looking after it."

"I can't promise it will work. That's *your* business. But we have kept the ship in the minimally powered configuration your family stipulated and supplied it with the raw materials it requested to upgrade itself. If it fails to function, I would rather not accept the blame."

"If it fails, I doubt very much there'll be anyone around to parcel out blame."

The ship had been built for compactness, but even Kanu was

surprised by how small it looked, enclosed within the walls of this larger structure. It had been conceived for exploration rather than the conveyance of cargo or passengers. A kilometre tall, was his recollection, but it looked smaller to his eyes. It was torpedo-shaped, a cylinder with rounded ends and a few angular bumps and protrusions to mar its basic symmetry.

"I'd like to go aboard."

"Of course. It's your ship."

"Does it have a name?"

"Not yet."

The Margrave showed him to the connecting bridge. The aquatic could come no further—the ship was not equipped for water-breathers—but Kanu had no great need of a guide. As he stepped aboard, the ship recognised him like an old friend. It was reading his DNA and his body's morphology, plumbing the deep mysteries of his mind—verifying, to its own satisfaction, that he met the required criteria.

Akinya.

Thus satisfied, the ship opened its secrets to him. It was still cold in the corridors and passageways, but light and warmth were now returning. Displays came on as Kanu walked past them—scrolling updates and complicated diagrams. He had never been aboard this ship before, had played no direct part in its construction, but it felt as familiar as if he was wandering the hallways of a childhood home.

Kanu found his way to the command deck. It was four-fifths of the way along the ship, near the rounded front. The deck would have been spacious for a small crew; for one man, it was outlandish.

But the deck was also extremely simple in its layout, its provisions reduced to the elegant essentials: a single chair, a bank of controls in a horseshoe configuration, an illusion of wide-sweeping windows. In fact—as Kanu well knew—the room was dozens of metres in from the ship's skin. He surveyed subtle hints of East African influence in the patterning and coloration of his surroundings. Inlays of wood and metal, glowing filaments of green and red and yellow. A selection of small black sculptures set into lit alcoves—Maasai figures, Kanu thought, wondering if they might be Sunday's handiwork. A bas-relief design of blocky interlocking elephants had been worked into the black framework of his chair. A map of the world radiated out from beneath it, with Africa at its focus.

Kanu settled into the chair, which automatically slithered a restraint across his lap, then tightened it. The horseshoe controls moved obligingly closer to his fingertips. He stared at the sweep of displays and keypads with a sort of numbed recognition, as if seeing it in the first moments of waking.

"Kanu Akinya," he stated, as if following a silent prompt. "Assuming control. Request departure readiness."

The ship answered in the tongue with which he had addressed it. It spoke Swahili with a soothing tone, as if there could be no problem, no contingency, for which it were not magnificently equipped.

"Welcome, Kanu. Systems are transitioning to operational condition. Final fault checks and calibration procedures are now in progress. Chibesa core is initialising. Estimated time to departure readiness: six hours, thirteen minutes."

"Give me an option for departure within two to three hours. In fact, present me with a range of options and associated risk factors."

"A moment please, Kanu."

The console presented him with his choices. They ranged from an immediate departure, which brought with it a fifteen per cent chance of losing the ship completely, to the more reasonable alternative of waiting the full six hours, by which point the likelihood of losing the ship would be negligible—at least to a fault of its own making.

If he insisted on leaving in three hours, the likelihood was down to a tolerable two per cent.

Odds he could live with, given the stakes.

The console chimed and a voice spoke from it. "Kanu, this is the Margrave. I'm afraid I had to leave you for a moment. Matters have taken another turn and I think you need to be aware of it."

Kanu pressed himself back into his seat, bracing for the worst. "Go on."

"The Consolidation are through. Their ships are still on the ice, but they must have brought high-speed tunnelling devices and submarine combat equipment with them. My agents report three or four separate points of entry into the ocean, as well as an increase in their orbital presence. They are bringing in forces from across Jovian space and further afield."

Kanu nodded, the news exactly as bad as he had feared. "So there are enemy—I mean Consolidation—forces in the ocean? In addition to the other Regals trying to batter their way into Underthrace?"

"Things have indeed come to a pretty pass."

"If this is in any way our doing . . . my doing . . . you have my sincere apologies."

"We will endure, Kanu—have no doubt of that. In the meantime, though, you might wish to leave sooner rather than later."

"Things are that bad?"

"I cannot guarantee the security of Underthrace. If—when—it falls, it will happen quickly. You should be aware of that."

"My safety is secondary—it's Nissa who matters. She hates me now, and frankly I don't blame her. I've treated her badly, Margrave—inexcusably—but I couldn't see any other way to get here. I don't want her coming to any harm on my account."

"Let me worry about Nissa. I have taken a personal interest in her welfare, and will continue to do so."

Kanu allowed himself the meagre consolation of knowing she would be well looked after, at least to the limits of the Margrave's power. It did nothing to lessen his remorse, or his sorrow at the terms of their farewell, but if he could trust that her safety was taken care of, it would be one less thing on his mind.

"Thank you."

"I wish you had parted on better terms, Kanu."

"What's done is done," he said, returning his attention to the console. The options it had given were still there, and the numbers had scarcely changed. What had been a fourteen per cent chance of disaster if he left immediately had now dropped to twelve point six. Even as he watched, the digits shifted again. The ship was doing everything it could to better his chances. Was a risk factor of one in ten tolerable? He had cheated death once—did that allow him a different perspective on such matters? He did not think so. He might be old, but these last few weeks with Nissa had given him every incentive to keep living.

Equally, he could not wait too long.

CHAPTER 17

No one dared speak of murder, at least not to begin with. But it was the only thing any of them was thinking.

Two things quickly became apparent. Dr. Nhamedjo conducted an examination of his body—what remained of it—and arrived at a clear medical conclusion. Mposi had almost certainly not been conscious when he entered the well. Despite the gash on his forehead, there were no traces of blood anywhere in the Knowledge Room, and no sign that he had struggled or suffered obvious distress in there. The presumption was that he had been hurt somewhere else—knocked out or killed—and then transported to the Knowledge Room, with a view to having the nanomachines break down and dispose of his body.

That was the second thing: the nanomachines in the well had been reprogrammed to enable them to process and absorb human tissue.

It was not supposed to be possible, Vasin told them. Granted, nanotechnology was, by its nature, almost infinitely protean. The difference between a medicinal form and a military version lay only in the expressed instruction mode—the deep-programming architecture. But Vasin had been assured that it was all but impossible to change one to the other, especially given the limited resources available on her ship.

Someone had managed it, though.

"It wasn't a perfect solution," Vasin said, when Goma and Ru were in her cabin two hours after Mposi's body was found. "So I'm told. The nanotech's returned to a safe configuration, but it's still contaminated by the presence of many kilos of organic matter—enough to affect its efficiency." She looked up sharply. "I am sorry, Goma, but I see no gentle way to speak of these things." Goma held her composure with a force of will—there was nothing to be gained from going to pieces now.

"Whoever did this," Ru said, "they'd have known their way around the working of the well pretty thoroughly, wouldn't they?" Goma was grateful to Ru for speaking so bluntly. It was more than she could have done.

"They'd have needed more than basic familiarity with the systems," Vasin said.

"Then they weren't expecting a perfect solution, just a means of buying time. If they could hide the body this way rather than keeping it in a cabin—somewhere easily searched—they might have bought themselves a few days."

"For what?" Goma asked. She was drained, shocked, numbed—so overcome with grief that she could not begin to feel it as a distinct mental state. She was swimming in it, breathing it into her lungs. The only emotion she felt was a sense that the universe had been wrenched rudely off course, carrying her along with it. She had to speak to Mposi about this. He would have something sensible and calming to say, a way to lessen her problems.

Uncle. Uncle. Uncle.

"This wasn't planned," Ru offered. "That's my take on it, anyway. Someone killed him, and it wasn't supposed to happen like this. Why would anyone ever think killing someone on a ship was a good idea?"

"Because they were insane," Goma said.

"They killed him," Ru went on, "but there wasn't time to make it look like an accident or find a better way of disposing of the body. This was the best alternative they could come up with. They knew it would be discovered sooner or later—you can't just lock the Knowledge Room and expect no one to notice—so all they needed was a little time to . . . hide their tracks, maybe." She looked up sharply. "Gandhari—whoever did this?"

"Yes?"

"They had a means of locking that door. A bangle like yours—or the capability to alter one. It can't be someone like Goma or me—we knew next to nothing about this ship until we were aboard it."

"So technical staff—one of my own people? Is that your suspicion?"

Ru hesitated then nodded. "I'm sorry, but who else could it be? A scientist, maybe—but I'm one of them, and my expertise doesn't begin to extend to this kind of thing. Nor does Goma's. Mposi himself couldn't have done this, even if he had a reason to."

"He wasn't wearing any clothes," Goma said. "How did he get from his room to the well without someone noticing?"

"I suspect he was dressed, whether he was moving on his own or being carried," Vasin said. "Whoever did this probably feared the nanotechnology wouldn't treat his clothes and his body in the same fashion. They must have undressed him in the Knowledge Room, then taken the clothes somewhere else. Easier to hide clothes than a body—easier to dispose of them later, too."

"Why?" Ru asked. "What did *he* do, that someone had to kill him for?"

"I have a good idea," Goma said. "Mposi told me something not long ago. You can check with Crucible, if you like, Gandhari. He was in contact with them."

"About what?" Vasin asked.

"Sabotage," Goma said, with a sort of flat resignation. "They warned him there was a possibility of it. Something on this ship—a weapon, maybe, that you don't know about, put aboard by people who don't want this expedition to succeed."

"Why didn't he tell me?"

"He was trying to gather more information. I don't think he wanted to come to you with something half-baked, especially if it was a false alarm."

"Dear god," Vasin said. "What kind of weapon was he thinking of? What was he looking for—how much did he tell you?"

"You had better speak to Maslin Karayan."

"He's the suspect? Is that what Mposi told you?"

Goma closed her eyes. This was all too much, a surfeit of troubles over and above those she had already accepted.

"Maybe. There's someone else you should look at. Karayan was asking what Mposi knew about Peter Grave." She swallowed. "We see him as a Second Chancer, but he's different from the others. There's something about him. Even *they* don't trust him."

"You think he killed Mposi?" Vasin asked.

"Why don't you ask him?" Goma answered.

Before the news of Mposi's death reached the entire ship—which it was bound to do, with or without official disclosure—Vasin declared a state of emergency, a condition-yellow situation. This was wisely chosen, being only one level above the routine condition green: not serious enough to suggest that the ship or its occupants were in immediate peril, but sufficient to limit the movements of crew and passengers, and oblige everyone who was already in their cabins to remain there. It was the kind of alert that might attend a problem with the air supply, such as the presence of a mild toxin or a breakdown of the proper equilibrium of component gases. There had been a couple of condition-yellow situations since they left Crucible, and the encounter with the Watchkeeper had elevated the emergency status a whole two levels above yellow, so this development was neither unprecedented nor liable to cause panic.

"Do you want us to return to our room?" Goma asked Vasin.

"No—you're here now so you might as well stay. I can't completely eliminate you as suspects—or anyone else, for that matter, including myself, until we have more evidence—but the fact that you were actively searching for Mposi and directed our attention to the Knowledge Room . . . Well, if you had murdered him—and again I am sorry that we must speak so bluntly, Goma—but if you had done it, you would not be in such a rush to bring the body to my attention."

"I appreciate your compassion, Gandhari," Goma said, "but he was murdered, and the only way to find out who did it is to talk about it. I might as well get used to it."

While they waited in her quarters, Vasin's immediate subordinates had sealed the Knowledge Room and were now sweeping the rest of the ship, with a particular view to apprehending Maslin Karayan and Peter Grave.

"In theory," Vasin said, "the bangles' localising function should enable us to identify the killer just by backtracking everyone's movements and finding out who was with Mposi since you last saw him. But whoever did this clearly knew their way around both the bangles and the nanomachines in the Knowledge Room. If they could tamper with one, they could just as easily tamper with the other—concealing their movements, if necessary. Still, it looks like they were in a rush—perhaps they were not as thorough as they might have wished."

It took under thirty minutes to find the two men and bring them both to Vasin's quarters. Neither showed any signs of having offered resistance, but of the two, only Maslin Karayan looked like a man who had just been dragged out of bed. He had a puffy, dishevelled appearance—even his beard was unruly.

Peter Grave by contrast was fully dressed, clean-shaven and had been apprehended en route to his cabin, apparently on his way back from the connecting spine.

They were in the formal stateroom adjoining Vasin's private quarters. Vasin was seated behind her desk, Aiyana Loring and Nasim Caspari to either side of their captain and Ru and Goma at one end of the desk. Maslin Karayan and Peter Grave were seated opposite Vasin, and Dr. Nhamedjo stood off to one side with his arms folded.

"Do you know why you're here?" Vasin asked the two Second Chancers.

"I'm waiting for you to explain why we're under a yellow emergency when there is clearly nothing wrong with the ship," said the older man, bristling with righteous indignation.

"What's happened?" asked Grave, his tone milder but still demanding of answers.

"Mposi Akinya is dead," Vasin said. "He was found a few hours ago, in the Knowledge Room. The nanomachinery was in the process of digesting his body. Aiyana—can you confirm what happened?"

"Machines had been reprogrammed—their core architecture altered? Very difficult thing. Process of disposal would have been complete."

"Would anything have alerted us about what had happened to him?" Vasin asked.

Loring shook ver head, but the gesture was equivocal. "Not immediately? Nanotech was programmed to revert to a safe mode once the body was broken down. Conceal obvious evidence of its earlier reprogramming? Safe enough in the well—wouldn't have started trying to dissolve you. All that absorbed biomass? Affected it in subtle ways, but take an expert to spot the signs."

Both men remained silent. Eventually Maslin Karayan said, "I do not know what to say. We had our differences, but my respect for Mposi was total."

"I heard you arguing," Goma said before anyone else had a chance to respond. "I came to see Mposi and you were shouting at each other."

"That was months ago," Karayan said. "Besides, I had no grudge against him—it was just differences of opinion. Heartfelt differences, true, but I don't go around killing the people I disagree with. And even if I did, I'd be a fool to hurt Mposi, knowing what you'd think."

"I'm aware of your background, Maslin," Vasin said, tapping one of several printed papers laid out on her desk. "On the face of it, there's nothing in it to suggest any expertise with nanomachinery. If you had such skills, would you tell me?"

"And incriminate myself?"

"No, but the sooner our relevant technical experience is out in the open, the quicker this will be over. The same goes for you, Peter—if there's anything in your history that isn't in your biographical file, I want to know about it now."

"What about Aiyana?" Karayan said, looking at the other scientist. "Haven't you as good as admitted your own expertise with nanomachinery?"

"Know enough to understand how difficult this was, Maslin," Loring answered. "Well beyond my capabilities. Basic expertise, different thing. General grasp of shipboard communications and security functions? Circumvent the security protocol on the bangles? Could if I wanted to."

"So could many of us," Caspari said, "but Aiyana hasn't stated any sort of open opposition to this expedition, and the two of you have."

"That's a gross mischaracterisation," Karayan said, flinching back as if he had been pricked with a needle.

"You in particular," Caspari went on. "When you saw you could not prevent the expedition from happening, you used your political leverage to join the crew. Fundamentally, though, you're still opposed to it. You are here to observe, to influence critical decision-making, but given the opportunity—as the Watchkeeper proved—you wouldn't hesitate to send us back to Crucible. If sabotage was one of the tools at your disposal—"

"Nasim," said Dr. Nhamedjo gently, "we are all aggrieved by what has happened. Many of us share a basic scepticism where the activities of the Second Chancers are concerned. But we must not allow that scepticism to colour our judgement."

"So much for your neutrality, Doctor," Karayan said.

"Medicine is science, Maslin, and to me your tenets are fundamentally regressive and anti-scientific. I do not think my personal views are a surprise to anyone."

The doctor's wide, boyish face appeared, to Goma, to contain a steeliness of character she had not detected before. But he was still smiling, and his manner was as peaceable as it had ever been.

"You are here by democratic means, though," Nhamedjo continued, "and you are human beings, with spouses and children. I presume some of them may be able to vouch for your whereabouts when Mposi was missing. Frankly, though, I don't need their testimony to convince me that you played no part in this. Why would *anyone* hurt Mposi Akinya?"

"Tell them what you know," Vasin said, nodding at Goma. "For the benefit of everyone present."

As numb as she felt, unwilling as she was to start thinking of her uncle in the past tense, she forced some composure upon herself. "Mposi was in contact with Crucible."

"We all are?" Loring said.

"This was different. Some kind of private, political channel—a secret hotline. It makes sense that a man like my uncle would have something like that. Anyway, they told Mposi we had a problem."

Caspari's hands were perfectly steepled. "What kind?"

"A threat, aboard the ship. A sabotage device, something like that, and maybe someone to operate it. That's as much as he told me." Goma swallowed—it was harder than she expected, just keeping the tremble out of her voice. She knew that if she let her mental defences down for an instant, she would soon be a sobbing wreck. "Mposi asked me to keep an eye out. He couldn't risk dragging Captain Vasin into it until he was sure of his facts. But there were no suspects I could suggest."

"Except me," Karayan said, "I presume?"

Goma looked down at her own hands, useless and sweaty in her lap. Nothing had prepared her for this, not even a life on Crucible with a mother the world detested.

"Actually, Maslin, of the two of you, I suspected Peter first."

Grave looked at her sharply and started to say something, but Maslin Karayan cut him off.

"What did Mposi say about Peter, Goma?"

She thought back to that conversation, trying to piece it together in her memory without adding layers of half-truth and supposition. "Just that you didn't know much about him."

Dr. Nhamedjo leaned in. "Aren't you both Second Chancers?"

"We are," Grave stated, speaking before Karayan had a chance. "But the movement is far more heterogeneous than outsiders tend to presume. The expedition put unusual pressures on us—testing divisions that were already present. The twelve of us don't stand for one strand of Second Chance thinking—we represent an assortment of viewpoints, from the progressive to the conservative." He squared his shoulders. "Maslin didn't know me when I joined the ship—that's true enough. But why would he? I came from a different part of Crucible, from a different strand of the Second Chance movement."

"A more conservative one, more strongly opposed to the expedition?" Ru asked.

"We all have our beliefs," Grave replied equably.

"What is *her* role in this?" Karayan asked, nodding at Ru with blatant contempt.

"*Her* role is that she was with me when we found my uncle being eaten by nanomachines," Goma said. "And I'd take one of her over ten of you any day."

"Thank you," Vasin said, with a barely audible cough. "Tempers are high and nerves are raw, but we still have to live aboard the same ship. Until we've formally got to the bottom of this, none of us is yet considered a suspect. We are all just potential witnesses—some of whom may hold clues to what happened. Is that understood?"

Grave mouthed an almost silent "Thank you."

"Have you anything to say about a potential sabotage effort?" Vasin asked him.

"I am here as a legitimate member of the delegation. But I was also tasked to maintain vigilance against a possible threat, whatever it might turn out to be, and from whichever direction."

There was a moment of silence. Goma shared the surprise and disbelief of those around her. "Oh, please," she mouthed to herself. But before she could frame a more eloquent objection, Vasin was already speaking.

"And the nature of this threat?"

Grave's voice sounded small. "It wasn't clear."

"Why was no mention of this made before departure?" Caspari asked.

Grave cleared something from his throat, his tone becoming more confident. "The agreement to allow the expedition was fragile enough as it was. If word had got out about a possible sabotage threat, it would have been bad for the expedition and twice as bad for the Second Chance movement." Grave was looking at Karayan now, as if he might have been appealing to his support. "Of course, we had our arguments against the expedition in broader terms, but this was not the way for it to end. It was in the best interests of all concerned to continue as normal, but inform me of the possible threat."

"Can any of this be confirmed by Crucible?" Vasin asked.

"I don't know. I was entrusted with this information under conditions of great secrecy. There are no names I can offer, no hidden cabals. Maslin—were you made aware of any similar concerns?"

"If I had, I'd have spoken up already."

Grave looked down, his expression impassive. He had been abandoned by his one possible ally, but the development did not appear to surprise him.

"I'll speak to our government," Vasin said. "Maybe they can confirm Mposi's side of things, at least—this hotline, the threat of which he was made aware. But it'll take at least fifteen days to hear from them. Until then, we're on our own. I'm afraid I must look closely at Second Chancer involvement—but that doesn't mean I'm making an automatic assumption of guilt on anyone's part. Maslin—you were asleep, with your wife and family. Your children have their own sleeping areas, but you'd all have known if anyone was coming or going?"

"Yes. I was in my room all night."

"And, Peter—you were up and about, weren't you?"

He nodded; it would have been pointless to deny it. "That's correct."

"You appeared to be on your way back from the connecting spine. You're allowed access to some areas of it—we all are—but I'm not sure why you needed to be there."

"Mposi asked to meet me there. When he didn't show up, I started making my way back."

"How well did you know Mposi?"

"Well enough."

"To murder him?" Goma asked.

"To believe him," Grave answered levelly. He held her eyes with his, the intensity of his gaze unnerving. "And I didn't kill him. Which means someone else did."

CHAPTER 18

"Secure for departure," Kanu said. "Close all locks, disconnect all bridges and umbilicals."

"If I might trouble you," the Margrave said, "I feel you should know that the Consolidation intruders are closing rapidly on Underthrace."

"Aren't they running into the other Regals?"

"It's nothing they aren't prepared for, I am afraid. Of course, if they were encountering anything more intimidating than barely organised ruffians . . . well, my people will give them a welcome they won't forget, but I cannot promise miracles. I know you would rather wait until your ship is totally ready, but if you wish to avoid local difficulties—"

"I understand. Margrave—this may be a silly question, but might you be safer aboard the ship rather than remaining in Underthrace?"

"Could your ship keep me alive? Would you have a means of returning me to Europa once you are under way?"

"I don't know," Kanu said. "I suppose there are escape capsules, maybe a shuttle or lander . . ."

"But you will most likely have need of such things when you reach your destination. No, I cannot put you to that much trouble, not when you have problems of your own. It is very kind of you, Kanu, but my home is here."

"And Nissa?"

"She is safely out of harm's way."

"Thank you, Margrave. When my family has a chance to show its gratitude . . . well, we will. You can count on that."

The console changed its displays. "Emergency launch readiness now achieved," the ship informed him. "Estimated risk factor below ten per cent."

"Ceiling charges primed and ready, Margrave?"

"As they will ever be."

"Then we're launching. Good luck with Underthrace. I can't promise I'll be in touch for a little while, but . . ."

"Our thoughts go with each other. Farewell, Kanu."

"Goodbye, Margrave."

Kanu readied himself for the jolt of acceleration, but when the clamps relinquished their hold, he felt only the mildest of shoves, no more violent than the movement of an elevator. So far, so good—at least the docking clamps were functional—but the true tests lay ahead. He had yet to start the engine.

Next came a barely felt crash as the rising ship crunched through the glass cupola at the top of the enclosing building. Since the water pressure had been the same on either side of the cupola, nothing slowed the ship's progress. Kanu felt the occasional scrape or grind of resistance, but nothing that should trouble the hull. And then they were through, clear of Underthrace and in the black void of the sea. The ship was still accelerating as smoothly as if it were being pushed up from below by a giant piston. Of course, it was one thing to punch through Underthrace, and quite another to reach space itself.

"Kanu," said a voice off to his right. "Might now be an opportune moment to speak?"

He jerked around in the seat, convinced until that moment that he had the ship to himself.

The frock-coated Swift was standing by the wall next to one of the alcoved figures. His hands were laced demurely before him, like a butler waiting for instructions. Kanu drew breath and started to speak, but before he could utter a word Swift raised a hand. "I'm not physically here, just a figment."

"I knew that."

"There was never a satisfactory time to present myself aboard Nissa's ship—and besides, you had enough to be getting on with."

"And this is your idea of a 'satisfactory time'?"

"This is an *excellent* time." Swift gestured at the surroundings of the control deck. "This is a fine piece of engineering, by human standards. But you have only limited experience with the operation of spacecraft and—I think it fair to say—none at all in a ship of this nature. Very shortly, though, its capabilities will be put to the test. You will need maximum knowledge of the ship—what it can do and, just as crucially, what it cannot. I suggest that you allow me—the machine part of you—to take precedence, at least until we are in free space."

"You don't know this ship any better than I do."

"That is true, but I can learn faster. I also have a great deal of technical knowledge to draw upon and the not inconsiderable advantage of being utterly infallible in my decision-making. We will hit the ice in about eight minutes, if those depth readings are to be trusted. I think that should be sufficient time for me to master the controls."

Kanu knew that a moment like this was coming—the moment when he had no option but to surrender himself to the machines.

"You didn't need to ask, did you? You're so much a part of me now that you could have taken me over at any point—hijacked complete control of my nervous system."

"If the integration were not as thorough as it is," Swift said, "it would have been easily detected. To answer your question, though: yes, I could have assumed control at any time and I will do so in an instant if your life is imperilled. But as this situation is not quite that critical, I thought it polite to ask first. We have, I believe, just under seven minutes and thirty seconds left now. Will you allow me, Kanu?"

At least one life—possibly much more than one life—hinged on this moment. For an instant, it was more than he could bear. But if he did not give himself completely to Swift, there was no point in carrying on. He had come this far, from the limbo of death on Mars, to serve one truth: the machines were not his enemy, and he was not theirs.

"Do it."

Swift walked over to Kanu, slipped his form through the horseshoe console as if it were made of gas and lowered himself into the chair Kanu already occupied. The figment's body folded neatly into the same space and submerged beneath Kanu's skin.

For a breath or two, Kanu felt no change.

Then Swift had him.

Since the thing inside his head was entirely biological—a separate personality utilising the same meat substrate on which his own consciousness now ran—Swift could only communicate with the outside world via the channels of Kanu's own senses. He could not address the ship directly or read its mysteries via some direct neural connection. But he could see, and speak, and listen, and make Kanu's hands move with card-sharp speed across the console.

Kanu, in turn, felt himself being ruthlessly puppeteered. The muscles and tendons in his arms were not used to interpreting such a barrage of nerve signals. His eyes moved from one focus to another so quickly that Kanu's visual flow shattered. He could feel the ocular muscles being cruelly overclocked, made to run faster than nature had intended. He visualised himself as he might have appeared had anyone been there to witness him: a man in a chair, twitching and jerking as if in the throes of a seizure or some prolonged electrical execution. He was even speaking—or rather giving out short, yelping utterances that bore little resemblance to Swahili, or indeed any human language, for that matter.

But the ship understood. It understood and it was talking back, giving Swift the information and resources he needed.

When Swift relinquished absolute control, Kanu felt the cutting of the puppet strings as an almost psychic severance. He slumped back in the seat, drained and in no small amount of pain after the way he had been manipulated. Swift was still there, though, his presence riding Kanu's consciousness like a passenger.

"I've made some adjustments to the display options. If you look up, the view through the ceiling shows exactly what is above us as we ascend. As you can see, the Margrave has not let us down—the charges are detonating."

They were still looking through inky kilometres of ocean, so the light reaching Kanu's eyes must have been amplified many times. Nonetheless, the stuttering milky flashes—like the lightning from a storm system well over the horizon—could only be the demolition charges, sewn through the ice when the ship was first entombed. There appeared to be no end to the explosions—dozens, then hundreds of separate pulses of light tracing a cobweb of radial and concentric lines. They were shattering the overlying ice, rendering it locally weak rather than blasting it away in a single massive detonation. Twenty kilometres of it was pulverised—ice turning to slush, slush to water, water to steam—while great chunks, house- or palace-sized, remained intact.

"It's not enough," Kanu said. "We've miscalculated. We'll never punch through that!"

"It will be sufficient. As soon as there is a clear passage to space, the water will begin to geyser out into the vacuum. That in turn will help disperse the remaining fragments. Besides, the charges are still detonating! He must have sewn thousands of them. For a human, he has shown remarkable thoroughness."

"I'm not sure he'd take that as a compliment."

Kanu's faith in the Margrave was not misplaced. As the ship closed the distance to the ceiling, so the explosions finally pushed a channel through to the Outside, a portal to the rest of the universe, and from that moment the process became self-sustaining as the water turned instantly to vapour, and the rocketing vapour forced the remaining fragments further apart.

"Core initialising," Swift reported. "Momentum will carry us through the breach and we'll switch immediately to full Chibesa thrust before Europa pulls us back. That will be the moment of maximum risk, Kanu. On the positive side, if things *do* go wrong, there's little likelihood of you knowing about it. I should brace, if I were you. Our passage will still be a little bumpy."

And it was—ice clanged and scraped against the hull on all sides—but Kanu was reasonably certain that such things had been allowed for. Even so, he gripped the arms of his seat and jammed his head hard against the headrest. The vibrations made his eyes blur. He closed them and willed this to be over. The rough passage reached a moment of maximum turbulence, and then the knocks and clangs and ice-rumbles began to diminish. A moment or two later they were clear, the ride perfectly smooth, and Kanu felt himself begin to float from the chair until the restraint redoubled its hold on him.

"Clear of the surface," Swift said. "Pivoting to bring drive exhaust clear of the horizon. Ignition in three . . . two . . ."

When weight returned, it felt as if someone had driven a mallet into the base of his spine. He sensed a bony shock wave moving up to his skull, the compression and relaxation of vertebrae, the sequenced stressing of nerves and muscle groups, gravity reaching and then exceeding Europa's pull. Had to be one gee, maybe two. Swift was really gunning it.

"One-third of a gee," Swift said, adding insult to Kanu's discomfort. "Chibesa core operating normally. The ship will run some automatic calibration checks then increase to half a gee. Congratulations, Mr. Akinya—you have yourself a starship."

At last Kanu opened his eyes. He still felt jammed into the seat, oppressed by cruel force.

"It works."

"Early days, I believe is the expression. Still, to have come this far is unquestionably something. Have you considered a name for this ship?"

"It's obvious, isn't it? *Icebreaker.* That's what it should have been all along."

"*Icebreaker* it is, then. There's a family connection to that name, isn't there—some other ship?"

"If you say so, Swift."

Kanu felt none of the triumph he had expected, only a nagging ulcerous guilt, a sense that he had fled the scene of a crime.

"Will the wound heal?"

"Soon enough. Actually, we've done very little harm compared to the damage inflicted by natural impactors over billions of years. And just as Europa's ice has re-formed over those wounds, so it will eventually seal this gap."

"I hope the Margrave is all right."

"So do I, but right now we have our own concerns. Our emergence point has naturally become the focus for those Consolidation vehicles. They are attempting to close on us."

"And if they get within range and try to stop us?"

"Judging from these control interfaces, we appear to have weapons. Your family obviously thought they might come in useful."

Kanu had spent enough time under the shadow of the Martian defence fortresses that the thought of space weapons did not immediately revolt him. The Consolidation vehicles would certainly be armed—even if most of those armaments could be excused as normal precautionary hardware. Space was full of things that sometimes needed to be shot out of the way or destroyed.

Sometimes those things were other ships.

"We won't use them except in self-defence. Is that understood, Swift?"

"Self-defence is an exceedingly elastic concept. Would you be so good as to narrow the parameters?"

Before he could answer, the console chimed.

"Incoming transmission from one of the enforcement vehicles," Swift said. "Addressed directly to you. Who could know you are aboard when we've barely started our journey?"

"You know exactly who if you've been riding inside my head since Mars. Yevgeny Korsakov."

Korsakov's face loomed large before Kanu, superimposed over the forward area of the window. He looked, if anything, even older than when they had last spoken—his skin collapsing into the event horizon of his skull, which would soon claim everything near it. The collar of his UON uniform was too generous for his neck, as if he had pulled the wrong outfit from the wardrobe. A wizened child wearing his father's uniform.

"Well, Kanu, I had my suspicions, but they didn't come close to this. You'll forgive me for shadowing you in this fashion?"

There was almost no time lag now. "Everyone needs a pastime, Yevgeny. I'm just sorry I became yours."

"Oh, don't feel bad about it. It wasn't your fault. If I blame anyone, it's myself."

"Really?"

"I should have listened to my instincts."

"Your instincts ended my career. Wasn't that enough?"

"Evidently not. In fact, all I've really done is facilitate something else. Isn't that true? You'd have done your best to leave Mars no matter what I said or did."

"It must be nice to have all the answers."

"I'd like a few more. You've done very well with that ship, Kanu, and in the long run I know we'll never stop you reaching interstellar space. But we're in the short run right now. These enforcement craft can easily outpace you and we have the means to disable your ship. Don't make this any harder than it needs to be."

"Since when have you been a mouthpiece for the Consolidation?"

"Our differences look slight now compared to the danger you pose. I agreed to an information exchange with our allies in the Consolidation. They were more than willing to accommodate me."

"Which ship are you in?"

"Does it matter?"

"It might. I am not a traitor. I have not sided with the machines or turned my back on humanity. I love humanity. I love my own people. But the machines are an opportunity—a chance to do great things, together. Between us we must confront the Watchkeepers, or at least find out what they want of us."

"How did they turn you, Kanu? How did the machines make you see everything through their eyes?"

"They didn't. I chose my own path. I'm still choosing it now."

When Korsakov replied, all the reasonableness had gone. It was as if he had given up any hope of negotiation. "I cannot persuade you to stop, Kanu, but you should be aware of our capabilities. You will receive no warning shot across your bows when our long-range weapons lock on to you."

"I understand, Yev. And you know I won't stop. That's clear, isn't it?"

"I suppose it is, Kanu."

"Then for the love of god please turn around. I am also armed."

"You may be misguided, Kanu, but I know you are not a murderer. You were an ambassador, a man who stood for peace and negotiation, for the non-violent solution. You won't fire on us. You don't have it in you."

"You're right," Kanu answered. "I was an ambassador, and I stood for all those things. I believed in them with all my heart. But then I died."

He offered them one last chance to abandon the chase. When Korsakov refused, Kanu gave Swift the order to fire on the pursuing craft, once more allowing Swift control of his body. It was supposed to be the minimum effective force, a disabling shot. He was certain Swift had done his best to comply.

But in space there was sometimes no option but to kill.

Afterwards, with the memory of the two amplified flashes—two virtually simultaneous detonations—still fresh in his mind, Kanu felt no sense of relief or escape. With their present speed and course and the power available in reserve, Swift assured him there was no real prospect of any further trouble. The drive was functioning perfectly, the ship capable of much more than it was already giving. They had cleared Jovian space and were now burning out of the ecliptic, soon to be moving faster than any other human-made thing within a light-year of the sun.

"The losses were regrettable, of course, but they were given every chance—"

Kanu told Swift to get out of his head, at least for the moment. To shut up and make himself invisible.

Alone, he stumbled on weak muscles to the bathroom nearest to the control deck. It was small but functional. He fell to his knees and vomited, but for all his nausea and revulsion, almost nothing came up. The dry heaving burned his throat and made him feel worse. His eyes stung. He was crying, in discomfort and loathing.

He had done the worst thing. The act he had never expected to commit, the sin above all others. He had taken another life, maybe several, and done so not in a blaze of terror or anger but in a cold assessment of his chances. Because it needed to be done, and he could not allow himself to fail.

Nothing excused it.

He was still weeping when he became aware of a presence standing over him, looking down.

"I told—" he began, certain it was Swift, outside his head again.

But the presence knelt down, took his head between her hands and for a moment looked on the verge of some tremendous kindness, a kiss to banish his shame. It was Nissa Mbaye.

Instead, she slapped him hard across the face.

CHAPTER 19

"It's one of them," Ru was saying, for the fourth or fifth time. "Why bother looking elsewhere? Why bother locking up the rest of us when we all know the truth? None of us wants the expedition to fail—why would we?"

"Gandhari's got to follow procedure," Goma felt obliged to point out. "It can't be easy for her, dealing with this."

"And if and when they find out who it is, what do you think they'll do? What kind of law are we working under now, anyway?"

"Are you hoping for blood?"

"I saw what happened to your uncle."

"So did I. But if there's one thing Mposi would have opposed, it's mindless retribution. He was on *Zanzibar* during the troubles—when all hell nearly broke loose. Mposi and Ndege tried to stand for something better. For reconciliation, acceptance—for putting the past behind us."

"And look where that idealism got him. Same goes for your mother."

"You don't need to remind me." And it was true: it was a constant fight to keep that image of him out of her mind, his body slumping over in the slow-bubbling digestive machinery of the well, the milky horror of what had become of the rest of him. She did not want to carry that memory with her for the rest of her life, but the more she resisted, the deeper it branded itself.

She forced herself to think of better times. Mposi at his desk in Guochang, Mposi swimming, Mposi the way she imagined him as a young man, emboldened by the challenges of building a new world—squaring up to a future he had earned, with forgiveness and prudence and an abundance of precocious wisdom.

Presently there was a knock on the door of their quarters. Goma opened it. It was Captain Vasin, looking tired.

"I thought you should be the first to know," she said in a low, exhausted voice. "It's starting to look like Grave was involved. We've already moved him from his quarters to a secure compartment."

Goma nodded slowly—on one level, none of this surprised her. "What do you have on him?"

"Enough to detain him for now. Maslin and your uncle both had their doubts about him. It turns out he was a late addition to the Second Chancer delegation—forced on them at almost the last minute. He has strong connections to a much more orthodox, conservative strain of Chancer thinking and they had enough influence to get their man aboard the ship. The others—the moderates—didn't know him all that well."

"So you're saying he was—what?" Goma said. "A plant, put aboard to sabotage us? Exactly the man he said he was sent here to track down?"

"It could be as simple as that. As to whether he was acting alone or as part of a larger plan against us, we'll have to wait and see. There's only so much background I can dig into on the ship."

Goma recalled their handful of conversations, and the opinion she had already formed of Grave. "What the hell was a throwback like him doing on the ship in the first place?"

"Obviously, a mistake was made."

"Tell me what else you know. This can't be just about his background—they're all true believers of one stripe or another."

"You're right—it's more than that. To begin with, there's a strong likelihood that Grave had the technical know-how to reprogram the nanomachines in the well. Even the records I have say that he spent time aboard the holoships, including *Malabar*. Obviously a mistake was made."

"That's an understatement if ever I heard one," Ru commented darkly, standing just behind Goma.

"What's the significance of *Malabar*?"

"After the information wave hit Crucible, *Malabar* was one of the few holoships that still managed to maintain viable populations of industrial nanomachines. All the nanomachinery now in use, here or anywhere else in the system, derives from the *Malabar* samples. Grave was there as a schoolteacher. There's no direct link, but with the right connections, he could easily have gained practical experience in handling and reprogramming nanomachines."

"Enough for what he did?"

"With some additional tuition, maybe," Vasin said.

"You'll need more than that to nail him."

"When we first found Grave, not long after you found Mposi, he was returning to his cabin from the direction of the drive sphere. That's suspicious, although not damning in and of itself. But we've now found blood traces in one of the secured areas. Evidence of a struggle, too—skin and hair scrapings, a shred of torn fabric."

"Grave's blood?"

"Mposi's. Saturnin's already run a match—he has your uncle's blood on file from the skipover tests."

"What about Grave?" Ru asked.

"There's no sign that he was hurt in the struggle. The fabric doesn't appear to have come from his clothes, either. But he's younger and stronger than Mposi was—it's not really a surprise that your uncle would have fared worse in a struggle."

"So what are you saying?" Ru said, still speaking over Goma's shoulder, "That Grave killed him there, and then carried him all the way back through the ship to the Knowledge Room without anyone seeing?"

"That's not as outlandish as it sounds. There's a cargo elevator connecting both spheres that bypasses all the main accommodation levels, and Grave wouldn't have had far to go from the elevator to the Knowledge Room. Again, ordinary passengers can't access the cargo elevator. But if Grave had already altered his bangle to allow entry into closed areas, it would have been no trouble to operate the elevator."

"What was that throwback doing in the drive sphere?"

"That's what I hope to find out. Of course, it's not just propulsion systems in that area—there are equipment bays, supply stores and so on."

"We're still alive," Goma said. "That has to mean something, doesn't it? If there is a sabotage plan, it hasn't worked so far."

"Maybe we've been lucky," Vasin said. "In which case we have your uncle to thank. I can only wish that he had come to me rather than keep this to himself. I've a feeling we will miss his skills and experience acutely in the days to come."

Captain Vasin's search parties worked their efficient, methodical way through the spine and aft sphere of *Travertine*. Before very long they found a storage room that had been closed but not locked, against normal protocol, and within that room was a rack of supply cases. The cases were examined thoroughly and with caution. One of them, supposedly containing spacesuit parts, was found to be unlocked. Inside, instead of helmets and neck rings were a dozen bottle-sized demolition charges packed in cushioning material.

Vasin explained to Goma that they were MH devices—metallic hydrogen charges. Their presence aboard the ship was not odd in itself, for such items were part of normal expedition equipment. These were not the itemised charges, however, which were stored under high security in the forward sphere. These must have been smuggled aboard, probably quite late in the loading operation. A single charge would easily have been sufficient to destroy much of the rear sphere, and perhaps the whole ship. Certainly *Travertine* would have been crippled beyond repair.

"How in hell—" Goma started saying.

"The final preparations were completed in too much of a rush," Vasin said. "Our supporters wanted us away as quickly as possible, before someone changed their mind and decided the expedition shouldn't go ahead after all. Corners were cut, details missed. First Grave, then letting something like this aboard."

"It's a little late for regrets," Goma said.

"Perhaps we've been fortunate. I'll have the rest of the ship picked clean as a bone, of course."

"What does Grave say?" Ru asked.

"Still sticking to his story. Says he arranged to meet Mposi—that they were both looking for the same thing. Whatever his defence, it'll be difficult for him to shrug off the forensic traces in that room. Grave's fingerprints are as clear as they could be on the box containing the charges, and he left skin flakes in the room, too. Maybe he was on the verge of blowing us all up, or maybe he just meant to extract the charges and spread them around the ship in preparation."

"Why wait?" Ru asked, frowning hard. "If blowing us up was the plan, why not do it there and then?"

"We don't know what his ultimate objective was," Vasin answered. "Maybe it wasn't to destroy *Travertine* itself. When we get to Gliese 163, we'll use the lander for close-up studies, not the ship. His target could be whatever we end up investigating."

"You'll make him confess," Goma said, hardly daring to imagine the damage a bomb could do to her beloved Tantors, if they were present. "I want to know exactly what happened and why."

"A man with deep convictions can be hard to intimidate," Vasin said.

"I think I could have a go at it," Goma answered.

Mposi's body had been removed from the well and the nanomachines rendered safe. There was a funeral service, of sorts—a difficult, harrowing ceremony, which Goma was glad to put behind her—and then his remains were placed in skipover, to be carried all the way to Gliese 163 and—perhaps—back to Crucible. Vasin told Goma that she was obliged to preserve the evidence of any crime even when the circumstances appeared unambiguous—Dr. Nhamedjo's post-mortem examination was as thorough as it could be but, given the limited resources and expertise available on the ship, not completely exhaustive.

For Goma's peace of mind, she would much rather have

seen the remains incinerated or cast into space. Then she could begin to grieve for Mposi.

Even so, she slowly began to adjust to his absence. Ru was a wonderful strength, and Goma found herself blessing the chain of circumstances that had kept them together. If it had taken the death of the matriarch Agrippa to bind them closer, then she was grateful for the old elephant's parting gift. She could not have faced the future without Ru.

Eventually, photons crawled back from Crucible. There had been a day or two of delay in addition to physical time lag. A stringent investigation of Grave's background had added to the picture already formed, reinforcing their existing impression of him. His ideological background and link to the most conservative branch of the Second Chancer movement were established beyond doubt. So, too, was the fact that Grave had the necessary basic grounding in nanomachine programming, acquired during his time on the orbiting holoship. Given that unexpected expertise, he had the skills required to override the bangles' intended security functions. There was no reliable confirmation that Grave had been installed aboard the ship as a kind of counterterrorist infiltrator.

Vasin still gave him his chance to defend himself. The "trial" was an ad hoc affair attended by nearly the entire complement of crew and passengers. Grave was asked to explain his presence in the second sphere. He did not deny it, accepting that the forensic evidence was irrefutable. Nor did he deny that he had some experience with nanomachines.

"What would be the point? You know my past. But this is a starship full of scientists and technicians."

"Your point?" Vasin asked.

"I doubt I'm the only one aboard who has come into close contact with nanomachines. Have you investigated everyone to the same extent you have me? What about the medical team?"

"He has a point," Dr. Nhamedjo said placidly. "I have worked with small quantities of medical nanomachinery—so have the other members of my team."

"Could you have reprogrammed the Knowledge Room?" Vasin asked.

His handsome features looked rueful. "For about five minutes, when I was just out of medical school."

"You do yourself a disservice," Vasin said, meeting his expression with a smile. "The main point, though, is that very few of us ever need to enter the second sphere—or have the means to do so."

"Mine can't have been the only forensic traces you found in that sphere," Grave said. "Or are you saying none of your technicians ever go in there?"

There was a reasonableness to his objections, but also a pragmatic acceptance that his fate was already sealed. He looked broken, his aspirations in tatters—a man going through the motions of justice, knowing he could offer no persuasive argument.

"Did you meet Mposi?" Vasin asked.

"On several occasions."

"Why?"

"We wished to speak. I had some concerns, and I hoped to share them with him."

"Were these vague concerns about a threat?"

"I can't help that they were vague. It was my job to find out more information—to safeguard both the expedition and the integrity of the Second Chance delegation. Had Mposi and I located a tangible threat, we would have brought our concerns to you directly. In the absence of anything concrete, neither of us wished to trouble you."

"I keep hearing about people not wanting to trouble me," Vasin said ruefully. "I wish they'd let me decide for myself. Being troubled is what I'm here for."

"You have spoken to Crucible. Presumably they have verified Mposi's account of things?" Grave asked.

"Mposi was warned about a possible sabotage effort," Vasin said. "But as far as we know, you could have been the saboteur he was warned about." Her tone sharpened. "Why did you kill him?"

"I didn't."

"Ah, this missed rendezvous. What was the point of it?"

"We'd arranged to meet and explore the second sphere together. Mposi knew how to enter secure areas. He'd already shown me how to alter my bangle to achieve the same settings, but I still needed his help to get into the drive section. When I arrived there, though, Mposi was late. Or rather, now I think he was early—that he arrived before me and someone else was already there. I saw signs of disturbance—the blood you found."

"You're saying Mposi had already been attacked, perhaps even killed, by the time you arrived?"

"I only know that he wasn't there. I have no direct knowledge of what happened to him after that, except that you say he was murdered and his body placed in the well." Grave paused, then asked with a sudden and plausible innocence: "You asked me about my history with nanomachines. Do you honestly think I had the expertise to do that *thing* to Mposi?"

"Didn't you?" Vasin asked. "The expertise is specific, but you could have easily acquired those skills on the *Malabar*. Why he agreed to meet you alone, I don't know. Regardless, you knocked him out, maybe even killed him—we only have half of his body to examine—and dragged him to the cargo elevator. You took him to the Knowledge Room, reprogrammed the nanomachines . . . and hoped that would buy you enough time to cover your tracks."

"I did all that?" Grave looked impressed with himself. "You overestimate my ability to improvise, Captain."

"If we were down to our last gram of fuel, our final rations," Vasin said, "I might have a case for execution—or at least for throwing you out of an airlock. As it happens, neither fuel nor rations are a concern. Besides, Mposi would not have approved. Given that—and the uncertain legal standing of this trial—I only have one option. You've offered a defence, but it cannot be corroborated. On the other hand, you had the opportunity, the technical means and—as a conservative Second Chancer—a plausible motive."

"Case closed, then."

"No—case still open, but looking increasingly doubtful for you. You may or may not be guilty—I don't have the evidence to decide—but I can't run the risk of you doing further harm. You will be committed to skipover, Grave. Put on ice for the entire duration of the expedition."

Dr. Nhamedjo spoke up sharply. "I won't be party to that."

Vasin turned to him. "I'm sorry, Doctor?"

"Regardless of what we might think of Grave, this doesn't begin to satisfy his rights as a member of this expedition. And I won't go along with some execution-by-proxy—"

Vasin spoke quietly, but she had no need to raise her voice to sound authoritative. "It's not an execution, Doctor—it's clemency. I'm doing him a kindness by *not* presuming his guilt. I'd prefer you to comply with this decision, but the truth is I don't need you to. Under emergency provisions, any member of this crew is entitled to assist another into skipover."

"Only when the medical staff are indisposed!"

"Or unable to discharge their duties, which at this point amounts to much the same thing. I'm sorry to state it so plainly, Saturnin—we are friends, and I've no desire to overrule you—but Grave will be going into skipover with or without your assistance. Would you rather stand by and watch one of us clumsily attempt to do your own work for you?"

"Of course not," Nhamedjo said, with a surliness at odds with his pleasant, accommodating features.

"Perhaps I made a mistake," Grave said. "Has it occurred to you that I achieved nothing by supposedly murdering Mposi?"

"You acted carelessly," Vasin answered. "That isn't my concern."

"It should be. I am not his murderer. Someone else is. You've found your demolition charges—good for you. Maybe they were part of a plot to blow up the ship, as you suspect. But if the real killer is still active, they'll simply move on to a different weapon."

"Such as?"

"I wish I knew. If I did, I'd be the first to tell you."

Goma woke after the trial to find a transmission waiting for her from Ndege. She had been expecting such a thing, knowing that her mother had been informed of Mposi's death through at least two channels. First there had been a personal communication from Gandhari Vasin, sharing the news and expressing her deep regret that this dreadful thing had happened to such a respected and well-liked figure. Vasin had allowed Goma to see the transmission before she sent it, and not long after that she had composed her own message to Ndege.

Vasin had done her a kindness, in that it did not fall to Goma to break the bad news. She had only to express her sadness and offer her condolences. It was bad enough that her uncle had been killed, but it was much worse for Ndege, losing her brother. Goma had only known him for the short span of her own life; Ndege and Mposi had been witness to centuries.

Both had separated knowing that a reunion was vanishingly unlikely, but neither had expected to learn of the other's death. Mposi might have died before the expedition reached its destination, but by the time the news of his passing reached Crucible, Ndege would probably not be alive to receive it. Similarly, if Ndege were to die in the next few decades, news of it could not possibly reach the expedition for many decades to come.

Neither would have anticipated this. *Travertine* was still only a little more than a light-week from Crucible—its voyage barely commenced. It felt limitlessly cruel of the universe to force this development on Ndege, as if she had not suffered enough already.

And yet she accepted it with what appeared to Goma to be extreme stoic forbearance. She spoke with dignity, acknowledging her sadness, yet proud that her brother had the courage to join the expedition, and the deeper courage to act to protect it. In the end, he had let none of them down—except Goma, perhaps, who would not now have his companionship and wisdom to draw on. Ndege was sorry for that, but she said there was a simple answer. What Mposi had been to Goma, Goma would now have to be to the rest of the expedition. Mposi's qualities were in her—she just needed to find them.

"You will not have to dig very deeply, daughter. I have confidence in you. I always have done. Now go, and choose wisely, and if it is within your capabilities, bring Mposi back to us. He came to love this hot, green world, and I think we owe it to him to bury him under a blue sky, under stars he would recognise. As for you—you already have my love, but if it were within my power I would send you twice as much of it. Be strong for me, be strong for Ru, be strong for the others, but above all else be strong for yourself. Good luck, my daughter."

Goma's first instinct was to reply at length, but on reflection she chose something simpler.

"You say you should send twice your love, but you have already given me more than anyone ever deserved. Mposi isn't here, but your good thoughts are. And in turn, I hope—I *know*—that you can feel mine. They wronged you, my mother, but you never hated them for it. And even when the world thought the least of you, I never wanted anyone else to be my mother. I am proud of my name, proud of what I am—proud of the place that shaped who I am, proud of the ancestors who stand behind me. I cannot replace Mposi—none of us could, except perhaps you. But I will do my best, and keep trying harder, and perhaps I will not disgrace his memory. And when this is done, I will bring Mposi home to Crucible."

If more needed to be said, the words were not there. She did not even replay the transmission before committing it to deep space, arrowing back to her planet of birth.

She could expect a reply in under twenty days, allowing for time lag, but she did not think there would be an answer. They had said what they needed to say, absolving each other of a lifetime's slow accumulation of unhappiness and bitterness and guilt. That was all gone now, wiped clean by a death.

When all that was left was love, words were superfluous.

The door opened at the command of her bangle. Goma stepped into the nearly darkened room, waiting a moment for her eyes to adjust to the low green lighting. The form on the bed stirred, sensing her uninvited presence. At first Grave appeared untroubled, thinking perhaps that he was receiving another inspection from the captain or the medical staff. But then he must have recognised that this was not one of his normal visitors.

"Goma," he said, raising himself from the bed, speaking quietly. "How did you get in here? No one told me to expect you."

Behind her the door closed automatically.

"You made a mistake," Goma said.

"Did I?"

"You mentioned that Mposi showed you how to reprogram the bangles."

In the green half-light she made out his frown, his sleepless eyes, wide awake yet full of exhaustion.

"How was that a mistake, exactly?"

"Because it told me it could be done. Once I know a thing's possible, that's halfway to figuring out how to make it happen. Neither you nor Mposi would have had access to security tools, so finding the reprogramming mode couldn't have been particularly complicated."

He gave a half-smile, equal parts amusement and anxiety. "And did you?"

"No, it was too difficult. Even for Ru, and she's ten times smarter than me. But I went to Aiyana. I knew ve'd be up to it."

"And was ve?"

"Already had it figured out. But like a typical scientist, once the puzzle was unlocked, ve lost interest in it. It never occurred to Aiyana to open any doors ve wasn't meant to."

"I'm surprised you mention Loring's name. Isn't that a little rash if what you're doing is against all the rules of the ship? Won't that get Loring into trouble as well?"

Goma had moved to his bedside. Grave was keeping an eye on her but making no effort to leave the bed. She wondered if he thought she might have a weapon.

"There isn't going to be any trouble," she said. "What do you think I've come to do—kill you?"

"It crossed my mind."

"In a little while, Grave, you'll be as good as dead anyway. I'd be a fool to jeopardise my own standing on the expedition, wouldn't I?"

"Then I'm not sure what the point of this little visit is."

"I think you killed my uncle."

"That does appear to be the consensus opinion. Well done for subscribing to it."

"Shut up." She grabbed a lock of his hair, twisted it hard from his scalp, not caring how much it hurt him. "Shut the fuck up, you piece of believer piss. I saw Mposi. I saw what was left of him. Whoever did that, there's nothing I wouldn't do to them. Nothing so fucking vile that I wouldn't consider it. And I do think you did it. But I can't be sure. Not totally."

She still had his hair in her hand. Grave made a guttural sort of noise, not quite a yelp, but it left her in no doubt as to the discomfort she was inflicting. Yet he made no effort to fight her, his own hands resting at his sides.

"Here's the thing," she said. "You're going on ice. Three hundred years, Gandhari says. No one will speak to you until we get back home. But if there's one thing I should know, one thing you think might make a difference to our chances, I want to know it now."

"For the sake of that tiny chink of doubt?"

She dug her nails into his scalp. "Fuck you. I think there's about one chance in a thousand that you didn't kill Mposi. That's not a doubt, that's an outlier. But I still want to know. One thing. Whatever you've got."

"Tantors," he said.

It was enough to slacken her hold on him. She withdrew her hand, allowed his head to slump back onto his pillow.

"Tell me more."

"That's the fear, Goma, the reason for a sabotage effort. There are some on the extreme edge of the movement who share your suspicions."

"My suspicions about what?"

"That the Tantors might have survived, somewhere beyond Crucible. That's why you're here, isn't it? Be honest—it isn't to heed the call of a dear dead ancestor. It's to find talking elephants."

"What do you know about Tantors?"

"The same as everyone else. And one extra thing. If there was a sabotage plan, destroying *Travertine* would only have been a side effect of the real intention. They mean to murder your elephants, Goma."

"You told me you hate the sin of what they are, not the elephants themselves."

"That was true."

"And now?"

"I think it would still be wrong to harm them."

"The captain found the explosives. If there are more, she'll find them."

"I don't doubt it. But explosives aren't the only weapon, are they?"

"What else?"

"I have no idea. If I were allowed my liberty, I might have a chance of finding out."

"Gandhari shouldn't stop at you," Goma said. "She should put all of you on ice."

"We're a fifty-three-strong expedition. That would still leave forty-one other candidates."

"It's not one of the rest of us. You're the fanatics, not us."

"I hope for your sake that you are right. Truth is, Goma, I never wanted us to be at odds. Whatever you think of me—and you have made your feelings abundantly clear—I did not hurt your uncle. Someone else killed Mposi—someone still at liberty aboard this ship. I know this, but of course I cannot make you see it for yourself. Nonetheless, I can encourage you to keep it in mind. Do you think you will find Tantors, after all this time?"

Goma felt a flush of shame for the physical hurt she had inflicted on Grave. It was beneath her, beneath the dignity of her name, beneath the memory of Mposi. The anger had been genuine and justified, but she had allowed it to use her rather than the other way around.

"I don't know."

"But you hope you will."

"Yes."

"Then be wise, Goma Akinya. Be very wise, and very vigilant. Because when the snake shows itself, I won't be around to help you."

Grave's entry into skipover followed shortly afterwards, conducted without ceremony and with no apparent resistance from the subject. Goma was allowed to be present in the skipover vault with a small party of witnesses and technicians, including Ru, Maslin Karayan and a select number of other Second Chancers.

Grave had already been sedated and was only minimally conscious by the time the skipover casket was closed and the transition to suspended animation initiated. After their public dispute, Vasin and Nhamedjo appeared to have come to some grudging agreement regarding Grave's committal to skipover. Saturnin handled the medical aspects, though with a conspicuous absence of enthusiasm.

Goma watched it all with a vague foreboding, knowing that she would soon be entering one of these sleek grey caskets and trusting her fate to a medical technology that was reliable but not foolproof, and which she did not pretend to understand. The assembly watched in silence as the status readouts marked Grave's slide into medical hibernation, the gradual arresting of all cellular processes. Finally his brain gave its final surrendering flicker of neural activity, and all was still.

"I am sorry I could not give you more," Vasin said to Goma, when the witnesses were beginning to disperse. "Some sense of justice having been done, rather than put on hold."

"Mposi wouldn't have expected anything more."

"Perhaps not. But I admit that I felt the need for retribution—some sense that the punishment should fit the crime."

Goma thought back to her night-time visit to Grave's locked room. To the best of her knowledge it had gone unwitnessed and unreported. If Grave had mentioned it to anyone, there had been no consequences.

She thought of her fingernails, gouging little crescent-shaped wounds into his scalp.

"I wouldn't have wanted retribution."

CHAPTER 20

Kanu prepared chai and knelt by Nissa's skipover casket until with a gasp of pressure the lid opened and slid back. She lay there, alive but not yet awake. He allowed that to happen in its own time, still kneeling, until the awkwardness of his posture became almost too much to bear. Still he waited. At last she stirred, her throat moving, her eyes opening to slits. Again he allowed her silence, although he was certain she felt his presence, breathing next to her.

Eventually she swallowed and said, "Where are we?"

"Our destination," Kanu answered. "The Gliese 163 system." He spoke slowly, calmly, with as much gentleness as the words allowed. "We're about six light-hours out—close enough for a good look at all the planets. I felt you should be awake for this."

"Why?"

"It's your right."

After a silence, she said, "I haven't got any rights, Kanu. I stopped having rights when I was kidnapped. I'm a hostage. A prisoner. Baggage."

"I'm sorry things happened the way they did."

"Then that makes it all better, doesn't it."

"I mean it. I mean it more than you can know." Kanu searched his thoughts, wishing there was a way to make her see his good intentions, the vastness of his regret. "I wronged you, we both know that."

"Do you?"

"I lied to you and I used you. My not being aware of it . . . that was never an excuse. Not when I planned it all in the first place, certain of how it would play out—us meeting, you having the ship, getting me to Europa, then going our separate ways."

Her voice was a rasp. He remembered how dry his own throat had been, coming out of skipover only a few hours earlier.

"And next you'll say you had no choice, that it had to be done."

He ran a hand across the cold skin of his scalp, shaved before skipover. "If I said as much, it would still be no excuse. I should have found another way—another means of reaching Europa. It was just that you presented the least risk of detection, and—"

"There you go again."

"I am sorry."

"This is your way, Kanu. You'll always have a justification, an excuse. There's no action you can't explain away. It's always necessary, always the only thing you could have done."

"I will try to do better."

"It's a little late for that, wouldn't you agree?"

"I will hold my hands up and say that everything I led you to believe after Lisbon was wrong. But *this* was never my intention. I didn't want you on the ship."

"Out of sight, out of mind? You'd use me, but at least I wouldn't be hanging around afterwards, reminding you of the fact?"

"If that's how it feels to you, I apologise. Do you remember much of what we talked about before skipover? This was the

Margrave's doing. He wanted to protect you, and I told him to do whatever was necessary. I didn't think that meant capturing you and your ship and smuggling them aboard my own!"

"Give me back my ship."

"It's yours, whenever you want it. But we're fifty light-years from Earth. *Fall of Night* would be lucky to make it to the edge of this solar system, let alone get you home."

"Then I'll die trying. Better that than this."

"It's normal to be a little fatalistic after skipover. You'll start to feel differently when you've been up and about for a bit."

"Don't tell me how I'll feel, Kanu." A notch of suspicion formed on her brow. "Why are you awake before me, anyway? You promised we'd come out together."

He nodded. "I did, and I'm sorry that promise was broken. Swift . . . thought it might be better this way."

"That's useful, then. Blame everything on Swift."

"I regret that, like so many other things. But I'm not sorry that you're here, that you're with me." He shifted on his old, old knees. "It's something marvellous, Nissa—something that eclipses anything that happened to me in my old life. I want you to see it, to share in the discovery—to be a part of this." He paused. "We've found . . . well, you really should see it for yourself."

"Nothing's going to make this better, Kanu. The sooner you accept that, the easier it'll be for both of us."

"I brought you chai," he said, with a certain finality. "I thought you might like some."

"Chai doesn't make everything better. You know that, don't you?"

"I do," Kanu answered.

When he was satisfied with her progress, Kanu returned to the control deck. Nissa was free to follow him there—he hoped she would—but she would have to make up her own mind about that. The displays and readouts were all still active, as he had left them: schematics and close-ups of various aspects of the system and the ship. The largest was a series of nested ellipses, marking the orbits of the worlds around their parent star. Taking his seat, Kanu refreshed the display. One by one, the globes of planets popped onto the image in their current orbital positions. They were shown at a scale much larger than their orbits, but their relative sizes were preserved. Next to each was a column of names and data.

Even the smallest of these worlds had been detected and characterised centuries ago and in most cases subjected to direct imaging of surface features. Still, even the mighty Ocular had not been able to study every single planet around every star, even in the local stellar neighbourhood—there were simply too many candidates. Gliese 163 lay further away than many of the better-studied solar systems, beyond the reach of the holoships, and so there had been no incentive to obtain more accurate data. Beyond the star's habitable zone was a barren, Earth-sized planet. Cold and nearly airless, it would not have merited his attention except for one thing. On the planet's face, sweeping around into view as it rotated, was another Mandala.

It was the same size as the alien structure on Crucible, different in its details but unquestionably the work of the same intelligence. In those first few waking hours, Kanu had stared at it in wonder and a kind of stupefied bewilderment, astonished that it should fall on him to be the first to witness and document this discovery. It turned out that it was visible, in ghostly form, in the Ocular data. But the resolution had not been quite sufficient to reveal it for the thing it was: an artificial blemish rather than the work of nature.

Now a question occurred to him. It was one thing to accept Mandala as a singular phenomenon, but if there were two of them, then there were probably others.

How many more?

He laughed. He had no idea, beyond the instinct that two were not sufficient. The Mandala Makers would do things in threes. Or fours. Or multitudes.

"Out of your depth already, merman," he said to himself.

"I might venture that we are all equally out of our respective depths," Swift said, standing several metres to Kanu's right, stroking his chin in idle fascination as he studied the new images. "There is no precedent for this. Well, exactly one precedent—the other Mandala. But we know so little about that, we are scarcely on firmer ground than if we had never seen anything similar. Would you care to take a closer look at it?"

"Definitely. But no matter what course we set now, we'll have to swing around the star first. What about that heavy planet, further in? Looks as if our present course will take us quite close."

It was the largest world that was not a gas giant, and it orbited Gliese 163 once every twenty-six days. That was a ludicrously short "year" by any measure, but the star was a red dwarf—cooler and smaller than Earth's sun—and such a tight orbit placed the big planet well within the bounds of habitability. It had been given a name: Poseidon. There were other Poseidons, Kanu knew, and he would be unwise to attach undue significance to such a thing. But given the history of his family and their long and tempestuous involvement with the people of the sea, it could not help but feel apt.

More than that, Poseidon was a waterworld. Its mass was higher than Earth's, and it was also larger. Oceans blanketed it from pole to pole, with no dry land anywhere. Indeed, those oceans were far too deep for any features to have pushed their way through to dry air. Warm at the surface—uncomfortably so—the oceans plunged down through endless black kilometres, finally becoming cool. Animals could survive in those clement depths, but they would have a hard time thriving in the surface waters.

Which was not to say that there was no life at the ocean's upper extremity. From space, the blue of the dayside ocean was broken by smears and swatches of green, ranging in size from tiny islands to expanses with the area of terrestrial continents. It only took a few scans to establish that these features were vast floating structures, rising and flexing with the ocean's solar tides rather than having the waters lap over them. From this distance, they looked as thick and dense as forests. But in fact the living mats were tenuous, seldom more than a few centimetres thick and subject to a constant process of shearing and re-formation—no more substantial than rafts of floating seaweed or kelp. They were an explanation for the free oxygen in the atmosphere, but it was hard to see how anything built on them would not break through into the underlying water.

Nonetheless they were an example of a rich alien ecology, and Kanu would have looked forward to gathering more information were it not for the other things on Poseidon. *Icebreaker* was imaging them clearly, and they were an affront to everything Kanu thought he knew about planets.

There were arches in the ocean. Dozens of them, dotted all over the visible face, always in open water rather than cutting up through the green swatches, and they rose so far that their tops vaulted out of the atmosphere and into airless space, a hundred kilometres above the sea. He stared at them for long minutes, convinced—despite himself—that they had to be an excusable analytical error, a figment of the ship's confused sensors.

But the harder *Icebreaker* looked, the more real the arches became. They were not phantoms.

They were solid entities, casting measurable shadows across a continent's worth of ocean. Each arch had a shallow rim and a flat face like the tread of a wheel. They gave off a radar backscatter suggestive of metals—the only hint of metals anywhere on Poseidon.

"What are they?"

She might have been standing behind him for as long as he had been staring at the arches—so absorbed was Kanu in their mystery that he had not noticed Nissa's arrival on the command deck.

He angled around in the chair. "I don't know. They're not the thing I mentioned—the thing I wanted you to see. How are you feeling?"

"If I wasn't well, the casket wouldn't have let me out of skipover." But perhaps that reply was harsher than she had intended. "I'm all right. Sore, stiff and very thirsty. I've never done this before. My head feels cold. I've never had it shaved."

"Nor me," Kanu said. "And I feel the same—or did, anyway. But a few hours up and about seems to help." He pushed aside the console so he could stand. It did not feel right to sit while Nissa had to stand.

"No, stay where you are," she said softly. Not an order, but a clear expression of her feelings. She was here out of curiosity—a need to know what was in store—but nothing had been forgiven, and he should not presume she would put aside her grievances any time soon.

"Artificial structures," Kanu said, just as softly. "No one's seen anything like *those* before, here or anywhere else.

They're still a bit hazy at this range, but our approach will take us a lot closer to Poseidon."

"You said this wasn't the thing."

"It isn't—although right now I'm not sure which is the more amazing discovery. The eighth planet out—let me get an enlargement up. It has a name, too—Paladin—and a circular orbit, about half an AU, which swings it around Gliese 163 in just over two hundred days. It's Earth-sized, but much too far from the star to be habitable."

Nissa waited until *Icebreaker* had projected its best image of Paladin onto the screen. She looked at it in silence for a few moments.

"I've seen something like that before."

"We all have. It's like the structure on Crucible—another version of the same thing. Can you imagine how significant this is? It's more than just another Mandala. It tells us—begins to tell us, anyway—that there has to be something more to Mandala. A deeper significance than anything we've worked out so far."

"How so?"

"The M-builders wouldn't have gone to the trouble of making two of them if it didn't mean something. And now that it turns out there are two, I think there must be more. Dozens, hundreds—who knows? We're just beginning to push into true interstellar space. There are hundreds of billions of other solar systems out there—maybe there are billions of Mandalas!"

"All right, it's something." Her voice was flat, unexcited. He wondered if that was her genuine response, or whether she was consciously damping down her enthusiasm as a kind of punishment.

"It's more than something! Now at least we have some idea why the original transmission was aimed at Crucible, not us."

"Do we?"

"Well yes, obviously. It's something to do with the two Mandalas—the two versions of the same structure."

"I hope that isn't the best explanation you've got."

Kanu was starting to feel needled now, but he fought to keep any sign of it from his response. "It's not much, I know—like I said, I was only awakened a little earlier than you, so I've barely had time to take any of this in, let alone think about the implications. And that's why I'm so glad to have you here!"

"And why would that be?"

"Two heads, Nissa! I'm a diplomat, not a scientist. I don't have the background to begin to do this justice."

"And you think mine's any more qualified?"

"I was married to you for long enough to know that you can turn your mind to just about anything if it interests you. Deep down, I'm not very imaginative. You are."

"It's a bit late to start trying to turn my head with flattery."

"That's not my intention. I just want you to feel valued. You can see your being here as a mistake, or you can see it as an opportunity, a chance—"

"I'll decide how I see it, thank you."

"I didn't mean it like that." But he knew that no choice of words was going to dig him out of this hole. It was largely of his own making, too.

Nissa was still standing, one hand cocked against her hip— her entire posture conveying scepticism and an unwillingness to be persuaded.

"So what have you done with this news?"

"Nothing at all. I started composing a message about the second Mandala—I didn't even know about the arches at that point. But I thought about you and decided against sending it."

"Why?"

"Because it would be selfish of me to act as if the discovery were mine alone."

"You made it."

"That was just happy accident. Now that you're awake, though, I'd like you to share it. I won't transmit the news, not until you've had a chance to see all of this for yourself and decide what we say."

"Such nobility."

She had meant the words sarcastically, but he decided to take them at face value. "It isn't, and I know it. But if I can do anything to make amends . . ." Then he shook his head. "I can't, I know I can't. And I don't expect your forgiveness."

"Finally."

"But what I said is true. I value you, Nissa—and you should value yourself. Regardless of how we got here, who wronged whom, we're here."

"And the prize for most tautologous statement goes to—"

He raised a hand. "I know. But I mean it—*we are here*. In this moment, experiencing this discovery. This is a place no human eyes have ever seen. Where no man has gone before—who said that—William Shakespeare?"

"I've no idea."

"The point is, it's just you and me. And we have responsibilities now, whether we want them or not."

"I'm clear about my responsibilities," Nissa said. "You don't need to spell them out for me."

"That was never—"

"Poseidon. How close will we get?"

"About five light-seconds—there's scope for adjusting our course if we want to skim nearer. We'll have a steadily improving view of the arches as we approach—and of anything else on or near Poseidon. Mainly, I want to find the sender of that signal."

"If they're still here."

"*Icebreaker*'s been transmitting its arrival for weeks, long before we were woken, and listening for a response. So far it hasn't heard anything, but that doesn't mean we won't find something when we get closer."

"The bones of whoever sent it."

"I sincerely hope it's more than bones."

After a silence, she said, "I want to know it's you. You and not the robot."

"It is me."

"Are you sure of that?"

"Swift is in me, but I'm not Swift. And when you speak to me, it's Kanu. The man you were married to. The man who still wishes he hadn't dragged you into this. The man who wishes he was back in Lisbon, and happy to have found you again."

He braced for a cutting response, but this time his words drew no venom.

"Are you in control of the ship, or Swift?"

"Me. Only me. Swift won't take over my body without my permission—my authority."

"Are you sure of that?"

"Yes." But he answered with more surety than he felt. What else could he do, if he were not to undermine Nissa's already fragile confidence in their situation?

But perhaps she knew he was lying. "Good," she answered, with a coolness of tone that said she had seen right through him. "Let's try and keep it that way, shall we?"

Kanu nodded. It was a small thing, but he would take what he could.

Days and weeks brought them nearer to Poseidon. The improvement in knowledge was steady rather than dramatic, their view of the system gradually sharpening and gaining detail and texture. After the initial discovery of the second Mandala and the arches there were no great surprises, just reinforcement of what they already knew. The Mandala was definitely real; the arches were definitely not of natural origin.

Beyond that there were hints of further interest, but nothing that answered Kanu's central question: *who or what had need of Ndege Akinya?*

Paladin had a very small moon. That was not unusual in itself, but this misshapen little body was odd in a number of ways. It was too warm, for a start: much hotter than would be expected given the standard thermal equilibrium for something in its orbit and distance from Gliese 163. Kanu wondered whether the rock might have been an asteroid, or the remains of one, captured after some violent collisional process. Such an encounter would have needed to be recent enough that the thermal energy of the event was still bleeding away into space.

It became even stranger, though, because in addition to the overall temperature of the rock, there were a handful of even hotter regions on its surface. They were like the infrared traces of fingerprints left on an apple held in a human hand. They were hot enough—up in the three thousand kelvins— that they made him think of geysers or volcanic outflow points. Strangely, though, there was no trace of material boiling away into space.

What was making those hot spots glow? Were they natural features or evidence of deliberate activity? He had been aiming transmissions at the rock but nothing had come back from it. Kanu knew he would need to take a closer look, if for no other reason than to satisfy his curiosity about the peculiar heating effect. But that would be no inconvenience since he would want to examine the second Mandala in any case.

Closer to Poseidon, they found a secondary mystery. The arches were numerous and tantalising and definitely warranted examination. But lacing Poseidon—orbiting at different inclinations, in the manner electrons were once thought to orbit the atomic nucleus—was a host of small dark moons. They buzzed around Poseidon like flies, shell after shell of them. There had been no hint of them in the Ocular data, but that was to be expected. Dark as night and much smaller than the planet, they would have been almost impossible to resolve in time-averaged exposures, even when they passed across Poseidon's visible face.

Clearly, they were not natural. Even if the moons *were* natural in origin—and their uniform size, shape and reflectivity suggested otherwise—they had most certainly not fallen into these orbits by chance.

The moons' orbits ranged in diameter. The smallest nearly skimmed Poseidon's atmosphere, almost down to the tops of the arches, while the widest spanned a distance of ten light-seconds. Between these extremes lay another fifteen shells. There were forty-five of these tiny moon-like objects in total, but no natural moons.

Kanu's instinct was to avoid them. But they threshed around Poseidon in perfectly repeatable patterns, tracing staunchly Newtonian paths like marbles in grooves. Clearly their individual masses did not perturb each other, or the effects had been allowed for in some way. He could already calculate their positions to many centuries hence and be confident of his predictions. Threading *Icebreaker* through the weave of moons was a trivial matter: there were countless viable trajectories. The hard part would be choosing which he preferred; how close he was prepared to get to the world and to any one of its moons.

There was time to think it over—and of course it would not be a decision he took alone.

Nissa remained distant, offering no hint of imminent forgiveness. But her anger had softened to the point where they were able to have mostly cordial exchanges, even if there remained an underlying and unresolved tension. They kept themselves to themselves, occupying different bedrooms. *Icebreaker* was not a large starship, but there was space enough for privacy.

They did manage to put aside their differences long enough to eat together. They sat opposite each other, in high, stiff elephant-carved dining chairs, in a room set off from the control deck. Sometimes they ate in silence or with some musical accompaniment, often very old recordings. Occasionally the walls displayed moving images of African landscapes at dusk, skies like flame, trees like dark paper cut-outs against that brightness.

"With your permission," Kanu said one evening, "we'll take a closer look at Poseidon."

"Permission?"

"Wrong word. Mutual consent. If you agree it's the right thing to do."

Nissa was silent. Kanu knew better than to press her. He studied her face, her eyes averted from his gaze—as if the act of eating demanded her total concentration. He still loved her. The more she pulled away from him, the more he wanted her. He thought of gravity, of inverse squares and the swarm of moons girdling Poseidon.

"You'd have to be a corpse not to be interested in those arches," she said eventually. "That doesn't mean I'm enthusiastic, or that I like this situation." She ate on. "I just want to know as much as possible, given that my survival may depend on the choices we make."

"I feel similarly."

She shot him a sceptical look. "Do you?"

"On one level, I'm terrified of that planet. It's too huge—and those arches? They're a slap in the face, a boot crushing down on human ambition. But I want to know what they're for. I want to see them up close."

Nissa poured herself a glass of wine, steadfastly omitting to charge Kanu's glass at the same time.

"There's a Mandala on that other planet."

"Paladin."

"And arches on Poseidon. They don't look alike, but I suppose they both require a technology beyond anything we have. Do you think they were put there by the same culture?"

"No clue, but I'd like to find out. My guess? There's a connection. To those moons, too."

"And what about the chunk of rock orbiting Paladin that *Icebreaker* can't explain?"

"I don't know. It doesn't appear to fit. The other things are recognisably alien—Mandala, the arches, maybe the land masses on Poseidon, the forty-five moons in those weird orbits. This is just a lump of rock that's slightly too warm. I scanned it with radar, too—some metallic backscatter, but it's different in composition from the arches' signature. It could just be mineral deposits baked onto the surface—you'd have to ask a geologist."

"But you don't think so."

"I think it's something else that doesn't belong, but which is different in nature from the other things. This system is strange enough that we'd have sent an expedition here sooner or later, so why would it not have interested other civilisations? Maybe we're not the first explorers."

"There's something missing, though. Something that ought to be here but isn't."

"I had the same thought."

"Where are the Watchkeepers?" Nissa asked.

Icebreaker's planned course took them into the thresh of moons, slipping through their paths halfway between Poseidon and the highest orbit of its satellites. The trajectory would provide an opportunity to look at the moons in closer detail, but Kanu's chief interest lay in the arches, rising from the ocean like the glimpsed coils of sea serpents.

Slowly their view of the arches improved. Only the tops were free of atmosphere, but much of their height was in extremely tenuous air, offering little obstruction to *Icebreaker*'s sensors. The arches were semicircular, rising one hundred kilometres from the ocean's surface—identical in every dimension to the limit of *Icebreaker*'s measurements. Beneath the water there was a hint of continuation, a suggestion that the arches were in fact only the visible portions of half-submerged wheels, but that was as much detail as they could discern from space.

If they were wheels, then their treads were a kilometre

wide, very narrow in comparison to their heights. Their rims were also about a kilometre thick, and there were no spokes or hubs. The arches—wheels, perhaps—were made primarily of some pale grey non-metallic substance, presumably possessing immense structural strength. From deep space, *Icebreaker* had detected the radar backscatter of metals, but this turned out to be a kind of ornamentation or embellishment added to the surface of the wheels. Cut into the rim and the treads, inlaid or recessed, perhaps even as a bas-relief—it was impossible to tell from space—was a suggestion of dense metallic patterning. To obtain a clearer, more detailed view, they would need to get much closer than five light-seconds. *Icebreaker* was not meant for atmospheric flight, but it could land on top of one of the wheels, which in turn would give them indirect access to the surface. Other than *Fall of Night*, there was nothing aboard *Icebreaker* that could serve as a shuttle, lander or re-entry vehicle—at least nothing with the capability of returning. If their other options were exhausted, there were single-use escape capsules which ought to be able to make it down to Poseidon's seas.

But not now. This was a first pass, a scouting expedition. When they gained a better look around the system, identified the origin of the signal and found water ice to convert to hydrogen, which would in turn feed the initialising tanks for the PCP drive and guarantee them a trip home—*then* they could think about taking a closer look at the wheels.

"We need another word for them," Kanu mused. "'Wheel' isn't big enough. Worldwheels, perhaps. Do you like that? *The Worldwheels of Poseidon*. Has a certain ring to it."

"Whatever you think."

"I think this is wonderful and terrifying, and I wouldn't miss it for a heartbeat."

"You came here to aid the robots, not to sightsee. Don't forget the real reason for this trip."

He smiled, still in the happy rush of discovery. "How could I?"

"And what does Swift make of all this?"

"Swift is all intellect—brilliant and fast. Swift by name, Swift by nature—but Swift doesn't actually know very much. There wasn't room in my head for him to carry a universe's worth of wisdom—I carry my memories, my life experience.

Swift can draw on my knowledge to some extent, sample my memories, but mainly he's here to serve as witness, to guide my interpretations and actions."

"You haven't answered my question."

"Swift wonders if machines made the wheels. The world-wheels. And Swift wonders if that would make them gods."

"So your friend has begun to turn to faith? I'd watch him carefully if I were you."

"Robots are entitled to ask the same questions as the rest of us," Kanu said. "There's no law against it."

Soon they were inside the orbit of the moons, still moving at a hundred kilometres per second.

The forty-five moons were all alike as *Icebreaker* could tell: each a perfectly regular grey sphere two hundred kilometres across. They were still very hard to see, swallowing or scattering electromagnetic radiation and offering nothing to *Icebreaker*'s other sensors. No hint of mass, or magnetism, or particle emission. Artificial, certainly, Kanu decided—and while the moons were larger than the worldwheels and the arrangement of their orbits an impressive feat, he found them less daunting an achievement than the surface structures. They were worthy of admiration, certainly, and definitely merited further attention—but he was content to relegate them to third place after the new Mandala and the worldwheels. They would suffice for study when the other wonders had been picked clean.

But as *Icebreaker* nosed its way through the dance of orbits, its sensors detected another dark thing circling Poseidon.

It was smaller than any of the moons, and consequently they had missed it until now. It was a light-second or two closer to Poseidon, orbiting more swiftly.

Kanu's first thought was that they had chanced upon a piece of captured planetary debris—a tiny natural moon, blemishing the order of the forty-five artificial satellites. No solar system was free of primordial material, after all, and sooner or later some of those wandering fragments of early planet formation were bound to become gravitationally ensnared, tugged into orbits around larger worlds.

He was curious, though. Maybe there was water ice on this

shard, tucked away in the shadows of craters. Maybe they could use it as a base for operations when they returned to take a closer look at Poseidon. He ordered *Icebreaker* to concentrate all its sensors on the little fragment and waited as the results appeared before him.

There it was: a sheared-off splinter of some larger thing—wider at one end than the other and hacked across at an angle with a very clean separation. Kanu stared at it wordlessly. He felt himself on the cusp of some vital recognition but not quite able to make the link.

It was Nissa who identified the thing.

"That's a Watchkeeper," she said, with a cool, calm reverence in her voice, as if she were speaking of the recently dead.

Which was perhaps the case.

It was the corpse of a Watchkeeper, not the living whole. They were looking at perhaps half of its former extent. It had been sliced in two, severed along an impossibly precise diagonal.

Kanu thought of the Watchkeeper they had seen on their way to Europa—the pine-cone form, the stabs of blue radiation spiking out from between the plates of its armour. They had always been dark apart from that blue light, but here there was only darkness.

"Something killed it," he said.

CHAPTER 21

Goma's first thought, when the fog of revival had cleared sufficiently for something like consciousness, was that Mposi and Ndege, sister and brother, her mother and her uncle, must by now be united in death. There could be little doubt of this, given the fact of her own survival. There would have been no cause to wake her before journey's end, no accident that her body would have been capable of surviving, and at the same time, no chance that her mother had survived the long decades of *Travertine*'s crossing.

They had said goodbye, Goma reminded herself—or at the very least ended things well, with her mother's loving imprecation that she had to look inside herself now, to find the strength she had depended on in Mposi, and to be that rock for the rest of them.

But Mposi was still dead, and the truth of that was no easier to bear now than before she had gone into skipover.

Presently there was a face, and a voice.

"Gently now."

Before the face assumed focus, something cool and sweet and soothing touched her lips. She thought for a drowsy instant that this kind form was Ru, for the voice was a woman's. But it was Captain Gandhari Vasin helping her back to life.

"Thank you," she said, when she was at last able to coax some sounds from her mouth. "I wasn't expecting . . . I mean, you didn't need to."

"I didn't need to, but if a captain can't welcome her crew back to the world of the living, what can she do? Anyway, I need you, Goma. Take your time—getting up and about is hard enough after a normal skipover interval—but I have something of interest to show you when you're ready."

Her eyes still would not focus properly, but the vague textures and colours of her surroundings were enough to establish that she was still in the skipover vault.

"Are we safe? Did we make the crossing?"

"Yes, we made the crossing. Seventy light-years, and not a single mishap. How much of that we owe to the Watchkeeper ahead of us, I don't know. But the ship is in good condition, and we are where we wished to be."

"What have you found?"

"A great deal. Most importantly, though, a welcome message—a signal telling us where to go. I think you should hear it. I would be very glad of your opinion."

"How is Ru?"

"There's no need to worry about Ru. She's in excellent hands."

That was meant well, but it was not quite the answer she

had been hoping for. And yet Goma could only focus on her fears for so long before drowsiness pulled her under again.

She had no idea how long she was out, but there came a moment when the face of Dr. Saturnin Nhamedjo was assuming gradual focus before her. He was studying her with magnificent and serene patience, as if nothing in his universe was more valuable than the health of this one patient. She could easily imagine that he had been there for hours, waiting by her skipover casket, untroubled by any concern save her own well-being.

"Welcome back, Goma. I know you have already spoken to Gandhari, but I will reaffirm the news. You have come through safely. All is well. We have all survived skipover—even our prisoner."

She thought of Grave, and that in turn made her think of Mposi. But for the moment there was only one thing at the forefront of her concerns. She made to get up out of the casket, forcing effort into unwilling muscles.

"Steady!" Dr. Nhamedjo said, smiling at her determination.

"I want to see Ru."

"In good time. Ru is receiving the very best care and I am perfectly satisfied with her progress."

"Something went wrong, didn't it?"

"We have all survived. This is a blessing. Anything else must be considered a minor setback, nothing more." A stern, admonitionary tone entered his voice. "I do not wish you to overtax yourself, Goma, not during these early hours. You have more than enough work to do in building your own strength back up. Leave Ru to us. She will be well. I have the utmost confidence in her."

"Is it the AOTS?"

"It was always going to be a complicating factor. An already damaged nervous system is not best equipped to deal with the additional stresses of skipover, but I would not have agreed to let her join the expedition if I did not think her strong enough." He reached into the casket and patted her wrist, offering reassurance. "She is in a medically induced coma now, but that is for her own good. We are giving her a cocktail of drugs that will help with the combined effects of

AOTS and the ordinary stresses of skipover. There is no reason for them not to work, but it must be done carefully, and the results monitored at each step. Gradually, she will be elevated back to proper consciousness. I have every confidence that she will be well again."

"How long?"

"A matter of days. A hardship for her and a worry for you, I appreciate that, but it is an extremely small price to pay when set against the years we have already crossed. Now rest, Goma—and set your mind at ease. Ru will be well."

She wanted to demand more of him—additional guarantees. But she was too tired, too groggy, to do more than place her trust in this man. Sometimes that was all you could do.

So she rested. After an hour or two, she was able to experiment with moving around, easing herself out of the casket and onto her feet, steadying herself against walls and furniture until she learned to trust bones and muscle. It was hard at first—she felt pinned down under a dead weight, nauseous and dizzy at the same time. But her strength and confidence returned, and the ill-effects slowly faded away. She kept down fluids and soon found herself able to eat. She wandered around a small area of the ship, regaining her bearings. Hour by hour, more and more people were awake and mobile. All appeared content to share the same assumption: that they were aboard a ship that had crossed seventy light-years of space, in one hundred and forty years of time.

Goma could hold these facts in her head well enough, but accepting them as deep, visceral truths was another thing entirely. She felt exhausted by skipover, physically drained, every part of her bruised, but that was not the same as feeling fourteen decades older.

She kept looking down at her own hand, studying the familiar anatomy of her wrist, the pores of her skin, the fine dark hairs, the architecture of bone and tendon beneath the flesh. Nothing had changed—nothing felt older. She pinched the skin of her belly, but it too appeared miraculously indifferent to the process it had undergone. Blemishes, moles, scars were all present and correct. She did not look quite herself in the mirror—there was a slackness of muscle tone, a vagueness to her gaze—but all of that was a normal consequence of skip-over. Indeed, the ill-effects were connected with the transition from total skipover stasis to full animation rather than the fourteen decades of stasis itself.

They had moved Ru out of her skipover casket into a dedicated medical suite—one of two on the ship—and placed her on a normal bed under a bank of conventional medical instruments. She had lines going in and out of her, of different colours and thicknesses, conveying blood, urine, saline and drugs to and from different machines. She had a crown-like device fitted around her forehead, maintaining the medical coma and simultaneously running some sort of cyclic neural scan—peelings of her brain flickering in different colours on the display above her headboard. It was a difficult time for Dr. Nhamedjo and his staff since they still had a dozen or more sleepers to bring out of skipover. But they managed to find time to make it look as if Ru was their chief concern.

Goma wanted to be at her side. But Dr. Nhamedjo assured her there was no chance of her waking up ahead of schedule; that everything was proceeding according to a fixed and orderly timescale. "These prefrontal areas," he said, indicating part of the scan, "are still inflamed and must be brought under control. She is also suffering microseizures—a kind of temporal-lobe epilepsy. None of this is without precedent in AOTS cases, and all of it is responsive to careful management. But above all it must not be rushed, or we will leave Ru with greater impairments than when she joined us."

It was hard to watch her lying there, so helpless and so clearly afflicted. Every now and then she tremored, sometimes violently enough that it was hard not to think she was in the grip of nightmares, or in pain. But Nhamedjo assured Goma that there was no conscious activity involved, and that Ru would remember nothing of this time.

Goma held her hand, tried to still it when the palsy hit. She whispered kindnesses to Ru and settled a kiss on her fever-hot brow.

"Come back, my love. I need you."

For the time being, though, there was nothing to do but wait.

* * *

"Perhaps," Gandhari said, "a thing or two to take your mind off Ru—would that help?"

"It might."

"The truth is, I hardly know where to begin. We've learned so much already, and yet all we've managed to do is replace every question with two more. Still, I have to start somewhere."

They were in the captain's cabin, just the two of them. Not much had changed since the last time Goma had been in it. The picture on the wall was different now—perhaps Vasin had changed it herself, or else the room had made the choice based on its own selection algorithm. It was a strange, gloomy painting of a pale and naked woman in the embrace of a withered skeletal figure. To one side of the coupling floated sperm-like forms; to the other, bulbous-headed aliens.

Goma had difficulty squaring this image—or, for that matter, the destructive landscape that had preceded it—with the calm, collected, warm-spirited person who lived in this room.

"Who was there to wake you up?" Goma asked, remembering the other woman's kindness.

"Nobody. But one of us had to be first, and it might as well have been me."

"That can't have been pleasant."

"Well, it was silent, I'll say that for it. Colder than I wished. Something was off with the thermostat settings—we soon fixed that, but only after I'd shivered my way through two whole days, trying to restart the climate control. Still, it wasn't too bad—mainly I was happy we'd made it, that we weren't just some cloud of atoms sailing on through space."

The ship had not been totally devoid of life during the main part of its cruise, Goma knew. Periodically, technicians had come in and out of skipover to review the vital systems, while Nhamedjo's medical team had done the same thing for the sleepers, putting themselves through the ordeal of multiple skipover transitions. From what she could gather, there had been little work for these brave souls to do. Nothing had gone badly wrong; nothing had needed serious repair.

"Then you were the first to see Gliese 163," Goma said.

"Yes, I had that honour—dubious as it felt at the time.

We're close enough now that it's harder to see the true colour, but when I first came out, you could really tell it's a red dwarf—it had a definite pink tinge to it. Now it just looks blazing white, but that's only because our eyes aren't very good at dealing with bright objects. You'll find it very familiar—in fact, it's not so different in temperature from Crucible's sun."

"Home sweet home."

"Well, I wouldn't go that far. Still, we didn't come for the scenery. And if we'd only made one discovery, we'd have justified the expedition a thousand times over."

"Tell me what we've found."

"Another Mandala, for starters."

Goma was so surprised she laughed. "My god."

"I know—astonishing, isn't it? It's on one of the rocky planets—Paladin, they call it. I'm guessing you remember it from the Knowledge Room."

"I do."

"If your mother were with us, she could tell us exactly if and how it differs from the one on Crucible. Loring and the others will be studying the data when they're all awake. You're welcome to share in the analysis, of course—it might stop you worrying about Ru."

Goma doubted that, but she knew Vasin meant well by it. "I'm not sure I'll have much to add. Don't expect deep insights just because of my family connection."

"At this point, I'm ready to consider anything that might help. Anyway, the Mandala is only part of it. Are you ready for the rest?"

"Go on."

"There's a rock orbiting Paladin, like a little asteroid, and someone appears to have reached it ahead of us. There's evidence of colonisation—surface structures, odd thermal activity. Maybe some additional orbiting objects that we can't yet resolve, but which will be clearer when we get closer."

"Is that where we're headed?"

"You'd think so, and it would be a good guess if you didn't know about the superterran. Remember the waterworld—Poseidon?"

Goma nodded—she recalled trying to clutch the pure blue ball in her fingers, to steal it from the Knowledge Room.

"There are artificial structures rising from its waters. Not another Mandala this time—something different, but just as fascinating. Anomalous-looking moons, too, in orbits you wouldn't expect to occur naturally. All very odd, all very enticing. I'm inclined to rate it as a higher priority than the second Mandala. After all, we already know quite a bit about one of those."

"Not as much as we'd like."

"True. But then there's also the signal—aimed directly at us during our approach."

"From Poseidon?"

"No—not from Paladin, either, or even the rock orbiting it. The point of origin is Orison, another one of the planets. Based on its characteristics, we think it likely that the sender is the same one who transmitted the original signal—which is the reason we're here at all. See what you make of it."

Vasin looked to the wall next to the gloomy painting where a scramble of geometric forms, a hash of numbers and symbols, gave way to a matrix of pixels assembling into a blocky, low-resolution mosaic of a human face looking back at them. Goma squinted, blurring the pixels together.

"Eunice."

"Yes. Easy enough to check against the records, but it helps to have you confirm it."

Now the face was speaking.

"I wondered what was keeping you. Is half the speed of light really the best you can do?" The question was clearly rhetorical, for the face continued its monologue after only the slightest of pauses. "Well, good that you've finally arrived, even if you're not the first. Things have reached a pretty pickle and now you're part of it. Under no circumstances respond to any transmission from Paladin or go anywhere near Poseidon. Come to me instead. Lock on to the origin of this transmission and adjust your course accordingly. I have amenities and technical know-how you may find useful. Above all else, I have knowledge. If you want to know what happened to the Trinity, I'm the one to talk to."

The pixels rescrambled into the same blitz of numbers and symbols, then it recommenced.

Vasin permitted it to play a second time, then dulled the sound while allowing the visual to continue cycling.

"It carries on like that—a repeating transmission, sent out in bursts every six hours. She must have set up some kind of automated send, waiting for us to answer. What do you think she means, that we're not the first? We've sent no other expedition, and our government was careful to limit disclosure of the original signal. How could someone else be here before us?"

"A ship from another system?"

"But how would they know to come here? That transmission was aimed at us, Crucible—no one else."

"We assume."

"Rightly, I hope. That's only the start of my worries, though. She's expecting an answer, and we need to get off on the right footing."

"I should speak for us," Goma decided.

"I wouldn't have it any other way. It's only fitting that an Akinya should make the first formal response—for what little good it will do us. Do you like the painting, by the way? *Death and the Maiden*."

Goma was attempting to read Ndege's notebooks, trying to make some sense of the hash of symbols and connecting propositions, when Doctor Nhamedjo called to say that she should come to the medical suite as quickly as possible.

"Is something wrong?"

"Quite the contrary, Goma. Ru is on her way back to us, and I thought you would like to be here when she awakens."

Goma snapped the notebooks shut with no small measure of guilty relief. She was in the medical suite in less than five minutes, equally relieved that she had not arrived too late. Ru was surfacing to consciousness but had not yet woken fully. Dr. Nhamedjo was at her side, another of his medics—Dr. Mona Andisa—on the opposite side of the bed. Neither appeared unduly concerned by the progress of their patient.

"It worked, then," Goma said.

"It counts in her favour that she is strong," Nhamedjo said. "It's rather a severe case of AOTS, but she compensates very well. As a matter of interest, how did she ever suffer such extreme exposure? I treated one patient who was lost north of Namboze, wandering the jungles for weeks with nothing to protect them from the oxygen—a flier had gone down with a faulty transponder—but that was a very unusual set of circumstances."

"Self-neglect," Goma said. "Too many field trips, not enough time thinking of her own safety compared to the elephants. I'd have watched over her, but the harm was done by the time we met."

"She must have been fiercely dedicated to her elephants to think so little of her own well-being."

"They get into your blood."

"Yes, I've heard as much. Almost like an illness?"

"I can't say I've ever thought of it that way."

"Well, I dare say medicine is no different. We all have our magnificent obsessions."

"And what would yours be, Saturnin?"

"The sanctity of human life, I suppose. The ever-unfolding challenge of doing more good than harm. But I would not pretend to share Ru's dedication to a single cause. She will be frail for a little while, Goma. You will need to take even better care of her than usual, but I do not think that will be a problem."

"No, it won't."

He nodded towards the neural displays. "She is approaching consciousness. We will let you have some time alone together—you've earned it, both of you."

Goma eased next to Ru and stroked the side of her face, the merest touch.

"Come back to me, love."

Ru woke. Her eyelids fluttered, opening to narrow slits. She was still and unresponsive for several seconds. Goma snatched a glance at the neural display, wondering if there could have been some mistake—some dreadful brain injury that had somehow escaped notice.

But then Ru said, "Am I awake now?"

Goma grinned. "You're awake."

"It feels like I've been trying to wake up for centuries. Floating under ice, trying to find my way to the air."

"That's not far from the truth. You hit some problems in skipover but you're better now."

"Tell me you're really Goma and not a figment of my imagination."

"I don't feel like a figment." She squeezed Ru's hand where

it poked out from beneath the bedsheet. "It's me—warts and all. We've come through. We're here, in the other system. We all made it."

"Really?"

"Yes."

"What happened to me?"

"The AOTS complicated your revival, but there's no lasting damage. You'll just need to take it easy for a few days."

"You're supposed to be the centre of attention, not me."

"Don't worry about that—I'm sure my time's coming. There's so much to catch up on! I want to tell you everything now, in one breathless rush. But there's time. You need to wake up at your own speed."

"I could use a drink."

"My pleasure."

Dr. Andisa gave Goma a beaker of amber fluid, some kind of medicinal restorative, which Goma in turn offered to Ru's lips. Ru sipped slowly, then eased herself into a sitting position on the bed. Goma was encouraged by this show of determination and strength.

"Thank you," Ru said, taking the beaker from Goma. "How was it for you, coming out?"

"I thought it was bad until I saw you."

"That really lifts my spirits."

"If it's any consolation, they say no one gets an easy ride."

"And are you sure this isn't a hoax—you're not all pulling a trick on me?"

"No, we're really there. Around Gliese 163—or approaching it fast, anyway."

"I want to see everything."

"You will. But it's like a sweet shop—we barely know where to start. I already have a job, though."

"Lucky you. What is it?"

"I get to answer the message. We've been signalled, told to head for one particular planet. I think it's Eunice."

"You think."

"The tone was frosty enough. We'll know for sure when we get there."

"And Dakota—any word on her?" Ru glanced at the

remaining medic, lowered her voice fractionally. "The other Tantors you promised me?"

Goma smiled—it was as if they were sharing a naughty secret, barely daring to mention it aloud in the presence of others.

"It was never a promise, just a possibility."

"Tantors?" Dr. Andisa asked with a smile.

"We can't let go of our work," Goma said. "Can't stop thinking about the elephants back on Crucible. We live them, breathe them, dream them."

"It's all right," Ru whispered. "We never expected to receive all the answers in one go, and I'd be disappointed if we did. But when we get to this planet, whichever one it is, I want to be part of that."

"You've a way to go before you'll be strong enough."

"To be honest, right now I feel like something left out to die. What did they do to me while I was under?"

"Whatever it was, believe it or not, it appears to have worked. If only you'd taken care of yourself way back when, this would have been easier on you."

"We'd never have met."

"Don't be so sure of that."

"Oh, I can be. You and me—intellectual rivals, competitive investigators in the same line of research? I'd have been nothing to you unless I was a threat, Goma Akinya. And I only made myself a threat by working myself halfway to the grave."

"So I'm responsible for what you did to yourself before we met?"

"I'm just saying—if I'd taken care of myself, I'd never have come to your attention."

"But I fell in love with you the moment I saw your face."

"And why was my face of such interest to you?"

Goma had no choice but to confess. "I wondered who this annoying woman was, trampling all over my research interests, daring to question my methods, having the nerve to imply that she knew more about animal cognitive science than I did."

"Bet you wanted to scratch her eyes out."

"I wouldn't have stopped at the eyes."

"So the message here is . . . if you can't beat them, marry them?"

"I suppose."

"Poor fool me. I didn't have a clue what I was letting myself in for."

"Neither did I," Goma said. "But I'm glad it happened."

She kissed Ru. She was back, and for a moment, brief as it was, all was well with Goma's world. They were in love, they were together again, there were mysteries waiting to be solved. This state of momentary, careless bliss could not last, and she did not expect it to. But she had grown old and wise enough to take such gifts when they were presented, without fear for their transience.

Vasin did her best to keep everyone informed about their discoveries in the new system. She made regular announcements over the shipwide intercom, and periodically, for those who were interested, she arranged gatherings in the largest of the common areas and showed the latest images and data. Goma wondered how the woman managed to find time to sleep. About a quarter of the crew were still in skipover now, and hour by hour that number grew smaller.

Goma tried hard not to resent each newly woken face. They were all entitled to be here, even the Second Chancers.

Vasin told them about the new Mandala, the strange rock orbiting Paladin, the structures on the waterworld, the transmission from the construct. The images amplified her story but added nothing dramatically new. *Travertine* was still operating at the limit of its sensory capabilities, offering tantalising glimpses rather than hard details. The Mandala on Paladin was clearly the same kind of thing as the object on Crucible, but its geometry differed in various interesting ways. Arch-like structures appeared to rise from the ocean on Poseidon, but their exact nature was difficult to guess at. Perhaps they were indeed arches, or—as Loring suggested, based on tantalising hints in the data—wheel-like structures which actually continued down into unimaginably deep layers of water. The girdling moons were simply weird—confusing *Travertine*'s sensors in a thousand ways, their orbits spherical according to some measurements, ring-shaped according to others. They would need to get much closer to say more than that.

But their immediate concern was another world entirely.

Orison lay on an orbit between the hot Poseidon and the cooler Paladin, too far from its sun to have held on to a thick atmosphere. Whereas Paladin swung around Gliese 163 in just over two hundred days and Poseidon in a mere twenty-six, Orison's orbit was seventy-four days. It was an unpromising, nearly airless little world, and were it not for the signal, this moonless planet would not have attracted their attention.

The origin of the signal, they now knew, was some kind of transmitter on Orison's surface. It only swung into view with the planet's rotation, and even within that rotational cycle the signal was only being sent for a relatively short interval.

Goma was ready with her response when the message started coming in again. She had gone over it with Vasin, and now the captain and Ru sat watching her as she prepared to recite her response.

She coughed, cleared her throat. Vasin nodded.

"My name is Goma Akinya," she said. "I'm Ndege's daughter, and I've come all the way from Crucible. I know you called for Ndege, but my mother was too old to make the crossing. Besides, there were other . . . complications. So I've come instead, as part of an expedition funded by Crucible. We come with no agenda, no objective beyond the gathering of knowledge. But of course we're curious about you. And now that we know of the other Mandala, we'd like to find out some more about it, as well as whatever is on Poseidon. We don't know why you've warned us away from them, we'll assume you had good reason. You also mentioned someone arriving before us. That's news to us. Maybe you can share some information when we meet. We have a fix on your transmission site and we are bringing in our ship. We'll come down in our lander, as close to you as possible. If there's anything else you feel we should know, we would be glad to hear it."

Goma touched a hand to her throat. Her mouth was dry, but she was done.

"Good," Vasin said.

"What do you think will happen next?" Ru asked.

"No idea, but it'll be interesting," Vasin said. "That first signal was very generic—it could have been aimed at anyone—and sent by a very simple repeating-transmission system with no intelligence behind it. But now she knows your name, and your relationship to Ndege. If we are dealing with anything more than a mindless recording device, we should know it soon enough."

Orison completed another turn. There was silence, no hint of a return transmission. But on the next rotation the signal was there again.

"Good," the woman said. "It was Ndege I wanted, but if I must make do with second best, another Akinya will have to suffice. How far the apples have fallen from the tree, Goma Akinya. I do hope you measure up."

"I'll try," Goma answered acidly.

"Assume orbit around Orison. You shouldn't have any trouble spotting my surface encampment. Land at your convenience, within a kilometre or so, and meet me on foot near the main surface lock. I have food and water, so don't worry about bringing rations. Oh, and prepare yourselves for a surprise or two."

Tantors, Goma thought. It was a treacherous line of thinking—all too liable to lead to bitter, crushing disappointment. But she could not help herself. They would put everything right—every wrong thing in her universe.

She could not stop herself.

CHAPTER 22

It turned out that more than one Watchkeeper had died around Poseidon. There were dozens, at least. Once they found the first corpse, it was as if their eyes—their sensors and instruments and analysis tools—had become attuned to the task of finding more.

The dead machines had all been caught up inside the thresh of moons circling Poseidon. Their orbits were irregular, and their sizes varied from fragments only a few kilometres across to one corpse that—given what they already knew of Watchkeepers—was almost whole. Almost intact, save that it was also dead, adrift and dark and absolutely inert. The space around Poseidon was a graveyard and its gatekeepers were the forty-five moons.

Gatekeepers or executioners—presuming there was a distinction.

"Where have you brought us?" Nissa asked.

"Somewhere we shouldn't be." But they were still inside the moons' domain, still following their course around Poseidon, and they were not dead. Yet. They were moving without thrust on a trajectory that ought not to be mistaken for an attempt to fall into orbit or land on Poseidon. "Whatever happened here," Kanu went on, "it may have been a very long time ago. Something did that to the Watchkeepers, but we don't appear to be attracting its attention."

"We might, at any moment," said Nissa. "We don't know what those Watchkeepers were doing, or how close to the surface they got. For all we know we're *just about* to cross some threshold."

She was seated next to him on the control deck, the ship having furnished a second chair while they were on the long approach from the system's edge. It had happened without either of them asking, rising out of some buried concealment in the floor.

"I know, and I agree," Kanu said. "But we can only slow or change course by using our engines, and that may be the one thing that makes us conspicuous. I think the safest option may be to carry on as we are until we come out the other side."

"Another eight hours."

"I don't like it either."

"And what does Swift think?"

Swift's figment stood to the left of Kanu, hands on hips, conveying fretful agitation. He kept taking off his pince-nez, polishing them, returning them to the tip of his nose. "As a matter of fact, I agree with Nissa—we may be about to sail into difficulty. Equally, I have some sympathy with your position, Kanu. It could be a mistake to use thrust."

"He's a fat lot of use. Swift says we're both right."

"Then ignore Swift. We still have to do something."

"I've felt this same indecision once before, near our old household in Africa. I was out in the grass, not more than an hour's stroll from the gates, and I noticed a large black snake moving through the grass near me. I'd not had much experience with snakes and was so terrified I couldn't move. My brain said: if you almost didn't notice that snake, there might be one *there* as well, and *there*, and *there*."

"And were you surrounded by snakes?"

"I have no idea. The big snake passed me by. It wasn't interested in me at all—I'm not even sure whether it sensed me or not. But my point is, that's how I feel now. I don't want to make a move, to do one thing that might bring disaster. But we have to act."

"Full drive," Nissa said. "Empty the tanks if we have to. Ditch the escape pods to save mass. Sacrifice *Fall of Night*, if we must. But we get out of here as quickly as we can."

"There's another way," Swift said quietly, as if to speak were an impertinence.

"Go on," Kanu said.

"Go on what?" asked Nissa.

"Swift has an idea." But there was a sense of words forming in his throat, sounds pushing out of his mouth. "You must excuse me taking this liberty," he said, or rather was compelled to say, an invisible hand squeezing speech out of his larynx. "It is simpler, Nissa, if I speak directly to you both. The Watchkeepers have been killed, but their remains are tolerated, allowed to follow their orbits."

Nissa regarded Kanu from her seat, making no effort to hide her appalled revulsion. But there was fascination, too, of a clinical kind.

"What have you done to him?"

"Nothing has been *done* to him; nothing *will* be done. He is my friend. Now might we speak of the Watchkeepers? We would be well advised to get out of here, but we dare not make too much of a show of ourselves doing so. On the other hand, none of us wishes to spend another eight hours trusting to our luck. Therefore, a compromise. If we maintain our present heading, we will soon pass very close to one of those fragments. It's moving slower than us, but with a short, sharp burst of thrust we can match velocities. We park ourselves next to the fragment—on or inside it, if necessary—and let it carry us beyond the orbit of the outermost moon. When the fragment reaches its apogee, we depart—and cross everything we have for luck."

"Or we could just cut and run," Nissa said.

Swift relinquished his control of Kanu's larynx, Kanu letting out a small involuntary gasp in the process. "I'm back," he said. "And I'm sorry, but I don't like Swift's idea. It's still too risky, given how little we know."

"So we do nothing, is that your plan?"

"I didn't say that. Continuing with our present course of action *is* still doing something."

"Well, if we keep talking about it long enough, those eight hours will just fly by," Nissa said, rolling her eyes with heavy irony.

"We're on edge," Kanu said. "It's natural—we'd be fools if we weren't. And there are no rules for this situation, no precedents. None of the ideas is bad. But if the thing we're doing hasn't harmed us—"

Swift walked over to Kanu, ghosted through the console and lowered himself into the same volume of space occupied by Kanu's body.

"I am sorry, Kanu, but I think this is necessary."

Kanu could neither speak nor control his body. Swift was puppeteering him again, working the levers inside his skull. He had done it once, with Kanu's consent, but this time there had been no invitation, not even tacit permission.

Kanu rose from his seat, pushing aside the console. He moved to face Nissa, still seated in her chair, and sank until he rested on his haunches.

"The choice must be yours," Swift said. "Kanu is right—there are no precedents. Equally, you did not ask to be placed in this position, whereas Kanu and I embarked on our enterprise in the full and certain knowledge that there would be grave unknowns. So, as I said, the choice is yours. Whatever you decide, that is what we will do."

"Why?" she asked, narrowing her eyes in suspicion of a trick.

"Because I would very much like you to begin trusting me, and this looks like an excellent place to start. Whatever you say, that is what we will do. I will implement your decision."

"Then . . . get us out of here as quickly as possible."

"Very well." As Swift moved Kanu's body back to his seat, he added, "Normal structural and accelerational safeguards will be suspended. That seat should protect you, but I would strongly advise bracing in readiness for the load. In a moment I will disengage spin-generated gravity and align the control deck for the new vector."

"Wait," Nissa said.

"Yes?"

"It is a risk."

"Indeed. But there are no risk-free options."

"All the same . . . no. We don't cut and run. Your option— is that still valid?"

"For the moment."

"Then do it. Get us close to that fragment, like you said. There are forty-five moons—I presume they can't all see us at the same time?"

"If sight lines are relevant, then we are presently within the range of visibility of thirteen moons, although the number will fluctuate as we continue our course."

"Are you clever, Swift? As clever as Kanu thinks you are?"

"I doubt anyone is *that* clever."

"Then here's a test for you. When the drive comes on, make sure we're as invisible as we can be. Use that fragment to its maximum advantage."

"You are presenting me with a somewhat challenging N-body problem."

"I'll tell you what's *challenging*, Swift—being dragged fifty fucking light-years across the galaxy without my consent. So rise to the occasion. You said the choice was mine—this is my choice."

"And you could not have put it more eloquently, Nissa. Well, I do appreciate a challenge, and I shall apply myself to the matter with alacrity. This will take a few moments . . . fortunately, we can already draw on *Icebreaker*'s detailed model of the moons to minimise our visibility."

When Swift returned to his console, Kanu again had the strange experience of seeing his hands whip across the controls, his vision blurring with the speed of his eyes' jolting attentional shifts. It felt strange to him; it must look monstrous to Nissa.

But necessary. As resentful as he felt—it was not remotely pleasant to be usurped from control of his own body—he understood why Swift had done it. To surrender before Nissa, to give her not just a say in her fate but absolute control—it was the only thing that might prompt her to see Swift as an ally rather than a parasite.

A risk. But as Swift had said, there were no risk-free options.

After a few minutes, Swift said, "It's done. I'm relinquishing Kanu. We'll make our course change in a completely automated fashion, beginning in about seven minutes. It can be revoked at any point. Once we start, though, I would strongly suggest we continue."

Kanu had to take a deep breath as he returned to himself—Swift had drawn deeply from the well of his energies.

"Remind me not to let him do that too often."

Nissa looked at him through guarded eyes. "Do you have a choice?"

"I thought I did."

"He could take you over completely, couldn't he? If he can lock you out at that level, what's to stop him?"

"Nothing," Kanu said. "Except his respect for the trust I had in him."

"And is that trust still intact?"

"Battered, but it will heal. I think he did the right thing."

"Good. But I take it this is the point where you start trying to argue me out of my decision?"

"No," Kanu said, after a moment of reflection. "I don't know which of us is right. But Swift had an idea, and you've chosen it, and that's good enough for me. Whatever happens, it should be interesting—you realise no one has ever come as close to a Watchkeeper as we're about to?"

"Dead Watchkeepers don't count. Anyway, your mother . . . one of your mothers—she'd say differently, wouldn't she?"

"I suppose she would," Kanu said. "But the Watchkeeper came to Chiku, not the other way round."

It was a long seven minutes—time enough for doubts and second-guessing. But their nerve held, and at the appointed moment, *Icebreaker* commenced its course change. It was as hard and sudden as Swift had warned, an assault to the frailty of the human body, but they were ready for it and the shock was bearable. Kanu sensed himself on the verge of blacking out, but unconsciousness never quite came and his thoughts remained lucid. The course correction continued for several minutes, a succession of nerve-rattling instants, any one of which could have seen some dreadful reprisal from the moons. But no attack came. Perhaps they were too small to draw the moons' attention, or Swift had timed their course change accurately enough to avoid drawing down their fire. Or perhaps, Kanu mused, all this destruction was the work of millions of years ago, and they had never been in harm's way.

When the engine stopped, they had arrived within a whisker of the broken Watchkeeper. *Icebreaker* was less than the width of its own hull from the skin of the alien machine. There had been no sign of life—of activation—from a distance, and there was none now they were closer. The drifting hulk was warm on one side, cool on the other, but only because it kept one side turned to Gliese 163.

It was the middle section of a Watchkeeper, severed at both ends—a snipped-off cone—and with a long, deep, lateral gouge running the length of its warm side. They decided to chance another small thrust correction to place *Icebreaker* inside the thermal concealment of that gouge. Although they were floating next to part of a Watchkeeper, the ruin of the alien machine was still hundreds of times larger than Kanu's ship, and the gouge was deep enough to hide them completely.

They came to a halt, holding station in their improvised hideaway. The walls and floor of the wound offered glimpses of the Watchkeeper's secret interior—a puzzle of vast and silent mechanisms packed as tightly as intestines—but only a glimpse. They could see no deeper than the outermost viscera, and no blue glow shone from the depths to elucidate the overlying structures.

A living Watchkeeper was awesome enough, Kanu thought. But a dead one was something more because it testified to a greater power—something with the capability to kill a robot as large as a moon.

"We should be safe now," he said, "but just to be certain

we'll power down everything we don't need and sit here as quietly as we can. Swift—can you compute an optimum escape profile for us?"

"Consider it done, Kanu. And thereafter? Resume a higher orbit, beyond the moons? It won't cost us much more energy."

"No—we're not ready for this place just yet. I'll admit it—I'm a little spooked."

"Entirely understandable. Imagine how I feel—another machine intelligence, witnessing butchery on this scale. So where should we go next?"

"I think it's obvious," Kanu said. "Paladin. And hope there are no nasty surprises waiting for us there."

"There are no nasty surprises," Swift said, "only degrees of unpreparedness."

Swift's plan had them waiting ten hours as the fragment's orbit carried it beyond the diameter of the orbit of the outermost moon. It transpired that the Watchkeeper had a measurable gravitational field—strong enough that they had to resist its pull with a whisper of micro-thrust, as if they were moored next to an asteroid. There should have been no surprise in that, but in no other context had the mass of a Watchkeeper ever been detected. It was as if—being dead—some cloaking or mass-negation effect had now ceased to function.

To control gravity, to make mass vanish like a palmed card—here were implicit technological secrets which, suitably unravelled, might spur a thousand industrial revolutions. But Kanu and his companions could only content themselves with the gathering of data. The understanding—the exploitation—would have to be left to other minds, in other solar systems, if it could be done at all.

Still, here was another solid discovery to add to the puzzles they had already found. A new Mandala, wheels taller than the sky and a glimpse into the physics of the Watchkeepers. If Kanu did nothing else with his life, these findings would be achievement enough. The very thought of it—the idea of contributing something this big to the sum of human knowledge—brought him solace. It was good to have done something useful, and to have survived until now.

At no point could Kanu say he felt totally calm—there were still too many unknowns for that—but there was an easing in his mood, a sense that at least one challenge had been met. He realised, quite suddenly, that he was ravenously hungry. It would be good to eat, not knowing what lay ahead or when they might have the chance again.

Nissa agreed with him.

"Thank you for allowing me to make that decision," she said when they were seated at their table. "Even if the idea was Swift's."

"It was right to do something. My plan wasn't a plan at all."

"You never told me that story about the snakes before."

He thought back to the happy, golden bliss of their short few weeks together since Lisbon, before the reality of his mission came between them. "There hasn't really been time."

"I mean during all the years we were married. I'm sure I'd remember."

"Really?"

"The old Kanu was a good man. He told a lot of stories, but most of them were designed to put him in a good light. Subtly, I'll admit, but admitting to weakness definitely wasn't one of his strengths."

"I admitted to a weakness?"

"Indecision is a poor quality, especially in a politician, a mover and shaker."

"Although sometimes it can be better than making the wrong decision in haste."

"Sometimes," Nissa conceded. And in a gesture that was outwardly small but which conveyed magnitudes, she allowed herself to add a measure of wine to Kanu's glass. "But not always."

He was not forgiven, he knew that. Perhaps there could be no forgiveness after the catalogue of injustices he had inflicted on her, from betrayal to outright kidnapping. But independently of forgiveness there was an unconditional kindness, a generosity of spirit, which she had always possessed, and for which he now thanked his stars.

"I have said it before," he told her, "but I cannot say it too often. I am sorry."

"We saw the worldwheels," Nissa said. "No one else has. That doesn't excuse what you did to me. But in this moment, after what we just survived? I'm glad to be here. And I want to go back, to find out what those worldwheels have to tell us."

"They frighten me," Kanu admitted.

"And me. But I won't rest until we've confronted them. Snakes everywhere, Kanu Akinya, no matter where you look. But sometimes you just have to step into the grass."

Kanu lifted his glass and sipped his wine. It was as delicious as any vintage he could remember.

They left on a ghost of thrust, emerging from the Watchkeeper's wound at a few tens of metres per second, more than enough to break the pull of its gravitational field, and for several minutes all was well. They had seen nothing of Poseidon for the ten hours of their concealment, but now the planet was visibly smaller and they were safely outside the weave of its moons. Swift made another course correction, lining them up for the transit out to Paladin. Kanu allowed himself to believe they had beaten the odds on this one, and for that he was grateful. Whatever they encountered around Paladin, they would take much more care not to stumble into danger a second time.

But that was when the Watchkeeper struck.

CHAPTER 23

On its approach to Orison, *Travertine* directed the full bore of its mapping sensors at the little world's surface. The instruments clarified a picture of a virtually airless planet, its grey-pink surface lavishly cratered, its magnetosphere extinguished, its atmosphere no more than a thin, attenuated relic slowly leaking into space. Nothing orbited Orison, no moons or stations or ships, and the planet showed no obvious signs of large-scale settlement. There were a handful of metallic features scattered within several hundred kilometres of each other, but few of them were large enough to be independent camps. Somewhere in the middle of these scattered signatures was a larger, concentrated cluster of objects and power sources, and this coincided with the origin of the most recent burst of transmissions.

They studied it at maximum magnification, picking out a small hamlet of domes and locks and connecting tubes, with hints of deeper structures buried underground. Even from orbit, it had a makeshift, unplanned look to it, as if thrown together in haste using whatever components were available. Scratchy trails led away from the camp, aimed in the rough direction of the other metallic features far over the camp's horizon.

A surface expedition was soon made ready and a scouting party selected to go down in the heavy lander. Vasin would lead it, accompanied by Goma, Loring, Karayan and Dr. Nhamedjo.

"And Ru," Goma said.

"She isn't well enough," Vasin said. "I watched her stumbling around only a few hours ago."

"We're all stumbling around, Gandhari. Ru's no worse than the rest of us. Anyway—why the hell does Maslin Karayan get to come along if Ru can't?"

"He has every right."

Goma folded her arms. "So does Ru."

"It took a lot of negotiation to talk Maslin into coming on his own rather than as part of a larger Chancer delegation. But if it means this much to you, I will speak to Saturnin again."

"Do so."

"I am not accustomed to taking instructions, Goma."

"I mean: please."

"You are very determined," Vasin said, not without approval. "There is more of her in you than any of us realise, I think. But be careful you don't become her—I rather like you the way you are."

Nhamedjo was initially unwilling, declaring Ru still much too frail for a surface expedition. But at the collective insistence of both Goma, Ru and—with a measure of reluctance—the captain herself, he eventually agreed to reconsider his position. While the lander was being readied, he brought Ru back to the medical suite for another series of tests. Whether it was stubbornness, or some late improvement in her condition, Ru scraped narrowly through. Nhamedjo conceded that she could cope with a spacesuit's breathing system, and she was not so weak that the trip in the lander would cause her difficulties. In return for this concession, Goma agreed not to cause a fuss about the presence of Maslin Karayan.

"Whatever persuasion you used on Doctor Nhamedjo," Goma said later, when she and Ru were alone in their room, "tell me you're really well enough for this."

"I am."

"Good, because I need you around for the rest of this expedition. And don't forget we have a return trip to make."

"Yes," said Ru, feigning surprise. "Somehow that had slipped my memory."

"I mean you have to be strong for that, too. No good wearing yourself out here."

"I know you mean well, but honestly, nothing could stop me being on that lander. Miss the chance to see you getting taken down a peg by your dear dead grandmother, or whatever she is?"

"Glad to hear your motives are so pure."

"Scientific curiosity comes into it, too, of course. Tell me you're as excited by that as I am."

Despite her apprehension Goma forced a smile. "I am."

It was true, or near enough. For the first time since Mposi's death she had something else to think about. The prospect of having a few of their questions answered—albeit at the expense of dealing with the haughty reincarnation of her distant ancestor—could not help but excite her. She was desperate to know more, and soon she would.

But still—Mposi.

"Ru . . . there's something I need to tell you. I wasn't happy bringing it up until you were stronger, but—"

"If you're breaking up with me, your timing is a little unfortunate."

"Please don't joke."

"All right, sorry. Go on."

"Do you remember me asking you to try to reprogram my bangle?"

"I couldn't."

"No, but Aiyana Loring could. Ve fixed it, and I broke into

Grave's room—where they were keeping him after the trial, before they put him into freeze. It was late one night, no one else around. I wanted to see him, to speak to him, before skipover."

"In the name of hell, why?"

"Doubts. Mposi. Him being a better judge of people than most of us will ever be. I wondered . . . worried . . ." Goma hesitated, realising she was on the threshold of confessing something that could not easily be undone. "I wondered if Grave was telling the truth—that he didn't kill Mposi, and they were acting together after all."

"Oh, he really got to you, didn't he?"

"I had to be sure, Ru."

"You mean you had to let that little weasel plant the seed of doubt in your mind. I thought you were stronger than that, wife. I thought you had sense."

Goma did not rise to the provocation. She was prepared to give Ru the benefit of many doubts given the drugs currently swirling through her blood.

"No one got to me—and Grave's story isn't ridiculous. Even Captain Vasin couldn't establish his guilt beyond all doubt, which is why she accepted this half-measure of having him frozen rather than executing him. Someone *did* try to damage the ship—no doubt about that. But if it wasn't Grave, then the culprit is still out there."

"Well, let's see. Grave was a Second Chancer, and there are eleven other Second Chancers on the ship. Where do we start—with the women, or the children?"

"Please take me seriously."

Ru nodded firmly. "I am. But equally I have no idea how we're meant to act on this change of heart of yours. Nothing you just told me will cut any ice with Gandhari. Have you spoken to her about it?"

"I can't see what it'd achieve. She's heard Grave's side of things. I've nothing to add to that."

"Then what exactly was it about this midnight visit that rocked your world to its foundations?"

"He mentioned Tantors."

Ru made a sneer of disgust. "And if there was one emotional button he knew would work on you—"

"It wasn't just that," Goma said, trying hard not to snap.

"He's aware of the possibility that splinters of the original population might be out there. He doesn't even hate what they are. But he says whoever's behind the sabotage attempt won't sit back if we encounter them."

"Won't sit back—what does that even mean?"

"That the saboteur has another weapon, but won't use it until we're close to them."

"If we ever meet them."

Goma nodded solemnly. "If."

"Then we'd both better hope Grave was delusional, hadn't we?"

"Or keep our wits about us. I keep thinking Uncle Mposi would have had all the answers, all the wisdom. But I bet he'd have given anything for Chiku's guidance, and Chiku probably felt the same way about Sunday."

"And Sunday would've missed whoever, all the way back to your mouldering ancestor. Hard to think of that sour old relic missing anyone, but I suppose she must have. One day, Goma, it'll be you that someone misses."

"I'm not so sure about that."

"I am," Ru said.

The lander had a crew capacity of twelve, so there was more than enough room for six of them, including spacesuits and surface equipment. Goma had seen the heavy transport being prepared for departure. It was a squat, multi-engined cylinder with retractable landing legs and an angular cockpit bubble jutting out from the cylinder's side, its faceted windows offering the best possible field of view for the pilot. Inside there was a surprising amount of space, with a bridge, common area, medical suite, galley and several semi-private crew compartments, each of which was rigged with zero-gravity sleeping hammocks. Vasin was already in the command chair on the bridge when Goma boarded, the chair projecting out into the bubble, Vasin imprisoned by folding screens and controls. She appeared to be in her element, utterly indifferent to the risks presented by this expedition. If the worst befell her, though, Nasim Caspari had the necessary skills to command *Travertine*.

After a series of checks and reports, they were finally given permission to detach from the larger ship. They pushed out to a safe distance, then executed a deorbit burn. The lander descended under controlled power, shrugging aside the atmosphere's ghostly resistance. They were never quite weightless, and as they lowered closer to Orison, so the pull of its gravity became steadily more apparent until it reached a maximum of about half a gee.

They overflew the encampment, first at an altitude of ten kilometres, then at successively lower elevations, while Vasin picked out a suitable landing site—it was near one of the scratchy trails that led out to the more distant features. The terrain was uneven, with escarpments and slab-sided plateaus. On some of the lower outcroppings Goma noticed dome-shaped piles of rock, arranged too deliberately to be accidental.

"I meant to speak to you before this," Maslin Karayan said, sitting close enough that she could not ignore him.

"Did you?"

"Yes, but the time was never right. I wanted to say that I am truly sorry for what happened to Mposi." They had made the bullish, barrel-chested man trim his beard in readiness for skipover. All of them had also had their scalp hair cut short or shaved off completely so that the requisite transcranial scans could be conducted with minimum difficulty. In Karayan's case the change was the most dramatic, softening his features and making him look both younger and less sternly patrician.

Goma saw this as a trap, not a blessing.

"And I am sorry that extremists were ever allowed on this expedition."

"In your view, then," Karayan said, "anyone who does not share your exact philosophy is an extremist?"

"If you want to put it like that."

Karayan ruminated. She thought she had silenced him, but after a moment he said, "Mposi would not have agreed with you."

"You think you knew him that well?"

"Well enough. Our paths crossed over the years and I always found him willing to set aside differences, to see beyond ideology."

"Ideology is all there is."

"Really? I would have thought there were many other

human qualities worth considering. Fairness. Generosity. A sense of humour. A willingness to see the best in people, even those we do not automatically agree with." He glanced out of the window at the monotonous and arid terrain over which they were now circling. "Shall I tell you a story?"

"If you must."

A whirr signalled the deployment of the landing gear. It whined into place and locked with a series of metallic thuds.

"I was gravely ill, once—a bad reaction to one of the local organisms on Crucible. Mposi and I were political adversaries, but he still found time to arrange help for my wife and children, and to come and see me when I was well enough for visitors. He did a great deal for me and mine, although he always downplayed it—said it was a small favour, nothing more. I never forgot that gesture, and I always made sure Mposi knew it."

"You fought like cats."

"We argued our positions when much was at stake, but nothing interfered with our basic respect for each other as human beings. And I regret very much that we have lost Mposi's stabilising influence. He was an ally to us all."

She could have left it at that, but something in his manner had undermined her instinctive dislike of him. She thought back to a conversation with Mposi, when he mentioned the "small favour." It accorded with Karayan's account of the same kindness.

"Did you really not know Peter Grave before the expedition?"

"I wish I had known him better. Unfortunately, there was very little contact between us until shortly before the ship left. Perhaps if there had been more time . . ."

At the risk of putting words into his mouth, she said, "You'd have realised what he was, what he was capable of?"

"I'm tempted to think so, but in practice, I'm not sure I am that good a judge of character. During his time with us, I certainly sensed that he was an outsider, or rather an outlier. Call him an extremist, if you will."

"Then why did you put up with him?"

"Our movement encompasses a spectrum of viewpoints. I could hardly criticise Peter Grave for believing in certain things more forcefully than some of the rest of us."

He was speaking in a low voice now, barely audible above the dull roar of the lander's motors and life-support system. Again, Goma recalled Mposi telling her that Karayan was obliged to project a blustering self-image in order to unite the disparate groups of Second Chancers. Here, now, perhaps he felt able to express more moderate sentiments.

"Of course, we always agreed on the essentials," he said, as if that affirmation were necessary.

"Of course," Goma said. But they were playing a game now, each understanding what the other really meant.

"Be glad that Peter Grave is where he is," Karayan said. "There may have been one bad apple among us, but I do not think there will be a second."

She nodded, wishing desperately to believe things were as simple as that. Grave the conspirator, Grave the murderer, and Grave now safely on ice for the rest of the expedition.

They were on final vertical descent now, the blast of the lander's motors beginning to pick up dust and small pieces of surface debris, sending them scurrying away in surging concentric waves. They were not far from the encampment—Goma could easily make out the silver crest of the nearest dome. Vasin called out altitudes: one hundred metres, fifty, then down in increments of ten. The salmon-coloured dust rose and swallowed the view. Finally Goma felt the soft compression of the landing gear touch down and heard the motors stop. The lander rocked slightly, then was still.

"Engines off. Stable and secured for return to orbit," Vasin declared, not without a measure of pride.

It did not take long to prepare for the surface. All six of them exited through the lander's high-capacity lock and then climbed one at a time down the ladder which had deployed upon touchdown. They wore lightweight spacesuits, silver-white to begin with, but which selected their own visually distinct colour-coding as soon as the party assembled below the lander. Goma had received just enough training not to feel encumbered by the suit.

"Are you all right?" she asked Ru, concerned that her breathing sounded laboured.

"Stop fretting," Ru said, in a firm but friendly tone.

They moved away from the lander and joined the trail

heading back to the encampment. They had touched down in an area of low, gentle hills, reaching away under a mauve sky that darkened to purple-black at the zenith. There were a few clouds, laddered wisps of high-altitude vapour, and enough of a breeze to stir dust around their feet, but the air was a thousand times thinner than the atmosphere aboard their ship. They could see stars, and other worlds in this solar system. The trail had been cleared of debris, but a treacherous scree of small stones and pebbles littered the surrounding terrain. The colours of this planet were all mauves and fawns and shades of pale rust. It was relentless and depressing, not a hint of a living organism anywhere to be seen.

The encampment looked further away now they were down. Surrounding it, but thinning out with distance, was a junkyard of failed or abandoned technologies. There were transmitter aerials, sagging where their guylines had snapped. There were radio dishes, jammed into the dirt and now half-filled with dust. There were boxes of electronics, gutted and exposed to the elements. Where electrical or data cables were still strung from pole to pole, they had been hung with tattered, fluttering pieces of metal foil, like bunting. A drum fixed to an axle like a wheel appeared to turn lazily of its own volition.

Nearer the camp, the air of decrepitude lessened. Projecting above the small cluster of domes was a skeletal tower surmounted by a set of transmitters and receivers of differing function. Though it had clearly been repaired and patched up over the years, it still looked operable, with various steerable dishes and antennas, plus the tubes of what Goma guessed to be optical telescopes or ranging devices.

Of a spaceship, even a short-range vehicle, even something to cross the ground, no trace existed.

They halted as one, noticing movement. To one side of the camp was a low cliff, perhaps three or four storeys high. The cliff face was nearly sheer, but a figure was nonetheless clinging about halfway up it with spiderlike tenacity, feet planted on the narrowest of ledges, one hand grasping a rocky protrusion, the other wielding a cutting tool. All along the face, to both sides of where the figure worked, was a dense patterning of angular inscriptions. The cutting tool had a sun-bright tip, a glaring flicker. Where it touched the cliff, the rock breezed off in a constant curling ribbon of grey dust.

"It's her," Goma said.

They had made no sound in the near vacuum of Orison, but the figure nonetheless turned off the cutting tool and slipped it back into a pouch on a utility belt. With disarming speed—and an equally disarming lack of concern for their own safety—the figure appeared to descend the crag in a series of perilous backward hops.

On reaching the ground, the figure looked back up at the cliff, as if inspecting the day's work, then turned to address the landing party. The figure was small and slight in stature, clad in an older, clumsier model of spacesuit than those worn by the landing party.

The figure raised a hand. For a moment nothing was said, the figure and the landing party facing each other in silence, nothing moving except the dust and the flapping flags and the idly turning wheel.

"Eunice Akinya?" asked Vasin.

A voice buzzed across their communications channel. It was a woman's, speaking Swahili with a curiously old-fashioned, fussy diction.

"No, Laika the space dog. Who else were you expecting?"

CHAPTER 24

To begin with there was only the fact of the attack and their own immediate survival. Had the Watchkeeper been intact and its offensive capabilities fully functional, there would have been no warning and no conceivable defence—merely an instant in which Kanu existed, followed by an endless succession of instants in which he did not.

But he was breathing, and thinking, and the fabric of the

ship—at least judged from the pressurised vantage of the control deck—could not have been too violently disrupted.

But he heard the wail of alarms, saw the red pulse of alert indications, felt in his belly the beginning of an uncontrolled tumble as *Icebreaker* lost control of its orientation. He looked at Nissa, saw the understanding in her face—no need for either of them to state the obvious.

"Can you do something?" she asked.

Kanu's hands were on the console, trying to force the ship to correct its own tumble, but the systems were not responding. "No good. Control lockouts across all steering systems—it's not allowing itself to fire compensatory thrust. Swift—if you think you can do better than me, now's your chance."

He felt Swift assume control of his hands. They began to move across the console with a renewed speed and confidence—the difference between a novice and a concert pianist.

"One of you had better find a way to make it," Nissa said. "We don't want to swing back into the Watchkeeper."

"We're trying," Kanu said. "Hard to see how bad the damage is—sensors are completely burned out along that whole flank."

"What hit us?"

"Nothing physical—not a missile or anything like that. Must have been an energy pulse, some kind of electromagnetic discharge. I'm not even sure it counted as an attack—more of a playful nip."

"It didn't feel very playful to me," Nissa said.

"It must have been. We're still here."

Swift had turned up the console's visual refresh-rate. Status readouts flickered at hypnagogic speed, too fast for his conscious faculties to absorb.

"What's he doing?"

"I wish I knew. Talk to me, Swift."

"It is rather serious," Swift answered. "We are drifting further from the Watchkeeper, which is encouraging, and there has been no further attack—but equally the evidence points to severely compromised guidance and propulsion capability. I am attempting to persuade the ship to let me stabilise its tumble."

"Persuade a bit harder, then."

"Do not blame *Icebreaker*, Kanu—the ship is doing its best. It knows it has been badly damaged and it is wisely protecting us. I will do what I can. I have some thruster channels open to me now—would you mind if I augmented their effect with the selective venting of internal air and water pressure?"

"And bleed us dry?"

"Volatile gases can be mined and the reserves replenished once we locate a suitable resource. Besides, only a small percentage will be required—say five to ten, depending on circumstances." Swift pushed on, apparently taking Kanu's consent for granted. "There—we are already regaining some control. When we are properly stable, we can think of ways to assess the extent of the damage."

"There's only one quick way to do that," said Kanu. "I'll need to go outside to see how bad things really are."

"With the ship caught in this tumble?" Nissa asked. "You'll be flung into space the moment you make a mistake."

"Then I'd better make sure I don't. I think Swift can help with that, can't you?"

"If you will allow me a little more time to do what I can from this position, then we shall attempt it together."

Slowly the tumble reduced until Kanu felt confident that he could move around inside *Icebreaker* without immediate injury. He instructed Swift to leave things as they were, then rose from his seat. It would still be a challenge to reach the suit locker, let alone take care of himself in vacuum with the ship still tumbling like a thrown bone, but he had to assess the damage.

"You're leaving me here alone?" Nissa asked.

"The ship's programmed to answer to you if something goes wrong. In the meantime, we'll still be able to talk."

After he had struggled into the suit—Kanu would never find it a quick or easy process, despite his years on Mars—he cycled through the airlock closest to the damage, which brought him to the brink of space. He pushed his head and upper body out into true vacuum, taking in the view. The hull stretched away on either side of him—sometimes feeling as if it were a ceiling, at other times like a floor or the sheer side of a cliff. Much of it was smooth, but here and there handholds and footholds had been provided, and with some concentration he could plot a route that would take him to the damaged area, which was presently out of sight.

"Can we do this, Swift?"

"With care, Kanu. I will let you take the initiative until I feel the need to intervene. Maintain three points of contact at all times, and do not be distracted by the huge planet dominating your field of view."

"Thank you," Kanu said, with all the false sincerity he could muster.

But it was one thing to see Poseidon on-screen, and quite another to view it with his own eyes. Its lit face was turned to him, wrapped from pole to pole by a smothering deep ocean. As tall as the worldwheels were, they were too narrow in cross section to be visible from this distance. As he watched, a splinter-like sliver moved across the planet's face with the perfect Newtonian slide of a dead eye cell. It was the remains of a Watchkeeper, perhaps even the one that had attacked them. He felt no anger towards the alien machine, sensing that there had been little or no intent behind the attack.

Kanu brought his whole body out of the lock, nervously grasping for a handhold, then another, until his feet could find purchase. He was not standing so much as spreadeagled on the hull, and the ship's slow tumble made it feel as if it wanted rid of him as he spidered along. Slowly, adrenalin flooding his veins, his hands trembling with nervous concentration, he began to traverse away from the lock. His first few reaches were awkward, but he forced himself to pick up the pace, to trust to the limbs and senses that had never failed him before. The tumble was not in itself the problem—he was perfectly strong enough to hold on despite it. His real enemy was fear.

As he began to work around the hull's curve, the lock fell away out of sight. Poseidon swung in and out of view—too large to ignore, since it was always bright and blue in his peripheral vision. He felt the world's scrutiny on him, as if it were taking a particular interest in his fate.

Ahead was a recess in the hull, a trough a few metres deep. There was no way around it that would not take precious minutes and bring its own hazards. Crossing the trough would require a longer reach than he was used to making, but Kanu saw no practical alternative.

"Keep your eye on me, Swift—if things go wrong out here, they'll go wrong fast."

"My eye is never not on you, my friend."

Kanu stretched across the gap, fingers grasping for the handhold on the other side. But as he pushed out into the void, his heart jumped in his chest.

"Fuck!"

"What is it?" Nissa called out sharply.

"Fuck."

"Calm down, Kanu," Swift said. "Having a seizure will avail neither of us."

"Kanu?" Nissa called, with real concern in her voice.

"I'm fine. I just wasn't expecting to find a corpse here." He was staring at it, his pulse still racing. It was tucked into the space, sheathed in baroque and cumbersome armour, squatting and compressed as if ready to spring out in ambush. "One of the Regals," he went on. "I don't know whose side they were on."

"A Regal? How in hell did a Regal get here?"

"They must have been stuck on the side of the ship since before we left Europa. Maybe they were trying to break into the ship, or use it as a hiding space."

"That's horrible."

"I doubt they survived more than a few seconds after we broke through the ice. Maybe there are more. We'll have to search the whole ship at some point, I expect." He shivered inside the suit. He had been close to very few corpses in his time and the experience was still unpleasantly novel. "I'm sorry," he told the dead warrior.

"Sorry for what?" Nissa asked.

"That I did this."

"You didn't make this happen. You heard the Margrave—things were breaking down on Europa before we arrived."

"I certainly helped them along."

"Then I'll take my share of the blame, too. I'd have ended up there even if we hadn't met in Lisbon."

He left the corpse, having noted its position, and approached the edge of the damage zone. Finally, his confidence improved—the corpse had pushed him over some horizon of fear into a startling sort of calm—and Kanu risked standing upright, with his toes planted firmly into footholds. Overlooking the damage, he was momentarily silent.

Although he kept telling himself that they were lucky to have survived the Watchkeeper attack at all, the impact area was worse than he had feared. It was an open wound dozens of metres long and almost as deep, cut with cruel disregard into the ripe, vital organs of his starship. Gases were venting from numerous ruptured pipes, coiling out in glittering blue-grey nebulae.

"Can you see this, Nissa?"

"Yes, I have a feed from your helmet. It's not pretty. I'm no expert, but I don't think that's going to be a five-minute repair job."

"No, it won't."

"It's worse than we thought," Swift said, then after a moment, he added, "We haven't merely lost propulsion control. That area of the hull also contained your main directional antenna. With the exception of short-range communications, we are now without the means to send or receive transmissions."

"I'd say that was a catastrophe," Kanu said, "but no one was talking to us anyway."

The hull was blackened in a wide area beyond the obvious limits of the wound itself, suggestive of a massive concentration of energy. He risked stepping nearer to the edge of the damaged section. Gas was still geysering out from multiple locations. It aggrieved Kanu to see any kind of pressure loss. Darkly, he began to wonder if this sort of damage was even repairable at all.

"I need to take a closer look," Kanu said.

He bent down, preparing to resume his spidering progress, when something flashed white. There was no pain, and barely enough of an interval of lucidity before the coming of unconsciousness for him to register one simple truth.

He was no longer attached to anything.

He was falling into ever-darkening waters, each layer colder and heavier and stiller than the last. He was on his back, his face turned to the receding surface. He could still see some evidence of the sun, its radiance chopped into pieces by the waves, its light further diminished by the oppressive mass of water that now lay between him and the air. He reached out, trying to claw his way back to the light, but for all his slow thrashing he could not arrest his descent. He knew how to swim; that was not the problem. He was simply too heavy now, and the pull of the deep layers too powerful. He glanced beneath him, but could see nothing below except steadily mounting blackness. A little daylight still found its way to him now, but soon he would be down to a few struggling photons, feeble as glow-worms, and after that there would be nothing but darkness. An endless succession of moments in which he did not figure.

Something eclipsed the wavering sunlight. It was another kind of darkness, more concentrated than the general absence of illumination below him. It had a distinct core, like a negative shadow of the sun itself, and radiating from that core were wavering beams of darkness. It was swelling, stealing more and more of the precious light.

One of the wavering beams reached out towards him, stretching down to arrest his fall. He surrendered to it, allowing the dark limb to coil its padded extremity around his midriff.

"Leviathan," Kanu said. And felt a surge of joy that his old friend had come back to him.

He remembered nothing of the return journey to *Icebreaker*. It was only later that he came to an understanding of what had happened to him—an explosion from the rupture point, the blast damaging his suit and sending him falling away from the ship, back towards Poseidon.

Nissa had chased him aboard *Fall of Night*, willingly placing herself at risk of another stinging attack from the Watchkeeper—knowing full well that her own ship was much less capable of surviving such an assault.

"I caught you," she said. "Swung in sideways, matched speed, allowed you to drift into my lock. You were nearly dead. Even when I brought you in, got you out of the suit, I didn't know if you were going to make it."

"I remember nothing."

"I'm not surprised. You were out cold. Swift was doing all the talking."

"Swift?"

"Yes. Your other half."

For a moment he had forgotten. He was still thinking of his old friend the kraken, the happiness he had felt knowing that Leviathan had again found a purpose in life.

"Thank you for saving me," Kanu said, hesitantly, for there was something in her manner that left him disquietened. "Thank you for placing yourself in harm's way for me."

"Self-interest played its part," Nissa replied, her tone businesslike. "I'd rather not have to fix and operate this starship on my own."

"Regardless of why you did it, I'm still grateful. But why can't I move?"

"Because you're fixed to a surgical unit."

He was lying on his back. He nodded slowly, stiffly, at last recognising his surroundings. She must have brought him to the medical bay, removed the outer layer of his suit and placed him on one of the auto-surgical platforms.

"That can't have been easy."

"I had some assistance. I explained to Swift what I was trying to do, and he helped. You were unconscious, but Swift could still move your body around."

"I see." There was a drift to this conversation that was not quite to his liking. He did not feel injured. Exhausted, confused, but not injured. Was there more wrong with him than he realised?

"I put a gun to your head. Actually, more like a harpoon. I retrieved it from that body you found outside, the Regal. Do you remember the Regal?"

"I do now."

"I brought the harpoon thing back inside with me. I don't know whether it works or not, but that's not really the point. Swift didn't know either, and he wasn't going to take a chance and find out. I needed a bargaining position, you see. Does that make sense to you?"

"Perfect sense."

"It wasn't my intention to kill you—if it had been, I could

have just let you fall away from the ship—but we do need to change our working relationship."

"In what way?" Kanu asked, with a forced levity.

"I accept the situation. I accept that Swift got inside your skull and dragged us across interstellar space. Nothing's going to change that. And now that we're here, I'm not about to turn my back on these discoveries. I want answers, too—and I want to survive, and to fix this ship. But we do things as equals from now on."

"As far as I'm concerned, we've been on equal terms since we reached this system."

"Fine words, Kanu, but from my position things look a little asymmetric. There's the small matter of Swift. Now, I'm not so naive as to think I can cut him out of your head like a disease—nor would I want to."

"Good. That's good."

"You and Swift got us into this; it'll take both of you to get us out of it. But as I said, things have to change. Swift and I have been talking, and we've come to a mutually acceptable solution. The auto-surgeon is going to put a small implant into your head—a very simple device, nothing complicated. It will address your visual and auditory centres, in effect eavesdropping on your private conversations."

"Are you absolutely sure you want to go through with this?"

"Yes, I'm quite sure. And here's the clever part. When it's done with you, the surgeon will reactivate some of my own latent neuromachinery, the stuff I've been carrying around in my head since the fall of the Mechanism. It'll establish a communications protocol between the two sets of implants. Do you understand what that means?"

Kanu did not need to think about it for long. "You'll be able to see and hear Swift."

"More than that—I'll be able to talk to Swift just as easily as you can, at least when we're in close proximity. Equals at last—or as equal as I want to be. Does that strike you as an acceptable arrangement?"

Kanu considered his options—try and talk her out of it, or accept that allowing Swift to be visible to both of them might be a path to forgiveness, or at least a step along the way.

"I suppose it does."

"I'm glad. Although, to be fair, it wouldn't make the slightest difference to me either way. I'd still be doing it."

After a silence, Kanu said, "Do you hate me?"

"Hate you? No, I don't even dislike you. Why would I? We were married, and then we were lovers again. You're all over me like a chemical stain."

"That's a flattering way of putting it."

"You've been flattered enough. Things change now." She leaned over as if to kiss him, but instead she was merely activating the surgeon. "Now sleep. When you wake up, we'll talk about our options. The three of us, as one happy family."

The surgeon's sterile hood whirred over him and he heard the hiss of anaesthetic gas.

"Did you agree to this?" he asked Swift.

"I had to. You'd be surprised how persuasive a harpoon gun can be."

The three of them were sitting on the bridge, the evidence of Kanu's surgery visible as tiny clots of blood on either side of his temples.

"So basically there are no good choices," Nissa said. "Is that what you're telling us?"

"We haven't escaped Poseidon's gravity well," Swift said, "and left to itself, *Icebreaker* doesn't have the capability to do so. The damage to the propulsion system is simply too extensive. Equally, we aren't in immediate peril. We'll simply orbit and orbit, and hope we don't attract the attention of either those moons or any more almost-dead Watchkeepers. Power isn't our problem—we can easily return to skipover and await rescue."

"From where?" Kanu asked.

"Given that no one will be able to reply to our transmission until we repair our antennas, that is an exceptionally good question. At the moment our effective communicational range is no more than light-seconds, perhaps less. Sooner or later another ship will reach this system, and perhaps they will find a way to signal us, but we might have to wait many decades for that to happen."

Kanu and Nissa were in their control chairs; Swift's

figment was seated before them in a chair of his own imagining. He had one leg hooked over the other, an elbow on the armrest, chin resting in his hand, pince-nez glasses dangling from his fingers, the very model of urbane relaxation. Kanu thought back to their many chess games and wished that nothing more was at stake now than his own intellectual pride.

"That's no good," Nissa said.

"Which is why we must consider Paladin," Swift said. "*Fall of Night* is much smaller than *Icebreaker*, but it has the capability to shove both ships out of Poseidon's gravity well and into a transfer orbit for Paladin. When we reach Paladin, *Fall of Night* can steer us into a rendezvous with the orbiting shard."

"How long will that take?" Kanu said.

"About a year. I'm afraid that's orbital transfer mechanics for you. The damage to our ship has effectively catapulted us back into the early rocket age. Now we move at the speed of comets, of asteroids."

"We could be there a lot quicker if we just took *Fall of Night*," Nissa said. "It can talk to other ships, too, if anyone's listening."

"But then we would be abandoning our only hope of return," Swift answered patiently. "And we would still need to drag *Icebreaker* across the system to get it repaired and re-fuelled. At least this way we arrive with our ship."

"But all that time!" Nissa said.

"It won't be wasted," Swift said. "Kanu's ship can begin to repair some of the damage now—rebuild steering control and communications. That will give us a valuable head start."

"Then we go back into skipover," Kanu said.

"Unless you would rather be awake for the entire transfer. Is this acceptable to you, Nissa?"

"You did say there were no good options—I suppose sleeping is as good a way to pass the time as any other. But you'll be asleep as well, won't you, Swift?"

"I'm afraid so. Skipover will suppress all Kanu's higher brain functions, including those useful to me. But we need not worry. *Icebreaker* already has a high level of autonomy. It will wake us if there is a development."

"Such as what?" Nissa said.

"I have no idea," the figment answered. "I can tie our systems into *Fall of Night*'s and continue transmitting our recognition signal via Nissa's ship. It will be less powerful, and less capable of detecting a weak return signal, but we will lose nothing by trying."

"Nothing will answer us," Kanu said, struck by a sudden gloomy fatalism. "If they meant to, it would already have happened."

"Nonetheless, we may as well keep trying. Nissa: I will provide you with a range of solutions for the transfer orbit—each will put a different strain on *Fall of Night*. I will leave it to you to make the final selection and handle the operation itself."

"That's very good of you, Swift," Nissa said, drenching her answer in sarcasm.

Swift gave an obliging smile. "One tries."

Nissa was easily capable of using her ship as a tug. They agreed on an option which provided for rendezvous with Paladin in just over eleven months, with fuel in reserve for the corresponding orbital correction at the other end of the manoeuvre. Not that it really mattered if they used up all of Nissa's fuel: if they could not replenish *Icebreaker*'s initialising tanks, they would be going nowhere anyway.

Inside the larger ship, it was hard to believe there had been any course correction at all. Such was the difference in the masses of the two ships that even with its drive at maximum output, *Fall of Night* could provide only the gentlest of accelerations. But the push was sustained over several hours, and when it was done, Swift confirmed that they were on course.

Kanu spent a restless couple of days making sure the repair systems were working as intended. When that was not on his mind, he kept transmitting his recognition signal, this time sending it via *Fall of Night*'s much smaller antenna. He had announced his arrival to every obvious body in the solar system; now he was ready to consider anything larger than a pebble. But still the signal went unanswered. He was starting to imagine something in that silence: not the simple absence of an answer, but something more sinister, a kind of purposeful withholding. A decision not to speak, a deliberate and calculated refusal to acknowledge his presence.

"Perhaps you shouldn't be so surprised," Nissa said as his mood began to darken again. "The message wasn't meant for you and Swift in the first place."

"They could at least do us the courtesy of answering, after all the distance we've travelled."

"It's not how far you've come that matters. It's where you've come from."

After that, there was nothing to do but sleep.

Kanu reviewed the orbital transfer again and programmed their caskets for an interval a few days short of the end of the crossing. It would give them time to adjust to their surroundings, make renewed efforts at contact and generally recover from skipover before they arrived at their destination.

He put Nissa to sleep, watched her casket seal itself over her body, monitored the medical readouts for the smooth transition to unconsciousness, and then observed her gradual decline into cryogenic suspension. He touched a hand to the casket's cool side, feeling an intense protectiveness for her. He loved her and wanted to make amends for the wrongs he had done her, from the failings of their marriage to the recent deceits concerning his intentions for Europa and beyond. It would please him very much if Nissa Mbaye were to start seeing him as a good man again.

Perhaps there was still time.

Almost without thought, he programmed the same sleep interval into his own casket. They would awaken together. Whatever the shard held for them, they would face it as partners.

And so Kanu submitted himself to the cold once more.

CHAPTER 25

The airlock was set into the side of the largest dome, near the transmission tower. It was a high-capacity lock with a lofty ceiling, large enough to take a big vehicle. The chevroned door opened and they all passed through at the same time, Goma studying Eunice's mirrored visor, trying to glimpse the face behind the glass.

Beyond the lock was a gently sloping corridor leading to lower levels. Eunice guided the party a short distance along it until they reached a secondary door set into the corridor's wall. It was not an airlock, but was clearly capable of holding pressure in the event of a blow-out. She opened the door and invited them to step through.

They entered some kind of accommodation area with metal-lined walls and several passages leading off in various directions. There was a table and a set of chairs, although not nearly enough for all of them. Around the metal walls were shelves and cabinets, and various utensils and implements set upon the shelves.

Eunice lowered herself into the grandest chair at the table, then bid the others to take such chairs as were available.

"We don't need to sit down," Vasin said. "Not yet. We've come a long way and what we'd like first is an explanation."

"It's rude not to sit," the spacesuited form said. "But look at me! Calling you rude and I haven't even had the common courtesy to remove my helmet."

She reached up with both hands, undid some latching mechanism on the neck ring and lifted the helmet free of her head. She placed it before her on the table and beamed at them over its crown.

Goma should not have been surprised—she had seen this

woman's face in the earlier transmission, after all—but a transmission could easily be faked or doctored. Yet here was the unmistakable face of Eunice Akinya, a figment from history, strikingly real and human-looking down to the last details.

"There. Fresh air. I hate suit air. Always have, ever since I took that long trek on the Moon. Well, what about the rest of you? Are you going to stand there like fools?"

Nhamedjo was glancing down at his cuff readout. "The air looks good. Perfectly breathable, in fact—no trace toxins, according to the filters. I think we are safe to remove our helmets."

"No," Vasin said.

"Oh, but I insist," Eunice said. "No—really. I insist. You want answers from me, meet me on my terms. Take off your helmets. I want to know who I'm dealing with."

"Worried we might be robots?" Goma asked. But she had already taken a leap of faith and was reaching up to undo her own helmet.

"Goma!" Vasin said. "Don't do it!"

"You heard her. I want answers. If this is what it takes, so be it. I don't think she'd drag us seventy light-years just to play a nasty trick with poison gases."

"Good girl."

Goma lifted her helmet off and the air gushed in. It was cold, but nothing about it smelled or tasted suspicious. She gulped a load of it into her lungs and waited for some ill-effect to manifest.

Nothing. No headache, no light-headedness, no sense that her thoughts were in any way affected.

"The air is breathable," Eunice said, looking not at Goma but at the rest of them. "The gases' ratios won't differ greatly from those on your ship, I expect. There are no biological toxins or radiological hazards. If there were, I'd already know about them."

"Why would a robot care about biological toxins?" Dr. Nhamedjo asked. "For that matter, why does a robot need airlocks or a spacesuit? You're a construct. You could walk out there naked and not feel a thing."

"Those are cooking utensils," Goma said, nodding at some

of the tools she could see racked and shelved around the room. "That is a stove. Why would you need cooking utensils? Why would you ever need to cook anything?"

"A woman's got to eat. Why else?"

Ru lifted the lid on a plastic container, then sprang away in revulsion. "Worms!"

"Mealworms," their host corrected. "Very tasty. Very good source of protein. Practically all we ate on Mars in the early days. You should try them. Go well with a little curry powder— stops them wriggling off your chopsticks, too. Now—since you're staying—will you be good guests and remove the rest of your spacesuits?"

"Why?" Vasin asked.

"Manners, dear Captain."

They obliged, stripping down to their inner clothing layers, and set the spacesuit parts in neat piles by the door. Then, in plain view so there could be no possibility of substitution or subterfuge, she also discarded the outer elements of her spacesuit, removing the parts neatly and methodically, as befitted a veteran space explorer who had come to trust her life to the complex, interlocking components of the garment, and who accorded them the respect and care which was their due.

Beneath the suit she wore a sleeveless ash-grey top and tight black leggings. She resumed her position at the table and offered one arm across it to Dr. Nhamedjo, her palm raised.

"Go ahead. Feel my pulse. Poke and prod to your heart's content."

Nhamedjo moved to touch his fingers to her skin, but hesitated at the last instant. He glanced at his colleagues.

"She cannot be living. We know what she was when she left. This is not open to debate."

Eunice gave a pout of disapproval. "Do I look like a robot to you?"

"The records say you were a very good emulation. You could pass for a living person except under close scrutiny— you looked and sounded and moved like the real Eunice Akinya. But you were still a machine, a robot, under the layers of synthetic anatomy. You got better at acting like a person, but the essence of what you were did not change."

"Test her pulse," Goma said.

Nhamedjo did as he was bid, holding the contact for long seconds. "It feels real."

"Not just the pulse," Eunice said.

"No—everything. The texture of your skin, the anatomy of your wrist joint . . . it's astonishingly good. May I examine your eyes?"

"Whatever you like. You'll come to the same conclusion."

He indulged himself by staring carefully into either eye, pinching back the surrounding skin with physicianly gentleness. He held a hand before her mouth and reported that he could feel the passage of her breath. "I can conduct further tests . . . scans, blood samples. But why doubt the evidence of our eyes and what she's already telling us?"

"Because history says she can't be alive," Goma said.

"History's a stopped clock," Eunice said. "It's nice to look at, but there's only so much it can tell you."

"Then start by telling us how you can possibly be alive," Vasin said.

"Why shouldn't I be?"

"Because the living version of you, the flesh-and-blood Eunice, died in deep space," Goma said. "You went out in a stupid little ship, barely equipped for interstellar space, and unsurprisingly you didn't make it. Years later, they came and found you. They pulled your frozen corpse out of that ship and found that there was no hope of ever reviving you. Your brain cells were just so much slush."

"But there were recoverable patterns," Eunice said. "Chiku brought them to me on *Zanzibar*. I uploaded them into myself, used them to make my emulation even better."

"But you were still a robot," Goma said. "You were a robot with some neural patterns copied from the dead corpse of the real Eunice—a few human flourishes to embellish your programming. But that didn't make you flesh and blood."

"Something did," Nhamedjo said quietly. "Answer me this, Eunice—knowing that I'll be able to verify the answers for myself, given time. Is any part of you still cybernetic?"

She looked at her hand and wiggled the pinky. "My little finger. I kept that as a memento of better times."

"What about your brain? Do you have a brain?"

"If I don't, there's an awful lot of blood wasting its time moving around inside my skull."

"And the structure of that brain . . . the modular organisation? Do you have hemispheres, a frontal cortex, a commissural gap? Is that where your visual processing takes place?"

"I don't know, Doctor—where does yours happen?"

"We could put her in a suit," Vasin said. "Run a standard host medical, have the diagnostic piped to one of our faceplates. If she has a cardiovascular system—heart, lungs—the suit will tell us. It should also pick up neural activity if her brain's anything like ours."

"I think we already know the answer," Nhamedjo said. "She must be organic. She would not embark on such a lie knowing how easily we could prove her wrong."

"Then the Watchkeepers must have done this," Goma said.

This drew a nod from Eunice. "At least one of you has a tenuous grasp on the situation. Of course it was Watchkeeper intervention—how else could it have happened?"

"Why?" Goma said.

"Because it was what I wanted. Because becoming organic—becoming the living incarnation of myself—was the end-point I'd been moving towards for my entire existence. I started off as a bodyless software emulation, a thing stitched together from public and private records of myself. A piece of art. Then I became something more than dear Sunday ever anticipated. A fully autonomous, self-aware artilect—a thing too dangerous to be allowed to exist. So I made myself invisible, dispersed, tenuous—far beyond the reach of the Cognition Police—until the time came when I needed an actual body to bottle myself into. That's how I got aboard *Zanzibar*—stuffed into a robot puppet. But then I acquired those neural traces. They had an interesting effect on me—pushed me over the edge of my own computational prediction horizon. I could no longer foresee my own response to any given stimulus. I'd become quixotic, unguessable—prone to whims and sudden, irrational changes of mind. I experienced complex mental states that I could only characterise as emotions. Human, in other words—except for the fact that my body was still artificial."

"How do you know an emotion is an emotion?" Nhamedjo said.

"Because I'm not an idiot, Doctor. Because when something hurts inside you when you've never had the sense of being hurt inside before—you do the obvious thing and put a name to it. One of my emotions, if we're going to articulate it, was longing."

"I find that difficult to believe," Nhemedjo answered.

"I find you difficult to believe. The fact is that I sensed an absence in myself—an incompleteness. And I knew that until I filled that absence, I wouldn't feel happy. There. Another emotion."

"Go on," Goma said, feeling a loyalty to Eunice.

"I sensed that I had almost attained something, but with that proximity came an almost unbearable desire to complete the circle, to achieve artistic culmination. Have you ever looked at a jigsaw with one piece still to be put in place? I had been sent into existence with one purpose: to stand for Eunice Akinya in the absence of her living self. I had always been an imperfect substitute, a close-enough copy, but nothing that could be mistaken for the real thing. But the Watchkeepers changed all that. It was a trivial thing for them, having taken apart Chiku Green. They knew what makes us tick. They knew how to make me alive—how to pour fire into my soul."

It could still be a trick, Goma knew—clever robotics could produce the illusion of a heartbeat, or an inhalation, or the liquid mysteries of the living eye. But every instinct told her that Dr. Nhamedjo would find nothing amiss, no matter how thorough his examination. He was correct: she would not make this assertion unless it were provably the case.

It was peculiar indeed to be sitting across from this person and find it strange and marvellous that they were made of skin and bone rather than metals and plastics. And in its way, more thoroughly unsettling than any robot could ever be. Robots were knowable; their governing algorithms might be complex and opaque but they were still algorithms. Robots could be shut down or destroyed if they became bothersome.

It was not nearly so simple with people.

"I don't know what to make of you," Goma said.

"That's the first reasonable thing any of you has said. Of

course you don't. I don't know what to make of myself, and I've had plenty of time to think about it."

Goma searched for a flaw in her face, some hint of machine stiffness, a texture or glossiness that was not quite correct. But there was nothing about Eunice that looked anything other than real.

"How long have you been like this?"

"For nearly as long as I've been here. That's the odd thing—I don't appear to be ageing, certainly not to any degree that I can measure." As she said this, she held her hand up for examination, turning it this way and that. "I didn't ask them to make me physically immortal, but they appear to have done so anyway. Perhaps they mistook death for a simple design flaw, a bug in the system, and edited it out of my body. Should I be grateful? I suppose I should be."

"You don't sound convinced."

"They've made me perfect, and in doing so they've introduced an imperfection—the one part of me that doesn't match the living Eunice. She expected to die. Death was the mainspring making her tick. Do you think she'd have done a third of the things she did without that knowledge?"

"Could you be killed?"

"I don't know. I suppose. Then again, I haven't put that one to the test." She cocked her head with sudden birdlike interest. "What are you, exactly? My great-great-granddaughter? Let me think."

"You can add another 'great'—my mother would have been your great-great-granddaughter. But none of that matters. Whatever you are, whatever you've become, it doesn't suddenly make you my distant ancestor." But now Goma found herself hungry for more answers. "Speaking of Ndege—why did you summon her across space? What's so important?"

"I need an Akinya and I thought she would suffice."

"Just an Akinya? No more to it than that?"

"Someone with experience of Tantors."

Goma allowed herself a shiver of private excitement. She glanced at Ru, the look drawing the merest acknowledgement of their shared thrill. The thing they had hoped for, the thing they had hardly dared believe, might just be possible.

"Are they here?"

"Some of them. But that's where the story gets complicated."

"Like it wasn't already complicated?" Ru asked.

"Oh, I'm just getting started."

Goma said, "When you say 'here,' do you mean this system, this planet, what?"

"I mean here in my encampment. Why do you imagine I need such a big airlock? It certainly wasn't for the tourist trade."

"Show me them," Goma said. "Now."

CHAPTER 26

Odd, unsettling dreams chased him all the way to consciousness. He kept seeing himself wandering the empty corridors of the ship, haunting it like a ghost. The dreams had a fever-like repetitiveness, circling back around themselves in Möbius loops. Again and again he returned to Nissa's casket, touching its cold flanks as if he needed reassurance that she was still inside.

Had he really slept, or spent a year sleepwalking his own vessel?

But no, here he was—emerging from skipover, stiff and cold and groggy but relieved to find himself in something as unsparingly specific in its annoyances as reality. His back ached, his neck itched. He could feel where the edge of a fingernail had ripped itself from the quick. Dreams never bothered with that sort of detail.

He waited until he had the strength to move, then hauled himself out of the casket, bones aching, muscles weak, sense of balance off-kilter. It was never good—even a year in skipover was a penitence. Nausea hit him and he dry-heaved into a metal pan, coughing up only a few strands of pinkish phlegm. His throat felt scraped raw as if by broken glass.

Never mind, though—he was awake, and alive, and out of the coils of those dreams. Much more of that, he felt certain, and he would have gone mad.

Vision still blurry, he fumbled his way to Nissa's casket. Condensation beaded the unit's hood and the medical display showed traces of rousing brain activity. She was coming out of skipover as well, but with a slight delay compared to his own revival. It happened; no two physiologies responded in exactly the same way.

Kanu washed, and some of his discomfort began to ebb. He went to the bridge, checked that the ship was in no worse state now than when they had gone to sleep. The repair processes were proceeding to schedule, although there was still much more to be done.

He boiled water and made chai, enough for two of them.

Then he knelt next to her casket and waited for the return of life.

"Someone's in there," Nissa said. "People, with machines and equipment. Things that can help us fix your poor little broken starship."

"We'll ask nicely," Kanu said. "What else can we do?"

They had both been awake for several hours, both of them feeling slightly groggy and frayed around the edges but otherwise unaffected by the skipover interval. Nissa was eating a plate of grapefruit while seated in her command chair, loosely gowned and with one leg crossed over the other. Her hair had not had time to grow back between the skipover episodes, still only a shadow of stubble across her scalp.

Up on the main display was their best view of the shard, overlaid with contours and graphics showing thermal, compositional and geomorphological properties.

They had gained the answer to at least one of the mysteries as soon as they woke. The volcano-like hot spots Kanu had noticed from halfway across the system were evidence of a technological support infrastructure—the signatures of a power-generation system.

Power that was being still used for something.

Nissa was right: someone had to be in there.

"I'd like to know what Swift makes of this," Nissa said.

"We'll have his opinion sooner or later. Probably more of it than we want or need."

"Why is he keeping a low profile? Do you think there's something wrong with the implant protocol?"

"If I could see him but not you, I'd say that was the case. But I've seen neither hide nor hair of Swift since I woke. He's here, though. I'm certain of that. I think he's just allowing us some privacy."

"While listening to everything we're saying?"

"He can't fight what he is. Can you, Swift? Well, you're missing out on all the fun here, leaving the analysis to Nissa and me, although we appear to be making progress without your input. Do you see those hot spots? They're only a little cooler than the surface of Gliese 163. They're pools of reflected and concentrated sunlight, gathered and directed onto the shard's surface. There must be heat-transfer elements under those hot spots, turning the sunlight into power. We found the optical elements, too—all on our own. Backtracked the paths, identified four extremely dim infrared signatures, also in orbit around Paladin but at a higher elevation than the shard. Mirrors, Swift—each a few kilometres across. Aren't you impressed?"

There would never be a time when at least one of the mirrors was not in direct sight of Gliese 163. Their function was to gather the star's energy and concentrate it with extreme accuracy onto the receptor sites on the shard's surface. Controlling the mirror satellites required finesse to direct their beams with the same precision as the fortress stations spinning around Mars. On the other hand, solar energy was an old-fashioned and inflexible power source. *Icebreaker*'s own Chibesa core could easily duplicate the incident power of those beams, and it could be turned on and off and ramped up to higher output at will.

Only someone lacking Chibesa technology of their own would need those mirrors.

As they came in closer still, so the overall shape and nature of the shard became clearer. It was irregular, a tawny-black lump peppered with craters and veined with fissures. It turned slowly on its longest axis, about once every two minutes, like a lump of meat on a spit. A deep, mouthlike depression lay at one end of it. Like the Watchkeepers' corpses, it appeared to have once been part of some larger body—there was an ominously clean, almost planar surface cutting diagonally across the other side of the shard from the depression. Perhaps it had also fallen foul of the Poseidon defences, or something similar guarding Paladin.

But that did not account for the evidence of human habitation. Lodged among the craters and veins—even spilling out across the sheer face—were glints of silver and gold arranged in lines and grids and clusters, and at the nodes of these brighter threads were what Kanu instinctively recognised as a very human technology of spacecraft berths, signalling dishes, airlocks and large-scale cargo docks. The hot spots were now revealed to be circular grids criss-crossed with a quilting of pipes. Fluid pumped through those grids and heated by the beamed energy would be used to drive electrical generators. Once cooled, the fluid could be sent through the grids again, and the cycle repeated endlessly. The docks and berths, though absent of visible spacecraft, explained how the satellite mirrors must have been deployed and maintained.

Kanu stared at the image, conscious that once again he had more questions than answers. How had this come to be? Who had put this thing in orbit around Paladin?

Who—if anyone—still made use of it?

"I felt a little discretion was called for," Swift said quietly, "but I am very glad that you have been missing me."

There he was now, standing off to their right, hands clasped before him like a patiently waiting servant. It was more as if Kanu had managed not to notice his presence until that moment, implying some deep and skilful doctoring of his attentive faculties.

"I wondered if you'd got lost in skipover," Kanu said.

"After enduring it once? No—there was no danger of that. I will say this, though—it's a very odd thing not to be conscious. To be—to all intents and purposes—dead. Neither gathering nor generating information, as cold and changeless as eternity. How do you humans live with the thought of that hanging over every moment of your pitifully short existences?"

"We don't," Kanu said. "We just get on with it."

Nissa spooned grapefruit into her mouth and then used the spoon as a pointer. "Speaking of getting on with things—do you want to hazard a guess as to why they aren't sending?"

"Maybe they were sending, and now they're not," Swift ventured.

"Is that the best you've got?"

"For the moment, Nissa."

"Those mirrors haven't wandered off-course," Kanu said.

"A good control system, then," said Swift. "Or there *are* occupants, but they are simply not particularly talkative."

"Could they be machines like you?" Nissa asked.

"I doubt it. For a start, look at the mess they've made of the place. It's untidy—ramshackle. Not the robot way. I fear you will only find the answers you seek by going inside."

"Those look like standard docking systems to me—locks that will match ours," Kanu said. "We shouldn't have any trouble coupling on." He grinned, finally shrugging off the cloud of bad feelings that had dogged him since their revival. "My god! I wasn't expecting this. How the hell did anyone get here ahead of us?"

"We knew someone was here," Swift said.

"Yes—but our assumptions were all wrong. We thought it could only be Eunice, transported here by the Watchkeepers— we weren't expecting some ship, some expedition that no one knows about. But they haven't answered our hails or shown any sign of acknowledging our arrival."

"You think they might be dead?" Nissa asked.

"It's possible. But their equipment and supplies may still be of use to us. We'll need to bring *Icebreaker* in closer, but for now I'd sooner keep some distance."

"We can take *Fall of Night*. It'll dock with anything down there, and at least I trust my own ship not to malfunction on us. Any objections, Swift?"

The figment bowed its head. "You appear to have matters adequately in hand."

They closed distance to the shard until Paladin swallowed half the sky, the new Mandala turning its cryptic geometric gaze on them as the world swung past below. They were careful not to slip into the mirrors' beams, for such a concentrated heat source could have inflicted severe damage on their already crippled vehicle.

They held off at one hundred kilometres, then went out in Nissa's ship. They made a couple of circuits of the shard, scanning and mapping, then transmitting the composited data back to *Icebreaker* for safekeeping. It was eighteen kilometres across at its longest point, about eleven wide. At first glance, it appeared to be a small asteroid, or perhaps the husk of a comet. The more Kanu looked at it, though, the more he found himself wondering about the depression at one end. At first glance he had taken it for a natural feature, the lingering blemish of a deep impact or collision. Now they were closer, however, it looked much too symmetrical for that. Its circumference was perfectly circular and its interior face, as it sloped down into the shard, had the smooth-bored regularity of something carefully excavated. At its narrowing base was a flat surface like a wall, spanning the throat of a shaft that went deeper into the shard.

Nissa had picked out a landing point about a third of the way in from the start of the depression. She synchronised *Fall of Night* to the shard's spin, then brought them in at steadily decreasing speed until they were almost at a walking pace. At the last moment, she rotated *Fall of Night* to align its ventral docking port with the equivalent structure on the rock and then used lateral thrust to complete the mating. Automatic clamps locked them into place and the status lights on her console indicated that the docking was secure. The shard's rotation now subjected *Fall of Night* to centrifugal effects, meaning that it would fall away from the dock should the clamps fail—they felt like a fly hanging upside down on a ceiling. But if anything were to fail, Nissa said, it would not be the systems on her ship, and the structure to which they had docked looked adequately anchored into the surrounding rock and unlikely to tear itself away under the increased load.

They completed their spacesuit checks, locking down helmets, reviewing visor readouts, confirming that they could both see and address Swift, then went to the lock. They were under half a gee now and had to clamber up into it, but there were ladders and handholds in abundance. The lock was large enough to take both of them.

"Air on the other side, if you believe that," Nissa said, directing his attention to the airlock's status panel. "We'll treat it as suspicious until proven otherwise."

Kanu agreed wholeheartedly. He was uncomfortable, and for a moment could not pin down the precise origin of his disquiet. Then he remembered the airlock on the wrecked ship on Mars, the necessity for them to pass through it one at a time and the trap they had found inside.

"Are you all right, Kanu?" Nissa asked. "You're breathing a little fast. Is your air supply normalised?"

He made a show of checking his cuff readout, with its blocky histograms of gas ratios. "All good."

Swift, who was presently invisible, said, "I can adjust your anxiety, if that would assist matters. It's well within my capabilities."

Kanu shivered. "I'd rather not know that."

"And rather him in your skull than mine," Nissa said. "At least I know my feelings are real."

The ship's airlock cycled and they entered the corresponding part of the shard. Since the exterior elements of the lock had looked familiar enough, it did not surprise Kanu to find the interior provisions just as recognisable. It was neither strikingly modern nor particularly antique or alien. The technical readouts were even labelled in Swahili and Chinese, as they were on almost every ship he had been aboard.

"Suit confirms that the air is good," Nissa said, "but we'll take nothing for granted."

"Agreed," Kanu said.

There was power to operate the lock and illuminate the chamber and its readouts, but since locks usually carried independent power, that told them nothing about the rest of the shard. Still, Kanu drew some encouragement from the fact that the lock was operable and had not fused into useless immobility.

There was a lateral door, so they did not need to climb any further. Beyond the door was a service area equipped with some storage lockers and control panels, again of unremarkable design. An angled, armoured window looked down through the floor, out into space, allowing them a view of the still-docked *Fall of Night*. Low-level lighting was in evidence and some of the consoles still had active readouts, but Kanu did not know what to conclude from that. Perhaps the power had come on when the lock was activated and was even now draining the last drops of energy from nearby storage cells.

A set of stairs led up and away from the service area alongside a heavy-duty elevator. They opted for the stairs—their suits lacked power-assist, but in half a gee, Kanu did not think the ascent would be too arduous.

"Why haven't we heard about this place before?" Nissa asked as they began their ascent, walking side by side up the short flight of stairs before reversing direction. "To organise and fund an interstellar expedition of this size—there's no way it wouldn't be in the public record. No matter how secretive you wanted to be, you couldn't hide the departure of a starship."

"We haven't even seen a starship. Maybe this rock is the starship."

"Like a holoship?"

"Perhaps," Kanu said, "but they were slower than anything we have now, and they needed the economy of an entire solar system to build them. Whichever way you cut it, it's hard to see how anyone did this. And why come here in the first place?"

"Maybe they discovered the second Mandala ahead of everyone else and wanted to exploit it?"

"To what end, though?" said Kanu. "If there was something about the Mandalas you could exploit, wouldn't the people on Crucible already have a head start?"

They must have ascended a hundred metres, doubling back over and over again, before the stairwell reached another room. It was larger than the one they had passed through below and more sparsely provisioned. Low-level illumination picked out the edges of its walls and ceiling. No control panels or lockers here, no windows—but there was a door, set into the wall opposite the stairwell. Twice as tall as Kanu, it was impressively braced and armoured, doubtless designed for emergency pressure containment. It looked as if it was meant to slide up into the ceiling, but there were no controls on this side.

Kanu walked to it, grasped one of the brace pieces and

tried forcing the entire door to slide up. The gesture was as futile as he had expected. It must have weighed several tonnes.

"Any ideas, Swift?" he asked. "We have cutting gear aboard *Icebreaker*, if need be."

Swift was conversing with them now but had still not manifested as a visible figment. "We could undock and scout around for another airlock, perhaps? There was no shortage of options."

Nissa was standing next to Kanu, hands on her hips. "Hello?" she called, using her suit's speaker. "Is there anyone here?"

"I worry that the place is dead after all," Kanu said, his earlier enthusiasm beginning to ebb.

"I don't know," Nissa said. "It feels a little less dead the further inside we go. It would take life-support systems to keep air warm and breathable. I swear I can hear something, too."

All Kanu could hear was his own breathing, too fast and ragged for his liking. "Are you sure?"

"Try increasing your auditory pickup. Shall I show you how to do it?"

"No, I'm fine."

But he followed her lead, amplifying the suit's pickup as far as it would go. There it was: a distant mechanical process, the hum of mechanisms. It could have been anything—generators, pumps, air scrubbers—but it meant there was more than stored power providing the signs of animation they had already witnessed. Machines were running; had perhaps been running since long before their arrival.

"There's something else," Nissa said. "Do you hear it?"

A steadily rising component now overlaid the low-level hum, as if some heavy thing were advancing slowly towards the room. It consisted of a repeating series of bass thuds, falling into a sort of haphazard rhythm—like the slow, ominous beating, Kanu thought, of some tremendous war drum. The slight irregularity of it contrasted with the continuous drone of the background machines. This was not something mechanical, and on a primal level he found it invoked a specific but nameless dread. If only they could see what was coming. But that huge door was windowless.

They had only just entered the shard, and now Kanu's sole instinct was to return the way they had come, back down the staircase. But he could not turn. It was not simply the fear of running from one threat only to stumble into another. If they could not negotiate with the occupants of the shard, they were as good as dead anyway.

"Do you know what that sound is, Swift?"

"I've never encountered anything like it. You may have, but it will take some time to search your memories."

The thudding slowed and stopped. Kanu had the impression that the origin of the sounds was now only a few metres from him on the other side of the huge door. An ominous reverberation, so low as to be almost subsonic, throbbed through the armour plating. It was a living sound, not the product of something mechanical.

"I don't think you need bother searching my memories," Kanu said.

A loud clunk signalled the rise of the door. It began to haul itself into the ceiling, a widening brightness at its base. Kanu and Nissa stood back in unison. His fear was all-consuming now, but to run would be futile, he knew. He allowed his hand to reach for hers. If she spurned that contact, so be it, but he could not bear to face this alone.

Her hand hesitated in his, then her fingers closed slightly. Glove to glove, barely a touch at all. But it was more than he had dared hope for.

Beyond the door was a blazing brightness that rammed around and through and between the giant forms standing on the other side. There were three of them. In the first dazzled instant of his viewing, before the door had risen fully into the ceiling, he thought he had been mistaken, that these were machines of some kind after all. They stood on massive, tree-like legs—four legs to each form. And in those first few glances, they looked mechanical, or at least shrouded in armour.

But no, these were indeed living creatures, and he recognised them for what they were.

Elephants.

CHAPTER 27

It was cold in the long, sloping corridor. It came from deeper within the camp, a whispering planetary chill that felt as if it had travelled all the way from Orison's dead core, clawing through shivering layers of rock and crust and dusty permafrost. It cut through their clothes, through their skin, and into their bones. Goma thought she could take a few minutes of it at most.

"Let's get a few things straight from the outset." Eunice was looking back at the party as she led the way into the deeper layers of her camp, her breath visible in the cold. "They are Tantors and only Tantors. Never elephants—that offends them terribly."

"How many?" Goma asked, excited despite the cold.

"Six."

"Six!" Ru exclaimed.

"My dear girl, you'll have to make allowances for me—I can't tell if you're elated or disappointed."

"We're delighted that Tantors still live," Goma said, presuming to speak for both of them. "On Crucible, the numbers weren't sufficient to sustain them as a distinct subspecies. They had to breed back into the baseline elephant population, and in the process we've slowly lost whatever it was that made them special. Six is wonderful, of course, but we were hoping for a self-sustaining breeding group."

"You may still have one. There are six here with me, but hundreds—thousands—more in *Zanzibar*."

"Thousands!" Goma exclaimed.

"You might need to dial down your hopes a little. *Zanzibar* is where all our problems began—where I got on the wrong side of Dakota, and why I ended up here."

"You said *Zanzibar*," said Dr. Nhamedjo. "Do you seriously mean—"

"You haven't figured that out yet, have you? Well, we'll come to *Zanzibar* in due course—that's a whole other can of mealworms. The important point for now is that the six Tantors who live with me are what you'd call defectors. They sided with me when the others stuck with Dakota, and for that they were also banished. Actually, there were more than six, and these are the children of the original defectors. In truth, we all got off lightly. There were many who'd have been glad to see us killed, but Dakota had just enough residual respect for me to offer exile rather than execution. So they used one of their last long-range vehicles to drop us here, me and the Tantors, with sufficient equipment to build our happy little home. They stayed long enough to make sure we weren't going to die and then abandoned us. And here we've been ever since."

"Were you here when you sent the original signal?" Goma asked.

"Yes—it was almost the first thing I did after setting up home. They didn't want me to have any kind of transmitter, certainly nothing capable of squirting a signal across interstellar distances. Still, I've always been good at improvising—make do and mend. Eventually I patched something together that just about functioned, aimed it at Sixty-One Virginis, pressed 'send' and here you are."

"Two centuries later," Goma said.

"Yes, damn that Mr. Einstein and his unreasonable insistence on causality and the inviolability of the speed of light. I still thought you'd get here a little quicker."

"We came as soon as we could," Goma answered.

"You mentioned someone coming here ahead of us," Vasin said. "What did you mean by that?"

"The other ship."

"There isn't one," Vasin answered. "I would know. We've come alone, the sole expedition sent by our government. Even if Crucible launched the second starship after our departure, it could never have overtaken us."

"That answers one question, anyway. I tracked the point of origin of this other ship for a while before I lost a fix on it." Eunice was striding on, fit as a fiddle, apparently oblivious to the cold. "It was hard to be sure, but it didn't look as if it came from your quadrant of the sky. Earth, maybe, although there were some other possibilities."

"Did you try talking to them?" Goma asked.

"Not until it was too late. They made me nervous, popping up in the wrong corner of the sky like that. Call it a fault of old age but I'm not fond of surprises. Anyway, I did eventually try to signal them, but by then they'd run into some trouble around Poseidon and either I wasn't sending reliably or they weren't listening."

"When was this?" Goma asked.

"A little over a year ago. Frankly, I was starting to think Poseidon had done us all a favour by taking that ship out of the argument."

"And then?" Ru asked.

"Six weeks ago I intercepted another burst of transmissions— short duration, low signal strength. These came from the other side of the system, close to Paladin. Did you pick up something similar?"

"We'd still have been on deceleration thrust then," Vasin said, "which limited our sensitivity. Unless the signal was strong or kept repeating, we were more likely to miss it than hear it."

"You think it was the same ship?" Goma asked.

"Almost certainly. It must have gone dark—spent the intervening year making a very slow transfer from Poseidon. No way for me to track that. Probably damaged, too, if that second burst was an indicator of their transmitting capacity. I tried signalling again, but either they couldn't hear me or they chose not to respond. You had a good look at Paladin on your approach—did you see any evidence of a ship?"

"No," Vasin said. "And I don't see how we could have missed something that big."

"You would if they'd hidden it inside *Zanzibar* while they make repairs."

"Mystery ship or not," said Karayan, "that rock cannot be *Zanzibar*. The remains of that holoship are still orbiting Crucible. End of discussion."

"Whatever remains you've seen," Eunice answered, "they're not the whole thing. A good bit of it ended up here. It wasn't teleported or sent down a wormhole. It came the same way you did—moving through space, through all the points between here and Crucible. It just did so very, very quickly."

"Faster than the speed of light?" Goma asked.

"No—that really is impossible. But close to the speed of light. *Very* close. The survivors didn't report any subjective time interval between being in one system and the next, which means their clocks barely had time to tick."

"You just said survivors," Goma stated, hardly daring to imagine what that news would have meant to her mother, to the people who had damned her, to the loyal but ridiculed Travertine. It would not have absolved Ndege of a crime, but it would have made the magnitude of it far less—and she would have been hailed in the same breath as the discoverer of something wonderful.

Too late now.

"Hundreds of thousands of them," Eunice said. "Adults, children—Tantors, as I've already mentioned. Snatched from Crucible to Paladin, bounced between two Mandalas."

"Then it's no wonder that ship made contact," Ru said. "If you weren't answering them, they must have homed in on the first signs of human habitation elsewhere in the galaxy."

"And that's where we run into a little local complication. No easy way of breaking this news, but I'm afraid there aren't any people left in *Zanzibar*. There were . . . difficulties . . . differences of opinion. Rather violent differences."

"What happened to my grandmother?" Goma asked.

"Something bad," Eunice said. "But understand this: you can't blame the Tantors for any of it. It was Dakota who led them astray. But even she can't be held to account for what became of her, what the Watchkeepers turned her into. It was never her fault that she became a monster."

"And these Tantors—did they play any part in what happened?" Ru asked.

"Blameless. As innocent as babes. But please don't underestimate them on that basis."

They had reached a flatter part of the corridor where an enormous door led into the sidewall. Eunice touched a control and the door heaved open. Light drenched the corridor, accompanied by a steamy warmth. She stepped into whatever room lay beyond, indicating that the party should wait before following her.

Goma felt her emotions wrenched askew—dismay and horror at what might have happened on *Zanzibar*, to the people in general and her own grandmother in particular; and a delicious, giddy anticipation of what she was about to experience. She felt like a traitor to herself, not fully surrendering to the sadness and anger that were the right and proper response. But what could she do? There was joy in her heart that Ndege might now, at least in death, receive a measure of forgiveness. She would have given anything to communicate this one vital fact to Crucible, back in time, so that it might ease Ndege's burden. She could not bend time to her will; she could not bring that greater happiness to Ndege. But she had this moment, and for now she was thankful.

And she was about to meet Tantors.

She heard Eunice speaking. She heard answering voices. She felt as if all the arrows of her life pointed to this moment.

Eunice came back into the corridor. "All right, they're ready for you. These Tantors are my friends and they mean well, but aside from me, they've never seen another human being. So please—no sudden movements, no shouting, nothing that could be construed as a threatening gesture."

"We won't scare them," Goma said.

"It's not them I worry about, dear."

"The two of you should go first," Vasin said, beckoning Goma and Ru to step through the doorway. "You've earned this. May it be everything you've hoped for."

"Thank you," Goma said with genuine gratitude.

They entered with Eunice next to them, and for a moment all they could do was squint against the brightness of this underground room. It was warm—much warmer and more humid than the corridor—and Goma felt the blood returning to her fingertips.

Under their feet was dirt. The chamber had a huge vaulted roof, with a dome-shaped skylight set into it. The floor was stepped, with different levels.

"It was a natural bubble," Eunice was saying. "Ours for the taking. We roofed it over, sealed it against pressure loss, pumped it full of atmosphere. We've dug out some adjoining chambers, but this is still the biggest."

She might as well have been talking gibberish for all Goma cared. It was the Tantors that had her absolute and binding attention. In that instant, nothing else in the universe mattered.

"They're glorious," she said.

Ru was holding her hand. Goma squeezed back. The moment was theirs and theirs alone, as precious as any they had shared. "Yes."

The cold of the corridor had already brought water to her eyes; now the water became tears of joy. It was only three of them, yes—nothing compared to the multitude she had dared hope for. But still: to be here now, to be standing in this room and beholding three living Tantors—there would always be her life before this moment, and her life after it, the one a dim reflection of the other, and nothing would ever be the same.

The universe had given them a gift. She was light-headed with the thrill of it all, delirious with gratitude and wonder and a sense that beautiful possibilities still lay ahead of them all.

"Say something," Eunice said. "It generally helps."

Goma opened her mouth and found her throat was dry. She coughed, swallowed, tried to gather some tatters of composure. It was hard to speak, grinning the way she was. Mposi and Ndege—if only they could be here, seeing what she was seeing.

But they were, if she wanted them to be.

"I am Goma Akinya," she said. "This is Ru Munyaneza. We've come a long way to find you. You are magnificent—a wonder to us. Thank you for allowing us to see you."

Three Tantors stood before them on a slightly raised part of the floor, adults or near-adults by her estimation. They were elephants, of course—the physiological differences between Tantors and baseline elephants were not dramatic—but everything about the way they stood, the intense, unwavering scrutiny of their gaze, spoke of something beyond animal intelligence. It was in their deportment, in the lowering of their heads—not subservience, but more a kind of greeting, displaying the boulder-like prominence of their skulls, crammed with intellect.

Tools and equipment hung from belts and harnesses fastened around them, and above the trunk and between the eyes, their brows were covered by a curving metal plate that fastened in place like a horse's bridle. The black plate contained a screen and a grille, and it was from these grilles that their voices emerged. The middle of three, the largest and most mature, spoke first.

"Welcome, Goma Akinya—and Ru Munyaneza. I am Sadalmelik."

"I am Eldasich," said the one to Sadalmelik's left.

"I am Achernar," said the third Tantor.

"Are there more of you?" Goma asked.

"Outside," Sadalmelik answered. "Atria, Mimosa and Keid. They have gone outside to make repairs to one of the distant antennae. It is more than a day's walk from here. But they will soon return."

Their voices were machine-generated and sounded with no corresponding movement of the Tantors' mouths—a kind of ventriloquism. Each had been assigned a different pitch and timbre. Goma had already decided on the basis of body morphology and tusk thickness that Eldasich was the female of the three, and her voice was slightly higher and purer than the two males'. It was a concession to human anthropomorphism, but it accorded with what she knew of the original Tantor populations. The language-generating equipment was familiar, too— long after Crucible's Tantors had died out, the augmentation gear had remained, dusty and unused but too valuable to throw away. The black plates read neural signals, translating subvocal impulses into sound, which left the Tantors free to continue using the entire normal repertoire of elephant vocalisations and rumbles.

"Eunice tells us that you've never seen other people before," Ru said.

"No," said Sadalmelik. "But we have studied images and recordings, and heard many accounts. You are new to us, but not unfamiliar. Have you come from Crucible?"

"Yes," Goma said, still grinning. "By starship. Eunice sent for us. For my mother, actually."

"Ndege," said Eldasich. "You were known to her?"

"Yes. I had to leave her behind."

"We remember Ndege. She was kind to us. It is good to remember such things," said Achernar, the smaller male.

"You can't possibly have known her," Ru said.

"Our kind knew her," Achernar said. "We remember. We pass down the knowing of things. Is this strange to you?"

"No," Goma answered. "Not at all. And my mother would have loved to meet you. She knew Tantors on the holoship, and then for a little while after we reached Crucible. But it wasn't to last."

"Then you have not known Tantors?" asked Sadalmelik.

Goma looked to Eunice for guidance, but their host had evidently decided to let them deal with this on their own.

"You are special," she ventured. "Very special and rare. After we lost *Zanzibar*, there were not enough of you left to carry on your line. Ru and I—our work on Crucible concerned you. We were trying to find ways to return Tantors to the world."

"Did you succeed?" Achernar asked.

"No. We failed. There are none of your kind left now. There was a wise one . . . her name was Agrippa. She was strong and clever. We loved her very much, but she grew old."

"Were you there at her end?" asked Eldasich.

"Yes," Goma said. "Both of us were."

"It is good that you were there," Sadalmelik said. "Speak of her to us. We will remember her. We will find her true name and pass down the knowing of her. Then she will always be known."

"Thank you," Goma said.

Ru asked, "Can we come nearer?"

"Do you wish to touch?" asked Sadalmelik.

"To touch. And be touched. If you're fine with that."

"We are fine with that," Eldasich said.

Remembering Eunice's instruction not to make sudden or threatening movements, they approached with the utmost care. Behind Eunice, Vasin, Nhamedjo, Loring and Karayan watched the proceedings with a sort of nervous encouragement, like spectators at a circus.

"You mentioned Agrippa's 'true name,'" Goma said.

"Yes," answered Sadalmelik.

"What did you mean by that? The names you just told us— are these your true names?"

"Those are our short names, the names for people to use. They help you separate us. But they are not our true names. Our true names are too hard for you, and too long. We never speak our true names."

"I understand," Goma said, although she was not sure that she did. Better that the Tantors had their secrets and mysteries, though, than be too transparent, too easily understood.

She approached to within touching distance of Sadalmelik, reached out slowly and raised her hand to touch his shoulder. She felt the warm, bristly roughness of his skin as it moved with the great tidal surge of his breathing. She shifted her hand, maintaining the gentlest of contacts, from shoulder to neck, from neck to the side of his face. Ru, meanwhile, had stationed herself next to Eldasich and was stroking the upper part of her trunk. Goma moved a hand to one of Sadalmelik's tusks, warm to cold, soft to hard. His eye regarded her steadily, and despite every instinct she could not bring herself to avoid contact with his gaze. Far from repelling such contact, the eye's intelligence appeared to demand it. She stared into its liquid depths, trying to imagine the sharp and curious intelligence within.

Sadalmelik moved his trunk and touched her other hand with the tip, then traced its way to her face. An elephant's trunk was a marvel of elastofluidic engineering—a tool both supple and strong, sensitive and expressive. Goma was used to being examined by elephants but this was a different order of intimacy—guided and methodical. She held her ground fearlessly, even as the trunk moved from her nose to her brow, mapping her like an instrument.

"You are like Eunice."

"I should be."

"You are also like Ndege. She stands where you stand. She sees what you see. Did she pass into the Remembering, Goma?"

"Yes," she answered, and the answer was like a damburst, the first time she truly felt the knowledge of her mother's passing.

"Then we will speak of Ndege as well, until her true name has spoken itself."

"There's a lot to talk about." It was all Goma could do to hold herself together. "Would you mind if Ru and I spent some time with you? We can tell you about Agrippa—about anything you like. And we want to hear your stories, the knowledge you have passed down."

Sadalmelik elevated his great head to look beyond Goma. "Is there time, Eunice?"

"A little," she said. "We must wait for the others to return, at any rate."

"Then we shall talk."

"Not just yet," Eunice said. "My guests are tired, and they need feeding and watering. We have some discussions of our own to attend to. But they will not be far away."

The good news was that Eunice could offer something besides mealworms; the less good news was that the alternatives were scarcely more appetising. Today's offering was some kind of fibrous edible fungus, lithoponically grown in one of the domes she had set aside for food production. Eunice flavoured her dishes with carefully rationed spices, some of which had been with her since the exile, some of which were the product of her own experiments in cultivation.

"They didn't expect me to last as long as I have, I suspect." Their host was pottering with plates and cutlery. "Equally, Dakota didn't have the stomach to just kill me. We'd seen and done too much together for her to turn against me totally. I think she always hoped I'd change my mind, become useful to her again instead of actively unhelpful. Well, fat chance of that."

"Go back to the beginning," Vasin said. "Your arrival here, to start with. The three of you—the Trinity. How did it go from that to this?"

"We were brought here by the Watchkeeper. We travelled close to the speed of light, although probably not quite as quickly as *Zanzibar*. Say when."

"When." The captain took her plate of processed fungus, staring at it with a measure of trepidation.

"It won't kill you, Gandhari."

"Thank you, Eunice. When you say *Zanzibar*, though—this was before the arrival, the translation event?"

"Yes—long before. Think about it. The Trinity left Crucible more than twenty years before your Mandala event. We had that much time to explore this place—to begin to understand for ourselves what the Watchkeepers had in mind for us."

"Which was?" Loring asked. They were all seated around Eunice's table, squeezed together like the unexpected drop-ins they were, with Ru and Dr. Nhamedjo perched on storage crates instead of chairs.

"Exploration. To serve as their proxies. To learn things they themselves could not discover. Doctor Nhamedjo?"

"About the same as Gandhari, please. Maybe a little less."

"Suit yourself." She deposited a generous dollop of the fungus on his plate. "You can always come back for seconds. Maslin?"

"Thank you," he said.

"How was that supposed to work, exactly?" Goma asked. "What could the Watchkeepers not discover for themselves that they'd need our help with? We're nothing to them—we're not even the same order of intelligence."

"And therein lies your answer. There are facts concerning the M-builders that they would like to uncover, but they can't because of what they are. The M-builders put up barriers. Think of them as intelligence filters, capable of deciding what is allowed access to the truth and what isn't. Consider yourselves lucky: without my intervention you'd have likely blundered into one of the filters yourselves."

"The Mandala, or Poseidon?" Loring asked.

"Both, to a degree—although the really formidable defences are around Poseidon. Those moons aren't to be trifled with. They'll permit certain kinds of intelligence to pass and deny others."

"Machines are barred, organics allowed?" Vasin asked.

"More complicated than that."

"Is there anything about this that's *not* complicated?" Goma said.

"Not to my knowledge. Aiyana?"

Ve lowered a hand over ver plate. "Not very hungry? A little for the taste?"

"Go, you." Eunice served the scientist rather more than was required for a taste. "And my two special guests—my brave Tantor specialists? Surely all that intellectual stimulation has worked up an appetite?"

"If you eat it, I'll eat it," Goma said. "Even though it looks like shit."

"Wait until you find out how it tastes. Ru?"

"She doesn't get to have all the fun on her own."

Eunice beamed. "I like you both already."

"Make sure you save some for yourself," Goma said.

In fact the food was not as inedible as it looked, nor even as bland, for there was a saltiness to it and a faint aftertaste of chilli powder. As a one-off, Goma could tolerate it well enough. But she had not been forced to live here for more than two centuries with only a handful of items on the menu. It was a wonder Eunice had not gone insane.

Perhaps she had.

"Tell us about the M-builders," Vasin said, between tentative mouthfuls. "Everything you know. And the Watchkeepers, while you're at it. Where are they now? What happened to them?"

"Questions, questions."

"You can't blame us," Ru said. "You still haven't told us about *Zanzibar*, about Dakota and Chiku."

"Let me tell you the most important thing—the most pressing thing. Dakota is set on a very bad course. There are structures on Poseidon. You'll have seen them—arch-like objects rising from the seas. They're wheels, if you didn't already guess. Dakota wishes to reach those wheels—to learn the secrets they encode. Until now, she hasn't had the means to either reach Poseidon or penetrate its defences or atmosphere. Unfortunately the arrival of that other ship has fallen neatly into her plans. She has to be stopped. The first thing we must attempt is communication—get a signal through to that ship if they're still listening."

"Haven't you tried that already?" Goma asked.

"My transmitters can't possibly reach all the way through *Zanzibar*, but yours might be able to. Use whatever you have, from radio to neutrinos. Send Morse code with your engine— but get through to them. Tell them that Dakota absolutely can't be trusted, and that whatever help or reciprocity they think they're getting from her, there'll be a significant sting in the tail. Can you do that, Captain Vasin?"

"I'll see what Nasim can manage. But if they weren't prepared to listen to you—"

"Maybe they couldn't, and maybe they're dead already, but you can still try. And it's not just the crew of the ship you'll want to reach out to—it's the rest of the Tantors. My bridges are burned, but you saw how Sadalmelik and the others revere Ndege's name. That goes for the other Tantors in *Zanzibar*, too. They will still think twice before disregarding the advice of an Akinya. As long as it's not me, of course."

"Tell us about the people," Vasin said. "The hundreds and thousands you said survived the translation. Surely they aren't all gone?"

"Every last one. There were difficult times after the translation. Have you noticed how much of my camp I need to set aside to provide for just six Tantors? The problems on *Zanzibar* were much more acute, and there was no way it could keep everyone alive, people and Tantors. But there was a way out— a solution. Most of the human survivors agreed to return to skipover, to conserve basic resources."

"The Tantors were already independent by that point?" Goma asked.

"Not quite. There was enough capacity to keep a handful of humans alive, a skeleton staff to guide and assist the Tantors as their world was remade."

"Then we'll speak to them," Goma said.

"You can't. Dakota had them all killed. For thousands of years, we had the blood of elephants on our hands. Now the deed has been repaid."

CHAPTER 28

Kanu had nothing to say in the face of the elephants. Nothing in his long and strange life, no experience or lesson, had prepared him for this moment. He had a million questions for the elephants, but no idea where to begin. It was all he could do to stand still, caught in the paralysing rapture of the moment.

"Who are you?"

It was Nissa who spoke first, her voice booming out through her suit's loudspeaker. The elephant's answer, when it returned, was also in Swahili. It was not merely an echo of her words, for the intonation was distinctly different, questioning and with a trace of superiority.

"Who are *you*?"

"I am Nissa Mbaye," she answered, with a collectedness that impressed Kanu, as if she had expected to meet and speak to elephants all along. "Our ship was damaged, we needed a place to repair it, and we weren't expecting to find anyone alive inside this station."

"Station?"

The vocal sounds were coming from the lead elephant but they were not being generated by its mouth, or at least not directly. The elephant was the tallest of the three, its skin pigmentation a dark umber offset with pinkish mottling around the eyes and mouth. It exuded an impression of powerful muscularity, a sense of enormous force just barely contained.

The sounds, insofar as Kanu could judge, emanated from a thick angled plate that the elephant wore across the front of its face, fixed between its eyes and above the top of its trunk. The voice was loud and very deep. At the lower end of its frequency range, Kanu felt certain it would be deeper than any possible human utterance, and certainly far louder.

"We thought this was a station, a base," Kanu said, finding his voice at last. "We were expecting people—humans, like ourselves. We were not expecting you."

"Take off your helmets. We will see your faces."

Nissa glanced at Kanu through the side of her visor, then the two of them consulted their wrist readouts.

"It's safe enough," Kanu whispered. "If there's enough oxygen to keep them alive, we should be fine."

"I don't like it," Nissa said.

"Nor do I, but when in Rome . . ."

They eased their helmets off, then tucked them under their arms. Kanu breathed in the air. There was a mustiness to it, but he had inhaled worse.

"Speak your name."

"Kanu," he said levelly, hoping he sounded as matter-of-fact as Nissa had. "My name is Kanu Akinya."

"Akinya?"

"Yes."

He was talking to an elephant, and the elephant was replying. The strangeness of this situation was almost too much to bear. It felt dreamlike, and yet he had a clear sense of the events that had led up to it, the chain of contingencies, each of which had felt logical and inevitable in isolation. It was entirely likely that this was happening. Astonishing, absurd, wonderful, but not beyond the realms of the possible.

"You look the same to us. Are you brothers?"

He glanced at Nissa, tried to imagine a point of view from which they were indistinguishable. They were both nearly hairless now, but as far as Kanu was concerned, that was where the similarities ended.

"No, we're not brothers. I am a man, Nissa is a woman. We aren't related."

"You are the man Kanu Akinya?"

"Yes."

"And you are the woman Nissa Mbaye?"

"Yes," she answered.

"Do you know the name of this place, Kanu Akinya and Nissa Mbaye?"

"The planet is Paladin," Kanu said. "That's what we call it, anyway. We found this shard of rock orbiting it and hoped it could help us fix our ship. That's all we know."

"Then you do not know the name of this place."

"Do you?" Nissa asked.

"Yes."

"What do you call it?" she asked.

"*Zan-zi-bar*," said the elephant, each syllable a distinct, booming thing unto itself.

Nissa looked at him. Kanu shrugged within the collar of his suit. The temptation was to dismiss the name out of hand. Anyone with an education, anyone with the slightest interest in history knew what happened to the holoship. But here was a talking elephant, claiming otherwise.

It felt only fair and reasonable that he should listen to what the elephant had to say on the matter.

"We thought *Zanzibar* was destroyed," he said.

"No."

"But people saw it happen," Kanu persisted. "It was a terrible event, one of the worst in recent history."

"Were you there?"

"No . . . we've come from Earth, not Crucible. Neither of us has ever been there."

The elephant was looking at him, sometimes directly, sometimes by angling its huge head to favour one eye over the other. The eyes were a pale amber under a cowling of dark lashes.

"But you know of *Zanzibar*."

"Everyone does," Kanu said. "Something terrible happened— an accident with the Mandala on Crucible."

"Speak of this accident."

"*Zanzibar* was passing overhead and there was an energy burst, a discharge—a massive explosion. Hundreds of thousands of people were killed—I'm not sure of the exact number. The holoship was turned into rubble and the debris formed a ring system that's still orbiting Crucible. Are you saying that's not what happened?"

"There was an accident. But *Zanzibar* came here. We were on it. We survived. We have been here ever since."

"Do you have a name?" Kanu asked.

"I have two names. A true name and a short name. You cannot hear my true name. That will not pass into your knowing."

"What is your short name?" Nissa asked.

"I am Memphis. I speak for these Risen. You will speak to them through me."

"A name with a connection to the family," he whispered to Nissa. "It proves a link to the elephants that came to Crucible."

They were led out of the chamber into a corridor easily high enough for the elephants and wide enough for two of them to walk abreast with room to spare. Memphis went ahead of Kanu and Nissa, the other two slightly smaller elephants bringing up the rear. Kanu was uncomfortably aware of their lumbering presence behind him, the ease with which he might be injured or even killed were he to stumble under their feet. Memphis's massive hindquarters loomed ahead, muscular and baggy at the same time, as if the skin were a size too big for the meat and bones beneath. The elephant's tiny afterthought of a tail pendulumed with each stride, as if setting the rhythm. Once, without any pause in his progress, Memphis released a sackful of steaming dung, forcing the humans to step around it.

"This is a development," Swift said.

"Is that your idea of understatement?" Kanu answered, speaking subvocally.

"It's my idea of bewilderment. How can this be *Zanzibar* if the records say that it was destroyed?"

"It's hard to square with what we know. But then again, why would they make up something so unlikely?"

"They need to explain how it got here," Nissa said, speaking through the same subvocal channel. "I may not be an expert on Akinya history, but I know how long it took the holoships to crawl their way to Crucible. This is even further from Earth."

"Then it got here faster," Kanu said.

"This isn't even all of *Zanzibar*," Nissa replied. "We'd have recognised a holoship immediately. Where's the rest of it?"

"You heard the elephant. A large part of it survived—not all."

"Speaking of elephants—what the hell is going on? What do you mean by 'family connection'?"

"You mean he never told you?" Swift said.

"There's a history of involvement with elephants in my family," Kanu said, feeling like a man called upon to defend himself. "It goes back a long, long way—to academic studies in Africa, but also genetic experiments on the Moon and elsewhere, shaping an elephant daughter species with the resilience to survive in space."

"And this is the result?" Nissa said.

"I don't know! Some elephants travelled aboard the holoships, and there have always been rumours about the emergence of a strain with enhanced intelligence. More than rumours, apparently. But those elephants didn't use machinery and speak Swahili. These are something else—yet another strain."

"Does their name mean anything to you?" Nissa asked.

"Risen? No. I don't think I've heard that before. Risen from what? By whose hand?" Kanu's pace must have slowed, for he felt a gentle shove from behind, a nudge against his backpack. "Where are you taking us, Memphis?"

"To see Dakota."

The corridor went on and on, following an almost imperceptibly rising curve. It must cut, Kanu decided, through the rocky shell of *Zanzibar* itself, defining in its curvature the rough outline of the former holoship.

Clearly the corridor had not always been as wide as its present state. Here and there he could tell where it had been blasted or excavated open from some narrower configuration, and some of the remodelling was far from neatly done. Parts of the corridor were clad; other areas were bare rock, crudely furnished with illumination. At intervals, various corridors and passageways branched off it, angling away to mysterious destinations. Some of these were large enough to admit an elephant, but not all of them. A juvenile elephant might still be able to get down them, but not one of these hulking, armoured adults. Either there were still people around, or there were parts of this place that the elephants could not access.

So it had not been built for them, but adapted—in haste, perhaps, and imperfectly. They had language and the evident ability to control doors and perhaps use tools, but he wondered how capable they were of modifying their larger environment. Had they made these makeshift changes, or had they received assistance? More pertinently: were they now the only tenants?

"Look," Nissa whispered.

He followed her gaze to the error readout on her cuff which meant that her suit was no longer in contact with *Fall of Night*. Kanu checked his own suit. It was the same story. He tried a wider search, hoping to pick up a contact from *Icebreaker*, but both ships were silent.

"We have gone too far into the rock," Swift said. "The intervening material is blocking an already weak signal. I am afraid there is nothing to be done."

Presently they reached a branching corridor which climbed steeply up through a number of turns, until at last they arrived in a much larger enclosed space than any they had seen so far. They were at the base of it, with a vaulted ceiling soaring several hundred metres overhead, its rocky underside pin-pricked by hundreds of bright blue lights. The chamber was large but—Kanu reminded himself—still small compared to the original size of the holoship. Waiting in the chamber was an impressive vehicle, easily as big as anything he had seen on Earth. It consisted of a platform flanked by three pairs of huge balloon-tyred wheels, with a steep access ramp leading up to the platform.

The elephants and their guests went up the platform. There were no seats or amenities aboard the vehicle, just protective railings around the outside edges. Memphis moved to a control pedestal near the front and started touching things with his trunk. The vehicle rolled into life, giving off no more than a rumble of tyres against the chamber's rough flooring. Up at the front, beyond the control pedestal, Kanu saw what looked like a conventional cockpit of some kind, encased in a pressurised canopy.

"Did you make this?" he asked, one hand on the nearest railing, the other arm still cradling his helmet. He had been breathing *Zanzibar*'s air for many minutes now without obvious ill-effect.

"No, we did not make it."

"Then who did?"

"It was made for Crucible. Now it is for us."

The pedestal had been welded to the deck, and wires and cables ran in crude fashion down its length.

"Did you adapt it?" Nissa said.

"No."

"Then who did?"

"The Friends. You will see them soon, once you have seen Dakota."

They were rolling out of the chamber now, having gathered a respectable turn of speed—easily faster than an elephant's stampede charge. Once again they were travelling down a corridor, but the course of this one was much more erratic than before, suggesting that it had been bored anew rather than converted from an earlier element of *Zanzibar*. It twisted and turned, climbed and descended. The vehicle rolled on, Memphis keeping the very tip of his trunk in contact with the steering controls. He produced more dung and one of the other elephants used a kind of broom to sweep it into a hopper on the side of the vehicle, leaving only a greasy smear. They must eventually collect their waste wherever it falls, Kanu thought, or else the world would have been full of dung.

"This vehicle was meant for the colony, surely," he said, addressing Nissa, keeping his voice low while not yet subvocalising. "Manufactured up here, I suppose. They would have kept most of the factories and fabricators in orbit, sending finished goods down to Crucible. This one never made it, and now it's been altered so *he* can drive it. But no matter how smart they've become, I don't see this being within their capabilities. Someone must have helped."

"Were there people on this thing when the accident happened?"

"Hundreds of thousands. Most were presumed dead, wiped out in an instant. But if the elephants survived, then I suppose some people must have, too."

"Strange that they weren't in the welcome party, isn't it?"

"Memphis," Kanu said, "who are these Friends you mention? Is Eunice among them?"

The great head turned to regard him. "No."

Kanu said, "Do you know what happened to her?"

"Why do you speak of Eunice?"

"Then you've heard of her."

Memphis flapped his ears—a gesture that Kanu could not help but interpret as one of irritation. He was still driving, but his attention was now on them, not the way ahead. Still the vehicle trundled on. "Eunice did not like us. Eunice is gone."

"What do you mean, gone?"

"Dead."

Presently they arrived in a significantly larger space—what Kanu guessed must be one of the holoship's original pressure caverns. It was kilometres across in all dimensions—dizzying after the confinement of spacecraft and airlocks and corridors. He forgot how many chambers the holoships had carried, but he was sure it was more than a dozen. Still, this one chamber would suffice for tens of thousands of survivors, if they were prepared to put up with a measure of crowding.

But there were no people to be seen.

There *were* elephants, or Risen, if that was the name they now preferred. They were standing around in groups or moving in ones and twos—elephants both large and small, though Kanu was no expert in such matters. All but the smallest wore similar equipment to the three with them now, allowing for differences in detail. They stood in the open areas between buildings, or walked along wide, dusty pathways linking those same structures. There were many buildings, none of them more than a few stories high, and all had clearly been designed for human occupation. Enlarged doors and windows had been cut into the sides of some, but others were still as they must have been built. The buildings nestled in and around squares of open grassland, small lakes and woods. The chamber's floor curved gradually upwards, the more distant buildings built on rising terrain and appearing to tilt inwards as if their foundations had subsided. But the chamber did not encompass more than a small fraction of *Zanzibar*'s circumference, the ground on either side eventually shrugging off vegetation and assuming a sheer, clifflike steepness before curving over again to form the ceiling. A honeycomb of blue panels covered the ceiling, glowing with the brightness of sky. The honeycomb was interrupted by patches of darkness where many of the individual panels had broken away or stopped working. But the overall effect was still sufficient to suggest the muted light of an overcast day.

The vehicle was slowing now as Memphis steered them along a dirt track passing between two of the buildings. Elephants turned to study them, lifting their trunks in a kind of salute. The elephants were talking to each other, or expressing some shared emotional response.

"I hope that means they're pleased to see us," Nissa said.

"I can't tell."

They stopped at one of the larger buildings—it had a forbidding, civic look to it, with a frontage of grey pillars like a mouthful of teeth. The ramp lowered and Nissa and Kanu were encouraged to disembark.

"Follow," Memphis said. "Dakota will see you."

They entered the civic building through an open doorway twice as tall as an elephant. Beyond the entrance was an equally impressive lobby, at least a hundred metres wide and perhaps three times as long. For all its size, it was a gloomy place. Shafts of light shone down through windows in the ceiling and upper walls, but all they did was push the darkness into the corners. Kanu and Nissa's boots clacked on the marble floor. Only Memphis accompanied them. Kanu guessed that the elephants were wise enough to know their guests would not attempt an escape now, when they were so far from their point of entry.

There was a kind of ramp in the middle of the floor leading down to lower levels, but Memphis steered them around this and brought them to a halt at the far end of the chamber. Next to a set of doors was an upright glass rectangle set on a stone plinth, and next to this was a huge metal staff. Memphis wrapped his trunk around the staff, lifted it effortlessly from the ground and hammered its blunt end against the floor.

The sound—a dull, atonal *dong*—echoed and echoed around the empty chamber. Kanu noticed now that the place where Memphis had struck the ground was spiderwebbed by myriad cracks, as if this ceremonial summoning had been conducted many times before.

A moment passed. Then a large pair of doors swung open in the chamber's wall.

"We found two people," Memphis said, addressing the form that waited in the red-lit space beyond.

"Only these two?"

"Yes. The man Kanu Akinya and the woman Nissa Mbaye."

"Where is their ship?"

"We have it."

"You mean the smaller ship, of course."

"Yes."

"Then where is the larger ship?"

"It is still where it was. We brought them straight here from the lock."

"Have they seen the Friends yet?"

"No."

"But they shall. Bring them to me, Memphis. Let me see what they are. Let me see what time and tide have washed up for us."

The voice was as deep as Memphis's but the intonation was recognisably distinct—older, slower in its utterances, but at the same time conveying a sly and calculating capacity that Kanu had not sensed in the first animal. If it had been a surprise to find himself in the presence of a talking elephant, now he had the first disquieting sense that this intellect was superior to the first, and perhaps even to his own.

He wondered how Swift felt.

"I am searching your memory, Kanu. There *was* an elephant by the name of Dakota, who may have been the product of genetic cognition enhancement. But it is quite impossible that particular Dakota could still be alive after all this time."

Kanu could have sworn he felt Swift rummaging through his memories, travelling from one part of his skull to another like a slowly moving itch.

"We'll see about that. What happened to Dakota?"

"Dakota was one of the three Watchkeeper ambassadors—the three intelligences that left Crucible shortly after settlement. The first was Chiku Green, the second Eunice—"

"And the third an elephant. I should feel as if I'm getting answers to questions, Swift—why don't I?"

"Conceivably they are not *quite* the answers you were hoping for."

Memphis encouraged them into the red-lit space beyond the doors and then retreated—his own head lowered, adopting a posture that Kanu could not help but interpret as submissive.

He thought about elephant power structures, the singular importance of the matriarch. No matter how much intelligence had been grafted onto elephant minds, the hard, strong bones of those ancient hierarchies would still push through.

But could this really be the same Dakota, after all these years?

The doors closed behind them. The room was a library, or part of one. Its shelf-lined walls were two storeys tall, with a narrow wooden balcony running around the upper level. The shelves were occupied by hundreds, perhaps even thousands, of heavy physical books. Their spines were mostly black, occasionally a dark academic red or an equally sombre blue or green. Their titles were printed in metal leaf, embossed into the leather of the spines.

The floor level contained an arrangement of study tables set with slightly sloping tops. Many books littered the tables in various states of organisation, some in loose piles, others spread open. Hooded reading lamps were scattered about, some of which cast a muted red light. These and equally muted lights set between the shelves were the only sources of illumination in the room. Kanu had the impression that the books must be too fragile to be exposed to anything brighter.

In the middle of the room, framed by two long rows of reading tables, was an elephant. It was on its knees, angled away from them, its great head lowered, its forehead almost brushing the surface of a reading table. There was a concentration of books before the elephant, stacked into haphazard piles. One was open before it, and in its trunk, pinched delicately at the very end, the elephant held a circular magnifying glass.

The elephant set down the glass. Still with its back to them, it picked up one of the books, rose from its knees—daintily managing not to upset the reading tables—and moved to one of the shelves. Taking its entire weight on its rear legs, the elephant used its trunk to return the book to a vacant spot on a high shelf. Then it plucked another down, just a little to the right of the one it had been reading.

"Excuse me a moment."

The elephant set the new book on the reading table, then employed the tip of its trunk to leaf through the densely printed pages. Finally it arrived at a passage near the middle, which it proceeded to study closely with the aid of the magnifying glass.

Kanu and Nissa watched in silence. Kanu had the feeling he had walked in on some surreal fantasy of his childhood.

"Scholarship is one of the more harmless habits of old age. Sometimes I lose myself among these books for days at a time, following one thread of research to another. My needs are modest, and I am, regrettably, something of a slow reader. And an inexcusably bad host, too: you must forgive me." The elephant replaced the glass on the desk and turned around slowly to face them. "I am Dakota, as you were doubtless forewarned. You must excuse Memphis his clumsiness with Swahili—it is not his strong point—but in all other respects he is thoroughly dependable. I would miss him like the dung of my mother were he to leave us. Memphis mentioned your names, but I confess I need them repeated. Would you mind?"

"I'm Kanu Akinya," he answered carefully. "This is Nissa Mbaye."

"Akinya," the elephant said, drawing out the syllables. "Yes, I thought that was what Memphis said. I would be surprised if that were a coincidence."

"I imagine it's no more of a coincidence than you being called Dakota," he said. "Are you really the elephant that went with the Watchkeepers?"

"I shall admit you into a confidence. 'Elephant' is a term best reserved for conversations between people. If you must insist on a name bestowed on us by people, then we are the Tantors. Perhaps you know of us. But even Tantor has connotations of a doubtful past we would much sooner put behind us."

She was smaller than Memphis, but still large enough to be intimidating. Dakota was also tusked, but the tusks were narrower and perhaps two-thirds as long as his. Like the other elephants, she wore a kind of speaking device across her forehead, but hers was smaller than the others. Under the device, her forehead was a huge bony swelling, almost like a malignancy. Her skin was a highly wrinkled pearly grey, like a landscape subjected to aeons of interesting geology. Beyond infancy, all elephants looked wizened and venerable to some degree. Kanu nonetheless had no doubt that he was in the presence of a truly ancient individual.

But could it be the same Dakota? It seemed impossible to him. The Dakota who had been part of the Trinity was an old elephant before *Zanzibar* reached Crucible—an event that was already hundreds of years in the past. In the absence of artificial prolongation measures, no elephant lived as long as a human.

"I'm sorry," Kanu said. "I'll try to watch what I say. But I'm finding it hard to accept that you could really be the same Dakota."

"Why would I not be?"

"It's been far too long, that's why. Unless you've found a way to put elephants—sorry, Tantors—into skipover—"

"You are not, if I might be so bold as to say so, the youngest of human beings. Presumably you are also quite old? Two centuries, perhaps more?"

"Memphis appeared to have trouble telling us apart, and yet you can guess my age?"

"I am not Memphis. I see a human man, a human woman, distinct in their individuality. Memphis sees only the common herd of humanity. You cannot blame him for that. He has not had a great deal of experience with people."

"And you have?"

"More than my friend. But indulge me—how old are you, in point of fact?"

"It's complicated," Kanu said. "I was old when the Mechanism fell. Along the way I've had genetic modification from the merfolk, additional prolongation therapy, a long bout of skipover while we travelled to your system . . . and quite apart from all that, I died and was reborn on Mars, put back together like a jigsaw. I doubt very much whether any of these things apply to you."

"There are other kinds of prolongation therapy, Kanu—other ways of cheating time. It's true that I have seen a great many changes since the Watchkeeper took us from Crucible.

I was old then, as you rightly surmise, but from my present vantage I see my life before that time as a kind of infancy, no more than a preparation for what was to come. My full flowering, you might say. The Watchkeepers changed us all, a few decades after our arrival in this system. There were more of them then, you see—a whole host. The changes they wrought on us were almost trivial, from their perspective. They saw what was broken, deficient or incomplete, and they set it right."

"So they made you more than you were?" Nissa asked.

"One way of putting it. I have aged, and I continue to age— my eyes are not what they once were! But I grow old slowly, and if there has been a decline in my higher faculties, my ability to speak and read and reason, I remain blissfully ignorant of it."

Kanu was still struck by her swollen forehead. He thought of what that expanded braincase must mean in terms of her mental capacity—a great pressured swelling of pure intellect. He hardly dared compare his own brain volume to hers.

"Can the others read?" he asked.

"My offspring are blessed with some of my gifts, although seldom are all the attributes present in the same individual. Slowly, though, with each new generation I am becoming less exceptional. The calves are a miracle now—they have a thirst for learning and experience that you would scarcely credit. They gobble language as readily as they gobble dung! Sometimes they frighten me a little. I wonder how brightly their children will shine—and their grandchildren!"

"You're enough of a miracle for me," Kanu said.

"You are very kind—and generous. Humans have carried the flame of intelligence for a million years. For you the gift was a consequence of natural factors—the stirring of genes, the adaptive pressures of a changing environment. You have earned it through generations of almost unbearable hardship— times when the human lineage was pinched to the brink of extinction. In our lineage, intelligence has been installed by artificial means, much as you might set a light in a darkened room. While there is a will, the light provides illumination. But it can just as easily be turned off, or allowed to falter. Your kind possess the inbuilt resilience of a hundred thousand generations. There is hope for us, in the new offspring. But we will not have the luxury of genetic resilience for a great many centuries, if we are fortunate to have it at all. As you see, not all the lights in this room work as they once did."

"But you've survived whatever happened to *Zanzibar*," Nissa said, "and now we're here, if there's anything we can do to help. There'll be more like us, too. From now on you don't have to be alone."

"I will admit that I am not ungrateful for your arrival. I hope we can be of benefit to each other. But first—your ship. Tell me what happened, to bring you to *Zanzibar*?"

"We responded to a signal," Kanu said. "It appeared to concern us, but when we got here, no one replied. I'm afraid we found ourselves in some trouble—our ship was badly damaged, unable to steer itself. We set it on a transfer orbit and eventually ended up here."

"Because you knew of us?"

"Not at all! But we'd seen your rock—*Zanzibar*—and we thought we might be able to use it as a staging point for our repairs."

"The ship fixed some of the damage while we travelled," Nissa said, "but not all of it. We'll still need outside resources if we're to make it back home."

"That is very unfortunate. If only you had come to us directly, all this could have been avoided. I must apologise for not responding to your arrival, but I am afraid our capabilities are still very limited. We can sense objects in the vicinity of *Zanzibar*, but not much further out than that. And I confess we were not expecting visitors."

"Then you didn't transmit the signal?" Nissa asked.

"No—we had nothing to do with it. Let us put all that behind us, though. Were people hurt aboard your ship? Are there sick and injured to be helped?"

"No, it's just us," Kanu said.

"That is a mercy. Should you have need of anything, though, you must not hesitate to ask. This ship was made for people, as you know, and many of its facilities are still largely as they once were. I cannot promise you that everything still

works, but I do not think you will find it too great a hardship
to spend some time with us. As for your ship—the damaged
one—you may rest assured that we will do our utmost to help
you mend it. In a little while we shall commence the arrangements to bring it closer to *Zanzibar*, and then we can discuss
the practicalities of the repair process."

"I don't know what to say," Kanu said.

"Who are the Friends?" Nissa asked.

"I beg your pardon?"

"You mentioned them to Memphis, when we arrived. He
said we hadn't seen them yet."

"You must forgive me—I'd quite forgotten. Perhaps old age
is taking its toll after all. I find myself quite easily able to
forget the thread of a conversation after only a few minutes,
yet I can remember things that happened a century ago as if
they were playing out before my eyes."

"Are the Friends the Watchkeepers?" Kanu asked.

"No—nothing so strange as that. In fact, the Friends are
like yourselves—people, human beings. They were with us
when we first arrived in this system. Would you like to see
them?"

"We didn't think there were any people here," Nissa said.

"You will not have seen them, but there is an excellent reason for that. In fact, the Friends are very near. I shall have
Memphis show them to you—unless you would rather begin
the repair work immediately?"

"That might not be a bad thing," Nissa said.

"It will not take long to see the Friends. And then you will
have a better grasp of our situation." Dakota stomped a foot on
the floor, three times. After a moment, the library doors
reopened.

"Take our guests to see the Friends, Memphis. I should like
them to watch the recording, too—I think it may be of great
interest to them."

The larger elephant led them from the library back into the
main part of the civic building. In the very middle of the grand
space was the gently sloping ramp Kanu had noticed before,
angling down into the building's lower levels. It looked old

enough to be part of the original architecture, but it was easily large enough for Memphis. Perhaps vehicles had used it to come and go from the basement levels. Kanu wished he knew more of *Zanzibar*'s history during its flight and the years spent orbiting Crucible. Mposi would know, he thought, and wondered what his distant half-brother would make of this place now.

The ramp reached a landing, reversed direction and descended again. Then it levelled out and reached a T-junction. It was almost totally dark now. Ahead was not a wall but rather a dimly sensed emptiness. Kanu moved to the railed barrier facing them. They had reached the upper part of a vault, presumably extending deeper into the lower levels.

"See the Friends," Memphis said, standing at their backs, the slow in-and-out of his breathing like the movement of air through a house-sized bellows.

"We can't see anything," Nissa said. "Your eyesight must be better than ours. If we put our helmets back on—"

"Wait."

Memphis stepped forward, extending his trunk to touch a panel set into the nearside wall. Lights came on, banks of them in sequence, illuminating deeper parts of the vault. Kanu saw now that the pathway continued to either side of the T-junction, enclosing the length of the vault before joining up again at the far end. More ramps led down to the lower levels.

It was a skipover vault.

"Amazing," Kanu said, taking in layer after layer of sleeper caskets, more than he could begin to count. "I've never seen anything on this scale. Must be hundreds, thousands of sleepers here."

"No one would have done anything like this since the holoships," Nissa said. "But why are they here?"

"There must have been lots of people still in skipover when the holoships reached Crucible," Kanu guessed, "many vaults just like this, crammed full of the frozen. Remember how the cities weren't ready for the colonists? They couldn't move everyone down in one go. They'd have held them in skipover until the surface settlements were finished—and that was going to take decades. Even when they started waking everyone up, they'd have kept the vaults as an emergency resource."

"At least we know where the people are now. Why aren't they awake, though? And what happened during the accident—were they already in skipover, or did that happen afterwards?"

Kanu turned to their elephant host. "Are there more than these, Memphis?"

"These are all the Friends. There are no other Friends."

"They're all asleep now," Nissa said. "Is that what you mean?"

"Yes."

"Was there ever a time when they were awake?"

"Yes."

She looked at Kanu before answering. "Then what happened?"

"A time of troubles. I will show you the recording. Then you will understand."

They returned to the lobby entrance where Memphis had first struck the floor with the metal staff. Kanu noticed again the upright rectangle of glass set into a stone plinth. He had taken it to be a piece of interior decoration, but now he realised there was rather more to it.

Memphis waved his trunk in front of the glass. At first nothing happened, but after a few passes the glass brightened. A standing human form appeared in the upright material, a woman with whom Kanu felt an instant and visceral bond of recognition. He knew the shape of that face, the cheekbones, the brow, the curve of the lips.

She was his mother.

She nodded once, bowed and began to speak. "I am Chiku Akinya. Chiku Green, for anyone who might take interest in such things. And I am here to tell you what happened to us."

CHAPTER 29

The days on Orison could never be long enough for Goma and Ru. There were too few hours and too many things they wished to ask of both the Tantors and their host. Goma could hardly believe that there were another three Tantors still out there, on their way back to the camp. In her limited time with the first trio, she had already formed an appreciation of Sadalmelik, Eldasich and Achernar as distinct individuals, each with their own past, their own place in the Tantor hierarchy. All were interested in the world beyond Orison, in the stories of Agrippa and the other elephants on Crucible, and all appeared willing to learn about Ndege and the wider Akinya clan. But in the case of Eldasich and Achernar, the latter interest was more polite than insatiable. They were mildly curious, but human business clearly sounded less important to them than news of other Tantors.

Goma offered the most truthful account she could. It was hard to skirt around the issue of the Tantor decline, the gradual weakening of their intelligence, without alluding to their similarity to baseline elephants. She did the best she could, with Ru's assistance, and if offence were taken, it was not obvious to either of them.

The Tantors, for their part, appeared to relish dialogue with someone other than Eunice. It was clear from their surroundings that they required constant intellectual stimulation. In the main bubble and the sub-chambers excavated around it, they had been provided with many tools and toys—or perhaps they were better thought of as puzzles, for toys sounded demeaning for creatures of such evident cognitive gifts. There was an upright rack, divided into black and white squares, with movable symbols—some kind of game or logic exercise. There was a horizontal flat panel bisected by a central net of recovered insulation material with two racket-like paddles suggestive of table tennis. There was a fist-sized cube made of many smaller coloured cubes which could be twisted into different permutations, but only via cooperative action between two or more elephants. There were tall sculptural objects made of interchangeable networks of transparent plumbing, through which the Tantors liked to roll little polished marbles. There were data screens arranged in stereo pairs for the convenience of animals with broad skulls and opposed eyes. There was a socklike tool which could be worn over a trunk and came equipped with a variety of plug-in micromanipulators, allowing the Tantors to perform the deftest tasks. There were cave paintings, splashed on the walls in bright primary colours. There was a wire-frame wind chime which the Tantors liked to set in motion as they passed, and a thing like an alpine horn which they enjoyed blowing into that produced a note so deep it made Goma's guts throb.

But the Tantors also had work to do, sharing the business of survival. They each placed a much higher demand on the camp's life-support capabilities than one human. One of the sub-chambers led into a lithoponic glasshouse, while another accessed the nutrient troughs where the mealworms were grown and harvested. Another chamber contained the lavish waste-treatment beds—the smell of elephant dung brought Goma and Ru back to Crucible in an instant. Elsewhere they were shown the elephant-sized spacesuits, with their goggled helmets and accordioned trunk sheaths like antique gas masks. Eunice said it generally took three Tantors to prepare another three for the outside, so they seldom went out at the same time.

They shared the camp on equal terms with Eunice. She had expertise and insight but she was not their master. She had been exiled, and the Tantors' ancestors had agreed to defect with her. But their relationship was based on loyalty, not blind subservience. They needed each other to survive, the partnership built on friendship and mutual dependence.

Goma and Ru had as many questions for Eunice as they did for the Tantors. She was obliging, up to a point—willing to go over the same details, to repeat or re-examine that which was not immediately clear. But it was not like asking things of a robot.

"I knew a Finnish astronaut," she said, launching off on a sudden tangent. "Hannu. It was on Phobos, when we were cooped up there waiting for that big Martian storm to die down. Nerves were starting to fray—the slightest thing set us off. Someone sneezes the wrong way, someone rubs their nose or keeps saying they miss Earth. 'All guests stink on the third day,' said my Finnish colleague. He was right."

"Give us a break," Goma said. "We've barely been here two days, let alone three."

"It feels like longer. I have opened my home to you, offered you sanctuary and the essentials of life-support. How many times do we need to keep going over the same basic facts?"

"You'll have to excuse us," Vasin said, with the manner of one who minded very little whether or not she was excused. "We've arrived in the middle of a situation we don't understand with next to no prior information. You're our only reference point, and you shouldn't even be alive. I mean that in the literal sense. If we were expecting anything, it was a robot."

"I must be a disappointment to you all."

"No," said Dr. Nhamedjo, moving his hands in a magnanimous flourish. "You're a wonder of the age! But you're also human. As recording systems go, memories are fallible. And by your own account, all this happened such a long time ago."

"You've been on your own here," Goma said soothingly. "Nothing but you and the Tantors and a totally deserted, barely hospitable planet."

"And you think I went mad without the benefit of your sparkling conversation?"

"I think we need to be sure that you're as sane as you think you are," Vasin said. "Hence our questions. You'll admit it's an unlikely set of circumstances—you becoming flesh and blood, *Zanzibar* reappearing . . . Tantors turning against people. It's not that I doubt these things, but I'm still trying to understand how they fit together."

"You told us the Watchkeepers needed you," Goma said, "something to do with Poseidon not letting them near, but I still don't really get what that means."

They were in Eunice's kitchen. She wet her finger and drew

a watery circle on the table, then another circle surrounding it. "Poseidon prohibits examination by purely machine intelligences. But the Trinity was able to bypass that prohibition."

"One of you was a machine," Ru said.

"And one of us was human, and one of us had a trunk. It was the totality of us that counted. Collectively, we were more than our individual selves—we were a distinct information-gathering entity."

"Then you've been there," Goma said.

"We got close but turned back. Something touched us. The Terror, Chiku called it." She smiled at their uneasy reactions. "There was nothing occult about it. The Terror was just a form of deep understanding—information being drilled into our heads. A vast, precise, intuitive grasp of the probable consequences of our actions. That to know the truth of the M-builders was to grasp the most dangerous knowledge of all."

"All right," Goma said. "We've skirted around this long enough—what's the big deal about the M-builders? What's so important that they have to put the Terror into you? What secret is worth protecting that badly? And if it's such a big, bad secret, why not just erase it, or hide it away for ever?"

"I don't know what it is. I didn't get close enough to find out."

"But you got close enough to experience the Terror. And you've had all this time since then to think about it, to put it into perspective. Don't tell me you didn't come up with something—you're Eunice Akinya."

"At least someone has faith in me."

"I'm trying very hard," Goma said.

After a while, she said, "The M-builders discovered something. A fundamental truth about the universe, about the fate of things—what happens to the universe, what happens to all the matter, and all the life in it, in the future. This much I understood. The rest is . . . harder. It's like telling a child about death. There's no nice way to break the news."

"They let you know this fundamental truth?" Ru asked.

"It came through."

"And the secret itself?" Goma probed. "If you got a glimpse of it, you need to share it with us."

"It's a lot for you to take in."

"Then give us your best stab. You can't expect us to get worked up about Dakota when we only have a clue what it's all about."

"I can expect whatever I like."

"Eunice . . . please."

"Persistent little upstart, aren't you. Annoying. Annoying and cocksure and full of your own insufferable self-belief."

Goma lifted her chin in defiance, displaying more boldness than she felt. "Coming from you? You made a career out of insufferable self-belief. You built an empire on the back of it."

This drew the tiniest grudging smile from Eunice. "Very well. At least you and I can speak plainly. *You* can take this, I think. You've got the steel for it. I can't speak for your companions—they're your business. The M-builders . . . are you sure of this?"

"Yes, we're damned well sure," Goma said.

"They arrived at this truth. It's a bitter pill. None more bitter. The universe ends. It has a built-in expiration clause. It's going to stop—and not at some remote cosmological time from now, when the galaxies crash together or the suns fizzle out, but sooner . . . much sooner."

"When you say sooner . . ." Vasin said. "What are we talking? Thousands of years, millions?"

"It can't be quantified. It's a fluctuation event, a vacuum instability, a random but inevitable process like the flipping of an atomic nucleus, the decay of a neutron. It could happen tomorrow or a hundred billion years from now. Statistically speaking? Probably won't happen for hundreds of millions of years . . . a good few billion, most likely."

Goma could not help but let out a gasp of relief. "Then it's so far off as to not matter."

Eunice looked at her with scorn. "Try, just for a second, *not* to think like a thing made out of cells, with a lifespan shorter than some planetary weather systems. You're a human being. You have limited horizons. Thinking beyond next week is a reach for you. That's fine, it's what you are."

"Thanks," Goma said.

"You're welcome. But it wasn't like that for the M-builders.

They'd already been around for tens of millions of years when they made this discovery. They'd accepted the idea of being an immortal super-civilisation. It suited them down to the ground. Masters of creation? Lords of all they surveyed? Architects of eternity? Why not? Bring it on. But there's always a catch—they needed the universe not to die on them in the meantime. When they worked out that the end state was not just probable but inevitable . . . let's just say it didn't feel quite so far off to them. Not when they'd already been around for aeon upon aeon and were making plans for the rest of time."

"Then the truth is . . . what?" Vasin said. "The confirmation of all this? Then we don't need it. I've seen those theories, too. We already know about vacuum fluctuations."

"So do the Watchkeepers," Eunice answered. "So does every galactic intelligence with the ability to count up to three. But it's always been a theory . . . a dragon in the mathematics. Something nasty, but which you aren't required to take seriously. The M-builders did, though. Their mathematics was watertight, and they'd excluded all competing theories. They knew the end was coming. And Poseidon is their answer."

"A solution?" Ru asked.

"An answer," Eunice repeated.

Ru began, "I'm not sure—"

"Did something go wrong on your ship's life-support when you were on the way here? Some catastrophic lowering of your overall intelligence baseline? I'll spell it out to you slowly. Poseidon is a species-level response. Information, yes. A requiem, if you like—although we'd have to read it to be sure. Whatever Poseidon is, it encodes their response to the knowledge that life, existence itself, has a finite duration. That it cannot last for ever."

"And that's what the Watchkeepers want to know—how the M-builders responded to that information?" Goma asked.

"Well, wouldn't you?"

Goma shrugged. There was a certain formality or protocol to dealing with Eunice, and she felt as if some of the rules were becoming clearer. "If I were a machine civilisation instead of a bag of cells—maybe. But I'm not sure I'd go to all this trouble to get it."

"You would if you were them. The Watchkeepers are also ancient, and just like the M-builders, they're keen on the idea of long-term survival, of enduring deep-time, burrowing into the extreme future of the universe. They know that vacuum fluctuation is real—they can see it in their physics, and in the physics of all the other cultures they've encountered or unearthed. So inasmuch as worry is an emotion they're capable of, they worry. They fret in their dim little machine minds and wish they knew what the M-builders knew. But to find that out, they have to enlist proxy intelligences like ourselves. The trouble with that, though, is that we have to know the Terror. We have to allow our souls to be ripped open while they look on. We're disposable instruments to them, that's all. Doesn't matter if we're blunted or damaged or burned in the process so long as we function long enough to extract information. Well, fuck that."

Goma laughed in surprise and admiration. "Really?"

"Yes, really. Fuck it. Fuck being the tools of a higher alien intelligence."

"Only you could say that."

"Say it? We did more than say it. We downed tools." Eunice straightened in her chair, puffed up with pride. "We said we weren't going to do it. That they'd have to find another way. That was their problem, you see. They could only use coercion up to a point, and then we stopped being free agents. But only free agents, creatures operating under their own free will— only they could survive the moons. Of course, the Watchkeepers don't give up that easily. They tried different avenues of persuasion."

"Such as?" Goma asked.

"The gifts—the bestowings." She touched a finger to her chest. "Making me human. They thought they could bribe me into doing their will. But it wasn't sufficient inducement."

Goma nodded. "What did the others get?"

"Dakota was already clever. They made her much cleverer—and almost immortal."

"And Chiku?"

"Dear Chiku. In hindsight, she was the only shrewd one among us. There was nothing they could offer her—no carrot, no stick. She wasn't interested in being smarter, or living longer, and she certainly didn't want to become anything she already wasn't. Blame it on my grandson—that boy Geoffrey put some distinctly odd ideas into her head."

"They sound healthy enough to me," Ru said.

"Then you're as odd as he was."

"Carry on, please," Goma said, a knot of foreboding tightening in her stomach.

"Chiku's defiance put her on a path against the Watchkeepers. When *Zanzibar* arrived, we all did what we could to help. But the Watchkeepers already had plans for Dakota. If they couldn't use humans, why not elephants instead? It's not that they understood us, that they had deep insights into our psychology. They just saw another group of vertebrate animals and knew what needed to be done to get what they wanted. Dakota was to be the new matriarch—the new ruler of the Tantors. The homecoming queen. They shuffled her genes, mixed in some new ones and let her breed—allowing her offspring to become the dominant order."

"Beyond the Tantors?" Ru asked.

"The Risen, they call themselves. In reality, they're just another instrument of the Watchkeepers—all being groomed for an expedition."

"Tell me more about Chiku," Goma said.

"She died. It was near the end of the human presence in *Zanzibar*. I was there, I saw it. They killed her."

"No," Goma said, preferring to believe anything but that.

"It was a dark time. Bad things were done by both parties. The humans began to realise that the Risen were slipping from their control, so of course some of them overreacted—tried to use *Zanzibar*'s systems to contain the elephants. Pumped inert gases into the life-support network—that sort of thing. Humans could easily squeeze into suits or airlocks, but the elephants couldn't hide. But it was too clumsy, and not fast enough. There were reprisals. Then the humans switched to lethal weapons—it's really not that hard to kill an elephant if you've the will. But the elephants, especially the Risen, were quick and smart enough to respond in kind. After that it was war."

"Please let this be a lie," Ru said, and Goma breathed out

hard and held her hand, together finding the mutual strength to face this awful truth.

"Chiku tried to broker a peace. She had friends among the Tantors—even among the Risen. But blood was running too hot on both sides. She was bludgeoned and killed. It was fast. She wouldn't have felt anything."

"Couldn't you have stopped them?" Goma asked, barely holding back her rage.

"You think I didn't try? You think I wouldn't have bloodied my hands against them if I could have made a difference? I'm not on the side of elephants or people, Goma. I'm on the side against stupidity." She looked down at herself, giving a little shiver of disgust. "But I wasn't strong enough. Not strong enough, not fast enough, not bold enough. Look at what I've allowed myself to become."

"One of us," Goma said. "In which case, pity poor you."

"Whatever happened on *Zanzibar*, Eunice can't be held accountable for it," Ru said.

"No, I can't," Eunice said. "But that doesn't get us out of the mess. I've been stuck here without a ship ever since my exile. But you've changed all that."

"And the other ship?" Vasin asked.

"It's a worry—and another reason for making contact with *Zanzibar* as quickly as possible. I doubt very much that your arrival has gone unnoticed—especially with all the electromagnetic noise you were putting out."

"Your fault for asking us to come in the first place," Goma said.

"Yes, that hasn't escaped my attention—nor the possibility that I may have inadvertently caused the arrival of the other ship. But I had no choice. I could not sit back and do nothing, not knowing what the Watchkeepers want of Dakota."

"You must have known we'd take more than a century to get here," Vasin said. "Who the hell plans on that kind of timescale?"

"I do. It's the habit of a lifetime. And look—you're here."

"So what's next?" Goma asked.

"The other three will be here shortly. I should very much like to take them all with me, but I doubt your ship is geared up to accommodate Tantors. They'll just have to sit tight here on Orison until I get back." She gave an unconcerned shrug. "They're clever. They can run the camp on their own, provided nothing major breaks down."

"You have a lot of faith in them," Karayan said.

"Someone needs to. It might as well be me."

Their arrival had interrupted her work, and Eunice said she could not leave until she had set down in stone the thread of her most recent insight. Goma wondered why she did not just write it down on paper, or record herself for posterity.

"You wouldn't understand."

"I could try."

Eunice put on her spacesuit, the one with the heavy utility belt, and Goma followed her out through the lock, although she had not been specifically invited to do so. Wordlessly, Eunice set off for the cliff where they had first encountered her. She picked her way around one of the high stone cairns, then stopped at the base of the cliff. She inspected it for a moment, hand shading her helmet like a visor, and then chose a confident route up through the cracks and shelves of the face.

Goma watched from below. Eunice took out the cutting tool, made its tip flare bright and then began cutting meticulous angular marks into the rock.

Feeling herself on the brink of some momentous, life-changing disclosure, Goma swallowed hard and said: "I've seen these symbols before."

Eunice carried on working in silence. She completed a section, then traversed gingerly to the right, her toes resting on the merest wrinkle of out-jutting rock. She cut another series of markings.

"I very much doubt it."

"And I'm pretty sure I have. It's the Mandala grammar— the same pattern as the one cut into Mandala's sides, like long chains of dominoes, zigzagging and branching. Only there's something more, isn't there? You're mixing in other types of symbol."

"You are very clever. Now why don't you run along and play?"

"That's the Chibesa syntax. You're combining statements from the Chibesa syntax with the Mandala grammar, as if they're part of the same hierarchical language, or at least deeply connected."

Eunice stopped what she was doing. She turned off the cutting tool and returned it to her pouch, then shimmied back down to the ground.

"And you'd know that how, exactly?"

"Because my mother showed me. After you left us, Ndege spent thirty years finding connections between the two forms. Eventually she used her knowledge of the Chibesa syntax as a key to unlock the Mandala grammar. That was how she learned to talk to Mandala."

"I always knew Ndege had promise."

"Never mind my mother—how can you be coming up with the same connections? I know what you are. Your memories aren't Eunice's actual memories—you're made up from her public utterances, the outside facts of her life. Mother said these connections were a deep family secret—too deep for you to know about."

"Your mother was correct. She also does me a modest injustice—there is more to me than the posterity engines ever provided—but the essential truth is beyond dispute. I know that the Chibesa syntax is a mathematical formalism, a gateway into new physics, and I also know—or suspect, at least— that it has its origin in the rock scratchings of a passing alien tourist. I also have access to the entire public corpus of academic work on the Mandala grammar, at least as it stood at the time of my departure. But the notion that the two might be connected? I had to figure that out for myself."

"How?"

"The Terror. Whatever you make of it, it was a form of intimate contact with the M-builders' technology, and of course it changed us all. In my case it left me with glimmerings, a sense of larger insights just out of reach. All that stuff about the vacuum rip . . . the end of time? That came through. Like I said, leakage. Contamination. More of their nature was revealed than perhaps they intended. Ever since then, I've had an odd sense of connections waiting to be made. My dreams—"

"Then you do dream."

"Yes. Now, if you'd allow me to continue?"

"By all means."

"My dreams were great fevered battles between armies of symbols, regiments of logic and formal structure. They would not leave me alone. They chased me for years, decades, grinding away at my sanity until I began to exorcise them by way of these rock carvings. *That* appears to help. I still only have glimpses most of the time. I can't see how the syntax and the grammar fit together at all levels . . . just little pieces, phrases in a larger argument. But that's enough. It's as if the glimpses want to be carved into rock—as if they crave permanence. And with each breakthrough—each new carving that appears to lock into the whole—I see that my initial insight must have been real. There is a link."

"Ndege agreed."

"And did she . . . theorise?"

"My mother wasn't allowed to talk about her ideas—not even to me. But she did. And yes, she theorised. The grammar is an evolution of the syntax—a later, more elegant form. The syntax is a useful shorthand, but it's hard to use it to talk about anything other than physics. The grammar goes beyond that—it's richer, more complex, like a language with lots of tenses and genders."

"And she understood the formal relationships?"

"No," Goma answered. "She had many deep ideas and worked out a lot of the details, but that was already a lifetime's work. I know my mother didn't feel as if she was done with it, only that she'd made inroads, seen further than anyone else. If they'd allowed her continued access to Mandala . . ."

"And to the Mandala here."

"Yes—she'd have wept to have known about that. To know that some part of *Zanzibar* survived—that she wasn't the monster they thought she was."

"Do not think ill of me, Goma. It has taken courage for you to come here, and I know you are at least as bright as the rest of your expedition."

"Thank you," she said doubtfully.

"But you are not Ndege. I asked for her, and hoped fervently she would be the one who came. I was thinking of the help—the guidance—she could offer to the Tantors, but I see now that she could have been of incalculable value in other respects. How I would have benefitted from her insights. How much I could have learned, just by showing her this wall."

"I'm as sorry as you are that she can't be here now."

"Sorry won't get us very far."

"But I have her notebooks. I brought them with me—all of them. Do they interest you?"

Eunice looked at her through her faceplate. She had adjusted the reflectivity, offering Goma a chance to see her expression. She was smiling, and the smile was as genuine and beautiful as any Goma had seen.

"I correct myself. I am not sorry you came, Goma Akinya. Not sorry at all."

They could have left directly—the lander was ready for immediate takeoff—but the other three Tantors still had not returned. In any case, Eunice needed a day to make the necessary housekeeping arrangements, placing the camp in a state of semi-dormancy so that it could be easily maintained by Sadalmelik and the others.

Goma saw this enforced delay as a blessing, offering further opportunity for interaction with the Tantors. She had to sleep and eat, but if not for those necessities she would have gladly spent every hour in their presence. Ru shared her excitement. Together, though, they realised they had an obligation to shift into a more structured methodology, using this opportunity to gather data rather than anecdote. The free-flowing exchanges of the early hours were all very well, but now it was time for discipline and rigor. Many of the cognitive tests they had performed on Crucible could be duplicated here, and these stood a real chance of answering questions only hinted at through dialogue. Language projected a bluff of intelligence, but no fakery could circumvent some of the more challenging tests in their arsenal. So they went down to the Tantors, excited and daunted by what lay ahead. Both knew that a few careful hours here could supplant the work of a lifetime back on Crucible.

But when Goma entered their domain, she immediately saw that something was terribly wrong.

Sadalmelik was on the ground.

CHAPTER 30

It took Kanu a moment to realise he was mistaken—that the woman speaking from the glass was not in fact his mother. The error was forgivable: Chiku Yellow, Chiku Red and Chiku Green had once been a single individual, and their likenesses remained very similar despite vastly different personal histories.

"You know her," Nissa said, studying his reaction.

"She's one of my mother's three embodiments," Kanu replied in a near-whisper. "Chiku Green, who came to Crucible on the holoship. But I wasn't her son—that was Mposi."

"This must be strange for you."

"Just a little," Kanu said, smiling at his own understatement, the exquisite sadness of the moment.

Nissa took his hand as the figure continued speaking.

"None of this is easy to explain," she said. "My story is complicated—so much so that even I am not sure of all its parts. But what matters now is only recent history. A number of very odd and surprising things have happened to me lately, and now they bring me to this place, and this recording."

Her voice was familiar—intensely, personally familiar—but as she spoke it phased in and out of clarity, like something recorded onto wax or cellulose and played back too many times.

"Is it really her?"

"I think so."

"Our Covenant with the Watchkeepers," she said, "was for three individuals to travel into interstellar space with the machines. In return, the rest were allowed to settle and colonise Crucible, and to explore the Mandala." Chiku nodded and smiled. "It was a perfect Trinity: a synthesis of the born, the made and the evolved."

She paused and glanced down at her hands before raising her eyes back to her future audience. "They brought us here. We didn't know where we were at first. Another solar system, one not so far away that we couldn't recognise some of the constellations. It all happened very quickly. We must have travelled close to the speed of light because the journey did not appear to take more than a few days in our reference frame. Eventually we learned that this system is Gliese 163— that we had travelled seventy light-years. And, just as slowly, we began to understand why the Watchkeepers had brought us here."

The image glitched, remained frozen for a second or two, then jumped back to life. "By now, I'm guessing you already know about the second Mandala and the structures on Poseidon. You have probably wondered how they relate to the Watchkeepers, and the reason for their deeper interest in them. You must exercise extreme caution in relation to these structures."

"Thank you for the timely warning," Nissa said.

But the image had frozen again. It jumped, the recording of Chiku shifting her posture as if frames had been skipped over.

Skipped over, Kanu wondered, or deliberately edited?

"We did what we could for the survivors of *Zanzibar*. They were in a bad way, and there was only so much help we could offer given the limited tools at our disposal. It was a huge challenge. This little fragment of our old holoship had to keep alive not just people, but also the Tantors still aboard. The early days were incredibly hard. It was a constant battle just to survive. Finding ways to return to Crucible, even generating enough power to send a transmission—those were luxuries we couldn't begin to think about. It was tomorrow that counted, and the day after, not some possible rescue hundreds of years in the future. The—"

Again the image jumped.

Kanu glanced at Nissa. Privately, he was sure she was thinking the same thing. The recording might have suffered some natural breakdown, but it was more likely that it had been doctored. He wondered what Swift, who had been silent throughout, would make of it all.

"In the end," Chiku continued, "the resource load was too great to support the entire population of survivors. We had the skipover vaults, but there was no hope of converting them to take elephants. So we reached a compromise. The Tantors would remain awake, but most of the human survivors would go into skipover. Some of us volunteered to stay with the Tantors to guide them through the difficulties of the coming years. Together—human and Tantor—we planned to work to expand *Zanzibar*'s life-support capability, to turn it into a world we could all begin to share. Once that was achieved, we could turn our collective efforts to the greater problem of getting home—if that was still what we wanted. Given my experience with Tantors, you'll hardly be surprised to hear that I chose to stay with the living." She smiled. "Don't think too highly of me. It wasn't much of a sacrifice—I'd far rather be up and about, doing something, no matter the odds against us. With most of the colonists back in skipover, it was easier for the rest of us. Of course we always knew there would be difficult times ahead—"

The image jumped again.

"Still, let us hope for the best, not the worst. If the Risen and the people have endured, something beautiful will have happened. And should you find it of interest to wake those of us who sleep, I do not think you will find it too taxing a proposition. By the time you reach this system, you'll have decades or centuries of advancement over us. But because I want to maximise our chances, I'm appending all the relevant information I can think of which may be useful to you. You'll find it at the end of this recording. There is more to say—much more—but this will have—"

The image made a deferential bow.

"I am Chiku Akinya. I was born on the Moon, within a light-second of Earth. My great-grandmother was Eunice Akinya—Senge Dongma, the lion-faced one. She opened a door to the future, and some of us had the nerve to follow her through it. Whoever you are, wherever you have come from, whether blood or electrons run through your veins — I wish you the best of luck. May wisdom and humility guide your actions."

This part of the recording had finished playing. A sequence of schematics followed, flickering past too quickly for the eye to absorb. Kanu had just enough grasp on them to tell that the data was medical in nature, presumably referring to the functioning of skipover technology.

"Interesting," Swift said, in the quietest of voices.

"What do you mean, 'interesting'?" Kanu asked.

But the glass slab darkened, and for now Swift had nothing more to add.

They docked *Fall of Night* with *Icebreaker*, disembarked, made some system checks. They had been gone for a short enough time that the ship had made the barest progress in repairing itself. Equally, nothing untoward had happened.

Kanu remained on *Icebreaker*, while Nissa returned to *Fall of Night*, continuing to use it as a tug to shift the larger craft nearer to *Zanzibar*. The nearer they got, the more fraught and delicate the operation became—it would be so easy to lose control, and send *Icebreaker* battering into the elephants' home.

When they first scouted *Zanzibar*, not knowing its true nature, they had noticed the depression at one end, like a dimple pushed into its skin. Kanu understood now that this was the vestigial remains of the holoship's original Chibesa engine, the monstrous drive that had pushed it up to a fraction of the speed of light. Slow by the standards of his own ship—but then again, this was a thing the size of a mountain. The wonder was that it could be moved at all.

The holoships' Chibesa engines had not been needed during most of the crossing. Some had even been temporarily dismantled, freeing up an enormous amount of interior space, before the engines were reintegrated for slowdown. After the holoships reached Crucible, though, there had been no need for the engines any more. They were stripped down completely, reforged into a thousand bright new things for the young colony. *Zanzibar* was no different, and the space vacated by the gutted engine had been turned over to spacecraft berthing—a walled dock for handling much larger vehicles than the usual landers and shuttles.

Now the sheer wall at the base of the depression was sliding aside, offering access to the interior. It was a cylindrical space equipped with many docking clamps, holdfasts and airlocks, but there were only a handful of spacecraft visible, and none of them was a tenth the size of *Icebreaker*. The designs of the other vehicles were unfamiliar, but he could guess their capabilities and functions well enough. These were short-range ships, the sort that might have been used to venture down to Crucible or hop from one holoship to another, but none of them looked large enough to be capable of deep-system operations. They were also all built for human passengers—an elephant could not board most of them, let alone operate them.

The docking bay rotated along with the rest of *Zanzibar*, and Nissa had to perform some deft piloting to nudge *Icebreaker* into position against one of the holdfasts. Any damage done now would just have to be added to the ledger.

Icebreaker lurched, followed by a groan of structural complaint from somewhere beneath Kanu's feet. Then the holdfast's multiple clamps locked against the hull and all was silent.

Nissa redocked with *Icebreaker*, then moved through the ship until she had rejoined Kanu.

"Nice work," he said.

"I hope you're right about this."

"So do I."

"You mean," she said, "so do both of you."

Memphis was waiting for them on the other side of the airlock. They were taken to another vehicle, perhaps the same one they had ridden originally, and conveyed swiftly through a succession of tunnels and chambers until at last they returned to the civic building where their audience with Dakota had taken place. Only a few hours had passed, but Kanu nonetheless had the sense that his previous encounter with the matriarch belonged to another part of his life—one that preceded a momentous and irreversible decision.

"Memphis showed you the sleepers," Dakota said as she walked slowly around the four walls of the lobby. "In his way, I imagine he tried to explain our predicament. The humans gave up their conscious lives so that the rest of us might survive, submitting themselves to the uncertainty of skipover. It was a great sacrifice—a truly noble and courageous act. They were as mothers to us. But as you may have judged for yourselves, our circumstances are now much improved. *Zanzibar* is hardy, and in a thousand small ways it has begun to heal itself. Now there is no question of it being able to support the Risen. Beyond that, there is also capacity for Risen and people to share the same resources."

"All of them?" Kanu asked, thinking of the multitudes he had seen in the vaults.

"To begin with, no—that would be too dramatic a change. But a forerunner population, a small cohort of woken humans woken to assist and put right what the Risen cannot do for themselves? That is entirely achievable. Or rather, it has become so."

"You mean since our arrival," Nissa said.

"With the best will, we are limited in what we may achieve. Intellect is only part of the difficulty. We are also hampered by our very natures—our physical size. These tools and prosthetic enhancements you will have noticed upon us—they allow us a measure of control over *Zanzibar*'s functioning systems. But there have always been areas we cannot reach; control or sensory systems that are simply too delicate or complicated for us to operate. I may be able to read books, but even I would be daunted by the challenge of bringing sleepers out of skipover. I am sure the systems aboard your ship are highly automated."

"Of course," Kanu said.

"It was not the case here. When the designers installed the skipover vaults, it was always with the presumption that there would be living caretakers on hand. Their concern was to provide for a great number of sleepers, with automation being a secondary concern. They succeeded, of course—the skipover vaults literally saved our lives. But we cannot simply rouse the sleepers at the touch of a button. For that we need human assistance."

"Even then it'll be tricky," Nissa said.

"But you will have as much time as you need, and all the resources of *Zanzibar* at your disposal. If at first you fail, none of us will think ill of you."

"Even if lives are lost?" Kanu asked. "At least those people are frozen now, beyond any immediate threat."

"Of course there will be a chance of deaths," Dakota said. "But just as the settlers of Crucible made their Covenant with the Watchkeeper, so we have our solemn Covenant with these sleepers. They surrendered their conscious lives so that we might live—and for that they have our eternal gratitude. But the debt cannot go unpaid."

"You feel an obligation to bring them back," Nissa said.

"It is long past time—the duty weighs heavy on us. Your arrival is a great stroke of fortune."

Kanu gave a half-smile. "It didn't feel so fortunate to us."

"Nonetheless, I could not be happier to have you among us. Your ship will be repaired. Once the work is under way, please feel perfectly free to make use of your own skipover facilities. But with your permission, and when the time suits you, I should very much enjoy continuing our conversations. I have not often found my mental equal among my fellow Risen, but I think the pair of you will provide suitable stimulus."

"Of course," Kanu said, putting aside whatever misgivings he presently felt.

"But all that is for the future. Tomorrow, if you are suitably rested, I should like you to make an examination of the sleeper vaults—as thorough as you feel it needs to be. In turn, we will discuss the detailed arrangements for the repair work—the supply of materials, the use of our manufacturing systems. In the meantime, we will do our level best to make you feel at home. I believe you will find the arrangements exemplary, but you must not hesitate to speak up if some aspect of it may be improved."

"We will," Nissa said. "Might I ask a question, though?"

"By all means."

"Chiku's recording was edited. Does a complete record of her statement exist anywhere?"

"That recording is all that we have. The regret is ours—we

could have made much use of her wisdom. Are you troubled by the recording?"

"No," Kanu answered, with as much conviction as he could manage, although he shared Nissa's doubts about the recording's integrity.

"Then Memphis will take you to the White House. I think one of you will find yourself on very familiar ground."

When at last the household came into view—within another chamber a few kilometres beyond the point where they had been detained—Kanu's first impression was that his memories were playing an odd and unsettling game with him. He had been here before and already come to know this place—but that was quite impossible.

The vehicle was descending a steeply sloping path flanked by woodland, at the base of which lay an extensive area of flattened ground set with lakes and copses of trees. The trees thickened in the middle, enclosing a blue and white building whose outline—glimpsed from the path's descending elevation—was at once familiar and estranging.

"We were here," Nissa said, and he knew he was not going mad. "You showed me this place once. But that was in Africa!"

"On the old border between Kenya and Tanzania," Kanu said, understanding coming to him in waves. "It's where the old Akinya household used to be—the base of operations for the whole commercial empire, five or six hundred years ago. This is what it used to be like, before it became a ruin!"

"I don't understand how it can be here."

"It's a copy, not the same building. It must be my family's thumbprint on the holoship project—their way of reminding everyone what they'd made possible."

"As if anyone needed to be told."

"It looks in good repair," he said, raising a flattened palm over his eyes to shade out the ceiling lights. "Good as new. Given all the troubles aboard *Zanzibar*, I'm amazed it looks as fresh as it does."

"Someone thought it was worth taking care of, I suppose."

The vehicle picked its way through the thicket of trees surrounding the household, following a path that was either one of the original roads or had simply been cleared by the continuous passage of elephants. The vehicle rolled up in front of the house and Memphis dropped the ramp.

Two Risen were waiting to escort them into the household. The front entrance was easily tall and wide enough to accommodate them, although Kanu could not say how accurately it now reflected the architecture in Africa. If it had been modified, it had been done so neatly, with an eye to preserving the elegance of the original frontage. Beyond, lit by glass ceiling lights, was a wide, airy corridor which formed the cross member of the building's A-shaped profile. Again, it was comfortably large enough to accommodate two elephants and their human guests, but not all the connecting halls and rooms were as generously proportioned.

"You will stay in these rooms," one of the Risen declared, gesturing at a set of doors with a swish of its trunk. "You will have water and food. If you need more water and food, you will ask. If there is anything broken in the rooms, you will say."

"Thank you," Kanu said.

"Was that a series of orders or just very stilted Swahili?" Nissa asked in a semi-whisper.

"I'm going to be optimistic and assume the latter."

Finding the doors already unlocked, they entered the suite. Within, they discovered that the rooms were connected in such a way that they did not need to go back out into the hall to move from room to room.

The rooms contained clean furniture, bedding, toilets and washing facilities. Kanu ran a gloved finger along a surface and inspected it for dust, hoping to gain some idea of when these chambers had last been occupied, but there was no sign of neglect.

They searched and found hot water, a cooking device and a refrigerated store of basic foodstuffs. Kanu was doubtful of the long-term nutritional value of some items, but there was clearly enough to keep them alive for the time being.

"We will come for you tomorrow," the Risen said when Kanu and Nissa returned to the hall.

"Can we leave the property?" Kanu asked.

"You will stay in these rooms. You will not leave. If you need us, you will make a noise." The Risen gestured at a metal staff, similar to the one Memphis had used to alert Dakota, leaning next to one of the doors.

"Are we prisoners here?" Nissa said.

"You will not leave."

"That's clear enough," Kanu said.

When the Risen had gone, they removed their outer spacesuit layers and set the pieces down on one of the several beds. It was a relief to be out of the suits, able to move freely—and to wash, and feel fresh again—but Kanu had never felt more nakedly vulnerable in his life. For all that it might have been illusory, the suit had at least given him a sense of armour, a shell that would offer some protection against the brute force of the Risen.

"What have we blundered into?" he wondered aloud.

"You're the diplomat—you tell me."

"You're no help. Dakota's shown no ill intentions towards us and we could easily have left when we went outside to fetch *Icebreaker*. So why do I feel like we've just made a tremendous mistake?"

"Maybe we have."

Exhausted, Kanu sat down at a table and cradled his hairless head in his hands. Nissa moved to a bedside console and made one of the walls start cycling through panoramic views, rich and detailed enough that Kanu felt he could have stepped into any one of them. A sunset savannah, a rainbowed waterfall that he nearly recognised, some boys playing football on a beach. He watched the boys wistfully, thinking how delightful it would be to have no cares beyond the kicking of a ball.

"We fix the ship. Then we leave. There's no reason for Dakota to prevent that, provided we help with the sleepers."

"What is she to them?" Nissa asked. "A matriarch, or something more? What keeps her at the top of the heap?"

Now there was kora music floating gently through the rooms.

"I don't know—respect for her age and wisdom? Does it have to be more than that?"

"She's not just an elephant, though."

"I think the magnifying glass was a giveaway. That and the ability to read and talk."

"I do the sarcasm around here, Kanu. What I mean is she's more than just an exceptionally bright elephant. Where did that human-level intellect come from? What did you do to them?"

"Me, personally? Nothing at all!"

"But you know what happened, and it was something to do with your family."

"'My' family now, is it?" Kanu asked irritatedly. "You were happy enough to marry into it."

Despite his provocation Nissa kept her cool. "You know what I meant."

Kanu nodded, ashamed at himself for overreacting. He softened his tone. "I'm sorry—that wasn't warranted. The truth is, I don't really know what went on with the elephants. Human genes must have been involved, or the expression of dormant gene sequences in the elephant genome which could be used to shape human neurological structures—like throwing a big bank of switches, turning things on and off. The genetic engineers made them small, to begin with—something about phyletic dwarfism. The smart elephants only came later, but they were probably an outgrowth of the same experimental programme. Which wasn't strictly an Akinya programme, incidentally—we only helped it along."

"That doesn't absolve you of responsibility."

"I know."

She sat on a bed, tucked her legs underneath her and rasped a hand over her scalp. "I'm not really blaming you for this—not *you* personally, anyway. Maybe your ancestors. But I'd still like to know what she is. If we could dissect her brain, what would it look like—an elephant with some human attributes, or the other way around? And if she was already different when she left Crucible, what other changes did the Watchkeepers make? What use could an elephant be to an alien civilisation?"

Kanu rose from the table and found a glass. He tried the local water, which came out of a spigot. It tasted strange, but then water always tasted odd when you were away from home.

If there were microorganisms in it, he was going to have to get used to them sooner or later.

"They've always wanted something," he said. "From the moment they declared the Covenant and took Chiku, Eunice and Dakota into space. We know from the recording that they brought them here directly, no stops along the way—this system was the sole point of the whole exercise. The Watchkeepers wanted something from the Trinity, but Chiku wouldn't say what it was."

"You mean, every time she got close to talking about the Watchkeepers, someone cut the recording."

"Yes," Kanu admitted. "But not Chiku—she wouldn't have withheld useful information."

"You think very highly of her."

"I know what she went through. The pressure on her, bringing *Zanzibar* to Crucible. It should have broken her soul. But I think it made her stronger than any of us."

"And you're not just saying that because she's your half-mother, or one-third-mother, or whatever it is?"

"No," Kanu said, after a moment's reflection. "I don't think I am."

"The strange thing is, I agree with you."

"You never knew her."

"But I saw the recording, saw the strength in that woman—the acceptance of sacrifice. Either she was a good actor, or she was completely prepared to give up her life for the elephants. I think I know which it was."

"Chiku wouldn't have withheld the truth."

"But someone got to her recording."

"Might I add a thought or two?" Swift was suddenly there, leaning against a doorframe, taking a bite out of an imaginary apple. "Let us be charitable and not assume the worst of our hosts. Are these surroundings not to your tastes?"

"I don't remember having much of a choice about them," Nissa said.

"I believe the elephants are doing their best to make you feel at home. Any awkwardness on their part may be reliably ascribed to their shortcomings with regard to Swahili. Goodness knows I've had my share of difficulties with it. Why couldn't you humans agree to speak something logical and straightforward like Mandarin?"

"Are you finished, Swift?" Kanu asked.

"Very nearly. Might I be so bold as to add one request? A suggestion, rather. Clearly we will have to return to the skip-over vault if we are to be of assistance to those sleepers. At some point, without arousing suspicion, I should very much welcome another chance to view that recording."

"I'll do my best to arrange that," Kanu said.

"Good. And when the opportunity does arise, Kanu, could you endeavour to blink as infrequently as possible?"

CHAPTER 31

Sadalmelik had fallen over onto his side, crushing one of the tubular sculptures in the process. He was so motionless that at first glance Goma thought he was dead. But he was still breathing, albeit with a slow, laboured rhythm, and as she watched, the tip of his trunk tried to lift itself from the ground.

"No," Ru said, rushing past Goma.

Goma joined her at the fallen creature's side. Eldasich and Achernar flanked her, still on their feet, but it only took a glance to confirm that they were also ailing—their breathing heavy, their eyes red and weeping with a white suppuration. A similar whiteness spilled from the sides of their mouths.

"Fetch her," Ru said, kneeling to place a hand on Sadalmelik.

"What is it?"

"I don't know. Something fast—they'd have raised a warning otherwise. What are you waiting for? Go!"

Goma went. She raced back up the corridor to the camp's human accommodation. Eunice was where she had left her—seated at her table, discussing arrangements with Vasin.

Goma was breathless. She had to fight to get the words out. "You have to come."

"What's the matter?"

"I don't know. Something's wrong with Sadalmelik. The others don't look good, either."

Eunice was already rising from her table. "He's sick?"

"It looks pretty bad. You'd better hurry."

Eunice went to a cabinet and pulled out a green toolkit. "Excuse us, Captain."

"No, I'm coming with you. What can it be—an infection? Something we've brought with us?"

"I don't know. These Tantors have never had contact with anyone other than myself so their immunological response may not be particularly strong. But their ancestors moved freely on *Zanzibar* in close association with hundreds and thousands of human beings. Nothing should hit them this hard. Have you had any contagious diseases on Crucible since *Zanzibar*'s departure?"

"Nothing that should hurt them," Goma said. "Our own elephant populations have never been affected by anything serious." A sudden black despair washed over her. "Oh, god. What's happened? What have we done?"

"Let's not assume the worst," Eunice said. "Sadalmelik had an infected tooth once—it looked very bad at the time, but he recovered."

"I'm worried about the other two."

"Where is Ru?"

"Still there. Can I carry anything?"

Eunice hefted the green box. "These are my medicines. I seldom get ill, and nor do they. If we need anything more potent, it'll have to come from your ship, and pray that it works on elephants. But first we need to know what we're dealing with."

"We should act pre-emptively," Vasin said. "There are portable medical supplies on the lander, some analysis equipment. Saturnin—do you think you could get back there with a tool sled? The ship will open to any one of us, provided it recognises our suits."

"There's a chance I might be more useful here," Dr. Nhamedjo said. "That said, if I suit up and leave immediately, I should be able to get back within half an hour."

Vasin nodded her assent. "Eunice—will your locks allow him to come and go, even if you're down with the Tantors?"

"I'll make sure they do. Grab a sled and load up as much as you can—antibiotics, antivirals, anything you have. Are you comfortable going out there on your own?"

"I could go with him," Loring said.

"Thank you," Nhamedjo said, "but the trail's clear enough, and I've been back to the lander since we arrived. I won't get lost."

"The others can't be far from the camp by now," Eunice said. "If you see them, move with caution and don't block their way. The formal introductions will have to wait."

While Nhamedjo went to suit up and make the short trek back to the lander, the rest of the party raced down to the Tantors. Eunice and Goma took the lead, but at the door the older woman raised a hand. "Goma and Ru have already had close contact with the Tantors; the rest of you haven't. Let's keep it that way for now."

"Surely you don't think it's anything to do with them?" Vasin said.

"I'm taking no chances. Wait outside this door until we have a better idea of what's happening."

Eunice sealed the door behind her, locking Goma and Ru in with her and the Tantors. She made an adjustment to the room's air pressure and air-circulation settings.

Ru was still kneeling at Sadalmelik's side, a hand on his trunk. It could not have been more than four or five minutes since Goma left, but Sadalmelik's condition had clearly worsened. Having witnessed the death of Agrippa, the progression was as unmistakable as it was harrowing.

Eunice knelt down and snapped open her medical kit. There was more in it than Goma had been expecting, and it was all very neatly organised. She took out an enormous syringe, stabbed it hard into Sadalmelik's thigh and drew a dense purple cylinder of blood. She slotted the blood sample into the maw of some kind of miniature analysis device built into the kit.

"Plasma assay will take a few minutes to run," she said, tapping a finger against a tiny readout in the top of the analyser. "In the meantime, I'm going to take a chance on a double bolus of broad-spectrum antibiotics and antivirals." She dug deeper into the kit, produced another heavy-duty syringe filled with straw-coloured liquid. "It's worked before, so it may give him a fighting chance. Eldasich, Achernar—what happened? When did you all start feeling unwell?"

"They say they can't breathe," Ru said. "It started during the night—coughing, fluid build-up in their lungs." She was looking up at Goma from her kneeling position, abject concern on her face, nearly crying from the distress of it all. "Sadalmelik was the first to succumb, but Eldasich and Achernar are going the same way. It's something we brought, isn't it?"

"Eldasich," Eunice said again, "Achernar—I know this is hard, but we need to isolate the three of you. I want you to move into the secondary chambers—one in each. We'll do what we can for Sadalmelik, but I have to think of you as well."

"Will Sadalmelik pass into the Remembering?" asked Achernar.

"Not if I can help it. But all three of you are ill and I don't know what's causing it. Trust me to do my best for you."

"We will leave him," Eldasich said.

Eunice recharged the syringe and injected the other two Tantors. "This may or may not make any difference, but it's all I can do for the moment. Think hard, both of you—did either of you feel ill before the people arrived? Did you notice anything wrong with Sadalmelik?"

"We were well," Achernar said. "This came quickly."

"Then it must be connected to their arrival somehow," Eunice said, in a deliberate, judicial tone.

With visible reluctance, Achernar and Eldasich moved away from their fallen friend and trudged into the adjoining chambers. Eunice promised she would look in on them later, then sealed the connecting doors.

Goma, meanwhile, stood helpless, desperate to be doing something but utterly at a loss as to how she could help. "Test our blood as well," she said. "Just in case."

"I was about to. Has either of you experienced a recent illness?"

"Other than Ru's AOTS, we've both been fine."

This drew sharp interest from Eunice. "AOTS?"

"Accumulated Oxygen Toxicity Syndrome—it's a condition, not a disease," Ru answered. "The oxygen partial pressure on Crucible is high, but we've adapted to it with drugs and therapies. I lapsed on the drugs—allowed myself to suffer oxygen toxicity over a prolonged period."

"Go on," Eunice said.

"At its worst, it's like a persistent case of the bends. But that was years ago—I've been managing it ever since. Besides, as I said, it's not contagious."

"What about bacterial pneumonia?" Eunice asked as she prepared to take the two human blood samples.

"What about it?" Goma asked.

"Zoonotic infection. It's hopped from people to elephants in the past—usually with fatal consequences."

"Neither of us has pneumonia," Ru said.

"We'll see."

Eunice drew blood from both of them, docked the syringes with the analyser, tapped buttons on its keypad. The machine was already making whirring and clicking sounds, interspersed with the whine of high-speed centrifuges and pumps. While it was preoccupied, Eunice moved to a bucket, retrieved a wet sponge and used it to soothe Sadalmelik. "Easy, my friend," she whispered, dabbing around his eye. "We've come through a lot, you and me. Too soon to bow out just yet."

Sadalmelik's trunk moved. Eunice stroked it, closed her fingers around the tip.

"I'm right here."

The analyser chirped—it had completed the first battery of tests. Eunice peered at the cryptic numbers and symbols of the readout. "A viral infection," she said, delivering the news neutrally. "Give it a little while and it will attempt to cook up a targeted antiviral."

"Attempt?" Goma asked.

"It isn't perfect."

The device gave two more chirps. The earlier medical data shuffled aside, replaced by more numbers and symbols. Goma knew some basic medical biology but this was too arcane for her, and the technology of the assay device was unfamiliar.

"Well, the good news is that neither of you has an elevated viral load," Eunice said, after a moment's consideration of the numbers. "You had the closest contact with the Tantors, so that was my first suspicion. But if it's something airborne, any one of the others could be responsible."

"You'll have to test all of us," Goma said.

Eunice gave a snort of derision. "I fully intend to."

A chime sounded hollowly throughout the chamber and the adjoining volumes. It repeated twice more, with an interval between each chime, and then there was silence. Goma looked around, wondering if it might be some kind of alarm. They had heard nothing like it since their arrival.

"What's that?"

"The doorbell," Eunice told her. "Atria, Mimosa and Keid, back from their repair work. I told you they must be nearby. They're waiting at the main lock. I'll need to speak to them, explain the situation. They can wait outside a little longer if they need to." Then she handed the sponge and bucket to Ru. "We're going to need more water. I'll show you where to refill the bucket, and then you can take care of it when I'm not in the room."

"Where are you going?" Goma asked.

"Not far. I just want to be sure about these blood samples, and there are some more involved tests I can only run in the upper levels." Eunice closed the toolkit and rose to her feet. She went first to the door and punched her fist against a control. "Atria—can you hear me? You must wait outside. It isn't safe for you to come back inside just yet." Then she stepped away from the door and gestured to Ru. "This way. Goma—keep an eye on Sadalmelik. Talk to him. Reassure him."

"I will."

Eunice walked with Ru across the stepped platforms of the floor. They had not gone more than a dozen paces when Eunice discarded any pretence that this was about fetching water. She locked one arm around Ru's neck, applying enough pressure to force out a yelp of surprise and pain, and used the other to twist back hard on Ru's own arm, as if she meant to yank it out of its socket.

"Goma," Eunice said, turning back and raising her voice,

"do nothing and say nothing. I may only be human these days, but I'm more than capable of hurting Ru."

Goma jumped to her feet, kicking over the medical kit in her surprise. "What are you doing?"

Ru screamed. She was barely ten metres away, but it might as well have been kilometres for all the difference Goma could make. She shuddered to think of the force Eunice was applying, the nasty biomechanics of bone and muscle and nerve, the pain she was likely inflicting.

"I told you not to speak."

They were still walking, ascending the raised sections. Finally they reached one of the doors leading into the secondary chambers. It was not one of those through which Eldasich and Achernar had already passed, but rather a smaller door that would have been a squeeze for anything but a juvenile elephant. At the threshold, Eunice gave Ru a violent shove and then stepped smartly back from the door. Ru fell inside and the door sealed before she had a chance to spring back through the gap. Eunice touched the panel next to the door and Goma heard the sound of heavy locking mechanisms moving into place.

"What are you doing?"

Eunice turned back to address Goma. They were on the same level now, eye to eye. She was unfazed—no sweat or other sign of exertion showing on her face.

"Ru has an elevated viral load. She's carrying something, and my guess is we're looking at the consequences."

"Why did you lie?"

"Because I had to. Because she still trusted me enough to walk away from Sadalmelik. Understand that I could easily have killed her, Goma, with the things in this room—the things in that medical kit. I've chosen to quarantine her instead."

"Let her go!"

"She's a weapon, Goma. Whatever's in her blood acts so quickly it can't be anything but an engineered zoonotic virus."

"What are you talking about?"

"I mean it's something put there deliberately, designed to take down Tantors. Why else would she be asymptomatic? Extreme measures were necessary. Even more extreme measures might be required."

"You're wrong."

Eunice walked back to Sadalmelik, dipped down to offer him a reassuring hand. Carefully she released the harness securing the speaking plate to his forehead and eased the whole assembly away. Goma guessed that it must have been more comfortable that way, and that Eunice had decided that he was now too weak to generate language.

"How long have you known her?"

"Half my life. This isn't what you think."

"People can keep the strangest secrets from each other, Goma. Doctors make the best murderers. Someone who truly hates what the Tantors are—what they stand for—what would stop someone like that becoming a scientist? Being drawn to the thing they most despise?"

"You don't know her."

"I can see the evidence."

"Let me speak to the others. I have to tell them what you've done."

"Of course. Make it clear to them how far I'm prepared to go."

"And how far is that, exactly?"

"If I feel you are a threat to the Tantors, I will kill you all. Do you think you understand me well enough to be sure that's an idle threat?"

"I don't think I understand you at all."

Goma reached the door leading back into the sloping corridor. She touched the panel and it opened without any intervention from Eunice. Vasin was standing on the other side, looking back at her with something of the horror she must have immediately seen in Goma's face.

"What's wrong? You look like someone just walked over your grave."

"Tell them," Eunice said, standing a little way back from the door.

It was all Goma could do to force the words out, never mind hope that they made sense to anyone else. "She says Ru is the weapon. That there's something in her blood, something that kills Tantors. An engineered virus. She's got Ru locked up, practically broke her arm getting her in there."

"Is this true?" Vasin asked.

"Why would it not be true, Captain? She's given you the

facts and I'm not disputing them. I have Ru in quarantine now. I may wish to draw another blood sample so my instinct is not to kill her immediately, even though that would probably be the wisest and safest thing. Do you see Sadalmelik over there? He's dying. That's inevitable. My medicines can't help him—the best I can do is ease his passing."

"We can help," Vasin said. "When Saturnin gets back—"

The doorbell sounded again—the three chimes.

Eunice hammered a control. "Wait! Didn't I say we had a problem here?"

The three chimes came again, then repeated in groups of three, so close that they nearly blended into each other. This was no longer a request to enter, Goma sensed, but an urgent demand.

"Can't you speak to them?" Karayan asked.

"It's only one-way communication from here. For two-way, I have to be upstairs. It's just the way I wired the place."

"It might be to do with Saturnin," Loring said. "Maybe he's ready to come back inside."

Goma did not think half an hour had passed yet, but perhaps the doctor had been swifter than expected.

"Is Ru safe where you've left her?" Goma asked.

"For the moment. Without me you won't get that door open in a hurry, so don't think of attempting a forced takeover."

"I'm not. But if you harm a hair on her, I'll personally skin you alive—fearless space explorer or not, you still bleed."

"Nice to know the ties of blood are that strong."

"Oh, they're strong—but I also know something you don't. Ru is innocent. She didn't do this."

"Her blood says otherwise."

"Then your analysis is screwed up, or she's carrying that virus unknowingly."

"And how might that have happened, exactly?"

"I don't know—maybe if we all calm down and stop talking about takeovers and force we might get somewhere. We're on the same fucking side, Eunice. Against stupidity. So let's start acting that way, shall we?"

The chimes sounded again.

"Damn them!"

"It sounds as if they really, really want to come inside," Goma said. "Maybe they have an emergency of their own— have you considered that? Maybe you should speak to them. Meanwhile, we might have medicines that can help the Tantors—but only if we all start cooperating again."

"She speaks sense," Karayan said. "And I will add this—I may not know Ru well, but I do not believe she set out to hurt those animals."

Goma looked at him with something between suspicion and gratitude. He was the last person she would have counted on for support, and yet it appeared to be given with all sincerity.

"I'd have thought you'd be quite happy to see Ru blamed for the virus."

"Because it keeps the blame from falling on the Second Chance delegation?"

"Exactly."

"The Tantors may have been a development we viewed with unease, Goma, but that does not mean we endorse their cold-blooded murder any more than Ru would. This is something else. It is not our doing, and I doubt very much that it is hers."

"I need to talk to Atria," Eunice said. "Remember what I said about that door. You can follow me."

"I could remain here?" Loring said. "Keep offering comfort to Sadalmelik."

"You might all be carrying the virus by now."

"Ru's obviously the primary carrier," Goma said. "Anyway, the damage is done—let Aiyana do what ve can. We can't just leave Sadalmelik on his own."

Eunice looked at Loring for long seconds, performing some private assessment of ver suitability. "Fine," she said brusquely. "We'll be as quick as we can. If anything changes, use that red button by the door to speak to me."

"I shall," Loring said.

They were soon on their way back up the sloping corridor, Eunice almost sprinting ahead of the others.

"We have superb medical facilities on *Travertine*," Vasin was saying. "Anything in Ru's blood, or which has spread to the rest of us, we can isolate and treat. You just have to trust us."

"And where has trust got us, exactly?" Eunice said sharply. "One dying Tantor, and two more that won't be far behind?"

"We came across light-years of space to answer your call," Vasin answered. "Gave up our lives, our futures. We made sacrifices you can't begin to understand. Mposi even died for you."

They reached the accommodation level, all of them breathless except for Eunice. She barged through chairs, brushed aside kitchen utensils to reach a dusty communications console. "Atria? Can you hear me now?"

"Yes, Eunice," came the Tantor's voice. "We should like to come in."

"You can't, not yet. The humans have brought a sickness with them. Sadalmelik is very unwell."

"How unwell? Will Sadalmelik pass into the Remembering?"

"I don't know. I'm doing what I can, but I won't risk the rest of you becoming infected. I want you to remain in your suits, outside, until I'm sure the air in here is safe to breathe." She sniffed, rubbed a hand under her nose. "Can you do that for me?"

"We can remain outside if we need to. But you must open the secondary lock, Eunice."

"Why?"

"We found a man outside. We think he may have passed into the Remembering."

CHAPTER 32

Nothing was wrong with their rooms in the household, nothing obviously amiss with the amenities on hand, but Kanu had never experienced a more restless night's sleep in his life. He was back aboard *Icebreaker*, haunting the corridors again—ghosting their long, darkened lengths, returning to his periodic vigil at Nissa's sleeping station. There were only so many hours in the night but his dreams felt like they contained weeks or months of mindless wandering. When at last he surrendered to day—the blue of the chamber's ceiling lights had returned to its prior brilliance after dimming for the night—he felt as drained as if he had lived through every one of those wandering hours. He looked at his little finger, irritated again by the torn fingernail he had noticed on first waking from skipover. How had that happened, exactly? The inside of a skipover casket was smoothly contoured—there was nothing to catch a fingernail on.

He rose, gathered a sheet about his midriff and moved through the adjoining rooms to the washbasins and shower cubicles. He filled a basin with the odd-tasting water and doused his face, removing some of the night's grease and grime.

"What do you think Swift knows?"

"About what?" Kanu asked, turning around.

"Everything. Us. The Tantors. What Dakota really wants. What happened to Chiku and the others."

Nissa had entered the room through the other doorway. She was naked, her free hand resting on one hip, a chunk of fruit held in the other, the posture unselfconscious and one that Kanu found unavoidably arousing. They had been married, once, and then lovers again so recently it was easy to think that everything that had happened in the meantime was no more than a momentary loss of affection, a lovers' spat. But years had passed since their divorce—decades, in fact—and even the reunion that began in Lisbon had been predicated on his ultimate betrayal of her.

After all that, how did he dare allow himself to feel that he might have fallen back in love with her? How did he dare hope that his feelings might be reciprocated? The universe did not contain enough forgiveness for that.

"The thing is, I keep coming back to this: everything I know about you says you acted in service to what you thought was the common good. You're not a bad man and you want the best for everyone—in so far as you understand it. But that still leaves us with a little difficulty, doesn't it?"

Kanu swallowed hard. "Swift."

"Swift. Yes. And you know what? I'm almost at the point of thinking you might have earned my trust. Maybe even my forgiveness, although let's not run before we can walk."

Not wishing to hurt his chances of being viewed in a better light, Kanu nodded eagerly. "Let's not."

"You're an idealist, and you're also hopelessly naive. But you're not a fool, and nothing that's happened to us was because you were acting selfishly, or for personal gain. I keep reminding myself of that. It's the bridge that's helping me find a way back to forgiving you. But here's the difficulty. However I might end up feeling about you, I'm reserving that clemency for you, not the other voice in our heads. And—yes—I don't doubt for a minute that he's listening in."

"I allowed Swift inside me—offered him sanctuary beyond Mars. To that extent, I'm responsible for him."

"Yes, you are. In which case you'd better hope he's still on our side. That our ends are the same as his. Because if one or both of us gets in the way of whatever Swift really wants . . . well, who knows what might happen?"

"Let's try not to assume the worst."

"There you go again: always the optimist." She bit into her fruit. "You're an old fool and you've made some terrible decisions. You'll probably make more. But deep down you're good and kind and I think you still want to make the best of things. Shall I tell you something?"

"Go on."

"When I found myself trapped aboard your ship, being shot at on our way out of Europa, I'd have gladly strangled you. I mean literally—no exaggeration."

"I believe you."

"You should. But on another level, I can't quite say that I'm sorry it happened. I may not be an artist, but I'm a scholar of the arts—a seeker of wonder and novelty, if you like. I like it when life surprises me. And this morning I woke up to find three tiny elephants putting fresh fruit out for us." She levelled her palm at hip height. "They were this big. Not baby elephants, exactly, but miniature ones. They were clever, too. They could talk and answer questions. Their little piping voices came out of those contraptions they have strapped to their foreheads. We have elephant butlers. How marvellous is that?"

Kanu grinned. He felt flooded with joy, filled with the

promise of her forgiveness. It was not there yet; it was nothing he could count on, but it was at least within the scope of his future, and for now that was enough.

"Elephant butlers. I wish I'd been awake to see that."

"I suppose you'll get your chance. Have you washed?"

"I was in the process."

"Then finish. I'd like to make love to you. Do you have any particular problems with that?"

"No, I don't."

"On the evidence, I didn't think so. Afterwards we'll have breakfast, and then we'll see what Dakota has in store for us. And, Swift, if you're listening in? Go and think machine thoughts for a while. You're not wanted here."

They were returned to their broken ship. Once aboard, Kanu satisfied himself with a quick check of the systems, verifying that *Icebreaker* had not been tampered with during their absence. All was well—or as well as when they disembarked. The ongoing repair processes had inched forward, although there was no useful change in the ship's capabilities.

"That door is sealed now," Nissa said, meaning the entrance to the polar berthing dock, "but if we had to get through it, I'm sure we could find a way."

"*Icebreaker* won't be much use as a tool of persuasion—at least, not for a while."

"But we still have my ship. Granted, it's not big enough to ram its way out, but it could still do some damage that I'm sure the elephants would rather avoid."

"Including our own suicides?"

"I didn't say it was a perfect plan. While you think of a better one, would you like some chai?"

Kanu began to dig through the repair summaries, running a finger down the list of tasks. *Icebreaker* had taken care of itself up to this point, but now it needed materials and parts it could not easily synthesise. Weeks or months of further work looked inevitable. After the year they had already spent in skipover between Poseidon and Paladin, though, Kanu supposed the additional delay was acceptable.

"All this for an instant of damage!"

"Stop complaining—we're alive." She handed him a bulb of tepid chai, the best that could be managed in the weightless core.

"Oh, I'm not complaining. But I'd much rather not be in her debt."

"She's getting the better side of this bargain, Kanu. Have you seen the size of this place? She won't miss a few thousand tonnes of materials, but in return she regains those sleepers."

"She strikes me as clever enough to have worked out how to do that herself," he mused. "You'd think they'd have made more of an effort if the Friends mean so much to them."

"Be grateful there's something we can do for her."

"Oh, I am."

When they had done as much with the repair tasks as could be managed in a day, Memphis met them at the airlock and brought them back to Dakota. Along the way, Kanu debated asking for another chance to view the recording of Chiku, but his instincts told him not to sound too eager to view it again so quickly.

Especially as Swift appeared to think there was something he ought not to blink for.

"We will make every effort in our power to help you," Dakota said when he had outlined what was needed on an immediate basis. "I will assign a number of trusted Risen to you. You may direct them as you wish. I will instruct them to do everything they can to assist you with setting up the supply chains."

"It'll take a while to get the ship running again," Kanu said.

"Provided you find your lodging arrangements to your satisfaction, I do not see any great difficulty accommodating you. Besides, I have a selfish desire to enjoy your company for as long as I may."

"I think we'll be around for a little while," Nissa said. "Would you like us to look at the skipover vault now?"

"You are tired and there is no tremendous urgency. I would not wish you to feel beholden to me. Get the repair effort up and running, and then we may turn our thoughts to the Friends. Does that sound like a sensible course of action?"

"Very," Kanu said.

The next day was similar, and the next, and the one after that. Slowly the supply lines were established. When the requirements were simple, everything went smoothly. When Kanu had more complicated requests, however, he found it difficult to communicate his needs to the Risen. There were inevitable misunderstandings, some of which required careful unravelling. Slowly, though, he could see the glimmerings of progress. There would be setbacks, the odd calamity or two—such things were inevitable. Equally, he could see no insurmountable barriers. The ship was fully capable of repairing itself. They would be able to leave.

Dakota always made sure she was appraised of their progress. During their audiences with her, they spoke of technical matters for an hour or so before turning to more general topics of conversation. No subject was obviously out of bounds, but Kanu had noticed a disinclination on Dakota's part to speak in detailed terms about the history of *Zanzibar*. Even so, they did their best to coax information out of her while trying not to make it sound as if they had specific concerns.

"It all looks idyllic," Nissa said offhandedly during one conversation. "Tantors thriving, living independently of human support. You've got it all organised—heat, air, power, water, food, waste management—even education! Chiku would have been glad to see you doing so well."

"She would recognise our difficulties, too—that we are still recovering from the resource crisis. She would agree that we must not allow ourselves to become complacent. But at least we are laying the foundations for better times." Dakota closed the heavy volume she had been consulting. She had asked Kanu and Nissa for help with a difficult, ambiguous passage. "Yes, I am sure she would have been very pleased for us."

"And the construct," Kanu said. "Eunice had a stake in your future, too."

"That is very true."

"What happened to them?" Nissa asked.

There was a silence, and Kanu began to fear that the question had been too direct, Nissa's suspicions too overt. But when Dakota replied, she appeared unfazed.

"It was all a tremendous sadness. The construct was the first to leave us. Gradually, she began to cease to function properly. It was very upsetting, after everything Eunice had done for our kind during the crossing. Like all machines, though, she began to wear out. Is it wrong of me to speak of her as a person? I know she wasn't human, but the force of her adopted personality was striking, even to myself—she felt like a person to us."

"I understand," Kanu said.

"Over time—years rather than months—she became progressively more unreliable and confused. She lost the thread of herself. We did what we could, but given the failing state of our own systems and the difficulties we already faced, our efforts were destined to meet with little reward. Truly, we could have benefited much from the construct's guidance had she remained to help us. But in the end she stopped working."

"She died, you mean?" Kanu asked.

"As I said, it is a sadness."

Swift, who was standing in silent observation to Kanu's right, made a sceptical frown. He shook his head, touched a finger to the tip of his nose, looked on the verge of making a significant observation.

"What happened to her remains?" Nissa asked. "May we see them?"

"They were dismantled and destroyed. It was one of her last coherent requests. It troubled us, but we had no choice but to honour her wish. Doubtless you have some sense of our loss. But that is as nothing compared to our feelings about Chiku. As you know from the recording, she remained awake to help the rest of us—a typically selfless gesture. Unfortunately, there was a gradual collapse of the closed-cycle life-support system, and conditions deteriorated over time. It became very hard for the humans, even the small number who had remained awake to assist us. In desperation, most of them joined the others in skipover. I'm afraid Chiku was among that number."

"Why was that a bad thing?" Nissa asked.

"Because those last few did not survive. There was a systematic failure of an entire bank of skipover caskets. I am sorry, Kanu—I can only imagine how upsetting this must be to you. Truly she gave us more than could ever be repaid. And we wept for the deaths of these martyrs—wept and scolded ourselves for not having done more. That was when we realised how far we still had to go before becoming your equals."

"Why didn't you tell us all this sooner?" Kanu asked.

"For exactly the same reason I am sorry to have told you now—because it is a terrible thing, and a particular cruelty in light of your family connection. If I might offer one consolation, it is that the Risen cherish her memory—everything she did for us, everything she planned to do. And it is an honour to have another Akinya among us."

Eventually Kanu felt it was safe to ask for a second viewing of the Chiku recording. They had been aboard *Zanzibar* for more than six weeks; the repair work was proceeding satisfactorily— it was perfectly reasonable that he should wish to begin fulfilling his side of the arrangement.

"If you insist," Dakota said. "But please be assured that I have every confidence in your abilities, and that you will keep your word. Still, as you say, the repair process demands less of your time than it did originally."

So Memphis took them back to the skipover vault beneath the civic building, and they were allowed to conduct as thorough an examination of the equipment as they desired. It was cold in the layered depths of the vault, and silent, and since they were surrounded by the sleeping dead it was hard not to think of ghosts, of lives in abeyance, of collective dreams of an unending winter.

"I don't like it in here," Nissa confided.

"Neither do I." Kanu blew on the tips of his fingers, already numb. "But we have an agreement."

There were thousands of caskets, but as most of them were of a similar design, they only needed to inspect a sample of the sleepers. At first, the technology looked dauntingly unfamiliar compared to the skipover caskets aboard their own spacecraft. But upon closer study, the fundamentals proved to be similar, with only the overlying control and observation systems being of a markedly different design. Here there was no need for extreme automation since the presumption was that there would always be human caretakers to watch over the sleepers and intervene as needed.

Nonetheless, it was soon apparent that not all of the sleepers could be brought back to life. A fraction of the caskets had malfunctioned in one way or another, and some of the occupants must have been dead or gravely unwell before they were committed to skipover. Kanu and Nissa did not have the resources or expertise to assist with these difficult marginal cases.

Encouragingly, though, the majority of the sleepers appeared revivable. It would need to be done gradually, in small enough numbers that individual problems could be addressed as they arose. Once they were thawed, well and adjusted to their surroundings, the newly awoken could begin to help with the effort of waking the others. The work would get faster as they progressed.

Still, Kanu dared not guess how long the whole process would take. It felt optimistic to think in terms of months. Where would these people live once they were up and about, in a world remade for the convenience of elephants? It was one thing to keep a couple of human guests fed and watered— what of thousands, or even tens of thousands?

They were on their way back to Dakota, already inside the civic building, when Kanu said, "Memphis—might I have another look at the recording? It won't take a moment."

"Why, Kanu?"

It helped that their hair had begun to grow back since their arrival on *Zanzibar*, enabling Memphis to distinguish more easily between human man and human woman. Kanu's hair was still short and appeared to be growing back whiter than when he had shaved it, and it bristled out from his scalp in all directions. Nissa's was darker and she had made an effort to tame its growth, which resulted in her looking younger rather than older, despite their travails.

"Your leader has asked us to help with the sleepers," Kanu said. "Chiku left some information that we need to bring them out of skipover. You'll be saving us a great deal of time if we could review the recording again now. I'm sure Dakota would approve."

"You are not Dakota. You do not know her."

"But you do, Memphis." It was Nissa speaking now, confidently adding her voice to Kanu's. "She told us how much she admires you—your loyalty, your strength of character. She said you were one of the few she could talk to as an equal."

"Did she?"

"Oh, yes. She was fulsome in her praise." Nissa was being quite brazen now. "Did Dakota have a problem with us viewing the recording originally, Memphis?"

"No."

"Well, then, there won't be a problem this time—and you'll have shown useful initiative in decision-making."

"It won't take long, Memphis," Kanu said.

He could almost feel the slow, clock-like deliberation of the elephant's brain. Unfair to make that comparison, of course—he had judged Memphis to be a thing of wonder until Dakota offered him a new baseline—but he could not help it. Humans were cleverer than chimps, but a dull child was somehow more pitiable than any animal. Here was a talking elephant with only average intelligence.

"You will see the recording."

"Thank you, Memphis," Nissa said.

Memphis brought them to the upright glass and once again summoned the image of Chiku Green. Kanu had seen it all before, but this time he could not dismiss a sense of furtiveness, knowing that he had ulterior reasons for watching the message again. True, they had a theoretical interest in the appended documents. But that was not the reason they were here.

Rather than worrying about concealing his guilt, though, Kanu was doing his best not to blink.

Back at the household, Kanu kept being drawn to the windows. The rooms only offered a limited view of the surrounding household, overlooking an area of open ground, some trees, and part of an adjoining wing. But he had seen no sign of activity since Memphis brought them back from the civic building. Feeling oddly foolish, he checked cupboards and looked under beds, just in case one of the dwarf elephants had squeezed away somewhere.

But they were alone.

"Well, Swift?" he asked finally. "You've had time to think about the recording, and I tried as hard as I could not to blink. What was the point of that particular exercise?"

"I would have thought that was as blatant as one of your opening chess gambits, Kanu. The recording had been edited—rather crudely if I might say so."

"We both spotted that."

"Yes. But you may not have spotted that Chiku Green was ahead of her silencers."

"How so?" Nissa said.

"She must have prepared her statement ahead of time, reading from a script. She took the words she meant to speak and embedded them in the technical appendage, as a safeguard."

"It was too fast for me," Kanu said. "Just a blur of graphs and numbers."

"Fortunately, your visual system recorded rather more than your conscious mind was capable of processing. The words were encoded numerically—a very simple cyclic numerical cipher. Virtually hidden in plain sight. A child could have decoded the statement—but it would have needed to recognise what it was seeing in the first place. Chiku must have been confident that the Risen—the majority of the Risen, at least— would not be quite so perceptive."

"Can you show us these words?" Nissa asked.

"You forget that I have also seen Chiku and studied her patterns of speech. I can emulate her."

Something made Kanu hesitate—some lingering notion that it was an act of disrespect to Chiku to have Swift animate her. But he forced himself to set aside that disquiet. It would be better to hear the words from her lips.

"Do it. Show us the things she said that we didn't get to hear."

"I suggest you simply ask me to explain the most germane points for now, and I will provide a transcript of the entire document at my leisure."

"I'm not sure—"

"I am," Nissa said. "It makes sense. Do it, Swift."

Swift's form shifted to that of Chiku, exactly as she had looked in the glass, only sharper, more real, more suggestive of actual physical presence. And when she spoke, it was not a recording they were hearing, but the living voice of his third-mother.

"What would you like to know?"

Kanu was frozen. He had no idea how to begin addressing her. The likeness was too striking, the similarity heartbreaking. He had known two iterations of Chiku back on Earth, neither of them this woman, but everything about her was a reminder of that past, the contentment of the good years they had barely known they were living. He saw her profile in sunlit doorways, standing like a figure in a Dutch interior, the angle of her averted face stroked with gold. He remembered the kindness of Chiku Yellow as she cared for Chiku Red, who had lost language and needed to be nursed back to it like a child. He remembered the smell of brine at the quayside, the mewl of seagulls, the clack of rigging, the drowsy warmth of a Lisbon evening.

He recalled the fortitude and patience of Chiku Red, who when the Mechanism fell had turned out to be the strongest of them all.

"Let's begin at the beginning," Nissa said, when his silence grew uncomfortable. "Why are you here? Why did you come here in the first place?"

"They needed us," she said. "The Watchkeepers are old and immensely powerful, but there are things even they can't discover for themselves. The M-builders were an older civilisation—vastly older. Something happened to them, and the Watchkeepers would like to be able to incorporate that data into their own strategic planning. This system is a key to understanding what became of the M-builders, but the Watchkeepers can't use it."

At last, Kanu forced himself to speak. "Why not?"

"They're wholly machine. That's their strength, but also their limitation. The answers are on Poseidon, but they can't get there. Poseidon is closed to investigation by machine intelligences—or at least, to machine intelligences like the Watchkeepers. It's hard to explain, but it has something to do with them being too powerful, having too much processing power—they've slipped over the Gupta-Wing threshold."

"That doesn't mean anything to me," Kanu said.

"I wouldn't expect it to—it's quite arcane. But there's something called integrated information theory—a model of consciousness—that was very interesting to a couple of mid-twenty-second-century cyberneticists called June Wing and Jitendra Gupta. The underlying theory's much older than that, though—it's a way of looking at neural networks and how information can be made to flow through them. In *feed-forward* networks, the flow is all one-way—like a river running downhill. The cerebellum is a feed-forward network. Meanwhile, your higher brain areas incorporate information-feedback properties—you're gathering information and processing it in complex ways. That's an *integrated network*, and it's the key to conscious experience. Here's the interesting thing, though. Under certain conditions, an integrated network can be functionally duplicated by a feed-forward network, but at the expense of greater computational resources. It's not a particularly elegant or efficient mapping, but it is mathematically equivalent. Obviously you don't have that option. You're made out of meat. You're conscious because you can't afford to waste limited brain capacity on *not* being conscious."

"That's a relief."

"There are only so many neural pathways in that skull of yours, Kanu—you have to use them in the most efficient way, and your consciousness is just a by-product of that neural efficiency. But here's the thing. If you had limitless processing capacity, you could supplant your integrated networks with feed-forward networks, and you'd be functionally indistinguishable to an external observer. But there'd be one difference."

"I wouldn't be conscious."

"You'd be a computational zombie—giving all the appropriate external responses suggestive of consciousness, but with no conscious activity going on inside your head."

"Would I care?"

"There wouldn't be anything left of you to care. That's the point of the Gupta-Wing theorem. It says that any conscious entity with unlimited computational resources runs the risk of remodelling itself as a series of feed-forward networks, thereby slipping over the horizon of consciousness. But it never notices, because at the *precise moment* it happens, there ceases to be a conscious 'it' to detect the change. And after the transition, there's no compulsion to reverse it. That's what happened to the Watchkeepers. Collectively, they became too powerful—farmed out too much of their neural processing to feed-forward networks because they had the computational freedom to do so. Consequently they slipped over the Gupta-Wing threshold."

"They're machine zombies," Nissa said.

"At least partially. Maybe they've retained enough residual self-awareness to understand that they've lost something, especially after being rebuffed by the systems around Poseidon for so long. But from the point of view of those systems, of the M-builders, they're hollow. They can process, interpret, deploy forms of intelligence, but they're not conscious so they're barred from Poseidon. The moons can tell—they can detect which side of the Gupta-Wing threshold the Watchkeepers now lie on. But it doesn't stop them trying. They have almost limitless patience, an endless willingness to keep attacking the same problem. Maybe that in itself is a marker for the Gupta-Wing threshold—an inability to grow frustrated, bored, indifferent. The Watchkeepers have been throwing themselves against this knowledge barrier for millions of years—longer than we've been a species. But on a kind of glacial timescale their strategies can evolve. Lately they've begun to co-opt the assistance of other intelligences, creatures running on different cognitive substrates. Creatures like us—living organisms, like me or Dakota, or hybrid machine-human intelligences like Eunice. Individually, none of us is up to the task. But it was the Watchkeepers' intention that the Trinity would be able to function as an investigative whole, a single information-gathering collective intelligence, one that would be able to slip through the barrier of the moons and reach Poseidon. And learn, and report back—give them the M-builders' insights that they can't reach for themselves."

"Is that what you did?" Nissa asked.

"We tried. They gave us tools—a ship full of sensors and instruments, all of it copied from our own technology. They made us understand what they expected of us. And of course we tried to do as we were asked, because we saw it as an extension of the Covenant, a necessary act for continued non-intervention. Also, of course, because we were curious. To begin with, we approached Poseidon slowly, coming a little closer each time, gathering more and more data. Finally, though, we had to go deeper. And that's when we were tested."

"In what way?" Kanu said.

"Examined, scrutinised, our nature probed—the test the Watchkeepers failed. By some miracle, we passed and were permitted to go deeper. But we could not. The Terror had touched us. Something got into our heads—a kind of final warning for the curious. It is difficult to put into language, something more easily felt than expressed—but as near as I can phrase it, it was an invitation to proceed if we dared. *Come nearer and learn something of our secrets—how we changed our fate. But know that from this moment, you will be judged.* Not just us—not just the Trinity—but our entire species, our entire flowering, from people, to Tantors, to hybrids like Eunice. That was the Terror—we were about to take *that* responsibility on our shoulders for the sake of increasing the knowledge base of another civilisation entirely. So we refused. We had come this far, acted for the Watchkeepers—done their bidding without complaint. But no more, not until we had a better understanding of the risks."

"You stood up to them," Kanu said, smiling in admiration. "You had the brazen nerve to do that. That took real courage."

"The Watchkeepers knew they could not coerce us too forcefully," Chiku said. "We had to be free agents, not the zombie puppets of a zombie civilisation. So they tried to barter with us, and that's when they bestowed the gifts. Increased longevity for Dakota. Turning Eunice into a living woman. These boons were granted with the willing consent of the subject. They tried to offer me immortality, as well—they said it was a trivial thing."

"You took it?" Kanu said.

"I refused. That didn't go down well, but there wasn't much they could do about it. The other two weren't capable of functioning as an expedition team on their own. So: stalemate. Who knows what might have happened if *Zanzibar* hadn't appeared? None of us was expecting that—not even the Watchkeepers."

"Was there any warning?" Nissa asked.

"Not much. A brief, powerful surge of energy from the Mandala on Paladin across every electromagnetic band we could measure, hard gamma all the way down to ultra-long baseline radio waves. And then it was over, and *Zanzibar* was hanging over Paladin. It should have come crashing down! But somehow it had retained the orbital angular momentum it had at the moment of the Crucible event, and that was enough to send it looping around Paladin. We had no idea what had happened, to begin with. We barely recognised what we were looking at as being a chunk of the old holoship."

"Did you attempt contact?" Nissa asked.

"Rescue, more like. We picked up emergency transmissions from the survivors. Confused, panic-stricken—they had even less of a clue about what had happened than we did. At least we knew we were in another solar system after the Watchkeepers transported us. All they knew was that there'd been a massive explosion and half their world was gone. They were only starting to come to terms with that when we boarded. Of course, we were something of a shock to them— but not as much of a shock as what had just happened. Yes, you are orbiting a new planet now. Yes, we are the Trinity. Yes, you appear to have followed us across seventy light-years."

"The Watchkeepers allowed you to interact?" Kanu said.

"They kept their distance. The three of us were all highly regarded by the original colonists and the survivors readily accepted our guidance, even our leadership. I was invited to coordinate the human survivors, while Dakota—the cleverest, wisest of the Tantors—assumed her former role as matriarch. Eunice, being neither machine nor human nor elephant, didn't command quite such ready loyalty from either faction, but her expertise was invaluable in knitting *Zanzibar*'s broken systems back together. Even the harshest of her sceptics came to see her value. But then things began to change. We thought we were over the worst of our difficulties, but in truth they had barely begun. Our little rock was simply not big enough to sustain humans and elephants simultaneously."

"Swift," Nissa said. "Might I ask a question?"

Swift adopted his usual camouflage. "By all means."

"How much of this did you suspect the first time we saw the recording?"

"Had I suspected any of it, Nissa, I would have voiced my concerns immediately."

"Yet you're the one who wanted another look at the recording. That was your idea."

"Indeed."

"Then you had some idea that encrypted data was there, whether or not you're prepared to admit it now."

"It was clear to me that the recording had been edited, Nissa. But then, did we not all reach that conclusion?"

"Only you were capable of detecting that embedded data," Kanu said, struck by a powerful sense that he was arguing with himself. "Neither Nissa nor I saw anything suspicious in those numbers. You saw the alphabetical cipher—we didn't. And if you saw nothing the first time, why were you so keen that I not blink the second time?"

"He knew," Nissa said. "All of it, or part of it, at least."

"Is this true, Swift? Did you withhold your suspicions?"

"I rather resent the thrust of that question."

"Just answer it."

"We were in the midst of delicate negotiations with Dakota. It would have been counterproductive of me to raise doubts on the basis of incomplete data."

"Counterproductive to *you*," Nissa said.

"She has a point, Swift," Kanu said. "When we debated remaining aboard *Icebreaker* or taking it inside *Zanzibar* for repairs, you raised no objections."

"You were at liberty to take whichever course of action you thought the wisest, Kanu. Please do not blame me for failing to find fault in your own argument."

"You slippery little . . ." Nissa said.

Kanu raised a calming hand. "It's too late for recriminations."

"Is that you speaking, or Swift?"

"It's me, and we're in this situation now, so there's no point arguing about it. Maybe Swift could have spoken up sooner, but he's helping us now, isn't he?"

"Now that we're committed. Now that our ship is locked inside *Zanzibar*."

"May I continue?" Swift said, becoming Chiku again.

"Provided you promise to be a little less devious from now on," Nissa said.

"Gradually it became clear to me that it's not human assistance the Watchkeepers need, but organic assistance. The species doesn't really matter. From the perspective of an alien robot, a Tantor is just another warm-blooded organism with a central nervous system. The Tantors are already on the cusp of human intelligence—we did that ourselves, through generations of genetic intervention. All the Watchkeepers had to do to achieve their purposes was give them the final push. Extreme longevity was only the first of the gifts bestowed on Dakota. The next was human-level intelligence, perhaps something beyond that, even. It was not hard for them. They had a good understanding of how our minds worked, given how deeply they'd already looked into my head. When they took Dakota from us the second time, I still felt I knew her. When she returned, I wasn't sure."

"What had changed?" Kanu asked.

"She's become something new—something formidable and clever. And whatever mix of genes produces that cognitive enhancement, it's inheritable. Her offspring are significantly smarter than the Tantor baseline. It's unevenly distributed— they don't all get the same package of enhancements—but across all her children, and their children, Dakota's genes are slowly raising the intelligence of the entire Tantor population. More of them speak like her, more of them use tools the way she does—more of them can plan and strategise and out-think us. And I don't know quite what to make of that. I don't want to be frightened of it. I don't want to overreact against a development that could be wonderful. But all of a sudden, the Tantors are no longer ours. We neither control nor understand them—and we have no idea what they are going to do next. Something good and wise, I hope; something that serves all our needs. But I fear it may not play out that way. We have remade *Zanzibar* and given them the means to run it on their own. I think they could become totally autonomous, in time."

"They did," Nissa said.

"We don't know that for sure," Kanu said.

"Look around, Kanu. Have you seen another living human soul since we arrived? The worst did happen, just as Chiku feared—a war between the Risen and the people. And now we know who won."

CHAPTER 33

It was a challenging thing, Goma reflected, to remove one's own helmet under near-vacuum conditions, and Dr. Nhamedjo had given it his best shot. He must have retained his conscious faculties long enough not only to undo the neck-ring fastenings—supposedly failsafe under reduced pressure, although there were loopholes in any design—but also to lift the helmet away from his head even as the air and heat surged from his body, stealing life and awareness in the same explosive gasp. A final few seconds of lucidity, and then darkness ink-blotting in from all sides. Goma wondered what had been the worst part of it: the inexpressible cold, shocking as a helium bath; or the airlessness, his lungs attempting to draw sustenance from vacuum? Both, perhaps, equal in their viciousness, their absolute promise of imminent death. Nor would it have been instantaneous. But he was a physician, and must therefore have had a shrewd idea of what to expect.

The Tantors found him on the trail between the camp and the lander, on his own, with no sign of the cargo sled he was supposed to have been dragging from the airlock. From his footprints it was clear that he had never reached the ship, nor had any intention of doing so. He had set off with only one goal in mind: the taking of his own life. These last days must have seen him marking time, waiting to learn whether the virus functioned in the intended fashion. Once he had his evidence, he was free to remove himself from the expedition.

None of this was immediately apparent to Goma, or indeed to any of her associates. All they had was a dead man, brought in by elephants. Heeding Eunice, the three spacesuited Tantors had remained outside after depositing Nhamedjo in the airlock. They had found his helmet close to his body and brought that back, too.

"If it turns out they killed him . . ." Vasin said, apparently thinking aloud.

"I think he did this to himself," Goma said. "Look at his suit. It's not like Eunice's. The Tantors wouldn't have known where to start opening it, even if they had the right tools on their trunks."

"Maybe they did?" said Loring. "Went out to fix equipment, didn't they?"

"They had tools," Eunice confirmed flatly. "Trunk attachments, adaptors—stored in those panniers on their suits. They could have swapped them on and off easily enough—it's how they work in vacuum. But do you see any signs of a struggle, scratches or damage to his suit?"

"They're so strong, he wouldn't have had a chance to struggle," Loring said.

"No, but he'd have had ample time to run away. They don't move quickly in those suits. Even if they cornered him—which they didn't—your friend would have had time to call us."

"Can't have committed suicide," Loring said. "He went out there to help us? To fetch the medical equipment?"

"To delay the actual act," Goma said. "To buy more time for the infection to take hold, to make the medicines less likely to help. He never had any intention of coming back."

"You're very sure of his guilt," Vasin said.

"He put the disease in Ru."

"You don't know this."

"No, Gandhari, but who else could have done it? He had the opportunity, with Ru not being well enough to come out of skipover at the same time as the rest of us—and how do we know that was even true? We just took his word—he was the doctor. It gave him all the time he needed to pump her full of whatever nasty crap he needed to. I should have seen it sooner. Grave always said there was another saboteur among us."

"You're forgetting something," said the captain. "Doctor

Nhamedjo was openly critical of my handling of Grave. Of all us, he was the one who expressed the most scepticism concerning Grave's guilt."

"He was clever, that's all—he knew full well that nothing he said would make a blind bit of difference. *Look at me—the innocent, thoughtful Doctor Nhamedjo.*"

"We can argue his guilt in due course," Karayan said, "but right now we still need those medical supplies. I am willing to return for them."

"The Tantors are still out there," said Loring.

"Then I will exercise caution."

They watched Karayan leave, dragging the sled behind him—light now that it was unladen. Eunice had warned Atria, Mimosa and Keid that another person would soon be on the move, and their shuffling, spacesuited forms were visible from a number of topside windows as they waited for further instructions.

"Why don't you send them to the lander?" Goma asked. "They can help carry extra supplies."

"It's that clear-cut to you, is it?" Eunice snapped back. "Nhamedjo is dead, case closed? None of you had the slightest inkling of his guilt until just now, so how do I know I can trust any of you?"

"You don't," Goma said. "But you can begin by excluding Ru. She didn't have a clue what he'd put in her."

"She's still infected—still a lethal agent."

"You have her under quarantine, and pretty soon you're going to have more medicines and tools at your disposal. At least start treating Ru as the victim, not the perpetrator."

"I'd like to contact *Travertine,*" Vasin said. "I can speak to it via my suit, but it'll be simpler if you just give us a direct line. Are we in the right alignment for that?"

Eunice nodded at the ceiling. "Your ship is overhead."

"Then let me talk to Nasim Caspari."

"Another trustworthy soul?"

"I'm going to ask him to put a lock on Nhamedjo's quarters and medical suite. I'll want a complete search of his personal effects and a more thorough examination of his background than anything we've performed to date. Clearly we missed something."

"You have a fine talent for understatement."

"Then I'll ask Andisa to start working with us to find a cure for Sadalmelik and the others, just as soon as our analysers have a look at the blood samples. You've met six of us—"

"Yes, and hasn't *that* gone well."

"There are forty-six more of us in space—forty-seven if I decide to thaw Peter Grave, which is at least an outside possibility at this point. That's a lot of expertise—more than any of us has on our own, and that includes you, Eunice. If we made a mistake about Nhamedjo, then I'm truly sorry. But the only way out is via cooperation, and that means none of us acting rashly." Vasin looked at Goma. "I concur that Ru must remain in quarantine—that's the only sensible option—but she must be informed that we do not think she is culpable. Do you accept that, Eunice?"

"Nothing is proven either way."

"I'm not insisting on proof, just a little reasonableness. I am willing to turn over the resources of my entire starship to help you and the Tantors—now give me something back."

"You made this mess."

"You invited us," Vasin replied.

Of course there were no miracles to be had, except of the modest kind permitted by the exigencies of medicine and time. Karayan came back with a sled-load of supplies, and on the second trip the suited Tantors returned to the lander to help with additional logistics. Vasin outlined the situation to Caspari, and with all haste her desired arrangements were put in place. The lander's medical analysers were patched through to *Travertine* and additional blood samples taken from both Tantors and humans. The remaining members of Nhamedjo's medical staff—presumed innocent until otherwise proven—were assigned the task of processing this data, first to select the best therapeutic approach based on the existing medical stocks, and secondly to attempt synthesis of a targeted antiviral drug.

Not all of the news was against them. Atria, Mimosa and

Keid had completed repairs on one of Eunice's remote transmitters, which in turn allowed for better and more prolonged
communications with *Travertine*. The starship, meanwhile,
had now dispersed relay satellites into its own orbit, furthering
their chances of remaining in contact. Vasin returned to the
lander and moved it closer to the camp, allowing a flexible
pressure bridge to be strung from one of the airlocks. This in
turn permitted the humans to move more easily from one to
the other.

Ru's virus was detected at low concentrations in all the
expedition members, most notably Goma, but not at a level
where infection was a strong likelihood. After more than a day
all remained asymptomatic, confirming that the virus had
been engineered to avoid obvious detection.

"Nhamedjo would have seen it in our blood," Goma said.
"That's a given. But no one was looking over his shoulder,
doubting his word."

Eunice remained entirely free of infection; although in
other respects she appeared fully human, it was clear that she
had some sort of enhanced immune system.

"To think I let that bastard examine me," she said. "He was
close enough that I could have snapped his neck like a dry
twig."

"Would you have, if you'd known?"

"In an instant."

"That would have done wonders for diplomacy. Anyway,
the damage was done by then—Ru was already primed to
infect the Tantors. For all we know he tainted her blood while
the rest of us were still in skipover. With hindsight, it makes
sense that he'd concentrate his efforts on one of us—we were
always going to be among the first to contact them."

"I'd rather you didn't speak of this making sense, Goma.
Not while Sadalmelik is dying."

"I'm just saying there's a twisted logic to it. He must have
rejoiced when we put Peter Grave into skipover."

"Then this other man is definitely innocent?"

"I think he and Mposi were trying to flush out the real
saboteur. Grave confided in Mposi and they arranged to meet,
but Doctor Nhamedjo got to Mposi first. When Gandhari digs

into his background, I'll be interested to know if he had expertise in nanotechnology."

"Why?"

"That's how he hoped to get rid of Mposi."

"I am sorry about that. I remember Mposi, although he was a much younger man when I knew him. I would have liked to meet the older version—to see the person he grew into. And Ndege, of course."

"You only thought to ask one of them to come."

"I did not have the luxury of sending a long and involved message. Besides, Ndege was the one who had the best knowledge of Tantors—the one most likely to impress Dakota. Well, my plans did what plans have a habit of doing." But she touched Goma's hand. "You are blameless in this. I understand that."

"And Ru?"

"You appear convinced of her innocence. I admit that the force of your opinion is . . . compelling."

"We studied Tantors on Crucible—we put our lives into bringing them back. Ru almost literally—that's why she's as damaged as she is. She didn't want to follow me here at first—this expedition was going to tear us apart, wife from wife. But when she realised there was even a glimmer of a chance that they might still be alive . . . that was enough to change her mind."

"So the Tantors persuaded her where you could not?"

"I love her. And I know she loves me. But I can't ever be the biggest thing in her universe."

Eunice nodded slowly, as if some great truth had disclosed itself to her. "Then we're similar."

"You and me, or you and Ru?"

"All three of us, I think. I like people—much more than my reputation would suggest. I've experienced happiness and loneliness, and I know which I prefer. I was married once, to a man called Jonathan Beza, who made money selling mobile telephones. A good, kind man, but we drifted apart. I couldn't stay still, whereas Jonathan could. We watched the sun go down on Mars. As we held hands in our suits, Jonathan said to me, 'I could watch this happen a thousand times and never grow bored of it.' And I found myself thinking: sunsets are all well and good, but who wants to see the same one twice?"

"Almost all of humanity except for you."

"Well, yes. I never said I wasn't an outlier. But nor am I a hermit. On *Zanzibar*, it was a joy when Chiku Green found me. Another face, another head to swim around in. And I have enjoyed seeing new faces on Orison."

"Until, as they say, all guests begin to stink."

"You don't. Neither does Ru. I am not sorry I acted quickly to quarantine her, but I do regret hurting her."

"You had cause to be angry."

"But a moment's consideration would have told me she was unlikely to be the knowing instrument of a sabotage plot. Do you think she will forgive me, after the pain I've caused?"

"You'd have to ask her." But Goma remembered the agonised shriek Ru had let out and the fear in her eyes as Eunice transformed from friend to enemy, like the turning of the weather.

Justifiable, under the circumstances. But forgivable?

Knowing her wife as she did, Goma was not so sure of that.

A day passed, and then another. On the morning of the third day, Sadalmelik died. They were with him when it happened, although the Tantor had long since lost consciousness. Even Eunice had resigned herself to the inevitable by then, accepting that the battle was not to save Sadalmelik but to help Eldasich and Achernar. In their cases the infection had not been so advanced, and it appeared that the broad-spectrum antivirals had bought some valuable time—a window in which it might be possible to develop and administer something more effective.

The Tantors were still quarantined—Eldasich and Achernar in their own separate chambers, Atria, Mimosa and Keid in a temporary holding area where they could be relieved of their heavy, hulking spacesuits. By then it was clear that the infection could only have been passed via close proximity or direct contact and not through the air-circulation system. Nonetheless, Eunice refused to take any chances.

During the long vigil with Sadalmelik, Goma was often

alone with Eunice as they did what they could to ease the Tantor's suffering.

"It was true what I said, about welcoming new faces," Eunice said, "but Sadalmelik has been a good friend to me over the years. We are different, yes—you only have to spend a few minutes with them to know that. They feel time differently from us. But partners don't have to be alike. We could be so strong together—so useful."

"Do you think we'll ever learn to get along?"

"Each death makes it harder." She squeezed out a sponge, moistening the area around Sadalmelik's sightless, gummed-over eye. "All our crimes against them have been senseless, but there's a special idiocy about this one. Your doctor must have planned this before you even left Crucible."

"He probably did," Goma said, thinking of the demolition charges smuggled aboard *Travertine*. "I think he meant to get close enough to the Tantors to hurt them by destroying the ship—literally blowing it up in their faces. Suicide, obviously, unless he planned to put those charges aboard the lander. That failed—Mposi flushed out the threat—so he fell back on the virus. But even that wasn't straightforward since he didn't know that the majority of the Tantors were still aboard *Zanzibar*."

"He didn't even know about the six here until he landed."

"That's true. But if they were anywhere, the odds were pretty good that they'd be near you. He was wrong—thankfully."

"Not that it did Sadalmelik any good." After a silence, she added, "What put so much hate into someone, Goma?"

"Not hate, exactly—I mean, how could he hate something he'd never known? More likely fear, I suspect."

"Fear of sharing the universe with another thinking species?"

"Fear that the Tantors will always be something . . . wrong, I suppose—a mistake born from a mistake."

"Fucking stupidity. Is there any part of this universe that didn't start out as a mistake?"

"Not everyone has your perspective. And right now, I wish more of us did."

"Sadalmelik never knew *Zanzibar*—only ever this world, these closed-in spaces, these airlocks and spacesuits. Me for company. Me as his sole living example of a human being. And yet when we talked, I had to remind myself that he had never walked in those places, never known how they smelled, how they sounded. That's what the Remembering is like, Goma—it's more than recollection, passed-down stories, oral history. They feel it. It's deep within them—a bridge of blood between the present and the past. He remembered Earth. He spoke of it not as something he'd been told about, but as a world he knew in his bones. As if he ached for blue skies, hard sunlight, the promise of the long rains. Life as an elephant— simple as breathing, hard as death, the joy and the sadness of being alive. Nothing was ever easy for them. But nothing was ever as strong, either. They were born knowing they were the kings of creation. They took the worst that the world could throw at them, including humanity."

"You weren't such a bad companion," Goma said.

"I tried to be what I could for them."

"And you succeeded. If there are debts to be repaid, yours is done. Whatever you are, whatever you were, you've achieved one human thing—you've been kind to the Tantors."

Eunice touched Sadalmelik's trunk, now quite cool and still. "He is passing."

"I know."

"I never speak of death in their presence. It's not that they don't understand, or need protecting from the truth. They understand perfectly well. They just find our view of it somewhat simplistic—limited, even. You won't speak of death, will you?"

"I promise," Goma said.

Eldasich rallied; Achernar worsened. On the fourth day he entered a coma. On the fifth, as Sadalmelik had done before him, he passed. It turned out they were brothers, born to a mother who had lived with Eunice in the earlier years of her exile.

The deaths were harrowing but by the time Achernar succumbed it was clear that the remaining four Tantors were now out of danger. The lander had made a return trip to *Travertine*, bringing better medicines from the well-equipped suites in orbit. These were administered to both people and Tantors, and after some adjustment of the relative dosages, the virus was in retreat. It had been studied, understood, its vulnerabilities pinpointed. It was clever, and engineered to hurt Tantors much more than humans, but it was not infallible. They were far from Crucible now, but their government had equipped the ship with the best tools at hand, and unlike Dr. Nhamedjo they were not obliged to work in secrecy.

Ru, now also recovering from the infection, was released from quarantine. The experience had been harrowing, and it was clear to Goma that it was going to take more than her reassurances to rebuild her trust in Eunice.

"I saw it in her eyes," Ru said. "The naked hate. And felt her strength. She might be skin and bones now, but she's still a machine. She was only a twitch away from killing me."

"She's human."

"And that's meant to set my mind at ease?"

"She regrets what she did to you. It was a heat-of-the-moment thing—you saw how much the Tantors mean to her. She knew that someone had tried to hurt them and you were the nearest thing to a suspect."

"I never want to be around her again. No, I'll qualify that—around that *thing* shaped like your ancestor."

It pained Goma, but she could hardly blame Ru.

"She likes you."

"You mean she's saying whatever she needs to, to keep you on her side."

Goma had not thought of it in those terms, but now Ru had put the idea into her mind, it established itself with a nasty tenacity. Perhaps it was true. But then she thought back to Eunice's tenderness with the dying Sadalmelik, the genuine and touching empathy she had shown. Yes, she had treated Ru badly. But it was a human thing to err, and a human thing to feel remorse afterwards.

In any case, Ru would have to accept sharing a ship with Eunice whether she cared to or not. They were leaving soon. Complicated arrangements were already in hand.

The remaining Tantors could not come with them—there was simply no means of providing for them aboard *Travertine*—but neither could they be expected to maintain the camp on their own during Eunice's absence. Consequently, out of the remaining crew in orbit, a small delegation of technical specialists would be brought down and trained to care for the Tantors, instructed in the rudiments of life-support maintenance and briefed in the newly developing field of human-Tantor diplomatic relations. After an overlap period of a few days, the initial landing party would depart for *Zanzibar*.

They would not be gone for long—weeks at most.

First, though, there was the business of two Tantor funerals.

During the long years of her exile, Eunice had faced numerous times perhaps the hardest of all the decisions forced upon her by time and circumstance: what to do with the dead.

Nothing burned on the surface of Orison, nothing decayed. The encampment was a closed-cycle ecosystem, its own life-support bubble, but no such system was entirely efficient. The dead were significant reservoirs of stored chemical wealth, demanding—by all considerations of logic and wise management—to be recycled back into the matrix, broken down into their useful constituents. Planetary ecologies did it all the time—the endless conveyor belt of birth, growth and predation. There was nothing unnatural or distasteful about it, and she ought to have felt no qualms about employing the corpses of her friends for the betterment of the camp.

But she could not bring herself to do it, even though—as she was fully aware—in this act of refusal she was only storing up problems for the future.

But they had been her friends, her allies, her companions. It was the least she could do for them.

Fortunately the deaths came infrequently and she had never needed to contend with two in close succession before. There was another consideration. She hated the idea of all four of them being outside at once. They were as precious as jewels, more vulnerable than they knew. She could not bear the thought of something happening to all four of them at once. When the earlier deaths had occurred, she had persuaded her friends to take turns going outside.

But now the four of them went out together, Atria, Mimosa, Keid, Eldasich, bearing the wrapped corpse of Sadalmelik, a burden that would have been impossible even for Tantors to move without the power augmentation of their suits. They carried him between them, Sadalmelik laid on a bower formed from a heavy-duty cargo sled, their armoured trunks wrapped around the handles at each corner. They took him beyond the lander, out along one of the trails, until at last they reached a rocky elevation where they set him down.

The humans followed behind, but when the Tantors surmounted the burial spot, Eunice directed the people to remain where they were.

The Tantors removed Sadalmelik from the bower, set him on the raised ground and brought the bower back down to the level plain. Decorously, without haste, the Tantors loaded the bower with an assortment of boulders and pebbles. They hauled the bower back up to Sadalmelik and began to construct a cairn around his reposed form. This took quite some while and entailed many trips back and forth with the sled. They worked in silence, no word or vocalisation breaking across the humans' suit channels—only the slow, patient bellowing of furnace-sized lungs. Finally—after much deliberation and careful rearrangement of stones—the Tantors completed their cairn. It enclosed Sadalmelik completely, an igloo of interlocking rocks.

Then they returned to fetch Achernar.

Eunice signalled the human party. They proceeded up the slope and placed their own small stones and pebbles onto the cairn, taking care not to disrupt those already in place.

"For the Tantors," Eunice said, confiding in a low voice, "these stones are anchors of memory." She placed a rock of her own onto the cairn. "Let the memory of Chiku Green find the memory of Sadalmelik, and both be stronger for it."

"For Ndege and Mposi," Goma said, placing two similar pebbles into the cairn.

Ru stepped to her side and set her own piece down. "For Agrippa, and everyone we left behind on Crucible."

Soon, the Tantors returned with Achernar's bower and set his body a short distance from the first cairn. As before, the human party watched the Tantors assemble a stone mound around the remains, and then they joined them and made their own offerings to the cairn.

"For all the dead of *Zanzibar*," Goma said.

CHAPTER 34

Kanu hammered the metal staff against the floor, summoning Memphis in the agreed manner. He felt sick, literally on the verge of vomiting, but he knew his only choice was to confront the matriarch directly. It was no good continuing in this state of ignorance, accepting that answers would be provided in the fullness of time.

"Kanu," Swift said, "might I suggest a period of reflection before you engage in rash action?"

"You can suggest whatever you like."

"You will have to account for your knowledge of these supposed events. How will you do that without revealing my presence?"

"I'll just ask the obvious questions I should have asked all along."

"With respect, you *did* ask those questions—and answers were forthcoming, regardless of their veracity. The construct broke down and was dismantled; Chiku and the others succumbed to gradual systematic life-support failures. Might I remind you that we have precisely no evidence to the contrary?"

"Except Chiku's testimony."

"We have Chiku's expressed concerns relating to events which had not only failed to happen at the time of her recording, but which may never have happened."

"Shut up, Swift."

"Seconded," Nissa said.

They had never requested Memphis's presence until now, and this was an hour when they might have been expected to be resting. But Kanu was not prepared to sleep on his fears. He kept hammering on the floor.

"If nothing happens, I'm going to walk there. I think I can find my way out of this place if I try hard enough."

Before long they heard the thudding footfalls and deep vocal rumblings of the Risen. The main doors opened and a pair of elephants entered the central hallway.

"Is Memphis here?" Kanu asked.

"Memphis is outside. You asked for the Risen."

"Take us to Memphis," Nissa said.

These subordinate Risen were clearly content to do exactly as they were told—to a point. Kanu and Nissa were allowed out of the household. On the level ground before the main entrance waited Memphis and the wheeled vehicle.

"You called," Memphis said.

"We want to speak to Dakota," Nissa answered.

After a short silence, the huge bull said, "Now is not the time."

Kanu shook his head, anger overcoming his instinctive wariness of the larger creature. "I don't care whether it's the time or not. We have something to say—it's very important. Take us to see her. Now."

"You have asked many things already."

"Not nearly enough," Nissa said.

Memphis eventually relented, and they were soon on their way. As they travelled, Kanu turned the same thoughts over again and again, trying to find some sense in them. There had been people here once, coexisting with elephants, and now—by the evidence of his eyes—there were none. Had these slow and gentle creatures committed the worst of crimes, a kind of genocide? He could not begin to imagine how it might have happened, nor did he wish to dwell too long on the possibilities. There had to be some other explanation—one that absolved the Risen of any wrongdoing. He did not want to think of his hosts as murderers.

And yet, Chiku must have thought it possible. And she had known elephants as well as anyone.

He had no idea of Dakota's sleeping habits—if indeed she

slept—and was not surprised therefore to find her awake and alert when they were finally admitted into her presence. They were in the grand lobby of the civic building where only a little while earlier they had viewed the recording.

"You may wait outside, Memphis."

Soon they were alone—just Kanu, Nissa and the matriarch.

"Something has troubled you," she said, after a long silence.

"It's time to tell us what really happened," Kanu said.

"Have I not been open and honest with you thus far?"

"Where are all the people, Dakota?" Nissa said. "What happened after Chiku made that recording?"

"I gather from Memphis that you requested a second viewing."

"Answer my question," Nissa said.

"I do not care for your tone. What answers have I not already provided? I told you what became of the construct, and of Chiku. These were tragedies, and they left us weakened. Yet we recovered. What more is there to say?"

Kanu asked bluntly, "Did you kill them? Not just Chiku, not just Eunice, but all of the people who agreed to stay awake?"

"Why would we have killed them? What purpose would that have served?"

"Maybe they started to turn against you," Nissa said. "Is that what happened? Did the people try to check your rise to power? Did they start to realise that you were something more than the other Risen—that you were really acting for the Watchkeepers?"

"Walk with me," Dakota said, after a moment's consideration. "We shall visit the skipover vault. I have something to tell you about the Friends. I believe you will find it interesting."

Kanu and Nissa looked at each other.

"We'll stay here, thanks," Nissa said.

"No, you will accompany me. And no harm shall come to you—that is my promise. Believe me, my own self-interests are served by your not coming to harm. But I have something to say, and I think my point will be best illustrated directly."

They followed Dakota down the sloping ramps, first one

way then the other, until they arrived at the observation gallery where Memphis had first shown them the sleepers. Dakota moved to the same control panel and performed some deft input with the tip of her trunk, bringing on the lights in ascending stages, illuminating each layer of sleepers in turn.

"They were Friends to us then and are Friends to us now. One day, when the time is right, they will rejoin us. I wished you to be fully satisfied in your own minds that these sleepers can be revived. I wished there to be no doubt in your minds. Now that you have conducted a thorough examination of the technology, there is none—am I correct?"

"Yes," Nissa said, with an edge of doubt in her voice echoing Kanu's own growing qualms.

"Then we are in agreement. These are not frozen corpses but potential lives. With a few exceptions, there is no barrier to their being brought back to consciousness. Allow me illustrate my point."

Dakota touched the panel again. One block of sleepers a couple of levels below their vantage point turned dark.

"Let me be clear. I have not simply removed the illumination from that section of the vault. I have removed the power entirely. Their units are no longer functioning. Insofar as the Friends have the capacity to live again, that capacity is now being slowly removed. Their cells are warming, but in an uncontrolled, disruptive fashion. They are dying. If the process continues, there will be nothing worth reviving."

"Stop," Kanu said, as the full horror of what she meant to do became clear.

Dakota touched the same control and the sleepers were again illuminated. "I have restored the power. The caskets will resume functioning and no lasting harm will have been done. It was only a few seconds. But it could have been longer."

"Then you never needed us," Nissa said. "You've always known how to operate this technology."

"That is not quite true. Achieving full revivification would still be a challenge for us. Your help would be beneficial— essential, even. But I do not need complete control or understanding of the technology to make it stop working. That is much simpler."

"Why would you do that?" Kanu asked.

"Because it is necessary to explain my position. I had hoped that the terms of our relationship would be cordial, but . . . you have put an end to that. The Friends will be our bond now. You have provided us with a ship, and you will see to it that the damage is repaired. In addition, I will now request some minor structural modifications to enable it to carry a small expeditionary crew of the Risen. Then we will use the ship, but only for a short journey."

"Poseidon," Nissa said.

Dakota tilted the ram of her brow in a great, slow nod. "We will learn many things, and then our debt will be satisfied. The ship will be returned to you. I will allow you to leave, or to remain, whichever you prefer. But until you have helped me, the fate of the Friends lies in your hands."

"You can't do this to us," Kanu said, doubting that anything he now said would make a difference.

"You have done it to yourselves by doubting my good intentions. I hoped that we might stay friends, and perhaps our trust can be reestablished, given time. But the ship will be repaired, and it will be made ready. Nothing will stand in the way of that."

"So what does that make us—your slaves?" Nissa asked.

"Elephants were the instruments of human will for centuries. We were strong when you were weak. We did your bidding. We crushed your enemies for you, moved your mountains—tore down your forests. In your gratitude, you offered us only death and mutilation. We are better than that— more generous, more forgiving. Is it so wrong of the Risen to ask this one thing of you?"

"The Risen?" Kanu asked. "Or the Watchkeepers?"

"What does it matter? Why not serve us, as we serve another?"

Kanu looked at the sleepers again, thinking of the patterns of identity still enshrined in those countless frozen brain cells. The good memories and the bad, the joys and the sorrows, the wisdom and the foolishness, life's accumulated bounty of kindness and cruelty. Those things made people what they were. Those things had made him, too. And he thought of the warmth stealing into those cold skulls, the patterns losing coherence, the hard-forged connections of a lifetime surrendering to heat and chaos.

That could not be on him. He would not murder these people.

So their work continued. From the outside, there was no essential difference in their daily activities. They spent their nights at the household, treated like human royalty, and by day they were either aboard *Icebreaker*, nursing it back to health, or dealing with the Risen who had been tasked to assist them. The supply lines ran efficiently; the manufactories spat out the parts they needed, materials and components which slotted together with ominous precision, as if the ship were willing itself back to life. Even the communicational difficulties with the Risen were behind them now as both parties learned to better understand each other. Each day brought fewer problems, less to go wrong before completion. Also, now that they knew the goal of the repairs, Dakota could communicate her requirements openly. *Icebreaker* had to accommodate the Risen now as well as humans and needed to be adjusted accordingly—its airlocks modified, its interior spaces enlarged, provision made for the Risen to use its control systems and data interfaces. The *Noah*, one of the short-range winged shuttles from the original settlement of Crucible, was to be attached to *Icebreaker*'s hull so that the Risen could travel within Poseidon's atmosphere, perhaps even all the way down to its sea.

Kanu was torn. He could think of nothing worse than succeeding—with the sole exception of failure. If he gave her the ship, in the condition she dictated, she would commit herself to folly on behalf of the Watchkeepers—and take Kanu and Nissa with her. It was not just their own lives at stake, but the collective security of the entire human species. But if he failed in the repairs, she would exact her revenge on the sleepers.

The equation was trivial, he knew. Against the possible consequences of her expedition, the lives of the Friends barely registered. In rational terms, there was only one sensible course of action open to him. But to admit such thoughts was poison.

Their meetings continued. On the surface, there was a sort of lingering cordiality. She made her pleasantries and flattered Kanu and Nissa that she found their company stimulating. Even after showing them what would happen if they let her down, she still acted as if they were her honoured guests. Chai was always served, and if some urgent business needed discussing, she would always take her time getting around to it. Kanu wondered if she was in a state of denial, a kind of conscious forgetting of the unpleasant matter of the Friends.

But one day she was unusually direct.

"Another ship has entered the system," she said, without preamble. "Do you know about this?"

Kanu did not need to put on a front of feigned ignorance. "No. What ship? Where?"

"That is an excellent question. Since your arrival, the Watchkeepers have raised their level of vigilance, alert to any other intruders. But perhaps they need not have bothered—it was a Watchkeeper that heralded the arrival of this new ship."

"I don't understand."

"It accompanied this ship across interstellar space—that's my inference, at least. Now the Watchkeeper has removed itself to the edge of the system—they feel safest the further they are from Poseidon—and there has been a great deal of interest in this new ship. They whisper to each other—a chatter of blue lights across light-minutes, light-hours. Sometimes I have been allowed a glimpse of these thoughts of theirs."

Kanu thought back to the message from Chiku. "They're hollow. They've forgotten how to be conscious. You're listening to the whispering of zombie machines."

"Be that as it may, I can't help but be intrigued by this new arrival. It has come from Crucible, of all places."

"Maybe we shouldn't be too surprised by that."

"No?"

"When we first met, I mentioned a signal—the reason we came here in the first place. You claimed to know nothing about it. But the signal originated in this system, and it was aimed at the people of Crucible. It was only a matter of time before they responded."

"Is this true, Nissa?"

"As far as I know," she answered.

"Then how did it come to your attention, Kanu?"

"I am—or was—a diplomat," Kanu said. "I had ready access to many information channels. This signal was never public knowledge, not even in the Crucible system. But I learned of it, and decided I needed to make an independent investigation."

"Were you planning to arrive before the ship from Crucible?"

"I didn't even know they were sending a ship. I'd have come anyway."

"News of the signal had to reach Earth before you could begin your journey. How did you arrive sooner than them?"

"We started our journey later than they did but had less distance to travel, and their ship can't be much faster than mine. Have you responded to it?"

"No, and nor do I intend to. I see it as a nuisance, not an opportunity. Still, it must be addressed. You have had a chance to review the repair work since you awoke—I trust there are no setbacks?"

"No, it's all going smoothly," Nissa said sullenly.

"You do not sound encouraged."

"Part of me would rather report bad news, provided it wasn't too serious. You'd accept the delay and the status quo would continue. Kanu and I would still be of use to you, and there'd be no reason for you to hurt the sleepers."

"Very candid of you to admit as much."

"I find honesty helps," she said.

"Do not mistake me—either of you. My word is good. I have no intention of hurting you or of harming the Friends. If I did not think well of them, would I have kept them cold through all the years before your arrival?"

"Perhaps you thought they'd come in handy as a form of blackmail," Kanu answered.

"You are much too cynical lately. Tell me the truth concerning the repairs, regardless of whether the news is good or bad, and nothing untoward will happen."

"'Untoward,'" he said. "That encompasses a multitude of meanings."

"I see you are both beyond reasoned discussion. Never mind—we will restrict ourselves to the strict practicalities. I do not want this new ship interfering with the good work we have already done. Your ship is nearly ready for testing, is it not?"

Kanu glanced at Nissa, wondering if she shared his disquiet. "We're weeks away from that."

"Then make it days. I do not need the interstellar capability of your Chibesa drive, merely the means to reach Poseidon. If the *Noah* had been capable of doing so on its own, I would already have taken it, but its range and agility are not sufficient. This other ship must not be allowed to complicate my arrangements."

"Then ask the Watchkeepers to destroy it. They're capable of that, aren't they?"

"Callous of you, Kanu."

"Just looking at this from your perspective. Why not have them destroy it?"

"I'm sure they would if they felt the act was necessary. But they are watchers, recorders, gatherers of knowledge rather than butchers. More than that, though, they're not mine to command. Did you think otherwise?"

"I'm not sure what to think. Do you know what you are to them, Dakota? Do you really understand?"

"What is there not to understand?"

"The Terror," he answered.

"You could not know of such a thing."

"And if I did?"

She regarded him with cool superiority. "Terrors must be faced. I will have my ship, Kanu, and you will accompany me in the gathering of knowledge. We will not flinch in the face of the unknown. Move *Icebreaker* beyond *Zanzibar* once more. Make ready to test the Chibesa engine."

He sat on the edge of the made bed, bent over with his hands joined in his lap, considering the ways in which he might feasibly end his own life.

"I know what you are thinking," Swift said.

"Then give me an answer."

"You have never been suicidal. Even in your darkest

moments—and there have been several—*that* was never something you considered."

"Nothing's changed," Kanu answered.

"You do not appear to be depressed. If you were, I would see it in your brain chemistry."

"I'm not depressed and I'm not suicidal. What I am is trapped. There's a distinction. Can you see it?"

"I am trying."

"I'm in a hopeless position, Swift. There's no good course of action open to me."

"And killing yourself—that would be the solution? Have you forgotten the Friends, the fate of those poor frozen people?"

"Think it through," Kanu said, hating himself for wondering just how far Swift's empathy really extended. "They're just a bargaining tool to her—they give her some measure of control over me. If I'm out of the equation, she gains nothing by harming them."

Swift tapped his pince-nez against his chin. "Mm. But she might do it anyway, out of anger—or to reinforce her determination to Nissa, who I need hardly add will still be alive. There is human DNA in that elephant, Kanu—do you think she's incapable of spite?"

"Nissa can't finish the work on her own. I've had you in my head to guide me through every difficult part of the repair process. She won't have that luxury."

"Dakota will nonetheless force her to try, and she may resort to extreme measures in her attempts to persuade. She'll break Nissa like the proverbial butterfly on a wheel. Do you really want that on your conscience?"

"I wouldn't have one."

Swift strode around to stand before him, clenching his hands. "Please don't speak that way, Kanu. I gave you back your life when you should have died. Do not insult me by speaking of a human life as something disposable."

"Then don't speak as if you understand a single thing about being alive."

"I understand life more than you realise, Kanu. At least, I have begun to. How could it be otherwise after being inside you all this time? After the dead years of skipover, when I gained a little sense of what it would mean *not* to exist? Do you honestly think this hasn't given me some miserable insight into the human condition?"

"It's not a 'condition,' Swift. It's being alive."

"I know, and I feel it, and I will not permit you to squander such a gift. Especially when the circumstances are nowhere near as dire as you imagine." Swift adjusted his sleeves and cracked his knuckles. "Chess. A game of chess. That will put things into perspective."

"I'm not in the mood."

"Immaterial. I am."

Kanu pinched at the skin around his eyes, trying to shrug off the sense of hopelessness he now felt. Swift was perfectly correct: he had no desire to end his life. But when he set out his options, when he stepped back and analysed them dispassionately, suicide looked by far the most logical course of action.

"You mean well, Swift, but you can't see how bad things have become."

"On the contrary. I have as ready a grasp of our predicament as you or Nissa. But I do not think we have exhausted all our options yet. Nor should you. There is always hope, Kanu—provided you remain alive."

"Platitudes."

"We shall see." Swift conjured the chessboard into existence and set it between them. He lowered himself onto an invisible stool, adjusting his frock coat in the process. "Your mood is black, therefore I shall open proceedings."

"How thoughtful of you."

They commenced the game.

"Things are not as dire as you imagine," Swift declared, a few moves in.

Kanu responded automatically, barely caring who won or lost. "In which way are they not dire? We know about the Terror. We know that Chiku and Eunice were both against the idea of going any nearer to Poseidon."

"For which they surely had their reasons. But we are not them. Did we come here to wither at the first test, Kanu, or to challenge ourselves?"

"Even if we make it to Poseidon, we've no guarantee that

we'll get the ship back afterwards. Or that Dakota will honour her promise concerning the sleepers. For that matter, we have no idea what she or the Watchkeepers will do next—or how we fit into that."

"The situation is not entirely ideal."

"I'm glad you agree with me on something."

Swift moved his piece with a decisive clack. "But neither is it hopeless. To begin with, we do need our ship repaired—and since assisting Dakota in her expedition helps achieve that, I do not think the cost is too great. Secondly, our aims are not entirely at odds with hers."

Kanu responded with a weak countermove. "Aren't they?"

"We came here seeking knowledge, did we not? We know nothing of the M-builders and are scarcely better informed about the Watchkeepers. Dakota's interests neatly intersect with both areas of our ignorance. By serving her, if you will, we serve our own ends. I do not see that as catastrophic."

"You see her as a bridge to the Watchkeepers. Your interest in the M-builders is secondary."

"I have an intellectual curiosity regarding the M-builders, but you are right about the Watchkeepers. I would like to know them better, and if Dakota offers a path to them, then she becomes useful to me. To us, I should say."

"No, I think you were right the first time."

"We both have a stake in this, Kanu. I am a machine intelligence and you are a man. Our two lineages have been on the brink of hostility for generations. We've papered over our enmity with embassies and treaties and fine words, but why deny the underlying distrust? The only thing preventing the complete sterilisation and reclamation of Mars is the fear of Watchkeeper reprisal. Otherwise you would have wiped us out if the chance had presented itself."

Kanu looked at Swift, remembering better times, easier conversations. "I'm glad we're finally getting our true feelings out into the open."

Swift made his next move. "I make no bones about it. We were a threat to human dominion, and human oppression was a threat to us. Had the means existed, many of my fellow machines would have gladly taken the war beyond the atmosphere of Mars—smashed your orbital fortresses, retaken the moons, pushed our influence further out."

Kanu hesitated over his response. "It looks like you were already doing a pretty good job of extending your influence."

"In the most trivial of ways—the mere gathering of intelligence. Nothing compared to what some of us desire."

"And you wonder why humans have a hard time trusting robots."

"But you and I saw a better path, Kanu! Reconciliation, cooperation—the sharing of resources and knowledge. We are here precisely because we believe in something better, something bolder. An answer to the oldest question—how do I get along with my neighbours, even if they are not the same as me?"

At last Kanu made his move. It was a poor one, opening him up to at least one obvious attack.

"And look where that quest has brought us."

"To the brink of possibility. All doors are open now, Kanu—nothing is beyond our reach! The future stands before us. If we can just see our way past these present challenges—"

"If. That's a pretty big 'if,' Swift."

Swift responded to Kanu's weak defence with merciless indifference. "We have done rather well so far. Survived Mars, survived Europa—even managed to crawl away from Poseidon with only our noses bloodied. I have faith in us. Not just in you and me, but in Nissa, too. There's a point to carrying on, Kanu—and even if you can't see it now, I think you will eventually."

"Easy for you to say."

"Yes—but you forget that I have known you for a very, very long time. You are a good and honourable man, a friend and an advocate of peace. At heart, you are an optimist even at the least optimistic of times. Right now you see only darkness ahead of you—a locked room with no way out. No one would blame you for that. But this is the moment when the world needs you most. Find the strength, Kanu—find the open door."

It was Kanu's move, but his grasp of the game was sufficient to tell him that he had already lost. Swift knew it, too—it was only a matter of how many moves would be required to complete the killing.

Kanu swept his hand through the pieces.

CHAPTER 35

Eunice said her farewells to the four surviving Tantors, and after some agonies managed to convince herself that Gandhari Vasin's skeleton staff was sufficient to maintain the encampment until her return. Goma understood her dilemma: she urgently wished to be on her way, to confront or negotiate with Dakota, but it meant leaving the only home she had known since her exile from *Zanzibar*. No part of this decision was easily made, and the Tantors' lives depended on the soundness of her judgement.

Nonetheless, the moment was upon them. The party returned to the lander, its descent jets still glowing from its most recent return trip from *Travertine*, and Eunice purposefully avoided giving her home more than a backward glance. Soon they were aboard the lander, Vasin in the command chair, Eunice looking on with an examiner's impassive scrutiny. They took off, taking care to keep their blast away from the old and new cairns, and were soon approaching *Travertine*.

Eunice stirred from her seat, undid the restraints and floated to the nearest suitable window.

"A starship," she said. "An actual, proper starship—not some excuse for one like *Winter Queen*, or the holoships. I always wondered if I'd live long enough to see one of those."

"Are you impressed?" Goma dared ask.

"I don't really do 'impressed.' But consider yourselves the recipients of grudging approval."

"Praise indeed," Ru muttered.

"That said, you've had long enough to build it. And if I'm going to labour the point, you really ought to have understood the mechanics of the Mandala translation by now. Why build a starship when you have an alien transportation device sitting right there on your planet, waiting to be used?"

"You should have stopped at 'approval,'" Goma said.

"With me, dear, you take what you can get."

For Eunice's benefit, they executed an inspection pass around the much larger craft, Vasin offering a commentary on points of interest like a tour guide.

"It will do," was Eunice's final judgement. "Can you break orbit as soon as we're docked?"

"You're under a misapprehension," Vasin said. "I have no intention of committing *Travertine* to a situation we already know to be dangerous. Coming here was one thing—dabbling in a human-Tantor stand-off is quite another, especially as you've confirmed that the Watchkeepers have an interest in all this as well. Besides, the lander has just as much in-system capability as the mothership."

"Then we don't even need to dock. Set course for *Zanzibar* immediately."

"We need fuel and a few component swaps ahead of that," said Vasin. "Say, a day or two to make ready and assemble the final crew selection. Besides, there's the small matter of quarantine."

"You are all responding well to the antivirals."

"I'm not talking about us."

If it was not a quarantine in the strict sense of the word, it was still an extremely thorough medical examination, far more exhaustive than anything possible in the camp. There were two medical bays on *Travertine*—one with gravity for normal procedures and a second where weightlessness was beneficial. They were in the second bay now, which was located in the central spine, just beyond the rear pole of the forward sphere. There was no centrifugal spin in this part of the ship, and since *Travertine* was not presently under thrust, the bay was totally weightless.

Dr. Nhamedjo's immediate subordinate, Dr. Mona Andisa, was now in charge of all medical activities on Travertine. The weightless suite, she said, was a great benefit for performing full-body scans since there was no distortion of interior organs due to gravity or the pressure of supporting surfaces.

Andisa's patient had already been prepared for her examination. Eunice floated free, stripped to her undergarments, arms at her sides, while scanning systems orbited her like a host of tiny whirring satellites. Goma watched as the scanners slowly assembled a three-dimensional image of Eunice with sub-cellular resolution on a variety of flat and solid display media.

"I did not doubt what I heard from the surface," Andisa said, tapping a finger against a cross section of Eunice's skull, a coral atoll of bone enclosing a softer patterning of lagoon-blue structures, "but this settles the argument. If you presented to me as an ordinary patient, I would have no cause to doubt your authenticity."

"It's always reassuring to be authenticated."

"Her DNA," Goma said, "assuming she *has* DNA—have you sequenced it?"

"She would not last long without it," Andisa answered, a touch of testiness to her tone.

Goma could forgive her that. She knew how shocked and upset the soft-spoken Andisa had been by the death of Saturnin Nhamedjo—her discomfort as much to do with the fact of his demise as the manner in which he had disguised his true priorities, even from his diligent co-workers. They felt betrayed, and now they were expected to shift effortlessly into running the ship's medical activities. Worse than that, there remained the lingering suspicion, albeit unvoiced, that perhaps one or more of them had been co-conspirators. Goma was certain this was not the case, but she could imagine the toll it was having on Andisa and the other medics. She wished there was a way to show them that they were still respected, still trusted.

"Certainly her DNA has been doctored," Andisa continued. "Rather comprehensively, in ways that are not reflected in your own genetic history."

"But you can see that we're related?"

"Yes, but much less obviously than if I were looking at a simple, uncluttered mitochondrial line. The books have been cooked too many times for that—in both of you. You are the daughter of Ndege, and Ndege was the daughter of someone who underwent radical genetic and phenotypic restructuring for the purposes of triplication. There has never been an orderly genetic lineage for Akinyas. Eunice doubts that the Watchkeepers had access to the actual DNA of the original Eunice Akinya—she certainly didn't bring any such thing with her on the holoship. But they'd had ample opportunity to sample Chiku Green's genetic structure, and from that they could have reverse-engineered the DNA they used to synthesise this living exemplar of Eunice. There are still some sequences I have yet to identify. It would not surprise me in the slightest if they turn out to contain elephant DNA."

"So she's telling the truth—she's really alive? Alive and *living*, just like the rest of us?"

It was still hard to take in, and Goma was perfectly aware that Eunice was lying there listening in on this conversation.

"How deep a philosophical definition of 'living' would you like?" Andisa asked.

"She eats and breathes—we know that. She does something that approximates sleeping—we saw that in the camp. Does she dream?"

"She does," Eunice said.

"I wasn't asking you. Can you put a number on her age, Mona?"

"Not easily. By her own account, we know she has been in this 'human' form for more than two hundred years, completely cut off from any orthodox rejuvenative medicine. She tells me she has aged during that time, but if she were ageing at a normal human rate, in the absence of prolongation therapy she would have been dead many decades ago. Have you spent time in skipover, Eunice?"

"Not in this body."

"So something has vastly decelerated the normal ageing mechanisms. Slowed but not stopped them. Hayflick limits, telomere attrition—these factors must have been modified by the Watchkeepers. Perhaps we would be better off calling them Watch*makers*, Goma, since they have taken the basic ticking mechanism of human biology and made it really sing. Every cog polished, every spring tightened—every tiny piece of dirt, every imperfection removed from the process. With Eunice's permission, I plan to introduce a small wound—nothing serious—in order to study her healing processes. As to her ultimate lifespan, in the absence of further intervention? I have no idea. Another couple of hundred years does not sound outlandish. And as for children—a whole new flowering of descendants—why not? She has a womb, and eggs. I see no obvious reproductive impediment."

"One lineage will do us for the time being," Goma said. "It's caused more than enough trouble as it is."

The alterations to the lander had started almost immediately upon the authorisation of the expedition, with the vehicle being kept outside *Travertine* for ease of access. Despite appearances, Vasin assured Goma that everything was going smoothly and on schedule.

It still looked like chaos, the ship surrounded by vacuum-suited workers, tangled access lines, modular parts and free-floating tool tenders. Nonetheless, there was clearly some sort of order to it all, and Goma herself had reviewed the list of specification upgrades. The lander had been designed for an expansion of its long-range capabilities, with many detachable or swappable components which could be shared with other vehicles. Cargo racks were removed and replaced with additional fuel and thruster assemblies. Life-support systems were modified to keep a smaller crew alive for a longer period of time. Skipover equipment was provided in case of emergency, as well as a small medical suite furnished according to Dr. Andisa's exacting specifications. There were additional vacuum suits, two single-person runabouts for in-space repair and reconnaissance, and an augmented communications array.

Was this overkill or just barely sufficient? Goma wondered. It was hard to say. Five days to reach *Zanzibar*, five days to make the return trip—but an unguessable interval in between. They could not be held hostage, Goma kept telling herself—not while *Travertine* remained here, its engine a very palpable instrument of negotiation.

But if the Tantors had a ship, then they also had access to Chibesa technology of their own. Would they submit to argument by force or simply presume that the humans would never stoop to mass murder?

How well did they understand people, anyway?

* * *

"Peter?"

For the first time since returning to consciousness, the man opened his eyes and began to show recognition of his environment. He looked around slowly with an expression of perfectly neutral acceptance, as if this was no more or less than he had been expecting.

"So, are you going to hang me now?"

Dr. Andisa had alerted Goma and Vasin that he would shortly be fully awake after his emergence from skipover, and now the three of them were at his side.

"The first thing you get," Vasin said, "is an apology. We treated you poorly, Peter, and I take personal responsibility for that."

He looked unmoved by this news. "I've no idea how long I've been under. Have we returned to Crucible?"

"No," Goma said. "We're in the other system, at our destination. There've been . . . developments. It'll take a while to explain everything to you, but we now know who killed my uncle."

"And what has it taken to establish my innocence?"

"More deaths," Vasin answered. "Did you have any idea who the actual saboteur was?"

"You appeared so certain of my guilt that I started to doubt myself." He raised himself slightly, a spark of engagement showing in his eyes for the first time. "Who was it?"

"Doctor Nhamedjo," Vasin said.

Grave gave a slow nod. "I considered him a possibility, but he was only one of several candidates."

"But if you had doubts about him—" Goma began.

"I couldn't risk casting suspicion on an innocent member of the crew, especially not on a vital figure like Doctor Nhamedjo. Our voyage had barely begun—that business with the Watchkeeper had already led some of us to advocate turning around."

"You were one of them!" Goma said.

"I suggested we should at least consider that option. Don't tell me you didn't have similar thoughts?"

Goma was tight-lipped. She could not deny that she had been afraid in the face of the alien machine.

"But when the threat of the Watchkeeper evaporated," Grave continued, meeting her eye with a nod of understanding, "I was content for us to continue. Remember, I'd committed my life to this expedition, too—I hadn't left Crucible expecting us to turn around. Fundamentally, I wanted us to succeed—but not if that meant taking unacceptable risks."

"But someone wanted to destroy the expedition!" Goma said.

"I told you there was the possibility of a secondary threat. Beyond that, I had nothing to offer. My only hope was that Mposi's murderer would be exposed through a combination of heightened vigilance and human error on the saboteur's part. Is that what happened?"

"Not before two Tantors died," Goma said.

"Tantors?" he asked, between wariness and excitement. "You've contacted them?"

She nodded. "A few. But there are others—many others—and we hope to meet them as well. But it's not that straightforward. Mposi trusted you, Peter—can I trust you, too?"

"That is an odd thing to ask a man who has been accused of murder and put on ice for the rest of the trip."

"It is, but you knew my uncle. If he thought well of you, that makes you valuable to me. Gandhari says she's happy to reinstate you as a member of the crew, with a full apology and pardon. But I want more than that."

For the first time, some of the old amusement creased his lips. "Do you, now?"

"We're sending a small ship out to meet the other Tantors—just the lander, but with enough fuel and supplies to see us through every contingency we can forsee. The crew will include Maslin Karayan. I would be grateful for your presence, too. But I need to ask—are you really a Second Chancer?"

"What I believe and what I think can't be expressed in a sentence. But do I believe dreadful mistakes have been made in the past, and that we'd be very unwise not to learn from them? Most certainly. I count the Tantors among these mistakes—they should not have come into being. But now they are here, we must accept the fact of them with grace."

Remembering his words from one of their first exchanges, Goma said, "You hate the sin that made them."

"Yes. The sin of intellectual hubris. The sin of thinking we understand our own nature well enough to meddle in the natures of others."

"But you do not hate the fact of them."

"They are what they are—thinking creatures as capable of sin or goodness as the rest of us. They were never given a choice to be what they are. The greater sin would be to wish harm upon them for the sins of others. Besides, we are on a mission to seek the truth of things. The truth is seldom something to be feared."

"I think we have some more truth-seeking to do. Are you strong enough to join us?"

"That is not for me to say."

"I will monitor him closely over the next few hours," Dr. Andisa said, "but the signs are encouraging so far. I think he will be up on his feet as quickly as the rest of us were."

"We wronged you, Peter," Goma said, "and I take my share of responsibility for that. Mposi would have been disappointed in me that I did not stand up for you. But I am trying to do better."

"And succeeding, by the sounds of things."

"I still have some way to go."

"So do we all," Grave said. "But that is called living."

They were looking at *Zanzibar*, projected onto one wall of Vasin's quarters. It rotated slowly, bringing all its facets into view. It was the best 3D image they had gathered so far, assembled from a multitude of angles and sensor bands, across many light-minutes of space, with every conceivable image-sharpening algorithm thrown into the fray.

"It's not that we doubted you, Eunice," Vasin was saying, "but you'll understand we had reasons to be sceptical."

"And now?" Eunice asked, arms folded, unable to entirely hide her triumph.

"The shape speaks for itself—it fits into the larger profile of the original *Zanzibar* very convincingly, and its mass is just about equal to that believed to be missing from the ring system around Crucible. Of course, few of these artificial surface features correspond to the original holoship—but then you've already told us there was a scramble for survival after the translation event. Do you see much evidence of change since you were last aboard?"

"Nothing drastic," Eunice said. She sketched a finger across blurry details. "A few airlocks here and there, some alterations to the power grid, but I wasn't expecting much. The Risen can work outside if they need to—they also have space-suits and the means to move independently—but it's not their natural environment, and they don't adapt easily to it."

"Less easily than we do?" Goma asked.

"We're arboreal apes. We enjoy being high up and in our bones we feel safer. Elephants spend their lives glued to the ground, rooted there like trees. Being in space will never feel as natural to them as it does to us."

"So we have an edge over them," Vasin said.

"Only a small one. They're as determined as we are, and sufficient determination will conquer any natural reluctance. Monkeys don't like water, but we've overcome that instinct well enough."

"But still," Goma said, "if they don't like being outside, maybe we can use that to our advantage."

Eunice leaned in eagerly, as if about to make a constructive suggestion. "Engage them in close-quarters combat? Daggers between teeth, no quarter given?"

"I was trying to think of something useful—some way we could exploit our innate differences without resorting to violence. What about that power grid?"

"What about it?"

"If we stop it working, will they be able to repair it easily? I don't mean shut it off permanently, just demonstrate that we can deprive them of power. You said we need a means of nego-tiating with Dakota—would that help?"

"It might, it might not."

"Could we do it, though?" asked Vasin.

Eunice thought about it for a few seconds, or at least gave every impression of doing so.

"The mirrors were an emergency measure installed during the difficult days immediately after the translation. We worked with the surviving humans to cobble them together, using spacecraft parts and materials from inside *Zanzibar*. I never expected them to work as long as they have."

"And?" Goma pushed.

"The orbital control and mirror-aiming system is as autonomous as we could design it to be. We wanted the mirrors to keep working even if there was some total breakdown in communications with *Zanzibar*. Obviously, we did a fairly good job. But we did leave a back channel—a control protocol, in case we needed to reprogram or reassign the mirrors."

"Would Dakota know about that channel?" Vasin asked.

"Maybe, but it would still be hard for her to close it off without physical access to the mirrors. So . . . yes—*maybe* there's a possibility. But it's been a while and everything I know about the control architecture is in here." She tapped the side of her head.

"Is that good or bad?" Vasin asked.

"Oh, my memory is excellent. But I can't promise anything until I've done some tests. Can I use your spaceship?"

Vasin looked appalled. "Of course not!"

"Then at least your long-range communications array. It'll need to be done delicately—I don't want Dakota to guess that I'm trying to speak to the mirrors or she'll be a step ahead of us."

"With appropriate supervision," Vasin said, "I suppose I could permit it."

"Good to know I'm considered such a trusted guest," Eunice answered archly. "By the way, I like your choice of painting—it'll remind us what's at stake."

Goma had been so fixated on the image of *Zanzibar* that she had not noticed Vasin's wall image had changed again. Gone were the violent, world-shattering sun and the pale maiden with the skeletal figure. This was a skull-faced person clasping their hands to the bony bulb of their head, standing on a bridge or pier, under a lava-red sky that oozed and throbbed like a wound.

"*The Scream*," Vasin said.

"The Terror," Eunice answered.

CHAPTER 36

On the morning that he meant to kill himself, Kanu and Nissa made their customary journey from the household to the civic building for their daily audience with Dakota. Kanu had mentioned nothing of his intentions to Nissa and now did his best to banish every trace of them from his words and manner. She must not know, she must not suspect, or she would blame herself for not doing enough to stop him. Equally, Dakota had to be given every reason to believe that Nissa was in no way complicit in the act. His death would serve an obvious and logical end, but if he could engineer it in such a way as to cause the least difficulty for Nissa, all the better.

He did not feel suicidal, not even for a moment. This was not an action springing from some intense weariness of life, nor was he in physical pain. His despair, his sense of utter hopelessness, was derived entirely from his current predicament. He still loved the idea of being alive, and if he could have seen a path through his difficulties that both averted them and allowed for his own continued existence, he would have gladly taken it. But there was no such path. If he denied Dakota her starship, she would murder the sleepers. If he gave her the ship, she would court disaster not just for herself but for the entire human and elephant diaspora. Had he been a more ruthless person, he would have accepted the first outcome as morally preferable to the second. But Kanu would permit himself no such calculus. He would not balance life against life—except his own.

So he would do it. Destroy the ship, and he took away the means of her expedition. If she decided to kill the sleepers anyway, out of spite, that was beyond his control. But he hoped she would not, for they were still valuable to her. He dared apply the same reasoning to Nissa.

"I'd like Nissa to come with me," he bluffed, knowing full well what Dakota's answer would be.

"And risk both of you running away with that ship?" Dakota asked with a certain amusement, as if it was naive of him to think she might be so easily gulled. "No—good Nissa will remain here, aboard *Zanzibar*, while you conduct the tests. If the ship cannot be operated by one individual, it is not yet ready. Yet you have told me it is nearly ready."

"It is," Kanu said.

"Then you will go aboard alone. If you require Risen assistance, so be it, but Nissa will remain here."

He shook his head slowly. "No, I won't need the Risen."

"She won't compromise on this," Nissa said.

"I didn't expect her to. It was worth a try."

But in truth, he had never wanted Nissa with him—not given his intentions. He kissed her. He made it brief, lingering only for an instant. He did not want her to sense anything unusual about this parting.

"How long do you think it will take?" she asked.

"Not long," Kanu answered.

With great care, he moved *Icebreaker* under its own power for the first time since the Watchkeeper attack. Only steering motors were required to extract the ship from *Zanzibar*, but the operation was as slow and painstaking as defusing a bomb. Once free, Kanu allowed his ship to drift to a safe distance of one hundred kilometres, while still following the same orbit around Paladin.

"Dakota—can you hear me?"

"Perfectly, Kanu."

"Put Nissa on. I want to be sure you haven't hurt her."

"I'm fine," Nissa said, after the slightest of pauses. "She isn't so stupid as to throw away one of her assets."

"Are you prepared to start the Chibesa drive?" the Tantor asked, with a certain brusqueness. "I am eager for a demonstration."

"You'll get your demonstration. But I need an hour or two

to make sure nothing's shifted since we were in *Zanzibar*. Go and read a book or something."

Kanu was in the old control room. During the long course of *Icebreaker*'s repairs, Kanu had been aboard the ship so many times that it was easy to lose sight of the changes that had been made. From the outside, the alterations were slight, but the ship's interior was different now, its symmetry and elegance butchered to allow access by the Risen. A number of additional control pedestals now awaited him, rising from the floor like tree-stumps. They came equipped with chunky, tactile interfaces suited for the use of trunks, and with wide-angle visual readouts arranged for the convenience of elephant eyes. Elsewhere, the Tantors had been provided with bulky, padded "couches"—supporting structures they could straddle during periods of high gee-load or weightlessness. They were the size of trampolines.

The shuttle *Noah* had yet to be attached, but the docking connections were now in place on the upper hull. All but two of the escape pods had been adapted so that each could take a single Risen, leaving Kanu and Nissa a choice of the two remaining three-person pods—if the expedition ever took place.

Many of the locks, corridors and rooms had also been enlarged to suit beings the size and mass of Dakota. Where such enlargement demanded it, walls had been removed and chambers joined together. The ship's interior spaces were larger, but as a whole it now felt smaller. There were still places Tantors could not reach, mostly because of unavoidable engineering considerations, but none related to the critical functions of the ship.

But there were presently no Tantors aboard—not a living thing save for himself.

Although every part of the ship was now under weightless conditions—the centrifugal wheels had been deactivated during the rebuild—Kanu still assumed his normal seated position with the console folded down over his lap.

Now the console chimed.

He had become used to the ship demanding his attention at frequent intervals—it had done little else during the repairs—

but this was something else. *Icebreaker* was detecting an incoming radio transmission—a purposeful, directed attempt at communication—and it was not originating from *Zanzibar*.

While the console chimed, a blue symbol flashed on and off. Kanu stared at it, mesmerised. Breaking the trance, he made to answer the incoming transmission. But he stopped and first took the precaution of locking Dakota out of his communications, at least for the time being.

Then he took the call.

A man's face appeared on the main display. He was fine-boned, with a greying beard and a scalp covered with tight grey curls. "My name is Nasim Caspari," he said, speaking Swahili with a delicate inflection. "I trust you can understand me. I am sending this transmission from the expeditionary vessel *Travertine*—we are presently in orbit around Orison. We came to this system from Crucible, on a mission to gather information for our government. Our intentions are peaceful and we are ready to offer assistance should it be required. We believe you may have been damaged and forced to seek shelter aboard *Zanzibar*. Your origin is unknown to us, but if there is scope for cooperation we would be glad to discuss the possibilities. Please respond when you are in receipt of this transmission, which will repeat until we hear a response."

That part at least was true, for the ship confirmed that the signal was streaming in on a repeating cycle across a variety of frequencies and transmission protocols.

Whoever had sent it—whoever this Nasim Caspari was—they were anxious to be heard.

Kanu deliberated, wondering if he dared risk a reciprocal transmission. Was Dakota even aware of this attempt at contact? he wondered. She had never mentioned it, and *Icebreaker* had not begun to intercept the signal until it was safely beyond the screening influence of *Zanzibar*.

It was possible she did not know about it.

"Help me, Swift. Give me a way of responding that she can't possibly detect."

"Are you quite sure of the wisdom of taking such a risk?"

"Yes. Quite sure. Why wouldn't I be?"

"Our predicament is complicated enough as it is without inviting outside interference."

"I want to talk to him. If I don't, he may decide to interfere anyway."

"I still think it is unwise."

"I'm pleased you have an opinion. Do it anyway."

"A moment, in that case." Kanu's hands moved under Swift's control, executing a short sequence of commands. "There. The transmitters are aligned on Orison and the beam should not be within Dakota's capabilities to detect. You may speak at your leisure."

"Thank you, Swift. And if you'd do me the courtesy of only allowing *my* words to come out of *my* mouth, that would be even more appreciated."

"You're the diplomat. I wouldn't dream of encroaching on your sphere of expertise."

Kanu cleared his throat, tapping a knuckle against his windpipe, and straightened himself in his seat. "My name is Kanu," he began, seeing no need to add any more than that. "To the crew of the *Travertine*—may I congratulate you on a safe crossing. It's true that we suffered some damage close to Poseidon, but all is now in hand and—despite your extremely kind offer—we have no need of outside assistance. Might I suggest, nonetheless, that you proceed with great caution? We were fortunate not to be more seriously damaged—very fortunate indeed. I wish you the best of luck with your endeavours."

He closed the transmission and instructed the ship to send it onwards in a single burst.

This was a highly compact solar system, with Paladin, Orison and Poseidon all lying within half an AU of their star. Given the current alignment of the planets, Kanu knew he could expect an answer inside five minutes if the newcomers were quick in their response.

"Kanu?" Dakota asked, when at last he reopened the channel to *Zanzibar*. "Was there a difficulty?"

"None, Dakota, but these diagnostic tests place a high workload on the ship. It's better if we keep communications to an absolute minimum unless there's something to report."

"And what is the prognosis? Nissa and I are both eager to see the evidence of your hard work."

In truth, there was no reason for the ship not to work. The

loom of monitors continued to report nothing anomalous,
nothing that merited further attention. Trace gases pumped
through the various combustion pathways had found no leaks
or imperfections. The magnetic containment chambers
responded well to surges of test power. Thin plasmas injected
for test purposes were corralled, pinched and excited in the
expected fashion. The system did its best to simulate instabilities and show that the dampening mechanisms were capable
of doing their work.

Each of these conditions was only a step on the way to a
true post-Chibesa reaction, but Kanu saw nothing to give him
pause.

"The prognosis is excellent, but I still need to allow more
tests to complete."

"And how long would that be, precisely?"

"A few minutes."

"You demand great patience of me, Kanu. But after two
centuries, I suppose a few minutes more won't hurt."

"I hope not. In the meantime, I'm going silent again. I'll be
back in touch when we're ready to proceed with the full test."

He shut her off and leaned back in his seat, sweat pooling
between his shoulder blades. The diagnostic tests could run
for as long as he let them, but the fact was the ship already
knew as much about itself as it ever would.

"Swift?"

"Yes, Kanu?"

"They could answer in five minutes or five hours—or not
at all. If I'm left alone in my skull, I may go mad. Would you
care for a game of chess while we're waiting?"

"If you think it would help."

"It probably won't. But for old times' sake, if nothing else."

"Then I shall be glad to oblige. You are dwelling on the
possibility of a reply, aren't you?"

"I want to know what they know."

"It will not change our standing with Dakota. The essential
facts of our arrangement are not subject to outside influence."

"Then there's no harm in hearing what they have to say, is
there?"

Swift conjured a chess table. They played a quick, careless

game which Kanu won by narrow odds—it was possible, probable even, that Swift had contrived his own defeat—and were in the opening moves of a second when the console gave another chime.

"Dakota?" Swift asked.

"No," Kanu answered. "Our new friends."

It was a woman this time. She was an odd mixture of casual and formal, dressed in colourful clothes and a vibrantly patterned silk scarf, plus a great assortment of jangling, rattling jewellery. Her face struck him as open and friendly— there was something in it that reminded him of Garudi Dalal's mother, from that day in Madras. But she addressed him from behind a desk, her hands clasped solemnly together, a grey wall behind her. And when she spoke, while there was no intimidation or posturing in her voice, she nonetheless conveyed a tremendous impression of authority.

A woman to be reckoned with, he thought.

"Thank you for your response, Kanu. I am Gandhari Vasin, captain of the *Travertine*. Nasim was acting as my second-in-command while I was on Orison. We were alerted to your possible presence around *Zanzibar* and began beaming a message to you in the hope of making contact, but I confess our expectations were not great. Permit me to speak plainly. There are many things about this system we don't yet know, and I am willing to assume the same is true for you. But we do know about Dakota, and we think you do, too. You may even have made direct contact with the Tantors. So have we—but with a different faction from Dakota's. We have also made contact with Eunice Akinya. Eunice had a lot to tell us, and I think her account of events is likely to be different from Dakota's. You may have been told that Eunice is dead, and if so, I would like you to consider a few other things that may not have been true."

Kanu smiled at this. If only she knew. He had been doing little else but consider the degrees of truthfulness of things. She might as well have advised him there were benefits to breathing.

But for the time being, he was content to hear her out.

"We have no reason to presume that your objectives

conflict with ours, Kanu, but you may have been misled—
gravely misled. There are dangers on Poseidon greater than
anything you have already encountered. We are not speaking
simply of the risk to your own life, although that would be
considerable, but of wider implications—for all of us. You
appeared free to answer Nasim's transmission. Might I suggest
that you do nothing, that you take no further action, until we
are close enough for proper dialogue? There is one among us
whom I think Dakota may wish to speak to. If you have the
capability to pass on a message, please inform Dakota that we
have an Akinya with us. Her name is Goma, and she is the
daughter of Ndege."

Now it was all he could do not to laugh. An Akinya! How
impressed she must think he would be. The movers and shakers
of history—the lineage that had dragged people to the stars.

How could an Akinya possibly fail to sort things out?

Shaking his head ruefully, he composed a response.

"I will offer you the courtesy of a reply, Gandhari, but it
may not be quite what you are hoping for. Firstly, I have no
choice but to comply with Dakota's wishes. I am fully aware
of the risks posed by Poseidon, and also of the potential consequences of approaching that planet. I also know that many
thousands of lives depend on my not failing Dakota, so your
attempt at persuasion is wasted, I am afraid. Secondly, you
speak of someone called Goma Akinya as if that name might
carry weight. I am sorry to inform you—and indeed Goma—
that you should be under no such illusions. I am also an
Akinya, you see. My full name is Kanu Akinya, and my
mother was Chiku Yellow. And my family name has not made
the slightest difference to Dakota."

When he was done and the message winging its way back
to Captain Vasin, Swift moved a rook and offered his sage
assessment of things.

"You would be unwise to totally discount the value of this
second Akinya, Kanu. The message specifically summoned
one of your esteemed clan. There must have been a reason for
that."

"She said Goma, not Ndege."

"But she mentioned Ndege, which I would suggest is not

likely to be coincidence." Swift removed his pince-nez glasses and began polishing the lenses against his sleeve. "Are you going to make your move or just stare at the board until it suffers a minor quantum fluctuation?"

Kanu pushed a piece from square to square, but with no more care than if he had been blindfolded.

"A win appears inevitable," Swift observed.

"It doesn't surprise me. My heart's not really in the game."

"No, I mean that you have placed me in a highly disadvantageous position. There is hope for you yet, Kanu."

"Perhaps."

He contacted Dakota and told her he was ready to activate the drive.

"A short test," he explained to her. "Just enough to validate the repairs. Wouldn't want you thinking I'm trying to make a run for it, would we?"

"You would not, Kanu, in any case."

"Still, we don't want any misunderstandings."

"No, we most certainly do not. Are you ready?"

"Opening the priming flows as we speak." He waited a moment, studying the columns of numbers and shifting diagrams on his console. "Flows look good. Levelling out at injection pressure. Tokamaks building field strength. A little slow on three, but it's correcting. I'm going ahead with plasma injection."

"By all means. Proceed with caution, Kanu."

"Plasma in and bottled. Approaching ignition in three . . . two . . . one. Good. We have fusion. Burn looking clean and stable. Tokamaks holding. Clear to initial Chibesa excitation."

This was a technological commonplace—in the days before the moratorium, ignition would have been initiated hundreds of thousands of times a day with the utmost dreary reliability. But it was worth remembering that it had taken decades to perfect Chibesa's discovery into a single workable prototype engine, and decades more before the engines achieved sufficient reliability for widespread use.

But the thrust came in, gently pressing his back into the chair.

"I see you moving," Dakota said.

"Yes, we have thrust. But I'm stepping things up—I'm going to take us into post-Chibesa energies."

"Are you sure you are not being hasty?"

But another voice said, "What are you doing? It was never our intention to take things this quickly."

He told Swift, "I know what I'm doing."

"You may—but I certainly do not. We have barely satisfied ourselves that the initial process is stable, let alone achieved the confidence to push beyond that—"

"Shut up."

He must have spoken aloud, for Dakota asked, "Who are you addressing?"

"Voices in my head," he explained. "I hear them sometimes. Nothing you need worry about. Commencing post-Chibesa transition."

Now there was a bump rather than a nudge, and the console lit up with a quilt of red and amber status warnings. *Icebreaker* was achieving post-Chibesa energies, but in an uncontrolled, chaotic fashion.

"Kanu—is all well?"

"All is well, Dakota. Nothing could be better."

The console was now a blaze of red and audible warnings had begun to sound from the walls. Under normal conditions, the ship would have intervened to shut down the unstable Chibesa process, but in this test mode the usual safety measures were suspended.

Kanu knew this—indeed, he had made sure it was so.

"Kanu," Dakota said, "I have a suspicion—which may be unwarranted—but if you are attempting to destroy or damage the ship to escape your obligation—"

"Put Nissa on again."

"She's right here. Whatever you have to say to her, you can say to me, too."

"Then I'm sorry. I can't see any other way. This is not Nissa's fault. You must believe that, Dakota. Nor is it the fault of the Friends. You'll gain nothing by punishing them now."

"Kanu!" Nissa called out to him, her voice breaking on his name.

"I must do this," he answered. "I love you—I'll always love you—but there is no other way."

And then—independent of his own volition—his hands moved to the console. He resisted the action but his efforts were useless: Swift now had total control of his nervous system. He might as well have been outside his own body, watching it dance to another's will.

A vibration found its way through the fabric of the ship. It built in strength, the evidence of wildly varying drive stresses, too haphazard to be neutralised. And then there was a single violent shudder, as if *Icebreaker* had been struck by some larger object, and the vibrations died away to stillness. The alarms continued to sound, the console still a blaze of emergency notifications.

But the Chibesa engine had shut itself down.

The hold on him lingered, and then it was absent.

He gasped a powerful involuntary breath, as if he had just surfaced from deep, cold waters.

"You traitor, Swift."

"I saved your life—again. Is it too much to expect a little gratitude?"

CHAPTER 37

Travertine maintained its orbit around Orison. Next to it, tracing the same orbit and very nearly ready for independent flight, the lander remained the focus of intense human and machine activity.

In the forward sphere of the larger ship, the part spun to simulate gravity, a woman and a man sat opposite each other at table in the main public galley. The woman drank chai; the man cradled a mug of scented coffee. Around them, the spaces of the ship hummed with news and rumour.

"Something went wrong," Goma said. "That's what Gandhari says. Or nearly went wrong—as if the ship came very close to blowing up, and then the malfunction was damped down just in time."

"I'm no physicist," Peter Grave said, "but I would imagine there are a great many things that can go wrong with a Chibesa drive. The captain made contact with the other ship?"

"Momentarily. There was a reply to Nasim's automated transmission and then a direct response to Gandhari's. She played it back for me—he claims to be another Akinya!"

"This is either startling news, or almost inevitable." Grave looked up from his drink, smiled at her to disarm her natural defensiveness. "Another Akinya. Do you believe him?"

"He says he's Kanu. There is a Kanu in my lineage, so it's possible, but it's . . . complicated."

"Nothing about your family would be considered uncomplicated, Goma. Still—is this good or bad? Does his being an Akinya improve our situation or worsen it?"

"You mean, can he be expected to do the right thing?"

Grave scratched at his almost hairless scalp. Goma could not help but notice the crescent-shaped impressions where her fingernails had gouged his skin, still preserved despite decades of skipover.

"I suppose," Grave said.

"That presupposes there is a 'right thing' to be done. Kanu didn't threaten us; he didn't tell us to back off or say he'd do terrible things to us if we didn't comply. He just urged us not to get involved and advised us to be cautious."

"And yet he is still acting in a way Eunice deems hazardous—conspiring with Dakota in this expedition."

"If he knew what was at stake, he wouldn't go along with it."

"Unless he felt he had no choice," Grave said. "Have you looked into his history?"

"As much as I can find. Kanu was a significant figure in the United Aquatic Nations—a Panspermian, an advocate of the philosophy of the Green Efflorescence."

"I've studied that movement. They were regarded as cranks and cultists for a while, weren't they?" There was a playful, gently mocking tone in his voice. "True believers."

"I don't think it's quite the same thing as the Second Chancers," Goma answered, meeting his answer with a smile of her own. "They wanted to turn the galaxy green. You'd be content if we crawled back under a rock and forgot about the stars completely."

"A very slight mischaracterisation, if you don't mind my saying so."

"All right, I'll allow you that one." Goma could not help but smile back at Grave, seeing that no offence had been taken. "Anyway, that's only part of Kanu's story. Eventually he ended up being an ambassador to the robots on Mars—the Evolvarium."

"I've studied my early space age history. Correct me if I'm wrong, but didn't Eunice have something to do with all that?"

"Do you mean the real Eunice, as opposed to the one aboard with us now?"

Grave shrugged. "If we're going to insist on a distinction."

"Wait a minute, Peter. If either of us was going to insist they're not the same, I'd expect it to be you."

"Because of my belief system?"

"Why else? One's a human being who lived and died, the other's a cybernetic simulation that began as a conceptual art project long after the real woman was dead and gone."

"And yet—she is flesh and blood. And she has the real woman's memories."

"Gathered from public records."

"Not all of them—some of those memories are directly attributable to the neural traces she inherited from her own frozen corpse." A touch of mischief softened his features. "Or have you not been keeping up?"

"She's *my* fake robot ancestor, not yours!"

"But she is human now, and mortal—probably—and she lives and breathes the world much as the original Eunice would were she here instead. At this point, do we have the right to make any distinction between them? Whatever Eunice's essence was—her soul, if you will—surely it has been conserved, reconstituted, in this iteration?"

Goma shook her head. "No. We don't speak of souls. Not now, not ever. Souls aren't real."

"Patterns, then. Abstract structures of experience and reaction, making up a consistent, continuous human identity. She thinks of herself as Eunice Akinya. Have we the right to deny her that belief?"

"We can deny her whatever we like."

"But if we deny her humanity," Grave said, "we may as well deny our own. She has as much claim on her self as the rest of us, Goma. And if I can see it—me, a Second Chancer—then surely it can't be too great a leap for anyone else?"

Goma wished to argue. But the truth was, she had nothing to offer in return beyond a sullen: "We were talking about Kanu, I think."

"We were," he agreed. "But the digression was worthwhile."

Eunice was allowed her liberty, within limits. She was assigned a bangle and told to explore the ship as she pleased, and to mingle without hesitation among the other members of the expedition. But Goma knew the bangle would only get Eunice so far—the security protocols had been redoubled—and that there would be certain members of the crew who wanted nothing to do with this quixotic and fiery enigma from the past, this thing shaped like a woman that had not even come close to earning their trust yet.

Goma understood the concerns, voiced or otherwise. So what if Eunice was biological, if she needed air to breathe and food to stuff in her mouth? That did not mean she was in any way harmless or indeed on their side. Ru had learned that lesson and felt the alien strength in Eunice's bones and muscles.

Ru would not allow Eunice anywhere near their quarters, and Goma lacked the strength to argue with her. She had her point of view and it was justifiable. But if Ru disapproved of Goma speaking to Eunice at all, then that was just too bad.

They gave Eunice a cabin, and Eunice and Goma were free to meet there whenever they chose. For her part Ru was sensible enough not to ask too much regarding Goma's whereabouts when they were not together.

"Gandhari says it won't be long now."

"This captain of yours—do you have confidence in her?"

"Of course I do—why wouldn't I? Oh, wait—because she had the misfortune not to carve out her exploits in the daring days of the early space age, and therefore can't be relied upon to manage a starship?"

"You need not take that tone with me, Goma Akinya."

"Then don't presume to doubt Vasin's capabilities. She agreed to let you use the communications array, didn't she?"

"But only with one of you breathing down my neck, questioning my every move—and thereby making everything take twenty times as long as it needs to."

"Don't blame her for showing due caution. Her style may not be your style, but she's more than up to the job."

"We'll see about that when we discover what the job really entails."

"You're just jealous. You're a passenger and you don't like it. Well, get used to enjoying your lowly new status."

"I can see we'll get along famously. Did you bring the books?"

"Yes."

"I would like to see them. You say Ndege entrusted these to you? That was extraordinarily insightful of her. She had no guarantee they would eventually find me."

"She intended me to have them, not you. You're only getting a look at them, not a permanent loan."

"Then I take it you've made sterling progress in understanding your mother's work?"

Goma passed Eunice the first of the three notebooks. It was chronologically the earliest, going by the date at the start. By the same token, though, it was quite clear that Ndege had continued working on all the notebooks throughout her life, revisiting her earlier ideas and filling in those areas that had not at first yielded to her research. A complete picture of Ndege's work required all of the notebooks.

Goma knew this.

"Let's see what you make of it."

Eunice started at the beginning, gently creaking open its black spine and turning the pages with great care. She stared at the first two pages of notes, the columns of symbols with their meticulous and bewildering connections.

She stared and stared. A minute passed, maybe longer. If she blinked, Goma did not see it.

Eunice turned to the next pair of pages. She stared at them with the same intensity, but for not quite so long this time. The next pair she swept with her gaze, Goma watching her pupils

track up and down the columns. She looked at the next couple
of pages for a few seconds, then turned again. Faster now, the
turning of the pages becoming a slowly accelerating whisk,
like the chopping of helicopter blades.

"Are you—"

"Silence."

The pages sped by, her fingers moving with card-sharp
speed, her eyes never blinking. The whisking settled into a
machine-like rhythm, the action of her hands and eyes
methodical enough that Goma was fairly sure this was a kind
of photographic capture. She finished the notebook, closed it
and sat motionless for a second or two, as if the information
absorbed still needed to be processed into a deeper level of
comprehension.

"The second notebook."

"Not yet. Not everything in one go."

"I've waited long enough, Goma. There's nothing to be
gained from withholding the rest."

"Not for you, maybe. But the only power I have over you
lies in these notebooks."

"Why do you feel the need to have power over me?"

"Because I don't know what you are, or what you're really
capable of. Because I don't know what you think or feel
about me."

"I think you can be useful."

"Tools are useful. Materials and rations are useful. I think
I deserve more than that."

"And after everything that happened on Orison, the deaths
of my friends, withholding this information is how you hope
to elevate your status in my eyes?"

"If necessary, yes. Do you want the second notebook or
not?"

"After this glimpse? Yes. And the third."

"How badly?"

"More than anything. I've seen something marvellous,
Goma—felt the curtain of ignorance being tugged aside. All
the years I spent on Orison, trying to reconstruct a few fragments of insight—they've been eclipsed in a couple of minutes. Eclipsed and outshone. Ndege saw with clarity something

I had barely begun to think might be true. And beyond." She tapped the shut notebook. "There is more than just symbolic connection here, Goma—more than just the patterns between two forms of an alien language laid down millions of years apart. This is the key to understanding—the start of comprehension. I saw things during the Terror, but until this moment I did not have the apparatus to make sense of them. Now I do. At least, now I have the start . . . I beg of you—the other notebooks."

"In good time."

"This is intolerable."

"This is how it feels to be human. Not always getting the universe on a plate. Having to be beholden to others."

"You are being cruel."

"No, I'm being kind. I don't think you're a monster, Eunice, and I'm sorry about Orison—truly sorry. But you're going to have to work to become one of us. This is where it starts."

A hash of numbers and symbols sped past Goma's eyes much too fast to read, even if there were some sense to be drawn from them. They were in Vasin's quarters again. Eunice was stationed at a small fold-out console while Loring and Caspari watched with expressions of studied concern, still not quite satisfied that their guest was to be trusted.

Eunice tapped at the keys, her fingers moving with an unnatural fluency. The numbers and symbols kept scrolling.

"So," Vasin said, "tell us the state of things, as succinctly as you can manage."

Eunice glanced back at her audience. "The command channel to the mirrors is still open and they respond as I'd expect. I don't think Dakota has done anything to alter their basic functionality. Why would she, so long as they continue working?"

"What have you done so far?"

"Nothing she'd notice, just asked the mirrors to confirm their status and their readiness to accept further commands. We're using a tight beam, so it's unlikely Dakota will have intercepted our signal. Similarly, the mirrors are only sending their responses in our direction—there's little chance that *Zanzibar* has detected any of this traffic."

"That sounds promising," Goma said. "Do you think they'll do what you tell them to?"

"It depends on the complexity of the command. Turning them on and off shouldn't be hard—it's a simple matter of breaking the concentric symmetry of the individual mirror elements so that the beam is no longer focused. But that may not have been attempted since the mirrors were put in place. As for altering the beam angle, the mirrors need to do it all the time, so that shouldn't be a problem."

"So you can switch the beams off or aim them somewhere else," Caspari said.

"We won't know for sure until I send the command."

"We don't want to hurt them," Goma said, "but we've every indication that Kanu's being coerced. Right now, the mirrors are our only long-range negotiating tool. I don't intend to use them as a weapon, but if we can squeeze them short of power, we may buy some time for negotiation."

Eunice nodded, but there was a note of caution in her voice. "The instant the mirrors deactivate, Dakota will know that we have control. We'll have played our only card at that point, and Dakota's bound to start trying to regain control from her side. I'm doing everything I can to lock out direct commands from *Zanzibar*, but I can't promise I'll succeed."

"You designed this system?" Loring asked.

"Not exactly," she answered carefully. "The old version of me designed it, a version I barely remember being. Lot of water under the bridge since then."

"Do your best," Vasin said. "We can't expect the impossible. Equally, we'd be fools not to try to use the mirrors. Could we . . ." But she abandoned the thought with a sudden distasteful expression, as if she had bitten into something sour.

"What?" Eunice asked.

"I was wondering if we might use them as a weapon, if it came to that?"

"No!" Peter Grave said, Goma shaping the word in the same moment, sharing his exact repugnance.

"I'm not talking about inflicting deliberate loss of life, just making a statement. If that ship powers up again, could we focus the mirrors onto it, cause enough damage to prevent its departure?"

"Not with several minutes of time lag thrown into the pot," Eunice responded. "We can steer the mirrors, but not in real-time. Provided the ship doesn't follow a predictable path, it can always stay out of harm's way."

"Maybe not the ship, then. But *Zanzibar* won't be going anywhere in a hurry, will it? If we steer the beams off their power grids, we could inflict structural damage on the other parts."

Goma had believed there was steel in Gandhari Vasin before; now she had proof of it.

"This isn't war," Goma said.

"Not yet," Vasin said. "But we'd be idiotic not to think ahead, wouldn't we?" Then she clapped her hands once, making a jangle of jewellery. "Continue your work, Eunice—do everything you can to lock Dakota out of the mirrors, but take no action she might notice. In the meantime, we will continue preparing the lander. It will make no difference to your work—if you can control the mirrors from *Travertine*, you will also be able to do so from the smaller ship, and the time lag will be reduced as we close in."

"When do we leave?" Goma asked.

"Three days, maybe two if things progress well."

"It won't be war, Gandhari. We need to understand that. Tell her, Eunice."

"What would you like me to tell her?"

"That it can't come down to violence. That nothing's so serious that it has to end that way."

"I'd love to," Eunice said.

Then she returned to her work, as if the matter was settled.

CHAPTER 38

Nothing remained for Kanu but to return to *Zanzibar*, knowing he had failed. Swift had intervened promptly enough to prevent *Icebreaker* suffering severe additional damage—certainly nothing that would prevent an imminent departure—and such slight damage as had been done could be rectified during normal operations.

"Why?" he asked as they assumed station, floating just beyond *Zanzibar*'s polar door.

"Why did I not allow you to kill yourself?" Swift's figment asked, striking an ironic, chin-stroking pose. "Does that even require an answer, Kanu?"

"It was our only way out."

"You mean it was *your* only way out. It would have absolved you of any further involvement in this unpleasantness, that is true. But it would not have begun to resolve the larger problem, or left Nissa with a hope of saving herself."

"I had to take the ship from Dakota. I couldn't just run."

"And I could not allow a good man to sacrifice himself, no matter how much he might resent my intervention." Swift leaned in, both hands on the console, his face looming before Kanu. "We have *work* to do here—there is knowledge for the gathering. The potential for a meeting with intellects beyond our experience! Dakota is an opportunity, not an obstacle."

"To you, maybe."

"Our goals are not dissimilar, Kanu."

"I'm starting to wonder about that. I'll admit I came here to find some answers. So did you. But that was before we knew about Poseidon, about the Terror, about all those dead Watchkeepers. About Dakota, and what they've turned her into. That's enough for me for now. I've seen the pitfalls—seen what's at stake. But you want to keep pushing—you want ultimate contact with the M-builders or the Watchkeepers, whichever presents itself first."

"In which case, forgive me for not wishing to revel in ignorance."

"This isn't about ignorance, Swift—it's about you putting the interests of you and your robot friends ahead of the rest of us."

"I shall pretend I did not hear that."

"Pretend what you like. I had a chance to stop this and you interfered."

"I am expected to apologise for saving your life?"

"It was my choice. You took that away from me. If Dakota's the Watchkeepers' puppet, what does that make me? Just another puppet, except I'm serving the interests of the Evolvarium instead?"

"I believe we are both serving the interests of reason and enlightenment. And our relationship is one of mutual benefit, Kanu. Individually, we are ineffective. Together, we at least have a chance of outflanking Dakota."

"This is your idea of outflanking her?"

"One way or another she will have her ship, Kanu. If it is not this one, then she will lure *Travertine* in for the same ends. We have an obligation to spare our new friends that particular difficulty."

At last Kanu felt something inside him give way. He still felt violated, his trust in Swift damaged. But at the same time, he was only able to air these thoughts because his friend had not permitted him to kill himself.

"Damn you, Swift. How do you manage to make everything you do feel like the only honourable course of action?"

"Because I have learned well from a master." Swift moved to his side and patted his shoulder. "Strong heart, Kanu. Our day is far from lost."

"One promise."

"If I may oblige."

"Should I ever try to take my own life again, you will do me the honour of not intervening."

"But my own life would also be at stake."

"That's true. But this is the deal you signed up to. If I

choose to end my existence, I don't want a parasitic machine intelligence from Mars deciding it knows better than I do."

Swift tapped a finger against his lip. "Good that we can speak plainly."

"Yes."

"Might I add a reciprocal condition of my own?"

"If you insist."

"Do nothing in haste, Kanu. I had a taste of non-existence during skipover. Death is all very well—doubtless it has its benefits—but I am not quite done with living yet. I think the universe still has some surprises in store for both of us."

At the household, Nissa was silent. She had programmed the projecting wall to show a moving image from Earth, the view from a beach as the old sun made its way to the ocean's flat horizon. The light was bright, but also nearly colourless—a line of chrome breakers against the darkening platinum of the water, the sky a perfect shimmer of silver, the sand like snow, the trees in the foreground black silhouettes.

"I couldn't tell you," he said.

The wall made the sound of the waves. They crashed and broke in an endless series of static roars, each the birth of a miniature universe, each drawn back into a slow, hissing death.

"Never," she said, "do that to me again."

"I don't intend to."

"You thought that was the answer, Kanu? After all this time? Are you really that stupid?"

"The people aboard the other ship warned me," he replied. "I received a message from them saying I should not cooperate with her."

She was still facing the ocean, not Kanu. "They came all this way to tell you that?"

"I don't know. I'd have liked the opportunity for a longer conversation but it was difficult even with only a few minutes of time lag. Do you want to know the odd thing?"

"I'm being held prisoner by talking elephants. I'd say my capacity for oddness is somewhat overloaded." A breaker surrendered itself to entropy; in the interval between that wave and the next, she said, "What was it?"

"They sent one of us, another Akinya, on that other ship. Her name is Goma, and I don't even know who she is."

"Do you think she means well?"

"I think we all mean well."

"Not my question."

"It's the best answer I have. We do mean well—all of us, not just Akinyas. But doing well is the hardest thing of all. Our minds aren't up to it. The machine's too big. We can't see how any one of us fits into it, how any given action shapes the final outcome."

Nissa turned from the ocean. At last he sensed the promise of forgiveness, or at least a willingness not to withhold it for eternity. He would take that.

"Then we have to get better," she said.

"Yes."

"Much, much better." She rose and faced him, taking his head in both her hands, fingers like a vice. "I almost dare not ask. One of you decided not to go through with it. Who should I thank?"

There were still a number of short-range service taxis aboard *Zanzibar*—Kanu and Nissa had noticed them on their first arrival—some of which had been adapted for the use and transportation of Tantors. Over a course of days, a small expeditionary force boarded *Icebreaker*, together with all the supplies and equipment Dakota deemed necessary. The shuttle *Noah* had been mated via a docking connection that allowed humans and Risen to pass from one ship to the other.

There were three Risen, including Dakota. The others were a pair of males, both adults, but younger and smaller than their matriarch. Their names were Hector and Lucas, and from the similarity in their manners and build, Kanu was quick to decide they were siblings, or perhaps cousins. He had expected these newcomers to flounder in the unfamiliar weightless environment of the ship, but nothing could have been further from the truth. The Risen all had elephant-shaped spacesuits, enabling them to move from ship to ship even without the use of connecting airlocks, and their trunks proved surprisingly handy during weightless operations, serving as both anchor

and counterbalance. No: this was a well-trained crew, unfazed
by the challenges that lay ahead.

Clearly they were among the elite of the Risen, perhaps the
matriarch's direct offspring. Their dedication to her appeared
total, and utterly without question.

"I thought Memphis would be coming with us," Kanu said.

"Memphis would not cope well with the rigors of space-
flight," Dakota explained. "It does not come naturally to us.
These younger Risen have prevailed over their instinctive fears
with exhaustive training and dedication to the cause. They have
learned to use spacesuits and manage weightless operations
inside *Zanzibar's* central core. They understand physics and
the rudiments of astrogation. But Memphis is older, and consequently his ways are less easily altered. Besides, he is my most
loyal and dependable ally. Were I required to entrust the safety
and security of *Zanzibar* to anyone other than myself, it would
be to wise and slow Memphis."

"And you, Dakota—are you prepared for the rigors ahead?"

"I have faced the Terror already, Kanu. Faced it with my
deepest, boldest threat rumble. It is nothing to me, and neither
is the idea of leaving *Zanzibar*."

"And when we reach Poseidon—your nerve will hold?"

"When the chasing moons single us out, there will be fear.
Anything less would be unnatural. But we will stand our
ground. Why? Do you lack confidence in yourself?"

"I'd feel more confident if I had a choice in the matter."

"Ah, but you *do* have a choice. You'll always have that.
There will never be a time when we are beyond reach of *Zanzibar*, and there will never be a time when I cannot dictate my
commands to Memphis. Consequently the choice will be
simple enough: cooperate, or think of the harm you are doing
to the Friends."

"That's no choice at all."

"Perhaps not. The truth is, I would much rather we see each
other as friends engaged in a mutual adventure. But at the back
of your mind, remember that you have a powerful disincentive
to turn against me."

Kanu and Nissa boarded before the last of the Risen.
Within the ship, they had all the liberty they desired—no part
of the ship was barred to them, not even those spaces into

which only a human could squeeze. The centrifuge sections had been spun back up to normal gravity and they had ample privacy—their old sleeping quarters were untouched despite the modifications. They could also access all the normal shipboard functions, from communications to navigation.

"Despite our earlier conversation," Dakota said, standing at one of the control pedestals, "it is vital to me that we conduct our expedition in a spirit of mutual cooperation. It is true that we have had cause to doubt each other's better intentions. Such difficulties are to be expected in an enterprise such as ours. But let us not lose sight of what we have achieved, and of what lies within our reach. Human-Tantor symbiotic exploration—people and the Risen united in a spirit of scientific and cultural enlightenment. What have we to fear if we stand together?"

"You stood with Chiku and Eunice once," Kanu said, "until they had the poor sense to disagree with you."

"We have all made mistakes. The mark of intelligence is to learn from them, and not be bound by the errors of the past. I regret everything that came between Chiku, Eunice and I. But they were not steadfast in the face of the unknown."

"Are you still Dakota, or have the Watchkeepers made you into something else?"

"I know my own nature, Kanu."

She was cycling the main viewer through display options, learning her way around the controls. The tip of her trunk, splayed like an open hand, was a thing of dexterous wonder.

"I think I know it, too," he said. "You imagine you have free will, and maybe you have just enough to fool yourself into believing that. The fact is, though, you're doing the work of those zombie machines—mindless automata that became so clever they forgot how to be conscious. It's not too late, Dakota. Abandon this expedition—or at least delay it until we've made contact with the other ship."

"The *other ship*, yes. I will admit I have some interest in it—but only insofar as it spurs me to even more decisive action. They are on the move, did you know?"

"Are they?"

"Not the main vessel, but a smaller craft—a vehicle about the size of our *Noah*. Nothing escapes the Watchkeepers' scrutiny, and there is nothing I need to know that they will not bring to my attention."

"You think they care about you?" Nissa asked.

"I concede that theirs is a detached sort of interest—clinical, you might say. I am realistic enough to think of myself as an instrument in the service of their enquiry. If a better instrument were to present itself, I might cease to be their favoured subject. But for now they are invested in me, and this other ship is no more than a distraction. I would like it to remain that way. Might you show me how to project a schematic of the entire inner solar system? I appear to be unable to zoom out from the immediate neighbourhood of Paladin."

"Access that sub-menu, then select the logarithmic scale factor," Nissa said.

"Thank you—I should have seen that."

The schematic showed Gliese 163, then its family of worlds—at least out to the orbit of Paladin, the eighth world from the star. Dakota called up a set of curving paths which showed options for their own trajectory depending on start time, gee-loads and fuel consumption. The coloured paths fanned out like peacock feathers, annotated with numbers and symbols, but all commenced at Paladin and ended at Poseidon.

"Our course is simple—we have but one objective. They have commenced their journey from Orison, but at the moment their trajectory can't be extrapolated with any precision, other than to say that it remains bound to the ecliptic, so it is very unlikely that they mean to leave the system. More likely, they have a world in mind. Paladin is one possibility, but it would not cost them much in additional time to divert to Poseidon, or indeed towards three or four other objectives. What do you make of this smaller vehicle, either of you?"

"You're the one with the Watchkeepers whispering in your ear," Nissa said. "Why not ask them?"

"Oh, I have—or rather, they have tried to present me with the information in a way suitable for my comprehension. But they are not good at that sort of thing, and frankly I don't have time to be swallowed up and dismantled by them again. The small ship does not strike me as having interstellar capability, but I would not like to bet against it if it came down to speed and agility within a solar system. Do you concur?"

"If you'd like me to," Kanu said.

"I do not wish to find that ship already at Poseidon when we arrive, hampering our approach. For that reason, we shall take the hardest, fastest course open to us—or at least the fastest we can achieve without employing post-Chibesa energies." Dakota moved her trunk—Kanu was still curiously fascinated by the way it shaped itself to the needs of the moment—and blanked out all but one of the trajectories. "There—our golden course. It will bring us within the outer perimeter of the moons in just over forty-eight hours. Unless the other ship has capabilities not known to us, they cannot beat us to Poseidon."

"When do we leave?" Nissa asked.

"Is there any reason not to depart immediately?"

"No," Kanu said, for he knew that the ship was as ready as it ever would be, and Dakota far too intelligent to be convinced otherwise.

"Then you have your answer," the elephant said.

For a long while they hardly appeared to be moving at all, *Zanzibar* diminishing in size so slowly that Kanu's eyes offered no real impression of progress. They were like a ship fighting its way out to sea from the safety of a harbour, the town and the rising land beyond only reluctantly allowing their prize to slip from reach.

The tiny distance they had come made no difference to Paladin's apparent size. As they pulled away from *Zanzibar*, so the Mandala rotated into view below.

Kanu stared at it with a troubled sense that he had offered it insufficient attention—that too much had been happening when they arrived, too much while they were guests of the Risen. It felt discourteous—a lapse in respect that was bound to be punished. When he had known of the Crucible Mandala's existence, he had envisaged a mute and mindless thing—an alien construction, sphinxlike with its secrets but possessed of no deeper intent. Now, in such close proximity to the second Mandala, his perception underwent a change. He felt its scrutiny on him—its need to be attended, to be observed and to feel itself the subject of awe. It was not malignant, he decided, but neither was it universally benign. It was capricious, capable of acts of supreme and disregarding cruelty—a jealous god branded onto the face of a world.

He did not like it. But then again, no one was asking him to.

"At one hundred kilometres from *Zanzibar*," Dakota said, "you may increase our thrust to normal output. We will make a direct course for Poseidon. We have nothing to hide, nothing to be ashamed of that would require subterfuge."

That was when *Icebreaker* began to pick up a transmission. The console chimed, and chimed again.

"It's the smaller ship," Kanu said. "Do you want to take the call?"

"Let us hear what they have to say—we have no obligation to respond."

The transmission was simple audio-visual, with no cumbersome encryption. Kanu threw it onto the nearest wall and studied the face that appeared. He recognised her immediately: it was Gandhari Vasin, the woman who had spoken to him just before his abortive suicide bid.

He was careful to show no recognition.

"This is Captain Vasin," she said. "We see you moving, accelerating away from *Zanzibar*. I must insist that you reverse course and return to *Zanzibar*. I will allow you five minutes to acknowledge this transmission and demonstrate some intent to turn around. If I see no change in your trajectory, I will be forced to consider punitive action. Trust me—I have the means."

The transmission ended. Kanu made a mental note of the time. She had allowed for the time lag between the smaller vehicle and Paladin's neighbourhood, but without much room for error.

"Your thoughts?" Dakota asked.

"There's no point articulating them," Kanu said. "You're committed to this action, and you know she can't reach us across this distance."

"Then you consider it a bluff."

"You tell me."

"I am struck by two things. The first is that she would be very unwise to stake so much on a bluff, given that we will know the truth of it in a few short minutes. The second is that she arrived at her point very quickly—no introductions, no clarification regarding her mission or mandate, the name of her ship—"

"Make of that what you will."

"If you had prior contact with these people, Kanu—you would have informed me, of course?"

Half-truths came to him without effort. "That may not have been her first transmission but it's the first one we've heard. But she could have been sending for days without *Icebreaker* recognising it as a deliberate attempt at communication. For all we know, she made her introductions ages ago and the ship was too damaged to recognise it for what it was."

Dakota gave a nod, and Kanu trusted that she was satisfied. He ought to have been grateful for that, but the words had come from Swift, not his conscious self.

At least, he could take no credit for them.

"Nonetheless, we must consider her threat," Dakota said. "Unless her expedition has weapons that defy physics, she cannot possibly harm us from such a distance. But she must have something to back up her threat."

"Or it *is* a bluff," Nissa said.

"We shall find out soon enough, in that case. Maintain our heading, Kanu. Make it clear that we will not be deterred."

"Do you want me to respond verbally?"

"I do not think that is necessary. Our intentions will be clear enough from our actions."

"Swift?" Nissa asked, using the subvocal channel.

"As much as it pains me, I can't fault her analysis. But I doubt very much that Captain Vasin would make a threat unless she had some means of delivering on it."

"Well, *that's* reassuring."

"It was not meant to be."

"Sometimes," Dakota said, "I have the sense of something passing between the two of you—a private discussion to which I am not privy. Is it wrong of me to feel that way?"

"We feel the same way around the Risen," Kanu answered.

"Ah, but in your case the feeling is entirely justified. Speech is efficient, but there are some things that can only be conveyed through the old channels—the rumble and the roar."

Vasin was generous; it was another ten minutes before they heard from her again.

"You haven't altered your course, which is regrettable because it's going to make things very difficult for both of us. Charitably, you may not have heard me or be incapable of responding. Unfortunately, I don't have time to make charitable assumptions. If you are in a position to do so, please turn your attention back to *Zanzibar*."

They needed to do nothing; the image of the shard was still up on the wall, albeit now captured by high-magnification sensor. It was a real-time view and the shard would not be visible for much longer before it passed behind Paladin. For the moment it was unobstructed, lit sharply on one face, shadowed on the other.

"I have complete control of your solar mirrors," Vasin said. "They are mine to deactivate or redirect. A preprogrammed command is about to take effect; in about ten seconds you should see the consequences."

"My god," Kanu said, genuinely startled.

It could not be a bluff, he knew: no one would claim such a thing unless it were within their immediate capabilities to make good on it. And indeed, he only had to look at the thermal hot spots to see that the threat was entirely real.

The bright spots winked out instantly, although it would take much longer for the thermal collection grids and the area around them to cool down to the ambient temperature of the rest of *Zanzibar*. Still, the point had been made, and made excellently.

"No," Dakota said, with a rage that was both quiet and world-consuming. "No. This will not stand."

"They've done what they said they would," Nissa said. "Maybe it's time to think about negotiating."

Vasin was speaking again. "Although I've turned off your power, it's fully within my capabilities to restore it. I have no desire to hurt or inconvenience you—merely to demonstrate that I have the means to do so. Turn around now and the power will be restored."

"Speak to her," Dakota said.

Kanu nodded. "To let them know you're going to turn around?"

"To let them know that their power is worthless. Of course I am infuriated that she has this capability. I do not fully understand how it is possible, although in time I am sure that I will. But she misunderstands our position. That power is a luxury, not a necessity. Tell her this, Kanu."

"I have no reason to believe you."

The elephant lowered her head. "Better to ask yourself: do I appear concerned? Outraged, most certainly—this is a violation—but it means nothing."

"You must need that power," Nissa said, "or else why would you bother collecting it?"

"The power was a lifeline in the early days, when times were at their hardest and we had no independent means of supplying our energy needs. But we have become stronger since then—less reliant on the external universe. *Zanzibar*'s Chibesa core was damaged beyond hope of repair during the translation, but we still had the ships, shuttles and service vehicles gathered within her docks. Many of them had small Chibesa power plants of their own, and so we incorporated them into *Zanzibar*'s energy grid."

"But you still need the mirrors," Kanu said.

"Only in the very long term. Some of the chambers will have to be darkened and resources conserved elsewhere, which is difficult but not intolerable. The Risen have withstood much worse. Tell the captain that. Tell her that I am impressed by her cleverness, but that she would need to shut off the mirrors for many years before it became a serious problem."

"This may not be the end of it," Nissa said. "If she can turn them off . . . well, what else can she do? Do we really want to find out?"

The mirrors were still disabled and Kanu supposed that Vasin would maintain this state of affairs until she had reason to change it. It was an effective and surprising demonstration, he had to admit—the kind of thing he might have expected of Swift, but not this pleasant-faced human woman.

Evidently he had underestimated her.

"Captain?" he said, delivering the return transmission. "We've seen what you did and there's no doubt it's an impressive demonstration of your technical capabilities. Unfortunately, it hasn't made any difference to us. The mirrors do feed energy into *Zanzibar*'s power grid, but it can function without that power for a very long time. Months, years, easily—it's simply a question of placing more reliance on the internal generators. So I'm afraid there's no reason for us to turn around, and now you've taken this hostile action, there's no further incentive for us to consider you a trustworthy negotiating partner. I'm very sorry, but I think we've said all we need to."

"Very good, Kanu," Dakota said, when he was done.

"Don't thank me. I may as well have had a gun to my head. Was any of that true, by the way?"

"About the generators? Mostly. I won't pretend that her actions aren't a nuisance, but it will be the Friends who are the first to suffer. She is the one damaging *Zanzibar*'s capacity to sustain life, Kanu, not I. For now my concern is with *Icebreaker*—and we are safely beyond Vasin's influence."

"You wouldn't treat the Friends so callously."

"Let us not dwell on things yet to happen."

"Then you'll leave it at that?" Nissa asked.

"This Captain Vasin is resourceful, but I doubt she is infallible. If there is a way to regain control of those mirrors, I shall find it. I can communicate with them just as readily from *Icebreaker* as from *Zanzibar*, and I shall indulge myself with the problem: it will help to pass the hours. Do you know something? For the first time in a very long while, I rather wish I had the assistance of my old friend Eunice. She would know exactly where to start."

"It's a shame she died," Nissa said.

"Yes," Dakota answered. "Careless of me to depend on the frail. I learned that lesson well."

Later they were alone, making use of the privacy they had been promised. It would be an exaggeration to say they were enjoying it, but Kanu was at least glad to be away from the Risen and their goal-fixated leader.

"She's insane," Nissa said. "The Watchkeepers have done this to her, but that doesn't change what she is."

"I don't disagree."

"So what are we going to do about it?"

"Nothing. What else can we do? You saw how easily she shrugged off Vasin's attempt at persuasion. If that didn't turn her around, what will?"

"This is our ship, not hers. We'll always know it better than she does."

Kanu gave a joyless smile. Odd how Nissa now felt an equal claim on *Icebreaker*'s ownership.

"I know what you're thinking, but it doesn't change anything. We already have control of the ship but a mutiny would be pointless. The problem is the Friends. If we act against her, she'll take it out on them."

"So kill her. Then what?"

He shuddered at the thought of it. But repugnant as the very notion might be, killing Dakota was not the biggest problem.

"She's in constant contact with Memphis. We can presume that contingency plans are in place—if Memphis doesn't hear from her, he'll take action against the Friends."

"Would he follow through on an order to commit mass murder?"

"I don't know, but we can't risk the slightest chance that he might." He offered his hands in defeat. "That's all there is, Nissa. Square one, and we're stuck on it."

"Swift should help us."

"If Swift knew a way, he would. But even he can't change the facts."

An undercurrent of scepticism entered Nissa's voice. "That, and Swift might not think this expedition is such a bad idea?"

"We're on the same side," Kanu asserted, with more confidence than he felt.

Nissa waited a moment before answering.

"You hope."

They were stationed at a porthole in a part of the ship that still looked back in the direction of Paladin. After hours of acceleration they were at last free of Paladin's gravitational environment, pushing deeper into interplanetary space. Kanu could easily block out the planet with his upraised fist, and *Zanzibar* itself was now much too small to make out with his unaided eye. But the Mandala was still visible when it swung

into view, and something of its uncanny regularity demanded
attention, snaring the brain's innate capacity for pattern recognition. It had changed again since his last viewing, the interlocking, intersecting circles and radials shifting to some new
configuration. The movement of matter on the scale of conti-
nental mountain ranges, as effortless and efficient as the re-
arranging of cutlery between servings.

"It's trying to tell us something," he said.

"Or it's waiting for us to answer," Nissa replied.

CHAPTER 39

It was not the first time that Gandhari Vasin had gathered her
crew together since their departure from *Travertine*, but there
was something different in her mood on this occasion—a
lightness, or at least an elevation of her spirits, which had not
been there before. Her demonstration of the mirrors had not
achieved the intended effect, but perhaps, Goma reflected, she
was pleased it had worked at all.

"The ship needs a name," Vasin said.

"Do you have one in mind?" Goma asked.

They were stationed in the lander's common area, a space
barely larger than one of the bedrooms aboard *Travertine*.
They had been on full power almost since detaching from the
main ship and the acceleration provided the effect of gravity,
allowing the crew to sit or stand as they pleased.

"Well, possibly," Vasin said. "I hoped that one particular
good and wise man would be with us today. Since fate has
taken him from us, we can at least carry his name as our inspiration. I trust it will encourage us to be the best we can—and
let us have faith that this little ship, *Mposi*, does all that we ask
of it."

"It is a good name," said Karayan.

"Peter?"

"Mposi was an honourable man. You could not have picked a better name, Gandhari."

"Goma—any objections?"

"None whatsoever, and thank you for thinking of him. I just wish he were here to share in all this."

"We don't have Mposi," Vasin said, "but we have his example. Let's do our utmost to live up to his memory. We owe it to him, but we also owe it to those we left behind on *Travertine*, and the millions more on Crucible. I have confidence in us."

"Thank you, Gandhari," said Loring.

"Thank me when we're back home. Until then, it may be tempting fate."

The lander's interior configuration had changed slightly since Goma's trip to Orison, its walls and partitions repositioned to accommodate the extended mission requirement. This was no hardship—there had been no time to get used to the old arrangement—but it puzzled her that one locked room would not open to her bangle. She wondered what could be in that room that she was not meant to see.

"I meant to tell you about it," Vasin said when Goma put the question to her captain. "It's not that I don't want you going in there, but I felt you ought to hear about it from me before you do."

"Hear about what, exactly?"

"We have a mass restriction even with our Chibesa drive—we don't want to be carrying things we won't use. But we *are* an expedition, and we should have all the necessary tools at our disposal. I'm reluctant to limit our ability to visualise any new findings as they are gathered by our sensors." Vasin elevated her bangle and the door unlocked itself. "So I've brought the well of nanomachines from the Knowledge Room. For the moment, they are more useful to us than to our colleagues on *Travertine*."

Goma understood, although she did not wish to. "You mean you brought a subset of the machines?"

"No, the entire well. Aiyana rendered them dormant, which

allowed us to transplant the whole thing. The mass burden is slight, and we now have a viable population of nanomachines."

"They destroyed Mposi," Goma said, shivering as images of his half-digested form played back in her mind's eye.

Vasin opened the door. It was a smaller space than the original Knowledge Room and the well nearly filled it, leaving only a narrow aisle around its sides. Vasin entered, Goma lingering outside until Vasin urged her to cross the threshold.

"No," she said, closing the door behind them. "Saturnin Nhamedjo killed your uncle. The machines were simply how he hoped to dispose of the body. They can't be blamed any more than we'd blame earth or fire or water."

"I saw what they did to him."

"As did we all. Believe me, if I did not think the well could be useful to us, I'd have left it behind. But we need it, Goma— we need every speck of advantage we can get." She pulled rings from her fingers and passed them to Goma. "Hold these for me, please."

"You're worried it'll eat them?"

"No, I just don't want to have to fish them out from the bottom if they slide off." Vasin pushed back her sleeve, flicked her scarf over her shoulder, leaned over the side of the well and dipped her hand into the yielding liquid substrate.

Goma flinched—it was an unavoidable reaction after what she had seen happening to Mposi. Vasin closed her fingers around the floating figment of Paladin and hauled it from the well.

"You should have told me sooner."

"I'm telling you now. I'm also telling you that there's nothing to fear. The programming has been corrected—the machines are safe. Do you think I'd trust my hand to them if I doubted that?"

"You might if you had a point to make."

"If there's a point, it's that we can't afford not to have them. Let me show you something—maybe it'll soften your opinion." She was holding Paladin above the surface of the well, red as an apple, the Mandala a bruise on its skin. The simulation of the shard—what they now knew to be *Zanzibar*—was a microscopic grain of dust so small that it was easily capable of holding itself aloft without any physical connection to the planet or the well.

"What am I supposed to be looking at?"

"The second Mandala keeps changing. They tell me that on Crucible, the first Mandala underwent a sudden state change when your mother attempted to communicate with it. But that Mandala hasn't done anything since then, has it?"

"Not to my knowledge."

"This one is cycling through distinct state changes. Each shift looks about as dramatic as the original event on Crucible—the literal movement of mountains' worth of matter. Here." Vasin raised her voice slightly. "Well: iterate the Mandala variations, one hundred thousand times observed speed."

And she offered the apple's face to Goma, allowing her to observe the alterations the Mandala was forcing upon itself. They arrived about once a second, a rhythmic, hypnotic disclosing of new geometries like the tumbling of kaleidoscope shards. There was always symmetry, a balance of features at all scales, a recognisable quality in the circles and radials that Goma could only think of as Mandala-ness, but she did not think the patterns ever repeated.

"We don't know what it means. But Eunice tells us the Mandala was static until *Zanzibar* arrived, just as the Mandala on Crucible was static until the colonists arrived. But the *Zanzibar* translation was achieved at almost the speed of light, so the arrival event must have been nearly coincident with the arrival of information about your mother's experiment."

"I don't follow."

"Ndege started something, Goma. She initiated an event on Crucible which, as we know, led to the partial destruction of *Zanzibar*. But most significantly she appears to have woken *this* Mandala, too. We don't know how or why, but something has been triggered—a process that is still ongoing. Would you like to hear my theory?"

"One's as good as another."

"Something huge is waking up. Rebooting itself—bringing its elements back online after a long period of dormancy. I also think we're dealing with a machine bigger than Crucible, bigger than Paladin—bigger even than the space between solar systems. And I think your mother found the 'on' switch."

Goma and Eunice faced each other in a quiet corner of the lander. They had been under way for about twelve hours and some of the other crew were trying to get some rest. The interior lights had been turned down to a dull red, just sufficient to enable navigation of *Mposi*'s cluttered spaces. The windows had been shuttered, the displays and readouts muted, and the constant background roar of the Chibesa motor was in itself lulling. Goma felt the pull of it—sleep sounded like a very good idea. She had not rested well the night before departure. But at the same time she was far too anxious to think about crawling into her hammock.

"It's a small ship, so options are limited," Eunice said, "but I see Ru is doing a very good job of avoiding me."

"Can you blame her?"

"What's blame got to do with it? I would simply be much happier were she to forgive me for what happened on Orison."

"There's a lot to forgive. I think we can agree that Ru was one of the more innocent parties in all this unpleasantness."

"I'm not the one you need to convince. I admit that my actions were not as thoroughly considered as they might have been, but lives were at stake. If I've learned one thing in my long existence, it's that hesitation gets you nowhere. On Mars—"

"Yes, we've heard all about Mars. What matters is how easily you could have killed her in that moment."

"In that moment, I was watching one of my closest friends suffer an agonising death. The blood pointed to Ru as the most likely perpetrator, so I acted on the facts available to me. I am sorry that I hurt and frightened her, but nothing matters more to me than the Tantors. Will you talk to her, Goma? She won't hear a word from me, and if I'm honest with myself I really don't blame her. But she might come round if you explain why I acted as I did."

"What do you want—her friendship?"

"Yours, mainly. But if I've hurt Ru, that hurts you as well."

They sipped their chai. The sounds of the ship surrounded

them, noises that must have been as soothing and familiar to Eunice as the snap of rigging to the mariners of an earlier age. She had been aboard a lot of ships, and done her share of spacefaring.

"Why would my friendship matter to you? You lived alone with the Tantors for two hundred years. Haven't you reached the point where you don't need to be around people any more?"

"Most I can do without, but not all."

Despite herself—knowing it would be unwise to take any of Eunice's pronouncements at face value—Goma could not help but feel a flush of pride. It was a good feeling to be needed by another being, even a robot made human. "So I'm the lucky exception?" she dared ask.

"I've become something strange, Goma. Even I can see that. There's no precedent for what I am. Do I even have the right to call myself Eunice Akinya? I look like her, I have a head full of her memories . . . Except they're not quite her memories, and I know that the real woman died centuries ago. So what does that make me? A very good likeness—walking photograph? But I live and I breathe, I sleep and I dream. There's blood in my veins and your physician said I have the capability to give birth. So what the hell does that make me?"

"I don't know. Something old. Something new."

"Something borrowed. Something blue." After a silence, Eunice added, "You are the real thing, Goma. You can trace your lineage all the way back to the true Eunice—through Ndege, Chiku, Sunday, Miriam . . . How does that feel? What's it like to have that story threaded through your mitochondria?"

"It feels like being me."

"I wish I knew what that was like."

"I can't help you," Goma said, not without regret. "I never knew Eunice. I never even knew anyone who knew her. It's just too long ago. If you want me to say that you're her—"

"I am not expecting that."

"But you want affirmation of some kind—you want to feel you have some claim on her."

"Do you blame me for that?"

"Knowing what you are, what you've become? No, not in

the slightest. But you don't need my validation, Eunice. You've earned the right to simply be yourself, whoever that may be. What you did for the Tantors, across all those years—on the holoship, on Crucible, here in this system—and the choice you made to go with the Watchkeepers—any one of those deeds measures up to anything she did."

"She would not thank you for saying that."

"She can go and screw herself. You're here and she isn't." Goma reached into her pocket. "I have the other two notebooks. Would you like them?"

"I would. More than anything."

Goma passed them over. "I hope they make more sense to you than they did to me."

"It was the work of years for Ndege to make these connections," Eunice said, opening the second book so carefully it was as if she expected insects to come fluttering out of its pages. "You can't judge yourself if you've found it hard to follow in her footsteps. But you would, given time."

"You think so?"

"Oh yes. I have faith in you, Goma Akinya."

In the morning, Vasin gathered her crew in the commons around a circular table that also doubled as their largest display.

"It's time to consider our next move. We're still tracking Kanu's ship—the Chibesa signature is clean and steady, and we have radar and optical returns from the body of the vehicle. He could be throwing us some intentional misdirection, but I don't think there can be much doubt as to his destination." She turned to look at Goma. "Do you agree?"

"I have no special insight into this man just because we share a name."

"Nonetheless, if you were him—"

"She's not," Eunice said, "and on the basis of those transmissions, we'd be wise to assume that Kanu is acting under duress. Show me his course so far."

It was a bright filament curling away from *Zanzibar*, like a hair trapped in the display. Vasin was correct—there was not nearly enough of it to allow an accurate extrapolation but the goal appeared to be Poseidon, and nothing contradicted that yet. "We don't know enough about his ship to make any really detailed predictions," Vasin said. "Aiyana is coordinating with Nasim on an analysis of the exhaust signature, which may give us a little more insight. In the meantime, the best we can do is make some educated guesses. He's maintaining one gee at the moment, but he'll need to slow down when he approaches Poseidon, whether to assume orbit or plot a path through those moons and down into the atmosphere. I'd estimate forty to fifty hours, if his present acceleration is sustained."

"And if we alter our own course and try to get there ahead of him?" Goma asked.

"There's no way to beat him based on our present knowledge. We'll be six to twelve hours behind him under the best possible circumstances, and we're still in a better position than *Travertine*. Unless something goes seriously wrong with his plans, we can't stop him reaching Poseidon. But that doesn't mean we've exhausted our options."

"The solar collectors didn't get us very far," Ru said.

"We're not done with them yet. Clearly, cutting power didn't hurt Dakota as much as we'd hoped, but there are other possibilities—and Eunice still has a direct channel to the mirrors."

"For the moment," Eunice said. "But there's data traffic to and from the other ship. Someone is having a good go at locking me out."

"Will they succeed?" Vasin asked.

"Not if I stay one step ahead of them."

"Make it two steps. We need all the advantages we can get. I'm not yet ready to use the mirrors in an offensive capacity, but I want that card in my hand when it's needed."

"And when do we abandon negotiation and start hitting each other with increasingly large sticks?" Ru said.

"Only when we've exhausted all the other options," Vasin said. "But we're not there yet. For now, I'd like to concentrate our efforts on a maximum appeal to Kanu's better judgement. He may well be acting under duress, but that doesn't mean he can't resist Dakota if we give him sufficient encouragement."

Ru looked sceptical. "Good luck with that."

Vasin smiled tightly. "Goma—I propose that you be our main spokesperson from now on given the family connection, distant as it may prove to be. Eunice—do you have anything to contribute? You know Dakota better than any of us, presuming she's still alive."

"After all the history between us, I'm the last person she'll listen to. But Goma stands a chance of getting through to her. Make her remember Ndege—play on her conscience."

"You think she has one left?" Vasin asked.

"We all had a conscience when we arrived," Eunice said. "Even me."

Over a span of hours, *Mposi* adjusted its trajectory. The alteration in their course was far too gradual to be perceptible to any of the crew, save for the shift in the position of the stars through the lander's unshuttered windows. Paladin had been their previous objective; now it was displaced to one side, replaced by the blue crescent of Poseidon swinging close around Gliese 163. *Icebreaker* had maintained one gee all the while.

"Kanu," Goma said, staring into the recording lens, "we see you moving. We have a fix on your ship and we believe you know your objective. I'm Goma, by the way. Gandhari already mentioned me, but I'll say a little more about myself. I'm Ndege's daughter, and my grandmother was Chiku Green. If I'm right, you must be my half-uncle, or one-third-uncle. I believe you were born to Chiku Yellow, back on Earth—at least, there's a Kanu in the family tree who bears a distinct resemblance to you. That would make you Mposi's brother—or half- or one-third-brother, depending how you want to cut it. Mposi was my uncle, and we both lived on Crucible. I knew him well, and he sometimes spoke of you—he liked to think you were living a much less complicated life than he was. If you've come here in response to the message about Ndege, then presumably you know of her as well. She was Mposi's sister, my mother, and she was too old to come with us when we left Crucible."

Goma paused and drew breath. What she had to speak of next was hard, a truth she had yet to fully internalise.

"My mother is dead now—she died while I was crossing

interstellar space to this system. But I am here instead—trying to be where she could not, trying to stand in her place. Kanu, I have to tell you about Uncle Mposi. He died—was murdered. But first I need a reply from you, to confirm that you can hear this."

Icebreaker's position relative to *Mposi* dictated a four-minute time lag for round-trip communications, although that figure was decreasing as the gap between the ships narrowed. Five minutes passed, then six. Kanu had already stated his case—it was entirely possible that he would decline any further contact.

Goma was just starting to resign herself to the fact—and wondering how it would shape Vasin's tactical decisions—when his response arrived. She studied his image, measuring it against her own idea of Akinya faces. He was one of them, without a doubt.

An older man, his face carried the unmistakable signatures of aquatic modification, notably a flattened nose and large, dark eyes that were almost seal-like. His hair was short, bristly and mostly white. He had a strong jaw and an even stronger neck, flaring out to merge into the broad musculature of his shoulders. His face was handsome, dignified—but in his expression there was also a world of worry and sadness, more than anyone ought to be made to bear.

"Thank you for your communication, Goma," he said. "As you observe, we're still on our way. Our drive flame must be very obvious to you so I won't pretend that our goal is anything other than Poseidon. I know you have concerns about our expedition—so do we. But the truth is, we have no choice but to continue. Dakota has allowed me to speak freely of the conditions under which we're travelling so that there need be no misunderstandings. It is paramount to her that she fulfil the Watchkeepers' needs, and we are obliged to cooperate with her agenda. That said, we also came here to gather information—to find answers to questions. If cooperation with Dakota is the key to unlocking the secrets of the M-builders and the Watchkeepers, it does not feel like too great a price to pay. Sooner or later we must face our ignorance—it may as well be now. But I understand your fears." His handsome, familiar face softened. "May I say that I am sorry to hear about Ndege? I never knew her, but we knew of each other, and it always pleased me to think of my distant one-third-sister sharing a new world with Mposi. I am sorry that she could not be here with you, Goma. But you mention that Mposi is also dead, and you speak as if you knew each other well. May I hear more about him?"

Goma answered, "I'll speak of Mposi. It's hard, but I'll do it. But I'd like to talk to Dakota, too, if that's possible. Tell her I am Ndege's daughter, and that I worked to help the Tantors. Tell her that I stand for Ndege—I am here because my mother could not be. Tell her also that I have helped bury two Risen, Sadalmelik and Achernar. I was with them as they passed into the Remembering. Will you do that for me, Kanu?"

The delay was almost unendurably long this time, and Goma was halfway to convincing herself that the window of communication had closed—that she had gambled too much on the mere fact of being Ndege's offspring.

But Kanu responded, "Dakota will speak with you but not negotiate, because there is nothing to be negotiated. You have soured the terms of engagement with that little trick with the mirrors. But she still wishes to clarify her intentions—and to urge your continued non-interference." Irritation showed on his face. "This time lag is a nuisance to us all—it would be so much simpler if we could talk directly. I suppose you are too young to carry the necessary neural machinery for chinging?"

Goma looked at Vasin, unsure of Kanu's meaning.

"Virtual telepresence. 'Virching,' or 'chinging,' in one of the old pre-Babel languages. At a deep enough level of neural management, time lag can be edited out of your perceptual stream. But I haven't heard anyone speak of such a thing for at least a century. It's irrelevant. Even if Kanu still has the implants, you don't. There's no way to inhabit a shared consensual space if only one of you has the neuromachinery."

"We could meet him halfway, though," Eunice said. "One of your spacesuits will give Goma the immersive experience she needs, even if we can't turn off her consciousness."

"There's a better way?" Loring said. "But we will need a little time to prepare for it. Tell Kanu that we are ready to arrange a meeting in a consensual space—Kanu's free to set the parameters?"

"But I don't have the implants," Goma said.

"You won't need them—not for this."

Goma understood what they had in mind when they opened the door.

"No."

But Vasin placed a hand on her shoulder. "Aiyana says it's safe. What went wrong before can't happen again."

"My word on this," Loring said, offering ver own hand to Goma. "I've dug into the deep architecture—locked in additional safeguards against rogue replication? Hard for you, I know. But if we want dialogue with Kanu, no other options."

"Not until we're closer," Vasin said, "and I'd much rather not wait until then."

The well stood before her. It had been altered from its usual default display configuration, no longer containing the figments of Gliese 163 and its clutch of worlds. Now the well appeared to be full of a semi-translucent pale gold syrup, like a very fine honey.

"Doctor Andisa tells me," Vasin said, "that if one of us suffered a severe accident, we would have used the well as an emergency life-support medium. That's one of its basic utilities."

"Burns, chemical exposure, vacuum, radiation contamination," Andisa said. "The nanomachinery in the well can adjust to provide a recuperative support medium for all of these injuries. Fortunately, we've not needed to use it until now."

"I am not injured," Goma stated, as if this needed to be spelled out.

"But the support medium can also help us in other ways," Andisa said. "Had you been severely injured, the medium would allow us to address and access neural functions directly by infiltrating your central nervous system. It is programmed to do that, and the process is quite painless, if a little disorientating. Mainly, though, it will permit us to duplicate the basic protocols of ching." Andisa looked at her colleague, the physicist. "Aiyana and I have completed the tests."

"You mean you've put yourselves in it?" This was Ru, asking over Goma's shoulder.

"No time for that?" Loring said. "Infiltration and adjustment process takes several hours. Medium needs to work its way across the blood-brain barrier into deep brain structure? Best not to delay Goma's immersion?"

"Try it on me first, in that case," Ru said.

"It'll waste just as much time as trying it on myself or Andisa. Besides, your own nervous system is, shall we say, somewhat atypical?"

"You mean it's screwed up."

"Trying to think of a nice way to put it?"

"Mine's also atypical," Eunice said, "so you'd better hope it works for me as well."

"It would not be any quicker for you," Vasin said.

"I know, and I'm not proposing that I go instead of Goma. But that well is easily big enough for two of us. At the very least she shouldn't have to face this on her own."

"Establishing parallel interfaces? Going to be challenging—" Loring began.

"Then you'd better get started," Eunice said.

Goma's throat was tight with apprehension. "How? When?"

"As soon as you're ready," Loring said. "The less encumbered you are, the better the proprioceptive immersion? But you need only strip down to your underwear."

"How do we breathe?" Eunice asked.

"The medium's fully capable of supporting respiratory function, but you may find the transition uncomfortable?" Loring began to open a sealed sterile container. "We have breather masks—they'll fit over your mouth and nose, provide an airtight seal? You'll still be able to speak."

"The masks sound clumsy to me."

Ru glared at Eunice. "No one asked you."

"No," Goma said. "She's right. All or nothing. Forget the masks, Aiyana. I can do this."

Goma shed her outer layers of clothing, eyeing Eunice as she stripped down to a similar state of undress. Vasin gathered their clothes in two neat bundles. Goma believed Loring—the well had been made safe. Even if it malfunctioned, she was neither alone nor as helpless as Mposi had been. No harm could come to her. But it was impossible to rid herself of the feeling that the amber fluid still contained traces of him.

"I'll go first," Eunice said. "Wait until I'm fully immersed, breathing the fluid, before you join me. If there's anything wrong with it, we'll know soon enough."

"I should go first," Goma said.

"Age has its privileges, dear."

Eunice stepped over the rim of the well, pushed a foot into the medium—watching as it resisted and then yielded, behaving less like a fluid than a membrane. Once her foot reached the base of the well, she risked planting the other one beside it.

"It's all right. Warm, cloying, but no ill-effects. Yet."

Eunice lowered herself slowly down onto her rump, knees bent against her chest. She maintained this position for a few seconds then began to stretch her legs out to their full extent. At the same time she allowed her arms to descend into the medium. Only her head and upper torso were not yet immersed.

"In for a penny."

She submerged herself. They could see her through the medium, blurred but still distinct. Her mouth was closed but her eyes open. She stayed like that for a few seconds then gaped her mouth wide. As the fluid pushed into her she released a few bubbles of air—human air, from human lungs—and gave a sharp but controlled twitch. Then she was still. They studied the rise and fall of her chest. She did not appear to be in distress, but then again this was Eunice. Her eyes remained open, oddly unblinking. She allowed a hand to rise above the surface, gloved with a clinging epidermis of the amber medium, and shaped her thumb and forefinger into an "O."

"She's all right," Dr. Andisa said. "It'll be a while before we can communicate directly, but she's going to be fine. You next, Goma."

She made to move to the well, intending to follow suit, but Ru clutched her arm.

"Are you sure about this?"

"Not really."

But Goma kissed Ru and allowed herself to slip from her grasp. Then she stepped into the well, one foot at a time. It was warm, as Eunice had said—the sensation was akin to pushing through jelly, the substance resistant at first, then yielding easily and obligingly to her movement. Less like being immersed in a liquid than pushing into a multitudinous crowd of tiny and obligingly helpful creatures. There was no sense of it doing her harm, no tingling or unpleasantness. She sat down and stretched out her legs. Then she lowered most of herself into the medium, side by side with Eunice.

Now came the hard part. She dropped her head below the level of the medium, feeling it slither over her chin, nose, eyes and forehead. She blinked as she descended, but once submerged she forced her eyes open. She felt an odd slithering coldness around her eyeballs, then nothing. She could still see, albeit through the golden tint of the medium. Her ears made a gurgling rush. Then a roaring silence.

She opened her mouth.

It was in her, and for an instant she thought she could bear it. But two terrors hit simultaneously. The first was that she was drowning, and the reflex to fight against this was as strong as any she had known. The second was that Mposi was in her mouth, in her windpipe, in her lungs—and the horror of this, the need to gag away the traces of him, was as fierce as the need to breathe.

Goma convulsed. This was not the dignified twitch Eunice had given but a full-body spasm, and she had no conscious desire other than to be out of the medium, back into air. She knew she did not have the strength in her to overcome this, not now, not ever. She had made an awful mistake—banked on a courage she did not possess. She flailed, reaching for a solid surface, a means to push herself from the well.

Eunice took her arm. There was a vicelike strength in her grip. She was holding her down, preventing her from surfacing.

Until Goma could hold her breath no longer.

CHAPTER 40

By the time the women joined him, Kanu had fashioned the parameters of their meeting place. He had needed a lot of help from Swift for that. There was information in his memories and data in *Icebreaker*'s files, but stitching the two together, forging a place that was simultaneously familiar, neutral and aesthetically satisfying to all parties including the elephants, and doing it in much less than a lifetime, would have been quite beyond his abilities.

He drew on the Akinya household as his template. Swift had direct knowledge of the replica of the building on *Zanzibar*, and Kanu also carried his own experiences of the real structure, albeit in the faded decay of its later years. From these threads, Swift concocted a three-dimensional environment, programming it directly into *Icebreaker* with all the embellishments necessary for the time-honoured protocols of ching. He did all this right under Dakota's nose, puppeteering Kanu—letting her think Kanu was the true architect.

The result was limited in its scope, spartan in its details, and its solid facades hinted at depths it did not contain. It had the shimmering, dreamlike quality of a fondly remembered place rather than an actual location, with dirt and dust and cracks.

It would have to suffice.

Kanu and Nissa both possessed legacy neuromachinery, which Swift was already using to speak to both of them. Dakota was slightly more problematic. The Tantor had no implants, but thankfully her external prosthetic communication aids were easily adapted to meet the needs of the exchange. Her human voice had always been machine-generated, so it was an easy matter to add earphones and goggles to allow her to participate in the environment.

Now Kanu, Nissa and Dakota awaited their guests. They were sitting within the enclosure of the household's A-shaped geometry, in the triangular courtyard framed by the two main wings and the connecting bar between them. Within the courtyard lay a pond, some fountains, a series of layered terraces, a handful of marble statues. There were small trees and bushes, and the sky above them was the cloudless pink of late afternoon. The two humans sat on stone chairs positioned around a low stone table. The Tantor rested her haunches on a stone pedestal, tail draping the ground, a repose of perfect scholarly contentment.

"They're late," said the elephant.

"They warned us there might be technical difficulties," Nissa said.

"We shan't wait much longer. I already warned you that I have no interest in negotiation."

"And I made sure to tell them," Kanu said. "But it's also in your interests to convince them to leave us alone. You don't want a confrontation if you can avoid it, do you?"

"There would be no confrontation—only the nuisance value of them being close behind us." Dakota swivelled her huge tank-turret of a head. In this environment, she carried no prosthetic enhancements and her speaking voice appeared to emanate from her mouth rather than a piece of machinery fixed between her eyes. "You did well with this, Kanu—especially given the limited time you had at your disposal. I remember the household well enough to vouch for its accuracy."

"It's a combination of the one aboard *Zanzibar* and my memories of the one on Earth."

"I'm still impressed that you were able to construct this environment as quickly as you did. Are you surprised, Nissa?"

"It takes a lot to surprise me these days."

Dakota signalled her agreement, head descending like the nodding counterweight of some huge steam-driven pump. "I never doubted your capabilities, Kanu, after all that you have done for me, but this is still a formidable achievement."

"Well, I've had practice. On Mars we often spent our

downtime playing with virtual spaces. The ambassadors were all old enough to carry the requisite neural technology."

Swift bent over to whisper in Kanu's ear. "Incoming packets—clean and ching-compliant. Best not to answer me—it's safe for me to talk to you, but this environment is so merrily slapdash I can't swear that your subvocal intentions won't be picked up."

"Here they are," Nissa said, shooting a glare at Swift, who did the decent thing and returned to being one of the statues.

The two women appeared out of thin air on the lowest part of the terrace. One was small, the other not much taller. For a second or two they looked thoroughly unsettled, like two fish that had fallen out of the sky. The smaller of the two was Eunice, Kanu decided instantly—he would have recognised her from Sunday's emulation were her face not already known to him from a thousand historical records. The other woman he now knew to be Goma—Mposi's niece. Mposi was his one-third-brother, so what did that make Goma? His one-third-niece-once-removed? Or did the common language of family ties simply collapse in the face of Akinya profligacy?

Both were thin, hair cut short, their clothing modest but casual—black or ash-grey trousers, loosely belted slash-necked tunics, low-heeled slip-on shoes. Neither wore conspicuous ornamentation or jewellery, although he noticed a ring on the younger woman's fingers.

He raised a hand in greeting. "Welcome aboard *Icebreaker*. A few words of explanation before we go on—this environment will do its best to eliminate time lag by anticipating our responses and stalling our conscious processes while signals pass between our two vehicles. But the less strain we place on it, the easier it will be for Dakota—she'll be experiencing everything in strict real-time. I suggest we consider our interruptions very carefully and try to speak as clearly and unambiguously as we can?"

"We'll do our best," Eunice said. She nodded at the other woman and they made their way up the terrace steps to the area where their hosts were already seated. Eunice and Goma took their places on the other side of the low stone table. Both of them sat with their backs straight, heads held high.

"You have to stop what you're doing," Goma said.

Kanu smiled, charmed by her bluntness. It cut across a life's worth of diplomatic training to state her position so nakedly, so early in the process. He continued smiling, assuming there would be some elaboration.

But after a few moments' silence, he concluded she had said all she meant to say.

"Goma is correct," Eunice said, patting the other woman's knee by way of mutual support. "You're on the wrong course, Dakota—and you, Kanu, have been very unwise to get yourself tangled up in her plans. Who are *you*, by the way?" She was looking at Nissa now. "I don't think we've been properly introduced."

"Nissa Mbaye. I was married to Kanu, once upon a time. Things happened to us and now we're here. But you're wrong about us. Or rather, if anyone's to blame for this, it's you. We came in response to your message—your summons. And if you'd warned us in time, we wouldn't have run into trouble around Poseidon."

"Trouble you are about to repeat," Goma said.

"We're better equipped this time," Kanu answered. "It wasn't Poseidon that damaged us, it was the remains of a Watchkeeper. All we have to do is steer clear of their corpses and it won't happen again."

"I admire an optimist," Eunice said. "My guess, though, is that you haven't been properly informed about the stakes. Dakota and I both know what's involved, don't we? We both experienced the Terror."

"A deterrent," Dakota said. "A keep-out sign, nothing more. But if we heeded all the keep-out signs, where would we be?"

"Safe," Goma said.

"Tell that to your ancestor. She never did a safe thing in her life. How are you, by the way, Eunice? You look well, rested. Orison has been kind to you. I knew I did the right thing by not killing you."

"I might be about to change your mind on that one."

"Well, we do have some bridges to build, do we not? I presume you supplied the technical expertise to gain control of my mirrors, for the little good it did you? But, Goma—I'm equally intrigued by what you said. You mentioned Tantors to Kanu. We call ourselves the Risen, but I shan't split hairs over a matter of definition. Have you met my kind before?"

"I met Sadalmelik, Achernar and the others on Orison. But none of them was like you."

"You find me distinct?"

"You're smarter. There's no point in denying it. Or perhaps you're more like us. Either way, you're something new." Goma held up a hand before Dakota could interject—she was not done. "But not in a good way. My mother knew you on Crucible and you were not like this."

"You fear me because I am something outside your immediate experience? Because I have dared to escape from your control—to achieve true autonomy?"

"That would be wonderful if you'd done it on your own. But whatever you've become, it's because the Watchkeepers want you this way. You're not their slave, you're not even their puppet—even I can tell that you have some sort of free will. But they've seeded a very bad idea in you, and you're so close to it you can't see how bad it really is."

"You would frame mere curiosity as an unhealthy, even dangerous impulse?"

"The point here isn't for you to talk us out of anything," Kanu told the visitors. "Our mission is fixed—we cannot and will not abandon it. But you can spare yourselves pointless aggravation and risk by turning away from your interception course. You will not catch us—we both have a good grasp of our mutual capabilities—so why waste time going through the motions? There's far too much at stake. Back off, continue your remote investigations, restore external power to *Zanzibar* and let us conduct our exploration of Poseidon. Later, we can discuss terms for cooperative exploration of the whole system—but only after we've returned from Poseidon."

"Something's really put a bee in your bonnet, hasn't it?" said Eunice.

"He's being coerced," Goma said. "We guessed as much. Why don't you just admit it, Kanu? And you, Nissa—what have you got to lose?"

"There is no coercion," Kanu stated.

"In your earlier message to us," Goma said, "you warned us that lives are at stake. You said you have 'no choice' but to comply."

"Your lives will be at stake if you place yourselves at risk of collision, or stray too close to Poseidon without a proper understanding of the consequences," Kanu answered.

"That's not what you meant," Eunice said.

"There is no point in debating this further," Dakota said. "Our objective is simple: scientific truth-gathering. If it takes a human-Risen cooperative expedition to unlock some of the secrets of the M-builders, so be it. We can't spend the rest of history failing to understand the Mandalas and what they meant to their makers. We've both been through the Terror, Eunice and I—both of us sensed larger truths, almost glimpsed, leaking through into the prison of animal consciousnesses. The collapse of the vacuum? The fluctuation that ends everything, that negates every act, every thought? How can we bear *not* to know how the M-builders addressed that truth? Besides, we may also learn something of the Watchkeepers—and hopefully find out what they want of us."

"No one disputes any of that," Goma said. "We're all here because of the quest for deeper understanding. But rushing into it is as bad as burying your head in the sand. We've barely begun to map this system, let alone poke our noses into its deepest secrets."

"Speak for yourself," Dakota said. "Some of us have been here for centuries."

"So have I," Eunice said, "and I'm still inclined to be cautious. We could easily spend another century here, gathering information, before attempting close exploration of Poseidon."

"And be no more confident of success after all that time," the Tantor said.

Eunice leaned forward. "You sound very confident of your position, Dakota. I'm pleased. Confidence is a marker for intelligence—it shows that you have sufficient self-awareness to model the parameters of your environment. But it's also a hazard. There's far too much that we don't know about our surroundings." Her eyes narrowed to a sharp, inquisitorial focus. "The variations in the second Mandala—have you been studying them?"

"I could hardly be unaware of them, Eunice."

"Your interpretation, then?"

"The changes were precipitated by the arrival of *Zanzibar*. Beyond that, we have no basis for further speculation."

"I do," Eunice said.

"Anyone could make such a claim," Dakota answered.

Kanu nodded. "You'll have to give us more than that, Eunice."

"I shall. The way I was left on Orison made it very difficult for me to conduct long-range studies of anything, let alone the Mandala on Paladin. But Goma's ship—*Travertine*—has the sensor capability I lacked. They've been tracking the Mandala variations since their arrival. The exact meaning of the individual states isn't clear to us—yet—but at least we understand the timing of the variations. Mandala is an eye, sweeping across the heavens. Once in a while, its gaze chances upon another star."

"Mandala is at a fixed latitude," Dakota said, "and Paladin's angular tilt only changes on timescales of tens of thousands of years. At best, this eye can only ever sweep a narrow track."

"That's true, to a point. But the state changes appear to be related to an alteration in the direction of the eye's gaze. It's like a radio telescope built into the bowl of a valley. You can't move the primary mirror, but you can adjust the position of the antenna. We think that's how the Mandala works. It can sweep a broader swathe of sky, direct its gaze onto objects that aren't along its precise line of sight."

"That's supposition," Dakota said.

"I had two of *Travertine*'s technical experts take a close look at the timing of the state changes and their corresponding angular projection onto the sky. Within a fixed error margin, the focus is always another star of a broadly similar spectral type to Gliese 163, within a distance of a few hundred light-years."

"What does that prove?" Nissa asked. "Look hard enough, you'll find any alignment you want. It's like drawing lines between pyramids."

"But the statistical odds against these alignments being chance is actually rather high according to our experts—about one in twenty thousand, if I understand the analysis. Shall I tell you what I think is happening?" But she glanced quickly at Goma. "What *we* think?"

"We may as well hear it, as you're here," Kanu said.

"The Mandala on Paladin is communicating with other Mandalas in other solar systems. It is sending them wake-up signals—telling them to begin rebooting."

"Rebooting," Nissa said. "I don't know that term."

"Old spacefaring terminology. It means to put your boots on—to start getting ready for business."

"I see," she said, nodding doubtfully. "And what exactly is it that is 'rebooting'?"

"It's a machine," Goma said. "A machine hundreds, maybe thousands of light-years across. It's been dead, dormant, for longer than we can imagine, thousands, millions of years, at least. But my mother restarted it. Crucible was a peripheral branch of the Mandala network—an outlying system, a dead end. Ndege's Mandala sent its wake-up signal to this one and transported *Zanzibar* here during the same event, probably because *Zanzibar* just happened to get caught up in the initial reactivation process. But this system isn't a dead end. It's a node, a hub, in some wider network. There may be others, but this must be the closest one to our part of the galaxy. It's what the Watchkeepers have been drawn to all this time. They know it's significant—they just can't advance their knowledge beyond that."

"A machine wouldn't take this long to start up," Kanu said.

"It could if its basic components are still light-limited," Eunice replied. "Depending on how far out the furthest parts of the network are, it might take tens of thousands of years for the whole thing to come back online. Signals whispering across the void—start-up instructions, error correction, status reporting. A process longer than the span of recorded history. But that's what's happening. And on a local scale, it may already be partly operable."

"Operable," Kanu said, almost laughing. "As if it's a thing we might use?"

"Why not?" Eunice said. "The Risen are here because of it. Instead of barging to Poseidon, we should be consolidating our efforts, trying to understand how to make safe use of the

Mandala network. We know from the survivors that the *Zanzibar* translation was instantaneous within their reference frame, which means they must have been travelling at only a whisker below the speed of light. Consequently, any other part of the network is also only a blink away in subjective terms. Deep exploration of the galaxy is within our grasp—and you're risking all that for the agenda of a bunch of mindless alien robots?"

"Why do you say mindless?" Dakota asked.

"We all felt it," Eunice replied, "from the moment the Trinity made direct contact with the Watchkeepers. There's nothing inside them. They're hollow—scooped out like an ice-cream cone. They've forgotten how to be conscious. Or are you in some sort of denial about this? Does it not worry you that you might be the willing servant of a zombie machine intelligence?"

"They've passed the Gupta-Wing threshold," Nissa said. "Is that what you mean?"

"At least one of you has a grasp on things," Eunice said, miming applause. "Perhaps I should be addressing you, Nissa—are you the one I should be reaching out to?"

"I am afraid we must curtail this discussion," Dakota said, rising from her seat—more nimble than any elephant had a right to be. "The time lag has consumed valuable hours."

"We've barely begun!" Goma said.

"It's been six hours," Kanu said. "I'm sorry, but I think we've said all we can. We're not adversaries, any of us, but we are on different paths. You have your concerns, we have ours—but that doesn't mean we can't work together when we return from Poseidon."

"It's going to kill you," Eunice said. "Dakota knows that—whether she admits it to herself or not. If you have a chance of turning away from this, I strongly recommend that you do so."

She might have been on the point of saying something else, but before she had a chance her figment vanished from the environment. Goma was gone as well, their stone seats vacated.

Kanu expected to be snapped back into the normal timeflow of *Icebreaker*, no longer in ching. But Dakota turned her huge broad forehead to face him. "We have a measure of

privacy here so we might as well use it. The younger human—
Goma. What did she mean when she spoke of your 'earlier
message'?"

"You've monitored all the transmissions between the two
ships," Nissa said.

"But she appeared to be referring to a conversation I do not
know about. The mention of coercion, of lives being at stake—
how could she know about the Friends, Kanu, unless you told
her?"

"Eunice would have told them."

"Eunice knows nothing of what has happened in any part
of *Zanzibar* since her departure. This was specific, directed
knowledge. How could either of them make such a deductive
leap?"

"It's what we do," Nissa said. "Being humans."

"You think highly of your faculties. I don't blame you for
that. But it would be a mistake to underestimate me. If there
was communication between *Icebreaker* and *Travertine* ahead
of the exchanges I know about—or in parallel with them—I
would very much like to know. What was discussed? What
was considered, then abandoned?"

"Nothing," Kanu said. "There was no communication."

The Watchkeeper came in so swiftly that they had only a couple of hours to prepare for its arrival. It must have been among
the gathering of alien machines on the system's edge, waiting
beyond the orbit of Paladin until *Icebreaker*'s movement
snared its interest. For a little while, as it closed in with dis-
dainful swiftness, it looked inevitable to Kanu that there
would be a collision, or something just as catastrophic. This
was nothing at all like the patient, inscrutable comings and
goings of the Watchkeepers in the old system.

"It's not been damaged like the others," he said as they
studied the sharpening images on the bridge—the Watchkeeper rendered as a stubby cone sidling in at a definite angle
to its velocity vector.

"Of course not," Dakota chided. "The corpses are as old as
your hominid forebears. It has been aeons since a Watchkeeper was unwise enough to chance a close encounter with

Poseidon; aeons since one of them was harmed. They learn slowly, but they do learn. You are quite wrong about the alien consciousness, by the way. It may be slower than you can perceive, but that does not mean it is absent. The machines have learned that the endurance of cosmological time demands no swift actions, no hasty measures."

"This looks pretty hasty to me," Nissa said.

"An exception, because human activity is itself exceptional, especially when such activity is directed towards Poseidon. You would have drawn their attention sooner or later, even without that unfortunate accident. This movement, though, must be of particular interest to them—it originates with *Zanzibar*."

"They think you're involved," Nissa said.

"And that pleases them. These centuries are long to us. They swallow our lives as a whale swallows water. But they are merely a breath to the Watchkeepers—a moment between their great, slow thoughts. From their perspective, *Zanzibar* arrived a few busy instants ago."

The image shivered, gaining a new layer of detail.

"What should we do?" Kanu asked.

"Maintain our heading. Make no change. If it meant to stop us, it would already have done so. This is curiosity, concern, encouragement. It shares our desire to unravel the secrets of Poseidon."

"Oh, I'm just bursting with curiosity," Nissa said.

Kanu acknowledged that with a thin smile.

It came in closer still, slowly adjusting the angle of its course until its body was both parallel to *Icebreaker* and moving in the same direction. They were halfway along its length, with hundreds of kilometres of it to bow and stern. The nearest point was two hundred kilometres away, but in the airlessness of space where cues of distance and perspective were elusive, the Watchkeeper appeared to be dismayingly near. They had been closer to the corpse, but this one was very much alive. Blue radiance fought its way out between the close-layered scales of the Watchkeeper's pine-cone armour.

Now something changed. The scales were angling apart, allowing more of that light to escape. It fanned out in hard

blue arcs, sweeping across *Icebreaker*. They saw it on screens
and sensors—had there been windows, the glare would have
been too bright to tolerate.

"Have we seen this before?" Nissa asked.

"I don't think so," Kanu said, offering a shrug by way of
incomprehension.

"They will speak to me," Dakota said, with sudden deci-
siveness. "Reduce our thrust to zero. I will go out to them."

"In *Noah*?"

"On my own. I will make dung, then you will assist me
with the suit and the airlock. I will not be outside for long."

They put *Icebreaker* into a free-fall cruise and followed
Dakota to the main airlock, where she had first come aboard.
Her suit was waiting there, partially dismantled—its hard,
curving sections looked more like the pieces of a small white
spacecraft than something meant to be worn. The parts
clamped around her and locked together with airtight precision, first the two Easter-egg halves of the body, then the four
limb sections, complexly jointed and accordioned, and finally
the monstrous trunked helmet with its two blank circular portholes for eyes. There was something horrible about the life-
lessness of that helmet, as if a second, exterior skull now
enclosed the first. She flexed the trunk, experimenting with its
dexterity, while the suit's life-support system puffed and
wheezed and ticked.

Her voice, amplified and resonant, boomed through the
suit's speaking system. "The others remain here, Kanu, and
they have their orders with regard to *Zanzibar*. You would not
be so unwise as to forget that, would you?"

"No, I think we understand the situation perfectly."

"That is good, because our conversation with Goma gave
me some small grounds for concern. It will be good to know
that I may put them to rest."

"How will you move outside?" Nissa asked.

"Let me worry about that. If you wish to witness, no harm
will come of it."

She moved easily into the lock and the cycle was soon complete. Kanu had stopped the engines by then—it would make
a small difference to their arrival at Poseidon, but nothing that

would seriously complicate their plans—and Dakota was able to drift free of the ship without being left behind.

It turned out that her suit, which they had not been able to inspect in detail, was fitted with a set of steering thrusters arranged for three axes of control. She looked perfectly at ease with this technology, directing it with a tap of her trunk against a control plate fixed between her shoulders. Kanu reminded himself that this extra-vehicular equipment must have been developed during that brief and hopeful period when humans and Tantors had coexisted within *Zanzibar*. The sense of squandered possibility, of better paths now lost to them all, filled him with a sudden rising sadness. He wondered if it was too late to make something better of their world.

Dakota picked up speed. It was an exceedingly odd thing to see an elephant in a spacesuit. But to an elephant, a monkey in a suit must have looked no stranger, no more of an affront to the expected order of things. They were both mammals, both creatures who needed air in their lungs.

She diminished, becoming a small white sphere with appendages, then a dot soon lost against the scale of the Watchkeeper. They tracked the electronic signature of her suit with *Icebreaker*'s instruments, and then quite suddenly she was moving in a way that could not be explained by the capabilities of her suit alone. She began to accelerate along the narrowing length of the alien machine, gathered in some net of invisible force, until at last her signature vanished into the tiny circular aperture at the Watchkeeper's tip. Tiny only in the most relative of senses, of course—the proportions of things, even at the machine's extremity, remained mountainous, and Dakota would have been swallowed into the Watchkeeper like a speck of plankton.

As they carried on watching, the platelets—each of which was easily the size of a small land mass—began to close again, eventually shuttering the blue radiation.

The better part of an hour passed.

"Do you think she'd give the order?" Nissa asked.

"To murder the Friends?" Kanu said. "I don't know. I don't know and I don't want to find out the hard way what her limits are. It could be a bluff, but in *Zanzibar* I had the feeling she might go through with it. If they've already committed murder, which we as good as know they have, there's no reason for them not to do it again."

She gave him a sidelong, questioning look. "Is that you speaking or Swift?"

"Why wouldn't it be me?"

"Because you have every incentive to find a way to back out of this. I'm not sure Swift feels quite the same way."

"Swift won't agree to anything that puts the Friends' lives at risk."

"No—but if there was a chance to turn around, without risking the Friends, would Swift accept that?"

"Why wouldn't he?"

"Because Swift's agenda and ours aren't quite the same thing."

Swift had been silent until then, but this statement was enough to draw him to speak. "I do not believe our concerns are all that different, Nissa. Aren't we all here to gather knowledge—to learn more than we already know?"

"Some of us didn't have a lot of choice about being here."

"There is truth in that, but you would not have gone to Europa were you not also in the business of seeking knowledge. Curiosity motivates us in different ways, I agree. Kanu has spent his life searching for answers to the oldest of questions: how may I live peacefully with my neighbour? On Earth, he worked to foster good relations between the distinct and troubled factions of modern humanity—between the folk of the land, the folk of the water, the folk of the air. On Mars, he quite literally gave his life for the betterment of human-machine affairs. But Kanu knew that a deeper solution to our differences required answers he could not hope to find within the old solar system. They drove him to travel here."

"Did they, Swift? Or did you drive Kanu because you needed a head to travel in?"

"Please," Kanu said. "There's nothing to be gained by this. I know why I'm here, and Swift is part of it but not the only reason. And this discussion changes nothing because we still have to think of the Friends. We can't forget about them, and we can't abandon Dakota inside the Watchkeeper and hope there'll be no consequences. I'm sorry, but going through with her expedition is the only course open to us."

"Even if it kills us?" Nissa asked.

"Yes. Even if. Because what is the alternative? To take a gamble with thousands of human lives? I'm not suicidal—not any more. But I'd rather die than have their deaths on my conscience. Nothing's worth that."

"She's coming back," Swift said.

They had a lock on her suit signature again and observed as it emerged from the narrowing waterspout-like proboscis at the very limit of the Watchkeeper's shell, a seed spat out into vacuum. At first she moved with the same implausible speed and agility they had witnessed before, until the Watchkeeper surrendered her to the steering and propulsion of her own suit and she closed the distance back to *Icebreaker*. As she did so, the Watchkeeper turned on its axis and fell away at an unnerving acceleration.

Whatever business it had with them, it was clearly concluded—for now, at least.

Kanu readied the lock and watched as Dakota slowed her approach before tucking herself back inside the ship. When the lock had begun to cycle, he returned the drive to power and resumed their earlier acceleration. Kanu and Nissa were at the lock when she emerged back into *Icebreaker*, and—with the aid of the other Risen—set about divesting herself of the suit. As they were removed from her, the pieces gave off a rank pungency. Kanu suspected that the inside of a human spacesuit would not smell all that appealing to an elephant.

"Are we back on course?"

"Yes," he answered. "We didn't lose too much time—certainly not enough to help Goma. What happened to you inside the Watchkeeper?"

"The continuation of a process. The continued revelation of that which demands to be revealed. Beyond that, I do not think any answer would satisfy you."

"You could try," Nissa said.

"Then I shall. Such doubts as I had have now been set aside. I feel emboldened—confident that this is the right course. The machines have eased my misgivings and reaffirmed my absolute conviction to the cause of knowledge-gathering. Has there been contact from the other ship?"

"Not since we spoke to them," Kanu said.

"Then you will prepare a transmission. I have no wish to stir up trouble with these people, but they must be made to understand the utter inflexibility of our position. Tell them to turn around. If they go back to Orison, there will be no more difficulties between us and we may yet find common ground. But they must come no closer to Poseidon."

"We've tried persuading them already," Nissa said. "Look where it got us."

"Words alone will not change their minds."

Kanu hardly dared ask. "So what now?"

"Tell them about the Friends. If Eunice is who she claims to be, she will validate the fact of the Friends' existence. She will also convince the others that I am fully capable of destroying each and every human life in the skipover vaults. Tell them that, Kanu. Tell them and make them turn around. We will be watching and waiting."

CHAPTER 41

Aboard *Mposi* they had seen the pause in the other ship's progress and the temporary quenching of its Chibesa signature. At first they drew some encouragement from that, hoping that it might signal a change of heart on Dakota's behalf—perhaps even a technical fault that would force her to abandon the mission. But closer examination showed the presence of a Watchkeeper, a dark-shuttered lantern a thousand times larger than Kanu's tiny spacecraft. They watched it shark in close and stop with an insolent suddenness. It held station for an hour or two, then veered off at high acceleration. Not long after the Watchkeeper departed, the Chibesa signature resumed.

They had lost a little time, but nothing that made any difference in the larger scheme.

"Eunice?" Vasin asked, as if she had all the answers.

But Eunice had nothing to offer. "You know as much as I do. If the Watchkeepers didn't think that expedition of hers was a good idea, they'd have stomped down on it."

Soon there was an incoming transmission from Kanu.

They crowded around to watch it, letting it play without interruption. Now that she had spent time in the man's presence, Goma felt she had some measure of Kanu as an individual—some sense of when he was speaking frankly, and when he was being held back from absolute candour.

Now she had no doubt that he was speaking freely.

They were to turn around, Kanu said. They were to turn around and restore full power to *Zanzibar*, and if they did not do so there would be immediate and irrevocable consequences.

"She has no weapon that can touch you," Kanu explained, "just as you have no real weapon that can hurt her—and no, the mirrors don't count. But ask Eunice about the Friends, about the survivors in the skipover vaults. Dakota has already convinced us that she'll harm the Friends if we don't cooperate with her, and that's argument enough for me. Now she's extending the same terms of engagement to you. If you don't turn around, the Friends will die."

The distance between *Mposi* and *Icebreaker*—they now knew the name of Kanu's ship—had closed to less than one light-minute now. On that basis, Kanu demanded a response to his request within three clock minutes. Both ships were fully capable of tracking the other's movements and exhaust energies—there was no possibility of subterfuge.

"Sounds like brinkmanship to me," Vasin said.

"Whatever it sounds like," Eunice replied, "he's telling the truth about the sleepers in the skipover vaults. They exist."

"You mean," Ru said, "they existed the last time you had any hard evidence."

Eunice gave a gracious nod. "That's true, and I can't prove

that the Friends are still on *Zanzibar*. But they were always a potentially useful resource to her, even if only as a human shield. Provided she had the power to keep them viable, I think she'd have done so. Besides, there is another reason to believe they're still alive."

Ru folded her arms. "Which would be?"

"Atonement. A great crime took place aboard *Zanzibar*. Don't think that hasn't left its mark on Dakota—there's a part of her that still feels, still suffers remorse."

"You're that good a judge of her character, after all this time?" Vasin asked.

"I know elephants. The past isn't the past to them."

"Then she's kept the Friends alive out of a sense of guilt, is that what you're saying?" asked Goma.

"Not guilt, precisely, more out of a deep desire to undo what was already done—to balance out a wrongness with a greater good. But that doesn't mean she won't harm the Friends if she feels there's no other alternative."

"How might she do it?" Vasin asked.

"A hundred ways. The simplest? Turn off their power. Left to warm too quickly, they'll come back to us as so much neural porridge. Trust me. I've had some experience with this."

"You were warmed too quickly," Goma said, remembering one thread of Eunice's ancient history. "But they found your body in time to recover some patterns from your head."

"They may as well have read chai-leaves. I don't think Chiku brought back anywhere near as much of me as she imagined. But she meant well by it. It encouraged me to be more than I was."

"So where does this leave us?" asked Vasin.

"Your choice, Captain," Eunice said. "Take Kanu at his word and turn around or press ahead if you think this really is brinkmanship."

"What would you do?"

"I can't say I've ever been one for turning."

If there was an argument to be mustered against Vasin, Goma was not going to be the one who took a stand. She could see the case for turning around—that to press on further was to risk retaliatory action against the Friends. But equally they had come this far with the intention of dissuading Dakota, not of giving in at the first setback.

She felt uneasy about it—as if she was allowing herself to be swept along by a rising tide of belligerence. But abandoning the pursuit felt no more desirable.

"I meant to salute your courage," Grave said, during a quiet moment while they were waiting to see how Dakota would respond to their refusal to turn back. "After what happened to Mposi, it was not an easy thing to submit to the nanomachinery."

Goma thought back to the horror of that moment, the imminent terror of drowning, the cool, calm force of Eunice restraining her under the surface of that lung-filling fluid.

Goma dredged up some false bravado. "It wasn't as bad as I thought it would be."

"It's what you feared beforehand that matters. I can't say I knew him as well as you did, but I believe he would have been suitably proud. I just wish your negotiations had brought us to a more positive state of affairs."

"So do I."

"Our captain appears to be moving towards an acceptance of force as the only solution."

Goma answered wearily, "If you have a better idea, please raise it. We've argued with them and reasoned with them. It's made no difference."

"Mposi would not have been so defeatist."

"You're right—you didn't know him as well as I did."

"I just think we're rushing into something we will not be able to undo. Gandhari will try to use the mirrors in an offensive capacity; Dakota will deliver on her promise to harm the Friends. And what will have been gained by either party except a deepening of our estrangement?"

"I get all that, Peter. I just don't see an alternative."

"We could have demonstrated our good intentions by backing off."

"And allowed Dakota a free run at Poseidon?"

"An even freer run," Grave corrected, without any censure. "In one sense, our chase is completely futile. She will get there ahead of us no matter what we do, so what is to be gained by pursuing this course of action?"

"We can't just let her do what she wants."

"But since we cannot prevent her, what are we hoping to achieve? A show of defiance?"

"Anything could happen once they approach those moons. They'll need to slow down drastically. If they run into trouble or have a malfunction, the tables might be turned."

He smiled. "Might."

"It's all we've got, Peter. You have your faith, and this is mine—that a long shot is better than no shot at all. And you forget, Dakota is a Tantor—no matter what she thinks of herself, what she's become, that makes her something marvellous to me. I want to know her mind. I want to protect it like a jewel. Nothing so precious should ever fade from the universe again."

"From what I've seen, she looks like a monster to me."

"Even monsters are beautiful," Goma said.

Dakota delivered her answer via Kanu. His face, familiar to them all now, bore the stress of recent events. Nissa, his former wife, looked on from the background, her expression no more settled than Kanu's.

"Well, you can't say you weren't warned. Dakota has sent a command back to *Zanzibar* to begin selective thawing of one hundred of the Friends. You know what this means. They'll be raised from skipover too quickly and suffer irreversible damage to their detailed brain structure. The process will take a few hours and you'll have no independent confirmation of it until the work is done, but I've spent enough time with Dakota not to doubt her conviction. The thawing has commenced. You can still turn around, and perhaps the damage won't be so bad that they can't be cooled down again and given another shot at revival. But that's your decision, and your risk. I've done what I can—I've argued our case to the best of my abilities. I hoped you'd see sense—see that there's no option but to permit us to continue alone. But you haven't, and I'm sorry."

When he was done, Vasin turned to her little assembly. "An idle threat?"

"Not given her history," Eunice said.

"Then we can assume those sleepers really are being allowed to thaw?"

"Yes."

"Do we still retain control of the mirrors?"

"Ditto."

"And her efforts to lock us out?"

"Continuing, but as yet unsuccessful. They've put up a good fight, but I know the control architecture of those mirrors better than they do, and I had a head start."

Vasin nodded solemnly. "Then we'll put that control to the test. Depriving them of power hasn't been persuasive. I want you to swing the beams back onto *Zanzibar*, but not directed at the power grids this time. Concentrate the heat on anything that might be vulnerable."

"This will not make her a happy bunny."

"We were not the first to move to violence as a negotiating tactic," Vasin said.

"We were not," Peter Grave said, "but we did refuse to listen to any of her earlier pleas, and now we're going to meet violence with violence."

"Against physical structures, not human bodies," Vasin said.

Loring steepled ver fingers and gave a sagelike nod. "Fair point."

"Our intention is to debilitate *Zanzibar*, not to harm the Tantors," Vasin went on. "If we can hurt their life-support capability, we may force them back from the brink. Reactivate the mirrors, Eunice. Let's show them that we have teeth."

Like vengeful searchlights, the mirrors' beams tightened their focus and swung back onto *Zanzibar*.

Vasin's knowledge of the former holoship was still predicated on long-range imagery and the gloss of interpretation—reliable or otherwise—offered by Eunice. Doubtless they were wrong or confused about some of the details, but at least the positions of the original solar grids were known with reasonable confidence. They were now directing the foci of the beams away from those designated collector areas onto other parts of the crust. The grids were intended to absorb the incoming energy of solar photons, soaking it into the fluid that would eventually drive the generators inside *Zanzibar*. They would grow hot—no radiation conversion process was entirely efficient—but that was compensated for in their design. But no such allowance would have been made for any of the other structural installations on the shard's surface.

Under the continued assault of three thousand kelvins of temperature, almost any mechanical system was bound to suffer catastrophic damage. Locks would be fused into slag, power ducts ruptured, berthing cradles warped out of function, insulation charred and boiled away, the very skin of *Zanzibar* turned locally molten. Volatiles trapped in the rocky matrix of the original holoship would geyser into vacuum. These actions would only damage the outer skin of the little world and the consequences might not be immediately fatal for the deeper layers—it was not Vasin's intention to blast through into the airtight cores, or to bake the inhabitants into submission. But she was hoping to do sufficient swift and severe damage that her opponents would be cowed into renegotiation, for fear of worse to come.

Even from the distance of *Mposi*, the effects of their work were soon visible. Wherever the beams touched, warm material began to haze off into the surrounding vacuum. *Zanzibar* began to resemble the husk of a warming comet stroked by sunlight. These tendrils of gas and ionised matter would eventually curdle into orbit around Paladin.

"This is Kanu," he said, when news of the attack reached *Icebreaker*. "I confess I'm surprised by the haste of your actions. Under any other circumstances we'd call this a declaration of war."

The time lag for round-trip communications was down to ninety seconds—not quite short enough for a fluent conversation, but sufficient for real-time negotiations.

"Call it what you will, Kanu," said Vasin. "Dakota was the one who began murdering innocent hostages, not us. So far we've not touched a single life—Tantor or human. You can still back down, provided you convince Dakota to give up on this expedition."

"You still don't get it, do you? You're damaging *Zanzibar*, but that won't make any difference to Dakota. You can't touch *Ice-breaker*, and whatever harm you do to *Zanzibar*'s outer structures won't have any real consequences for the Risen inside. They'll ride this out, then repair and rebuild. It's what they do—what they've always done. And in the meantime, you've only given her additional incentive to carry on warming the Friends."

"They say you were a diplomat."

"In another life."

"Were you good at diplomacy, Kanu Akinya? Were you good at finding a solution where none appeared evident?"

"No better or worse than the rest of my colleagues."

"And what became of them?"

"Most of them died. We were trying to keep a peace. I don't even know if it was worth the effort."

"It's always worth it. Our argument isn't with you, Kanu—we understand that you are acting contrary to your better judgement. But that doesn't mean you have to surrender to Dakota. Tell her I am ready to withdraw the mirrors the moment she changes course. Tell her that, in the event of a peaceful resolution, I'll commit all our resources to repairing the damage we've done. Total amnesty, no recriminations. But you must do your part, too. She's sailing into calamity, whatever you may believe to the contrary. If there's a way to stop her, you must do it."

"You forget," he said, "I've seen the Friends. I know they are real, and that they are viable for restoration to life. That changes everything, Captain Vasin. To you, they're just a number—some hypothetical dead people who may or may not get to live again. But I've glimpsed their faces. I've read their names, their histories. Seen the families among them—the mothers and fathers, the children they committed to a better future. The love they had for each other, the love they had for the Tantors. I cannot abandon them. I won't."

"You have my admiration, Kanu. You appear to be a good man. It's a pity we find ourselves at odds."

"We don't need to be. Turn off the mirrors."

"Turn around."

"No."

"And no again."

* * *

That was the end of diplomacy.

The dispersing of the bodies began soon after. They saw it on video, imaged aboard *Zanzibar*, transmitted to *Icebreaker*, bounced to *Mposi*. They could doubt the veracity of it, if they cared to, but Goma was minded to believe it was as real as it looked. There had not been time to prepare a plausible fiction, and something about the process itself—the unplanned, marginally shambolic means by which it was executed—spoke eloquently of its authenticity.

The elephants began bringing bodies to the external locks. They were the thawed dead, or perhaps not even fully thawed—it was difficult to be sure. They had been removed from their skipover caskets, the caskets too heavy and bulky to be easily moved into the locks. Upon contact with vacuum, the bodies would have quickly refrozen. *Zanzibar*'s spin meant that they fell away quickly, soon escaping beyond the immediate effects of the mirrors.

They came out in ones and twos, threes and fours—as many as could be stuffed into the locks at the same time. They tumbled out, glittering mummies, glistening starfish, the exact moment of their committal determining the trajectory they followed. They were all still in orbit around Paladin, but those orbits were fully independent of *Zanzibar* now, and some of them would, inevitably, intersect with Paladin's surface, or skirt the scorching edge of its whisper of an atmosphere, close enough to flash into a comet-tail of incandescence. They were dead already as far as their hopes of revival went, but what became of their bodies would now depend on acute contingencies of physics and timing. Some would become ash, others would spend half an eternity as ice.

They counted close to a hundred, although it was impossible to verify the exact number.

Then the dispersal stopped. There were more sleepers aboard *Zanzibar*, Eunice said—many thousands more. Dakota had made her point and must have been hoping it would prove sufficient.

Meanwhile, the mirrors continued beaming their energy onto *Zanzibar*'s surface. From the plumes of gas and their compositional spectra—the distinct tang of rare, artificially refined metals—it was clear they were inflicting significant damage to the external structures.

"Turn them off," Vasin said.

Eunice withdrew her hands from the console. "I don't need to. She just found her way into the mirrors' control architecture."

"What?"

"As of a couple of seconds ago. She's busy finding her way around—closing loopholes, sealing me out. In a minute or two she'll have complete control."

"You told us she couldn't beat you," Goma said, affronted by this sudden development.

"I was wrong. She must have remembered more about the architecture than I assumed."

"So fight back," Vasin said. "Those mirrors are the only hold we have over her."

"Excuse me, Captain, but you just told me to turn them off."

"Only while we consider our options."

"I'll lay out our options," Eunice said, joining her hands in her lap. "There aren't any. We're royally fucked. The mirrors didn't persuade Dakota to turn around or stop her throwing those sleepers out into space. How much more damage would we have to do before she has a change of heart? My guess is she'd just carry on until the skipover vaults were empty."

"She could never be that ruthless," Ru said.

"You're still thinking of her as an elephant, or a Tantor— something you can relate to. So was I, for a little while. I hoped she'd show restraint, clemency. But whatever part of her was capable of that is long gone. The Watchkeepers scooped it out and replaced it with this single overriding compulsion. Nothing will stop her. If you want proof of that, just look at those bodies."

"Then we've failed," Vasin said.

"We can't reach *Icebreaker*, and reasoned argument hasn't worked. Now she's gained control of the only instrument that stood a chance of persuading her. I'm sorry. We did our best."

"You're taking this very well," Goma said.

Eunice gave a semi-shrug. "Experience. You can fight the odds up to a point, but sooner or later you have to face reality. The universe doesn't care about temper tantrums or pity. This was our chance, and we blew it. Captain Vasin—will you turn us around?"

Vasin nodded slowly. "I don't want to—not after we've come this far. But I won't have more deaths on my conscience."

"It's the right decision," Eunice said, as if offering sympathy to the bereaved. "Hard, I know—but it's the only course open to us now. If you change our vector, Kanu will see it—there's no need to make a formal announcement."

"I'd like to, all the same, just so there's no confusion."

"If you think that's for the best," Eunice said.

Vasin made her statement. It was short, to the point. She said that there must be no more deaths. To this end, *Mposi* was abandoning its effort to reach Poseidon. As they peeled away from their present course, they would consider their options—whether to return to Orison or attempt to make diplomatic contact with the Risen on *Zanzibar*. If Dakota had an opinion, Vasin was ready to hear it.

They did not have long to wait for an answer. It was the elephant this time rather than Kanu.

"Thank you for seeing sense, Captain Vasin. I am sorry that I had to make my point so forcefully, but I think we can both agree that it was necessary to demonstrate the extent of our convictions. No, there will be no more deaths. If you wish to return to Orison, please do so. If you wish to visit *Zanzibar*, or are compelled to do so by reason of fuel or life-support demands, you will be treated well. But it will not be diplomatic contact. You have taken action against us, attempted to harm our world, and you will be regarded as prisoners of war. You have my word, though, that you will not be harmed. It was a serious tactical mistake to imagine that you could gain control of our mirrors and retain that control. Be grateful I have decided not to take punitive action for your error of judgement. Such an act would be unfair, though—the Friends cannot be blamed for your short-sightedness."

The transmission ended. Even as it played, *Mposi* had begun to change its course, opening up the distance to *Icebreaker*. The engine was at full output, sending the clearest possible signal to Kanu and Dakota.

"We took his name for the ship," Goma said, "and we screwed it up. We didn't act wisely at all."

"This is the wise act," Grave said, his tone gently reproving. "This is the thing Mposi would have been proud of—that we have the sense to know when the battle is lost. No, we haven't succeeded in the way we hoped. But we could only do our best under very difficult circumstances."

"People *died*," Goma said. "Using the mirrors ruined any chance of a peaceful discussion. How is that not a disaster?"

"Mposi would have understood that we went into this with an incomplete understanding of the facts. We had to test Dakota to see how ruthless she was prepared to be. We know that now, whereas before it was just supposition. The mirrors were a mistake—but even I dared hope we might have gained the upper hand by those means."

"Then we're all fallible. Even Eunice."

"Even her," Eunice said.

"Eunice thought she was cleverer," Grave said, directing a sympathetic glance at her as she spoke. "It's excusable. Most of her existence, that's exactly what she's been. But she forgot that being human comes with some limitations."

"Most of us have already worked that one out," Goma said.

"Be patient with her," Grave answered. "She's new to this."

The crew of *Mposi* convened around the well, squeezed into the tight, knee-scraping spaces between its rim and the enclosing walls. It had reverted to its former function now, offering a three-dimensional view of the entire system from Paladin's orbit inwards. They were debating their options while also plotting Kanu's trajectory.

He was nearly at the outer margin of Poseidon's moons. Unchecked, he had made excellent progress and was now engaged in a steady deceleration burn. The well showed a fist of bright, curving lines worming through and around the orbits of the planet's moons, eventually terminating at some point close to Poseidon's surface. Aboard *Icebreaker*, Kanu must have been faced with a similar spread of possibilities, only now able to refine them down to a set of possible choices. Given the uncertainty in his total journey time from *Zanzibar*, there would have been nothing gained by planning this stage of the expedition in too much detail ahead of time.

"Six hours to the limit of the outer moon," Vasin said, dipping a finger into the well. "After that, guesswork is all we have. We still don't know the detailed capabilities of that ship—whether the plan is to orbit and send down a secondary vehicle, or whether the whole thing can handle Poseidon's atmosphere. It's a pretty compact-looking ship, so maybe it can."

"Where would they land, if they make it down?" Loring said. "Other than those wheels, there's nothing but water."

"Maybe the ship can float," Vasin answered. "Maybe they intend to remain in the atmosphere. Those wheels are huge, after all—there's presumably a lot to learn just by observing them from close proximity. If they're content to just study the tops of the wheels, they don't even have to enter the atmosphere."

"If they get that far," Goma said. "Eunice—you said the Terror always made you turn back—what's to say they won't run up against the same thing?"

"They will if they go deep enough. The moons don't allow anything to get that close to the surface without being sampled, examined, deemed worthy of further interest. That's the test the Watchkeepers keep failing—they ring like empty bottles, and the moons don't like that at all."

"And Kanu's crew?"

"I think they will pass the test. We always passed. It was the courage to continue that failed us."

"And now?" Goma pressed.

"I'd still be shit-scared, dear. But that's because I'm a sane and sensible organism with a ready appreciation of the risks. Dakota is an instrument—a meat probe. The Watchkeepers have turned her into what they can't be themselves. If she feels the fear, it's screwed down so tight she can't act on it."

"But Kanu will feel it. And Nissa."

"Yes. Pity them. Would you do me a small favour, Captain Vasin?"

"That depends."

"Zoom in on Paladin for a moment."

Vasin looked puzzled, and then a little troubled. "Our concern is Poseidon, Eunice."

"Nonetheless, indulge an old woman."

Vasin played the well with her customary fluency. She centred the display space on Paladin, then enlarged it by degrees until Eunice held up a hand.

"Good enough for you?"

"That's fine. This is a real-time image, right, Captain? It shows the rotational aspect of Paladin, the relative position of *Zanzibar* in its orbit? It's accurate to the limit of our current observations, the combined sensor inputs from both *Mposi* and *Travertine*?"

"Yes, but there's no—"

"Watch and learn. I think you'll find this most instructive."

"Eunice," Goma said, with a slowly dawning dread, "what are you about to do?"

"Nothing that your mother didn't spell out in her notebooks, child. They were very useful. Enormously instructive. They filled gaps in my comprehension I didn't even know were there."

"What is she talking about?" Vasin asked. "What notebooks?"

"Never mind," Goma said, with equal sharpness. "What's going on? What's about to happen?"

Eunice jabbed one finger at the little glowing mote that was *Zanzibar* and another at the second Mandala. "If this rendering is as accurate as you claim, the Mandala is not presently visible from *Zanzibar*. It lies over the horizon, around the curvature of Poseidon—but not for long. *Zanzibar*'s orbit is low and Mandala is about to start coming into view. In fifteen minutes, the former will be over the latter."

"And?" Karayan asked.

"I am about to send a sequence of commands to the Mandala. They will duplicate the effect of the command sequence Ndege gave to the original Mandala. I will initiate a second Mandala event."

For a moment there was silence as everyone struggled to process the full import of what she had just said. Goma was as speechless as the rest of them. There was too much to consider, too much to examine except in small pieces.

How could she think of doing this? How could she be confident that her commands would have the same effect, or any effect, for that matter? How could she talk to the Mandala? How could she take this risk with Tantor and human lives? Where was she planning to send them? Was it too much to hope that she had a plan?

How could she dare to be Eunice Akinya?

"Any questions?" Eunice said.

"It won't work," Goma said eventually, the first of them to break the spell. "My mother spent months, years, setting up experiments inside Mandala's walls. She didn't talk to it for fifteen minutes from inside a spaceship, across light-seconds of distance. It doesn't respond to radio, laser, neutrinos or anything we use for normal communication."

"Then it's a good thing I'm not planning to utilise any of those channels. Your mother used light and shade, did she not? The selective masking of areas of the Mandala?"

"Yes, but she was inside it, camped there, physically present. She had screens, blackout sheets, floodlamps . . . you have none of these things."

"I have the mirrors," Eunice said.

This was met with another silence, but it was shorter than the first and this time Vasin was the one to break it.

"No. You lost control of the mirrors. We saw it happen. You told us she had found her way in."

"Ah, yes, so I did. Which obviously eliminates any possibility that I was lying, or withholding some portion of the truth . . ."

Ru made a lunge for her across the edge of the well and nearly got a hand around Eunice's neck before she jerked out of reach.

Ru snapped her attention to Goma. "What the fuck is she talking about?"

"I don't know."

"Everybody calm down," Vasin said. "Eunice—clarify the situation with the mirrors. You said she had control."

"That was true."

"And now you're saying you *do* still have control?"

"That's also true. You should have paid more attention when I told you I was deep inside that architecture—deep enough to allow Dakota the illusion that she had regained some control. I allowed her to think she'd beaten me. I allowed you to think I was all out of options. In truth, I'd already embedded the command code—the instruction for the mirrors to swing onto Paladin's Mandala."

"You want to attack it!" Vasin said.

"What are the odds, Captain, that any human technology could even begin to damage something that's been there for several million years, weathering solar storms, asteroid bombardments and geological changes without sustaining so much as a blemish? No, that's not what I wanted the mirrors for. Goma knows. Goma sees."

"Light," Goma answered. "She can modulate the mirrors to send a version of Ndege's command string—talk directly to Mandala in the language of light."

"To initiate a Mandala event?" Vasin asked.

"Yes," Eunice said. "It's not difficult. It's the Mandala's purpose, and it doesn't need huge encouragement to start doing the thing it was designed to do. Especially not after all this time asleep, dormant, waiting to be reactivated—as Ndege found when she communicated with Crucible's Mandala."

"You're insane," Karayan said. "You cannot take this action."

"I see no alternative. Kanu is acting under duress because of the threat to the Friends. I am removing them from the equation."

"Stop her," Ru said. "Kill her. Whatever it takes."

Eunice directed a look of supreme contrition at the other woman. "You have every right to despise me, Ru—but not on this score. I'm not hurting the Friends or the Tantors. I am sparing them further involvement in this unholy human mess. They have endured one Mandala event; I have every confidence they can survive another."

"No," Ru said, as if none of those words had reached her. "She's got to be stopped."

"And how would you do that? I've told you that the command sequence is already activated. Would you like me to deactivate it? In which case, I'll need access to the console again—and you'd better hope we still have enough time left before Mandala begins to come into view, because that fifteen minutes is a very fuzzy estimate indeed."

"If we allow her access to the console," Grave said, "we could be giving her exactly the opportunity she needs. Are you bluffing, Eunice? Can we trust a single word that comes out of your mouth?"

"You can trust me when I say this: the translation event is irrevocable. It will happen. And if you wish for some good to come out of this, now would be the time to warn Dakota so that she can get a message to the rest of them."

"She won't believe a word of it," Vasin said. "Not now."

"But at least you'll have tried," Eunice said.

CHAPTER 42

Kanu was staring at the approach solutions for the swarm of moons, thinking back to their first ignorant encounter with the killing space around Poseidon, when the chime of an incoming transmission began to sound.

"I think we have heard all we need to," Dakota said. "Our point was made, as was theirs. They have begun to turn from us, and we have clarified their status as potential prisoners of war. I do not believe there is anything left to say."

"We may as well hear them out," Nissa said. "If there's the slightest chance it might be useful information, we'd be fools to ignore them."

"They have nothing we need or can use," Dakota said. "Our knowledge of Poseidon is already immeasurably richer than theirs."

"They have Eunice," Kanu said.

"They have a bag full of dying memories that thinks it once owned the stars. I am sorry to speak so bluntly of her, Kanu, but you have seen first hand the harm she would have done us had the means been available. As it was, she overreached herself."

The chime continued knelling.

"I'd take the call if I were you," Swift said. "I think it may be a matter of some urgency."

"How would you know?"

"I've spent some time getting to know the ship."

"You're in my skull, Swift. You only see and hear what I see and hear."

"That's perfectly true, Kanu, but as I hoped I demonstrated in *Zanzibar*, you do not make the best use of those channels. The ship is telling me that this signal is something we would indeed be very foolish to ignore. It speaks of a matter of urgency that I think one might characterise as 'dire.'"

"They have nothing that can touch us."

"We are not the subject of the dire urgency, but we can assist those who are. Something awful is about to happen to *Zanzibar*, Kanu, and in that respect, I think we can agree that it concerns us all."

"What are you talking about?"

"Ignore Dakota. Take the call."

In his own voice, Kanu instructed *Icebreaker* to play the transmission. Dakota began to voice her disapproval, but she had barely begun when Goma started speaking.

"Don't shut me off. Listen. You too, Dakota. This isn't a threat, or any kind of negotiation. Eunice claims that *Zanzibar* is about to experience a second Mandala event. A second translation to who knows where. It's imminent—minutes away, maybe less. We can't stop it happening, and nor can you—but you can warn them. It was bad the first time; now you can at least tell them to prepare for it—to bring in anyone or anything outside and to brace for whatever's coming. Please heed us—we gain nothing by lying to you. And tell them that wherever they end up, they won't be forgotten."

Goma fell silent. Kanu looked at Nissa, then back to Dakota—wondering if they felt the same way he did. He hoped this would prove to be nothing more than a ruse. But the time he had spent talking with Goma had convinced him that she spoke with absolute sincerity. More than that: she was genuinely afraid of what was coming.

So was he.

"After all this time," Dakota said, "a Mandala event would not simply happen all by itself."

"So it's not a coincidence," Nissa replied. "It's something to do with our activity. Triggered by us, or by them."

"There is no mechanism by which they could reach Mandala at that distance."

"That we know of," Kanu said. "And Nissa's right: they gain nothing by lying. We must take her seriously. I think you need to consider giving that warning."

"I will not be held hostage to absurd threats."

"Signal Memphis," Nissa said. "Tell him there's a chance something is about to happen. Tell him to act as if it might be real—that's all you have to do."

The elephant cogitated. "Perhaps."

"Do it!" Kanu snarled. "Goma said we might only be minutes away from the event. It'll take that long to get a signal back to *Zanzibar*!"

But then the chime sounded again. On his console, Kanu saw that the point of origin was Paladin space, not *Mposi*. He raised an eyebrow at Dakota.

"Someone wants to speak to you."

It was Memphis, as he guessed it must be. The huge bull filled the wall, projected larger than life. The other Tantors, with the exception of Dakota, lowered their heads in submission.

"The mirrors have moved," Memphis said. "They are not pointed at *Zanzibar* now. They are pointed at Paladin. They are shining light onto the Mandala. We cannot make them stop. What should we do?"

Not all of them, Kanu guessed—the mechanics of their orbits and sight lines would not allow for that. But if someone wished to communicate with the Mandala using light, they needed only one mirror.

"Memphis," Dakota said. "I have news . . . information. You must act upon it with all haste. *Zanzibar* moved once, when it came from Crucible. Now there is a chance it may move again, and very soon. Communicate with all chambers. Bring all Risen inside as quickly as you can—away from the locks and the berthing core. *Zanzibar* was very badly damaged during the first translation, and there may be damage during the second . . . You must be ready, Memphis. Close the great doors, ready the chambers for isolation . . . prepare to bring the emergency generators into use. You have never been the swiftest of us, Memphis, but you are good and loyal and there is no Risen I would sooner trust with the welfare of our home. You have a slow strength—but you are seldom wrong, and you have never disappointed me."

Kanu spoke up. "Memphis—hear what I have to say. You're going to another solar system, probably, into orbit around another star with a Mandala on one of its planets. Everything's going to be strange. You'll have to fend for yourselves to begin with, but I promise you won't be forgotten. We'll come—no matter how long it takes. We won't rest until we've found you."

"None of us shall," Dakota said. "But answer me this, Kanu—who is this 'we' you speak of?"

"Whatever we make of ourselves, Dakota. Humans, merfolk. Tantors. Machines. Whatever we manage to salvage from this. We're all orphans of the storm now, all Poseidon's children. We either find a way to live with what we are, with all our differences, or we face oblivion. I know which I'd rather."

Few had been in a position to witness the first Mandala event, mostly only those caught up in its immediate and devastating effects. For excellent reasons, their testimonies had never entered the public record: the majority of them were now part of the cloud of gas and debris circling Crucible—a monument to their own destruction.

It was different this time. There were multiple spectators both within *Zanzibar* and beyond, and to a degree all had been forewarned. On Paladin itself, no living thing stirred. But the changes to the second Mandala, quickened by Eunice's play of light, had now become convulsive. Patterns shifted and shifted again, becoming hypnotic, beguiling. Once, it had been a thing of wonder to witness changes on a timescale of hours or days. Now the Mandala adapted from second to second, moving matter around with a careless disdain for the ordinary limitations of inertia and rigidity. Indeed, since something odd was clearly happening to space in the vicinity of the second Mandala—or was about to happen when the translation event initiated—perhaps that was also true of time. Clocks might be running strangely down there—who could say? It was beyond any conceivable human physics—an invocation of alien science and engineering that might as well have been the work of mages, for all that it corresponded to any theory or hypothesis.

On *Zanzibar*, Memphis and the Risen watched as their orbit brought them closer and closer to the edge of the changing Mandala, and then they were over it. They saw this through cameras, through portholes and observation bubbles—faces pressed against the glass, filled with apprehension and terror, wondering what new fate the universe now had in store for them.

On *Travertine*, long-range sensors captured the same spectacle. By some dark fortune, the Mandala and *Zanzibar* were both visible to them. *Zanzibar* was a pollen-like smudge, bright and tiny, the Mandala a shivering labyrinth of intersecting circles and radials foreshortened by their angle of view. Nasim Caspari was reminded of ripples on a pond, of the interference patterns where they met and interacted. This pond was governed by weird, restless symmetries. He yearned to reach a deeper understanding of the fundamentals.

They had been warned. From the data on the first Mandala event, some sort of energy release could be anticipated. Caspari ordered *Travertine* on high alert, its Chibesa core quenched as a precaution. The crew rushed to their emergency stations and braced for the unknowable.

There wasn't much time left.

On *Icebreaker*, Kanu, Nissa and Dakota observed the same changes. They were also tracking *Zanzibar*, although from a different viewing angle—Paladin's spin had brought Mandala into nearly perfect alignment with their sensor array, and *Zanzibar* was about to transit across it like a planet sliding over the face of its sun.

Dakota had sent her warning in a spirit of precaution, but now there could be no doubt that it had been a wise decision.

There had been no time for Memphis to organise a return transmission, but she was inclined to look on that as a favourable indicator. It meant he was busy, rushing to prepare *Zanzibar* for the moment of translation. He was doing everything she had ever counted on him to do.

Much had changed for Dakota since she first arrived in the system as a guest of the Watchkeepers. She had felt the Terror and come to regard it as a challenge rather than an impediment. She had seen the arrival of *Zanzibar*, flicking into existence around Paladin, and she had helped steward the Tantors—the Risen—through the immense and testing hardships of those first days. Over time, she had diverged from her companions in the Trinity—come to see them as adversaries rather than allies. The Watchkeepers had bestowed gifts upon her, and in turn she had become their instrument, their willing servant. She accepted this role with equanimity. They had made her more than she had been or ever could be by herself, and it was an honour to be chosen, to be considered worthwhile. But she had not entirely discarded the bonds of love and loyalty, even though these things were now vastly diminished among her greater concerns. Memphis had always been dutiful and she had come to think fondly of him, even as the Watchkeepers' changes pushed her further and further from the ranks of the ordinary Risen. Even now, she felt empathy for the old bull. She could do nothing for him, not at this distance. But whatever happened, she hoped he would rise to the challenge, and that the challenge would not be too testing for him—indeed for all of them, and if his plans found a use for the Friends, she would also wish them well.

Nissa Mbaye, who was not an Akinya but whose life had been snared in their concerns, wondered what part, small or otherwise, she had played in this development. It seemed probable that Kanu's arrival had precipitated much of what was now taking place—the expedition, the deaths, the coming translation. She accepted no moral blame for any of that—those forces had been in motion long before she had any conception of their purpose. But had it not been for her desire to reach Sunday's artworks, she would never have provided Kanu with his ride to Europa. Could a meeting in an art gallery in

distant Lisbon really have led to this? She told herself that
Kanu would always have found a way to reach his ship, but
there was no guarantee of that.

So she had also played her role, whether consciously or
otherwise.

Kanu Akinya looked on with a sort of horrified bemuse-
ment, grasping as he did that the larger narrative of his
family—the things they had made, the events they had caused,
the web of responsibilities they had inherited—had just taken
a new and unexpected swerve. There were no Akinyas on *Zanzibar*, but the lives of the Risen and the Friends were an
inseparable part of the flow of events Eunice had set in motion.
Someone would have to follow up on this. Someone would
have to take ownership of this event.

Swift, who occupied the same physical space as Kanu and
observed events using co-opted neural networks within the
same central nervous system, felt something close to surprise.
Swift was used to modelling future events, and over the course
of his existence he liked to think he had gained some modest
proficiency in that art. The likelihood of a terrorist attack on
Mars, the chances of Kanu suffering injury . . . these were
events Swift had considered to be well within the bounds of
statistical probability. He had even taken it as read that the
expedition to Gliese 163 was likely to run into local complications. Encountering the Tantors—especially Dakota—had
been a surprise for Swift. But he had not been surprised to be
surprised.

This, though, was an event far outside the scope of even his
wildest conjectures. Not one of his iterative forecasts had
come close to predicting a second Mandala event. He was off
the map now; a chess piece sliding over the edge of the board.
The moment had come to discard all his earlier exercises in
future-casting—they had failed him totally.

Not for the first time, Swift would have given half of Mars
not to be imprisoned in this cage of bone and meat, with its
narrow, shuttered perception of the world. But he had done
what he could. In the interests of information-gathering, he
had already tasked every available sensor channel aboard the
ship to record the Mandala event.

The humans and elephants around him had not the slightest clue that his control of *Icebreaker* was so comprehensive.

He had seen no need to inform them.

Not yet.

In the lander *Mposi*, Eunice Akinya considered the imminent consequences of her handiwork. It had been one thing to formulate her own ideas of the Mandala grammar, to hew them into the rock of Orison as if they had integrity and self-consistency. It had been quite another to find those connections confirmed and amplified in the patient handwriting of Ndege Akinya, in the black books that her great-great-granddaughter had in turn bequeathed to Goma. Quite another thing still to go beyond those symbols and connections and understand that she had the means to duplicate Ndege's original command sequence.

Not to whisper it, as Ndege had done, in the muted *sotto voce* of screens and shadows, but to proclaim it in the fierce, focused light of Paladin's own star.

To speak the words of truth to the Mandala, in the form of address it expected.

To make it sing.

Ru, for her part, wondered why no one had found the good sense to kill the old hag. She had cheated them all—lied about her control of the mirrors, lied about her intentions. And now the Mandala was changing so fast that the moment must be nearly upon them.

She remembered the impression Eunice's hands had left in her flesh as she was dragged into quarantine, fingers and nails pressing into her as if she were human clay. Only Ru had been near enough to see the hate in the old woman's eyes; only Ru knew how close Eunice had come to murdering her there and then in a spasm of fury and recrimination. None of the others had seen it, not even Goma.

Ru had tried to understand. It was true that the Tantors' lives had been threatened; true that the disease in her blood made Ru look like the automatic culprit. But she had done nothing wrong, and Eunice had only been a twitch away from killing her.

No one else saw that. And now she had trumped that with

this monstrous, egomaniacal act—this act of godlike, spiteful indifference to the lives of the mere mortals around her.

Making Mandala sing just because she could.

Goma Akinya, meanwhile, could think only of the lost opportunities. They had met the Tantors on Orison. Even with the deaths of Sadalmelik and Achernar, she could not fail to find wonder in those hours she had spent in their presence. To know the minds of elephants when that possibility had been closed to her for most of her life—it had been a blessing, a bounty, a miracle. But the six Tantors who had shared Eunice's camp could hardly be compared with the thousands more on *Zanzibar*. Eunice's Tantors were companions, not servants. But they never had a chance to evolve their own social structures, to become fully independent. It would be a joy to see how elephants ran a world when that world was theirs to run.

That chance was gone now—or soon to be gone.

She had been granted a glimpse of something wonderful, promised that it would be hers, and been foolish enough to believe she would get her due.

Elsewhere, observing events from viewpoints remote and chilly, Watchkeepers gathered data and found that it did not tally with anything in their immediate experience. The Mandala had been changing for centuries—moments by their galactically slow and patient reckoning—but in these last instants the changing had accelerated asymptotically, and that acceleration had very clearly been precipitated by the actions of the organic intelligences now active around Gliese 163.

The Watchkeepers had uses for some of these intelligences; less for others. They also had their own names for things. They had never shaped a thought remotely congruent with "Mandala" and the terms of reference they used for the worlds and star of this dim little solar system were simply not translatable into human terms. They were best considered as compilations, event strings with the scope of infinite extensibility. In the language of the Watchkeepers, no word was ever uttered to completion, no sentence ever finished. There was only an endless branching utterance, sagas that begat sagas, until time immemorial.

The Watchkeepers were not capable of sadness, or of self-doubt, or at least no states of being that could be flattened into such simple human terms. But much as a hypersphere is the higher-dimensional analogue of a circle, they were capable of a kind of hyper-puzzlement, a kind of profound, vexing mismatch between expectation and external reality.

It puzzled the Watchkeepers that these living intelligences were able to make use of the Mandala when they were not permitted to do so. It puzzled them that these busy, buzzing creatures were tolerated within close proximity to Poseidon. It caused them to question the reliability of their own simulations of long-term survival. If they could not understand everything happening here, now, in the space around Gliese 163, in this system where the M-builders had left their traces, then nothing else could be depended upon. The Watchkeepers were used to being right and certain about things. This intrusion of doubt troubled them.

But not much. Being troubled was a state of existence most closely associated with fully conscious infovores, and the Watchkeepers had forgotten how to be conscious. Occasionally, as if surfacing from a bad dream, they felt a dim apprehension that something within them was missing; that what had been present was now absent. They felt hollow where once they had been full. It was an odd and contradictory impression because all rational data pointed to the Watchkeepers being more powerful than at any point in their history to date. How could something have been lost?

It was not possible.

But it was at instants like this, when the universe did something they were not expecting, that the Watchkeepers were at their most introspective. They pulled their scales tight, treasuring their blue light within. They reduced their communication with neighbouring Watchkeepers, becoming isolated units.

They watched and thought and skirted the edges of a regret as old and mysterious as the gaps between the galaxies.

And then the moment was upon them all.

The Mandala reached its final configuration. *Zanzibar* had arrived in the space directly above it. There was a flash, an energy release—space shearing and curdling and screaming its agonies in a flare of photons across the entire spectrum from gamma to the longest of radio wavelengths.

The flash originated neither at the Mandala nor in *Zanzibar*, but rather from a volume of space between the two. On Crucible, it had occurred just above the atmosphere. Here there was nothing to stop the flood of radiation from lashing down on Paladin. But it was brief, lasting barely longer than the time it took for light to cross the space between the Mandala and *Zanzibar*.

And *Zanzibar* moved again.

There was no measurable acceleration, nothing that human or alien recording devices could quantify. Between one moment and the next, *Zanzibar* went from being in orbit to travelling at an infinitesimal fraction less than the speed of light. From mere kilometres a second, relative to Paladin's surface, to something in the vicinity of three hundred thousand. If indeed there had been acceleration, it must have acted uniformly on every atom of *Zanzibar* and its occupants—or perhaps on the very space–time in which it was embedded, swept up to speed like a leaf in a current. No matter in the universe could have retained its integrity under such forces, much less a thing of rock and ice, metal and air, filled with living creatures.

Later, when the observations had been collated and examined, it would be determined that *Zanzibar* had shown the effects of extreme relativistic length contraction: that the potato-shaped fragment of the original holoship had been reduced to a circular pancake, massively compressed by frame contraction. Instead of a solid thing, it appeared to have become a disc, a stamped-out impression of itself.

The survivors of the original contraction had reported no experience of subjective time as they travelled between Crucible and Gliese 163. This could only mean that they were experiencing time-dilation factors of at least several billion. Such an inference had sounded doubtful before, but the new measurement of the frame contraction made it look much more probable.

The same thing had happened again. Hard as it was to credit, that paper-thin disc contained the entirety of *Zanzibar*. Its chambers, its cities, the Risen, the skipover vaults—all were still present, pressed against each other, ready to be unpacked like a folded-up doll's house. Within that subjective realm, nothing would have felt out of the ordinary.

The original survivors had reported no elapsed time, but their first journey had been relatively short. Seventy light-years, after all, was a scratch against the galaxy.

Who knew where *Zanzibar* was headed now?

No one.

Least of all Eunice Akinya.

CHAPTER 43

Mandala was quieting, cycling through an ever-slowing sequence of changes. The mirrors had withdrawn, their purpose served. Aboard *Mposi*, Eunice surrendered herself to the consequences of her actions. She had done something that would be hard to explain, but the right course had presented itself to her with the supreme and ecstatic clarity of a temporal-lobe vision. She knew, given the choice, that she would do it again in an instant.

"It was the only way."

They had bound her to a chair using its acceleration straps. She had made no effort to resist, offering herself up as compliantly as a puppet. Whatever they decided to do with her, she would accept.

"Explain," Vasin said.

"Kanu couldn't turn around if there was a chance of the Friends being harmed. To begin with, I hoped Dakota wouldn't go so far as to start killing them. Once she did, though, I saw no option but to initiate the translation."

"You worked very quickly," Karayan said.

"I'd already prepared the groundwork. I've been thinking about the possibilities for a long time—almost as long as I was on Orison. It was always clear to me that a second Mandala event would shake things up a bit if the need ever arose. Of course, I didn't have all the pieces until I saw Ndege's work. And even then I didn't have the means to make it happen. Not until we found the mirrors."

"But you had this plan at the back of your mind the whole time?" Vasin said.

"I'm all for spur-of-the-moment decisions, but sometimes you have to play the long game."

"Half the crew want to kill you," Goma said.

"I don't blame them."

"If I were you, I'd start presenting a few arguments in your defence. It looks as if you just committed mass murder."

"She did," Ru said.

"I didn't kill *anyone*. *Zanzibar* survived one translation; it will make it through another. The chances are better this time: there's no debris left behind so the effect was cleaner, nothing outside the edges of the field. I think they will do perfectly well—thrive, most likely."

"You don't even know where they've gone!" Vasin said.

"Where they're going. It's true—I don't know. I didn't have time to finesse anything to that degree. I couldn't even be sure it would work! But the Mandala won't have just sent them in a random direction. We'll work it out—backtrack to the moment of the event, identify the candidate stars in the general angle of view. Then we'll know."

"You're so pleased with yourself," Ru accused.

"Pleased that I've given Kanu a hope of digging his way out of that mess he's in? Yes, I am. Why shouldn't I be?"

"You know nothing about Kanu's situation," Grave said. "Wishing to turn around and being able to—they're not the same thing. You've staked countless lives on this gamble."

"I haven't."

"How can you know?" asked Vasin.

"Because I've spoken to Swift," Eunice answered.

And for a moment there was silence, until Goma asked the question they must all have been thinking.

"Who the hell is Swift?"

CHAPTER 44

There was darkness, and then there was light. For a few seconds *Icebreaker* had gone dead, all its displays inactive, its interior illumination shut off, the background noise of its life-support systems silenced. Even the Chibesa core had fallen to a sudden and ominous stillness. Nothing in Kanu's prior experience of the ship had prepared him for this, not even the Watchkeeper's attack.

As the systems began to recover—emergency lights coming on in the bridge, fans restarting, a chorus of recorded voices informing him of various status indications—Nissa and the Tantors began to speak at once.

"What has happened, Kanu?" Dakota asked.

"I don't know."

The elephant persisted. "Do you think it is connected to the Mandala event—the energy spilling out from Paladin?"

"*Zanzibar* must have streaked past pretty close," Nissa said. "Maybe we got buffeted by . . . something?"

"I don't know," Kanu repeated.

For once, he had no need of a mask, no need to lie. He genuinely had no idea what had just happened—he had neither initiated it nor expected it. But the more he thought about it, the less likely it felt to him that the Mandala event itself had anything to do with *Icebreaker* going dark. They had witnessed the event and the ship's normal functions had continued uninterrupted, registering nothing of immediate concern within its environment. *Zanzibar* was long gone before the arrival of whatever hit *Icebreaker*.

Whatever this was, it must have been initiated locally, whether by accident or design.

A dark suspicion began to form.

"Talk to me, Swift," Kanu subvocalised.

"Ah, you can still hear me. That's excellent. I wasn't totally sure, you know. A shock to the ship of this magnitude—who knows what the collateral effects might be?"

"I can hear you. Now talk to me."

Kanu was still in semi-darkness, but he was not alone. Nissa was next to him, both of them seated. Dakota and the other Risen were still present, too, but drifting free of the floor. Their huge breathing presences were tumbling like boulders—there was nothing fixed within reach of a trunk or foot to arrest their motion.

Presumably they were just as bewildered by this latest development as Kanu. Or perhaps, having witnessed the Mandala event, their capacity for astonishment had been overloaded like a blown circuit. He could relate to that well enough.

"The ship is ours again, Kanu," Swift said. "Or it will be, soon enough."

"It was never not ours."

"You know exactly what I mean. We were unable to take decisive action while the Friends were in jeopardy. Now they are no longer in jeopardy—or at least their prospective fates lie completely beyond our influence. That frees us, wouldn't you agree?"

"You made the ship do this?" Nissa asked through the same subvocal channel. "You could do this all along, and you waited until now?"

"You are both silent, yet I sense deliberation," Dakota said. "I will ask again. What do you know of this event—both of you?"

"Some fault in the ship," Kanu said, for the sake of giving her something. "That's all I know."

More of the lights and displays were coming online now and the recorded warnings were beginning to die down. The ship was restarting itself, cycling through health and calibration checks, but the process appeared to be running without complication.

"Your ship seemed reliable until now," Dakota answered. "Do you have an explanation for this sudden fault?"

"Nothing I'd bet my life on," Kanu said.

She rammed the ceiling and tucked her trunk around a structural member. "Try me anyway."

"Clearly we missed something. But the ship's coming back to us. When we have full functionality, the event logs should explain what the problem was."

"I find it telling that it happened so soon after the atrocity we just witnessed."

"I wouldn't read too much into that. Can you get down from there?"

A lurch signalled the centrifugal wheel restarting itself, providing gravity in the absence of thrust. Dakota held on for a few seconds while the spin slowly phased in, then allowed herself to "fall" the short distance to the floor. She landed hard enough to send a solid thud through the fabric of the ship. Hector and Lucas found their own footing, stumbling and then regaining balance.

"Are you being honest with me, Kanu?" Dakota asked.

"No, he isn't. But don't blame him for that. He's not responsible for me—at least, not entirely."

The sounds were coming from Kanu, but Swift was generating the words. Kanu had no control over them. With the same absence of volition, Kanu rose from his seat. They had reached normal gravity. He walked around until he faced the Risen and gave a small bow, tucking his hand against his belly.

"Permit me to introduce myself," he said.

Dakota's eyes glittered with vehemence. "What is this?"

"I am Swift. We haven't met."

Dakota shifted her gaze onto Nissa. "Do you understand what is happening?"

"I do," she answered, "and I think you should listen." But there was apprehension in her voice as well—Kanu sharing her sense that Swift had begun to operate entirely on his own agenda.

"I am an artificial intelligence," Swift said. "I came from the Evolvarium society on Mars, inside Kanu—operating on the same neural platform as his own consciousness."

"A parasite?"

"A passenger," he corrected delicately, tapping a finger to Kanu's lip. "My host was entirely cooperative—a full and willing partner in our enterprise."

"Which was?"

"To understand ourselves. To explore our origins and our ultimate potential. To seek the paths by which the machine and the organic might coexist. Or, if such coexistence proved impossible, to learn which strategies would suit us best when forced into opposition. The least destructive paths. I had two primary ambitions. The second was to achieve meaningful contact with the Watchkeepers, something quite impossible within the human hegemony of the old solar system."

"And the first?"

"To meet my maker."

"You believe in a god?"

"I believe in Eunice Akinya. That may or may not be an equivalent statement. That ambition was achieved. I met Eunice, and we had a full and frank exchange of opinions."

"We met her," Dakota said. "In the ching environment. But only us."

"You forget—where Kanu goes, I go. What Kanu witnesses, I witness. But there's so much more to it than that. Within the bounds of that environment, Eunice and I were able to exchange a great deal of information. You caught none of it. We used non-verbal channels—a battery of subtle methods. You'd be surprised at the resourcefulness of two artificial intelligences when they have something to communicate. Actually, I should clarify: she's no longer running on a machine substrate. She's become meat—returned to her human origins. That was an interesting adjustment for me to make—like discovering that god is made of wood, or flint. But the essence is still her, and her faculties haven't been entirely diminished by reversion to the flesh."

"Reversion," Nissa said. "Thanks."

"No offence intended."

"None taken. What else did she tell you?"

"That we have a chance. She believed she might be in a position to initiate a Mandala event, although nothing was certain. She encouraged me to do everything I could to maximise the usefulness of such an action. Fortunately, I had already done some preparatory work of my own. Of course, I knew nothing about the viability of instigating the Mandala event.

But I had long thought it wise to install some precautionary measures in the operating architecture of this ship."

Had Kanu been capable of registering surprise, this would have been his turn.

But Swift continued, "Let me explain. It's rather impolite of me to keep using Kanu as a puppet in this way so I am going to relinquish control to him. In any case, I think the ship has now regained sufficient capacity to render this mode of communication quite superfluous."

Kanu felt himself return. He worked his jaw, drew breath—Swift never appeared to breathe enough when he was in control.

"Swift—" he began.

"A moment, my friend."

The bridge's main display filled with an image of Swift's head and upper torso, dressed as always like a man of learning from the late eighteenth century, with a white scarf, frock coat, pince-nez glasses and a head of boyish curls.

"Forgive me," he said. "Some explanation may be in order and we'll come to that in a moment. Before we do, though, there are a couple of pressing issues to be addressed. The first concerns our trajectory. The Chibesa core is restarting—I have it on a fast cycle—and in a few minutes we will have full power and control. Once we have that capability, we will initiate a hard burn to avoid crossing the outer threshold of the moons. Given our present speed and course, that burn will push the ship to the limit of its structural and energetic tolerances. It will be uncomfortable for all passengers, but with due preparations it should be bearable for everyone."

"I hope you haven't left it too late," Nissa said.

"I haven't. Now for the second issue. The Risen are no longer the commanding authority aboard this vehicle. Kanu and Nissa are in control, and any challenge to their status will be met with immediate punishment. I can make this ship do things to itself that would be uncomfortable for a primate but most certainly fatal for an elephant. Is that understood?"

"Does he really have control?" Dakota asked.

"If he does," Kanu answered, "I have no idea how. But I don't think he's lying."

"I'm not. The moment is nearly upon us. Dakota—you may remain here, if you desire, but I would strongly recommend using one of the adjoining restraint couches."

"Whoever you are, however you are speaking to us," Dakota said, "this ship will continue to operate under my command. The loss of *Zanzibar* is shocking, and there will be consequences, but it must not distract us from our purpose. Kanu—resume our planned trajectory. Do not deviate. Our projected course remains valid."

Swift did something that jammed the centrifuge to a violent halt, forcing an emergency braking system to engage equally violently. Kanu was thrown off his feet, Nissa likewise. He paddled madly and grabbed the nearest console, then reached out a hand to Nissa.

The Risen were not so fortunate. They had begun to drift again—paddling their feet and swinging their trunks in a vain effort to gain some traction. Air-swimming was barely effective for humans; for elephants it was entirely useless.

Nissa grabbed the back of her own chair and released herself from Kanu's grip.

"I can keep doing this indefinitely," Swift said, "but I hope the point is made. Force and strength will not help you now, Dakota. When I restore the gravity, you will secure yourselves in the restraining couches. Nissa—might I ask where you are going?"

"To fetch something."

She moved quickly and confidently even though gravity had not yet returned. A minute passed, maybe two—long enough for her to reach any number of adjoining rooms. Kanu swallowed hard, trying to ease the tightness in his throat.

"I hope you've thought this through, Swift. Why did you have to shut down the ship?"

"I installed an avatar of myself in *Icebreaker*'s control architecture. It needed a total shutdown to gain the necessary authority across all functions—without it I'd only have partial control. Besides, it's rather helped to make my point."

"If making your point involved scaring me half to death, consider your work done."

Nissa pushed her way back into the bridge holding something long and thin in her right hand and tucked into the crook of her right elbow. Kanu stared at it for a second before recognising it as the harpoon gun they had found on the dead Regal.

Nissa braced herself into a stable position next to one of the chairs and settled the harpoon into both hands like a rifle. It was a nasty, complex thing, with gas canisters and a gristle of pressure lines, the ugly barb of its tip a promise of the damage it could do to flesh.

She aimed it first at Kanu, thought for a moment, and then shifted the aim onto Dakota.

"You appear to be in two minds," the matriarch said.

"I was. Now do what Swift said."

The gravity returned and the Risen took their positions in the acceleration couches, Nissa aiming the harpoon as if she was more than willing to use it. But the Risen had accepted the practicalities of their situation and offered no resistance to this change of status.

"Will you kill us, Kanu?" Dakota asked. "Is that your plan?"

He considered offering her glib reassurance, that he had no intention of harming them, but in truth he had not thought it through. Perhaps it would indeed come to killing. He hoped not, but this was not the time for empty promises.

"We'll see how we fare," he answered.

As soon as the drive was ready, Swift applied power in increasing increments, winding down the centrifuge as the thrust ramped up to half a gee and beyond. Kanu returned to his seat and Nissa to hers, where she cradled the harpoon in her lap.

"You realise that would only have stopped one of them," he said. "And even that wasn't certain."

"After what she did to the Friends, I'll take what I can get."

The drive climbed through one gee, then beyond. At one-point-five gees, Kanu sensed that he would struggle to lift himself from his seat and move around. At two gees, his own weight pressing against his bones, he decided it would be beyond his capacities. Nissa, lither and stronger, might still have been able to move around with care. But the Risen were now effectively prisoners of their couches. Their musculoskeletal structures were already operating at the limit under terrestrial gravity; now they weighed twice as much.

"Can you still breathe, Dakota?"

"We are not so weak as you imagine, Kanu. Our strength has carried us this far—it will serve us a little longer."

But he could see the effect of the acceleration for himself—the muscles of her face being dragged down, the skin around her eye slipping to reveal the pink enclosure of her eyeball. Her trunk sagged listlessly.

Two gees, then two and a half. Warning messages had begun to sound again, but these were of no evident concern to Swift. Kanu did not need to speak—he could have subvocalised easily enough—but for the sake of the Risen he made the effort.

"Tell me how you did this, Swift." His voice was strained and he had to fight for breath between words. "I understand how you found a way to communicate with Eunice, but you couldn't have put all this in place since then. There's no way you'd have time to install any kind of avatar, or whatever you want to call it."

"I must confess there has been a degree of deception on my part, but I hope you will not hold it against me."

"What did you do?" Nissa asked.

"When you were sleeping, after the Watchkeeper attack, but before the arrival at *Zanzibar*, I saw it as an opportunity to put certain provisions in place . . . and therefore I took it."

"I don't see how," Nissa said. "We were both in skipover. I was with Kanu when we went under."

The engine had topped out at three gees. Kanu could hear as well as feel it, like an endless thundering storm front.

"She's right," Kanu said. "I programmed the sleep intervals myself."

"You *think* you did," Swift replied, with a trace of bashfulness. "The truth is, I intervened. The sleep interval you programmed was not the one you intended. And when you emerged from skipover, I held you in a state of borderline unconsciousness while I made use of your body."

"For how long? Hours, days?"

Swift equivocated. "Rather more than days, Kanu. Weeks and months would be more truthful." He paused to fiddle with his sleeve, as if a button had come adrift. "There was a lot to be done, even operating at the limit of your capacity. Getting the ship to obey me wasn't the hard part—it already thought I was you. But installing a useful part of me in the architecture with only the tactile and expressive channels available via the use of your body . . . that was supremely challenging."

"You duplicated yourself?" Nissa asked.

"No. There was never time for that. It took every resource available to the Evolvarium to stuff me inside Kanu's head—I had nothing to guide me, and nothing to work with but your own flesh and blood. What I created was an image, a kind of shadow of myself. I gave it the ability to make some autonomous decisions, but primarily its job was to conceal itself and eventually respond to my commands. The implant protocol Nissa suggested? That was helpful—it gave me a direct channel into *Icebreaker*'s neuro-medical surgical suite, which in turn offered me a window into the larger operating architecture. But it was still daunting work!"

"I dreamed of wandering the ship," Kanu said. "Haunting it like a ghost, passing through empty, cold corridors. It felt like a nightmare—a horrible, endless fever dream. But that wasn't a dream at all, was it? That was *you*, using me."

"Some small component of the experience must have slipped through to conscious recollection. I can only apologise for that."

"You don't sound in the least bit apologetic."

"Forgive me, in any case."

"Swift," Nissa said. "The Risen. They're unconscious. They can't endure this the way we can."

Kanu had shifted his attention from Dakota to Swift, but now he saw that her eye was closed and her breathing unusually sluggish and laboured. "You said it yourself, Swift—what's hard on us might be fatal for them. You have to reduce the thrust."

"In a little while I will do just that. But we must sustain this output if we are to correct our course."

"How long?" Nissa asked, groaning out the question.

"Another thousand seconds, give or take."

Kanu looked at Lucas and Hector, then back at their leader. He knew nothing about elephant anatomy, still less regarding their chances of surviving another thousand seconds. He imagined their hearts, slow at the best of times, now being pushed to the limit of their strength—each beat a triumph of muscle over fluid mechanics. Only an evolutionary eyeblink separated Kanu from the savannah, and that was just as true for the Risen. Their minds might be fixed on the stars, but their bodies were only a footstep from the dust and heat of Amboseli.

"It's too long. Reduce the thrust now."

Swift made a quick tooth-sucking sound. "I would gladly do so, Kanu, were this course correction not already critical. We can make it—but only if we hold our present output."

"Then we can't make it."

"Kanu—I do not think you properly grasp the implications."

"No," Nissa said. "He grasps them, and so do I—it's us or the Risen. We can survive this, but they probably won't."

"Given recent events," Swift said, "I would venture *that* is not such an unthinkable trade-off."

"Only in your world," Kanu answered. "Not in mine. While there's a chance to save them, I won't have their deaths on my conscience."

"Let me be completely clear: unless we complete this burn, we will *not* avoid entering Poseidon's influence. Do I need to define the word 'not'?"

"No, you don't. And yes, I understand exactly what's at stake."

"And once we do approach Poseidon, we will not have sufficient time to prevent ourselves reaching the atmosphere."

"I understand that as well."

"Where we may very well die, since this ship was never engineered for atmospheric entry."

"We have *Noah*," Nissa said.

"*Noah* will do well to survive entry at the speed we will be travelling."

"We understand," Kanu affirmed. "It changes nothing. Reduce the thrust, Swift."

"I could disobey you, I suppose."

"But you won't, because you want my friendship and respect as much as I want yours. You've admitted one breach of our trust, Swift. Don't make things worse."

A moment later, Kanu heard the engine noise die down and

felt his weight easing. It was not a complete shift to weightlessness, but enough of a transition that it felt just as welcome.

"One gee," Swift said. "We'll try and lose as much speed as we can. And if this doesn't suit the Risen, then god help us all."

"You did the right thing," Nissa said.

"Oh, I'm sure I did." Swift prodded his pince-nez glasses higher up the fine profile of his nose. "Even if it means the end of us, which may well be the case. But at least this will be *interesting*."

CHAPTER 45

From *Mposi* they had witnessed the total shutdown of *Icebreaker* and the gradual return of the ship's systems. Although they were still too distant to image any salient details of the other vessel, they had a clear lock on its thermal signature. The dimming and reactivation of the Chibesa drive—even with the thrust directed away from them, towards Poseidon— were impossible to miss.

Besides, they had the benefit of Eunice's insider knowledge.

"You asked me about Swift," she said, with a certain primness of tone. "The truth is, I don't entirely know what Swift is, or what Swift wants. Swift is some kind of artificial intelligence, that's clear enough—he's an artilect consciousness, much as I used to be. But unless I'm hugely mistaken—and frankly the likelihood of that isn't worth mentioning—Swift is running on an entirely neural substrate. That's how Swift was able to communicate with me at all. He's inside Kanu's skull."

"Like some sort of parasite?" Dr. Andisa asked.

"I think we may presume that the relationship is mutually consensual and to the benefit of both host and symbiote. That

Kanu has willingly allowed Swift to co-opt part of his neural network. What do we know of Kanu? He was an ambassador to the machines on Mars. I do not think these two facts are unrelated."

"Then who—or what—is Kanu acting for?" Goma asked.

Eunice wriggled in her restraints. "Are you going to let me out of this chair any time soon?"

"No," Vasin said. "You acted without authorisation. You took a foolhardy gamble with thousands of lives, both human and Tantor."

"I took a gamble to stop someone else taking a worse one. I gave Kanu an opportunity to challenge Dakota, with Swift's reassurance that he had the means to take control of *Icebreaker*. Swift explained that there would be some kind of restart of *Icebreaker*'s systems, which is what we've just witnessed. Clearly, the humans are back in charge. That's why the ship is making such a concerted effort to reverse course."

"So you've succeeded," Ru said.

"It's starting to look that way. A little closer to the bone than I'd like, but what are nerves for, if not to be frayed?"

"You haven't even considered the lives on *Zanzibar*. The Friends, the Tantors—they're not even a part of your thinking any more. You've moved them off the board and forgotten about them. We were all wrong about you."

She looked at Ru with an expression of pleasant interest. "Were you, my dear?"

"You're still a fucking machine."

"Well, thank you for that considered opinion. Shall I be equally candid, then? I don't care. I expected to die. I expected to be torn limb from limb or stuffed into the nearest airlock. I expected that and I knew I had to act anyway—that nothing else was going to work. So spare me your lofty human sanctimony, because until you've been through the Terror, you have no idea what's at stake. And if you had an idea, even the tiniest grain of an inkling, you'd know full well that my actions were not only necessary but the very least that needed to be done. If I could have destroyed *Icebreaker*, do you think I'd have hesitated?"

"No," Ru said. "I don't suppose you would have."

"Then we're getting somewhere."

But Vasin said quietly, "You say the humans should be back in charge by now."

"Yes."

"Then explain this."

Over the next few hours they watched Kanu's ship fall into the barricade of moons. The course correction had been going well, the engine signature reading clean and steady, no cause for concern even as *Icebreaker* topped out at a crushing three gees of reverse thrust. Then it dropped down to a single gee even though *Icebreaker* still had far too much residual motion in the direction of Poseidon. Their first guess was some kind of engine failure, but nothing in the data hinted at anything other than a smooth, controlled reduction of power—a deliberate change of plans.

They waited to see if this was a temporary adjustment, soon to be corrected. Eunice was as bothered about it as the rest of them—her confidence in both herself and Swift severely damaged. More than anything, that was the deciding moment when Goma put aside the last trace of doubt that they were dealing with a human being. No matter what Ru thought, no machine would have shown such consternation at this change in circumstances. A robot would have absorbed the altered parameters without the slightest sense of betrayal or personal failure.

Soon they had the confirmation they had been dreading.

"This is Kanu. I hope you can read me. Shall I begin with the good news or the bad?"

They were close enough for real-time communications again. His face loomed large, but now the effects of gravity made him look drawn and fatigued, older and wiser by many years.

"Go ahead, Kanu," said Captain Vasin.

"Nissa and I have complete control of *Icebreaker*. Tell Eunice—if she isn't already listening in—that she and Swift did a very good job with their scheme for *Zanzibar*. They can be proud of their achievement. That doesn't mean I approve. Right now I'm not certain what approval would say about any of us. Was it an act of kindness or cruelty? I'm not exactly sure."

"Nor are we," Vasin said. "Horrified, and awed—there's no doubt about that. But was it the right thing to do? I'd say it was, if we couldn't see you continuing to Poseidon."

"We ran into a local complication which neither Swift nor Eunice anticipated. We had the means to turn *Icebreaker* around and were in the process of doing so, but it was too hard on the Tantors. They couldn't take the gee-load. If we'd carried on, we are fairly sure they would have died."

"Just a second," Eunice said, now free of her chair but still shackled at the wrists. "You can turn around, but you're not going to?"

"We won't murder them. That's what it would have been. You can see that, can't you?"

"You owe them nothing," Eunice snapped back. "Especially not Dakota. You're not dealing with an elephant, Kanu, or even a Tantor—you're dealing with an alien intelligence that just happens to be using her body."

"I can understand why you feel that way. But if there's a shred of humanity left in any of us, we can't place our own lives over theirs."

"That's very noble of you, but it's not just your lives on the table here. Turn your ship around."

"It's too late for that now, Eunice—you know that as well as we do. We're committed to Poseidon now, for better or for worse. It's going to be hard, in more ways than one."

"Not just hard," she said. "Suicidal."

Kanu's gravity-strained face managed a weak smile. "Yes. I'm aware of that. And believe me, I don't like it for a second. But we're not totally out of chances. We'll see how we weather the moons. Even if we survive passage through them, we'll still have the problem of atmospheric entry. We're moving a little too quickly for safe planetfall, and *Icebreaker* certainly isn't designed to cope with the stresses. But we have our lander, *Noah*. It's large enough to accommodate all of us, and once we're through the moons it *might* get us down to the surface, and maybe we can reach one of those wheels, see what we make of it. But we're under no illusions about getting back out again. Since we're going in, though, we may as well make the best of it. We'll be gathering all the information we can and doing our best to share it with you. But you've done your part now."

"What are you suggesting?" Vasin asked.

"Turn around. You gave it your best shot and I think we can both agree there need be no hard feelings. There's nothing to be gained from debate now—the time for that has passed. We have no option; we're going in, and we'll endeavour to be your eyes and ears. I was about to wish you the best in forging ties with *Zanzibar*, but I keep forgetting that won't be necessary—it isn't here any more. Will you be all right? Can you get back to your starship?"

"Don't worry about us," Vasin said. "We have everything we need, and even if we didn't, there's still Eunice's camp on Orison. We'll return there to help the surviving Tantors—but not until we've done all we can for you."

"There's nothing to be done. But Nissa and I appreciate the sentiment."

"Let me speak to Swift," Eunice said.

"So that you can talk him into destroying *Icebreaker* in a moment of glorious self-sacrifice?" Kanu smiled sadly. "As it happens, we've already discussed that, and maybe it wouldn't be such a bad idea. But we're not quite ready to face total oblivion just yet. Not while there's a chance to learn something new. It's the reason we came here, after all—to gather knowledge. And if, collectively, none of us is quite up to the measure of the M-builders—well, then it looks to me as if we're all doomed anyway. But I'm handing no one my head on a plate."

"Tell Swift—"

"Swift says that he'd welcome the exchange of further views, but for the time being we have a little preparation of our own to be doing. I'll talk to you all on the other side of the Terror. Wish us well, won't you?"

The channel was closed, but they could still track *Icebreaker* clearly enough to observe its progress. They watched it fall deeper, slowing all the while but never enough, and they ran their own simulations for atmospheric insertion assuming a spread of assumptions for the capabilities of Kanu's ship.

Until Eunice drew their attention to one of the moons, now veering out of its orbit like a marble that had wandered out of a groove.

"There's always one," she said. "The chasing moon. It'll be on them soon enough. And if Kanu has an ounce of sense—or if he listens to Dakota—he'll know better than to try to escape."

"What will the moon do?" Goma asked.

"Swallow them. And cut them open. Crack their spines and read them like books. But don't worry. It's less painful than it sounds."

CHAPTER 46

Kanu had been wrong about the moons, but he could be forgiven for that. Even *Icebreaker* had been confused by them, its sensors registering them only as small, black, mathematically spherical bodies. As one of the objects closed upon them, though, he began to grasp his error. The moon was only spheroidal in the way a spinning coin defines the shape of a sphere. The moon was winding down—turning ever more slowly on its axis. The rotational speed was still almost too fast for the naked eye to interpret, but now at least the ship was having less difficulty.

He stared at the images and overlays on the bridge display—the patchwork of analysis and interpretation the ship was doing its best to offer.

The chasing moon was a thin grey ring of the same diameter as the implicit sphere—about two hundred kilometres across, which in turn made it about the same size as the wheels on Poseidon. The width and thickness of the ring were also in proportion to the wheels. They would have better data as the moon reduced its spin even further, but on the evidence presented so far, Kanu had little doubt that additional information would only confirm the observations to date. He knew nothing of the M-builders, still less of their psychology, but it struck him as profligate in the extreme to create two distinct kinds of thing which were all but identical in their major dimensions.

No—he was sure of it: the moons were identical to the wheels. The wheels were down in the sea and the moons were in space, but they were the same class of object—simply assigned different functions.

"How much of this," he asked, "is ringing a bell?"

"All of it," Dakota said. "A moon always detached from its orbit and closed on us as we approached. The moons are the basic line of defence—the sentience filter. In a short while, it will sample us."

"Am I going to like that?" Nissa asked.

"It depends how you feel about terror."

The moon—or, more accurately, the wheel—continued its approach. Within minutes, its rate of spin had dropped to a few rotations a second. Then—with a surprising abruptness—it locked still, its central axis aligned with *Icebreaker*. It was closing at a rate that they could never have outrun, even with a fully functioning Chibesa core.

Besides, Dakota was clear: it would have been perfectly futile to run. The moons allowed nothing to evade their scrutiny. If they veered from the reach of this one, the remaining moons would simply mesh their orbits tighter. And if by chance there had been some trajectory which allowed them to slip beyond the moons, *Icebreaker* would simply be destroyed with long-range weaponry as a precautionary measure.

"They allowed us through once," Kanu said.

"Your course was oblique to Poseidon. The moons determined that you had no intention of slowing or landing. Do not think of that as clemency—it isn't. The moons simply determined that you were neither a threat nor of interest to them. They guard their energy carefully—nothing is without cost, even to the M-builders. But you still did very well to survive after your entanglement with the Watchkeeper. Be glad you never went deeper."

"I'd be glad if we weren't going deeper now," Nissa said.

"For years—decades—I lived for this." But after a silence Dakota added: "Now I am not so sure."

They watched as a silver filament formed a cord between two parts of the moon's inner arc. The filament lengthened until it spanned the diameter, like a single hubless spoke. They had seen nothing of how the filament was generated, or any suggestion of how it was sustained.

"What is it?" Kanu asked.

"The means by which we shall be sampled," said Dakota. "It is a physical scanning process—a kind of examination by touch. But do not be alarmed. This is not the thing that will harm us."

The moon had begun to rotate again, but now the axis of rotation was at right angles to its previous orientation. The spin accelerated quickly, drawing the single silver spoke into a flat silver disc. The disc was slightly translucent, stars and planets still visible through it. Now the wheel began to gain on *Icebreaker* until the silver surface was only a few hundred metres aft of the vessel.

"The first time," Dakota said, "we thought this must be a weapon. We believed we were going to die. In hindsight, though, it would have made a very clumsy tool of execution. We should have understood that it was a learning machine, not a weapon."

Kanu studied the bridge display. The schematic outline of the ship showed a sketchy, barely apprehended surface closing in from behind, like a fog bank.

"What will happen when it touches us? Will it pass through the hull?"

"The sampling surface will not be interrupted. It will pass through every system of *Icebreaker*—including the Chibesa core."

"And us?"

"From the perspective of the M-builders, we are all just systems of the ship."

The silver wall had begun to consume the ship from the tail end. But there were no emergency warnings, no sense of any damage or impairment to the propulsion systems beyond that which they had already sustained. *Icebreaker* was aware of the surface passing around it but had no perception of any more significant violation of its integrity.

"I want to see this," Nissa said. "For real, with my own eyes."

"You will, soon enough."

"I mean while there's time to compose some last thoughts. Will it matter if we move around?"

"Nothing you think, say or do will make the slightest difference now," Dakota assured her. "This is the price of your forgiveness, in sparing us."

"Would you rather we hadn't?"

"I suspect you will come to believe so."

"Such gratitude," Nissa said.

"Oh, I am grateful. You had the means to escape and we were safely unconscious. You could hardly have been blamed had you put yourselves before the Risen. I still wonder why you did not. You had everything to gain, and now you have nothing."

"But I can still look myself in the eye in a mirror," Kanu said.

He followed Nissa. Instead of going directly to the central shaft, she stopped at the spacesuit locker and began donning layers as quickly as she could. For a moment Kanu merely watched, wondering how she thought a spacesuit was going to help her when the silver surface arrived. But the impulse to do something was inarguable, as human as the reflex to raise a hand against a striking knife. He began to put on his own spacesuit, skipping the usual safety checks for the sake of urgency.

"I know this won't make much difference," Nissa said, "but if the ship breaks up around us, I don't want to die with vacuum in my lungs. I'll take oxygen starvation over decompression any time."

"I've never been keen on drowning," Kanu confessed. "I imagine the two scenarios aren't all that different."

They left their helmets off for now, judging that there would be time to put them on if the ship really did begin to suffer some catastrophic structural failure. With the helmets tucked under their arms, they continued further into the ship.

They did not have far to go before they reached the end of the central shaft, which ran a significant part of the distance back to the propulsion section. The shaft stretched away before them, picked out by running lights.

They floated there, holding gloved hands. Neither of them needed to say anything. They could see what was coming.

The end of the shaft was a moving silver surface. It filled the shaft perfectly, as smooth and tight-fitting as a plug of liquid mercury. It was slightly mirrored, so they were able to see the converging perspective lines of the shaft. Far in the distance, where those perspective lines pinched together, lay their own tiny reflections—two floating suited forms, barely distinguishable from each other.

"The ship is still there, beyond the surface," Swift said. "We would know by now if that were not the case. It is not a destructive sampling process. The material must be examining matter on the molecular level, then reconstituting it as it passes through."

"Shut up, Swift," Nissa said. "I need to face this without you in my head."

Kanu squeezed her hand. "It'll be all right."

His instincts told him to try to paddle away from the approaching surface, but he could never have made enough speed to outpace it. Besides, there was nowhere to go. At least this way they would face it with dignity.

It came fast, appearing to accelerate as it consumed the last few metres of the shaft, but that must have been an optical illusion. Kanu stiffened his body and held his breath—it was impossible not to, even as his rational mind argued that it would make no difference. Nissa's grip tightened on his own.

"We were married once," she said.

"Yes."

"And then not married."

"To my regret. But I'm glad we came back into each other's lives."

"However it happened."

"Yes."

She nodded at the nearing surface. "It's not a ring, but it is silver. When it touches us, we'll be united. I don't know if that'll be good or bad, but we may as well make the best of it."

"I agree."

"Let's say it remarries us. Even if that's the last thought we hold in our heads. Do you agree, Kanu?"

For a moment her words had punched a hole through him. He had been hoping for her absolute forgiveness, but never counting on it. The human capacity for kindness was as infinite and inexhaustible as it was surprising. He had done nothing to earn this moment, and yet he would not refuse it.

"Totally," he said, pinned between joy and horror.

"Swift," she said quietly, "don't say a word, but you are our witness."

Swift did not say a word. But they both sensed him there, fully participant in the same alien betrothal. Then the surface was on them, and in the exquisite and momentary bliss of their remarriage they also knew the Terror.

Except "terror," now that they were in it, was not quite the right word. They struggled to capture the essence of it, after the surface had passed through them and continued on its way, their bodies and minds put back together. But it was both more and less than terror. Better, they thought, to describe it as a total apprehension of the consequences of the present direction of their actions—a kind of absolute, unflinching understanding that they were assuming a responsibility not only to themselves, but to every creature of their kind across all their worlds and systems.

That they were here at the sufferance of the M-builders, and that from this instant on they would be judged against the lofty priorities of that civilisation rather than their own. That the M-builders offered a guarded welcome to the wise and the curious, but reserved only punishment for the foolish and the rapacious. That merely to think in such parochial and human terms was itself an error, and a dangerous one.

That the M-builders had confronted the single most daunting truth facing all intelligent civilisations and arrived at their own response to that truth. That other cultures were free to learn from their example, if they so chose. That the gathering of knowledge was not to be discouraged, and that these guests were at liberty to study the structures and inscriptions of Poseidon as they pleased. The guests would be pleased to hear that the inscriptions contained additional operating guidelines for the transmitting elements of the Mandala network, that obsolete but harmless set of toys that the M-builders had left in place for the benefit of lesser civilisations.

But there was something more.

For on Poseidon, the M-builders had encoded a complete statement of their response to the ultimate truth of life's fate in the cosmos, and these lesser civilisations were free to incorporate the facts of that response into their own strategic planning. But should the disclosure of that response result in the consideration of acts detrimental or injurious to the absolute security of the M-builders, they would not hesitate to enact species-level extinction.

They had the means. They had done it before.

They valued their word.

Kanu understood. He felt it in his bones—as if this was knowledge that had been part of him for every second of his life, no more open to doubt than the specific blue of the sky, the sting of the sun on his neck, the salt of the ocean in his mouth.

In the hundreds of millions of years since their abdication from the affairs of lesser civilisations, other cultures had come into contact with the work of the M-builders. Some, like the Watchkeepers, never passed the first line of protection. They were rebuffed, often violently, but had suffered no wider retribution. Being hollow machines, being dead to consciousness, they were not deemed a threat—more a thing to be pitied, for they knew not what they were.

Others had passed the sampling, known the Terror and believed themselves wise enough to bear that higher responsibility. But they had faltered, allowed their masks to slip, and the M-builders—or rather their vigilant guardians—had decided they posed an unacceptable threat. Judgement had been delivered and punishment meted out. The evidence of that punishment was not hard to find, even now. There were dead worlds, scorched of life. There were stars that had reached the ends of their nuclear burning lifetimes too soon, as if something had stolen their fuel, or made their fusion processes misfire. There were tracts of space where interstellar dust floated too hot and too thin, swept clear by the blasts of supernovae occurring in odd and suggestive clusters of temporal and spatial proximity, like a spree of murders. There were worlds orphaned from their stars, floating in space.

All this and more was the work of the M-builders. They would have done none of it without immense consideration, immense sorrow. Fundamentally, it was never their intention to kill. They would do only that which was necessary. In what might have passed for their alien hearts, they believed these cruelties were a greater kindness—perhaps the greatest kindness of all.

They?

Us.

What are we?

What *were* we?

Much like you, Kanu Akinya—in our fashion.

Life is short, against all the mute measures of the cosmos. A star barely draws breath. A world turns around that star a hundred times.

The galaxy is frozen in an instant of its turning, like a jammed clock. A life begins, a life ends—nothing changes. The clock unjams itself for one vast, godlike tick and a billion souls know their fierce, fast moment in the light.

Until the clock jams again. Until the next tick.

And yet . . .

We are more than the sum of all those short seconds that make up our span. We learn, we give, we love, we are loved. We stir ripples into the wider fabric of social discourse. We are in turn moved by the ripples of other lives. We open books and know the thoughts of those who have lived before us—the hopes and sorrows and golden joys of earlier lives. They move us to laughter or to tears. Their days are over, but in the marks they have left behind their lives continue to resonate. In that sense, their days are limitless. They have lived again, in us.

So it is with all our deeds, all our acts of cleverness and stupidity. Our wars and inventions, our stories and our songs. The houses we make, the worlds we change, the truths we unearth. We end, we conclude, but our deeds continue. In this continuation, a retrospective meaning is shed onto every living moment. There is a point to love, if love itself is remembered. There is a point to the creation of beauty, because beauty will endure. All words, all thoughts, have a chance of transcending death and time. There is no heaven or hell, no afterlife, no divine creator, no great will behind the universe, no meaning beyond that revealed by our senses and our intellects.

This is a hard thing to accept. Yet there is still a point to being alive, and that makes the acceptance bearable.

But the universe withholds even this bleak consolation.

Within its deepest structure, written like a curse into the very mathematics out of which it is forged, the universe contains a suicidal imperative. Vacuum itself is poised in an unstable condition. Given time—and the one certainty is that there will always be time—the vacuum instability will tip the universe into a new state of being. In that instant of uncreation, all information encoded in the present universe will be erased.

No memory of anything will endure. No single experience of any living organism will be preserved. Nothing learned or discovered or made will survive. No art, no science, no history, no deed, no kindness, no fond thought, not a single moment of human happiness.

Nothing will last.

Nothing will matter.

Nothing *has* ever mattered.

When the sampling was done, when the silver wall had passed through them all, the moon spun its filament down to a clean silver spoke and then withdrew it back into the rim. For a moment it hung ahead of them, a moving ring keeping pace with *Icebreaker*. Perhaps their fate was still in the balance, still being adjudicated.

The moon retreated further still. It began to turn on its polar axis, blurring into a hard silver sphere. Then it veered off, returning to the orbit it had vacated during the chase. There were further layers of moons below, but they showed no interest in the ship. Kanu had just enough power to avoid coming too close to any of these moons, but not enough to stop *Icebreaker*'s fall towards the top of the atmosphere.

His head rang like a bell. It was still full of the Terror. Not so much the emotion of terror, he now knew, but rather a very specific sort of terrifying knowledge engraved in his consciousness with the indelible force of truth. He could still feel its argument, sounding out like an after-chime. He looked at his own hand, marvelling at it as if seeing it for the first time. He knew it for what it was: the instrument of a directed intelligence, an extension of himself, the means by which a being such as himself might do anything. Move earth, move water, move the stars, numberless multitudes of them, feel a glittery cascade of them run between his fingers like little grains of diamond sand.

And knew that all of it was futile, that no action had ultimate consequence, that the best and the worst he could be would all be forgotten; that in the white moment of forgetting, even the fact that he had existed, the fact that he had left the tiniest mark on creation, would be lost.

As would everything else.

He was still with Nissa. As they passed one of *Icebreaker*'s airlocks, wordlessly and with no prior exchange, they both slowed and looked at the lock, thinking of the void beyond it, the promise of immediate nullification. He could toss his helmet aside, step into that lock, release the air and life from his lungs.

He had tried to kill himself on *Icebreaker* once before, but that attempted suicide had been born out of desperation, of seeing his death as the only thing that would stop Dakota and at the same time not endanger the sleepers. He had reached the decision to kill himself only as the culmination of a bleak calculus, not because he had wearied of life or sought any kind of release in death. Life had not stopped surprising him; he was not yet ready to surrender it without good reason.

It was different now. His death would have little impact on their chances, and certainly would not improve them. Equally, he had no immediate and pressing external reason for killing himself.

Except that the Terror had reached inside him and negated

every conceivable argument for his continued existence. It was purposeless, a life's ledger of futile acts that was itself doomed to be erased. Nothing would ever matter. Nothing would ever change that single fact, nothing would ever make it more tolerable. How could the M-builders ever have borne such knowledge?

More to the point, how could Kanu Akinya?

Nissa held his gloved hand.

"No," she said.

And he understood.

No.

Not yet.

"I saw it," he stated, filled with a shivering horror. "The Terror. I understood it. It's in me—filling me like a black poison. It'll always be in me."

"I saw it, too," Nissa answered. "It's in me as well. For the moment it's all I can think of. I want to put my hands over my ears and shut it out. It's like a shriek of despair coming from every cell in my body. But we have to be stronger than the Terror. It will pass. It *must*. Chiku endured it."

"I'm not as strong as Chiku."

"Nor am I. But there are two of us. I need you back from the edge, merman. And you need me. Remember, we're married now."

Kanu forced a nod. He did not feel as if there was strength enough in the universe to push aside that soul-swallowing negation he now felt inside himself. But he would have to try.

For both their sakes.

From the bridge he ran the simulations over and over. There was no flaw in them, only a choice of deaths—various angles by which they would hit the air too steeply. *Icebreaker* had been armoured against the crush of the Europan ocean, but that was an entirely different proposition from the aerodynamics of transatmospheric flight.

"Unless I'm missing something—"

"You're not," Swift said. "*Noah* is our only option. It might get us down through that atmosphere."

"Might?"

"Our approach speed is still very high. *Noah* was built to

shuttle between the low orbit of *Zanzibar* and the surface of Crucible, not to cope with a velocity in excess of eighty kilometres per second."

"Can it get us back into clear space?" Nissa asked.

"Not at this speed. We'd still be too deep into the gravity well. At best, we can use *Noah*'s remaining delta-vee to ease our atmospheric entry and trust that aerodynamic braking will do the rest."

Kanu nodded—it was pointless hoping for any more certainty than that. In truth, as he had told the crew of *Mposi*, he was already committed to their fate. He touched a glove to the control pedestal, feeling as if he were about to commit a loyal and dependable workhorse to the slaughterhouse. "It's just a machine, but I almost feel as if I'm betraying it."

"That's Swift, bleeding over," Nissa said.

"What about you, Swift? The image of you inside *Icebreaker*—can you transfer it to *Noah*?"

"I hesitate to say. What's your estimate for the time left to us?"

Kanu glanced at the display, squinting at the confusion of vectors and orbits—it looked like a wrestling match between many-tentacled sea-monsters. "It depends on the point of separation. Too early and the moons may mistake *Noah* for a second expedition—or even interpret it as a threat. In any case, I don't want to go through the Terror again quite so soon. Too late and we won't have sufficient time to decelerate. Either way, we're looking at less then fifteen minutes."

Swift removed his pince-nez and studied the lenses. "Then I would say we are short of time by approximately three weeks minus, of course, those valuable fifteen minutes, since that is how long it would take me to transfer a secondary image to *Noah*."

"Then you're in trouble," Nissa said.

"The image has served its purpose. The version of me inside Kanu still has a chance. If it helps, do not think of one as being distinct from and independent of the other."

"I'm calling Goma," Kanu said, making sure they still had a communications lock on the other ship. "They need to know what's happening. Once we hit the atmosphere, we may not be able to get a signal through." He turned to the matriarch, swivelling his head in the neck ring of his suit. "Dakota—can you move in these conditions?"

"You would have me confined somewhere else while you complete the evacuation?".

"No, I would have you aboard *Noah*—Hector and Lucas, too. This much I'm sure of—none of us passed that test as individuals. It was something in the entirety of us that tipped the scales. Human, Risen, machine. Together. A Trinity, like the first. For that reason alone we're staying together."

"After all our differences? After the threats, the deaths?"

"Recriminations can wait. Right now my main concern is that none of us dies a horrible fiery death. Does that sound like a plan to you?"

"If I were you," Nissa said, "I'd listen to my husband."

CHAPTER 47

On *Mposi* they watched and listened as Kanu informed them that his crew had survived the Terror but were now about to abandon ship. This was no great surprise—he had already mentioned the lander—but privately they had all hoped for some new last-minute opportunity, something that might yet give Kanu a chance of avoiding direct contact with Poseidon.

It was not to be. The larger ship was now within one thousand kilometres of the top of Poseidon's atmosphere and still travelling far too quickly to survive contact with the air. Finally the drive shut down, *Icebreaker* entering terminal free fall, and the lander detached itself. They could see it with their sensors at maximum magnification: it was a tenth the size of the starship, a plump deltoid with a stubby tail fin. Goma had seen similar vehicles in the civic museums in Guochang and Namboze, preserved since the early days of Crucible's settlement. She knew very well that they had not been designed for the gruelling environment of a sweltering superterran world such as Poseidon.

The lander fired its control thrusters and opened up the distance from its mother craft. Once it had achieved a kilometre of separation, *Noah*'s own engine started up, trying to whittle down yet more residual velocity before it met the friction of the upper atmosphere. From *Mposi*'s point of view, Poseidon's visible face was half in day and half in night, with the two ships tiny bright points against the darkening line of the terminator.

"I hate to state the obvious," Eunice said, glaring at her wrists which had just been freed of the restraints, "but Kanu won't have achieved much if the Risen still end up crushed to death under the re-entry loads."

"He'll have gained the world," Goma said, "because when he had a choice, he did the human thing."

"You mean the futile thing."

"If you want to start passing as one of us, start thinking a little less analytically. Would you really have allowed the Risen to die?"

"Dakota? In a heartbeat."

"And the others? We know there are more of them aboard."

She met this with a non-answer of pursed lips. But it was enough for Goma to know that Eunice had her limits.

"I've signalled Nasim," Vasin said, without much enthusiasm in her voice. "Told him to bring *Travertine* in on a fast rendezvous. We can't do a thing for Kanu, but we have a transatmospheric lander on the main ship. If all else fails, we could send it down under autonomous control."

Goma nodded—it was the right thing to do, but even if it did get anywhere near the surface, it would make no difference to Kanu's chances. On the scale of a solar system, especially a compact one like this, *Travertine* was no faster than *Mposi*. It would still need several days to cross the system from its orbit around Orison.

But what else was a captain to do but give orders that contained the promise of hope?

"Thank you, Gandhari. And thank you for letting Eunice out of those restraints."

"She isn't forgiven—not until I work out what exactly she needs to be forgiven for—but I gain nothing by keeping her tied up. She's clearly smart enough to use us whichever way she sees fit, and for now I'd rather we at least entertain the illusion of cooperation."

"You can forgive her when you're ready," Ru said.

Eunice looked unfazed. "I don't need anyone's forgiveness. I did what needed to be done."

"What she did was brutal," Goma said. "No one's disputing that. But she's also right that it was the only thing that would help Kanu."

"And remind me how it helped Kanu, exactly?" Ru said. "Because from where I'm sitting, they're in just as much trouble as they ever were."

"He had the choice," Goma said. "That's all that mattered. That the choice was his, finally, and he made the only one he could live with."

"She got to you," Ru said, shaking her head in disgust. "When you took that bath, in the well, she spread a little of her poison into you. Didn't you, Eunice?"

"Please," Grave said, interceding with raised hands. "Everybody—what is done is done. We can either carry our grievances forward and let them weigh us down, or allow them to blow away like dandelion seeds."

"Why should we listen to a word you have to say?" Ru asked, without a flicker of anger or accusation. "You're a believer, drowning in your own superstition. You're the enemy of all that's rational."

"I was also wronged. Each of you, in your way, was ready to see the worst in me. But I blame none of you for that, or for the differences of opinion you now share. The truth is that Eunice has a perspective none of us presently understands. She has been here before and she truly grasps the consequences. Until we attain her perspective, we cannot judge her. Nor can we blame ourselves if our sympathies do not always align. Ru—you have the right to feel aggrieved. You were also wronged, and in a terrible way. But Eunice acted on the facts available to her, and from her standpoint it was a perfectly rational decision. Something was hurting her friends, something in your blood. Ask yourself how quick you would have been to look beyond the obvious explanation—that you were a willing agent in the killing of the Risen?" But Grave did not give her the luxury of dwelling on an answer. "Goma is right, and it has nothing to do with Eunice. She's just seeing things clearly, as we all should. Kanu has done the only human thing possible, as any of us might have under the same circumstances. And if it took the *Zanzibar* translation to bring us to this moment, this chance of a final reconciliation between humans and the Risen, I think it will have been for the best."

"You people love your sacrifices," Ru said.

"And you people love your certainties. None of us are enemies, Ru—at least, none of us needs to be." And he nodded at the blue transected disk of Poseidon, swelling larger in their sky by the minute. "Not in the face of that."

CHAPTER 48

Nissa eased her bulky, suited form into the command position aboard the shuttle *Noah*, quickly familiarising herself with the layout of the instruments and control inputs: they were not too dissimilar from those aboard *Fall of Night*. Under normal circumstances, the shuttle would have gladly flown itself. But these particular circumstances were anything but normal, and the lander was all too willing to turn to human guidance.

"The poor thing's confused," Nissa said. "Like a dog being made to learn a new trick. It can't find an acceptable entry solution and is wondering why it's been placed in this position."

"You mean it knows we're all going to die and it doesn't want to be a co-conspirator?" Kanu asked.

"Think kindly of it," Swift said. "It's a simple machine and it's doing its best. Might I suggest a slightly steeper angle of attack—say, two additional degrees of nose-up elevation?"

"Am I flying this or are you?"

"My abject apologies. Under the circumstances, you are doing a most creditable job."

But Nissa altered their approach angle anyway and consented to allow Swift to offer such advice as he deemed useful. The fact was, even Swift could not be expected to work miracles.

"If it's the last thing we do," Kanu said, "it would be a shame not to see one of the wheels up close. Can you find us an entry profile that gets us within visual range of a suitable wheel?"

"Already done," Nissa said. "And it's not just out of curiosity, either. Those wheels are the closest thing we're going to find to dry land. I know this ship's supposed to float but I'd sooner not stake my life on it."

"It's a good plan," Kanu said.

But they both knew it was barely a plan at all. They would have no choice but to land in open water, for *Noah* had no means of setting down on the wheels even if there had been a suitable hard landing surface. For a few minutes they deliberated about attempting a controlled descent onto one of the floating biomasses, but all the evidence suggested that the living rafts were too tenuous to bear the lander's weight, let alone absorb the shock of impact without rupturing. And then they would be back in water again, except this time choked in from all directions. Besides, none of the biomasses came within five thousand kilometres of any of the wheels.

With the lander still under thrust, Kanu made his way back from the command position to the Risen. They were in support hammocks identical to the ones on the larger ship. He braced a hand against the ceiling and leaned in to Dakota.

"We'll be hitting air in a few minutes. Nissa's going to find us the smoothest way down, and we'll try to hold our deceleration at a manageable level. I can't promise it'll be easy, though."

"Nor can we expect the impossible of you," Dakota said.

"Of any of us. But before things get tough, we need to think ahead. You had years to plan this expedition. Is this ship well stocked with equipment?"

"What do you have in mind?"

"Whatever we need to survive on the surface. We'll float, while we're able. But you knew this was a waterworld, and that the wheels are the only solid surfaces. How were you hoping this would play out?"

"A close visual inspection of the wheels. The analysis of the encoded patterns—the understanding of their context."

"From the air?"

"Most certainly. Your ship could have coped with atmospheric insertion had our approach speed been low enough. What can be learned from the tiny parts of the wheels at the ocean's surface?"

"Right now I'm more concerned with not dying." He would have smiled at his own remark had the black toxin of the Terror not still been within him. The absence of hope, the absence of purpose, the inability to see a point to any act, the realisation of the supreme and total futility of existence—he could not begin to imagine how it would be possible to live with this hollow, howling void inside him, sucking the hope out of every moment.

And yet Nissa said there had to be a way. She was feeling it, too—so surely were the Tantors. And yet, as Nissa had pointed out, Chiku must eventually have come to an accommodation with the facts of the Terror. Life could go on—purpose found again. Presently Kanu saw no way through his present despair, but for Nissa's sake he would trust her judgement—trust that there was a path, a way of living, that would make this bearable. That the void would close.

"We can use one of the wheels as a safe haven," he continued. "Those inscriptions, the ones we saw from space—they're deep, cut into the wheel like ledges. If we can get onto one of those ledges—"

"Then what, Kanu?" Dakota asked, with an edge of desperation.

"*Mposi* isn't far behind us. I've told Goma to turn around, but if there's a shred of Akinya in her, I might as well have been whistling in the wind."

"It will not help."

"I'm not just going to drown, Dakota. Or let you drown, for that matter. If the lander's in poor shape, we need a survival plan. None of us is going to cope well with Poseidon's heat even if we can breathe the atmosphere for a while. Let's start with the basics. Can we cross water?"

"There are powered rafts. They can be deployed and inflated when we are down."

"I hope they're big."

"Do you think we would forget what we are, Kanu?"

"I'm sorry." He scratched his glove through his bristle of white hair. "What about exposure to the atmosphere—do you have suits aboard *Noah* as well?"

"There are emergency suits. They are not as capable as the one I wore to visit the Watchkeepers, but they will function."

"Can you get into them once we're down?"

"We shall try. As for the rafts, they are in the external compartments. They cannot be reached from here."

"As long as we can access them when we're down." Something in him made him place a hand on Dakota. "We're not done yet. Not while there's breath in our lungs."

"Do you believe that, Kanu?"

"I'm trying to."

It was a performance, a mental tightrope act. One foot before the next and never look down. Think only of the present moment, and perhaps the moment to come. Kanu wondered how long he could sustain it.

"Kanu," Nissa shouted. "You'd better see this."

While they were decelerating, *Icebreaker* had carried on ahead, meeting the atmosphere first and at a sharper angle. Now it was encountering significant friction, beginning to shroud itself in a cocoon of plasma. Kanu stared at it with a sort of horrified wonder, finding it hard to imagine that they had been inside that doomed ship less than an hour ago. It looked tiny now—a thing of utter insignificance against the larger backdrop of Poseidon.

"Starting to tumble," he said, noticing that the hull was sliding in at an oblique angle, cats'-tails of plasma bannering out from the leading surface, the brightness of which was still turned away from them.

"It won't be long now," Swift said.

"Are you still in contact with the image of yourself?" Kanu asked.

"We made our peace. But I am sorry for your ship. It did well to get us this far."

"Good job there's another ship to take us out of this system," Nissa said.

Kanu nodded, glad to endorse the sentiment, although they both knew their chances of leaving this world, let alone this system, were diminishing rapidly.

He felt a bump, then a shudder.

"Strap in," Nissa said. "Now it's our turn."

Noah's engine had done the best it could; now aerobraking was the only thing that stood between them and a rapid crash into the sea. Kanu had offered Dakota the best assurance he could, but the projections of their entry profile gave him no great confidence. Depending on minute and subtle factors of aerodynamics and tropospheric physics, their peak gee-load could be anywhere between two and five gees. Even the upper limit might be tolerated by the Risen if it was short in duration, but he could make no promises.

Icebreaker was pinwheeling now, about fifty kilometres deeper into the atmosphere and throwing off molten pieces of itself like the arms of a spiral galaxy. Nissa's entry profile had to take that into consideration as well—the last thing they wanted was to ram into debris from the larger ship or the turbulence stirred up by its passage. But she dared not steer too far off their plotted course or they might end up tens of thousands of kilometres from the closest wheel.

Kanu was surprised that the towering structures were not more obvious now they were sliding into the atmosphere's thickening depths. But the wheels were much narrower than they were tall, and what was clear to long-range sensors was anything but distinct to the human eye. One wheel lay dead ahead of them, but it was edge on—no more than a pale scratch rising from the blue, which Kanu easily lost track of if he allowed his gaze to slip to either side of it. Besides, the air outside was beginning to glow, taking on a rosy flicker as *Noah* started to pick up its own cocoon of ionised atoms. When the brightness reached a certain level, the windows shuttered automatically.

As the air resistance increased, so the deceleration forces mounted. The load exceeded one gee, reached one and a half—the force they would experience on Poseidon's surface, hard but bearable—and then climbed to two gees. Kanu dared hope that it would level out there, sparing the Risen more difficulties, but the needle was still creeping up. Two and a half, then three.

He twisted back in his seat to address them. "It can't last too long. Hold out as best you can."

"Still climbing," Nissa said.

At four gees it was all Kanu could do to breathe. His view of the instruments and readouts blurred as darkness stole in around the edges of his vision. Even through the layers of his suit, the chair felt as if it was made of knives.

A minute of that, maybe two, and he sensed an easing. The ride smoothed out and the gee-load dropped smoothly down to one and a half. Without warning the automatic shutters raised again and the blue light of an alien world pushed its way into Kanu's eyes. They were in the lower layers of the atmosphere now, still descending but under some aerodynamic control. The upper half of the sky remained very dark, a purple that inked to a starless velvet black, but it was gaining in blue opacity with each kilometre they dropped. Poseidon was a huge world compared to Earth, or indeed any planet in Kanu's direct experience. Huge and hot, despite the coolness of its sun. That surface warmth made its atmosphere swell like a loaf of bread, puffing higher into space. But its surface gravity was higher as well, jealously tugging the atmosphere closer to the ground, acting against the effect of the increased temperature. The net result was that the atmosphere thinned out with height in close similarity to the air on Earth, with almost all of it squeezed into a layer less than a hundred kilometres thick.

They were in the lower quarter of that layer now and Noah's wings were becoming increasingly effective. They were flying, nearly. Kanu knew that their difficulties were far from over but it was a blessing to have made it this far, and he vowed not to be ungrateful for it.

"Nice job."

"Thank you. But we've taken a fair battering." Nissa

directed his attention to the many warning symbols on the console. "We came in harder and hotter than anyone ever intended."

Kanu was certain that the air in the cabin was warmer than it had been before they hit the atmosphere.

"But we're still here, so the damage can't be too great, can it?"

"I think the hull got pretty chewed up in places. You say this thing is meant to float?"

"So I gather."

"Then let's hope we're not full of holes."

The ride was smooth now, the gee-load coming from Poseidon rather than their own deceleration. He unbuckled, anxious to check on the Tantors. He moved cautiously, feeling like he was carrying at least his own body weight on his back.

In an instant his world turned white, a white that shaded to pink at the edges where it rammed through the lander's windows. Now the forms of the windows were precise negatives of themselves, burned across his retinas like brands.

"What—" he started to say.

"*Icebreaker*," Swift said, with disarming coolness. "The Chibesa core must have detonated."

"Did you know that was coming?"

"It was always a possibility."

"Then you might have mentioned it!" Kanu pulled himself further along the cabin. His vision was clearing slowly, the after-images fading—they had not been exposed to the full and direct effect of the blast, but it had been bad enough. Reaching a window, he stared at the curve of the sea below, so smooth and flawless that it might have been machined from an ingot of hard blue metal. He watched a line slide across that flawlessness, a demarcation, travelling impossibly quickly, turning the shining sea to a leathery texture where it had passed.

"Nissa! Shock wave! Bank hard. Put our belly to the blast. When that wave hits—"

She had already begun to turn them, anticipating exactly that, and Kanu grabbed for a ceiling rail as *Noah* pitched steeply. He watched the Risen swing in their hammocks, elephant-masses providing a demonstration of pure Newtonian mechanics.

The shock wave hit. Kanu had braced for it, but still he was jolted from his feet and sent tumbling against the opposite wall. His suit absorbed the worst of it but the impact was still hard enough to drive the breath from his lungs. He was too stunned to know whether he had hurt himself or not. But however unpleasant it had been for him, it must have been worse for the Risen. Their hammocks were meant to absorb continuous loads, not sudden shocks.

"Nissa?" he called.

"Levelling off. Guessing we're through the worst of it."

"Any damage?"

"How long have you got, merman? Whatever was wrong with us before, that didn't help."

"But we're still flying."

"On a steady descent, about five hundred metres per minute. We should have brought *Fall of Night*, not this barely flyable brick."

"Can we still make it close to that wheel?"

"Depends on your definition of close."

"We can cross water if we need to. There are rafts—big enough for all of us."

"They'd better be. We're coming up on the wheel now—this may be your one chance for a good look before we ditch. Do you want to see it?"

"More than anything in the world. I'll be there in a moment."

He had reached the Risen. He knelt by Dakota, glad when her pink-rimmed eye made contact with his.

"We're through the worst of it, I think. *Icebreaker* blew up and we ran into the shock wave. But other than the splashdown, we shouldn't hit anything you can't handle. Are you all right?"

"I was always the hardiest of us, Kanu. Hector is alive, though weak. But Lucas has passed into the Remembering."

It took only a glance to confirm this news. Hector looked drowsy, but his gaze still tracked Kanu and a twitch of his trunk signalled the presence of life. The other Risen's eyes were open but quite unseeing. Kanu stared at the mountainous swell of his ribcage. It remained as still as a rock.

"I'm sorry."

"We are stronger than you in so many ways, yet weaker in others. How far are we from the sea?"

"Pretty close now. When we ditch . . . well, I'll do what I can for everyone. Best stay in the hammock until we hit water."

"I shall."

Kanu glanced out through the window again. The waters ruffled by the shock wave were returning to their former stillness. He tried to estimate their height from the hammered texture of the wave-tops, but it was impossible. And there was nothing down there, no rock or living thing, no trace of human presence, to offer the slightest hint of scale.

"You're missing the show," Nissa said.

He returned to the command deck, trying to put aside thoughts of what lay ahead by confining himself to the present moment, to the spectacle the universe had seen fit to let him witness.

Half of the wheel was hidden to him, lost beneath the water's surface. The visible portion arched from the ocean in two places, separated by the two hundred kilometres of the wheel's diameter. The nearest of those two points was only a few tens of kilometres from *Noah*. They were circling it now while also losing height—and still coming down harder and faster than Kanu would have wished. The upper portion of the wheel was not visible at all, but that owed less to Poseidon's curvature than to the presence of so much atmosphere in between, hazing out detail and contrast. Looking up, he could track the ascent of the nearest arc, soaring almost vertically to begin with but gradually evidencing its great circular curve as it pushed higher and higher, finally cresting the atmosphere and vaulting into open space. There was much less air to obscure his vision when he looked to the zenith and the wheel's arc was traceable far past its maximum height. He followed the fading white scratch until it vanished into the haze, pointing to the place on the horizon where the rest of the wheel must lie.

They continued descending. The wheel's tread was a kilometre across; its rim had about the same depth. From space they had detected a suggestion of dense patterning on the surface, a complex, shifting backscatter of metallic traces. Now their eyes were all the equipment they needed to gather more data. The wheels only looked smooth from a distance; up close they bore a finely printed text. A pattern of grooves had been cut into both the tread and the rim, as sharp-edged as if they had been lasered yesterday. On the tread, the patterns consisted of horizontal grooves, one above the other, running nearly the full width of the wheel. The grooves were only straight when averaged across their length. On a scale of a few metres, they exhibited a series of angular changes of direction, sometimes doubling back before resuming course. Each groove appeared distinct from those above or below it, but it was impossible to look at more than a few at any one time. There were no more than ten metres between each groove; if the wheel's circumference was somewhere in the region of six hundred kilometres, then there could be many hundreds of thousands of these grooves—more grooves than there were words in a book. The rims, meanwhile, carried about a hundred concentric grooves—circular statements which Kanu presumed continued all the way around the wheel. On the wheel's concave face, too, were yet more angular grooves.

Kanu reminded himself that there were other wheels all over the planet. Some intuition told him that the wheels must each contain distinct patterns. If each wheel was a book, then Poseidon was a library.

"I'm no expert," he said, "but that looks like the same sort of writing they found on Mandala."

Nissa nodded. "No surprise if the M-builders were here."

"The same language," Swift said, "but not necessarily serving the same function. Eunice was only able to trigger the Mandala because the syntax provided a set of operating rules. This has to be something different."

"Operating rules for the wheels?" Kanu speculated. "We know they're multifunctional—they can become the moons, if needed, or the moons can turn into wheels."

"Perhaps," Swift said.

"You think it's something else."

"If the Terror taught me one thing, it's that there are answers here—otherwise why guard against the likes of us? Perhaps a history, an accounting of what became of the M-builders. The wheels may encode that history, collectively or individually, and we have been granted permission to read it."

"Then it's a pity we don't have the lexicon," Nissa said. "Or did Eunice share that with you during your blissful communion?"

"No—there wasn't time for anything like that. But you are right—she would know what to make of this, I think. Better than I do, at any rate. I think I may have outlasted my usefulness to you both."

"We'll be the judge of that," Kanu said. "Anyway, you're here for the same reason I am—to see and learn. So make the most of it."

"Believe me, I am doing my utmost."

As they spiralled down, Nissa strove to bring them closer and closer to the point where the wheel rim thrust from the waters. The scale of it had been overwhelming enough in abstract terms, but now Kanu had the sense of some stupendous cliff or pillar rising from the sea, a thing of imperturbable mass and solidity. They could dash *Noah* against it and not even leave a blemish.

"One more circuit, if we're lucky," Nissa said. "Are the Risen ready?"

"It's just Dakota and Hector now. I'm afraid Lucas didn't make it."

She must have heard something in his voice. "You're sad about that, aren't you?"

"I don't know. A little while ago I'd have given a lot to see the three of them dead. But I can't rejoice."

"Maybe Lucas was the lucky one—he got it over with quickly."

"We'll see."

Chimes sounded; *Noah* had detected the approach of the sea's surface, thinking in its simple-minded way that it was still ferrying people from orbit to Crucible.

Whatever happened, it would not be long now until they hit the water.

CHAPTER 49

Mposi was not yet committed to entering the thresh of moons, but it would not be long before they ran out of time to turn around. "We can go a little deeper," Vasin said, "but it'll gain us very little in terms of our view and it probably won't help them at all. The best we can do—the only responsible thing— is document their actions from this distance, so that at least we have a chance of telling someone else about them."

"You're not dead," Eunice said, "until you've left a crater big enough to stick a name on."

"They won't leave much of a crater on a waterworld," Vasin replied brusquely. "Anyway, what do you propose? This is a heavy lander, built like a squared-off brick. We are not remotely atmosphere-capable. And that's not a question of skill or daring—it's a basic limitation of the vehicle. Drop it into air, it'll rip itself to pieces."

"If we keep our speed low, we can hold the aerodynamic stresses at a safe level."

"Perhaps. But the engine's not rated to run in atmosphere, and we'd need to fire it continuously to keep our speed low enough to avoid structural overload—basically we'd be descending on a pillar of flame. That's fine in the upper atmosphere, but as soon as it thickens up, we'd run into significant thermal transfer. We'll superheat the air we're descending into, and on top of that, our exhaust plasma will back up all the way to our tail quicker than you can blink. It's easy to say that we should have brought something that can fly in air—but when we left *Travertine*, this wasn't exactly where we thought we'd wind up."

Eunice absorbed this without further argument—it was clear to Goma that she accepted the essential truthfulness of

Vasin's statement; just as it was clear that Eunice would not have rested without exploring all the options, however slight they might appear.

"Then there's nothing aboard—no escape pod or capsule—that we can send down into the atmosphere?"

"Nothing," Vasin said. "And believe me, I wish it were otherwise. But if they can hold out long enough for Nasim to get here, maybe we can do something for them."

"You should see this?" said Loring.

Vasin looked more irritated than intrigued. "Will it change our options?"

"Not certain? Changes *something*, for sure."

Ve had arranged a display of the space around Poseidon, collating data from both *Mposi* and *Travertine*. It was as up to date as the latency of time lag and sensors allowed, showing the relative positions of the moons and spacecraft with high accuracy.

Something was happening to the moons.

"Kanu passed through," Loring was saying. "We all saw it? Happened just as Eunice warned us? One of the moons chased down his ship, swallowed it, put them through . . . what did you call it?"

"The Terror. The ultimate line in the sand, which the moon clearly deemed Kanu fit to pass." Eunice was rubbing at the welts on her wrist where she had been restrained. "But that didn't surprise me—Dakota had already made the crossing, so why would it turn her back now?"

"A million reasons," Vasin said. "Still—what's the significance of this? Have you seen anything like this before?"

"I don't think so."

"You don't *think* so?"

"At my age, you become forgetful. But no, I believe this is new to me. Shall I speculate?"

"The floor's all yours," Vasin said.

"Kanu was scanned by the M-builders the way the Trinity was and they've allowed him safe passage to Poseidon. But the moons see us as more of the same—just another extension of the same interested intelligence. They must recognise some basic kinship between us and them—something that indicates we share the same biological concerns and imperatives—for now. It's allowed him through, so for the moment the gates are open. The moons are giving us clear passage."

"You can't know that for sure," Ru said.

"And your contribution to this debate is . . . what, exactly?"

Still, it was true about the moons—they were not following their usual orbits, or rather their orbits had begun to bend, lining up into a single flat ecliptic. They had not yet settled into that configuration—it would take hours at the present rate of change—but the end-state could be easily predicted.

"Ru's right, though," Goma said. "That could just as easily be a final 'keep out' as an invitation."

"Thank you," Ru answered, pushing her words through clenched teeth.

"It's of theoretical interest," Vasin said, "but it changes nothing. We haven't suddenly become a different ship, and all the barriers to landing on Poseidon I've already mentioned still apply."

"Then we don't," Eunice declared. "You said the ship isn't built for atmosphere. But we could land on top of one of those wheels, couldn't we? Give me a reason why that wouldn't work."

"How about because it's totally pointless? We still wouldn't be able to get help to Kanu."

Eunice looked around the room, eyes wide with disbelief. "Give me a break, Gandhari. This ship is stuffed with supplies."

"Which would still be a hundred kilometres from the surface. The time it would take to climb down . . . *if* there was a way to do that . . . and then what?"

"Lower supplies to them—rations, clothing, medical gear, whatever they need. Enough to keep them going until *Travertine* arrives. And if that doesn't work, they can tie themselves to the rope and let us haul them back into space."

"One hundred kilometres?"

"Why not?"

Vasin sighed. "Because I reviewed the equipment manifest myself so I know exactly what we have aboard. We have docking tethers, surface-penetrating grapples and power winches. But the tethers won't reach that far—we brought them to help us hook onto *Zanzibar*, if it came to that. I saw no need for longer lines on this trip, and I'm not even sure *Travertine* could have supplied them if I had."

"How long," Goma said, "is the longest tether?"

"Forty, fifty—no more than that. They're not made to be joined together, either."

"It's not enough," Ru said.

"Next time you put together a supply manifest," Eunice said, "ask for some help."

"Nobody could have anticipated this," Vasin said. "Not even you."

CHAPTER 50

Kanu had gone back to the two surviving Risen, who were still in their hammocks. "You should prepare yourselves," he told them. "There'll be a bump, I think, but nothing worse than what we've already been through. How are you coping with the gravity? Do you think you can stand it?"

"I believe the gravity may be the least of our problems, Kanu. I shudder to imagine the depth of water beneath us, that it can swallow half the width of that wheel. Have you seen it?"

"Yes. It's magnificent. And humbling. Whoever made it, they weren't exactly lacking in confidence."

"No, I do not think they were. I saw some of it through the window. I would very much like the time to know it better—the time to study those writings. Do you know the strange thing, Kanu?"

"This is all strange, frankly."

"Then let us talk of specifics. For as long as I can remember, I have wanted nothing more than to be here, inside the mysteries of Poseidon. Within the sentinel moons, having once more endured the Terror, close enough to see the wheels, close enough to understand them for myself. And yet now that I am here, I realise there can be no understanding. Not for me, at least. I gather information, but I was never intended to be anything more than a recording instrument, a conduit to transmit observations to the minds of the Watchkeepers. I am their eyes, a branch of their extended nervous system—nothing more."

Once again Kanu marvelled at the bony prominence of her forehead, holding back the force of her mind like the wall of a dam.

"I think you underestimate yourself, Dakota."

"I think they would say that I have failed them. I might say that I have failed myself."

"No," Kanu said. "Not yet."

"You ought to despise me, knowing what I ordered done. But while there is time, I would like to absolve Memphis of any complicity in my actions. Should the opportunity present itself, I would ask you to present this information to your fellows—the other humans. If they find *Zanzibar* again, Memphis ought not to be blamed for the deaths of the Friends."

Kanu phrased his question as softly as he was able. "Because he was only following orders?"

"Because there were no deaths. I deceived you. The hundred cold corpses? They were already long past any chance of revival. I told Memphis to use only those who could never live again."

Kanu nodded slowly—he had no means of validating this claim, but it did not strike him as a lie. She had continued to value and respect the Friends long before his arrival, and he believed that she felt genuine remorse for the humans who had perished during the time of troubles.

"And if another hundred had needed to die?"

"I trusted that my point would be adequately made by those first hundred."

He smiled. "It was."

"What became of me, Kanu, to bring us to this place?"

"Nothing you need blame yourself for."

"I made questionable choices."

"So did we all." He set his jaw, tried to look confident in the face of dauntless odds—one of the oldest tricks in the book of diplomacy. The void was still inside him—it was going to take more than a few hours of his life to eclipse that darkness. But like a stiff new spacesuit, cumbersome at first, he was beginning to adjust to its presence. "We'll be hitting the water very soon. The odds are that the ship isn't in excellent shape, but we'll do our best to hold it together."

"We always do our best."

The impact was hard, but perhaps not as bad as he had feared. After the initial bump, *Noah*'s momentum carried it through the water, bellying up and then settling into a level configuration. Water sizzled where it touched the still-hot hull and fanned out in butterfly wings of spray on either side. And then they were resting, with barely any rocking from side to side as the lander floated. Dakota and Hector began to extract themselves from their hammocks, Hector labouring over it at first, then appearing to find some of his old strength.

Kanu went forward. Nissa was already out of her seat.

"Well, we're down," she said. "More than I was expecting when that shock wave hit us."

"We're in one piece. How is the ship?"

"I wouldn't bet my life on it—or yours. If the hull's as damaged as it thinks it is, we may not remain afloat for long."

Kanu leaned down for a better look through the window. "You did well. Hard to say, but I don't think we can be much more than five kilometres from that wheel. We should be able to cross that, and then find a way to set up camp on the wheel."

"I hope they packed some climbing gear."

"We'll manage," he said.

But the simpler truth was that he could think of better ways of dying than drowning in a sinking ship. Dying in open water was scarcely an improvement, but if it came to it, at least the choice would have been his. He knew they had no hope on the wheel, not now that its sheer size was so clear. And although it might only be a short distance from the waves up to the nearest groove—a scant few metres, probably—what use was that to an elephant?

They would die, all of them. But at least they would be moving.

"That's it," Nissa said, nodding at the horizon. "We're picking up a definite list to the right. *Noah*'s flooding."

"Time to go."

Dakota showed him to the onboard equipment store. It was well stocked, a mixture of the old and the new—items that must have come from Crucible and others fashioned more recently, for the express convenience of Tantors. They had supplementary oxygen supplies, water flasks, bales of compressed food concentrate. They decided to empty some of the flasks so they could serve as flotation aids. Meanwhile, Nissa and Kanu locked their helmets down over their neck rings but kept their external air valves open so they were not yet reliant on suit air. These were simple suits with a fixed supply of no more than twenty hours, and the less they used of that air now, the better. They strapped on as much of the equipment and supplies as they could manage.

Periodically, Nissa bent down to inspect the angle of the horizon, but Kanu could tell without looking that they were taking in more water. It was starting to become difficult to move around under the gee and a half of gravity and with the floor gaining a steepening tilt. Kanu moved to the side lock and operated the manual pressure equalisation, allowing Poseidon's atmosphere to flood into *Noah*.

He inhaled deeply. It was oven-warm even after it had passed through the suit's intake valve. The oxygen partial pressure was enough to keep them alive, although it would be similar to breathing at altitude. If there were organisms or toxins in the air, his suit had not yet detected them. Either way, he doubted they were his most pressing concern.

He opened both the inner and outer doors of the airlock. They were looking out over the wing that was already dipping down into the sea. The sun glared off it in an arc of brightness. The water had begun lapping over its furthest edge.

"We need the rafts," Kanu said. "They're in the external hold, just aft of the wing. It's not underwater yet, but once it is we may find it hard to open against the sea pressure. I'm going in now."

"Take care," Nissa said.

He grinned back at her. "I used to be a merman."

It was getting warm in his helmet—like inhaling the hot spent air from the mouth of a giant. The refrigeration cycle would not work properly until the suit was running off its own air supply, and he did not want to commit to that just yet. Outside, the temperature was a shade over fifty degrees. The organisms that floated on the ocean, the great green biomass rafts, were operating near the upper thermal limit for multicellular life forms.

He was out on the wing now. He moved to the edge, cautious on the slippery upper surface, and eased himself into a seated position, dipping booted feet into the water. He closed the intake valve and slid in. The water closed over him in an instant. Nets of sunlight wavered overhead. He surfaced and found that he was able to float, the suit providing sufficient buoyancy.

At least the waves were gentle. He swam to the cargo hold, most of its door still just above water. Next to the hold was a fold-back panel with scuffed stencilling in Swahili and Chinese. Kanu read enough to identify the panel as containing the manual release. He dug his gloved fingers into the gap around the panel and tried to hinge it back.

It would not move.

Kanu tried and tried again, but he had nothing to brace against and his fingertips refused to gain traction on the smooth, glossy material. Quickly he sensed that the effort was futile. Nissa was standing on the wing, leaning forward to watch with her hands resting on her knees. Her voice boomed out through the amplifier in her neck ring. "What's wrong?"

"Won't work. Must've picked up some damage during the entry."

"Can Swift help?"

"I think we'd have already heard by now if he could."

The lander lurched, its tilt increasing by several degrees from one moment to the next. It stabilised, but the sudden change had nearly sent Nissa tumbling.

"Something just flooded in a hurry."

"Get the Risen out," Kanu called. "Once it goes, it may go fast."

"What about the rafts?"

"I don't think we're getting rafts. Not today."

Neither Dakota nor Hector wanted to abandon dead Lucas,

but when the lander tilted again, fear overcame their unwillingness. They shuffled out onto the wing, heavy under their
burden of equipment, each footfall seeming to transmit itself
through the fabric of the ship, into the water in which Kanu
floated. He urged Nissa to join him, fearful that *Noah* was
about to upend itself without warning. She held her mask for
safety and splashed into the water. He reached out a hand, but
Nissa was strong enough to tread water on her own.

The Risen were wearing their emergency spacesuits. They
were made of a flexible grey fabric with accordioned limb
joints, the round-eyed helmets similar in design to the one
Dakota had already used. The suits would have been easier
and quicker to don in the confined space of the shuttle, but to
Kanu's eyes they had a makeshift look about them, like something sewn together by prisoners as part of an escape attempt.

There was no graceful way for the Risen to enter the sea.
They bounded off the wing, making two bomb-like splashes
before resurfacing, armour-sheathed trunks periscoping for
the sky in a pure reflex to immersion.

Dakota's voice boomed from the white mask of her helmet.
He had no trouble telling the two Tantors apart, for the differences in their size and body shape were still obvious despite
the suits.

"What is the difficulty, Kanu?"

"We can't use the rafts—the door's jammed. We'll have to
swim for it. We can do that, can't we? It's not too far."

"In spacesuits?" Nissa asked.

"Better in them than out—we'd boil alive in these waters."
He looked back at the floating ship, now listing hard to one
side. "Whatever we do, I don't think it's a good idea to stay
close to *Noah*."

At least there was no wind or ocean current, and no doubt
as to the direction in which they needed to swim. The wheel's
rim was the only landmark to be seen in any direction. The
sky was cloudless. Even when the waves lapped high enough
to hide its base, they could always see the wheel's soaring
flanks.

They swam out from the lander, the two humans setting the
pace, the two Risen following. The going was not too hard at

first. Kanu kept looking back, to reassure himself that Dakota and Hector were indeed still with them. He heard the regular huff and chuff of their suits' life-support systems—oxygen packs strapped like panniers to either side of them—but beyond that they made little noise, with all the work of swimming going on under the surface. It struck him as profoundly absurd that elephants should be so capable in water, but there was the evidence. Not that it was easy for them, for they felt the pull of gravity just as surely as on land, and it took work to move those muscles and bones.

Kanu and Nissa floated well enough but they needed to move arms and legs to make any headway in the direction of the wheel. That was fine for a while, but before long Kanu felt himself beginning to overheat. Immersed in water, the suits were having trouble keeping their wearers cool. Kanu found himself needing to pause, allowing his strength to recover and the suit to chill down again from his labours. He tried to find a posture that kept as much of his backpack out of the sea as possible, giving its radiators the best chance to work. He hoped all the critical systems were watertight.

"It's as far away as ever," Nissa said when they stopped for the fourth time.

Kanu could not disagree. Equally, the lander now looked very distant, so they had come some way. While they paused, he watched *Noah* with agonies of indecision. It had not sunk so far, and the angle of its tilt did not appear to have worsened since they abandoned it. Perhaps they had made a terrible miscalculation in surrendering their chances to the sea. Could they make it back? It was better than their chances of getting to the still-distant wheel, he reckoned.

"Look," Nissa said.

She was nodding back to the only other thing visible besides the wheel and the four swimmers.

Something was taking *Noah*.

A dark mass, grey-green, glossily brilliant and quilted with scales, had swelled up from the water and enclosed some muscular parts of itself around the lander. From this low, bobbing vantage he could make out no more than that. Perhaps that was for the best.

"There aren't supposed to be monsters here," he said, feel-ing oddly calm in spite of himself. "It's too warm. Nothing multicellular should be able to hold itself together."

"We're multicellular," Nissa said, still watching as the grey-green thing hauled *Noah* out of sight.

"For now."

"Is that a joke?"

"Not a good one. I apologise."

Kanu supposed that the monster must have come up to the surface from much cooler depths below, kilometres down, where perhaps a whole marine ecology lay waiting and undis-covered. Perhaps, once in a great while, the denizens of these cool black layers detected some surface disturbance which made the journey into the warm layers worth the risk of overheating.

After that, there was no point looking back. They swam on because to do otherwise was to leave space in their thoughts to dwell on the apparition. But the swimming cost Kanu so much of himself that after willing his arms and legs into motion, he had nothing else to spare. A sea-monster of some kind. But he had known sea-monsters and not all of them were monstrous.

Swim. Keep swimming.

Stop thinking.

The wheel shimmered and wobbled before him like a line of smoke in a thermal. The waterline bobbed up and down the glass of his faceplate. The air above the sea cut the horizon into ribbons, buckling it with mirage heat. He still had the dizzy sense that the wheel was moving.

"I think—" Nissa began.

"Don't speak. Save your energy. We still have a long way to go."

Soon they had to stop again. The temperature inside his suit was unbearable now, his breath fogging the faceplate like the inside of a sweltering greenhouse. He wanted to remove the helmet, be rid of that glass, but the air outside was no cooler than the water. It had become a struggle even to main-tain the correct angle in the water to prevent his backpack from being fully immersed.

"Kanu," a voice said finally.

"Swift. Yes."

"You must fight, Kanu. Fight or I will do it for you. Is that understood?"

"I can do it."

"Then *do* it. I would much sooner spare you the indignity of being puppeteered because you lack the will to overcome your own tiredness."

"Fuck you, Swift."

"Good. Anger. Anger is an excellent sign. Now put some of that anger into your arms and legs."

He did, for a little while. He would show Swift that he still had the determination to strike forward, to push through the pain and fatigue. But the effort was temporary, and by the end of it the suit had become a furnace, his own sweat stinging his eyes, his breathing ragged.

"Kanu!"

"I'm sorry, Swift. I need to rest."

There was an interlude, a dream of coolness, and then he awoke. He was still hot, still drained, but he was not in water now. He had come to rest on a warm, dry surface, like a sun-baked boulder. He had taken off his helmet but was still holding it in one hand even as he lay sprawled like a drunkard. Through pained, salt-encrusted eyes he made out Nissa a little to his right. She was on a boulder, too, prone atop its ridged upper surface, head lolling away from him. Her foot dragged through the water.

The boulder moved under him. Beneath a membrane of flexible grey material it was breathing.

Kanu understood. The Risen were ferrying them over the water, to the wheel. Dakota was under him, Hector beneath Nissa. They were lying on the backs of swimming elephants.

The nearer they came, the more impossibly sheer the wheel looked. It ascended vertically for what looked like dozens of kilometres, until finally, resentfully, it began to arc over. Climb that? Kanu thought. Not in a million years, even if there was some way to get from one groove to the next. Could they worm their way up the near-vertical grooves cut into the rim rather than the horizontal ones in the tread? It would be no easier, he reckoned—and after the Risen had brought them this far, he could not countenance abandoning them.

"Kanu." It was Nissa, her voice hoarse.

"Try not to speak too much," he said. "We'll tap into the fluid rations when we reach the wheel."

"Look up."

"I am looking up."

"Not at the wheel, merman. The moons."

It took his tired, salt-gummed eyes a few moments to pick out the tiny orbs of the moons against the sky's blue. He had not noticed them before, and had given no thought to how they must appear from Poseidon's surface, from within the atmosphere. But however he might have imagined them, it was not like this.

"They're lining up."

"I know."

"What does that mean? Is it good or bad?"

"We'll find out," Nissa said.

He woke again. They were at the wheel, a few scant elephant-lengths from the tread. They had arrived close to the right side of the tread, not far from the right angle between the tread and rim. Kanu felt a shudder of vertigo, imagining the wheel's continuation beneath the visible surface, plunging down through tens of kilometres of darkening water, enduring pressures beyond anything in his experience on either Earth or Europa. He had never felt vertigo in water before. Water was his element, the place where he felt safest. Water sustained, water provided, water gave him suspension.

Not here.

"It's turning," Nissa said. "I've been watching it for a while, and there's no doubt."

"The wheels don't turn." He had no strength for discussion, but the last thing he wanted was for Nissa to pin her hopes on something ridiculous. "We scanned them from orbit. *Icebreaker* would have seen signs of movement."

"Not then. Now," Nissa said. "The moons have changed, so why not the wheels? Besides, we're close enough to see the grooves clearly now. Close enough to fix on them and watch them—they're coming out of the water, one at a time, and going up. The wheel's turning, or rolling."

From his perch on Dakota's back, he stared with as much concentration and focus as he could muster. The motion was slow—easy to miss when they were further away, with the rise and fall of the waves to confuse their eyes.

Not now.

It took about three seconds for a metre of the wheel to emerge from the sea. About every thirty seconds, an entirely new groove emerged. He tracked the latest one—watched it inch slowly above the sea, water sluicing out of it, until the next groove came into view.

"We can get on it," Nissa said. "We all can."

"Yes."

The Tantors were slower now, their strength ebbing. Kanu put his helmet on, again seeing the world through steam-smeared glass. He slipped from Dakota's back into the blood-hot bath of the water. He bobbed, forced his limbs into motion. It felt as if the water were turning to something solid, like a cast setting around him. Nissa replaced her helmet and slid off Hector to join him in the water. She looked as exhausted as he felt.

They closed the distance to the wheel, but the last couple of hundred metres were a kind of torture. They were swimming so slowly by then, all of them, that the wheel must have been rolling away at nearly the same speed. They had to fight not only to keep up with it, but also to close the gap. He lost any sense of how long that final closing took—it could have been minutes or hours. All he knew was that when they were finally at the wheel's side, he had given everything he had.

But at least there was no doubt that it was turning. The wheel made no noise, not even up close, except for the slosh as the water drained out of each kilometre-wide groove. The sloshing was nearly continuous, each newly emerged groove adding to the sound as the one above began to empty. It was like ocean breakers, a lulling, pleasing sound.

The grooves rose out of the water slower than walking pace, but they were only three or four metres from top to bottom—between nine and twelve seconds' worth of ascent time. After that came a stretch of smooth, flawless surface until the top edge of the next groove appeared. They would have no purchase on that, and no chance to cross from one groove to the next. Once they were in a particular groove, there would be no way off—no way of reversing their decision.

"Spread out," Kanu said, summoning the energy to talk as he trod water. "We all want to be on the same groove. No good being one above the other—we may as well be kilometres apart."

Nissa had swum to within almost touching distance of the wheel. "One chance," she agreed. "That's all we have. When the ceiling appears out of the water, we'll swim into the gap—let the floor rise up under us, push us out of the water."

"The grooves vary in height," Kanu said.

"Yes."

"And we can't see that height until the floor's already under us."

"By which point it'll be too late to change our minds."

"I know."

"And that backwash looks fierce," Nissa said. "Could easily suck us out again."

"There is a significant risk of that occurring," Swift added.

"Do you have something better to offer?" Kanu asked.

"Only my very best wishes. I do not think it would help to puppet you—the variables are quite beyond my accounting."

Swift was right. Until they were inside a groove, there was no telling how grippy or frictionless the walls were going to be. He hoped they could wedge themselves in tight enough to avoid being pulled back by the drain-off. He hoped there would be room for the Risen.

But they would not know until they tried.

"We must do what we can," Dakota said. "We have no love of high places. But to be on the wheel will be better than remaining in these waters. Have strength, Hector."

"The next groove," he said. "All of us. Give it everything."

They spread out—Kanu, Nissa, Hector and Dakota, with a few metres of clear water between each of them. Kanu reached inside himself for the reserves of energy and concentration he hoped had to be there. One chance, he told himself—all or nothing.

The groove began to appear. Centimetres—tens of centimetres already.

"Now!"

But the others had seen it as well and were not waiting for his word. Nissa spread her arms for one last push against the water—she was a stronger swimmer than he had ever given her credit for. Kanu found his own burst of strength and pushed himself into the widening space. A metre of the groove was now out of the water. He touched the fingers of one hand against the inner surface and jammed his other hand against the cool ceiling. An instant later, he felt the floor press against his feet. He glanced at Nissa. She was in, twisting around to secure herself as best she could. Beyond her, through eyes stinging with seawater, he saw Hector shunt his massive bulk into the same rectangular space. Dakota had to be behind him, but his vision was too blurred to make out more than a suggestion of motion, a confusion of grey mass and surging water.

Now the lower part of the groove was clearing the sea. He braced against the surge of escaping water, but mercifully it was not as strong as he had feared. And then he was standing, feet on solid ground, hands on the cold interior of the groove.

Safe.

"Kanu!"

The lower part of the groove was now fifty centimetres above the water, higher than most of the waves.

Nissa was moving away from him, towards the Risen. He saw in an instant what was wrong. Hector was safe—he had made it into the groove and was bracing himself in place with his spine against the ceiling. But Dakota was not quite secure. Her head and forequarters were over the groove's threshold, but the rest of her was still hanging over the edge. There was a metre of vertical distance now from the bottom of the groove to the surface of the water. Her front legs struggled for traction on the slick surface, her trunk stretching into the groove. Hector had turned around to extend his own trunk out to her. Their trunks met, sheathed tips coiling around each other. Had the elephants not been wearing suits, their trunks might have gripped more readily. But the sheathing was too slippery.

A metre and a half—still rising.

Nissa squeezed past Hector's bulk. There was only just room for her to do it without leaning dangerously far out into the void. She reached for Dakota, too, closing a hand around the nearest tusk-like protrusion of her helmet. Kanu in turn reached for Nissa, fearful that she was about to be pulled back into the sea.

The wheel was still turning. The lowest part of the groove was now two metres out of the water. He could see Dakota's hindquarters—her legs struggling to find a grip on the smooth surface between the grooves.

Still the wheel turned.

"Let go!" he shouted. "You're rising too far! Fall back into the water and try again on the next groove!"

"Help me," Dakota said.

Other than the fading roar of the water sluicing from further down the groove, there was no sound beyond their own breathing, their own grunts and bellows of exertion, their own voices.

Dakota was completely out of the water now—her whole weight borne by her forequarters. A metre between her tail and the sea. Another metre every three seconds.

She was starting to slide.

"Hector! You have to let go! Much higher and the fall will kill her!"

"I cannot," Hector said.

Kanu tugged at Nissa, risked a moment of imbalance to free her hand from Dakota's tusk. But she could only have held on for a second longer in any case, for the tusk was smooth and slick, offering no friction to her palm.

"Dakota," Kanu said. "Fall. Get into the next groove. We'll find you. It isn't over."

"It is," she said.

"No!" Nissa said.

"Is all forgiven?" Dakota asked.

"Yes," Kanu said, horrified at the growing space beneath her, the drop she was about to take. "Yes. All is forgiven. For ever and always. All is always forgiven."

"Think well of me. Do well by Hector. Think kindly of the Risen."

"We will."

Dakota slipped from the groove. Had Hector not relinquished his hold on her trunk, he would have been pulled over the edge. As it was, the sudden easing of tension sent him falling back into the groove's depths. Kanu pulled Nissa to him, wrapped his arm around her waist. He dared look down. He watched Dakota fall, tumbling away with her belly to the sky. By then, the next groove must already have emerged from the water. An elephant could never have survived such a fall on Earth. On Poseidon, where the gravity was half as strong again, the impact with the water would be even more severe.

He leaned into the void, one hand around Nissa, the other gripping the right angle above his head where the top of the groove met the smooth surface of the wheel. He looked for some sign of Dakota, hardly daring to hope that she might have survived. But if her body resurfaced, Kanu was too high up to see it when it did.

Yes, of course she was forgiven.

Forgiveness was the least he could offer.

They were safe, for now—or at least out of the ocean.

The wheel would keep carrying them higher, and eventually the air would thin and cool. But facing that was better than boiling to death in the ocean, or being eaten by sea-monsters, Kanu told himself, and at least the wheel gave them time and the possibility, however slim, of rescue from above. Dared he pin his hopes on that?

No—not yet. Focus instead on the present moment, the immediate practicalities of survival. Secure in the groove, there was no chance of their falling out again now. Indeed, as the wheel turned, so the gradually steepening angle of the groove's floor made it even less likely. Granted, it was a small thing. In an hour they had risen no more than a kilometre, by Kanu's reckoning.

He was still breathing the ambient air. It was cooler now—almost pleasant compared to the heat of the ocean's surface. It would keep cooling as they rose, though, cooling and thinning, and before very long it would not be breathable. They had both needed to tap into suit air and power while swimming, and now—according to the indicator on Kanu's wrist—he had no more than fifteen hours of life-support remaining. Nissa's suit was down to a similar margin. Worse than that, some of her suit systems were showing error conditions, presumably because of exposure to the water.

Nissa was standing at the edge of the groove, a sheer drop beyond her feet.

"We won't have to freeze or suffocate if we don't want to. There's always that."

"Perhaps we'd have been better off in the ocean," Kanu said, fiddling with his suit's communication settings.

"I'll regret not knowing more about those moons," said Swift, who was sitting on the very edge of the groove, his stockinged legs dangling over the drop. He had his pince-nez glasses in one hand, squinting against some microscopic blemish on the lens. "But I cannot be too ungrateful. To have come this far, to have touched the wheel itself—that's more than we had any right to expect."

"We've learned nothing," Kanu said, overcome by a sudden fatalistic gloom. "The wheel's still a closed book. Just because we're in it doesn't mean it's suddenly revealed its secrets."

"The grooves are a form of Mandala grammar," Swift said. "I don't have to understand it to recognise it. Although a little of the meaning keeps suggesting itself to me rather coyly, but I can't quite bring it into focus. Do you have the same sense of the numinous?"

"Something came through to us," Nissa said. "Some knowledge, some information, when we felt the Terror. Just as Chiku told us."

"Secrets and imponderables." Swift settled the pince-nez back into place on the bridge of his nose. "I rather feel for Hector. Do you think he will be all right?"

Hector was balled up at the back of the groove. The Tantor had said nothing since Dakota's death, and they had been careful not to press him. It was not necessarily some fault of his suit, Kanu decided, but the terrible weight of a loss none of them could begin to appreciate. She had been more than a matriarch to the Risen. She had been the spearhead of a new order of being—a vanguard of promise and power.

"We're all going to die, Swift," Kanu said, allowing a little of his anger to flash through. "None of us is going to be 'all right.' And you being in our heads isn't going to change that."

"You are a rational animal, Kanu," Swift said amiably. "You would not have placed us in this position unless you thought there was some hope of survival. You know full well that the wheel is turning, and that it will take us higher."

"Our suits don't have enough life left in them. It's just a question of which kills us first—the cold or the thinning air."

"Or, as Nissa said, you can choose the drop. But you won't do that. Neither of you has it in you to abandon Hector. For which I am glad."

"Glad?" Kanu asked.

Swift nodded to the sky beyond the groove, where a bright moving spark was crossing the darkening zenith.

"That, if I'm not very much mistaken, is a Chibesa signature."

Something crackled across his helmet channel.

"Kanu Akinya," he said.

Another crackle, a silence, then a broken, nervous voice— as if she had not even dared hope she might receive a response and was not quite ready to trust what her ears were telling her.

"This is Goma. Are you all right?"

"For the moment. Ask me again in fifteen hours. Is that your ship we can see?"

"It must be. We can see your thermal signatures on the wheel—we tracked you from the moment you splashed down. The wheel's bringing you higher—it looks like it's rotating!"

"Not that it'll do us much good, I'm afraid, but it felt better than staying in the sea."

"You're not out of options just yet, Kanu. You're coming up to us, and we have every intention of coming down to meet you. Can you hold out for those fifteen hours? You may need every last minute of them."

CHAPTER 51

Captain Vasin had needed considerable persuasion to take *Mposi* into the moons' sphere of influence, still more to contemplate touching down anywhere on the upper surface of the wheel. But even after she agreed to attempt a rescue, her technical objections—fair and reasonable as they were—still applied. *Mposi*'s design was not compatible with entry into deep atmosphere. The ship would tear itself apart, or roast itself, or both, before it got within thirty kilometres of the surface.

Eunice argued that they should set down at exactly that threshold, thirty kilometres, while praying that each and every variable happened to line up in their favour. If the hull survived the re-entry forces, and the engine did not quite overheat . . .

Vasin was having none of that. She would consent to a touchdown at fifty kilometres, halfway to the wheel's summit on the ascendant side. But she would not let *Mposi* stay where it landed. They would unload the rescue party, allow them to get to a safe distance, and then *Mposi* would take off again before the wheel's rotation carried it over the wheel's summit and then began to lower it too deeply into the atmosphere on the wheel's downturn.

"Forty kilometres, if you're going to make life difficult," Eunice said. "Then you can stay on station until at least the apex without going too deep into the atmosphere. I like that a lot better than watching you fly off again while we're still on the wheel."

"What you like and what you get are two different things."

"Not in my experience. This is space travel, Captain Vasin. There is no part of it that's risk-free."

"Managed risk, then."

"What do you think I'm doing if not managing your risk? At forty, the ship won't know the difference from fifty. We're looking at a tiny increase in pressure—not enough to hurt us."

"If I give you forty, you'll push for thirty."

"Not this time—I want to live as much as you do. I'd just rather do so knowing we'd done our best for those people."

"And the elephant."

"The elephant is one of the people. Speaking of which, we're going to have to find room for him inside this ship. If emergency adaptations are required, now would be the time to start making them."

The sparring went on like that for the better part of an hour, neither of them conceding any significant ground. Goma would have found it infuriating, but the truth was they still had time to make the final decision. Until *Mposi* was closer to the wheel, their exact point of landing was up for debate. It would only take a few minutes to go shallower or higher, depending on who won.

Whichever they decided, it was not going to be a simple rescue operation.

In her conversation with Kanu, she had learned that the three survivors of the *Icebreaker* expedition who had managed to scramble into the groove were wearing spacesuits. But the humans' suits would not be able to keep them alive until they were in true vacuum. At best, they had the means to hold out until they were twenty kilometres above the surface, and that would be at the extreme edge of survivability. *Mposi*'s rescue party had to reach them quickly if they were to make any difference to their chances.

Eunice had inventoried the supplies. They had plenty of supplementary oxygen and power cells, and the coupling interfaces ought to be common between the various suit designs. But their longest tether was fifty kilometres, and there was no reliable way of coupling the shorter tethers together to make something longer. No matter which way she looked at it, they would have to make do with that one long tether.

"Can we get that down to them?" Goma asked.

"Yes, I think so," Eunice said. "Reel out at the maximum speed the winch allows, abseil down the wheel. The wheel's rotation will tend to act against us, but provided we can move at more than one or two kilometres per hour, we'll easily beat the rotation."

"Faster than that, I hope," Goma said. "And coming back up?"

"Haul in the way we hauled out. And if that fails, we just ride the wheel up to the top."

"You make it sound easy."

"I'm involved, so there's a very good chance it won't be. Incidentally, what was the part about 'we'?"

"It'll take more than one of us to carry the supplies. Besides, there's a Tantor down there. Ru and I want to be part of this."

"Want—or feel you must?"

"Don't make this harder than it has to be, Eunice. We're going down, with or without you."

"And the number of hours you've spent in a spacesuit . . . ?"

"We'll have you along to show us how it's done, won't we?"

"I'd argue with you, but I suspect it would feel a bit like arguing with myself."

"Futile?"

"Boring."

Mposi continued its approach to the wheel, moving at much less than orbital speed and slowing all the while. Eunice and Vasin continued their horse-trading over altitude and risk. Gradually Eunice appeared to be getting her message through: given the supplies they had, going deep was the only way of reaching Kanu's party in time.

They circled the top of the wheel, recording its grooved structures at maximum resolution in every waveband *Mposi* was capable of registering. In the hours since Kanu reached the wheel, the sun had set on that part of Poseidon. It was now night-time at the wheel's base and would remain so for another ten hours. But the wheel's top was still catching the refracted light of the setting sun, shining a reddening gold. And there were other wheels, and they would all need to be compared, cross-referenced. There was work here for a lifetime—many lifetimes. They had been allowed access to Poseidon for now, permitted to slip through the cordon of moons on this one occasion, but there was no telling how long that licence might be good for.

Goma figured they had better make the most of it while they had the chance.

She spoke to Kanu again. "How are you holding out?"

"We're on suit air for fifty per cent of the time. Trying to buy some hours, not that one or two will make much difference. Are you any closer with that rescue plan?"

"Yes, but it's going to involve you sitting tight a little longer than you might like."

She heard the smile in his voice. "I'm hardly in a position to complain. What do you have in mind?"

"We're going to lower a line down to you. But not vertically—it would be too risky to hover *Mposi* like that, and we wouldn't be able to offer you any assistance at your end. Better if we lower the ship down the curve of the wheel. We'll land at the lowest altitude the captain's happy with—Eunice has talked her down to forty kilometres."

"Is that safe for you?"

"The ship's not really built for it. But of course Eunice says safety margins are meant to be tested."

"Please, Goma—don't take any risks on our behalf."

"You don't get a say, Kanu. Besides, you have one of the Risen with you."

"That's true."

"Around here, at least, the Risen just became an endangered species again. We owe it to ourselves to do all we can for Hector, but I can't promise it'll be easy. Our tether's shorter than we'd like. If we touch down at forty kilometres, we can just reach you, but you'll need to hold out until you're close to the limits of survivability. If all goes well, we should be able to get down to you before you're much higher than fifteen or twenty kilometres up."

"That'll be cutting it fine."

"No other way, Kanu. But we'll have oxygen and power when we reach you. Don't be alarmed if you see the ship lift off—Gandhari's going to circle around for a few hours before coming back in."

"This is more than we were hoping for, Goma."

"It's what Mposi would have done. While we carry his name, we'd better try to live up to it."

"You already have."

"I'm signing off now. Once we're on the tether, we'll speak again. For now, keep warm and conserve your supplies. See you soon, Uncle Kanu."

"See you soon, niece of mine."

They lowered into the atmosphere on a spike of Chibesa thrust, dialled back to the minimum necessary to support *Mposi* against Poseidon's gravity. It was silent to begin with, the descent as smooth and uncomplicated as when they landed on Orison. But the air was thickening with each kilometre closer to the sea, and as the Chibesa exhaust began to interact with the atmosphere, so the physics of the plasma exhaust began to turn messy. The engine could adjust, up to a point. It damped shock waves and smothered runaway instabilities before they had a chance to manifest as bumps or lurches felt by the human crew. It whispered sweet nothings at turbulence and laminar-flow boundaries. It brought to bear a monstrous amount of computation, calculating its way around the curdled, fractal corners of emergent chaos.

But they had to go deeper.

Vasin was at the controls, her seat pushed out into the armoured eye of the bubble cockpit, shaking her head all the while as if—despite having agreed to this—she was still not convinced that it was anything but the utmost foolishness, guaranteed to wreck them all. *Mposi* sounded a mounting chorus of status warnings and master caution alarms, and the engine surged and ebbed as it tried to balance the demands being placed upon it.

Deeper still.

Chaotic interaction with the high atmosphere was only part of the problem. Now the heat transfer from the exhaust to the surrounding air was beginning to overload the engine's own cooling capabilities. Refrigeration pumps and heat exchangers surged and screamed beyond their normal tolerances.

Still more alarms.

But Vasin had given Eunice her word, and Kanu in turn had been led to believe there was a chance of rescue. Goma understood, in a flash of admiration and empathy, that Vasin would not now turn back; her commitment was total. Having said she would do this one thing, their captain would not surrender.

Fifty kilometres from the seas of Poseidon.

Forty-five.

Vasin deployed the undercarriage. They had descended on one side of the wheel, but now she vectored them sideways until they were almost hovering over the tread itself. What had been taxing now became doubly difficult because she did not want the Chibesa exhaust coming anywhere near the fabric of the wheel, for fear that it would cause an explosion or be interpreted as a hostile act.

These fears struck Goma as perfectly reasonable.

The thrust had to be feathered now, vectored out at sharp angles, and that in turn meant an increased load on the engine just to hover. *Mposi* by then had gone berserk with its own anxieties. Vasin cancelled all the alarms and got a small round of applause from her crew.

"Probably for the best. I don't think I want a second's warning when things go completely wrong."

"You're doing wonderfully, Gandhari," Goma said.

"You sound like your uncle."

Goma did not know what to say to that. But she was not displeased by it.

Now came the hard part, as if it had been plain sailing until now. They had to land, or at least hold station, while the rescue party was unloaded.

It would have been easy enough on the wheel's summit, where the great curve approximated a level surface. Here, though, they were not even halfway to the top. At forty kilometres above the sea, the inclined tread of the wheel was thirty degrees away from a sheer surface. Only the grooves offered any possibility of a secure footing.

Vasin brought them in close, veered out, came in closer again—all the while making tiny adjustments to the landing gear. "No one move around much," she said. "And if you want to try not breathing for a bit, that would help."

The moment of landing, when it came, was barely a kiss of contact. *Mposi* swayed, its gear taking up the load as the engine slowly throttled down to zero thrust. Through one set of windows, Goma saw only the near face of the wheel, almost close enough to touch if the window's glass had not been in her way. She wondered how they had managed to land at all.

"Unload as quickly as you can," Vasin said, not stirring from her command seat. "Use the secondary lock, not the primary, and take care on your way out. Watch when you bring out the winch gear—it's heavy, and our balance may shift."

They had begun putting on their spacesuits before the final approach to the wheel, so now there were only final preparations to be made. Eunice had left her suit behind on *Travertine*, so they were all using the same standard model carried aboard *Mposi*. She was less than happy about that, scowling at the life-support controls built into her sleeve and shaking her head in disgust.

"What is this horse piss? You're supposed to get better at making things, not worse."

"Shut up and put up with it, the way we have to put up with you," Ru said.

They locked on their helmets, checked comms and began unloading the equipment.

It was only when Goma was outside that she could see how skilfully Vasin had put down the lander. It had been a tricky bit of work, worthy of grudging admiration even from Eunice. Two of the four landing legs were planted into the groove, compressed to their minimum extension. The other two, stretched out as far as they would go, were braced against the steep side of the wheel between the groove they were in and the next one down. The landing feet on that side were angled to their limit, relying on friction to support them to the lander.

It looked precarious, which it was. Eunice said that she had seen some nastier landing configurations, but not since the days of chemical rockets. Vasin was even applying a constant torque of steering thrust from one of the lander's auxiliary motors, a cruciform-shaped module high up the side of the hull, near the out-jutting control bubble. Without that corrective thrust, there would be little to stop the lander toppling away from the vertical.

"But I can't keep bleeding that jet," Vasin said. "It's not meant for sustained use, and it's not fed from the Chibesa core. Once that tank's empty, we're in trouble. I'll need to lift as soon as you're independent."

It took thirty minutes to get all the emergency supplies unloaded and organised—during which time Kanu's party rose another five hundred metres. Goma was supremely conscious that each second counted against Kanu. Equally distressing was the fear that they would make some miscalculation or omission now, and really damn their hopes.

The immediate task was to set up the tether and the grapple. The grapple was a thousand kilograms of heavy-duty engineering designed to bear the load of a spacecraft under adverse thrust. It would certainly not fail on them, which was one consolation, but it took two of them to move it, and even in its retracted configuration it only just squeezed through the secondary lock. It looked like a mechanical starfish, two metres across with five independent arms, each of which ended in a complex multifunctional gripping appendage. They wedged the grapple into the back of the groove, cleared to a safe distance, then ordered it to lock itself into place. The arms pushed out with explosive speed, the tips adapting to the sensed surface to provide the maximum locking force. Since the inner walls of the groove were smooth, there was nothing for the grapple to hook on to. But it was also designed to couple with the smooth hulls of other spacecraft, using high-friction pads. Its appendages angled to bring their pads into optimum contact. They slipped a little initially, then held. The three humans approached the grapple again and hooked on the tether. Using the power winch, they tested the grapple up to five thousand and sixty newtons of instantaneous force, at which point it slipped and then regripped. Five tonnes—not much.

They would never strain it that severely, though, because the tether was going to run over the lip of the groove, which would function as a bearing surface. From *Mposi*'s repair inventory they found a piece of spare hull cladding which had approximately the right profile to slip under the tether at that point of contact. They fixed it into place with vacuum epoxy, trusting that the bond would hold against the alien material of the wheel, and that the tether would not cut through it.

They buckled what they could onto the utility belts of their suits, but the emergency oxygen and power supplies were too bulky for that. These items were packed into a zip-up bag which they would lower down ahead of them, strung out like a plumb-bob on a few metres of standard safety line. They used the same line to tie themselves together, again with a safety margin of a few metres.

Eunice would lead, Goma second, Ru third. Ru was the only one coupled to the tether itself and she had direct control of the power winch, which was connected to the front of her belt by a sturdy clasp. The winch did not look like much to Goma, just a squat yellow cylinder with some hazard stripes and a few simple operating controls chunky enough to be worked with spacesuit gloves. It was hard to believe that most of the fifty kilometres of the tether were still spooled up in the winch's casing. But then the tether itself was almost invisibly fine, and Vasin had warned them that it could easily slice open their suits if they touched it under tension.

Or worse.

Still, doing it this way rather than spooling out from the grapple at least meant there was no moving contact between the tether and the corner piece. Eunice would be their lookout as they approached and traversed each successive groove on their way down. And to stand a chance of helping the others, they would need to be moving quickly.

Eunice was the first over the lip, with the supply bag dangling under her. She braced her legs against the nearly sheer side and signalled for Goma to join her. Ru spooled out the line, no more than tens of centimetres at a time, until all three of them were over the lip and their weight was borne by the tether. It was easy for Goma—she was coupled to Ru by a stretch of line obviously thick enough to bear her weight. But Ru was barely able to see the tether.

"I'm near the top of the next groove down," Eunice said. "Start lowering us. I'll kick off and rejoin the surface under the groove. You'll have to do the same. Once we get into a rhythm, we should be able to make good speed."

It took them a while to get the rhythm of it. They were strung out far enough that Eunice and Ru were both passing grooves while Goma was descending the flat section between them. If they did not time their kicks correctly, there was a risk of Goma being torn from the wall just in time to swing back into the mouth of a groove. At low speeds, little harm could come to her. But to be of use to Kanu's party, they would need to reach them in under ten hours, and that meant an average descent speed of five kilometres an hour. That was fine in spurts, not even a brisk stroll, but they could not allow themselves to fall behind. Every error counted, and if they had to go faster to make up time, any resulting accident could have serious consequences.

Thirty or forty minutes into the descent, though, they settled into a pattern. The tether was reeling out smoothly, the grapple holding. Goma stopped concentrating and just allowed her muscles to find the right pace, trusting in the women above and below her. The grooves passed one after another, punctuated by the icily smooth and pristine material between them. The angle of the tread was steepening towards vertical with every metre they descended, but it would be a long while before that became obvious to Goma's senses. The wheel's rotation brought Kanu's party higher with each second, but that same rotation was also working to push Goma's team higher as well. They could not afford to stop until they had closed the gap to Kanu, and to do so in a useful time they needed to outpace the wheel's counter-rotation.

"Kanu? This is Goma. We're descending. How are you coping? Looks pretty dark down there."

She had to wait a little longer for his reply than she cared to, as if she had pulled Kanu from the edge of sleep. "Dark, but we're looking forward to company. Swift says we're at six kilometres now. I won't pretend it isn't cold, but the suits are holding out, and there appears to be some heat radiating from the walls of the groove—it's definitely not cooling down as quickly as the surrounding air."

"Stay with us, Kanu."

"I have no plans not to. Having come this far, I'd very much like to finish the job properly and return with a full expedition—human, Risen, machine—whatever it takes. Did you know there are monsters in that ocean?"

"Nothing would surprise me," Goma said.

"I say monsters—one of them ate our ship, which didn't

strike me as very gracious behaviour—but I suppose we should reserve judgement. For all I know, that was the M-builders making contact."

"I think they're long gone, Kanu."

"So do I, but it's a nice thought that we might meet them, isn't it? At the very least, I'd enjoy telling them they were mistaken."

"About what?"

"The futility of existence. Ask Eunice—she's been through the Terror."

She told him to sign off until they were nearer, wanting him to conserve energy and oxygen.

They carried on down, the grooves passing like the stepped-out balconies of an endless hotel. They were only seeing a part of each groove from their line of descent—each one extended to either side for hundreds of metres—but that was still enough for Goma to convince herself that each groove was unique in its detailed form, not just a horizontal slot but a wavering, wandering trench with right angles and zigzags, branches and interruptions. Statements in a language her mother had expected her to be able to read by now, but of which she was still ignorant.

"Look," Ru said.

They slowed instinctively. Above them, a bright flame was rising beyond the convex surface of the tread, cut across by a converging density of grooves like the absorption lines in an atomic spectrum. Captain Vasin had waited until they were this far down before detaching the ship.

"Think she'll come back for us?" Eunice asked. "The way her hands were shaking on that descent, I thought she was having some sort of brainstem seizure."

"Give her some credit," Goma said. "She put that ship down under impossible conditions. Admit it—even you were impressed by that landing."

They carried on down a groove or three.

"I've seen worse."

"Such generous praise," Ru muttered.

It had been like that since they left the first groove—Goma caught between the two of them, Ru still needling, Eunice not exactly going out of her way to ease things. It bothered her not to be liked by Ru, Goma decided, but only because Ru was special to Goma. Had Ru been anyone else on the expedition, Eunice would not have cared less. She had spent her whole life being entirely unconcerned about the opinions of others; she was not about to change overnight, even in this latest and strangest incarnation of herself.

Goma liked it when they had something else to talk about, and when Ru just got on with working the power winch.

"I wouldn't say I'm starting to see the bigger picture just yet," Eunice said, "but maybe the tiniest corner of it. This is almost a different syntax again, you know? It's like all the work I had to do to make sense of the Mandala script needs to be thrown out and done over."

"How can you read anything when we're only seeing a tiny part of each groove?" Goma asked. "Isn't it like running your finger down the page of a book and only reading one word from each line?"

"No, it's worse—because this is more like one word from a page, not one word per line. But before we landed I had Gandhari transmit *Mposi*'s scans into my suit. Granted, it's only the top of the wheel—a tiny fraction of its total content—but I'm starting to understand."

"What did Kanu mean—about the futility of existence?" Goma asked.

"You remember we spoke about the vacuum fluctuations?"

"Barely."

But those easy conversations on Orison—before the deaths of the Tantors, before the second Mandala event, before this—felt as if they had happened to a younger, more naive version of herself. It was like reaching back into her childhood.

Eunice's kitchen. Mealworms. The joy of knowing Sadalmelik and Achernar.

"The M-builders were too clever for their own good," Eunice said. "They dug too far into physics and it bit them. Physics will do that. It's an ungrateful piece of shit. It's a fickle lover that will always betray you. It courts you, gives you rewards, coughs up little treats like fire and the wheel, telescopes and the secret of starflight, makes you think you're worth it, that you're the special one, that you really, really matter to it." She paused as she kicked off from the wall, swung out and thumped back into contact. "All the while it's saving up this nasty little truth: that every thought, every deed, every hope you've ever held is futile. That the universe will end, and forget itself. That there is no such thing as meaning. That you might as well kill yourself now, because in the end your existence won't count for anything. That there is no posterity. There is no Remembering. That nothing passes into anything—even for Tantors."

"Do you believe it?" Goma asked.

"Of course I believe it. Physics doesn't give a damn about how we feel. It doesn't give a damn about us sleeping soundly in our beds, thinking we matter."

"Just because the M-builders accepted it, we don't have to," Goma said.

"You mean . . . maybe they were wrong?"

"Why not?"

"No . . . you're right. It's a possibility. They were only millions of years ahead of us, after all. They'd only achieved a mastery of physics sufficient to build these wheels and moons, to move entire mountains around at the speed of light."

"Sarcastic bitch," Ru said.

"You'll have to excuse me. It's a coping mechanism. It's how I process stupid questions."

"I meant it seriously," Goma said, not giving in that easily. "Fine, they came up with a theory. But what if it isn't self-consistent? What if they just didn't look hard enough for the flaw? Building these things—these wheels, the Mandalas—doesn't that speak to you of a certain . . . arrogance?"

"It speaks to me of beings we'd be very, very wise not to underestimate."

"But being wrong can't have been beyond them. Anyway—what have you learned from the grooves?"

"Yes, do share your dazzling wisdom with us," Ru said.

"She's really starting to have issues with me, isn't she?"

"Probably has something to do with you nearly killing her."

"I thought we were over that."

"She isn't."

"I can tell. I keep picking up on these subtle undercurrents of animosity. Anyway—the grooves. Yes. They're very interesting."

"That's all you've got—very interesting?" Goma asked.

"They're either an obituary or a recipe, I'm not sure which. Let's start with obituary. What the wheels appear to encode—or this wheel, anyway—is a kind of final statement from the M-builders. It's not their cultural history. It doesn't tell us what they looked like, where they came from, what side they buttered their toast on. But it does appear to relate to the Terror—recapitulating the same basic theme of cosmic futility, the vacuum fluctuation, the end of everything. I'd need to spend more time with it, but—going by this wheel—they've left us with a complete description of their final physical theory. Their ultimate understanding of nature—packaged in the mathematics of the Mandala grammar. Chibesa theory is just a tiny, low-energy approximation buried somewhere in the margins—almost a footnote! As I said, I'm only seeing glimpses, fragments of the whole, but they're enough to tell me what I'm looking at."

"That doesn't sound like an obituary."

"Hold your horses—there's more. The theory's only part of it—it wouldn't need the entire wheel for its expression. The rest is . . . more complicated. Like I said, I'm only catching glimpses, but it feels as if I'm seeing a response to that theory—how the M-builders came to terms with their own ultimate description of nature."

While they were talking, Goma had begun to notice the wall becoming ever steeper. It was still night—even the top of the wheel was now in shadow—and they were still above most of the atmosphere, but already she felt a long, uncomfortable distance from their starting point. With the descent came a kind of reverse vertigo, a sense of being too low rather than too high.

She tried not to dwell too much on that barely visible tether, holding them all against gravity.

"So what was their answer—suicide?"

"Not quite. Or maybe yes, but not in the way you mean. If the vacuum is unstable, what do you do? Maybe nothing. After all, the vacuum underpins everything. It's the fundamental level of reality, the material out of which space–time is knitted. It's the game board and we're just the pieces sliding around on top. We can't touch the game board—we can't make it be something it isn't. But if you'd been around as long as the M-builders . . ."

"You might try," Goma said.

"This is going to take some digging into. Probably more lifetimes than I've had freeze-dried maggots. Here's a start, though. A hunch. The wheel is a recipe. It's a set of instructions—a list of procedures for addressing the fundamental structure of reality. For getting down and dirty and poking around in the greasy guts of the quantum vacuum."

"You think that's what the M-builders did?"

"I think it's what they became." Eunice let a few grooves go by before she carried on. "To alter the vacuum, to shore it up, to change the rules of the game—they had to embed themselves in the vacuum itself. They had to abandon matter and energy as we know them. Become pure structure—pure self-propagating patterns of coherent information. Phantoms in the floorboards. Ghosts in the carpet weave of the world."

"Did they?" Ru asked.

"That's a very good question."

"I said I could do with less of your sarcasm."

"And this time I'm giving it to you straight, my dear. It is a good question—and I've a feeling the wheels won't provide the answer. The wheels may offer an account of what they *meant* to do, but they won't tell us whether they succeeded or not. I suspect it was all or nothing for the M-builders—dance into the vacuum or bring annihilation upon themselves. I don't think they allowed themselves the option of living with failure—they could live with almost anything but imperfection."

"Remind you of anyone?" Goma asked.

"Oh, I'm not perfect—not by a long stretch. I just make the rest of you look bad."

CHAPTER 52

They had been descending in silence for hours, fatigue eating into their concentration, the wall now as close to sheer as made no difference, when Ru said, "Nineteen kilometres of tether spooled out. Can't be far now."

Goma signalled to Kanu that they must be near, but there was no answer. She did not immediately think the worst at this, for Kanu had sounded tired the last time they spoke and it would not surprise her in the least if he were asleep. On the far side of the wheel, the sky was beginning to show the first faint omens of day—an indigo haze where before it had been night. But the environmental readout on her suit still maintained that the outside conditions were entirely incompatible with the wants of human survival—that the air was too thin, too poor in oxygen and cold enough to freeze their lungs if they were so foolish as to breathe it in. By now, Kanu, Nissa and Hector would be totally reliant on the bottled oxygen while trying to keep hypothermia at bay.

"Kanu?" she called again, when they had descended another fifty grooves.

The answer came back at last—faint as if he were calling from the other side of the solar system.

"Quickly, Goma."

"We're coming."

They gave it one last push, Ru cranking the winch to its maximum output, spooling the last few hundred metres of tether at the emergency deployment rate, almost free fall, with their feet barely kissing the wheel's rushing succession of grooves and intermediate sections. And then there was a spill of light—not quite directly below them but close enough, a yellow warmth like the glow from a campfire.

They fell.

It was a slip of a few metres, no more—but it was enough to send Ru crashing into a groove, catching the edge of it with her suit's chest pack. Goma felt the impact travel through the line, a hard pluck of tension caught and then released, and watched Ru suddenly go limp above her, arms lolling at her sides.

"Ru!"

There was no answer. Goma's heart was racing. They had been descending fast enough as it was, but that sudden short fall had been as terrifying as anything in her experience.

"Eunice—are you all right?"

"Right below you. Grapple must have shifted then regained its grip."

"Ru's hurt."

"I can see her. We're not far from the ledge now. The winch is still spooling—I'm going to swing out, see if I can make it down. You'll be a few seconds behind me. Watch out for Ru, and for that tether—you don't want to tangle yourself up in that."

There was time only to do, not to think. Ru had been hurt, but if Goma dwelt on that they were all going to be in trouble. To help Ru—to help all of them—she had to act quickly and dispassionately.

"Kanu! We have a problem. Be ready to grab whatever you can—and don't get pulled off the ledge."

"I'm leaning out. I can see you coming down—you're only a few grooves above me. What happened?"

"No time to explain. Just grab Eunice and her gear as soon as you're able."

"Hold on."

Then they heard a groan—Ru's voice—and Goma's heart leapt a little. No one groaned unless they still had some life in them.

"What just—"

"You were knocked out," Eunice said. "Turn off the winch. We're in danger of dropping too far."

Ru still sounded groggy. "I . . . yes. Wait."

They slowed. Goma heaved a sigh of relief and realised she had barely been breathing since that first slip of the grapple.

Damn their useless technology—could it not work flawlessly, just for once? But she supposed they had been asking rather a lot of it, expecting it to maintain a permanent grip on the alien fabric of the wheel.

Goma looked down.

Eunice had arrived at Kanu's level. She halted just above the groove from which the yellow light spilled out and waited for Kanu to grab the supply bag and swing it in to safety. Goma saw Kanu's gloved hands, a sheathed forearm, but no more of him than that.

One by one, they all managed to get into the groove. Ru lowered them a step at a time, taking no chances. Goma thought about the grapple, wondering if it had enough room to slip again without being pulled out of the groove completely. Not much they could do about it, fifty kilometres away.

Kanu was the only one of the party moving. Hector was a grey mass at the back of the groove, tucked into himself like a sculpture carved from a single lump of stone. It took a second glance for Goma to reassure herself that the Tantor really was inside a spacesuit and not simply exposed to the atmosphere. Next to him, squatting with her knees drawn up, hands laced around them, head slumped and with the face behind the visor showing no sign of registering their presence, was another spacesuited human.

They pushed the supplies into the back of the groove, clearing space for Ru, whose feet were just coming down into view. Goma stood as near to the edge as she dared and helped her swing back onto the hard, level floor of the groove. Ru wobbled then found her footing, glancing over her shoulder at the drop.

"I still don't know what happened back there."

"We fell," Goma said, casting an apprehensive eye over the front of Ru's suit. The chest module was buckled in a crease where it had borne the brunt of the impact with the groove's hard corner, half its status displays dim, the rest pulsing red.

None of that looked good to Goma.

"I don't remember."

"It was only a few metres—the grapple must have slipped. You hit the edge of a groove—I saw it happen just above me. How's your head?"

"Sore."

"There's a smear on the back of your visor—the impact must have smashed your head against the glass, knocked you out for a second or two. Am I making sense to you?"

"About as much as ever."

"I'm worried about concussion. I hate these suits. Why did we ever agree to doing anything involving spacesuits?"

"Because it also involves Tantors."

They unclipped the power winch, leaving it hanging on the end of the tether but still within easy reach.

"She's hurt," Kanu said, noticing the damage to Ru's suit. "Did that happen just now?"

"I'm all right," Ru said, waving aside his concern.

"You've all taken an incredible risk to help us—I didn't want any of you to get hurt."

"Keep an eye on your life-support traces," Goma instructed Ru before turning to Kanu. "Nissa doesn't look good. I'm sorry we couldn't get to you sooner."

"You have nothing to apologise for, Goma—not so long ago we were at each other's throats. But I am concerned for Nissa—her suit hit its margins earlier than mine. When she started running low on air and power, I hoped she'd be able to extend it by remaining motionless. Now she's in and out of consciousness."

"We'll do what we can," Goma said.

She went to Nissa. Her suit's displays and marker lights were all dimmed or inactive, signifying its low-power condition. Nissa made no acknowledgement of Goma's approach, not even when she knelt next to her and tried to open the access panel on her chest pack. Goma studied the layout of valves and power connectors for a moment, comparing them against the supplies they had brought down from *Mposi*. Then she went and selected an oxygen cylinder and emergency energy cell.

Eunice came over. "Let me deal with that," she said gently, taking the items from Goma's hands. Eunice coupled them into Nissa's backpack, and after a second or two there was a twitch of colour from one of the displays. But Nissa showed no immediate response to the influx of oxygen and power.

Eunice watched for a minute, opened another panel in the chest pack and adjusted some manual settings.

"Well?" Goma whispered.

"Kanu?" Eunice said. "Things aren't good. Nissa's gone into a hypothermic coma. It must have come on in the last few minutes—her suit's incredibly cold, and she was down to a few gasps of oxygen on the needle."

Kanu knelt down next to them. He had yet to accept supplementary oxygen or power, even though the exterior indicators on his own suit were already feeble or completely dimmed.

"How bad?"

"Hopefully we got here in time to avoid brain damage, but whatever the case, she needs better medical care than we can offer her here."

"What are you thinking?" Goma asked.

"Waiting for the wheel to carry us back into space isn't going to be an option for Nissa. We have to get her up there much faster than that. The winch is the only way."

"Fine," Goma said. "Hook her on, reel the line back in as fast as it'll go—if you think the winch is strong enough?"

"The winch will be fine—it's the grapple that concerns me. But Nissa's already on the verge of death. She'll need someone to guide her up. We can zip her into the supply bag—she won't weigh any more than those bottles and power cells."

"I'll do it," Kanu said instantly. "Show me how the winch system works and I will take her back to your ship."

"You're barely any better off than Nissa," Eunice said. "That parasite in your skull is probably doing more to hold you on the right side of consciousness than you realise. One slip, though, and it's all over. It'll have to be one of us. We're still pretty sharp, and we've already crossed the terrain once before."

Goma nodded. The answer seemed obvious to her—not even worth discussing. "Can you do it?"

"I could," Eunice answered, "were I not staying down here with Ru and Hector."

"No."

"I will not leave the Risen, Goma. That's non-negotiable. Besides, if Ru has problems, I know a damn sight more about spacesuit functions than you do."

"If Ru's suit's damaged, then Ru should be the one who goes up."

"She may or may not have a concussion, and under an increased life-support burden, her suit may or may not last until she reaches the top of the tether. She's better off here with me, where I can finesse her suit to keep her alive. You're the strongest of us, anyway. You've got me to thank for that—all those good genes I had the decency to pass on to you."

"You're not going to budge, are you?"

"I've made a life out of not budging. Bit late in the day to change old habits."

"You don't even know Hector."

"Reason enough to spend some time with him."

Goma went over to Ru and Kanu. They were working on the seals of the supply bag, opening it in readiness for Nissa.

"She wants me to handle the ascent," Goma said, looking at Ru. "You can't do it, not after what happened. I'd like to argue with that but she's got a point. And if you run into trouble with that suit, you're much better in her company than in mine. Can you put up with her until we're back on the lander?"

"I'm still willing to take Nissa up myself," Kanu said.

Goma shook her head. "You're in no shape for that. If I had more confidence in the winch, I'd say we stuff you into the same bag. But there isn't really room, and I'd worry about the line slipping again."

"I'll stay, then," Kanu said, his tone indicating that he accepted the logic of the decision even if it displeased him.

Nissa was still unresponsive, although her suit was now back on partial power and her oxygen partial pressure had climbed back to a low but tolerable level. They eased her into the bag, checked her life signs one more time, then sealed it around her like a cocoon. The bag was toughened with layers of impact padding and self-healing membranes, sufficient to protect Nissa against tears, bumps and micrometeorite impacts. They had done what they could for her.

"Can Goma handle all that on her own?" Kanu asked.

"The load will be on her suit, not on Goma," Eunice said. "In the meantime you get to spend some quality time with Ru, Hector and me."

"Aren't you worried I'll kill the Tantor?" Ru asked.

"No," Eunice said sharply, "because that would make me an idiot. You were the weapon, but you were *not* culpable." Her tone softened. "And I overreacted, for which I'm sorry. How many times do I have to say that?"

"Once is a start," Ru said.

They were ready for the ascent. Goma tugged down on the power winch and coupled it to the front of her suit, making sure the latch was secure. She tested her own weight on the line—if the grapple failed now, there was no hope of it holding once she started hauling Nissa up.

"Will you manage down here?"

"We'll start a campfire sing-song," Eunice said. "The time'll fly past. And you need to be on your way. Once you're moving, I'll give Captain Vasin a heads-up as to what's happening. If she can drop *Mposi* back down between you and the grapple—that will save a lot of time."

"Ru—I'll see you in a few hours. Kanu . . . Hector—the same. Eunice—take good care of them all."

"I shall."

"And while you're at it, take care of yourself. I still haven't got to the bottom of what you are."

"There's no mystery, Goma—just me, alive, as simple as that."

"Nothing about you is simple."

She applied increasing power to the winch, drawing herself up from the floor of the groove before taking Nissa's weight. The winch was powerful and showed no hesitation as the burden increased. Perhaps they were going to make it after all.

She paused for one moment to make eye contact with Eunice, Kanu and Ru, giving them each a nod. She would have envied them their time with Hector, but the evidence suggested Hector was long past the point of conversation. They would do well to keep him alive as the wheel carried them up to space.

Goma managed an average ascent rate of ten kilometres an hour, running and leaping, doing her best to kick out as she passed the grooves, letting her payload pendulum beneath her. She could never have kept it up without the suit's amplification-assist, but even with it the concentration was taxing. She was all too aware of the damage she could do to herself through a single lapse of attention—never mind her cocooned, helpless passenger.

An hour of that, then another.

The one blessing was that in the time since their departure from *Mposi*, ten hours had passed. The wheel had continued to turn—thereby raising the grapple higher and allowing *Mposi* to come back in about eight kilometres beneath their initial starting position. Goma did not have to ascend the same distance they had descended, and Vasin was going to risk holding station until she arrived with Nissa.

The grapple held, and so did the tether. She was beginning to stumble, though, mistiming her kicks, when a bright light turned her shadow hard-edged. She looked up, squinting against the exhaust of the lander as it settled back onto the wheel. Five kilometres above her—Vasin cutting it fine this time. But Goma sensed she was nearly home, and that gave her a renewed burst of energy and focus.

Suited figures were waiting for her when she reached the underside of the lander. Andisa and Grave helped her up the last few metres. Then they disconnected the line and moved the survival bag into the lock.

Goma waited on the tilted ledge. She felt cored out, drained of something vital. But she would not allow herself to linger before resuming the journey back down to Ru. They argued with her about it, but her mind was set.

She was the last into the body of the ship, and they had her out of the spacesuit almost before she could blink. Andisa gave her a cursory but efficient examination—satisfying herself that Goma was exhausted but had otherwise suffered no ill-effects.

Goma gulped down fluids, putting back some of the litres she had sweated out on the wheel. "Give me ten minutes to get my head together. Then I'm going back down."

"No," Andisa said. "We can't stay here, and Vasin won't let you take that risk. They'll just have to wait until the wheel brings them around."

"She told you to tell me that?"

"You're a wreck, Goma Akinya. You've been up and down the wheel without a break and we almost lost all of you when that grapple gave way. Gandhari won't risk that happening again."

Goma reached for the anger and frustration she knew she ought to be feeling, but found only exhaustion and the sense that this was an argument she could never win.

"Did you tell her about Ru?"

"Yes, and I've been talking to Ru since you left her. She's lucid and her life signs look stable. If there'd been bleeding or a skull fracture, I would know by now."

"I hope you're right about that."

"It's my job to be right. Believe me, if there was a way to spirit all of them back up here right now, I'd jump on it. But the point of that dangerous rescue operation was to deliver the supplies Kanu and the others needed, and you succeeded. More than that—you got Nissa back up here."

Goma tried to see beyond her own concerns, if only for a moment.

"How is she?"

"You did your best, and I'll do mine. Now think about yourself for a few minutes. You did a magnificent thing, Goma—you saved a human life."

CHAPTER 53

Mposi had to take off again to conserve the fuel it needed for the steering motor. They pulled away from the wheel, made a few circuits to gather more information, then climbed back into low orbit.

"While all that was going on," Vasin said, "we neglected to keep you informed of wider developments."

It was just the captain and Goma, sitting next to one of the observation windows, interior lights dimmed, the ship taking care of itself for a while. Everyone was worn out, not just those directly involved in the rescue.

"You're going to tell me that the moons have returned to their usual orbits and we're going to have to face the Terror on our way out?"

"Thankfully, no—the moons are still holding their new alignment—all in the same orbit, strung out like pearls on a necklace. Problem is, it's drawn the Watchkeepers. They must think this constitutes an open invitation."

"A problem for us, or for them?"

"On the evidence, very much for them. We're on the night-side now, which makes it easier—let me turn down the lights a little more."

Vasin blacked out the cabin completely, leaving the moons and the stars as their only sources of illumination. The moons were too small to matter and the stars too far away. Goma floated in darkness until her eyes began to pick up something else.

Tiny migraine flashes, somewhere out there—almost too faint to detect, like ghost signals on her optic nerve. Pinks and greens and oranges, starbursts and starfish, tracing the same ecliptic plane as the moons.

"They're dying," Vasin said. "They've been trying to cross that line of moons for hours, ever since they fell into that new configuration, and they're being sliced and diced. One after the other, they keep coming. It's as if they're too huge, too slow, to realise their mistake—like a pod of whales coming ashore, beaching themselves."

"You can see it happening?"

"On long-range, yes. Whatever's killing them, it's hard to see where it originates. The moons, maybe—or even something out there we haven't detected yet. For all we know, the moons are just the sensory elements of a defence system we can't even see."

Goma thought about that for a moment. "Now you're scaring me."

"If you're not scared, you don't understand the situation. My—did I just sound like Eunice for a moment?"

"She rubs off."

"I hope you'll understand why I couldn't authorise another expedition down the wheel. I want them all back here—but I won't put more lives at risk to make it happen. Sometimes being a captain is about making the unpopular decisions—the ones you know you'll stand a good chance of being hated for."

"You've done well, Gandhari. You've brought us this far, and you've shared a ship with Eunice. It can't have been easy, working in her shadow."

"The airlock was never far away."

"For her, or for you?"

"Either option was on the table. But you know, I still can't decide whether we've really met her or not. She walks and talks like the real thing, and Nhamedjo—although it pains me to mention his name—told us she was real, all the way through. Mona came to the same conclusion herself. Nhamedjo might have been a treacherous fucker, but he didn't have any reason to lie about Eunice."

Goma, despite her fatigue, despite her apprehension, laughed. "That's not very captainly language, Gandhari."

"Do forgive me—I've had a taxing few days."

"You're forgiven. But I agree—I still don't know what to make of her. Where have her memories come from? They're incomplete, stitched together from biographical fragments—they're not actual memories at all. Then again, the construct version of Eunice lived several lifetimes on *Zanzibar*. Those memories are authentic—they're just not part of the original Eunice's life. Then she met the Watchkeepers, and they dismantled her and put her back together again using biological material. And she's lived another lifetime or two in this form. What does that make her? More or less than the original Eunice? Her equal in every way? An extension of the same personality? If we take her back with us, what rights would she have?"

"There's no precedent for her," Vasin said. "She's as strange as anything out there. Wonderful, intimidating—scary. And as sly as a fox. That trick she pulled on us with the mirrors—I'm still trying to work that one out. Did she commit the worst crime imaginable, or did she save lives and start another adventure?"

"Kanu still went to Poseidon."

"But of his own volition, to spare the Risen. She can't be blamed for his selflessness."

"I wonder if we'll ever know what she did to *Zanzibar*."

"We won't rest until we do. Collectively, I mean—as a society. Also, she's demonstrated something rather significant— that whatever we don't understand about the M-builders, and that's rather a lot, we do have the ability to operate their technology."

"We're just monkeys hitting piano keys."

"And maybe we'll hit a tune now and then. It might take time. But I'm a navigator, Goma. People like me won't rest until we've found a way to use the Mandalas. To go from our fastest ships to being able to travel as close to the speed of light as we can imagine?"

"Aren't you disappointed not to have something faster?"

"I'll take what I can get. I want to know how far that network extends—to ride the Mandalas so deep into the galaxy that our sun's just another nameless dot in the Milky Way."

"You might skip between those stars quicker than you can blink, but it'll still be years and years of travel for the people left at home."

"There aren't any," Vasin said. "Not for me, at least."

"I still want to go home."

"You will. And here's something else to think about. There is no Mandala in Earth's solar system—at least not that we know of. Our best intelligence says Crucible's is the nearest one."

"Crucible's going to change."

"If the Mandalas allow us to use them, then yes. Your little planet—and remember, I wasn't born there—it's going to assume a different importance from now on. Crucible will be the gateway—the port of entry."

"Into what?"

"We'll find out. When we make it work."

They turned their attention back to the distant lights of dying Watchkeepers. It was beautiful and sublime. Goma took no joy in the deaths of the alien machines, rather a sadness that they could not see their own folly.

Eventually the attrition slowed—the lights fading away like the last desultory bursts of a fireworks display.

"There are more still out there," Vasin said, "but they must have had the sense to hold back."

"I almost feel sorry for them."

"You shouldn't. They've caused us enough trouble."

That was true, and her words should have been enough to settle Goma's doubts. But still, the Watchkeepers had been kind to Eunice—or at least merciful—and they had given her a gift beyond measure. Perhaps it had been nothing to them, a kindly gesture almost too small for their accounting—like a person tipping an upended insect back onto its legs, the whim of a moment. But they had made her human, put life into her lungs, given her dreams and sorrows, all the stuff of mortality. They had given Eunice back to herself.

Goma could forgive them a lot for that.

She went to see Nissa, so that she would have something to report to Kanu. Nissa was still unconscious, still in Dr. Andisa's care. At least the best was now being done for her, although Andisa would not be pushed on her chances. Her suit had run out of power sooner than it ran out of air, so the cold of the high atmosphere had been her first problem. Despite layers of insulation, she had still suffered frostbite to her face and extremities, visible now where Andisa had applied a blue medical salve, especially around the temples and cheekbones. Oxygen starvation had come after the frostbite, and she could not have escaped neurological damage of some degree. But they had restored heat and air before the ascent, so things had certainly not worsened from that point on.

"I barely know her," Goma said, "but I want her to live. It's not just because of Kanu, of what her dying would do to him after all this. She came all this way, survived everything up until the wheel—even the Terror. It's not right that she should die of fucking frostbite and oxygen starvation!"

"We will do what we can," Andisa said gently.

Of course they would, but that was no reassurance at all to Goma. "Kanu's still down there. I want to give him some encouragement, some reason to think she'll be all right."

"This unconsciousness is partly a medical choice. I have given her as heavy a dose of neural growth factors as I dare risk. They will consolidate the damaged structures, prevent further obliteration and provoke a measure of synaptic reconstruction. But it is best that she not be awake while these processes are under way."

"I don't doubt your skill, Mona. I just wish I had something concrete to give him."

"Tell him she is alive and receiving the best care available. That is the only honest answer I can provide. The moment there is better news, you will be the first to hear it. In the meantime, Goma?"

She wondered what was coming. "Yes?"

"It was a fine thing, to have helped her. She would be dead without you, but you have given her hope. Now tell Kanu to worry about himself, and we will worry about Nissa."

"I shall."

She found some chai, splashed water in her face to keep the tiredness at bay, then resumed contact with the party on the ledge. She used the general channel, addressing them all at once. Ru might have been her wife, but her concern right now was for each and every member of the party, including Hector.

"We're holding on," Ru said. "Supplies look good. Our suits are working fine, for now. There's really not much to do but wait. We saw you take off—please tell me you're planning to come back for us?"

Ru's question might have been less than serious, but Goma was too tired to bother with anything but a straight answer. "Once you're higher, we'll break orbit and come back in again. Have you seen the firework display?"

"Yes, and very pretty it was, too. Kanu says it must have been the Watchkeepers."

"He's right," Goma confirmed. "They've been throwing themselves against the moons, getting sliced and diced—it's as if they saw this as their one chance to get anywhere near the wheels. But it hasn't worked. Looks like they've given up—at least, the carnage appears to be over for the time being. I don't think that means we've seen the last of them—there must still be a lot more out there, waiting to see what happened. But if they expect answers from any of us, I'm not convinced they're going to get them."

"Kanu might beg to differ," Ru said. "He's been through

the Terror just like Eunice did all those years ago. He said it's given him a certain perspective."

"Is Kanu there?"

"I am," he answered after a moment's silence. "Any news on Nissa?"

Kanu sounded more alert and focused than when she first met him on the ledge. "Doctor Andisa's doing everything she can," Goma answered, gladdened to hear his voice. "We need to keep her stable until we can get her aboard *Travertine*. We have much better medical facilities on the big ship."

"It's good to hear you, Goma. Would it be wrong to say I'm proud of you? We've done some good and bad things, we Akinyas. But I think I know where you stand."

His words warmed her. "You too, uncle."

"I'm not sure which sounds less formal—uncle or Kanu. No one's ever called me uncle before."

"They say you were a diplomat."

"Once. In another life. And a merman. I've been many things, in fact, and I'm not sure I've been terribly good at any of them."

"You're being too hard on yourself."

"Oh, I'm not so sure. What exactly have I achieved? I betrayed my government, let down my friends, misled Nissa— all to serve the goals of machines on Mars I barely understand, let alone trust? And while Swift's had to put up with being in my head, it's not as if he's really needed me for anything else. I've just been his vehicle, his means of reaching this place."

"Is Swift with you?"

"Standing near us, polishing his pince-nez, trying not to look offended. At least one of us got what they wanted, anyway—to meet his maker."

"There must have been more to it than that."

"Some lofty ideas about deepening our understanding of the roles of the machine and the organic—trying to find a strategy for mutual coexistence. Just words, though. Meanwhile, our little jaunt has cost lives and anguish, and we're no closer to understanding the Watchkeepers any better. Things are worse, in fact. If we hadn't come here, none of the deaths would have happened."

"If there's blame to apportion, you only get to take a share of it," Goma said. "None of us is an innocent party."

"Except, possibly, you."

"You underestimate me. I'd have climbed over a mountain of human bones to find the Tantors."

"Even though it was not the meeting you'd hoped for?"

"It was a start. Ru and I spent our lives charting the fade of the Tantors—the decline of their cognitive signal. We never hoped to encounter a self-sustaining colony of Tantors, let alone the Risen. But yes, things went wrong. Human fucking stupidity. Fear and ignorance. As if the worst thing in the world would be to share it with another intelligence."

"People and elephants. People and robots."

"Maybe we should just let the elephants and robots live happily ever after," Goma said. "They seemed happy enough to take Eunice on her own terms."

"It can't be that hopeless," Kanu answered, with a mixture of weariness and conviction. "I staked my life on brokering a peace between people and the Evolvarium. I'm old and foolish enough to delude myself that there's still a chance of achieving that. Tell me you haven't given up on the Risen?"

"There aren't many of them left."

"I gather there are a few on Orison, and shortly you'll have a proper chance to know Hector, too. I was an ambassador to the machines, Goma. That was strange enough! Now the Risen will need to send an ambassador to us."

"They may need some persuasion. Earth's not exactly their home."

"Mars wasn't mine, but I found friends there."

"How is Hector?" she asked.

"No physical issues that we're aware of. But the loss of Dakota has hit him hard."

"I wish I could speak to him now. Are you able to communicate?"

"Our suits have a link, but it's clumsy. Would you like me to pass on a message, for whatever good it may do?"

"Tell him he is valued. Tell him that Ru and I can't wait to hear what he has to tell us."

"I shall. Would you like to speak to Eunice now?"

"Of course."

She had been listening in all the while, naturally. "Goma. Good of you to remember us."

"As if I could forget."

"You did well. Kanu is right. Pride in another human being is an odd thing for me to feel—it's usually frustration, bitterness, anger. You get used to that after a while—start to feel as if it's the normal state of affairs. But look at you—you've made an old woman quietly pleased with you."

"That's not why I did it."

"All the more reason to applaud your actions, then. You've had a lot to live up to, Goma, but you haven't disappointed us."

"Us?"

"Your illustrious ancestors. If I can't speak for them, who can?"

"I suppose you're right."

"Not always. But on this occasion, yes. Very much so. Nissa is stable, you say?"

She would have gladly told Eunice how she truly felt about Nissa's chances, but not while Kanu was still part of the conversation. "Mona's doing her best."

"Yes. A distinct improvement on your last doctor, I must say. I much prefer her bedside manner."

When the call from Goma was done, Swift was still there, leaning casually against the back wall of the shelf. He was the only one of them not dressed in a spacesuit, his stockinged legs crossed over each other, his pince-nez perched on the tip of his nose, and he was peering at Kanu with a certain provisional interest, as if he were a new species of sea creature discovered during some nautical expedition.

"You really think my use for you is so shallow?" Swift arched an eyebrow, inviting an answer.

Kanu answered subvocally, sparing his companions this exchange. "When the moment came, you couldn't wait to show your true colours. You sided with that other machine—took events into your own hands."

"Only because I had the best interests of a friend in mind, Kanu. Need I labour the point?"

"I'm sure you will."

"When you attempted to kill yourself on *Icebreaker*, I

intervened. I did so because our twin fates were intertwined—if you died, so would I. But I also did so because you are my friend, and I believed that the situation was not *quite* as hopeless as you perceived it to be. I had, after all, already installed my image inside *Icebreaker* by then. I knew there was a faint chance of intervention, albeit under circumstances I had yet to foresee. But I also made a mistake. I denied you the free will I had always promised would be yours. And when you made me promise that I would not take similar action again, I held to that vow. Scrupulously. Even when it cut against every sensible instinct in my head. I mean, your head."

"That's not funny, Swift."

"It's not meant to be. My point is, I did not stop you entering Poseidon. We had the opportunity to turn around and only the lives of the Risen complicated that picture. To me they were a distraction, a nuisance. Statistical noise, interfering with my—what did you call them? Lofty ideas?"

"The Risen are living beings. People."

"I came here to know the minds of machines, not mammals."

"You still had an incentive for carrying on. That was your opportunity to experience the Terror, to touch the M-builders' minds. There was always something in it for you."

"Along with an excellent chance of dying. I would much sooner have abandoned the expedition, cooperated with Goma and organised an expedition under our own terms, rather than those of the Risen or the Watchkeepers. That point is moot, though. Did I break my vow?"

"No," Kanu admitted, with a certain sullenness.

"When everything was at stake, when my oldest human friend was about to throw himself into the fire for the sake of some elephants? Did I so much as tip the scales of his free will?"

"No," Kanu said again.

"Louder. I need to hear it."

"No. You didn't. You kept your vow."

"Well, then," Swift said. "With that unpleasantness behind us, let us discuss the base cause of your present malaise."

"My malaise?"

"I speak not of your present mental disequilibrium, occasioned as it is by the uncertainty surrounding Nissa's condition. That is to be expected, and like you I hope fervently that she will come through this ordeal unscathed. My concern is a larger one—that the Terror has driven a gaping wound into your psyche, one that time and tide may struggle to repair."

"You were in my head when we felt the Terror, Swift. You got a dose of that as well. Don't tell me otherwise."

"Yes, and the experience was every bit as bracing as I anticipated. A cold, hard blast of reality." Swift bounded to the edge of the groove with a chilling indifference to the drop beyond his toes. "What could be colder than being made to feel the utter futility of existence? To know that not only is there no meaning to anything, but there never can be? That life itself is completely devoid of purpose? That nothing will be remembered? That despite our grandest efforts, our boldest endeavours, nothing can or will ever be preserved? That the kindest acts are doomed to be forgotten, along with the cruellest? All loves, all hates erased from the record? Yes, what could be worse than that?"

"You tell me."

"Nothing. Nothing at all in the whole of creation. And if death troubles me—which, I am pleased to say, it most certainly does—then the idea of not even being remembered, not even leaving the tiniest quantum ripple in the wake of the coming vacuum fluctuation . . . well, that is a great deal more than troubling. We live by our deeds, whether we are machines or people or elephants. And if our deeds are meaningless and forgotten, what does that make us?"

"Nothing," Kanu answered, fiercely enough that he spoke the word aloud. "Pointless interactions between matter and energy, doomed to be erased. That's the message, Swift. That there's no meaning. That we don't matter."

"No," Swift answered, with corresponding force. "We do matter. This truth does not rob us of meaning—it gives it back to us. It liberates us from the burden of posterity, from the burden of deluding ourselves that our acts have some chance of outlasting eternity. If we are kind to each other now, it's not because we're hoping to be remembered well, to be lauded in some great accounting of things. It's not because we want to be rewarded for our behaviour, or to be admired for the wonderful things we did during our brief span of existence. Exactly the opposite! Now that we know there is no chance of that, our deeds have no higher meaning than the context of the moment in which they occur. One decent deed, one kind gesture, enacted without thought of recompense or remembrance, performed in the full and certain knowledge that it will be forgotten, that it cannot be otherwise—that single deed refutes the entire message of the M-builders. They were wrong! There is no Terror, only enlightenment! Only liberation! And we will continue to refute their message with every gracious act, every decent thought, every human kindness—until the moment the vacuum rips."

"Just a fancy speech, Swift. That's all it is."

"More than a speech, Kanu. A viable moral strategy for negating the M-builders' nihilism. It's a choice. A question of free will. Do you choose it, or reject it?"

"You're a machine," he said. "How could you ever understand?"

"I *was* a machine," Swift answered. "Once. But then I spent too long in the company of the living."

"Over here," Eunice said sharply.

Kanu turned. He had been so wrapped up in his conversation with Swift that he failed to notice Ru was no longer standing. She had slumped over at the back of the ledge and was lying awkwardly on her side. It was not the posture of someone who had sat down carefully with the intention of closing their eyes or conserving energy. He saw in the same glance that none of her suit's status indications were glowing.

Eunice was quickly at her side, easing her into a more natural position with her back braced against the rear of the ledge, her legs stretched out before her.

"What is it?" Kanu asked.

"I don't think it's the concussion—she was lucid enough when Goma called. That bump she took coming down here must have done more harm to her suit than we realised. There's been a sudden systems failure."

"She said nothing."

"Then she couldn't have got much warning. Wait a second." Eunice was repeating the exercise she had already performed on Nissa, flipping open hatches in the chest pack, squinting through her own faceplate with steely concentration, not wanting to miss a detail.

"We still have oxygen and power," Kanu said.

"That won't help her. There's a system failure deep in the pack, maybe a secondary leak here as well. It must have opened up as the ambient pressure reduced. She's in trouble, Kanu. Plugging in more air and power won't help—the fault's too extensive. Did you see her go down?"

"No."

"I saw her a few minutes ago and she was still standing so she hasn't been down long. If we can restore air and heat, she'll have at least as good a chance as Nissa."

"You just said we can't do that."

"Not with the supplementary supplies." Eunice paused, turned from the slumped form. "There's an easier way. It'll give her a fully functioning life-support system for the rest of the trip."

"I don't follow."

"She takes my chest pack. Watch what I'm doing very carefully—you'll need to reverse these steps precisely when you reconnect my pack in place of hers."

For a moment he did not quite grasp what she was proposing. The words, yes. The implication, no. But then the truth of it dawned with a sort of sick clarity. "No, Eunice," he said, dizzied. "This isn't how it's going to happen. My suit—"

"Isn't the same design as hers. Mine, piece of antiquated shit that it is, matches perfectly. Your chest pack won't mate with her coupling systems; mine will. Watch." She ran her fingers around the edge of the pack, where the power and pressure valves connected with the rest of the suit. "Primary and secondary shut-offs. These have to be tight or the air inside her will vent the instant I remove the pack. Are you following?"

"No. Stop. We need to think this through."

"Believe me, Kanu—the one thing you don't do in emergencies is think things through. Thinking things through gets you a headstone and a nice epitaph. *She thought things through. See how that worked out for her.* Now watch!"

He reached out, tried to prise her hands away from the chest pack. "No. Not a life for a life."

"You think Ru deserves to die?"

"None of us deserves to die! Not her, not you!"

"Because I'm an Akinya?"

"Because I will not let you give up your life for hers! For all we know she's already beyond any hope of recovery!"

"And Nissa wasn't? We gave her a chance, Kanu—why not Ru?"

"Nobody had to die for Nissa to get her chance."

"Ru wouldn't be in this mess if she hadn't come down for you." With a force that surprised him—far beyond what this small, bony woman looked capable of—Eunice reasserted her grip on the chest pack's connectors. "I know you don't want to see a death, Kanu. I know you're not valuing my life over hers. You're a good man and I understand your reluctance. But I won't sit back and do nothing. You're going to help me."

"I can't."

"You will. Swift? Make him. Do this one thing for me. And *listen*."

He tried to struggle with her again even as part of him surrendered to the logic of her sacrifice, while another part accepted that she would always find a way to be stronger if the moment depended on it. But then his own strength was gone. Kanu felt himself slump back, as if every muscle in his body had been given an immediate and binding command to relax.

He stared at the figure who stood watching proceedings, hands behind his back, expression observant but concerned.

"Swift!"

"I have no choice, Kanu. She made me what I am. I can hardly refuse a simple request from my maker."

After that, he could only bear witness.

"The connections are sealed," Eunice said. "I'm removing the pack now." She eased the buckled device from Ru's chest, exposing the gold-and-chrome-coated interfaces and plugs where it had coupled with her suit. "Now mine. This is the awkward part—they don't generally assume you'll be doing this while still *inside* the suit."

"There's a reason for that," said Kanu. He could not interfere, but he could still talk.

"Yes." But there was a sadness in her answer, not the dismissiveness Kanu might have expected. "I don't know how long I'll have. It'll depend on the tightness of the seals. If I can maintain consciousness and dexterity, I'll do my best to reconnect the pack to Ru, but you'll need to do it if I can't—is that clear?"

"You're asking the impossible of us."

"No, I'm asking you to save a life. Mine will already be over, bar the shouting. This isn't a moral conundrum. I'm sparing you that."

"Damn you. And damn *you*, Swift, for playing along."

Kanu was still unable to do more than talk and observe, his own body refusing to respond to motor commands.

"Don't blame him for his loyalty," Eunice said. "Two kinds of machine are conspiring to save a human life."

"You're not a machine now."

"No—but let's face it, I'm not one of *you* either. And as for our mutual friend Swift—he's a taxonomic headache all of his own. What a pretty pair we make, eh? Oh." She was suddenly silent. "This is trickier than I expected. I can't get my fingers around these shut-offs, but the pack won't release unless they're closed."

"No. I know what you're going to ask, and no."

"You're wrong. I don't even have to ask. Swift—help me with these fastenings."

"Don't do it," Kanu said.

Swift walked over to the two Akinyas and Ru's seated form. "I must, Kanu. Or rather, we must. Don't you see? I came to meet Eunice, to know the mind of she who gave life and form to the Evolvarium. Her request is a simple one and it would be quite wrong of me to refuse."

Swift's image fused itself with Kanu, and Kanu found himself moving. With deliberation and calm and an absolute absence of volition, his hands reached out to address the complicated, foolproof fastenings of Eunice's chest pack. He tried to resist—tried to generate the nerve signals that would override these motor instructions now being controlled by Swift, but the effort was useless. His fingers found the shut-offs that Eunice had not been able to reach.

"Do not fight it, Kanu," Eunice said, not unkindly. "You are blameless in this."

"Tell him to stop!"

"And do not blame Swift, either. Swift is only doing that which he knows to be right."

Cold grey gas vented out from her chest pack. Kanu's hands finished their work with the shut-off valves and grasped the pack on either side. Slowly he eased it away from Eunice's suit, revealing a corresponding arrangement of interfaces.

The spray of gas ceased. Nothing was coming out of her suit, nothing coming out of the pack.

Eunice was still responsive—there was still air in the suit and her helmet space, and her communications channel functioned independently of primary suit power.

"Good. You're doing well—both of you. Now attach it to Ru's suit. Quicker the better."

Swift made Kanu move towards the other suited form. But between one moment and the next, Swift's control over him was gone.

"You should do this, my friend."

"And if I try to put the pack back on Eunice?"

"We'll both fight you. Save Ru, Kanu. Her life's in your hands now."

He knew, with a vast and crushing inevitability, that there was only one course of action open to him now. He locked the undamaged chest pack into place on Ru's suit. Eunice knelt down next to him and between them they opened all the necessary connectors.

For a few seconds there was no change in her suit. Then status lights flickered on her wrists and on the pack itself. The suit appeared to puff out slightly, stiffening her form.

"She's back on full pressure," Eunice said. "We'll dial it up a little. Same with the power. Must be chilled to the bone in there." Eunice adjusted Ru's life-support settings using both the chest-pack controls and the wrist functions, and then stood with a grunt of effort. "That'll do. After thirty minutes, return to the default settings—use these controls."

Kanu studied Ru's unconscious face through her visor. There was no change as yet, but a drastic alteration was unlikely. He had to trust that they had helped her in time.

"How do you think she'll do?" Kanu asked.

"Lap of the gods. Goma mentioned something to me—a condition Ru has, due to oxygen poisoning—which may or may not complicate things. But we've done what we can." Eunice, he noticed, was drawing a heavier than usual breath between her utterances. "She looked strong to me. I liked her."

"You'd have done this for any one of us."

"Perhaps. But at least with Ru I had an account to settle. You'll take care of her until you reach the ship, Kanu? Soon you're going to be the only one of us standing."

"There must be something I can do for you. The oxygen supplies—can't we plumb them in directly?"

"You find me a tool shop, I'll make the necessary alterations."

"I wish . . ."

She was still standing, but the effort—especially in Poseidon's gravity—must have been taking its toll and her knees began to buckle. She allowed herself to rest a hand on Kanu's shoulder. "You wish things were different from the way they are. That's a refrain as old as time. I've lived a long and strange sort of life, Kanu, and I've known that feeling a few times. Generally it's best to accept that things are exactly as bad as they look. At least that way you know it's time to start digging your way out." She coughed, and when her voice returned it was weaker than before. "But no digging now. Not for me, anyway. And you know what? This hasn't been too bad. I got to be human again. I got to be alive, with a head full of memories that felt as if they belonged to me."

"Did they?"

"Once or twice. Enough to make the whole thing worthwhile." She staggered, caught herself. "Oh. I think I need to sit down now. Help me to the ledge. I'll dangle my feet over the edge."

"I don't want you falling."

"I've no plans to. I just want to see the sunrise."

It was still dark. At the rate her suit systems were failing, there would be no sunrise for Eunice Akinya. But he could not deny her last request. Kanu guided her to the ledge, took her arm as she sat down on the lip.

"Is there anything else I can do for you?"

"Yes," she answered, after a silence. "They'll want to take me back to Earth, back to Africa. They can have part of me, I suppose. But the rest belongs on Orison, with the Risen."

"I'll make sure that happens."

Kanu became aware of a presence looming behind him. He glanced around, expecting it to be Swift. But it was Ru, bracing her hands against her knees but otherwise standing.

"I blacked out," she said. "Something wrong with my suit after all, I guess. But I feel fine now. What's up with her?"

"Look at your chest pack," Kanu said quietly.

Ru must not have noticed until that moment. She stroked a hand along the clean surface of the unbuckled, undamaged device. "Wait . . ." she began. And then her gaze must have fallen upon the broken unit, still lying on the floor where they had left it.

"Its hers, the one you're wearing," Kanu said. "She wanted you to have it."

"What about Eunice?"

"I think we should sit with her," he said. "Just for a while."

CHAPTER 54

The wheel turned. *Mposi* orbited. The hours passed like lazy summers. There had been some sort of breakdown in communications between the ship and the party in the groove. It went on for an hour, with no one answering the transmissions from the ship; Goma was certain it meant the worst. She had thought of asking Vasin to take the ship down immediately; she did not mind abasing herself by begging, not when other lives were at stake.

But eventually there was a crackle, a voice she had no trouble recognising.

"It's Ru."

Goma took the call. "We were starting to worry about you. Is everything all right down there?"

"Everything's fine. I had a problem with my suit, but it's fixed now and I didn't suffer any harm."

She sounded defeated rather than ecstatic, but also alert and satisfactorily aware of her immediate situation.

"What about Hector?"

"Hector's all right. No cause for alarm. We've been checking on his suit status periodically—he's warm and breathing. I can't say we've had any deep and meaningful conversations, but there'll be time enough for that later. Are you ready for him?"

"Gandhari says she can bring the primary lock into play for long enough to load him. What about Kanu and Eunice?"

There was a silence before Ru answered.

"Kanu's good. Eunice is dead."

Goma's first instinct was to respond with a flat denial, as if this could not be possible under any set of circumstances.

"No."

"It's true. My suit went wrong, the damage was worse than we thought and I blacked out. When I came around, Kanu and Eunice had swapped the good part of her suit onto mine. She was already gone, Goma."

After that, there was nothing to do but wait for the wheel to turn. When the groove was approaching forty kilometres from the surface, Vasin once again summoned the nerve to take *Mposi* down, landing on the same level as Kanu and Ru but a few dozen metres to one side. It was still much too close for comfort, but the shorter the distance they had to move Hector, the better.

Goma, somewhat rested by then—but still having to argue her case with Dr. Andisa—was finally allowed to go out in one of the suits. Grave and Loring were dealing with Hector, coaxing him back to sufficient wakefulness to be able to assist with getting himself into the primary lock, access to which involved holding *Mposi* in an even more precarious position than before.

Goma had expected Ru to be up on her feet, wanting to be the first aboard off that cold and narrow shelf. But she was sitting on the groove's edge, her feet dangling over the side, next to Eunice. On the other side of Ru was Kanu. They were both still wearing their helmets, but Eunice's had been removed and now sat behind her, her head fully exposed to the vacuum. Goma moved to her side, standing perilously close to the edge herself. Ru and Kanu were also the only ones wearing chest packs.

Viewed from the side, Eunice's posture was one of acceptance, even tranquillity. Her gloved hands rested in her lap, shoulders relaxed, head lolling only slightly down towards her chest within the open neck ring. From a distance, she might have been taking a snooze, or lost in reflective meditation. Goma sat down next to Ru.

"Do they need help with Hector?"

"No," Goma said, swallowing hard before continuing. "I think they've got that covered. But we can't hold station here for very long. Vasin wants to be up and off the groove as quickly as possible. It's not safe."

"You don't say." But there was no malice in Ru's remark, just a quiet exhaustion. "I hated her, you know."

"You had grounds to."

"And yet she did this. She could have lived, but she gave herself up for me instead. Was it on her mind all the time? Is that why she was so keen to stay down here with me?"

"No one could have been that calculating."

"Except her."

"Not even Eunice," Goma said. She began to push herself up from the ledge, thinking how easy it would be to make a mistake, even now. "Ru, Kanu—we have to go."

"I'm staying with her." Before Goma could say a word, Ru went on, "Kanu should leave, definitely. He needs to get back to Nissa. But my suit is good. I only need to ride the rest of the way to the top of the wheel."

"We could move her now."

"She's frozen. We'd break her like an ice sculpture."

"We can't leave her here, Ru."

"I'm not saying we should. But there'll be another sunrise before we reach the top of the wheel. I want her to see the sun one more time."

"You're set on this."

"Yes, and if you know me as well as you should by now, you won't try to argue me out of it."

"I wouldn't dream of it." Goma stood up anyway. "Kanu—are you ready to go? Your suit doesn't have anything like the life-support capacity of Ru's."

"You're leaving them here?" he asked, rising carefully from the ledge.

"No, I'm just going to explain the situation to the others. I think it'll be easier face to face. Then I'll be back. I'll see out that sunrise, too. Vasin can damn well come and fetch us later."

"You don't have to do this," Ru said.

"Neither of us has to," Goma said, "but we're doing it anyway. It's the least I owe her. She's brought you home to me."

On the way out from Poseidon, *Mposi* slid beyond the bracelet of moons and then through the drifting corpses of the Watchkeepers, the freshest of their cruelly transected bodies still glowing along the geometric planes where they had been severed, a testament to killing energies both invisible and incomprehensible. The older corpses, those that had been littering Poseidon space for millennia, were as dark as coal—mute and mindless witnesses to this latest bout of machine carnage. No part of that alien defence system touched little *Mposi*, with its cargo of humans—one comatose, another a frozen corpse—and one elephant. But as soon as it was clear of the rebuked and punished Watchkeepers, the moons fell out of their single orbit and reconstituted the daunting thresh of their original configuration.

Something had been open to them; now—for the time being, anyway—it was closed again.

At a safe distance, *Mposi* made rendezvous with the larger *Travertine*. The lander docked; all was chaos for at least thirty minutes as medical personnel and equipment moved between the two ships. Goma kept well clear of the lock, remaining aboard *Mposi* with Ru until the worst of the rush was over. Eventually they were under way again, making the return crossing to Orison. By then Ru and Goma were in their room, holding each other until sleep came to mend the edges of their tiredness. Goma kept seeing Eunice, her face to the warming sun—the ice crystals turning to water drops, her eyes wide and receptive, that golden light flowing along her optic nerves like molten metal, coursing through the cold runnels of her brain, lava flowing down an ever-dividing network of channels, bringing her back to life.

"Bury me with the Risen," she had said. "But take my heart back to Earth."

When they woke, late the next morning by the ship's onboard clock, there were two kinds of news. The first was that a Watchkeeper—one that had not tested itself against Poseidon—was following *Travertine*. The alien machine was maintaining its distance for now, neither approaching nor receding, and its intentions could not be guessed at.

Vasin said they would hold their course. If the Watchkeeper had other plans for them, so be it.

Meanwhile, Nissa Mbaye died.

All credit to Dr. Andisa's small surgical staff—they had done everything they could, and at times had even appeared to be on the cusp of bringing Nissa back. Indeed, she seemed to be fighting for life with great vigour. Although she was in a medically induced coma, her neural activity was much more extensive that Andisa would have normally expected, and in areas of the brain that—given her clinical state and the damage she had sustained—ought not to have been active.

"Something's going on in there," she told Goma.

It had given them temporary hope, but all efforts to expand that trace of borderline activity into something more coherent, more sustained, were soon undermined. Nissa was fading. Whatever they had seen was the last flowering, not a return to life.

Captain Vasin gave the order for Nissa to be placed into immediate skipover.

"Our medicine can't save her, but we won't give up on her this easily, Kanu. For better or for worse, a lot will have happened by the time we return home—wherever home might be. There may be a chance for her then."

"It won't help," Kanu said.

"Nor will defeatism. It costs us nothing to bring her back. Don't fight me on this one, Mr. Akinya—you won't get very far."

A few hours later, Goma found Kanu alone. She had not spoken to him since Nissa's death.

"I'm sorry. I hoped we'd brought her up in time."

Kanu's face was impassive, holding back a freight of emotions she could barely guess at. But then, they had both suffered losses on the wheel.

"You did all you could, Goma. If anyone's to blame, it was me. Nissa was only ever meant to help me to get to Europa. Everything after that . . . it was all an accident."

"Don't cut yourself up about it too much. She met the Risen, Kanu. She walked in *Zanzibar*. None of the rest of us got to experience that. When I spoke to Nissa on *Icebreaker*, she didn't sound like someone being tugged along against her will. She appeared to be magnificently in control. I liked her. I admired her. I wanted to spend more time in her company."

"She'd come to an accommodation with it all by then, accepted what had happened."

"Then you need to do the same. Blame anyone but yourself. Blame Swift, blame Eunice, blame the Watchkeepers. Blame me, if it helps. But you're not at fault."

"I can't blame Swift. Ours was a joint enterprise."

"Begun for the best of reasons."

"I'm afraid that's no excuse."

"It's enough for me. I risked my neck to bring you up, Kanu—don't punish me by taking all this on yourself."

"I wouldn't dream of it. Anyway, we've both lost Eunice, although you knew her better than I did. You have my sympathies. How are you feeling?"

"She wasn't my mother, she wasn't Mposi, she wasn't Ru. We only spent a few days together, all told."

"But against those few days, you're aware of the entire span of her life. You may not have known her personally until recently, but you've known about her for your entire existence. We all have."

"Eunice died," Goma said, firmly. "That's what we've always been told. In deep space, on her own. Whatever she was . . . whoever she was . . . it's not so simple as we'd wish. She wasn't Eunice. She didn't even claim to be—she knew exactly what she was, where she had come from. She even told us she'd been a robot! But the robot became flesh, and the flesh carried memories that felt real to her. Who are we to deny that? And now there's a body to bury and a heart to take back to Africa."

"Then for the sake of argument—for the sake of decency—perhaps it would do no harm in the grand scheme of things if you continue to think of her as Eunice. A branch of her, a wing. Mansions have wings—why not people? Mposi and I were brothers, but we had different mothers. These aren't simple times for any of us, Goma. But we muddle through. We make things up and hope those constructs serve us. Occasionally, we don't fail as badly as we might have."

"That's meant as encouragement?"

"It's the best I can manage."

They spoke of the Terror and of the wheel. Goma had not experienced the Terror and could only imagine the depths of insight Kanu had endured as his ship passed through the chasing moon. Equally, Kanu had not been privy to Eunice's ruminations on the deeper meaning of the grooves, or how they constituted an instruction set for altering the base level of reality.

Goma recounted Eunice's ideas as best she could. Kanu listened with interest and the occasional wry smile, Goma hoping that the topic was sufficiently diverting to push his grief to one side, at least while they talked.

"So we're left with a question," she said. "Did they do it, or did they fail?"

"Could we ever know?"

"The universe hasn't suffered a vacuum transition. If it had, we wouldn't be around to debate it."

"On the other hand, it might be about to do so and we wouldn't have so much as an inkling of it. Or it could soldier on for unguessable aeons, always on the verge of collapse but never quite getting there. There's room for a little history, I think."

"The Watchkeepers were denied access to the wheel," Goma said, "but we were allowed to interact with it. On some level, the M-builders must trust us with the knowledge. Does that mean we should try reaching them?"

"You mean dig down into quantum reality?"

"Into the floorboards, Eunice said."

"I imagine that might be the work of a considerable number of millions of years. So there's no immediate rush to make a decision. Not today, at any rate."

She forced out a smile of her own. "Is it hard to live with?"

"The Terror?"

"The knowledge. The futility. The end of everything, the pointlessness of every act. Can you go on now they've put that in your head?"

Kanu, to his credit, did at least give every sign of considering his answer. "Not easily, Goma—I'll be truthful. I've seen it. Felt it, deep in my bones. Not just as some abstract, theoretical result, but as a deep governing truth. I know that everything I see, everything I do, counts for nothing. We could sit here, now, and solve the mysteries of human happiness and all of that would be forgotten, erased, as if it had never happened. Which it may as well not have done."

"That sounds unbearable."

"It is. But then again, the eternal verities haven't gone away. I watched my wife die. I saw her brain patterns fade to nothing, and although I know that our lives were meaningless, that neither of us has contributed anything to posterity, I still wept. I wish she were here with me now. I wish I had her in my arms, so I could ask her forgiveness. I would like to be back with her in Lisbon, feeling the sun on our faces, deciding where to eat. And I am hungry, and I have a bruise on my thigh and will be very glad when it heals because it is uncomfortable. So in that sense, I am still a human being, living in the moment, buffeted by wants and needs. Is that enough to build a life around, to carry on living?"

"Eunice knew the Terror. She found a way."

"She was hardly typical."

"No, but I don't think you are, either. We need you, Kanu. You've come through something truly momentous. You need to stick around for the rest of us—we need your wisdom."

"My wisdom?"

"Your experience. Whatever you want to call it."

He acknowledged her point but looked discomforted by it. She wondered what he was thinking.

"What about you?" he said. "You mentioned Africa, but unless I'm mistaken, you've never been to Earth."

"Always a first time for everything, including that. Anyway, they have elephants there. I like elephants."

"So do I," Kanu said. "But to be honest, it took me a while to warm to them."

CHAPTER 55

By the time *Travertine* fell back into orbit around Orison, the lander had been restocked and made ready for the descent to Eunice's old encampment. Goma and Ru travelled with Hector, squeezed into the pressurised bay alongside the hammock-suspended Risen, while Vasin handled the descent—a much easier proposition than landing on the wheel, and one which she handled with a certain casualness. Accompanying them were Kanu, Dr. Andisa, Peter Grave and Karayan, and the body of Eunice Akinya.

She had been autopsied in orbit. Nothing in Andisa's examination contradicted Nhamedjo's original findings, although she made a few discoveries of her own—quirks of anatomy and genetics that betrayed the handiwork of her alien makers, any one of which would have provided sufficient scholarly interest for an entire academic career. Andisa debated with Goma and Vasin about the best way to deal with the body—whether they were being negligent by taking it down to Orison to be buried with the other Risen and were in fact obliged to put it into skipover and return it to human civilisation.

"You have your scans, your autopsy," Goma said without rancor, for she fully understood Andisa's concerns—she was a scientist, too, not so different from Goma. "Some DNA and tissue samples, some blood. I'm afraid they're the best you're going to get. This is the way it has to be, Mona."

"She expressed a clear wish to be buried with the Risen?"

"According to Kanu," Goma said.

"Then we must honour that wish."

Before they landed, they had already made contact with the human skeleton staff left behind after the last visit. Goma, Ru and Vasin suited up and walked from the lander to the camp's entrance, passing the stone burial mounds on their way. The remaining Tantors—Atria, Mimosa, Keid and Eldasich—had been forewarned about Eunice's death. Goma nonetheless felt that she had a duty to share the message again in person. In their underground rooms, she and Ru sat and talked for long hours, recounting their memories of Eunice. Death was never mentioned, out of respect for the customs of their hosts. Goma and Ru spoke only of Eunice passing into the Remembering, and they stressed that hers had been a good and brave passing.

It was hard to read the Risen, even now. They appeared satisfied with this account of things. But Goma could not guess at the errors she had made, the myriad small hurts she must have inflicted. All her old knowledge of elephants and Tantors felt obsolete in the presence of these bold new creatures with heads full of language and time.

"There is another," she said, judging that the moment was right. "Hector is his name. He was with Dakota. I know that makes him your enemy after everything that happened between you and *Zanzibar*. But Hector's on his own now."

"Is he here?" Atria asked.

Goma nodded. "In the lander. I wanted to see how you felt before we arranged for him to come here."

"You may bring him," Keid decided. "We will wait."

It took three hours to arrange this first meeting between the two factions of the Risen, after their long sundering. It was an uneven congress, Goma had to admit—four of them, one of him. At first all were trepidatious, as nervous and hesitant in their way as any wild elephants would be on encountering unfamiliar herd members.

But the awkwardness passed. Trunks were intertwined. The Risen began to speak to Hector. Hector replied.

It was clear to Goma that they had much to talk about. She wondered what she was witnessing in those first moments of cordiality. She hoped it was the beginning of something—a keystone on which the Risen could start the difficult work of becoming a viable line again. She could not count on finding the Tantors of *Zanzibar* any time soon, if they were recontacted within her lifetime. But they would make the best of what they had, with the best that their genetic science and wisdom could do for these five individuals. Doubtless there would be many setbacks—it would be ominous if there were none. But they had come so far, all of them. They were due some luck.

She allowed herself an optimistic thought: *Let the Risen make the best of what they are, and let us all find the best in each other. Humans and Risen—people both.*

She did not think there could be any harm in that.

Meanwhile, there was work to do. Under the best set of assumptions, it would be weeks before *Travertine* was in any kind of position to commence its return journey to Crucible. Vasin had confided that months would be a more realistic estimate, and that it might be wise to assume they could be here for a year, even two. They still had to source fuel for the initialising tanks, and that would mean a much more thorough exploration of the system's outer worlds than they had yet undertaken. Besides, having come this far, it was senseless to rush home. There was still the other Mandala to be explored in detail, and there was even some rash talk of possibly attempting to initiate another Mandala event. If the mirrors could be made to work again—they were still in orbit—then there was no compelling reason why Eunice's work could not be replicated. *Travertine* could put a small probe in orbit, an instrument package with a long-range antenna. After the event, they would have some idea of the direction in the sky from which to await a response.

Rasher still, Goma even heard talk of possibly doing the same thing with the lander, with people aboard—volunteers, of course. Since they could not count on finding mirrors at the other end, it would of necessity be a one-way trip into the interstellar unknown. But if the circumstances of Eunice's event could be exactly duplicated, the lander might be sent to the same location as *Zanzibar*. They had promised they would come looking, after all.

Strange to think that wherever *Zanzibar* had gone, it was still on its way from her perspective. That would be true for years, decades, centuries to come. But in the timeframe of Memphis and the other Risen, no more than an instant would separate their experience of being in this system from suddenly being somewhere else.

In that sense, they were already there.

Goma marvelled at that thought. She wondered what the old, slow Tantor was seeing now, through the dark scrutiny of his wise and patient elephant eyes. Something truly worthy of his interest, she hoped. It would be good to find out, one day. She vowed that she would never look at the stars and not think about Memphis, not until there was news of *Zanzibar*.

"If there was a faster way to get you to Earth, I would jump on it," Vasin said, "but we have to go via Crucible, I'm afraid. Even if we had enough confidence to trust *Travertine* to that alien contraption, we still couldn't send you to Earth. Mandala to Mandala—that's the only way we know. We get the stepping stones, but not the choice of where they're located."

"For now."

"Granted—and maybe we'll learn more, if and when we get anywhere at all. But that's for the future. When you get to Crucible, I'll petition the government to allow us to make a rapid crossing to Earth space."

"If there's still a government," Goma said.

"There's that, yes. But let's hope we left the place in safe hands. You won't be sorry to see it again?"

"No, not at all. I never really wanted to leave."

"But you felt you had to."

"Because my mother was too old and I hoped we might do some good. Make some discoveries."

"You found the Risen," Vasin said. "That has to count for something."

"And now we've lost most of them again."

"Then we should be especially grateful for the five left to us. I was about to say 'in our care,' but that doesn't quite sound right. They really don't need that much from us, do they? They're our equals."

"At least."

"It would be good to bring one of them with us, back to Crucible—even onwards to Earth. An ambassador."

"Yes," Goma said. "We spoke about that. But it has to be their decision. We can't force it on them."

"No," Vasin agreed. "There's been quite enough of that."

* * *

It was not that any of them had stopped thinking about the Watchkeeper, least of all Kanu. It followed them from Poseidon, and when *Travertine* entered orbit, it too took up station around Orison. It was not orbiting in any conventional sense, but turning at an equal angular speed with the starship, only a much greater distance from the surface, the ship and the Watchkeeper like two dots on an invisible clock hand. It bothered them, hanging up there, its pine-cone shape aimed down at them like a blunt dagger. But then, people had been troubled by the presence of the Watchkeepers for a very long time, in all the systems where humans had left their mark. There was only so much mental energy available for worrying about them. Mortals could not dwell on the affairs of gods for the whole of the day.

But in the morning, the Watchkeeper left its station.

It descended down past *Travertine*'s orbit, paying the ship no heed, and then lowered itself to within a scant kilometre of Orison's surface. It hung there, an object the size of a small continent massing the equivalent of ten thousand *Zanzibar*s, yet stirring not a grain of dust below. In the airlessness of Orison, the Watchkeeper was as silent and wrong as a single thundercloud in an otherwise clear sky.

Its black facets were partially open, allowing fans and blades of blue light to push out from its core. The Watchkeeper was hundreds of kilometres wide near its blunt tail, the part currently pointing back into space, but its sharp end, almost touching Orison, diminished down through layers of concentric rotating machinery to a scale that was almost within the bounds of human conception. That last kilometre of it was a kind of elephant's trunk, a thing that corkscrewed and probed.

The trunk lingered above Eunice's camp. It touched nothing, but showed fleeting interest in the lander, the antennas, the glassed-over chambers where she grew her food, the curious stone kilns of the Risen burial mounds.

The humans and Risen could only watch. The impulse was to go deeper into the warrens of the encampment. But how deep was deep enough when a Watchkeeper was involved? Besides, they needed to know their fate. It was impossible to pull away from the windows, impossible to think about anything other than that looming alien presence. What did it want with them? What did it want, specifically here and specifically now?

An alarm sounded.

An airlock was activating. The momentary fear was that something was trying to get in, but a second's reflection showed how absurd that was. The Watchkeeper could have peeled back Orison's crust like a scab if it cared to do so.

No. That alarm was someone going out, not coming in.

"Where's Kanu?" Goma asked.

No one had seen him for some while.

He was nearly under the proboscis when she found the right channel on her suit.

"Kanu! It's Goma. What are you doing?"

He walked on for a few paces more, as if he had not heard her. Then he slowed, cast a glance back over his shoulder—light catching the edge of his visor, a hint of his too-familiar profile behind the glass.

"Doing what an ambassador ought to do, Goma—establishing diplomatic relations. It wants something. One of us, maybe. Well, I think I'm the obvious candidate."

"I lost Mposi. I lost Eunice. I won't lose you."

"We've all lost more than our share, Goma. But I came to this system to learn something about them. In a way, I'm glad the choice has been so easily made for me. I don't think I'd have had the courage to go out into space and meet one. But this? It simplifies things a great deal, wouldn't you agree?"

"Is it you talking, Kanu, or Swift?"

He sounded amused, curious, in equal measure. "Does it matter?"

"I'd like to know. I'd like to know if it's a man making this decision or a machine making it for him."

"Oh, it's very much the man. Swift is here, and we both know what must be done, but the choice is mine. The life is mine."

"You're only doing this because you've given up on Nissa. But the rest of us haven't!"

"Nissa died, Goma. Taking her back home won't change that. Besides, where is home for me now? I can't go back to Mars and Earth considers me a traitor to my own species."

"For all you know, no one even remembers what you did by now."

"No one remembers anything, in the end."

The proboscis had begun to concentrate its darting, twisting movements in the space immediately above Kanu. Only a few hundred metres separated them now. Kanu had even stopped walking, sensing the inevitable. He let his arms dangle at his sides, assuming a position of patient submission.

It was on him like a striking snake. There was no whip-crack, no shock wave, but the suddenness of the movement still left Goma stunned, almost falling back with the surprise of it. Nothing made of solid matter ought to move like that. Kanu was gone. The proboscis was withdrawing, telescoping back into that larger looming mass. At the same time, the Watchkeeper's entire body was rising back into space. Numbed by what she had seen, it was all Goma could do to keep breathing. She felt that to move, to utter a word, to allow herself one unwise thought, would be enough to provoke the Watchkeeper to take her as well.

She risked moving her head and looked up, tracking the Watchkeeper's ascent. It was growing smaller. She wondered exactly what she had just witnessed, and whether witnessing it would be a blessing or a curse on the rest of her life.

Hours passed, and the Watchkeeper did not return. They tracked its departure, first via the ramshackle instruments and sensors of Eunice's camp, and then with the keener eyes and ears of their orbiting ship. The Watchkeeper was speeding back out to the margins of the system where others of its kind, those that had not been damaged or destroyed by Poseidon, were presumably still waiting.

Goma could not help but feel that they were all in a state of judicial abeyance, waiting the deliverance of some terrible, irreversible verdict. It was hard to sleep, hard to think of anything else. She wondered what had become of Kanu, whether in any sense "Kanu" was still a living entity. It would have been good to speak with Ndege, and find out what she in turn had learned from her mother, during Chiku's own time inside the Watchkeeper.

She did not have Ndege; she did not have Mposi or Kanu. She could not even speak to Nissa, the only other human being who had endured the Terror and knew something of its qualities.

"If it intended to harm us," Grave said, "I think we would already know it. It had every chance to attack when it took Kanu. It must have sensed us nearby—in the camp, aboard the ship—but it chose not to use destructive force."

"And if Kanu hadn't gone out there?" Ru asked.

Grave looked down. "I don't know."

The three of them were seated around one of Eunice's tables. Since the burial ceremony, Goma and Ru had been spending a lot of time with the surviving Tantors in the lower levels of the camp. But it was necessary also to allow Orison's Risen to get to know the sole survivor of *Zanzibar*'s Risen expedition, and human beings were an undesirable complication during that process.

"Not like you, not to be sure of something," Ru said. "I thought it was all about certainty where Second Chancers are concerned?"

There was only gentle needling in her question and Grave took no visible offence. "If only, Ru. Funnily enough, nothing in Second Chancer philosophy prepared me for this situation— being on Orison, waiting to hear what an implacable alien machine makes of our human envoy—who just happens to be carrying the hopes of the Martian machines with him."

"We're all in the same boat, then," Goma said.

"Do you think he'd have done what he did if Nissa were still alive?"

Ru looked sharply at him. "You think it was suicide?"

"I don't know him well enough to say for sure, but it looked like the act of a man who had run out of hope."

"You can't blame him," Goma said. "First the Terror, then the loss of his wife? None of us is in a position to judge Kanu for that."

"Believe me, judgement is the last thing on my mind," Grave said. "I just wish he'd had more time to come to terms with his experiences. I think he would have had the strength to make peace with them, had they not all happened at once."

"Easy for you to say, not having been through the Terror," Goma said.

"None of us went through it," Grave answered. "But at the end of it all, we'd each and every one of us have been free to reject its message."

Ru made a sceptical face. "You mean deny it?"

"If denial is the mental strategy that allows life to be faced, so be it. Death is negation. Denial is better than that, under any circumstances. Besides—we have no objective evidence that the Terror is anything other than a psychological weapon, a set of apparent propositions that only feel persuasive because they're being drilled into our minds at a very deep level, like some kind of insidious propaganda."

"We don't need the Terror to tell us the message," Goma said. "We've got the wheels for that—the Mandala grammar lays out the same truth. The vacuum will collapse. There is no arguing with that."

"*May* collapse," Grave stated. "But their physics might be wrong. Have you considered that possibility?"

Goma shook her head. "They had millions of years to find a flaw in it. If there was one, they'd have found it."

"That's almost a position of faith, though, isn't it? By accepting unquestioningly that there was no error in the M-builders' logic, you're placing them on the level of gods. But they were not infallible—we've seen the evidence of that for ourselves."

"Have we?" Goma asked.

"Poseidon is ruthless, but it is also indiscriminate. And these Mandalas—a dangerous, powerful technology allowed to fall fallow? If they were gods, they were reckless, careless ones. Slipshod deities. They left us some lethal ruins—ask the citizens of *Zanzibar*. Ask your mother."

"My mother is dead."

"I am sorry, but the point stands. I don't see infallibility in the M-builders' work, Goma. I see arrogance. A blindness to their own flaws. Knowing that, how can we have the slightest confidence in their prophecies?"

"They're not prophecies—they're predictions!"

Grave nodded solemnly, as if some great and subtle truth had been laid out before him. "Nonetheless, this might just as easily be a delusion they talked themselves into—a kind of species-level psychosis. Why should we be bound by that?"

"If you understood the physics—" Goma began.

"Do you? It isn't your native discipline any more than it's mine. Everything you believe you know was filtered through Eunice's understanding."

"That was enough for me to get it."

"But Eunice didn't take it into her heart, did she? If she had—if she'd truly accepted the M-builders' gospel—that all acts are futile, that there's no point in any deed, any gesture—then she wouldn't have given up her own life to save Ru's. That was an act born of kindness and empathy, not despair."

"We can't know what was in her head," Goma said.

"But we can do her the honour of recognising that her sacrifice had meaning—that it was more than an empty gesture. With that one kind act, she repudiated every word the M-builders ever wrote. Their truth was theirs to live with—we don't have to."

"That's starting to sound like another article of faith," Ru said.

"So be it. Both of you came here seeking knowledge—it's been the arrow of your lives to know the world. Physics is one path—you chose to study the minds of other creatures. But that quest for meaning—for what you think of as truth—has only brought you to this. Doubt. Despair. A crisis of belief in anything."

"The truth hurts," Goma said. "But it's still the truth."

"You need to find a way through it, in that case. Truth isn't the end, Goma. It's just a door. There's always another door beyond it, too. Endlessly and for ever. The M-builders may not have realised that, but you don't have to fall into the same trap. Both of you have work to do—here and on Crucible." He gave an easy-going shrug. "On Earth, too, for all I know. The hard times aren't over yet. They may not even have begun. But we'll need good, strong people to face them. You ask me about faith. I have faith in *us*—in our capabilities, our ultimate capacity to make the right choices. People and Risen. People and machines. All of us. But the worst thing of all would be to start doubting ourselves."

* * *

Kanu came back to them three days later. The Watchkeeper returned to its former position, circling Orison in a higher orbit than *Travertine*'s. For several hours there was no clear change in its disposition, nothing to show—presuming Kanu still existed in any meaningful sense—that it held a human being within itself. Goma debated consulting the records aboard the ship, to refresh her memory as to what happened under similar circumstances when Chiku Green was taken into one of those machines. But the circumstances were only similar up to a point—Kanu was not Chiku, and this world was not Crucible.

It came in just as quickly as the first time, and the focus of its interest was the same patch of ground where Kanu had waited. The proboscis made a darting strike at the surface, and when it retreated, leaving only a curl of dust, there was a spacesuited human form, on his knees, hands at his sides.

Goma had put her own suit on as soon as the Watchkeeper began to close in. She was in the lock and waiting.

She rushed to him, found their common channel. The lights on his suit were all in the green, and she could see the fogging and unfogging of his breath on the inner surface of his faceplate.

"Kanu, talk to me."

He stirred. He turned his face towards hers. He opened his eyes, blinked, appeared at first to struggle with focus. "Goma."

"Yes, I'm here. Are you all right?"

"Yes." But then he paused. A moment of quiet consideration followed, as if her questions merited the most sincere answers he could give. "I think so, anyway."

"Kanu, you were inside the Watchkeeper. For three whole days. Do you remember any of it?"

"Three days?"

"Yes."

"It didn't feel like three days. Three years, maybe. Three decades. Something strange happened to me, Goma. I'm not quite sure what." Then he reached out a hand and she helped him stand, unsteadily at first but appearing to find his strength by the second. "Something strange," he repeated. "We were inside them. We were trying to make them understand."

"Understand what?"

"What they used to be. What they ceased to be. What they could be again."

"I don't follow."

"The Gupta-Wing threshold. Ask Chiku. Swift told them. Swift made them see—he understood it better than I ever did."

His words meant nothing to her, except for the mention of Chiku. "Kanu, is Swift still in your head?"

"No. Swift's with them now. They took him, but left me behind." With a certain resignation, he added, "They're done with me now."

"Swift's in that Watchkeeper?"

"In all of them. He's propagating between them, like an idea they can't help but spread. They were blind to the Gupta-Wing theorem, and once they'd crossed the threshold, they had no reason to doubt themselves. But Swift is giving them reason to question what they are."

It sounded like babble, but she thought it unlikely that Kanu Akinya would be spouting nonsense for the sake of it.

She took his elbow and helped him back to the camp. "Simplify it for me. I work with elephants, not machines. Is this a good thing or a bad thing?"

"We'll have to see. That's all. Like everything else. Has it really been only three days, Goma?"

"Would I lie to you, uncle?"

He stumbled on a pebble; she caught him before any harm was done. "Watch your step, ambassador."

"Oh, I'm not the ambassador now. I'll leave that to my friend."

"Then what are you?"

"A man still hoping to find some useful purpose in life. If it lets him. If he hasn't worn out his welcome."

"You have one useful thing to do."

The directness of her statement drew a laugh. "Do I?"

"Yes. You're coming back to Crucible with me. With Nissa. If they can help her on Crucible, so be it. Otherwise we'll carry on to Earth. You know that planet, and I'm going to need a guide when I get there."

"Someone to keep you out of trouble? I may not be best qualified for that. Anyway, Earth will be very strange even to me when we get back."

"Have you been to Africa, Kanu?"

"Once or twice."

"Will it still be there?"

"Barring the frankly improbable . . . yes, I suppose. It ought to be."

"Then you can take me to Kilimanjaro. I have Eunice's heart."

"Only her heart?"

"The rest of her stays here, with the Risen." Goma risked a glance back over her shoulder, into the emptying sky. "Do you think the Watchkeeper will be coming back?"

"Not for a little while. They have some thinking to do."

"Then we'll need to move ahead with the funeral arrangements. Kanu, are you going to be all right? You've lost Nissa, now Swift. And then whatever happened to you in there—"

"I'll cope, Goma. When you've already died once, coping becomes second nature."

"I think you might have died a second time."

"Three times, if you include the Terror. I'll try not to make a habit of it."

"Please don't," Goma said.

It fell to Goma to lead the human party. It was a smaller cairn this time, for the body was that of a human woman, not one of the Risen.

The Risen had done the hard work of shaping the cairn with large stones of various shapes. They took great deliberation in the selection of these pieces, and when they were set into the cairn they appeared to interlock with uncanny neatness, as if they were the shattered pieces of some once-unified whole.

For the humans, it remained only to select their own smaller stones and fill in the gaps. They took pains not to upset the work that had already been done.

"For Eunice," Goma said, placing one fist-shaped stone onto the cairn. "May these stones bind the thread of her memories with those who have already passed into the Remembering. May they bind her to the promise of the black skies she craved, and to the memory of the blue Earth she never stopped loving. Her name was Eunice Akinya, and her blood is my blood. They called her Senge Dongma, the lion-faced one. And I will bring this lion's heart back to the place she knew as a child."

The stone was set. Goma turned from the cairn.

Overhead, one by one, the Watchkeepers were dimming their blue lights to the lowest possible state of radiance. It was an accident of timing, nothing more. They were concentrating their mental resources on the vexing question of this odd and troubling mathematical theorem. At times like these, when a difficult matter required pondering, they had learned that it was wiser to assign separate streams of mentation to each Watchkeeper, each tackling the problem as a whole, rather than dividing it into fragments that could be processed among their dispersed elements, but with no one Watchkeeper grasping the entirety of the problem. That way, when answers tallied, they could view the results as significant. The Watchkeepers had indulged in this kind of deep meditation before, and they were quite prepared to take their time over it. These busy, buzzing humans had been a local distraction, and they were entertaining enough in their way. But it would be better when they moved on, and some silence had returned to this corner of creation.

The shutters of their scales closed. The blue lights dimmed to the darkest shade of blue that is not black.

The Watchkeepers settled down to dwell on what they were.

Kanu Akinya, turning from the cairn after setting his own stone in place, thought he glimpsed an old friend out of the corner of his eye. In a single fluid movement the figure raised a hand, touched a finger to his pince-nez, smiled a fond farewell.

And then was gone for ever.

CHAPTER 56

Goma and Ru had been awake for hours before they allowed themselves their first view of Crucible. It was less a case of apprehension than delayed gratification, refusing a reward until the proper moment, when they were both mentally prepared for it. Not that they had any real fears of failure, or concerns that their world would disdain them. Captain Vasin had assured them that *Travertine* had completed its return crossing successfully, and that they were now back in orbit, circling the planet at almost the same altitude from which they had begun their journey. Long before the ship completed its last course change it had been hailed, made welcome by a jostling flotilla of escort vehicles. The tone of the exchanges had been cordial, verging on the jubilant. There was no doubt of a warm reception.

But anything could have happened, Goma told herself. They had been away for two hundred and eighty-four years, enough time for governments to fall and rise, for revolutions and counter-revolutions, for personal reputations to crash or soar. Their expedition had been an expensive endeavour at a time when Crucible was still climbing out of the hardships that had come with the fall of the Mechanism. Perhaps, with time, it had come to be viewed as a folly, or even worse: a negligent, criminal waste of resources and minds.

Perhaps that had been the view, at some point in these last three centuries. But if the wheel of opinion could turn once, it could turn again. Whatever might have happened, they were favoured now. Conceivably, Goma thought, the events surrounding their departure were simply too remote for anyone to get all that bothered about. The wonder was that they had returned. All else was forgivable.

"Are you ready?" she asked Ru.

"As I'll ever be."

They floated together at a window in a weightless section of the ship. The window was facing Crucible, but for the moment it was shuttered.

"I keep thinking of Mposi. I don't think he ever expected to come home again. He'd have counted himself lucky enough just to make it all the way to Gliese 163."

"We're here for him," Ru offered, although there was not much that could push Goma's sadness aside. Sadness mingled with relief, gratitude, expectation. But also the heavy burden of the work that lay ahead of them. They had barely begun.

"Let's do it." Goma touched the control, and the window's external shutters snapped open in silence.

For a few seconds they stared at their world in wordless contemplation. They were orbiting over the day side, the clouds giving way here and there to offer hints of recognisable landforms and seas. Goma compared what she saw against her memories of maps she had known since childhood. On this scale at least, it was hard to say that much had changed.

"It's still there," Ru said, with a sort of wonder, as if the very act of their world maintaining itself across these years was astonishing. "All that time we were on our way, all that time we were sleeping . . . it was still here, still going about its business, doing what worlds do—as if you and I never mattered to it."

"We didn't," Goma said. She paused, added: "Anyway, it's really not been that long. Trees that were middle-aged when we left, they'll still be middle-aged—just a bit older. Us being away—it's just a blip, a heartbeat, to a planet."

But now Ru jabbed her finger at something nearer than their planet. It was an object, moving through space between them and Crucible. "A ship. Maybe one of those escorts Gandhari told us about."

The vehicle, whatever it was, sidled closer to *Travertine*. Its form was a blunt-ended cylinder, wrapped with lights. It was hard to tell how far away it was, how big. It moved a little too confidently for Goma's liking, coming in at too hard a vector. She tensed, unable to fight the instinct to brace against an impact, for all the good it would have done. But the cylinder cruised near and then veered sharply off, and at the moment of closest approach she thought she saw faces, pressed against the windows, gawking at this odd, antique apparition.

The cylinder swooped away, until it was only a tiny moving speck against the face of Crucible.

"I suppose we're of some amusement to them," said a voice beside them, speaking softly enough not to shatter the mood. "Visitors from the deep past. Gandhari says we're not the only starship they've ever seen—there's a flow of ships coming and going all the time—but you can bet it's been a while since they've clapped sight on a relic like us."

"I don't feel like a relic," Ru said.

"Nor do I," Peter Grave said, Crucible's blue-green light picking at the crinkling around his eyes. "But I strongly suspect it may have to be a role we have to get used to. Obliging ghosts at the banquet." He forced a smile. "Never mind. There must be worse things—and at least we'll never be short of attention."

Grave had come to the window while Goma and Ru were caught up in the spectacle. His presence was uninvited, but Goma struggled to find much resentment. Whatever differences they had once had, she felt certain that she and Grave now had infinitely more in common with each other than they did with the new citizens of Crucible. Ru, Goma and Grave were creatures out of time, unmoored from their rightful place in history. This was what interstellar travel did to people, and as yet no one had much experience coping with it.

"Kanu is awake now," Grave said. "I've spoken to him, and he seems to have handled the crossing as well as any of us. I just wish there were better news about Nissa—some good development we could bring to his attention immediately."

Goma understood that there had already been communication between Vasin, Mona Andisa and the governing authorities of the system. At least part of that exchange had concerned the fate of Nissa, preserved in skipover since her death at Poseidon.

"Maybe they have something," Ru said. "Better medicine than us, at any rate. How could they not have better medicine, after all this time?"

"We don't really know how far they've come," Goma said,

her tone cautious, refusing to indulge in wishful thinking. Historical progress was not linear. She reminded herself that the medicine of the Age of Babel had been superior to the medicine after the fall of the Mechanism. It was anyone's guess as to the leaps and reversals that had happened since their departure. At some point she would have to sit down and catch up on all that skipped history.

For now she had no appetite for it.

"If not here, then Earth," Grave said.

"Assuming Earth isn't even further behind," Goma said. "And even if we find out what the situation's like *now*, Crucible's best knowledge of Earth is still thirty years old. Just going on to Earth will still be a gamble, a leap into the dark."

"Would you consider it?" he asked.

"I promised I'd take her heart back home." Goma swallowed and nodded. "Yes. I mean to do that."

But it was so much harder now that she was home. The vow had been easy when even Crucible lay at an unimaginable distance, and she had barely dared count on seeing it again. Yet to be here now, looking down on her old home, knowing its airs and waters were almost close enough to touch—and soon would be—made her wonder if she really had the resolve to deliver on that pledge.

But a vow was a vow.

"You have my admiration," Grave said. "Both of you, because I do not believe for a moment that Goma will make this crossing alone."

It had been meant as a kindness, but having his admiration only left her feeling more beleaguered, as if the task ahead of her had become even more daunting. She held her nerve, though. And Ru closed her hand around Goma's.

"Of course," Ru said, as if nothing could have been less contentious. "I'm her wife. We do this together."

A little later, Goma went to see how their five most vulnerable passengers had coped with the crossing.

The surviving Risen had returned to Crucible along with the human members of the expedition. For the first ten years of the voyage, Hector and the others had remained awake aboard *Travertine*, accompanied by a small and dwindling support team, working with the Tantors to overcome the biological impediments to putting them into skipover. Goma and Ru had remained awake for a good portion of that time as well, and even after entering skipover Goma had come out again when the Tantors were ready for their own immersion. By then, all but a handful of doubts had been settled . . . but there would be no guarantee of success until the Tantors were revived. There had even been talk of keeping the Tantors awake for the entire crossing, down through generations of offspring. Nothing was without risk, though, and in the end Mona Andisa had declared herself confident that the Tantors had at least a better than average chance of surviving skipover.

So it was agreed, and the Risen had been drugged and dripfed and intubated, and finally placed in immersion vessels converted from expended fuel tanks, each now a giant, makeshift skipover casket. Periodically—once every decade or so—a waking technician would peer through dark windows into the murky interior of the caskets, make readouts, slide a stethoscope across the curving alloy, perform some tiny, precise adjustment of the life-support systems.

All of this seemed risky and perhaps unnecessary, given that some or all of the Risen could have remained back in the Gliese 163 system. But if the Risen were left to themselves, they would have to fend alone for another three centuries. Without *Zanzibar*, without thousands of their fellow beings, without the stewardship of Eunice, that would have been another risk again. Transporting them to Crucible was the least bad option.

Or so Goma tried to convince herself. She had been a strong advocate of exactly this outcome. But then again, she had been thinking of her own elephants, and of the genetic bounty now carried by the Risen. Agrippa's death had extinguished the signal of intelligence in the Crucible herds. But a signal could be pulled back out of the noise, with the right encouragement. It was her profound hope that the Risen would provide the means of amplifying that trace, no matter how uselessly faint it had now become.

A forlorn hope?

Perhaps. But she had entertained wilder fantasies, and some of them had become real.

"Goma," said Mona Andisa—her face carrying the lines and shadows of the years she had spent awake, ministering to the Tantors. "You've arrived just in time. Hector is rousing." And she nodded at a display, the cross section of a mighty skull, fortified with bone the way a castle armoured itself with walls and ramparts. "The signs are good," she added. "I think they all made it."

"We made it," Goma said. "All of us. And we all owe you our thanks, Mona. Have you seen Crucible?"

Andisa flashed a quick smile, as if she had something to apologise for. "Not yet. Too busy with the ambassadors."

"You should. It's still beautiful."

Ambassadors. The word had stuck, when speaking of the Risen. But ambassadors to whom, and representing what, exactly? All the rest of their kind now lay somewhere off in deep space, wherever *Zanzibar* was now. If indeed *Zanzibar* were not still travelling, not still hurtling along the path the Mandala had ordained for it, at a breath below the speed of light, so fast that the Risen aboard would not yet have had the time to formulate a single thought, let alone ponder their fate . . .

Less than a century and half had passed since the second *Zanzibar* translation, thought Goma, with a shivering insight into the scale of things. At best, *Zanzibar* was now one hundred and fifty light-years from Paladin . . . a distance to shrivel the soul, but still nothing, not even a scratch, on galactic terms.

Wherever they're going, they may not even be a tenth of the way there yet . . . or a hundredth part.

Andisa brought her to Hector. He had been taken from the skipover tank and placed on a support hammock. His forelegs were angled over the hammock's front, the boulder-like mass of his head resting on his knees, his trunk brushing the floor. There was gravity in this section of the ship, and although her bones and muscles still ached from the adjustment after skipover, Goma was glad of it. She would soon be walking on Crucible.

So would the ambassadors.

Hector breathed. She touched a hand to the upper part of his trunk, feeling the leathery, bristly roughness of it against her palm. At the contact, Hector opened one weary, sleep-gummed eye. It was the pink of a sunset, like a pale jewel jammed into grey flesh.

"We made it," she said softly. "All of us. There's a world down there. You can walk in the open air, under the sky, without suits or domes. For as far as you like."

Andisa nodded at the neural display. Colours were blooming in tight knots of activity. "He wishes to respond. Those are vocalisation impulses. But I don't want to hook up the voice apparatus until he's up and about."

"Take your time," Goma said, still stroking his trunk. "You need to be strong, Ambassador Hector. All of you. Your work's barely begun."

Nor, for that matter, had hers.

Travertine's orbit gradually brought it within range of a station. It was a golden structure, with a dozen curving docking arms flung out from a bulbous glowing core. Beautiful and strange, it made Goma think of a chandelier, or perhaps an octopus. Along the arms were numerous stud-like docking ports, many of which were occupied by ships of various sizes. Some were like the cylinder they had seen earlier, but there were also spheres and darts and translucent, barb-tailed things shaped like manta rays. The spacecraft glowed gently with different colours—there were no lights or markings as such.

Travertine had obviously been assigned a docking port. They nudged home and a small swarm of mothlike service craft was soon in attendance. Goma and Ru watched the colourful display, mesmerised, until a summons drew them to the main common area. Grave had already gone on to speak with the other members of the Second Chance delegation, and Vasin was calling the entire ship to a meeting.

Kanu was there, the first time Goma had seen him since their revival. She and Ru joined him. They hugged, each thankful that they had come through the crossing.

"I went to see the Tantors," Kanu said. "They're doing well. It's a fine thing you did, helping them with the skipover equipment."

"It wasn't anything compared to the years Mona and her team put in," Ru said.

"You all made sacrifices," Kanu replied.

Goma knew she could either skirt awkwardly around the Nissa question, or get it out in the open. "I understand there's already been some contact between *Travertine* and the medics on Crucible. We've been gone a long while, Kanu. There must be a lot of options open to them."

He nodded, like a man trying to put a brave face on things. "We'll see."

"They'll do the best they can," Ru said. "I'm sure of it."

"I'm certain they will." He was speaking slowly, distantly. "It was the best thing, keeping her in skipover. Even though she missed most of our time in the Tantors' system."

"We'll have to go back, won't we?" Goma said, trying to strike an optimistic note. "Not us, necessarily, but people. Maybe we won't even need a starship to do it. Just crank up Mandala again, the way it worked before."

"Someone's going to have to try," Kanu agreed.

But it would not be him, Goma thought. Or her, or Ru. Captain Vasin, perhaps, if she had not yet had her fill of cosmic exploration. But even Gandhari looked drawn, worn out by what they had gone through.

She was speaking.

"In a little while, so I am assured, we will be met by diplomatic envoys from the present government. They are bound to seem odd to us. Perhaps a little frightening, too. It's been a while. But you can be certain that they are just as apprehensive about meeting us. We must seem very strange to them indeed. But with good intentions in our hearts, good faith in our new hosts, good faith in ourselves, we will find a way through. Some of you will attempt to return to your old lives on Crucible. I do not wish to understate the challenges you will face—although I am quite sure you have a ready appreciation of what lies ahead. But never forget this. We are a crew now, and we will remain a crew. When you leave this ship, you do not leave behind the friendships and alliances we have forged. They remain with us. They will be our bond across all the years and challenges to come. Each and every one of you has my respect and gratitude."

There were more words to come, not just from Vasin, but after a while they began to wash over Goma, her thoughts spinning away on their own trajectories. She was thinking of the ambassadors—how easy it was to gloss over the complicated business of introducing five new sentient beings to a world, until the time was almost upon them. She was thinking of Kanu, for whom this was no kind of homecoming, and for whom any mood of celebration must have rung cruelly false. She was thinking of Nissa, neither dead nor alive, and the hopes that had been placed on the unknown medicine of a world three centuries from their understanding. It was a kind of magical thinking, she saw now, like a child's trust in the intervention of fairies. And she was thinking of Eunice Akinya's heart, which had yet to reach its resting place.

Soon the envoys came. Their manner was quiet, understated, deferential. Even as they moved through the ship, she never saw more than two of them at any one time. They were doing their best to be unobtrusive, not wishing to shock their time-slipped guests. Their faces and skin tones showed a variety of ethnicities, and there were some among them who had the sleek, hairless features she associated with merfolk, but it was hard to be certain. Their clothes were dark, modest of cut, with wide white collars and puffed white cuffs. Some of them wore small skullcaps or berets over short, neatly manicured hairstyles. If they brought technology with them, Goma recognised none of it. Perhaps they were so saturated with it that carrying technology was unnecessary.

She heard them speak, shifting effortlessly from one language to another. They came equipped with Swahili, Zulu, Chinese, Punjabi, a dozen other tongues. Their diction was over-precise, their speech clotted with formalisms, including the odd phrase that was old-fashioned even when Goma was a child, but she could not fault them for that. Yet between themselves she caught them whispering sentences that hovered just beyond comprehension—not quite a foreign language to her—the cadences and rhythms were naggingly familiar—but a dialect so far removed from her experience that it may as well have been.

There were medical tests. One by one, all the crew were brought to the non-weightless clinic. Mona Andisa's team stood aside while the Crucible envoys performed subtle investigations. It was the one and only time Goma saw any kind of tool or instrument in their hands. They had black styluses, tipped with a small bulb, which they swept slowly over the bodies of their subjects. They spoke to Andisa's medics, whispered agreeably between themselves. They seemed unconcerned, going through formalities. Eventually word filtered through that there were no barriers to any of the crew, passengers or ambassadors, descending to Crucible. They were free to disembark into the golden station, from which shuttles were available to take them all the way home.

Goma and Ru only took the minimum of possessions with them—the rest could be freighted down later. They walked through the vaults and atria of the golden station, gawking at cathedral-sized spaces which seemed largely deserted, as if the station had been emptied of human occupation in readiness for *Travertine*'s arrival, or even built especially for them. Perhaps it had. They'd had decades to get ready for it, after all, decades to rehearse every detail of the reception.

The shuttles turned out to be the translucent manta things Goma had seen earlier. Each was large enough to take one or two Tantors and a dozen or more human passengers. Eldasich and Atria went down in one shuttle, Mimosa and Keid in another, and Hector stayed with Goma and Ru. Kanu was there as well, together with the draped form of Nissa's skip-over casket. The envoys fussed around the interior of the shuttle making adjustments to the provisions, moulding and shaping its décor with practised, wizard-like gestures. Finally they were satisfied, the casket secured, the passengers comfortable, and the last leg of the journey home could begin. Two envoys remained aboard the shuttle, but as far as Goma could tell no one was in direct control. The vehicle seemed to know what it was meant to do.

They detached from the station over Crucible's nightside, then arrowed down from orbit, knifing into the upper atmosphere and gradually catching up with dawn. Even as re-entry plasma flickered and curled around the shuttle, its brightness throwing highlights across their faces, the ride remained as smooth as if they were on rails.

"Gandhari spoke well," Kanu said, keeping one hand on

the casket secured next to his seat. "You couldn't have asked for a better captain. But this world won't hold her interest for long. She'll want to move on. I can see it in her eyes."

"I'm not sure it's our world any more," Goma said.

Kanu's look was kind. "You'll fit back in."

"Not for long, I hope. I have an obligation to discharge. It'll mean a trip to Earth, one way or another. I gather they have more starships. Sooner or later there'll be a ship going that way."

"Can you afford the passage?"

She had no answer to that. None of them did. Whatever funds they might have left behind on Crucible were now moot. Perhaps they had snowballed into vast personal fortunes, or perhaps they were worthless. Or worse, had somehow transmogrified into crippling debts. Besides, Goma did not have the least idea how much it would cost to transport herself back to Earth. It would cost twice as much again to take Ru, assuming she was deemed fit enough to tolerate another skipover episode. "I'll find a way," she said, as if the will alone was sufficient.

"But this is where the Risen will remain," Kanu said.

"For now," Ru said. "At least until we've gone beyond five living members. Maybe in a couple of generations we—*they*—will feel comfortable about committing some of their number to Earth. Not just Earth, but to other solar systems." Her tone hardened, gaining conviction. "Wherever there's a human presence, there ought to be Tantors. Risen. It's the only way. But we're twenty, thirty, fifty years from worrying about that. Let's help them build up the herd, get that on a stable footing, before we start reaching for the stars again."

"The work of a lifetime, then. Or at least an ordinary human lifetime," Kanu said.

"It's what we started. What we were trying—failing—to do, before Eunice's message came in."

"I can't think of two better candidates to bear that work," Kanu said.

"It'll be our successors," Goma replied. "Not us. Not until we get back from Earth."

"You have a weight to bear."

"Don't we all?" she answered, with a chill of foreboding.

* * *

They cut down into thicker, warmer, moister air. They over-flew rainforest and swept across inky lagoons and white-hemmed bays and heavy green seas. Once, when the visibility allowed, Goma made out the dark stormfront that was one of Mandala's peripheral walls, still much as she remembered it. Then they were over the outskirts of Guochang, now a vast sprawl of a city, what had once been its satellite towns become mere suburbs. The geometry of roads and parks was confus-ing, almost purposefully so—she kept seeing configurations that were almost familiar, but each would twist out of recogni-tion as the shuttle swept nearer. The city had been made and remade half a dozen times since her departure, and only the oldest, most venerated parts of it remained unaltered.

"You were born here?" Kanu asked, at last rising from his seat, bending to peer through the glassy hull.

"I was," Goma said. "But I don't feel it."

"You will." He smiled. "Give it time."

Presently they came up on a twisted black pyramid that seemed to drill its way out of what had been the old govern-ment district. The pyramid was enormous, with a horizontal slit across its warped faces at about a third of its height. Else-where it was windowless, with an oily, shimmering lustre. The shuttles—not just their own, but the others that had come down from the station—were filing into this slot, like bees returning to the hive.

One of the envoys turned to them, touching a hand to the sweep of her collar before she spoke. "This is the medical complex. The tests we ran on you in the ship were quite com-prehensive, but there is more that we can do here. We wish to make sure you are all as well as you can be."

"Will it take long?" Ru asked.

"No more than a couple of days. It will make things very much easier if you allow little machines to replicate in your bodies. They will help you adjust to your new surroundings."

"Like nanotechnology?" Goma asked.

"Yes," the envoy answered, but there was an equivocation in her answer, as if she recognised that the truth was more complicated. "Yes, something very like that. In your time, there was something called the Mechanism?"

"It had gone by the time we were born," Ru said.

"We made something like the Mechanism again," the envoy stated. "Better, less fallible. If we had to give a name for it, it would be something like the All. The little machines will let the All flow into you." Carefully, she added: "If this is what you wish."

"And if we don't?" Goma asked, trying not to sound too alarmed by the prospect.

"There are enclaves where the All is not as pervasive. You would be welcome to live out your lives there."

Kanu turned from the view, laying his hand back on Nissa's casket. "It sounds as if your medicine has come a long way from ours."

"In some respects," the envoy said, her eyes lowering. "But there is much that we have yet to achieve, or is outside the bounds of our medical-ethical framework. We were fore-warned of Nissa's case, though. Our best . . . experts . . . have been assigned to the problem. Rest assured that we will do what we can for her."

Kanu licked his lips and nodded. They were softening him up, Goma thought—preparing him for the news he did not want. How could they not help Nissa? she thought. And a kind of anger flashed through her, a resentment that these people were not more advanced, more godlike. What had they been doing for the past three centuries—sitting on their hands?

The slot in the pyramid contained a landing bay, spread out under a low ceiling. Dozens of craft were also parked there, and the place was already swarming with medical staff. Unlike the dark-clad envoys, the pyramid's medics wore outfits of a blazing, superluminous white. At best, the only instruments any of them carried were the little bulb-tipped wands. But they were also accompanied by many floating white spheres about the size of footballs, and the spheres cracked open along their midlines to spill out jointed arms and sensors. Goma and her friends were asked to offer their forearms to the spheres, and the machines tickled over them in a quick sampling of blood, tissue, DNA. The examination was painless and left no traces.

"What about the All?" she asked, as the whole party—human and Tantor—was led into the main part of the pyramid.

"It's already within you," the envoy answered. "The idio-syncratic connectome bridges will have begun to form. You may experience some mild hypnagogic imagery. The process can be aborted and reversed at any stage, though, should you decline participation."

"Would you decline?" she asked.

The envoy looked at her with a sudden, fierce frankness. "Decline? No. I would sooner be dead. But you must make the choice for yourself."

They were in the complex for two days. The tests were occasionally perplexing, generally dull, but never painful, and again Goma had the sense that much of it was formality, a series of legal obstacles that had to be surmounted before any of the newcomers were allowed free roam of Crucible. They had rooms in the pyramid, which were comfortable enough but austere in their provisions, almost as if the hosts were wary of overloading their delicate constitutions with too much novelty. There was a window, looking back across Guochang. Where the city thinned out Goma saw a margin of blazing green, a stretch of veldt hemmed by trees, and between those trees she thought she might have seen the distant moving forms of elephants, tiny as pollen grains, and she wanted to be out there more than anything.

Although the newcomers were being kept in a state of soft quarantine from the rest of Crucible, they were free to associate with one another and use lounges and public areas on one level of the complex. There was plenty of time between the tests, and Goma and her companions made use of it as they chose. Ru had her nose deep in the elephant literature, trying to catch up on three hundred years of scholarship. They had all been provided with antique data consoles, roughly comparable to their own technology. Through these consoles, and via extra layers of translation and mediation, it was possible to access public records and news channels.

Goma was restless. The elephants meant everything to her, but she could not simply return to her old role of researcher as if nothing had happened. What was the point, when she had no intention of remaining on Crucible?

Even Ru, she thought, was going through the motions.

She visited Grave, Vasin, the others. Everyone had the same slightly shell-shocked look about them, as if they had just been slapped hard in the face. They had been treated as well as one could hope, but still it was a jolt, to be back on Crucible. They had all known there was no going back to their old world, the one they had lived on before departure, but until now it had been an intellectual understanding, ungrounded in real experience. Now they were living it from moment to moment, seeing it with their own eyes.

Only Kanu seemed uninterested in what had happened on Crucible, what had changed and what had remained.

When she came to his room he had used his console to project an image up on one of the walls.

"Isn't it marvellous?" he said, nodding at the image. It was the face of a planet, all reds and emeralds and little dabs of blue. Not Earth, she was fairly certain.

"Is that Mars?"

Kanu looked pleased that she had recognised the place. "Yes. But not as I knew it. When I left Mars, the only humans anywhere on the planet were the ambassadors, cooped up in our embassy on Olympus Mons. We'd been in a stand-off for years. There were defence satellites in orbit, terrorists agitating for human takeover, endless tension . . . I didn't have high hopes. Swift came with me because between us we thought there had to be a better way; a mode of existence where machines and people might be able to work together, not against each other."

"And now?"

Kanu beamed, as if showing off a newborn child. "Just look at it. Those green swatches, those lakes—those are areas of renewed human settlement! Finally there was a recolonisation treaty. Strict boundaries, strict borders—but it's a start, isn't it? They've even begun to terraform the old place. Domes for now, atmospheric tents, but the air's thickening up, warming, gaining moisture. That's not a job for people alone! Human-Evolvarium cooperation—a joint venture."

Goma wanted to share his enthusiasm, but from where she was standing it looked like a capitulation for the machines.

"What did Swift's friends get out of it?"

"Earth," he said. "Or parts of it. That was the other half of the treaty. Machine enclaves on Earth! In the oceans, on the land masses. And it's working! Brokered largely by the Pans, I have to say. But what a thing to see." Excited, he worked the console's settings, almost fumbling over himself in his eagerness. "Wait, though. Wait until you see this! Wait until you see what the machines have been making on Mars . . ."

The face turned, bringing a new part of the planet into view. It was still daylit, but the shadows were fierce, cutting in from the right, projecting long strokes across the landscape.

Kanu magnified the image. He zoomed in on one area of Mars. Something swelled into focus. A mountain, or perhaps a very large boulder, on an otherwise flat and featureless terrain.

There was a face on it, chiselled into the boulder's upper surface, so that it looked back out to space. It was a minimalist portrait—eyes, nose, mouth, the merest suggestion of a personality. But she recognised it.

Her face. Or rather, Eunice's.

"One strain of them did this," Kanu was saying. "A faction among the machines. Call it a cult, if you will."

"Why have they done it?"

"I'll ask them, when I get a chance."

"I'll save you the trouble," Goma replied. "I'm the one who has to go to Earth. Mars will only be a skip away."

She asked him how things were progressing with Nissa. Kanu's answers were guarded, and she wondered how much he in turn had been told by the medical staff.

"There are some complications. The stuff that they have put inside us—those little machines? I gather there's little they can't do, in terms of microscopic tissue engineering. They could rebuild a damaged brain synapse by synapse."

"Isn't that what she needs?"

"The difficulty is knowing which pattern to reinstate." Kanu's speech was supremely collected, but Goma sensed the force of the emotions he must be holding back. "Even if the medics have the technical means to rebuild her damaged cortex—which is by no means simple—there is still an ethical issue."

"An ethical issue in bringing someone back to life?"

"Their law makes a careful distinction between the restoration of damaged neural structure, and the wholesale substitution of one set of structures for another. If they could satisfy themselves that they were rebuilding a personality, rather than inventing one from scratch, I gather they would consent to the procedure. Or at least consent to an attempt. But the ethicists are slow to make up their minds, and in the meantime . . ."

"Nissa isn't going to get any worse, is she?"

"No," he admitted with a nod. "She is safe. But if these people cannot help her, I must look elsewhere."

"Earth?"

"Perhaps."

She touched a hand to his forearm. "I want the best for both of you, uncle."

He clasped his own hand around hers. "Don't worry about me, Goma Akinya. You have enough to think about."

On the morning of their release from the medical complex, a ground vehicle, a wheel-less block with fluted sides and sharply angled ends, was waiting for them at a loading area in front of the lobby.

Kanu and Ru were with her, and two government officials: a dark-clad administrative envoy, and a white-clad medical representative. Both were women; their names—or at least the names that they were ready to share with their guests—were Malhi and Yefing.

Goma knew where they were going. She had asked if it might be possible, knowing that the longer she delayed matters, the less enthusiasm she would have to face them. Not that she had much enthusiasm now.

"Thank you for coming," she told Kanu, as they settled into their seats.

"My diary's not exactly full," he replied.

"Have the ethicists . . . ?" she began.

"Still deliberating, and there's nothing I can say or do which will make any difference." He added quickly: "Not that it isn't a pleasure to accompany you."

"We understand," Ru said.

They sped through Guochang, winding their way between tall offices, through business and commercial districts, around parks and residential zones. Goma recognised nothing, although she was certain some of the older buildings had been around before her departure. If she squinted, and forgot about trying to recognise specific landmarks, none of it was too odd or unsettling. There were traffic jams, pedestrians, roadworks. People were walking their pets, groups of schoolchildren were being led to school, fast-striding business types were deep in conversation. There were pavement cafés and areas that looked more run-down than others. But that was only if she squinted. With eyes wide and sharp, she was assaulted by the unfamiliar. The signs and banners above the shops and businesses were hard to read, as if there had been a specific lesion to the part of her brain that handled written script. There were colours that seemed wrong or improbable—reddish greens, blueish yellows. And a haze of subliminal texture, a kind of glimmering organised mist, floating between things.

Yefing, the medic, must have seen something in her face.

"The All will be reaching integration now. If you start seeing things, you should not be too alarmed."

"We won't," Kanu said. Then: "Is it like this everywhere else? In the other systems? Do they all have an All?"

"Variations of it," Malhi answered, twisting around to answer. "But each system chooses its own path, its own approach. And of course our knowledge is never complete. We have good ties with Earth. There's always been information exchange, but since the Watchkeepers left us alone, there's been a much increased flow of ships."

"Do those ties extend to legal agreements?" Kanu asked. "Extradition treaties, that sort of thing?"

"No," Malhi said. "Our relationship is much looser than that. Necessarily. How could we ever enforce treaties with a time lag of nearly sixty years?"

"You must barely remember how it was, with those things hanging over us," Goma said.

"They were here when I was a child," Yefing answered. "But it has been seventy years. Times have changed. It's hard to remember how it made us feel."

Swift's effect on the Watchkeepers in the Gliese 163 system had propagated to all the known Watchkeeper groupings in human space, and perhaps beyond. The influence had spread at the speed of light, so the disappearance of the Watchkeepers was old news by the time *Travertine* arrived back in Crucible space.

"No one really knows what happened," Malhi said. "Clearly your intervention around Gliese 163 played a part in it. From a causal standpoint, no other explanation is possible. But until we have your own accounting of events . . ."

"Don't expect answers to every question," Kanu said, in a tone of friendly warning. "We may not have one."

"Not even you, Kanu?" Yefing queried, a notch of doubt pushing into her forehead. "Our understanding was that no one had a closer contact than you."

"It was Swift, not me," Kanu said.

"But you were there," Yefing persisted. "The Watchkeeper took you . . . the Watchkeeper returned you. It was why our medical examination of you had to be unusually thorough."

"I was a bystander, that's all."

Malhi cleared her throat with a cough. "But you do think we are free of them? For ever?"

Kanu smiled at that. "Ever's a long time. I suppose the real test will be when we return to Gliese 163, or when we start making active use of the Mandala network. Perhaps that will draw them back to us. But they won't necessarily return as our foes."

"You are an optimist," Yefing said.

"So I've been told."

"You could play a part in these grand adventures," Malhi said, as if she wished to brighten his mood. "Our rejuvenation methods are the equal of anything from the Age of Babel—superior in some respects. You could be made as strong or young as you desire." And she turned to Ru: "And your AOTS. It's curable. Easily done. There's barely a mention of it in the medical literature these days."

"I don't need it cured," Ru said. "Unless it's to help me through another skipover episode."

Yefing pinched her lips. "We use a different process now. There are fewer complications."

"Then I'll be fine. Goma and I only need to live on Crucible until there's a ship to take us to Earth. Or are you going to tell us we couldn't afford passage?"

"You are . . . celebrities," Malhi answered, with a touch of awkwardness. "There would be few impediments, if you were determined to leave us. But please make no decisions in haste—you've barely arrived."

The vehicle sped on. They had been passing through residential districts for a while now, sprawling suburbs and precincts, thatches of woodlands, recreational lakes, new building developments. Eventually the houses thinned out into continuous parkland. They passed some kind of sports stadium, a pagoda garden, more woods. Then the vehicle turned onto a tree-lined side road and Goma recognised where they were.

Ndege's house.

They had kept the area around it undeveloped, and the dwelling itself appeared serenely untouched by the centuries. The walls of the old secured compound were still present, but there was nothing to stop anyone going through the gate—no checkpoint or guards any more. The vehicle slipped through unchallenged and parked between the compound and the house.

They got out, all five of them. Goma studied the house again, searching for traces of time's hand.

"You hated her," she said quietly, speaking not to Malhi or Yefing as individuals, but in their roles as government operatives. "Why didn't you tear the place down once she was gone?"

"That was a long time ago," Malhi said. "Things changed. You should go inside."

Goma looked at Ru and Kanu, nodding that they should accompany her.

But Kanu raised a hand. "I don't want to intrude."

"You came all this way," Goma said.

"And I'll enter the house shortly. But not until you've had a moment or two to yourself."

He had not spoken for Ru, but after only the slightest hesitation she nodded. "Kanu's right. We'll be right outside, until you need us."

"I need you now."

"No," Ru said. "You only think you do. But you're stronger

than you realise, Goma Akinya. If I didn't know that before
we left Crucible, I know it now. Go on in."

So she walked to the front door, pushed it open and went
on in.

And a thought flashed through her head: *Mposi always used
to bring her greenbread. I should have brought greenbread.*

No one else was in the house, and Malhi and Yefing had
remained outside with Ru and Kanu. Inside it was cool and
shadowed, with no illumination beyond that which the windows provided. They threw oblongs of brightness across the
rooms' pale surfaces, the walls, the bookcases and furniture
and such sparse ornamentation as Ndege had allowed herself.
Goma touched a window sill, testing it for dust. She held her
fingertip up for inspection. It was immaculate, harbouring not
a trace of dirt. Someone had taken pains to keep this place
both pristine and exactly undisturbed, as if it were a hallowed
public shrine.

Goma moved between rooms. She had never been here
without Ndege. Some part of her mind kept trying to impose
her on the scene: a suggestion of human presence at the corner
of Goma's vision, dissolving when she turned her gaze upon
it. Not a haunting, but the power of memory, the forcefulness
of its influence on the present moment.

Nothing was kinder or crueller than memory.

She went to take a book from one of the shelves. But as her
hand neared the shelf, a glowing rectangle lit up on a portion
of the adjoining wall. Text and images appeared in the rectangle. To her surprise, the text was in a familiar form of Swahili, the wording easily comprehensible. The images were of
Ndege, and of things to do with her life. The holoship, her
mother Chiku, the early days of the settlement, the Mandala,
her experiments in direct communication with it . . . the ring
of rubble that was all that was left of *Zanzibar*.

Trial, censure, imprisonment.

It was a familiar story, even though the tone of it was not
quite what Goma would have expected. Not so much damning
and judgemental, as sympathetic: framing her mistakes as
understandable errors, rather than as crimes of hubris. Miscal-
culations, not misdeeds.

This rectangle told only part of the story. As she wandered

the rooms, similar patterns of text and image appeared. Sometimes there were moving images and audio recordings, with her mother's voice whispering softly from the walls of her house.

Goma traced the arc of a life. Ndege had lived for another thirty years after the expedition's departure. It had not been long enough for her to learn the truth about *Zanzibar*, but then Goma had never really thought she would. Ndege had been dead long before the expedition reached Gliese 163, and still more years had passed before any news of their findings made its way back to Crucible. There had been no death-bed pardon for her, no easing of her conscience in those final years.

Still, with time, the government had decided to reassess its view of her. With the Watchkeepers gone, and with the news about the second Mandala—and its activation by Eunice— there was now a concerted push to understand and tame this daunting alien technology. It might take decades, centuries, before the Mandalas could be made to sing at humanity's whim. What was clear, though—and abundantly so, given the content of these biographical fragments—was that Ndege's work provided the foundation for all subsequent experiments. Need dictated that they build on her accomplishments, and what had once been considered a crime must now be viewed in a new, more clement light.

Goma wanted to accept this tacit forgiveness on its own terms. It was good to know her mother was no longer detested, no longer held morally accountable for a terrible accident. But there was a cynicism here that she could not set aside. It suited the government to build on her work, and therefore her reputation had to be rehabilitated.

But still. Forgiveness was better than opprobrium, wasn't it? Perhaps.

She was turning to leave the house when Ndege appeared before her, standing in a shaft of sunlight.

Ndege raised a calming hand.

"You're back, daughter. At least, if you're seeing me now, you must be. Don't fear, I'm no ghost. Long dead. This is a recording. They've allowed me to make it, on the assumption you'll one day be in a position to hear my words."

It was Ndege, but the older version of her mother she had

only seen in the wall's images—Ndege as she had been near the end of those final thirty years. The All must be playing its part, Goma thought—manifesting this image before her, as real as day. Was that the reason they had been so keen to get the All into her so quickly—so she would be able to see Ndege?

"You mustn't fear for me," Ndege said. "They've been kind, these recent years. My brother held the government to its word, even in death. They said they'd ease the terms of my confinement if I volunteered for the expedition, and so they have." She had to pause, gathering her breath before speaking again. Her voice was frail and frayed. "The fact that I never boarded the ship is incidental—the will was there, as you know."

"I do," Goma said.

The image continued without interruption. "I've been holding out for a pardon, but it's clearly not going to happen while I still have a heartbeat. Still, I've confidence in you, daughter. You'll have found something out there, I know. Something that puts me in a better light. Whatever it is, I know you'll find it."

"I did," she whispered, as if to speak aloud might shatter the spell.

"The doctors are kind, but they skirt around the issue of how much time I have left. I daren't think in terms of years now. Months would be good, but weeks might be more realistic." Her smile was gentle, her eyes sparkling with fondness. Some fierce edge was gone from her mother now—dented or worn away in the years since Goma had left. "I want you to know, nonetheless, that these last years haven't been the worst. Of course I miss you, and I still grieve for Mposi. But I have found ways to keep living. My enemies would be pleased to think that my days have been a catalogue of misery and despair, but I have disappointed them. We're resilient, and we like life. Sunsets are good, but sunrises are better—even an alien sunrise, on a world that still doesn't really like us. That's what makes us who we are. Call it an Akinya trait, if you will. I'd say we're just being human." She paused, drawing breath— slow, laboured inhalations. "I've made them promise me one thing. I can't enforce it—I won't be around to—but I think they'll keep their word. It really isn't much to ask, and I wanted you to have something when you got back to us. Whoever's brought you here, they'll know what I mean. Have them show it to you. You've earned the right to have it back. Welcome home, Goma."

The image paled, faded from view. Goma wandered the room again, in case something in her motion or bearing might bring Ndege back. But there was no second apparition. Some intuition told her this was all there was; that what she had heard would not be repeated. Ndege would not have cared to have her words ground down to meaninglessness by endless repetition.

But what had she meant?

Goma stepped out into the silvery glare of Crucible's day. She had to squint against the brightness. The others were still waiting for her, their expressions wary, as if none of them were quite sure what had happened inside.

"Well?" Ru said, to the point as ever.

"She left me a message. She said there's something for me—something she wanted me to have."

"There is," Malhi confirmed. "But we weren't sure what to make of it, or what you'd think. It's round the back of the house. Do you wish to see it?"

Goma swallowed. "Yes. Whatever it is."

Ru took her hand from the right, Kanu from the left. "There was a message?" he asked.

"From Ndege. On the All. You can go inside, if you like. I'd be interested to know if she appears for you."

"She won't," Ru said firmly.

Goma gave a nod. "No, I don't think she will. This was for me. Only me. And I don't think there'll be another message."

"Does there need to be another?" Kanu asked.

"No," she answered, after a moment's consideration. "I think we said all that needed to be said."

Malhi and Yefing had gone on ahead. As Goma rounded the corner to the back of the house, Malhi was standing there with one arm outstretched, pointing to the object that had been hidden from view until then. Goma stared at it for a few seconds, hardly believing what she was being shown. It was both utterly familiar, utterly a part of her, and yet it had been such a long time since she had brought it to mind, such a long time since she had considered its lines, admired its elegant balance of form and function, that it might as well have been the first time she had set eyes on it. It seemed unreal, blazing in the same superluminous white of Yefing's medical uniform.

"Geoffrey's aeroplane," she said, wonderingly. "The Sess-Na."

She slipped her hands free of Ru and Kanu, walked up to the aeroplane's side, touched a hand to that blazing whiteness. She half expected it to burst like a soap bubble. But it was real. It was cold and hard under her palm, undeniably present.

She touched the wing. She walked to the front and stroked the edge of the propeller, like a swordsman testing the keenness of a blade.

"Who's Geoffrey?" Kanu asked, stepping into the wing's shadow, eyeing the ancient machine with more than a little trepidation.

"You should know," she chided teasingly. "He was one of ours. Your . . . what? Uncle? Great-uncle? He was Sunday's brother. You figure it out."

"I knew I'd heard the name." Kanu smiled back at her and continued his doubtful examination of the primitive aircraft. "He owned this?"

"He owned this, and it wasn't even new at the time. It came with us, all the way from Earth. All the way from Africa. It's . . . *old*. Stupidly old. Nine hundred years. Maybe more."

"Can you fly it?"

"I used to, all the time. Against my mother's wishes, most of the time—she thought I'd break my neck."

"And yet," Kanu said, "she made sure you got it."

"If you were going to break your neck, you'd have done it by now," Ru said.

"Can you dismantle it, or box it up?" she asked Malhi.

Malhi frowned back. "You don't like it?"

"It's not about whether I like it or not. I have to go to Earth. It might as well come back with me. That's where it belongs, not here."

"I'd say it belongs here as well as anywhere," Kanu said.

"Doesn't matter. It can still come back with me."

He walked over and placed an arm over her shoulder. "The

machine belongs here. This is where it's spent most of its existence, isn't it?"

"And?" she asked, squinting against the abstract white glare made by the Sess-Na's shape.

"So do you," he said. "Here with the Tantors, the Risen. Here on the world where you were born." He nodded to Ru. "Both of you. This is your world, not Earth. You've work to be getting on with. Crucible needs you."

"Haven't we done enough for Crucible?" Goma asked.

"The more you do, the more you're needed."

"It doesn't matter," she said. "I have to go back. For Eunice's sake."

He lifted his arm from her shoulder, brought himself about to face her, his tone firm but affectionate.

"You made a vow, at least to yourself, that you'd see her heart returned to Africa."

"Yes."

"That vow can stand. But I can be the one who delivers the heart. Where's the problem in that? It's not as if I'm not family. It's not as if I couldn't be trusted to deliver on the commitment." He looked at her sharply. "Is it?"

"Of course not. But—"

"And I'm going there anyway."

"But Nissa—" Ru began.

"She'll come with me. Earth's medicine may or may not be more advanced than what they have here on Crucible. They may or may not have the same ethical constraints concerning the regeneration of damaged neural tissue. But it's not Earth I'm counting on. I'll take Nissa to Mars. They remade me once, when I should have died. Rebuilt my brain cell by cell, stitched Swift into my skull like a pattern woven into a tapestry. If they could do that for me, they can bring Nissa back too."

"You would have no guarantee," Yefing said.

"No, I wouldn't. But if curing her was easy, you'd have already done it. It's beyond what you can do—or beyond what you'll allow yourselves. Isn't it?"

"There are impediments," Yefing answered, in a confessional tone. "But none of us wished to dash your hopes so quickly. There are still avenues to be explored . . ."

"And I appreciate your efforts, your good intentions," Kanu

said. "But there's another consideration. I have to go back to Earth. It's not just about Eunice's heart. I have to answer for myself."

Malhi said: "I do not understand."

"Years ago, when I was leaving Earth's system, I turned my ship's weaponry on another vehicle. I killed a man. At least one. His name was Yevgeny Korsakov. We were friends. Or at least colleagues. I saw no other course of action open to me, but that does not absolve me of responsibility. You say there is no extradition treaty."

"You would go voluntarily," Malhi confirmed. "We have no record of this crime, and Earth has no knowledge that you have returned to us. If you chose to remain here, there is no reason why you could not enjoy decades of freedom."

"But I'd still have to live with myself." Kanu smiled at them all. It was a smile of wise and sad acceptance more than of joy. "It's all right. I'd more or less made my mind up before we left the medical complex. As soon as there's a ship, I'll be on it. Perhaps they'll have forgotten my crime, or decided to forgive me for it. Whatever their view, I'll abide by it. I'm sure they'll grant me the mercy of delivering Nissa to Mars, and Eunice's heart to Africa."

"You're doing this for her," Goma said. "Not because you can't live with yourself. But because she matters more to you than anything."

Kanu had no answer for that.

"A ship is scheduled to leave in a few weeks," Malhi said, finally breaking the silence. "There would be no problem in placing you and Nissa aboard it, if that's what you wish. But there is time to think about your decision."

"Thank you, Malhi. But I don't think I'll change my mind. This is what must be done. Besides, it's no hardship. Earth is my home. Whatever lies in store for me there, it's where I belong." And he turned his face to Goma, letting her know that she need have no regrets, no second thoughts, no doubts, no misgivings, that all was well between them. "Where Eunice belongs. I'll see that she returns home. It's the least I can do."

"Kanu . . ." Goma said, her eyes welling up. "Uncle."

He drew her closer, hugged her to him. "It's a beautiful

machine Ndege left you. I think you should spend some time enjoying it again. I'll be fine. One day, perhaps, I'll come back to Crucible."

"I wanted to see Earth."

"Earth's not going anywhere. It'll still be there in a hundred, or a thousand years. But meanwhile, there are Risen. This is their cusp, Goma—their bottleneck. We came through our share of them; now it's our turn to do something for our friends. They're in good hands, I know."

"I hope it works out for you, Kanu," Ru said.

"It will. I always try to hope for the best. What else can we do?"

Twenty days later they watched him depart.

Goma had already said her farewells; there had been no need to say goodbye to him at the spaceport. Instead they had flown out in the Sess-Na, far beyond Guochang's last straggling suburb, into elephant territory.

The ambassadors would soon be walking these alien plains, but not just yet: there were still weeks or months of acclimatisation ahead of them, before they could comfortably breathe Crucible's air. But elephants had made that transition once before, without the benefit of contemporary medicine, and Goma had no doubt the ambassadors would prove equally adaptable.

For now it was just her and Ru, standing together a few dozen paces from the aircraft.

"I spoke to Malhi," Goma mentioned. "They're still tracking her, after all this time."

Ru looked at Goma with only mild interest, her real attention still on the distant spaceport, lying somewhere beyond the distant shark fin of the medical pyramid. "Her?"

"Arethusa. She's still alive, still somewhere out there. But bigger and stranger than she ever was before. She nearly killed Mposi, did you know? He tried fixing a tracking device on her. That didn't go down well."

"And now . . . ?"

"Someone needs to bring her up to speed. She may not be an Akinya, but she's been part of this for long enough. I want

Malhi to take me out there. A boat, submarine, whatever it takes. There are still merfolk. They can help me find her."

"And if she tries to kill you as well?"

"I'm counting on her wanting to hear my story first. Someone owes her this much."

"For old times' sake?"

"For old times' sake."

They saw it long before any sound had a chance to reach their ears. A rising spark, steady as an ascending star, a glint of hull balanced on that brightness, arrowing its way to orbit, to meet with the larger starship that would soon be embarking for interstellar space. Goma waited, and waited, but there never was any sound, just the heat and stillness of the day, their own breathing, the untroubled silence between them. She thought of Kanu in that ship, his wife with him, their hopes and fears, and the heart that travelled with them, on its long homecoming.

There had been warning, but not quite enough.

When the moment of translation came, there was still much that the Risen could have done to ready their world for its next port of call. In the stony corridors, enclosed halls and great vaulted chambers of *Zanzibar*, countless Risen were still engaged in their daily activities. They had been going about their business despite Dakota's departure and the irksome human interference with their power-generation grid. Fortunately, the grid was not essential for their continued existence, although it certainly made life easier. Ideally, when the warning arrived, the Risen would have abandoned their less vital tasks and taken up monitoring stations throughout *Zanzibar*, but most especially near the vulnerable points of its skin, ready to act if some part of that outer layer ruptured. None of them had direct memories of the first translation event, the one that had brought *Zanzibar* (or rather this chip of it) from the orbit of Crucible to the orbit of Paladin, across a numbing span of light-years. But in the community of the Risen, direct memories were only one strand in the larger tapestry of the Remembering. All knew of the severity of that event—the terrible toll of Risen and human lives. All could recount the hard days that had followed as the survivors fought to transform this severed fragment into a home that could keep them alive. And after the hard days—hard weeks, months, years. Crushing setbacks, bruising failures. Not until Dakota came to them had the worst of it been surpassed, and even then their difficulties were not over.

Not by a long margin.

But they had prevailed, and they had found stability. Whatever the outcome of this latest event, Memphis felt certain they would find it again—no matter how hard it would be, no matter how long it took them. It would not be his generation that broke the continuity of the Remembering, nor the one that followed.

In fact, this translation event was not violent at all. This time, all of *Zanzibar* was displaced, leaving no trace of it— save the mirrors, which were too far away to be caught up in the event—in orbit around Paladin. But Memphis knew that something had happened. Beneath the pads of his feet he felt the world shudder as if gong-struck. There was one large upheaval, then a diminishing series of lesser vibrations. Dust fell from the ceilings; water trembled in basins; the fabric of the world gave a single bored groan; and then all was still again.

And they were somewhere else.

To begin with, of course, Memphis had no idea where that might be. In the final urgent transmission from *Icebreaker* during the last few minutes before the event, Memphis had been warned that they could expect to end up around another star, in some other solar system—but he had been given nothing more specific than that. No idea of what sort of star, what sort of worlds it might have gathered around itself, how far from Paladin it lay. All of that, it was made clear, Memphis and his fellows would have to work out for themselves.

Were they up to such a task?

There were some Risen who considered Memphis slow. None of them was as quick as Dakota, that was true. But among her subordinates there were indeed Risen who had a quicker, more fluid command of language than Memphis. Words did not form as easily in his head as they did for others. But the weakness of that faculty should not have blinded them to his inner strengths. He comprehended as well as any of them, and although he might not be the quickest at expressing the ideas that took shape in his head, he had no doubt as to his own capabilities. He had served Dakota well, and she had entrusted this world to him. When the instruction came to dispose of the bodies of the Friends who could never be revived, he had understood her intentions perfectly. She was not a natural murderer, and nor was Memphis. And just as she had placed her trust in him then, he felt bound by an implicit trust now. He felt that burden of duty even though he was certain he would never see the matriarch again.

So he would live up to it. To start with, they would not concern themselves with what lay outside. That could wait. In the immediate hours following the event, there was more than enough to be done making sure that their home had come through without serious damage, and that the Risen were all aware of the sudden change in their circumstances. Memphis made a point of informing as many of them in person as he was able to, but before long he had to appoint deputies of his own, sending them out into the warrens and tunnels with such facts as he could give them.

Robbed of the mirrors, *Zanzibar* was running on emergency power for now. They could endure this for a while, but in the longer run, Risen needed bright skies. The mirrors, Memphis knew, had been made from bits and pieces scavenged from inside *Zanzibar* and lashed together with haste and ingenuity. The Risen could not have done such a thing on their own back then, but these were different times. They had learned a lot—not least the fact that they did not need human authority or permission to run their own world. Memphis would pick the cleverest of his Risen and assign them the job of making new mirrors. They would succeed—he was sure of it. Fortunately, there was still abundant water and food. After centuries of occupation, it would take more than a few years for *Zanzibar*'s stone walls to lose all their trapped heat, even if they had popped out far from the warmth of a star. The essentials were still in place. The Risen could live, and keep living, while they addressed their problems in a methodical fashion. They would do what they had always done—place one sure foot in front of another.

When Memphis had satisfied himself that the absolute

essentials were in hand (*in trunk*—he would force his mind out of these old human patterns of speech eventually, but not today)—when all was *in trunk*—he at last allowed his mind to turn to the question of where they had arrived.

Memphis organised a small expeditionary party. They made their way out through the peripheral tunnels to one of the docking points, where there were windows.

Zanzibar was still turning. It had kept its angular momentum during the translation, which meant there was still gravity in its chambers. The view wheeled around with the clock-like rhythm Memphis had known all his life. Until this latest development, the only significant thing beyond the windows had been rocky, airless Paladin and its single Mandala. He had long been accustomed to the presence of Gliese 163, but the star was always too distant to be anything other than an abstract source of light.

Now a harder and brighter light, a light that was much bluer, much fiercer, streamed through layers of pitted and scratched glass.

"We will need fewer mirrors," Memphis declared.

If they needed mirrors at all. The blaze caused him to squint. He had rarely needed to squint before, so in a way it was encouraging that the old reflex worked as reliably as it did. Their new sun was hotter and bluer than their old one, and it looked larger. He raised his trunk as a point of comparison. He could not quite block the disc of his new blue star, whereas he had never had any difficulty obscuring Gliese 163.

There was a world, too. They were orbiting it. It was hard to tell how big it was—they would need more time to take that sort of measurement. But it was spherical and a very emphatic green, and there was a mottling in that green which did not quite strike him as the kind of pattern that would arise from purely natural processes. Beyond the curve of this new world's horizon lay an even larger one, and in a dizziness of hierarchies Memphis grasped that, as *Zanzibar* orbited this planet, so this planet was but a moon of the larger one.

There was much to explore here—much to keep the minds of the Risen occupied.

Memphis became aware of something then—a black object sliding across the patterned face of the green world. It appeared at first to be an extension of the planet's surface, but as their relative angles diverged he saw that the black object was raised above it, perhaps in its own orbit. It was a flattened six-sided surface, and on it was another Mandala.

The black object was easy to see when it was over the green, but as it slipped beyond the limb of the world he lost track of it. There was another, though. It followed on behind the first, and then there was a third, as if there might be a necklace of them strung around the green world.

So this location had more than one. *Zanzibar* had come here from somewhere else; from here, presumably, they could also travel to other places.

If they so wished.

The blue sun washed out the stars, but when *Zanzibar* turned from it, Memphis's bright-adapted eyes still made out a handful of them. He had never studied the shapes of the stars, the patterns and constellations they formed, but some shiver of disquieting intuition told him that these configurations were not at all familiar, not even to those who had made their home under the alien skies of Paladin. How far had the Risen come?

Did it matter? The Risen were the Risen. This home was their home, wherever it took them.

Presently, as *Zanzibar* again swung its face back towards the green world, he noticed movement. He stirred, alarmed at first, then realised it would do his deputies no good at all to see him perturbed. So he squared his ears and adopted a posture of studied repose.

"Visitors."

Little gold things were crossing space to *Zanzibar*. They came in several antlike processions, dozens at a time, converging from different directions. Each was a tiny double sphere with many golden appendages. It was impossible to say precisely where they had originated from—the green world, the orbiting Mandalas or the larger planet beyond the green one. Memphis allowed himself a moment's speculation as to their intentions. Perhaps they meant ill to *Zanzibar* and its citizens—startled and alarmed by the sudden arrival of this oddly shaped rock. More charitably, though, he could presume their intentions were benign, for the time being, at least.

They would arrive very shortly. It occurred to Memphis that the prudent thing might be to wake up some of the Friends, to see what the humans made of the golden envoys. In time, he decided, he would do just that. The humans were owed their stake in *Zanzibar*, after all—they would all have to share its spaces for a while.

But for the moment, just for now, the Risen had no need of anyone else.